WIDDERKIN

My deepest appreciation goes to:

My family;

*Nicola, my editor, for her wonderful expertise,
advice and professional manner;*

*Luke, for the insight and skills shining clear
with this third design and typesetting project;*

All the readers for their comments and support;

*Philippe, Dathi and Marlin, for their special mix of
cameraderie, ideas and encouragement.*

Widderkin
Peter Wood

Published by Diaspora Press
First published November 2021
Email: palantir@diasporatales.tech or visit diasporatales.net

© Peter Wood

Printed in Melbourne by Tenderprint Pty Ltd
Editor: Nicola Markus
Designer/ Typesetter: Working Type Studio (www.workingtype.com.au)

ISBN: 9780994618863 (paperback)
ISBN: 9780994618870 (ebook)

The author acknowledges Australia's First Nations Peoples — the First Australians — as the Traditional Owners and Custodians of this land and gives respect to the Elders — past and present — and through them to all Australian Aboriginal and Torres Strait Islander people.

A catalogue record for this book is available from the National Library of Australia

WIDDERKIN

PETER WOOD

Diaspora
PRESS

To Robert

WIDDERKIN

HEIR & OPAL

PROLOGUE

Gliding effortlessly in wide, lazy surveillance circles, the Courser veered for a different view of the sprawling heart of the High Realm. Concepts of magnificence and grandeur were for other minds, and the keen eyes regarded the panoply of ramparts, courtyards and tall spires with indifference until movement stirred a primal hunting drive. Recognition of the being below quashed the thought of prey and the pattern of watchful oversight resumed with a long sweep of the High Castle perimeter and a thermal lift past the massive central tower. Keen avian vision registered the purple glow from within a balcony, again with indifference, and moved on. In contrast, the watchful mind riding the Courser noted the signature of the powerful privacy ward with interest and wondered what deep matter the High King might be addressing.

*   *   *

The shimmer surrounding Aglaron and his advisors deepened in hue.

"What do you mean you can't? You must."

"We can't. Not without causing damage. High King, your son has extraordinary natural defences and directly overwhelming them could cause irreparable harm."

Aglaron gestured at the deep purple shielding. "Forget protocol and speak plainly. None can hear us."

Maynor, Lord of Power, ruler of the First Outer Realm and strategic advisor relaxed slightly, then waited while his liege contained his emotions.

"You are certain, Maynor? The succession for the Over Realm is at stake."

"I'm certain. This relationship with his guide and companion was successfully hidden for almost a decade and the bond they established can only be broken by an intrusion of great power—power strong enough to leave permanent damage and limit his future development."

"Then we must use some form of persuasion. If he changes of his own accord, we will need no mental interference."

Uirebon, Keeper of Lore and Elder for the Over Realm, shook his head emphatically. "Keryth cannot make that choice, Aglaron. His bond with

Pethron is so deep the inclination must be inherent. His will is strong, yes, but will cannot prevail."

"Inherent? It can't be. My family is free of Widderkin."

"Not quite. There was your cousin."

Aglaron paused to recall. "Seven centuries ago. And recalibration worked perfectly. It always works."

"And it would work for Keryth too, but at a cost you can't countenance. I agree with Maynor on that."

Aglaron clenched his fist. "Can we nurture the deception? They've successfully managed for all this time."

"We could, but discovery would be inevitable and then we are seen as condoning the practice."

"I know, I know. I'm venting my frustration. To retain sovereignty and order I may have to banish my own son. How can I do that?"

Uirebon and Maynor waited silently while the High King wrestled with his inner conflict.

"Maynor, you said you can't directly override his defences. Is there some indirect method?"

Maynor and Uirebon exchanged a glance of relief.

"Yes, there is, but it involves tedious preparation and great power and is rarely used. Moving Keryth to the Human Realm to live as a mortal for five years would give us time to slowly and carefully effect the change you seek."

"Keryth! A mortal for five years? Worse than banishment."

"Not so. He would live a life of challenge and fulfilment from the human point of view we give him. Elves who have undergone the process almost invariably report a strangely powerful longing to repeat the experience."

Aglaron listened to the structure of the plan then silently wrestled with his decision.

"The future of the Over Realm is at stake. With Lady Narello growing in both power and ambition, Keryth will require all possible strength and ability to cope with the succession. He must not be damaged. Conversely, none of the five Realms will accept Widderfolk for any Court position, let alone as High King. We have no choice.

Make it happen."

Chapter 1

Kieran cursed his headache and wished it would go away. The doctor said it was a kind of migraine and had given him tablets to help. Useless.

But he took one anyway. Maybe if he didn't, he'd feel worse.

No matter what, he knew his night was wasted and he'd be lying around the place till he fell asleep.

Bed! Easy chair! Which one? He chose the chair and closed his eyes.

Shutting the light out was the only relief from the strange way everything looked. The colours weren't right and all seemed dull.

He couldn't read a book—the words floated around—and watching a screen of any kind was impossible when the colours of anything moving left a blurry trail behind them.

Studying for the Maths exam was now a write-off. Not only because it was hard to look at the coursebooks but also because he couldn't concentrate properly.

The tight feeling in his head hampered concentration, so two hours in the morning was the best he could hope for now, and that might cost him his chance at acing the course.

His best lecturer wanted him to try for an open scholarship at the start of next semester. That was a tempting idea, but he had to make a decision by the end of the coming week, and it would also mean using most of the semester break for swotting time.

If he won it, he'd be able to rent an apartment and move out of his tiny college room.

An hour passed and Kieran opened his eyes. The room still looked like a faded colour photograph, so he drank some water, stripped off and climbed into bed. Hopefully sleep would come early and mask the discomfort.

It took another hour of fuzzy thinking and fighting the pressure in his head before he slipped into a fitful dream state and, finally, a deep sleep.

At eight o'clock the next morning he dragged himself out of bed.

So much for the early study.

Now he had to make his lethargic body start functioning properly with only an hour and a half before his exam started.

First step was ten minutes of slow jogging around the college fitness track. The cold crisp air was a wake-up in itself, the white mist of his breath making him think of a dragon sending smoke and fire from its nostrils. That was a good sign. Images usually poured into his mind when he was fully awake. Next step was a speedy shower and a light breakfast of herbal tea and toast.

This left fifteen to twenty minutes for music. Nothing seemed to set his body going like music, and this morning he chose a medley of lively Irish dancing tunes.

With earphones in place—he'd be howled down if he played music aloud at this time of the morning—he pressed the Play button and closed his eyes.

They opened quickly though, as he rose to his feet and started moving. The music sparkled in his mind, so much so that he almost felt like a puppet with the music pulling the strings.

Life and vigour poured in, and soon he was improvising steps, moving his lithe and nimble body to match the message from the player.

Whoops! Time to go! Jeans, runners, shirt and a warm jumper went on, and fifteen minutes later Kieran was sitting, waiting for the signal to start reading the exam paper resting on the desk in front of him.

Yes!

His spirits rose as he read through the questions in the fifteen-minute preparation time.

Maxima and minima, 20% and a real cinch. Anti-differentiation, 20% and he'd done an example almost identical only a week ago.

Complex numbers, 20% and it was his best topic.

Logarithmic equations, 10%, was the one he'd wanted to work on last night. The short-answer section looked okay but he'd find out later.

Bummer! The main problem wasn't one he recognised. Well, he'd tackle that section last.

The three hours flew and so did Kieran's pen. The only question he couldn't finish was the logarithm problem, but he did what he could with that by showing workings for the parts that he knew and thought must be relevant.

He was pleased with what he'd done, and then secretly felt even better when he heard other students complaining bitterly about how hard the questions had been.

Kieran's day was a long way from over because there was still a Literature exam on Wednesday afternoon, then Physics on Friday morning, and he was aiming for another nine hours of study before he went to bed.

He grabbed a sandwich pack from the canteen, relaxed in a sheltered courtyard and enjoyed the warmth of the winter sun while he ate. Then he headed for the college pool.

Twenty minutes of easy swimming would be a good break before he set his brain in harness again.

In this first semester of college, Kieran had discovered how much he enjoyed swimming, and with free student access and the pool being only a five-minute walk from his room, he'd gradually built up his swimming fitness till he was using it almost every day.

The pool was busier than Kieran had expected, and he recognised a few people from the Maths exam.

Rhys was a quiet guy who attended one of Kieran's tutorials. He had a smile for everyone but kept very much to himself. Kieran liked him and always said hello when their paths crossed.

Mark Geston was there too. He was confident and popular but something about him grated. Kieran tried not to have anything to do with him, though that wasn't easy because his room was only two doors down the corridor.

After ten minutes, Kieran pulled himself out of the pool and, with a practised twist of his hips, sat on the edge tiles next to Rhys, who was obviously taking a breather.

"Hi twin! What did you think of Maths this morning?"

Kieran liked calling Rhys *twin*. It always set him smiling and it was appropriate at the moment, because they were wearing the identical light blue bathers that had started it. Colour, make, and style were alike. The only difference would be size, to fit Rhys's larger body.

"Don't talk about it, Kieran! It was a nightmare and I'm worried whether I did well enough to get through. I suppose you thought it was easy?"

"It wasn't too bad."

"Well, you must be a genius! I'm fed up with studying but I've still got Literature and Physics left. At least they're not on the same day."

"Hey! You *are* a twin. They're the same exams I've got."

The smile lit up again as Rhys slid into the water. "Ten more laps and I start on Literature. See you!"

Kieran dived in after him but without a thought of trying to keep up. He swam because it was fun and easy, whereas Rhys obviously liked serious training. After a couple more laps, thoughts of how he should be planning his study started intruding enough to see him head for a quick shower.

* * *

On Wednesday afternoon, Kieran walked out at the end of his Literature exam feeling pleased with the way it had gone, and headed for Mr B's office.

He had received a meeting request the day before and was curious to find out what he wanted.

It was probably to talk about the scholarship, but Kieran would be happy to talk to him anyway. If only the other lecturers were as friendly and interesting.

"Kieran! Thanks for coming! I guess you know what I'm going to say, but entries close on Friday and I wanted to make one last effort to persuade you. I guess you've decided against it since you haven't done anything, but you do have a good chance. Don't tell anyone but I've checked the exam you did on Monday and you only missed on one question."

"The log one?"

"Yes! Look. What if I give you a couple of days' help in the break? You've got too much ability not to make the most of it."

"Mr B, I'm dropping the forms in to administration tomorrow. You don't have to give up your time."

"You are? That's great! Look, I've got some spare forms here so why don't we sit down and fill them in now?"

Five minutes later they were finished and Kieran complained that he'd just signed away two weeks of his break.

"Don't worry! The last week will make up for it."

Wondering what he meant, Kieran cast a puzzled glance at Mr B.

"You're going with the outdoor group in the third week. Since I'm one of the leaders I saw your name on the list. We're going to some great places."

Kieran's face lit up. "You're one of the leaders? Maths lecturers aren't meant to like climbing mountains."

"Well this one does and I'm really looking forward to it. Now! How does Monday sound for a coaching session?"

Kieran protested, saying he couldn't use Mr B's holiday time, but he was easily overridden and left a load of extra textbooks in case he got the chance to look at them over the weekend.

Well, it would be Physics and nothing else till Friday afternoon, but Kieran left feeling amazed at the way Mr B was helping him and wondering why.

Back in his room, Kieran mentally planned his time ahead.

A swim first then five hours of Physics between six and eleven, with some short breaks, and then, hopefully, he'd manage another twelve or thirteen hours tomorrow.

He slipped into his bathers, pulled on his tracksuit, and headed for the pool. He emerged half an hour later with his body relaxed and his mind clear.

After a quick meal at the college canteen he settled at his desk and started thinking. He'd needed that break after the Literature exam to help get his mind ready.

He was very conscious of changing to a different pattern of thought. From imagination to fact, and from inspiration and creativity to logic and problem-solving. He was intrigued with the sensation of being able to switch his brain to different purposes.

Four and a half hours later, Kieran wondered what had happened to the time. Oh well! He'd covered the entire topic of waves and wave motion.

Maybe it was that fascinating section explaining sound and music that made it pass so quickly.

It was eleven o'clock now. It would be great to put on a CD, but if he was to start at seven in the morning he couldn't afford the time, so bed it was, with a mental command to wake at 6:30 a.m.

The next day disappeared with the same focused concentration on the changing topics, and when he went to bed he had to force his mind to slow down or he knew he wouldn't sleep.

He used his black method. He'd learned it in a tutoring group when the tutor was late and the topic of sleeplessness had somehow arisen.

Solutions ranged from sleeping tablets to sex, hot milk to alcohol, and reading to yoga, but one girl had described her idea of sending a black wave through every muscle in your body and then using it to block out every racing thought.

Kieran had been intrigued and it had been so effective that it wasn't till the next morning, when he woke, that he realised he'd gone out like a light after trying it.

*   *   *

"Hi twin! How was Physics for you?"

The quiet smile blossomed, making Kieran's grow as well.

"Hi Kieran! It went well. I like Physics, though, so that makes it easier to remember."

"What about Lit?"

"Lit's my favourite and I know what the lecturer wants in the answers so I should get a good score."

Rhys pulled himself out of the water and sat on the tiles next to Kieran, who watched the play of his muscles and then the quick sideways glance as he settled.

"At least we've got a break for a while."

"Ha! Lucky you! Mr B talked me into trying for that maths scholarship so I'll be swotting for another two weeks."

"Two? Are you giving the last week a miss?"

"I have to. I'm going to the Grampians with the Outdoor Ed group and it sounds like it's going to be great."

Kieran stopped speaking because of the look Rhys was giving him.

"What?"

The smile that Kieran liked appeared.

"Twins again. I'm going on that trip too."

"You are? Your name's not on the list."

"I wasn't going but Mr B organised it for me when a spare place came up. He found out how interested I was when he was helping me a couple of weeks ago."

"He's helping you? Rhys, this is weird. He's helping me too."

There was a pause before they spoke together. "Twins!"

They talked about the trip and when Rhys slid back into the water Kieran spoke on impulse.

"Rhys! Why don't you come over to my room one day next week and we'll check out the maps and organise our packs?"

Rhys looked uncertain about this, but Kieran pressed him and they ended up arranging it for the second week. Rhys started on his training again and Kieran headed to examine the textbooks Mr B had given him.

*   *   *

"Kieran! Come in!"

Kieran looked around in amazement. This wasn't a house. It was big enough for three houses, and there were stairs leading to a second storey. Mr B led the way up and through a large living area. There were photos and sketches hanging on the walls and Kieran felt the hairs rise on the back of his neck at a glimpse of a wilderness photo showing a mountain with rays of sunlight streaming through a misty cloud bank, lighting a huge buttress of rock. He stopped and stared.

"You like that one Kieran?"

"Is it real?"

"Well, it mightn't have the same lighting—that was a lucky fluke—but you'll see for yourself when we get to Gariwerd. It's called the Fortress, and if the weather's kind we'll be camping there for two nights."

Kieran wanted to stay and look at all the pictures but it wasn't the right time and he followed Mr B into a roomy study where they sat at a big desk.

"Did you get a chance to work through any of the textbooks?"

Kieran had checked them all, and he'd also used the information sheet that came with the application form to sort out which areas he already knew and which areas he'd need to work on.

"Yes! And I've started on this graphing section, but I'm not sure how much of it I should do."

He handed Mr B a sheet of paper that showed five of the topics he wasn't familiar with, and other topics indicating how much attention he thought they needed.

"Kieran, are you sure this is right? Four of these areas weren't covered on the course yet you've put them as ones you know."

Kieran felt proud of himself. "They were in the textbooks and I worked through them early in the semester so they'd be easier, but then we didn't do them."

"You did? Well! I never did topics I didn't need when I was studying. In that case, let's see where you are with the graphing and then we'll do the hardest topic first."

Kieran answered some questions and watched Mr B sketch quick graphs, which he said were the basic references, then saw how different parameters affected them.

"So, can you see how the whole topic is based on just five main shapes? If you remember the rules for each, then all you'll need is practice with the different ways they dress up the problems."

Kieran had always thought he worked best by himself but this was a real eye-opener.

He knew he'd eventually have figured this out though it would have taken three or four times as long, and he'd also learnt some general tactics that weren't in the books.

Mr B made him feel good about what he was doing, too, and Kieran suddenly realised that every time a new idea clicked for him, Mr B was just as pleased as he was.

"Kieran, let's stop for food. Do you always work like this? It's half past twelve and we've covered two topics already."

Mr B went downstairs and Kieran spent ten minutes looking at the pictures in the living area before sharing a meal of cold chicken and a couple of rolls with various fillings.

The afternoon session was even more productive. Kieran's brain worked faster and faster to cope with all the challenges Mr B threw at him.

"Enough. We have to stop. You've worn me out. I've never worked with anyone who can learn like this. Do you think you'll remember everything we've done?"

"Yes! I've got a really good memory, and it works best of all when I've been concentrating like this."

Mr B arranged for another session on the coming Thursday and Kieran set off for college after trying to say thanks but not feeling he'd done it well enough. Following a swim and a meal at the canteen, he put in another four hours working on problem examples in the textbooks before heading to bed.

He had to use the black wave again to slow his mind and he noticed he needed to make it blacker and stronger than usual before it worked properly. He woke early the next morning though, ready and keen to get going. The day with Mr B had made the chance of getting the scholarship more real, and now he committed himself to working at it as best he could.

He didn't quite become a hermit because he came out for meals, a daily swim, and the morning run around the exercise trail, but otherwise he stuck to his program of 14 hours' study each day for the next ten days.

Mr B gave him three more sessions. The first was to finish the last uncovered topic and work through the logarithm topic.

For the second session he'd prepared a range of problems for every required topic, and on the Wednesday in the last week he had the scholarship exams for the last five years.

"I can hardly believe I'm saying this but we're going to do every one of these exams today."

Kieran didn't believe Mr B either for a start because there was a three and a half hour time allowance for each exam. As well as that, the questions were designed in three sections of increasing difficulty, with the last section being so long and complex it could take the whole time by itself. It worked, though because Mr B sat with him and listened to an oral answer for most of the questions.

"Just tell me the process, Kieran, and if it's the right technique we won't even write it down."

This way, question after question was ploughed through in a quarter of the time. Occasionally, Kieran had to write a summary of his technique and logic, and in the difficult section Mr B marked some questions to be tackled later. It took longer to finish than their previous sessions, but Mr B was excited at what they'd done and urged a continuation when Kieran said he was worried about the time.

"Don't worry about how long it takes. You won't be getting home till later tonight anyway."

He laughed at the surprised look he was given.

"We're going out for a meal. It's my thank you for an unforgettable experience."

"You're thanking me? I've learnt everything twice as fast because of you, Mr B."

"Call me Peter, please, and I'm serious about thanking you. I've never seen anyone learn things the way you do and it was exciting to watch. Do you always study like this?"

"I've been getting better, but I don't remember being able to concentrate so well before I started college."

It was good to be able to talk to Mr B. He was really interested, and Kieran had been wondering if other students studied the way he did. It certainly didn't happen in the tutorials because there were too many distractions.

"Well, it's a special gift, Kieran. We've covered half a semester's worth of work in a week and a half and I know you're going to get the scholarship. You can't miss with what you've shown today."

They left the study, sat in the living area next door and, after some general conversation, Mr B asked how Kieran liked to relax when he'd been studying hard.

"I like swimming, but the college pool closes early during the semester break so I either go for a run or put some music on and dance."

"Swimming? Let's go then. I love it too, and I feel like some exercise."

"Now? The nearest public pool is too far away and the college one is closed."

"Not for us, Kieran. I used to coach the swimming team and I have a key."

*   *   *

The High King pushed all thought of Court matters aside and gave full attention to his advisor.

"Your report is not as I expected, Uirebon. There is much that concerns me, and much I don't understand. Keryth's vision is affected and the head pain is so debilitating he can do nothing for hours at a time. During all the months of preparation and treatment there was no mention of any discomfort, let alone this disabling pain."

"Yes, my Lord. The effect is unpleasant and completely unexpected, and only presented when Keryth fully assumed his new persona in the Human

World. After thorough and very careful observation, Lord Maynor has determined there is no harm and that the effect passes completely with sleep or rest."

"Do we understand why it manifests with Keryth and not with Pethron?"

"We believe it must result from the powerful defences your son has inherited. In contrast with Pethron's seamless preparation, Keryth's was complex and difficult, as you know. Have you ever examined his mind shields?"

Aglaron made no attempt to hide his amusement. "My stubborn son, Keryth! Our wills have surely clashed but I have had no cause to pass his personal shields."

"His growing resistance to Maynor's ministrations will require the assistance of a triad of power to ensure success with the next reinforcement."

"A triad … and another reinforcement? This increase in frequency is also a divergence."

"Necessitated by Keryth's increasing strength of mind, but a short-term problem which augurs well for his future capabilities."

"Yes, I agree … Why has Pethron been brought into such close association? The report shows the Widderlink we wish to heal has resurfaced."

"Without effect, my Lord. Strictures of the situation allow companionship and nothing more."

"How so?"

"Pethron's role as an instructor bars him from any strong relationship with a younger student."

"Younger? Keryth is the Elder."

"The human persona developed for Pethron gives him an aspect of seniority, and the authority inherent in his position augments that seeming. The close association is necessary. It is the truest indicator we can devise for monitoring the progress of Keryth's treatment which, as you know, is designed to gently and steadily reduce the existing Widderlink, not bludgeon it harmfully from existence."

Aglaron gave a noncommittal nod. "And when will Maynor make the next treatment?"

"Not for several days, my Lord. The power requirements were a great strain and his triad of power must also be sealed to secrecy."

"Good. Convey my appreciation for his efforts, Uirebon. Apart from the head pains, Keryth appears to be happy and successful in the Human World."

* * *

It was unusual to be swimming with no one else around and Kieran felt like he shouldn't be there till Mr B explained that he did this three or four times a week.

While Mr B was unlocking the pool and turning on some lights, Kieran ran to his room, dumped his bag and grabbed his bathers. Mr B was already in the water by the time he returned and once Kieran dived in, they swam a couple of laps together.

Mr B climbed out but motioned Kieran to keep going, saying he'd join him again for the next lap.

Halfway down the lane Kieran realised Mr B was walking alongside, watching with a big smile. When he reached the end, Mr B asked him to swim back again.

"I'm checking your stroke. It's the coach in me. Can you do backstroke for this lap?"

Kieran set off, very conscious of Mr B's attention. He swam faster than normal, then stopped at the end of the pool and pulled himself out of the water. Mr B sat down beside him and dangled his legs in the water.

"Who taught you to swim?"

"No one. I just like it."

"Well of course I believe you, but I don't quite understand. Can I show you a few things? I have a strange feeling about the way you swim and I think you could be awfully good at it."

They moved to waist depth, and for half an hour Kieran learnt and practised the backstroke. Straightening his body, the angle of his hands into the water, how far to reach back, coordinating his breathing, the angle of his feet and the rate of kicking, all this and more Mr B showed him with increasing excitement.

"Kieran! This is amazing! Swim a lap for me and try to remember everything. Not flat out, but not slow either."

Once again Mr B followed at the side of the pool, but with so much to concentrate on, Kieran hardly noticed him.

"Oh my! How are you doing this? You're a natural. I'm the best swimmer at college, but I think you'd be even better if you trained seriously."

Kieran didn't believe this.

"Mr B, just about anybody's faster than me. I see them every time I'm here and they power past me."

"You're ten metres faster than you were half an hour ago. They won't be going past you in the backstroke anymore. How would you feel about a few more sessions to take you through the other strokes? I swim here at least three nights a week so there's no problem time-wise."

Kieran couldn't say no. Apart from Mr B's company, he liked the feeling of achievement he was getting. Mr B took him to a nice restaurant and the evening went by in a flash. The strangest moment happened when he asked Mr B if there was anything he could do as a thank you.

"Well, yes, there is, and it would be good practice for next year when you'll have to help with tutorials. If you could manage an hour a week to work with another student it would be a great help. I don't seem to have enough time to do everything myself and he's asked for help with his Maths."

"Of course I would. Is it someone from my group?"

"You won't know him. He's had a hard life and keeps to himself, but I really like him. I think you will too. He's coming with us to Gariwerd, so that will give you a chance to get to know him."

"Peter! You're talking about Rhys, aren't you?"

The unreal feeling that Kieran was experiencing was now mirrored by the surprised look on Mr B's features. "How did you work that out? I've never seen him in anybody's company at college."

"He told me he's worried about his Maths, and he also said you found a place for him on the trip. We're meeting on Friday to look at the maps and organise our packs."

"You're friends? Well! Isn't that a coincidence? But I've never seen you going around together."

Kieran sensed Mr B's puzzlement.

"We're not really friends. We were talking at the pool and found out we're both going on the Grampians trip, so I asked him over for an afternoon."

"Well, fancy that! I think you might get on really well so it's your job to tell him you're his official Maths coach … as long as you still want to go ahead."

Back in his room, Kieran listened to music then decided on an early night so he'd be ready for one more big push to finish off his effort for the scholarship.

Lying in bed, he thought about the day. It *had* been quite special and he wondered how he'd be able to thank Mr B properly. It wasn't just his help. It was the way he'd given it, and then at the restaurant he'd acted as if they were friends. Now Kieran was looking forward to the Grampians trip on Saturday because he'd be seeing more of him.

*   *   *

On Friday, Rhys turned up in the early afternoon. When Kieran opened the door he saw that he was nervous, so he pulled the maps out and started talking about them straight away. Rhys relaxed and Kieran found he was being told things he didn't know were happening.

"Chimney Pots? Hollow Mountain? Where are they? The only place I know about is called the Fortress and I saw a picture of it at Mr B's place. Boy! The names sound interesting, don't they?"

They pored over the maps, worked out distances and looked at some pictures Rhys had on a travel brochure that Mr B had given him.

"What you think of Mr B, Rhys?"

"He's the best lecturer in college."

"That's for sure! He used up four days of his holiday to help me with the scholarship, and guess what? He took me swimming one night and I kept wanting to say 'Triplets' to him."

"What do you mean?"

"He wears the same training bathers we do. The same colour and everything."

"He likes swimming, then?"

"Likes it? He's brilliant! He said he used to be coach for the college team and he showed me how to do the backstroke properly."

"Backstroke? That's my best style."

"He's given me a special job, too, and I'm really pleased about it. I bet you can't guess."

Rhys made a few attempts, and then Kieran gave him a clue.

"It's for someone at college, but Mr B can't find the time."

Rhys looked at Kieran for a while. "I can tell by the way you said it that you mean me."

"I'm your official coach, Rhys. I thought I was in the Twilight Zone when Mr B said it was you. He said one session a week but we can make it more if you like."

Rhys had a strange look on his face. "You don't have to, Kieran. I can get through by working harder."

"But I thought Mr B said you'd asked for help?"

"I wouldn't like to take up your time."

"You'd actually be helping me. If I get this scholarship, I'll have to take tutorial groups next year and it would be good practice. Anyhow, would you like me to help you?"

"Yes, I would!"

Kieran laughed. "Great! I'll be a real slave driver and make you work for hours and hours so you know everything perfectly. I won't let you go till you do."

"You won't let me go? How could you stop me? I'm stronger than you."

"Ha! That wouldn't matter. I'll chain you to the desk. I know! I'll get one of those special slave driver whips."

"That wouldn't work. I'd be so scared I couldn't think properly, and then I'd never learn anything."

"Oh, yes you would! I'll prove it. Tell me the worst topic in Maths and I bet I can help you."

"It's those logarithmic equations."

"Oh my God! Guess what, Rhys … twins again! They were the only things I didn't get right in the exam. I know them now though. Mr B took me through them. Come on, slave! We'll spend one hour and see how much you can learn."

"What? You mean now?"

"Too right! And if you don't learn anything you can get someone else. Otherwise, you're stuck with me."

With false groans about wasting good holiday time on college stuff, they sat down at Kieran's desk and got to work.

"Okay. Here's the basic things you have to understand before you can put it all together. Let's see how well you know them."

It took almost the whole hour and they didn't get nearly as much done as Kieran had expected, but he was still happy and rather surprised at how good he felt each time he got Rhys to understand something.

"So? Did you learn anything?"

It was really a stir question, because they both knew the answer was yes.

"Nothing! It's worse than ever! We'll have to spend another hour so I can get back to where I was."

Kieran loved this answer because it showed that Rhys wanted to keep going and also that he had a good sense of humour.

"Oh no! That's terrible! All right then. We'll start again right now and work for another hour and a half."

For a split-second, Rhys's mouth opened in surprise, till he worked out that Kieran was stirring him back and the smile that Kieran liked lit up his face. "So what are you, then? My twin or my slave driver?"

Whoops! An either/or question. Which one was best? The answer came with hardly a thought.

"How about both? And you can be the same for me."

"What? How could I be your slave driver?"

Kieran hadn't thought about it but that answer came straight away too.

"We'll go swimming, and you can make me do some training. Mr B said I should practise."

"Okay! Do twenty push-ups!"

"Now?"

"Yes! Come on, slave! We'll spend an hour and see how much you can do."

Kieran laughed to hear his own words thrown back at him, and when he dropped to the floor, Rhys's smile was breaking new boundaries. Rhys dropped down and did the push-ups too.

"Twenty sit-ups!"

"Yes, sir!"

This nearly got the laugh he was aiming for. Twenty sit-ups were so easy that Kieran did another ten as well.

"Let's go to the pool and you can boss me properly."

"I haven't got my bathers with me."

"You can wear mine and I'll wear a pair of shorts. They might be a bit small, but they're stretchy enough."

Rhys looked dubious, but when Kieran offered to go over to Rhys's room to get his, he decided to take up Kieran's offer.

"As long as you don't mind if I borrow yours. It's over half an hour of walking to get to my room and back."

They grabbed a couple of towels and headed off.

"Oh my gosh! These are smaller than I thought. I hardly fit into them. Can I try the shorts?"

The shorts definitely didn't work. They were tight around the waist for Kieran, and Rhys laughed when he couldn't even pull them right up.

"You're too skinny."

"No, I'm not! You're too fat!"

"Show me this backstroke you've been boasting about."

Kieran loved it when Rhys teased him.

They warmed up for a couple of laps and then the big competition was on.

Kieran could hardly believe it when he almost kept up with Rhys, who was also very impressed.

"Hey! I didn't think you were that good. What did Mr B show you?"

Kieran went through some of the things, but Rhys said he already knew them.

"All right! Freestyle now."

Kieran went back to feeling like a tortoise when Rhys powered off and left him for dead. They didn't do any more races, just swam some laps and mucked around. Kieran swam backstroke almost all the time, because he liked the feeling of being nearly as good as Rhys.

Back in his room, Kieran took everything out of his backpack. Well, it wasn't really his. It was from college, along with the sleeping bag, a special thermal pad, and a good coat in case it rained. They tried out the pad, watching it gradually inflate, then fluffed up the sleeping bag. Kieran climbed into the bag and lay on the foam pad.

"It doesn't feel very soft!"

Rhys took a turn in the sleeping bag, and as soon as he was on the pad Kieran sat on him, then kept him trapped when he tried to escape.

"So! You're stronger than me, are you? How are you going to get out of this?"

Rhys rolled over, got his arms free of the bag, then used his weight and strength to pin Kieran beneath him.

"That's how! And now we'll see if you can escape."

Kieran couldn't.

He wriggled and strained but Rhys seemed to be ready for every ploy. In the end, Kieran used trickery when he discovered that Rhys was ticklish.

"Cheat! Keep those hands away from me."

Rhys was now smiling so much that Kieran knew he didn't mind being tickled.

"What? These hands? The hands of torture! All right, I'll keep them away as long as you come and see a movie. I've got one of those receipts that lets two people in for the price of one and it's wasted if I go by myself."

For a moment Rhys gave him a dubious look, but when Kieran reached forward he shrank away in mock terror and agreed.

"Okay! But there aren't any good movies on, are there?"

"*The Mysts*! It's meant to be unreal!"

"Oh my God. It's happened again. I've been dying to see it. I've read the book three times but they say the film is just as good. We'll get back too late though. It lasts for three hours."

"I looked it up. There's an early session at six o'clock, so that's not too bad."

Rhys was looking eager now and he chatted excitedly about the book and some of the characters in it as they made their way to catch a bus.

"It's the best book I've ever read and I didn't like it when they said they were making a movie, but the fan-sites on the web all say it's worth it. Have you read it?"

"No, I don't seem to have enough time to do much reading, but I'll get around to it."

"You can borrow my copy! It'll save you buying it."

They shared a pizza for an early meal then sat engrossed by the classic story of dragons, wizards, elves and other mythical beings. In places it was sad and Rhys was so involved that Kieran heard his small sob and felt like hugging him. When it finished, they sat for a few minutes to return to the real world, before heading back to college.

"Wow! That was amazing, Rhys. What did you think of it?"

"Unreal! The book's better though."

"Better?"

Back at college, they parted company to go to their different resident halls.

"Kieran, I had a great day. Thank you for all the things we did."

Kieran didn't quite know what to make of this. The way Rhys had said it was kind of more formal than just a thanks.

"Hey! It was the best day I've had all year. Except for when you bullied me, of course. I'll see you in the morning."

That got the smile going and Kieran went to his room very pleased with himself.

He'd got Rhys smiling so many times that day and, in fact, even laughing, and then there was the work they'd done together on the Maths and the excitement they'd shared with the film.

He couldn't wait to read the book, except that it would have to wait till after the scholarship exam.

*   *   *

At 6:45 a.m. Kieran swung his backpack into place and headed for the student centre. There was just a hint of daylight showing in the east and his dragon fire puffed with every breath as he walked with hands tucked snugly in his pockets. The first person he recognised in the activity near the college minibus was Mr B, and after a quick hello and friendly smile he was dragooned into carting supplies of food and other gear which had to be loaded. On his third trip out he saw Rhys standing quietly to one side so he grabbed him to help. Fifteen minutes later everything was organised and it was time to leave.

"Quick, Rhys! Grab a seat at the front so we get a good view."

This worked out and the bus moved slowly past friends and well-wishers and headed for the open road. Mr B was moving from seat to seat, talking to everyone, and by the time he'd worked his way to the front, the bus was on the freeway and approaching the great bridge over the Yarra River.

"Squish up, Kieran. There aren't any spare seats so I hope you don't mind if I sit with you till Ballarat."

Kieran certainly didn't mind. There was something about Mr B that made it good to be near him. As soon as this thought entered his head, he realised it was the same with Rhys. The next thought nearly made him laugh aloud and he had to whisper to Rhys: "Hey. Look at us. The triplets!"

Rhys's smile grew.

"What's so funny? Are you going to let me in on the joke?"

"It's not really a joke … um … Mr B?"

Kieran felt awkward, but Mr B picked up on it straight away. "Peter!"

"Rhys and I have been calling ourselves twins because our bathers are identical, and then the other night yours were the same so we changed it to triplets."

As soon as he said it it sounded rather silly, but Mr B seemed to enjoy the idea.

"Triplets hey? I must admit I was quite surprised, too, when you walked out in my bathers. I had one of those funny moments and couldn't help glancing down to check I was wearing them. So, how's the swimming going? Have you done any practice yet?"

"I can nearly keep up with Rhys for the backstroke. He walks all over me for the other styles though."

"Well, I expect you'll catch up to him in a few weeks after we get back."

The conversation turned to Kieran's scholarship work and then to the days ahead at the Grampians. Rhys was quiet, but when Kieran mentioned that they'd seen *The Mysts*, Mr B wanted to know more about it.

"I've thought about seeing it, but I don't want to spoil the book."

"Ha! Talk to Rhys then. He's read it three times."

"Three? I can top that, Rhys. I'm up to five."

Suddenly Rhys was no longer quiet. Mr B read the same kind of books as he did and they compared notes and argued about different authors Kieran had never heard of. Time passed quickly, and they were soon approaching Ballarat.

"It's my turn to drive after we stop for a quick snack. I've been thinking about your triplets idea and I'm wondering if you'd mind sharing one of the three-man tents with me?"

The more of Mr B's company the better as far as Kieran was concerned, and Rhys looked pleased too. Ballarat was the last large town they'd see and Kieran's attention focused on the new scenery they were passing: sections of natural bush with gums and wattle, some pine plantations and then an area called the Western Plains which was all farming country. Kieran drank it all in. He loved the names of the places they passed— Smythesdale, Carranballac, Westmere—and couldn't get over how small they were. Some of them had only one or two shops.

"Look, Rhys. That sign says there's a town called Snake Valley."

After an hour's driving, their excitement lifted when the first distant views of the Grampians ranges appeared and then they stopped for a fifteen-minute break at a large lake. Kieran wandered near the water's edge and his eyes were drawn to a flock of waterbirds bobbing in the ripples about twenty metres away.

"What are you smiling at, Kieran?"

"The little black ones, Mr B. They look like robots with their heads jerking backwards and forwards."

"They're called coots. Here, have a closer look."

Kieran took the binoculars Mr B was offering, held them to his eyes and saw a blurred mess. When he moved his head away Mr B saw his look and showed him what to do.

"Just turn that ring on top and what you're looking at will snap into focus."

Kieran experimented for a minute and realised that somehow he'd never actually used binoculars before. The birds snapped into view and Kieran watched till they suddenly went berserk.

"Holy Hell! Look at that."

Some birds had dived under but most were scattering with a great flapping of wings, skittering across the surface. Forgetting the binoculars, Kieran watched as a huge hawk coursed through the milling flock. A few moments later there was a spray of feathers, a short, high-pitched scream, and then powerful wing beats as the predator flew off with its prey. A thrill of awe at the sudden savagery held Kieran rooted to the spot. The waterbirds settled as if nothing had happened and Kieran turned to listen to Mr B and Rhys.

"Wow, that was amazing. Why did they all stay together like that? If they'd flown away, they might have escaped."

"Who knows what a bird thinks, Rhys? The theory is that it's a herding instinct. Evidently, when they're by themselves they feel more vulnerable and it's easier for the harrier to focus on them."

"Harrier? I thought it was a hawk. What's the difference?"

"That white flash on its rump, and its size, tell me it's a swamp harrier."

Kieran listened to all this with fascination. "Do you know what these other birds are as well?"

"Most of them. I got interested in photographing them at one stage and I'm often out in the bush, so I carry a field guide with me ... Have a go at learning from it. It's much easier than you'd think. I bet you can see thirty different kinds in the next half-hour."

They only had another five minutes till they left but Kieran realised there were birds everywhere, and with help from the binoculars they found eleven types before they climbed aboard the bus. Mr B gave them the field guide and, with their eyes searching keenly in a friendly competition to find the next type, the tally quickly passed the thirty mark. Kieran's attention gradually wandered, though, as the mountains they were approaching grew larger and more prominent, and his eyes were drawn to new aspects. When they stopped at a small town nestled at the southern end of the range, he couldn't take his gaze off the nearby mountain.

This was a half-hour stop for an early lunch, and when Mr B said it was the last town for another five or six days, everyone took the opportunity for a final fast-food fix with pies, chips or a hamburger. Kieran and Rhys sat at a courtesy picnic table outside the cafe with four other students, where they could view the closest mountain and the ranges stretching into the distance behind it. Evidently it was called Mount Abrupt and, according to Mr B, there was a tagged bushwalker's track to the top if you knew where to look. Rhys started pointing to something when movement in a nearby tree grabbed everyone's attention.

"Hey, look! That kookaburra's watching us. Break off a bit of sausage from your sanger, Kieran, and see if he's interested," Shannon said.

That was highly unlikely, and Kieran was starting to say so when the kookaburra launched from its perch and startled everyone by landing on the table and standing quietly with its head cocked to one side. Shannon must have been right, so, without any sudden movements, Kieran carefully broke away a small piece of meat and placed it on the table timber. For several seconds, the kookaburra's head tracked this way and that, then, after a confident hop, its hunting beak made a determined jab before, with a great flutter of wings, it returned to its perch.

"Wow! Unreal! I've never seen one come so close to people. Did you see the blue on its feathers?"

"The cafe people probably put meat out to attract it for the tourists, Shannon, and that's made it really tame."

After another forty-five minutes the minibus reached their first major destination and the group set off to hike the Chimney Pots Trail. The information sign suggested an hour and a half, but it was almost three hours before they completed the loop. Kieran discovered how much Mr B liked exploring, because they checked every sidetrack and rocky outcrop, scrambled to every vantage point for a view of the valley below and left the track to examine every interesting feature. Kieran loved every bit of it.

There was another burst of driving before they reached the camping spot, and Mr B kept checking the map as the bus made its way through scrub and bush. Sometimes the track was gravel, sometimes sand, and sometimes so rough they almost had to slow to a walking pace. They were soon used to seeing wallabies and kangaroos bounding off to the side and, at one stage, some emus caused excitement when they ran alongside the vehicle for forty metres before heading into the scrub.

The minibus crossed a timber bridge over a small creek, pulled off the gravel and stopped fifty metres along the dirt track where there were some grassy clearings amidst a stand of wattles. There was a busy time while the tents were set up, wood collected and a campfire started.

Kieran listened carefully when Mr B gave hints about where to place the tent so no spark from the campfire would blow on it, so it wouldn't be flooded if it rained, and so your head wasn't downhill when you slept.

The sun was low in the sky by the time everything was organised, and Mr B said he was going for a walk to watch the sunset. Everyone was mostly occupied with the tents and sitting around the campfire, so only Kieran, Rhys and one of the girls went along. Kieran had decided earlier in the day that he was going to stick with Mr B because he always seemed to have a reason when he did things.

It surely paid off this time.

After walking for a good ten minutes. they reached a jumble of rock which rose above the scrub and trees. A quick, easy climb took them to the top of a large flat rock, and as Kieran lowered himself to sit beside Rhys with his legs dangling over the edge, he gasped and felt a shiver of awe. In front of them was the buttress of rock in the photo, but it looked so different. The light from the sinking sun gave the whole mountain range a soft glow, which made it stand out sharply against the darkening eastern sky. Gradually, the intensity of the glow increased till the great red ball of the sun disappeared below the horizon. Kieran's head turned from the sunset in the west to the mountains in the east, then back again and again as he tried to take it all in. Mr B put his camera away and smiled at them.

"Well, that was a real show, wasn't it? There are often great sunsets here but we were lucky to get such a good one at this time of year."

Rhys stood up but Mr B told him to wait.

"Something else is going to happen, Rhys."

The sky rapidly darkened further and the winter chill strengthened while they sat watching the stars appear and the mountain blacken. The Fortress, as Mr B called the great buttress of rock, became more and more menacing, and Kieran pondered the thought that they'd be camping at its base for the next two nights.

"Yes, here it is. I was starting to think I'd got the time wrong."

Kieran didn't understand till he saw a faint nimbus of light turning the outline of the Fortress into a silhouette. It brightened quickly and Kieran's first thought was that there must be a massive wildfire lighting everything up. An arc of bright whiteness appeared at a speed which astonished Kieran, and the full moon rose in the sky.

"There we are. Show's over. Let's get some food."

Mr B led the way back along the rough track with the aid of a small pocket torch and soon they were enjoying the welcoming warmth of the cheery campfire. Several hours later, when the meal was over, the discussions done and the campfire reduced to glowing embers, Kieran saw with astonishment that the moonlight was so bright he could see quite clearly, and the leaves of the trees glistened like silver.

It felt strange climbing into his sleeping bag so early, and even stranger lying so close between two other people, but the air was so chill outside it felt very snug. They talked for over an hour, mostly Mr B answering questions about his life and other adventures he'd had, but he was also keen to hear their thoughts about the day. Rhys said it was all good, but that the sunset was the best.

"What about you, Kieran?"

"It was the same for me, Peter, but watching the harrier made me think the most."

The silence told Kieran that Rhys and Mr B were both waiting for him to explain.

"I was on both sides. I wanted the coots to get away and at the same time I wanted the harrier to catch his prey, and I keep thinking how suddenly the bird's life stopped."

"I thought about it, too, Kieran. It was the way something savage was kind of beautiful at the same time."

Mr B spoke up now. "I think everything is beautiful, Rhys. It's only things that humans do that are sometimes ugly."

The conversation continued till Mr B said goodnight and went quiet. Kieran thought for a while, then went to sleep.

*   *   *

Great peals of laughter woke him next morning and made him wonder what was going on. Birds! Sounding berserk with all their calls. The laughter was kookaburras, of course, but they sounded so close. Kieran rolled onto his side and saw Mr B looking at him with a smile on his face.

"Morning in the bush. Leave the hustle and bustle of the city for peace and quiet in the country, and get woken at the crack of dawn."

"Are they always this noisy?" Kieran whispered back.

"Mostly when it's a fine, clear day."

Kieran pulled his jeans and a jumper on because he badly needed to relieve himself, but a couple of minutes later he dived quickly back into his sleeping bag.

"It's frozen out there. The grass is white."

"Good, a nice, clear day."

For half an hour Kieran relaxed cosily in his sleeping bag, listening to all the sounds, but then he got restless and when Mr B got up so did he.

"Here, make yourself the most popular person in the camp."

Mr B took a cardboard box with some newspaper and dry twigs and leaves from the minibus, started the campfire, and left Kieran to build it up. Soon, the delicious smell of sizzling bacon wafted through the camp and people started appearing from their tents.

"Kieran, see if Rhys wants coffee or tea. If we give it to him while he's still in bed we can stir him for the rest of the trip."

As soon as Kieran unzipped the tent a soft voice said, "Coffee please, and I've been awake as long as you have."

An hour later everyone was packed and ready to go. Kieran felt like an explorer with his pack on his back, and excitement and anticipation built as they took their first steps along the single-file walking track.

The day was unforgettable.

The air was crisp and clear, and Mr B stopped at every vantage point to look at the views and talk about the features. The Fortress itself looked more awesome the closer they got. Soon after midday, the trail headed down a long steep gully, followed a small creek upstream for several hundred metres and ended beneath the Fortress. That was such a good name for it and Kieran looked in amazement at the vast mass of rock stretching up hundreds of feet and the overhang angling in at the base.

After some lunch, the rest of the afternoon was spent exploring, with the highlight being a great split in the rock which disappeared into darkness. In the evening, after eating, Kieran sat listening to the talk, watching the shadows flicker on the stone walls and the soft glow of firelight on the nearby tree trunks. It was glowing on Rhys's face too, and Kieran kept glancing at him. He was quiet, and Kieran wondered what was going on in his mind. He'd obviously enjoyed all the things that had been happening but he'd hardly said a word to anyone apart from Kieran and Mr B.

Mr B was quiet too, even though he was talking and interacting all the time. With a sudden insight, Kieran realised that Mr B had built an understanding with every person on the trip since they'd started the previous morning.

Shannon, a third-year student, held everyone's attention when he collected a bundle of sticks about the length of a walking staff then made another fire and started one of the sticks burning at both ends. When he was satisfied with the glowing coals, he took it up and started twirling it like a band-leader's staff or a calisthenics rod. The effect was spectacular. When the stick was moving fast enough, the afterimage made a bright fiery circle in the dark. He was skilful with the twirling, sometimes doing it over his head and sometimes to the side, and when the coals died down or flew off the end of the stick he'd replace it in the fires for a while and start again. He made a dramatic finish by flinging the spinning fire stick high in the air and trying an unsuccessful catch. He still got his cheer though, and then he set more sticks burning for everyone else to have a try.

The firesticks finished, and for a while there was laughter and chatter, toast cooked on the end of sticks, marshmallows burned crispy on the outside and lots of warm drinks, but then the increasing cold sent more and more people to their tents.

Mr B set a stubby candle on a plate, and Kieran was surprised at how much light it gave off.

"I often like to go camping by myself, Kieran, and at night-time I lie in my tent and read by the light of a candle. You should try it, Rhys. Reading book two of *Myst* in the bush when the wind's rushing through the leaves of the trees all round is quite an experience."

Away they went, talking excitedly about which books would be good to read under different conditions. Kieran listened to the eager tone in Rhys's voice and decided on the spot to give him a book when they got back from the trip. He'd have to talk to Mr B about it. Yes, that was it. He'd talk to Rhys and get one for Mr B as well.

"Are we talking about books too much, Kieran?"

"No way!" laughed Kieran. "I love listening. You make me think of old philosophers or a couple of wizards arguing about their spell books."

This got silence for a moment.

"Turn him into a frog, Rhys."

"Maybe he already is one?"

"Yes, disguised as a handsome prince."

"Could be! Who's going to kiss him to find out?"

"… Turn him into an owl. Wasn't Arthur an owl in *The Once and Future King*?"

"I think it was a falcon. Do you remember what fewmets is?"

"You remember fewmets? Wow."

"You could turn him into a pumpkin, Peter."

"A pumpkin? You think he's disguised as a royal coach?"

Rhys laughed. "I didn't think of that. I thought he might be a Halloween mask. Watch this. Sit up, Kieran."

It was the old torch-under-the-chin trick, though they both said it worked better because the flickering candle flame made the shadows move.

"You're right, Rhys. That's definitely a Halloween mask. My blood's freezing at the sight of it."

"Perseus."

Half an hour later Mr B said good night and all went quiet.

＊　＊　＊

The next day they climbed to the very top of the Fortress. It took an hour of scrambling up a trail blazed with strips of blue plastic ribbon, and then they were treated to a great panorama: peaks of the ranges running north and south, and to the west a great plain of bush and scrub with a patchwork of farmland scattered here and there. For three or four hours they explored the great masses of rock, climbing to vantage points and taking in the rugged scenery.

Mr B's camera worked overtime, and Kieran discovered he was good at climbing and scrambling. Mr B and Kevin, the physical education leader, decided to make the return to camp more of an adventure by leaving the tagged trail and finding a way down the southern side. The bush was so thick, and the ridges of rock and gullies seemed to run in the wrong direction so much, that after an hour and a half of hard work some people started wondering if they were going the right way. When they reached a small creek and started following its bed they knew it was the way back to the tents. Everyone dumped their daypacks and relaxed at the campsite before starting the campfire, collecting firewood and making hot drinks.

There was almost an hour left before darkness, and having heard about yesterday's sunset, Kevin was heading down the creek and up the steep gully to a viewpoint on the inward trail with anyone who was interested. Kieran and Rhys were getting ready to go when Mr B beckoned to them.

"Do you think you can stand missing out on the sunset?"

"What do you mean?"

"There's something special I can show you if you like."

That was enough for Kieran, and a glance showed the same interest on Rhys's face. They waited till everyone had gone, heading down the creek.

"You have to keep this secret. Okay?"

Kieran nodded and now felt that wild horses couldn't keep him away. They reached the spot where the track turned off and went up the gully but, instead of following, they continued down the creek for another hundred metres, scrambled to a large rock on the right-hand side, and climbed along a ledge till they reached a flat platform set into the wall of rock. It was a neat spot, with a drop-off of about ten metres straight down and the overhanging rock making a natural shelter, but apart from its general interest, Kieran couldn't see anything special. They'd observed features similar to that all day.

"Have a look around and see what you can find."

It sounded like Mr B was setting a challenge. To the north was Mount Thackeray with its rough, craggy cliff faces and below was the gully of the creek, littered with great clumps of weathered rock. During the day Mr B had talked about a pair of special peregrine falcons which lived in this gully, so Kieran looked higher up the overhang of the rock, searching for a nest, but he couldn't see anything. They both glanced at Mr B but he just said to look harder.

"Not in the distance though."

It was very puzzling but eventually Rhys made an exclamation. "Is this it?"

"Good work, Rhys. Yes, this is it."

Rhys was staring closely at the face of the overhanging rock and Kieran and Mr B moved next to him. Faint, but quite definite when you looked closely, were a number of stylised markings on the rock.

"What shapes can you see, Kieran?"

"They look like handprints."

The penny dropped and Kieran remembered some information from when he'd been looking at the map to see where the Fortress was back at college.

"They're First Australian, aren't they? Is this the Cave of Hands? I saw it on the map."

"It's not the Cave of Hands, Kieran. That's a couple of kilometres along the road from where we left the minibus, but I think it must be connected. I looked up what I could at the State Library and it seems the hand symbol had two meanings. It was mainly used as a sign that a young man was being accepted as an adult and they had a big ceremony where the young man could make his own mark, but I read one book where it said that sometimes special leaders in the tribes would use it to link themselves with ancestors living in the Dreamtime."

"Dreamtime? That's a kind of idea of Heaven, isn't it?"

"It's much more than that, Rhys. Most people think it's a few simple stories explaining how the world started, but anthropologists who've studied it say it's amazingly complicated and very difficult to understand."

"I wonder which meaning these paintings are?"

"Well, I reckon it might be the second one, because I can only see three symbols here and the Cave of Hands has marks everywhere."

"Wow! Imagine it. If I put my hand there I could be linking up with everyone else who's been to this rock. I wonder if it's many people?"

"I wouldn't like to guess, Rhys. I don't understand why people don't make more of a big deal about it, but the First Australian culture is by far the most ancient that exists on Earth. There's evidence it could be a hundred thousand years old, and the Canberra University has carbon-dated bones and artefacts at even earlier than that. It makes the world's other old cultures seem like the blink of an eye."

Kieran watched Rhys slowly reach out and cover the marking on the left. He felt an urge to touch the symbols too, so he positioned his hand directly over the painting next to Rhys's.

"Hey, there're three symbols and three of us. What a fluke. Come on, Peter. You too."

Mr B laughed and placed his hand over the remaining symbol. "What? Triplets is it, Rhys?"

The rock was cold and hard. Kieran closed his eyes, thought of count-less dark hands doing the same thing, and wondered what they'd all been thinking at the time … He must be imagining things. Was the rock getting warmer? He opened his eyes and glanced from Rhys to Mr B.

"Um! This doesn't make sense, but does the rock feel different, like its warming up?"

"It is, Kieran. Your body's thirty-six degrees and the rock's about twelve or thirteen degrees, so energy is transferring from your hand into the rock the whole time you're touching it."

All that made sense, except it was happening the other way round. When he concentrated, it didn't really feel like warmth either, but what-ever it was it felt good. Sensation flowed through his arm, extended right through his body and faded away, leaving him wondering what was going on.

"Are you all right, Kieran? You look like you're blushing."

"Yes, I'm okay. But this rock does feel strange."

Mr B and Rhys stared at him. Then the moment ended and they all lifted their hands off.

Rhys smiled. "Maybe someone from ten thousand years ago was talking to you?"

Kieran smiled back. "I didn't understand them, then."

The three of them sat talking quietly, watching the changing light as the shadows lengthened in the valley below and the rock faces of Mount Thackeray absorbed the colour of the approaching sunset. Mr B started to worry about the dark.

"Come on. The moon will be out later, but it will get pitch black till then and I didn't bring my torch."

They reached camp before the others, set the fires, started boiling some water from the creek, then watched the light from several torches appear and disappear as the sunset-watchers moved slowly up the creek towards them.

Halfway through his meal, Kieran felt one of his headaches starting. He managed to finish eating but it steadily worsened till all he could do was sit quietly and listen to the voices all around. It worsened so much he felt like screaming at it to go away. The campfire became a strange blur and he wasn't game to stand up and move. The disorienting colour trail from the fire every time he turned his head made him feel nauseous and he knew he needed to lie down.

"Rhys, will you help me? I need to get to the tent."

"What's wrong?"

Rhys was on his feet in an instant and Kieran could sense his concern.

"It's one of my stupid migraines. It'll be all right because it always goes away, but I can't see properly at the moment."

Kieran closed his eyes and relaxed as the security of Rhys's strong arm slowly guided the way to the tent and his worried voice warned of obstacles. They unzipped the tent. Kieran pulled his boots off, crawled into his sleeping bag and arranged himself comfortably on his thermal pad.

"What's happening?"

It was Mr B's voice now.

"It's all right, Peter. I've got a migraine. It'll be gone by the morning. If I lie down and keep my eyes closed it helps me get through it."

"Have you got medication for it?"

"I didn't bring it. It's too soon after the last time, but it doesn't really help anyway. Don't worry. My head feels tight, then I get sleepy, and when I wake in the morning, it's gone."

There was silence for a moment.

"It doesn't sound like we can do much to help you. Would you like a warm drink?"

"Yes, thanks."

"Rhys, get yourself organised in the tent and start giving Kieran a head massage while I get the drink."

There was silence for a moment, from Rhys this time.

"Ah! How do I do that?"

"Lie down. Rest Kieran's head on your chest and try whatever feels good for him. Massage his temples, the back of his head, his eyes, and his hair. He'll tell you what works best and that's what you do the most. I'll be back soon with the drink."

Rhys moved into position and Kieran settled his head back.

"Kieran, this is all right, isn't it? I don't know what I'm doing but Mr B thinks it might help."

"It feels better already."

It did too. Rhys's chest was moving with his breathing and seemed to communicate a sense of security.

"How will I start?"

"Anything."

Kieran felt gentle fingers working through his hair. It was good.

"Try my temples. Both at the same time. That's where it feels tightest."

Rhys's hands moved and, after an uncertain start, began to make rhythmic circles. "What's that like?"

"Don't stop. It really helps."

The gentle contact continued and in an instant of shock, Kieran recognised that a sensation of warmth-but-not-warmth was building in his temples.

"Rhys! I ..."

The sensation exploded ...

Kieran sensed movement and opened his eyes as a match flared and Mr B's candle lit up. Kieran turned his head to see better then relaxed against Rhys's chest again and the movement caught Mr B's attention.

"Hey, sleepyheads. Are you awake enough to have your drink?"

While sitting up in response to this a series of questions chased through his mind.

He'd been asleep?

Rhys was asleep?

His headache was gone, the candle flame looked crisp and clear, and it must only have been a matter of minutes since Rhys was massaging him.

What had happened?

Accepting the warm mug, Kieran took some welcome sips. Rhys stirred. His eyes blinked open and tracked back and forth between Mr B and Kieran.

"What happened?"

"You fixed my migraine."

"You zapped me."

"So did you. Do you feel all right?"

Rhys thought about this. "The same as normal. How long have I been asleep?"

"I'm not sure. It must have been only a few minutes."

Mr B's head was switching back and forth to match the conversation.

"Hey! Earth to Mars! I'm totally left behind here. What are you two talking about?"

"He's a human battery, Mr B! I started rubbing his temples and he knocked me out. Except it didn't hurt."

"It was the same for me. When Rhys rubbed my temples, I went to sleep in a second and now I feel better."

"Slow down! Slow down, both of you! I had to heat some water, but I've only been gone five or six minutes maximum. You were both asleep, which surprised me, but Kieran woke up as soon as I came into the tent. You woke up straight after that, Rhys. Now, tell me what happened to you first."

"I've said it, really. I rubbed Kieran's head and then he said to try his temples because they felt tight. He said he liked it so I kept going, then all of a sudden some kind of shock wave went through me. The next thing I knew, you were both looking at me."

"Hmm. All right, Kieran?"

"It was the same for me. Rhys saying it was like a shock wave is a really good description for the part where I went to sleep, but just before that I had a strange kind of feeling. It's weird, but it was like the feeling I had at the hand paintings when you thought I was blushing. Sort of warm, but not really. Peter, it's fixed my migraine. I can't believe it. It always lasts for hours and I have to sleep overnight for it to go away properly."

No one said anything for a while. Rhys started humming *Twilight Zone* music and then everyone smiled. They went through it again and Kieran had to explain more of what he'd felt at the hand paintings.

"Well, I've never heard of anything like this. I know that sometimes people get zapped with that faith healing stuff but not the person who does it, and the warmth thing happens with reiki healing, but yours sounds different, Kieran."

"You're a super healer, Rhys!"

Mr B laughed. "Maybe you're both getting the flu and passed out at the same time?"

He pressed his hand against Rhys's forehead, pronounced his temperature normal, then turned to Kieran with the questioning look.

"Well, here goes!"

He held his hand on Kieran's forehead now … and after four or five seconds started quivering and shaking. He stopped, though, and told the rather stunned pair that Kieran's temperature felt normal too. Rhys's mouth opened for a second and then he started laughing. Kieran did, too, and Mr B sat there looking as if he was pleased with himself but trying not to show it. The laughter made Kieran relax and he could see that Rhys felt the same way.

"Rhys! Give Kieran another massage. Let's see if it happens again."

The pattern was irresistible. Kieran turned his head so that Mr B couldn't see, gave a wink, then snuggled into place with his head on Rhys's chest. Gentle fingers started their work and Kieran waited for about thirty seconds before making a dramatic moan and flopping his head from side to side. He heard the same sound from Rhys and then they both lay still, waiting for the reaction.

"Oh no! You poor guys. What am I going to do?"

Mr B carried on with his mock worry and panic till Kieran was nearly bursting with the effort not to smile.

"I know. I'll pour some cold water to wake them up."

Whoops! Would he do that? Kieran knew Mr B kept his canteen near the tent entrance.

"I'm awake. I'm awake."

"Me too. I had a quick recovery."

They talked some more about what happened then Mr B said he was going for his own hot drink.

"Finish giving Kieran that head massage, Rhys, then I think it might be a good idea for him to have an early night. There. Nanny has spoken."

Kieran almost started to say it didn't matter but changed his mind when Rhys began working on his temples.

"Try those other things I mentioned too. Three or four minutes for each, but keep coming back to his temples if that's what relaxes him most."

Mr B left and Kieran lay back, quietly enjoying Rhys's ministrations. It gave him a sense that they were close to each other in a personal kind of way. *What was Rhys thinking?*

"Rhys, I feel like I'm cheating you because my head isn't aching at all."

"I'll keep going. Mr B's ideas always seem pretty sensible to me."

"It is good. If you get a headache I'll do the same for you. Okay?"

The massage was so relaxing that Kieran felt his eyes gradually closing and by the time Mr B got back he was deeply asleep.

*   *   *

The next day was easy but still interesting. There was the hike back to the minibus, then a drive of over an hour to the next campsite. This was all on back roads and the first section skirted the base of the Victoria range. After passing some farmland, they were back in the bush again till they reached the far northern end of the whole Grampians area where they set up camp at a place called Mount Zero.

The following day was loaded with excitement and wonder.

The excitement came after climbing a steep track to reach a mass of rock called Hollow Mountain, where the morning's activity was a mixture of abseiling and exploring the cracks and fissures which formed an inter-connecting set of caves through the top section of the mountain. Kieran loved the abseiling for the adrenaline rush it gave, but he thought wriggling through clefts in the rock to a narrow ledge with a view of the valley below then chimneying up a cleft to find a platform with an overhanging rock ceiling was more like an adventure.

The wonder came when half the group went with Mr B on a five-hour hike across a large area called Flat Rock, through a jumble of gnarled and eroded boulders to a feature called the Amphitheatre where they walked with their heads raised to look at sheer rock faces and cliff walls. The track wound upwards till it eventually turned to follow the wild terrain along the crest of the range where it petered out and disappeared. Now they followed small cairns of rock which showed the way from lookout point to lookout point, from hidden path to rough rock walkway and even, at one stage, leading to a cleft in the rock which could only be crossed via a fallen tree trunk. Now their heads were constantly lowered to peer down the gullies and over the rocky ledges to the valley below. Kieran stayed as close to Mr B as he could because he looked at everything, had fascinating explanations about many things, and made whatever was happening more interesting.

"Look, Kieran, here's a special one for your list."

They'd stopped for five minutes to enjoy the view from a rocky ledge, and Mr B pointed to the sky in the south. Two large birds gliding and circling above the rocky peaks gradually moved closer and closer.

"What are they?"

"Wedge-tailed eagles! Watch how long they fly without flapping their wings."

Closer and closer they came, working their way along the line of the range, wheeling and circling, sometimes near the rocks and sometimes out over the plain. Six pairs of eyes were fixed on the aerial display and as they approached Kieran suddenly realised how big they were.

"Look at the size. The swamp harrier was nothing like that."

"Watch them while you can, Kieran. There are only two eagles in all the world that are bigger than these. Some of the females get close to three metres when their wings are spread."

To bring his point home, Mr B made three large steps from the rock he was sitting on.

"There, that's close to three metres. Isn't it unreal?"

It was hard to believe, and Kieran could see similar expressions on the other faces. In a great sweep, the eagles approached till their features and markings stood out clearly. One was larger than the other and looked almost black. For several minutes they stayed close and Kieran wondered if they were curious. It felt like they were because he could see their fierce eyes.

"Kieran, they're looking at us. Put your arm out like they do in the falconry stories."

"You and your novels, Rhys. They're wild birds."

Shannon jumped up, climbed on a boulder and stuck his arm out, and then Rhys did the same on an even larger rock.

"Come on. Get into the spirit of it."

The look on Rhys's face and the sound of his voice was so persuasive Kieran clambered up next to him and held out his own arm. The great eagles wheeled and shot past only ten metres away.

"Wow, look at that!"

Kieran could hear the awe in Rhys's voice. Rhys dropped his arm but Kieran didn't, and they watched the eagles bank in another wide circle and head back towards them. The larger, dark one was higher in the sky but the other came gliding in from below Kieran's eye-level. With a vast shock, Kieran realised it was coming straight at him. In total disbelief he watched it looming and for several seconds it was as if every bit of motion drained from the world and transferred to the oncoming force. The eagle swept up and, with a sudden wing beat, passed directly over Kieran's head with hardly a metre to spare, leaving him with a thudding heart and an image in his brain of fierce, piercing eyes fixed on his own.

Kieran swivelled to watch the diminishing shape but then a great commotion brought his attention back. His heart lurched because Rhys was lying at the base of the rock. Everyone converged on him, but he'd climbed to his feet by the time they arrived.

"God! It frightened me so much I jumped off the rock."

Mr B was holding his arm by now and wanted to know if he'd hurt himself.

"Ah! My backside."

He rubbed his right buttock and walked around for a couple of steps. "It's all right! But I might end up with a bruised rear, I think. Where are they?"

When Rhys looked around, so did everyone else but the eagles were gone. Everyone talked excitedly about what had happened but then they headed on their way because Mr B was starting to worry about the time.

The last section of their walk was the roughest they'd seen so far and Kieran thought they would have taken hours longer to get through if the little cairns of rock hadn't been pointing the best way. As it was, they spent most of the time climbing low rock walls, picking their way through deep gullies and trying to avoid the clutches of the tough, prickly vegetation. Mr B led all the time and somehow seemed to work out where the next cairn marker was likely to be. Kieran followed him and whenever they came to a climbing or scrambling section Mr B got him to show everyone the best way to tackle it. Rhys kept close, as they were now in the habit of sharing anything interesting with each other.

Back at the campsite the two groups swapped stories. Kevin had taken the keen abseilers to one of the biggest cliffs and they were all excited about having had to use the longest rope for a ninety-metre drop. The evening meal and talking went on for a couple of hours, but then the deepening cold sent most people to the shelter of their tents and the snug warmth of sleeping bags. Kieran thought it was marvellous: sharing the conversation and company with a flickering candle casting a glow on their faces, Mr B's head uncovered, and Rhys's peering out from his down hood. Rhys agreed with Kieran that while the morning's abseiling had been exciting, seeing the eagles was the highlight of the day. Rhys was convinced that the eagle had meant to land on Kieran's arm.

"You could see it slowing down. It was me falling off the rock that frightened it away."

"I don't think so. The slowing down must have been when it changed from gliding to flapping its wings, because it suddenly saw us right in its path."

"That can't be right, Kieran. Eagles have the most amazing eyesight you

could ever imagine and I'm sure it would have been aware of you standing on the rock the whole time you were there. How's that bruise feeling,
Rhys?"

"Sore! But it's all right."

"Give yourself a massage. That'll fix it in a second."

"Comedian. Hey!"

Kieran squawked when Rhys squished him and dug an elbow into his
ribs. "Help! I'm being attacked by a mummy."

"What?"

Everything stopped for the explanation.

"Look at him. With his sleeping bag hood all tied like that, he's an
Egyptian mummy."

This got a laugh. Then away they went:

"King Tut."

"Books of the Dead."

"The Mummy Returns."

"Curse of the Pharaohs."

"Quick. Close your eyes, Kieran. If you look at that face your flesh will
dissolve next time the sun's rays hit you."

"I'm coming to get you."

Rhys rolled over and brought his face close. Kieran screwed his eyes
shut and laughed.

"I saw it, I saw it. It was horrible. One look at that face nearly frightened
me to death."

The mummy made weird moaning noises before digging into Kieran's
ribs again.

"Help! What's it doing? It's trying to rip my heart out."

This started a discussion between Mr B and Rhys about Egyptian
priests who could reach in through a person's chest to pull out a heart for
sacrifice.

"That's not Egyptian, Rhys. That's Aztec. They used to drink the blood
from the hearts of victims and throw the bodies to the crocodiles."

"I wonder why they had pyramids too?"

Kieran listened to all these ideas. He'd have to read more books
himself. It felt friendly with Rhys digging into his ribs but that ended after
a discussion about how to protect against the mummy curse. Mr B and
Rhys decided that smothering his face in sunscreen before he left the tent
in the morning was the most practical.

"But we'll have to keep putting it on all the time and what if he brushes
it off by accident?"

"He'll have a permanent grin then, won't he? We'll cure him though. After we've had breakfast we'll search under rocks or bark for a nice big beetle. You can hold him down, Rhys, and I'll stuff it into his mouth, alive."

"A beetle?"

"Yes, it should be a scarab, but an Aussie beetle should do the trick, since it was an Aussie mummy. There are big black ones around here that would be perfect. When his teeth crunch, the green slime will ooze out and fill his mouth."

"Don't worry, Kieran. It might sound revolting, but we'll make sure you swallow it all."

"It's not that revolting, Rhys. It'll be like eating dry cornflakes with a new flavour. We'll get him to practise at breakfast tomorrow morning with cornflakes from the minibus."

"What about the green slime?"

"I know just the thing."

"Hey! What about the mummy? We'll have to kill it off or it'll just curse me again. I don't want to eat beetle slime every day."

"You can't kill a mummy, Kieran. It's already dead."

The talk went on for another enjoyable hour before Mr B blew the candle out, protesting about noisy students keeping him awake all night. Kieran groaned and protested about noisy lecturers keeping everyone awake with their blinding candles.

In the morning, Kieran woke to the feeling of soft fingers stroking sunscreen on his face.

"You idiot, Rhys."

"You're all protected now."

And after breakfast Mr B carried it further. "Open your mouth, Kieran. Time for your rehearsal."

Crunch! Crunch! It was revolting, but worth it for the look from Shannon and the smiles from Rhys and Mr B, to get through the spoon- ful of dry cornflakes with a squeeze of lime-flavoured toothpaste.

CHAPTER 2

The expedition progressed with a busy time of organising packs and the drive to a new area where the next hike started. After half an hour of walking beside a small creek, past a beautiful waterfall and up a steep scrambling trail, a strikingly desolate scene opened in front of them: a scene of charred trunks and isolated boulders, blackened remnants of vegetation and bare, scorched ground. Cameras and minds recorded this strange, fire-scarred environment which stretched to the base of the huge bluff looming ahead. The trail became meaningless, and after half an hour of meandering from one point of interest to the next, a strange group reached the rocky base of the bluff. Mr B and Kieran, as leaders, were the biggest mess, but everyone looked ready for combat, with blackened clothes and charcoal-smeared skin. Every brush against the vegetation had left dark smudges of burnt ash.

After exploring some rocky overhangs it was time to tackle the bluff itself. Anyone who was worried about the climb was given the option to go with Kevin via an extended, easier route, but no one was interested in that so Mr B led a slow and careful scramble up the sloping rock face. Erosion and weathering meant there were ample hand and foot holds but every now and again a tricky section would demand extra attention and care. Kieran discovered he had a real gift for being able to pick an easy course and felt flattered when Mr B deferred to him in pointing out the best way to suit everyone.

The top of the bluff was magnificent with 360° views. Two mountain ranges stretched in jagged arcs to the south, with a natural lake in the valley between. Mount Stapylton and Hollow Mountain showed in the north, and far below, to the east and west, stretched a great plain of mixed bush and farmland. Rhys stood with Kieran and they traced their route back and down, then traced the path of the wildfire and tried to work out where they'd left the walking trail.

"Tents, everyone. This is our camp for the night. We'll get set up and if anyone is interested we can make a trek to the top of Mount Difficult."

Twenty minutes later the tents were all set and seven of the group were gathered for the trek. Kevin returned from the rocky cliff's edge to their sheltered gully and spoke with Mr B, who then went to the high point with him.

"Trek's off, everyone. We've got a storm coming. If we want to do any cooking we'll have to start the fires now."

They moved the tents, they started the fires, and Kevin and a team of students rushed to collect a good supply of wood.

"We could have an interesting night, Rhys. Does lightning make you nervous?"

"No. Not really."

"Well, it might tonight. Let's watch."

The sight grew more and more spectacular as the storm swept across the plain, closer and closer. Distant bolts of lightning intermittently highlighted the black cloud mass with a random web of angry fire, and the trees rustled a warning of the stirring air. The whole group watched from the highest vantage point with murmurs of awe at the fiery pathways forged in the sky then exclamations when the distant rumbles changed to angry shouts. The light dimmed rapidly as the forerunner clouds raced overhead and Kieran jumped in fright when a huge river of flame struck at the burnt landscape below and a thunderclap so loud he could feel it shook the mountain.

A misty white curtain obliterated everything from view and a spattering of early raindrops sent everyone scurrying.

"Mr B, this is so scary."

"I know. We all wanted to camp on top of a mountain, but we didn't plan on something like this."

The three of them sat in pitch dark, speaking in loud voices over the battering rain, waiting and watching for the next burst of instant daylight and its accompanying sound, till the angry storm front passed, leaving just a constant drumming on the tent fly. The candle flickered to life and Mr B checked to see if water was finding its way in, but there was no sign of any. Kieran listened to the rain for a while, curled in his shell of comfort and warmth, and eventually went to sleep.

The rain stopped by morning, which was a great relief, and by the time they'd made their way down the trail, past the now-rushing waterfall and along the busy, busy creek to the minibus, the cloud cover was breaking and the sun finding its way through.

Half an hour of driving took them to the next destination, an area called Wonderland, and after three hours of exploration they headed for their last campsite of the trip.

The minibus pulled up and the prospect didn't look very interesting at all—just a walking trail heading into the bush—but after loading their backpacks they were soon making their way single file along the base of a great wall of rock.

"Here we are. We've got a roof over our head tonight. You can forget your tents if you like but I don't advise it."

The roof Mr B was talking about was solid rock, stretching up forty metres above the platform, which undercut six or seven metres into the base. Kieran was very tempted to try sleeping out, but he helped Mr B and Rhys put the tent up anyway, all the while listening to comments about volunteering for cryogenic experimentation and how he'd have to be thawed out over the fire in the morning.

"You're a wimp, Rhys."

"I know. But I'll be a warm wimp."

Mr B collected one of the collapsible water carriers. Kieran grabbed another, and thirty metres farther along they collected a supply from a little stream trickling under a jumble of rocks.

"This is why we didn't have to carry water from the minibus. There's always water here."

Kieran was more interested in the rock jumble which sloped upwards between the walls of a gap in the great buttress.

"That's the way to the top … We'll have a look when everyone's settled in."

*   *   *

"What was it?"

"A honeyeater. A white-eared one, and you don't see them very often."

It had been strange. The whole group finished setting up and scrambled to the top of the Bandolier, and Mr B and Kevin were pointing out different features: the Moora Moora water reserve, the wide valley and the section of the Victoria Range which hid the Fortress. Kieran was sitting on a rock next to some scrub, following it all and taking in the details when he heard a close-by rustle and flutter. His eyes tracked, caught the movement, then fixed on a small form peeking from the top of one of those prickly bushes. It hopped from branch to branch with busy, quick movements, its dark head and sharp, pointed beak cocked from side to side, apparently curious about the intrusion into its domain. Kieran held still, hoping not to frighten it away while he rapidly took in the dark head, olive back and yellowish underneath. Mentally, he coaxed it closer, hoping for a clearer view and watching every little movement. With a noisy flip-flap it launched itself and, to Kieran's startlement, landed on his shoulder.

Oh my, this was amazing.

There were tiny tugs at his jumper, a hop, several tugs at his hair, then an extraordinarily pleasant sensation as it stayed for a time on the top of his head. Kevin's voice stopped and Kieran saw from the corner of his eye that the others were looking at him. He didn't move, though, hoping to prolong his little visitor's stay. There was another tug, a flutter of wings and a flash of olive as it disappeared into the brush. Kieran searched for a moment for any last sign then turned his head to the now-obvious silence and the array of surprised and curious looks.

There was quite a discussion, which eventually reached the consensus that the tugs to Kieran's hair and jumper meant it was searching for nesting material.

"Animals like him."

"You think so, Rhys?"

"Well, they come close to him, instead of being scared, like the kookaburra, and I still think the eagle was going to land on his arm before I frightened it."

"Maybe he looks like food?"

"Maybe he smells like nectar?"

"Maybe he gives off good vibrations and attracts them?" Mr B laughed and agreed. Kieran shook his head as the crazy ideas went back and forth and kept him smiling as the group made their way down the gully. He wished this wasn't the last night of their expedition.

The evening meal was fun, and then everyone sat around and talked for ages. Kevin's group, who'd done the abseiling, wanted to try it in the dark, to descend from above and drop to the ledge near the campfire but it was just talk. Shannon wanted to know if this spot would have been an Aboriginal shelter in earlier days and Mr B explained that the whole Grampians range was an important area and that they'd find out more about it the next day when they visited the First Australian Visitor's Centre in Hall's Gap.

"I'm certain it would have been, Shannon, but we'll ask the Elder when he gives us his talk."

"An Elder? A real one?"

"The Centre arranged it when we made our inquiries about visiting. We're very lucky, really, because there's someone from Mparntwe visiting relatives who moved to live here, and he's meant to know a lot about the Dreamtime."

"What's Mparntwe?"

Kieran was curious, too, and he was glad Rhys had asked.

"It's the traditional name for Alice Springs, which is quite a coincidence because it's where we're going for the next college excursion in two months' time."

"In Central Australia? Isn't that too far for a college excursion?"

"Not really, Rhys. We'll be flying, so it won't take much longer to get there than it did for this excursion."

"What about all the equipment?"

"We'll be taking our personal packs and a tour company in Alice Springs will look after the rest."

"There haven't been any notices about it."

"There will be in the week after we get back to college. And if you're interested, anyone who came on this excursion will have priority if we get too many wanting to go."

Kieran was definitely interested and he thought Rhys might be too but he was shaking his head.

"It will cost too much. It'll have to, with the air flights."

"No it won't. Part will be paid by the Student Council, and the college knows that so few students could afford it that the excursion wouldn't go ahead unless they helped out as well. The overall cost won't be much more than this one so if you'd like to go I suggest you put your name in and start saving a few pennies."

"Will you be going?"

"Absolutely. Professor Miles knows that I'm more interested in our First Australians than any other staff member, as well as having experience with student excursions, so I was the first one he asked."

Kieran vaguely knew Professor Miles as someone from the anthropology department.

"There are some wonderful hikes and things to see, Rhys, so don't miss out."

Rhys looked at Kieran, who nodded enthusiastically. If Mr B was going, it was sure to be interesting.

"I'd like to go, but if it's only two months away I wouldn't be able to save enough money without getting a job of some kind, and I'm not going to do that because I need all the time I can spare for my study."

Mr B gave a serious-looking nod.

"Apply for it, Rhys. There's always some way to manage."

"What does 'Elder' mean?"

"It's someone who's very respected in the First Australian community, Kieran, often because they're a natural leader, but sometimes because they have special knowledge or wisdom. I've never spoken to one before, so tomorrow will be quite special."

Shannon went to build up the fire but Kevin stopped him because the time was getting on and the next day would be very busy and long. After making a hot chocolate drink with water from the billy, Kieran and Rhys moved to their tent. They talked about the day for a while and then some more when Mr B arrived after checking everyone was okay. Sleeping outside the tent would have been interesting but Kieran decided that being inside was definitely more friendly and companionable.

*   *   *

Kookaburras woke him in the morning and then there was all the activity of getting breakfast and packing the tents and all their gear for the walk down to the minibus. Rhys wanted to make a quick trip up the gully again to see what Moora Moora looked like in the early morning light but there wasn't enough time, and after half an hour of walking down the trail they were back on the minibus and on their way to Hall's Gap.

*   *   *

He wasn't old. Not really old at any rate. Probably middle-aged. Kieran laughed at himself for having the perception that an Elder would be an old person. The group was gathered in a conference room and Mr B and Kevin had just come in with two members of staff, who'd shown everyone some big photos of the local rock art, and another First Australian who'd made the media presentation in what they called the Dreamtime Theatre. The Elder was darker skinned than any of them and something about him demanded attention. After being introduced he spent some time looking at each person before he spoke.

"Welcome to Country. My people greet you and hope you have enjoyed your stay. Can anyone tell me what season of the year this is?"

Shannon called out that it was autumn.

"Not here. We use more sensible names."

The Elder paused to look for any other response and, in the quiet, Kieran raised his hand. He'd seen this on the wall in the Dreamtime Theatre before the lights went out.

"I think it might be cockatoo time."

"Excellent. I think you might have tracker's eyes … How many of you have seen the big black cockatoos flying overhead and calling with their creaky-door sound?"

There were nods and a general murmur of assent.

"Gariwerd people have six seasons. The one we're in now—Cockatoo—as well as Honey-bee, Nesting Bird, Wildflower, Butterfly and Eel season. Have your teachers told you anything about the Dreamtime?"

There were more looks and nods but no one said anything till Rhys spoke up.

"Mr B told us a bit about it when we were sitting around the campfire. He said it's very complicated."

The Elder nodded, then asked what parts of Gariwerd they'd visited on the trip and listened to the various place names as they were called out.

"There are Dreamtime stories that involve every one of those places. My favourite is the one about how Roses Gap was formed."

Kieran listened, completely fascinated, to the story of Tchingal, the huge emu, and how he chased Waa, the crow, for picking at his egg and made a huge gap in the mountains to get at Waa when he hid in a crack in the rocks. There were more stories and then an explanation of the relationships between First Nation people and how they were divided into two major groups called moieties. Mr B asked a question about why the rock art was so important and whether it would die out with the coming of modern times when people weren't living off the country like they did with the old ways.

"That is a very good question, Mr Teacher, but you are only partly right. Yes, the majority of First Australians now live in towns and cities but there are still many who visit these places to maintain the images and, in most areas, we have a core of people who pass on the local knowledge and heritage."

He looked to the Centre staff, who all nodded. One of them said the Gariwerd area had fifteen people sharing and recording their local Dreamtime stories.

"Are there special places that they don't know about?"

All eyes turned to Rhys and the Elder answered.

"There are many places like that. Why do you ask?"

Rhys turned to Mr B who nodded for him to go ahead.

"We think we found one. Not far from the Fortress."

A rapid interchange passed between the Elder and the staff in a language none of the listening group understood. The Elder held one hand up, signifying Rhys should say no more, then asked to talk with him when the session was finished.

* * *

"The Fortress area is one of the most important in the whole of Gariwerd and we know a number of places which are kept secret. Can you explain the exact location for us?"

"Mr B took us there so he can tell it better."

Kieran nodded. He and Mr B had been asked to accompany Rhys when the Elder learnt that three of them had been to the special spot. Mr B's description was careful and pinpointed the exact location in the minds of the two Centre staff who were with them. There was more talk between the staff and the Elder, but Kieran couldn't understand anything from their conversation.

"Why do you think that might be a special place? Mudgee knows the rocks you speak of but they are not known in the local story."

"They must be. They were faint, but we could definitely see the hand shapes on the rock."

"Hand shapes?"

Mr B took over.

"Rhys is right. I found them by chance on a previous trip and wondered if my imagination was seeing something, but Rhys and Kieran both saw the same thing."

"Kieran even thought the rock went warm when he touched it. That was definitely imagination, but it made us think about it."

Kieran wished Rhys hadn't said that, but then the three of them were astonished at the excited exchange between the Elder and the two staff, and then involved for nearly another ten minutes with questions about the details of their actions at the site and all their feelings and thoughts.

"Thank you, Rhys. We believe you have found something very special indeed, and tomorrow a group of us will investigate the rocks your teacher describes. His directions sound accurate but can you give your own version as a backup?"

Rhys did that, and then Kieran was asked the same thing. The Elder went away somewhere while the two staff explained that if anything came of their investigation they would be acknowledged for their part in it. The Elder returned and formally gave Kieran a short stick with a number of symbols burnt into it.

"When you travel to Mparntwe, present this message stick to my people and they will know you are especially welcome. Other Elders will talk with you and make sure you have an interesting time."

*   *   *

Oh no! Not now.

Kieran fumbled for his cell phone and, through the fog of migraine and unstable vision, pressed the speed dial for Rhys's number. The answer wasn't immediate, not this early in the morning, but eventually it came.

"Hello?"

"Rhys, it's me. Do you think you could come over and help me? I've got the worst migraine ever and I can't even stand up properly. I'd lie in bed and sleep it off, but the scholarship exam starts in two hours."

"What? You can't even stand? You want me to get a doctor?"

"No, a doctor will just make me stay in bed. Can we try a head massage, like at the Fortress? It's my only chance to do the scholarship."

There was a silence before Rhys answered, "I'll be there as soon as I can."

Kieran closed his eyes and waited. In the quiet the throb in his temples was more noticeable and again he felt like yelling at it to go away. The knock on the door came sooner than expected, and walking to unlock it was so disorienting he had to crawl then haul himself up by feel to unsnib the lock.

"You look awful. I really think we should get a doctor."

"Help me back to the bed first, Rhys."

Rhys's strong arm was supporting him in a flash.

"When I open my eyes everything's double vision and weird, and I get so off-balance I can't stand up. I took a tablet but it's useless … Can we try the massage thing, please? It might help, and if it doesn't I'll get a doctor."

Rhys didn't say anything, just positioned himself on the edge of the bed and rested a hand on Kieran's forehead.

"You don't feel hot. Where do you want me to start? Rubbing your temples like the other time?"

"Yes, please."

"Both temples at the same time?"

"Yes."

After a few moments of gentle rubbing, Rhys asked if he should keep going or try something else.

"Stay like that. It's where the throbbing seems to be and it feels good."

Rhys's fingers worked, and then hesitated. Kieran surfaced at the cessation of the comforting attention.

"What?"

"Your skin's starting to feel warmer."

Kieran pressed his own fingertips to his temples. "It feels normal to me. It might be from the rubbing."

Rhys resumed his ministrations and gave a laugh at Kieran's murmurs of appreciation.

"Yikes! I'm sure you're warmer."

Kieran automatically opened his eyes to check Rhys's expression then hastily scrunched them shut again.

"You're going to zap me again. I remember this feeling from last time."

Kieran started to answer, but didn't. Rhys was right, and exactly like last time the strange sensation of heat but not heat welled … and welled … and welled.

*   *   *

What? Now he was being crushed?

Kieran opened his eyes and abruptly smiled. Rhys was sprawled right across his chest, holding him trapped.

Oh my! No throbbing. No trouble with his eyes. Rhys really had fixed him.

Kieran took proper stock of himself and laughter and amazement built together. Apart from being trapped, he felt good. No, not just good, really good.

Rhys was breathing slowly and steadily and he appeared to be relaxed and asleep. Kieran lay still, remembering that Rhys had taken a few minutes longer to wake last time. What *was* the time? Ten to eight. A quick calculation showed about fifteen minutes of missing time and forty minutes till he needed to head for the exam room. Four minutes passed before Rhys stirred, opened his eyes and stared, then sat up abruptly.

"You did it again! Are you all right?"

"Totally, apart from being crushed by a great lump for the last twenty minutes. What about you? Do you feel different?"

Rhys looked at his hands. "They must have burns on them somewhere but they don't."

"Rhys, you fixed me. I can't believe this. You're amazing!"

"Not me. You're the one with a million volts zapping out of you. I said you're like a human battery and this proves it. Kieran, you better get up and get ready."

Kieran looked at his clock: 8:05 a.m.

"We'll talk about it later. Do you want some toast?"

Time was now pressing, and Kieran rushed through a shower, dressed in his black jeans and white T-shirt with the dragon image, gobbled a couple of pieces of the toast, then headed out with Rhys beside him.

"This is amazing. I was so miserable and now my mind's as clear as anything. I feel like I'm going to do really well. You must have pushed extra energy into me."

"As if … You'll do well because you studied so hard."

"I'm going to make sure you get top marks for your Maths and Physics."

"Physics? I don't need help with that. I'm already passing. You just want to do more slave driving."

"Only if you want to."

* * *

Tan was looking distinctly worried, and Kieran felt sorry for him. There were two others doing the exam but they meant nothing to Kieran as they were from different class groups and he only knew them by sight. There was still an hour to go in this three-hour sitting and any apprehension of his own had disappeared in the fifteen-minute pre-reading time, when he worked out that he wouldn't even have to tackle the only two questions in the third section that looked puzzling. The third section was always the most difficult and today was no exception. Except that, in a complete departure from all the previous exams, the instructions said to attempt only four of the seven questions being presented. Now the only concern was time, and even with this he was ahead of his early plan. An undercurrent of excitement started to bubble, but he pushed it aside and focused on the question in front of him.

"Ten minute warning, students."

Kieran looked up, startled. He was almost finished. There was only a graphical representation still to do and Mr B's method meant it would be straightforward.

There was a five-minute warning while he was carefully finishing all his labelling, and all that was left was to check that every page was named and in proper order.

* * *

"Are you all right? Is your head aching? Can you see properly? How did you go?"

Kieran smiled at this criss-cross of questions coming from Mr B and Rhys, who were waiting at the door.

"I'm totally all right. And it went really well. I even finished the whole third section."

Mr B shook his head. "You couldn't have. You never managed with any of the practice tests, and anyway, it's designed so you can't."

"They changed it so you could choose any four out of seven questions."

"You had enough time to do the whole four?"

"Only just. I nearly got finger cramps from writing so quickly but that's Rhys's fault for giving me so much extra energy."

Mr B looked back and forth between them. "Amazing. Will we celebrate tonight?"

"Before I even get the results?"

"Were your four questions right?"

"Yes."

"Then we'll celebrate. You'll have that tutoring job next year and, Rhys, you're being coached by an honour-level student."

"An honour-level slave driver you mean."

"Kieran, explain what happened with this head massage business. Rhys says you both passed out again but it cleared your migraine."

"And my eyes. He's got magic fingers."

*   *   *

"That's crazy. He was there in the room with us all the time. He knows I couldn't have, and why's he getting you to tell me all this? He should be doing it himself."

It was a week after the scholarship exam and Mr B had just told Kieran the senior maths lecturer was claiming he must have cheated somehow because his results were too good to be true.

"He knew I'd been coaching you, Kieran, and that it was on my recommendation you'd entered. He discussed it with me and we decided you'd accept it better from me."

"I don't accept it. It's completely untrue."

"After all that effort and your level of achievement I don't accept it either, but word came in from several students that you knew the questions before you went in."

"That's crazy too." Kieran's anger began lifting to a new level … "Did that come from Tan?"

"No, it didn't. Why?"

"We had a big talk the day after to compare notes and I *did* tell him I knew all the questions, but I meant I knew how to do them, not what they were. He understood that, because he said the first two sections were all right but he only knew how to do two questions from the last section and he only had time to do one of them."

"Where were you? When you spoke about it I mean."

"Waiting in the hallway for the door to get unlocked for our Physics class."

"So there would have been other students there?"

"The whole class. The lecturer was five minutes late and we couldn't get in."

"Hmm, that has to be where it came from then."

It didn't feel right to Kieran. "If they heard us they knew what I meant. I think they've changed it on purpose to make it sound bad."

Kieran searched his memory for who had been standing close by when he and Tan were talking.

"It was Mark Geston, wasn't it?"

"… What? I can't say, Kieran. It was in confidence."

Mr B's startled look said it all though. *What was with Geston?* He was always giving Kieran a rough time. Rhys too.

"The other problem is your perfect score. It's never happened before, and because of this accusation of dishonesty he wants you to face a panel of four lecturers. I'd really advise it, Kieran. If you do go ahead they'll see the competence I've explained to them, and if you don't the cloud of suspicion will deepen."

"It's wrong, Mr B, but I don't have any choice, do I?"

*   *   *

The High King puzzled at his Lore Master's report.

"Interference? To the workings of a triad of power?"

"Your son has befriended a fellow student who can channel our energy projections. It's known to occur with a small number of humans but seeing it actualised is almost unheard of. The combination of the right human, one of our people infused with power, and the laying on of hands is a combination we haven't seen since the Crossover."

"The laying on of hands is an act of faith, Uirebon, and your report makes no mention of any involvement with a human religion."

"There is no involvement. The human friend was massaging Keryth's temples in the hope of relieving his headache, and the contact channelled the energy the triad was applying."

"All that power? Does it transfer to the human?"

"Harmlessly, and then dissipates almost immediately."

"Amazing, Uirebon. Our triad will be recovering from the backlash for days and the human is unaffected. How will you resolve the situation? We can't allow any interference with Keryth's treatment."

"Resolution will require a second triad working in conjunction with our first when they recover."

Aglaron nodded as he fully understood the requirements in any attempt at safely affecting a human mind.

"What of this slur on Keryth's honesty? Is it just some misguided human heading for troubles he can't imagine, or is there more to it?"

Uirebon raised his eyebrows. The High King was showing his usual perceptiveness.

"Maynor has taken it on himself to personally manage Keryth's sojourn in the Human World and this is one of the challenges you requested. He will afford protection in the event of any overreaction by Keryth."

"Overreaction? Surely not? Keryth has always managed the Game of Will with finesse and understatement."

"The human involved has a dominating personality and he sees Keryth's independence and disregard as a threat to his position as leader of the pack."

A hint of amusement lightened Aglaron's demeanour.

"The bonds of conformity have never had much hold over Keryth. You think this human will evoke a strong response?"

"Most certainly. He has physical strength, a highly confrontational manner, and a strong disposition to impose his will on those around him."

Aglaron nodded.

"Good. I will watch with great interest to see how Keryth's human persona affects his way of dealing with this."

A twinkle of light flashed from a ring of control on Aglaron's little finger.

"Arrange a far-seeing, Uirebon. Narello is making further extensions to her border and I wish to understand her motive."

*   *   *

Kieran sat up with the groan, wished he hadn't, collapsed back on his bed, then, when the appearance of Rhys sitting on the nearby chair registered, ignored his nauseous feelings and struggled upright again.

"Rhys, what happened?"

"You passed out in the residence lounge. You said it was your allergy to alcohol."

Memory flashed of being violently ill on the lounge room floor and gales of laughter coming from a group of nearby students. That wasn't what he'd meant.

"Not to me, to you. The tissues? And your face is bruised."

"It's all right now. My nose was bleeding but it's nearly stopped."

Kieran tried to make a link between his passing out and Rhys's nose bleeding and felt shock and dismay.

"Did I do it? Was I violent or something?"

"What? No! That was Geston and his group. They were going to give you a Mohawk haircut and shave off your eyebrows. I had to stop them."

"What?"

"You passed out, Kieran, and they knew it was going to happen because they had scissors and a razor there ready. When you threw up they all laughed, and then when you rested your head on the table they were all watching. I was trying to wake you up when they grabbed me and pulled you onto the floor. Geston was saying you were a cheat and a misfit and a smart alec and they were going to put you in your place for being a disgrace to the college."

Kieran stared in disbelief. "You fought them?"

"I had to. They wouldn't let me go, and when they put shaving cream on your eyebrows Geston took out the safety razor. I had to kick one of the guys in the stomach to get at him."

"You got Geston?"

"Just long enough to stop him. They all ganged up on me then and that's when my nose got hit. They were holding me, and the guy I kicked punched me twice before I got away again and chased after him. They all ran off then, except Geston."

"He stayed?"

"Only till I told him his nose was next. I think I scared him because I had blood on my face and hands and the top of my shirt … I was losing my temper because they've been picking on you too much."

Kieran struggled to take it all in. Quiet, gentle Rhys fighting off a whole group? Yes, he was strong enough. His endurance with swimming and the ease with which he could overcome Kieran when they had a friendly wrestle was evidence of that, but the capability of enough aggression to scare off Geston was not something Kieran would have expected.

"Geston was scared?"

"He looked like he was. My temper's bad if I ever let it out, Kieran, but it was all wrong. Getting at you through your allergy could be really danger-ous. People with peanut allergies have to go to hospital sometimes, or even worse."

"Are you sure they knew? I've never told anyone."

"They had the scissors and razor there, so it means one of them got to your drink. Do you still feel bad?"

"It will last a while, but when I feel ready I'll go for a long walk and that will clear it out of my system."

"I'll come with you to make sure you're all right."

"How did I get back here?"

"I carried you. You told me before you flaked out that the only thing you needed was to go to bed, so that's what I did, and then I waited for you to wake up."

Kieran stared as another realisation hit him.

"You put me in my tracksuit?"

"I couldn't find any PJs and the trackie was on the floor beside your bed. I had to, Kieran. Your clothes were revolting because when they put you on the floor it was right where you'd been sick. They did that on purpose too. I reckon they should get kicked out of the residences."

Kieran went quiet while he watched Rhys dab his nose with a tissue.

"I know when they messed with my drink. There were two others waiting while I made it, and I remember someone in the room dropped a bottle or glass and the sound of it breaking made everyone look round. It must have been on purpose to distract me."

Kieran swung his feet to the side of the bed and tried standing up. Not the best, but walking it off would work.

"I'll go by myself. Walking in the cold air might start your nose bleeding again."

"No way. I'm staying with you to make sure you're all right. You might flake out again."

Kieran knew he wouldn't flake out, but he didn't argue because Rhys's company was important at the moment.

*   *   *

"Chunder features! Want another drink?"

Derisive laughter followed the jibe when Kieran walked into the lounge and every face watched in expectation that he'd back off and leave. After all, there were six of them and he didn't have crazy Rhys to protect him. Kieran's only response was to fix his gaze on Geston.

"Nothing to say? Cat got your tongue? Get him a drink … and make sure none of it spills on him."

One of the hangers-on moved to the drinks machine and there were smiles all round at the implication that the drink would indeed end up in his hair or his clothes.

Kieran said nothing.

"We hear you missed out on the scholarship."

More snickers confirmed in Kieran's mind that Geston was behind the accusation he'd cheated, and the gloating tone of the question lifted his determination yet another notch. He made no response though, and continued his silent watching. After a slight frown of puzzlement Geston made several more disparaging remarks then took the now-ready drink and closed the distance between them. With blatant deliberateness he upended the mug onto Kieran's hair. The hot liquid soaked his scalp, stinging as it made its way down his neck to his shirt.

The strange lack of reaction checked the few laughs, and there was a moment of silence before Geston gave a mocking grunt.

"Weak as piss. Fill the mug up again."

Kieran shifted his attention slightly and the guy taking the mug off Geston saw something that made him jump backwards in alarm. He took another look, and then, with his hands held protectively in front of him, he backed farther away before rushing to the door.

"Hey? What?"

Geston's voice sounded in the general startlement at this sudden and inexplicable behaviour. There was no laughter now. Every set of eyes was fixed on Kieran.

Geston broke in yet again. "Ricky, man! Chunder features here hasn't had enough."

Kieran switched his attention again and allowed a little more force and intent to show. As if struck by a physical blow, Ricky felt the strength of will suddenly directed at him and every skerrick of his group bravado vanished. In a wash of fear that froze him on the spot, every hair follicle tightened and his face flushed with an overpowering surge of adrenaline while he tried to avoid the gaze.

"Hey!"

Ricky was released. His legs gave way, and as he collapsed in the nearest chair he watched three of his friends rushing to get out of the room while Mark stood motionless.

"Don't … ever … hurt … Rhys … again."

Mark passed out and it took several minutes before Ricky could move from the chair to help him.

* * *

"Are you okay, Kieran? There's a weird story spreading that you attacked people in the lounge."

"Weird's right. I don't even know what happened myself."

Kieran was sitting at his study desk, trying to understand the reactions to his confrontation with Geston and work out what he should do about it, when Rhys's knock on the door interrupted his puzzled thoughts.

"Did Geston start something again?"

"Is your nose hurting much? I was thinking about it the whole time we were walking and when I was by myself it made me so angry I had to go to the lounge. I knew they'd be there and I had to tell them to leave you alone."

"It's okay if I don't touch it. The bleeding stopped ages ago … but why did you go when Mr B said to stay away from them? It's a wonder they didn't finish shaving your eyebrows or cutting your hair off."

"I think they were going to but everything went crazy."

"Crazy?"

"I was already mad at them for hurting you, and then Geston tipped a mug of drink in my hair and something snapped inside."

"You lost your temper? That's what I would have done."

"Sort of, but not really. All I did was look at them. That Ricky guy who's always with them collapsed on a chair, and when I told Geston not to touch you ever again he flaked on the spot."

"Flaked? Like unconscious?"

"I think so. I left because I was feeling strange."

"You just looked at him and he passed out?"

"And the others all ran like they were scared."

"Wow! Did you feel hot?"

"What?"

"The same as when you zap me."

"… No, it was nothing like that."

Rhys went quiet, but then he laughed. "I'd better be careful about slave driving you at swimming or you'll give me a look and I'll flake out."

"Idiot! I'll give it to you now."

Rhys shuddered and cowered away, but he couldn't stop grinning. Kieran felt tension he hadn't realised was still there drain away.

"I know! It's your Greek ancestry."

"Greek? Rhys, I'm not Greek."

"Yes, you are. Your great, great, something or other grandma could freeze people on the spot and you've inherited it from her."

"What are you raving about?"

"You know. Medusa! You've got snakes in your hair and they come out when you're angry. I saw them when you gave me the look."

"I didn't give you any look."

"I know. D'you reckon you could though?"

"What? And make you scared of me if it works? No way."

"Try it. You need to know if it's real or just a weird fluke where they all psyched each other out somehow."

"Really try it? On you? What if it *does* work?"

"Stop and give me a smile instead. You've got good smiles."

Kieran was dubious but, after more coaxing, tried his evil eye on Rhys. Nothing happened. Rhys kept carrying on that he was quaking in his boots, his blood was freezing in his veins, and wanting a mirror to see if his hair was turning white, but they both kept smiling at the strangeness of the experiment.

"Kieran, how am I meant to get frightened when you keep smiling?"

"And how am I meant to stop smiling when you keep saying your muscles are turning to jelly and your knees are knocking together?"

"All right. We'll both be serious."

Still nothing happened.

"Stop thinking it's me. I'm Geston and I've just poured drink over you. Remember the feelings you had, then bring them into your mind and act it out."

Kieran did just that and a tinge of the determination and anger he'd felt surfaced.

"Go away, Geston! I don't want you coming anywhere near us."

As soon as he said Geston's name Kieran felt he was being overdramatic and looked for the resultant smile. Instead, Rhys was staring at him.

"What?"

Rhys stared a bit longer, then shook his head and leaned back. "Whoo! Just as well you stopped."

Rhys was carrying on with the joke and Kieran laughed … till he saw his expression.

"That was … scary. Kieran, it worked. It really worked. I felt like I was going to panic."

"You're not joking?"

"I was till that last bit. Before that you looked like you were acting. What did you do different?"

"Just what you said. I remembered when he poured the drink over me and a bit of the same feeling came back."

"A bit? No wonder those guys ran. Try to do it again."

"Right now? What if you panic again?"

"That'll prove it's real."

It didn't take much effort, and after Rhys's quick recovery, they puzzled it over for ages.

*   *   *

The maths coordinator gave an affirming nod. "You certainly understand the graphical representation techniques, Kieran. How would you apply them to this problem?"

He passed a printed question over, and after a quick perusal Kieran looked up.

"This was a section C question from four years ago and the answers come from finding the two maxima and an inflection point. You should ask me original questions so I can show you my understanding and not just my memory."

"You remember the methods used for all the previous section C questions?"

"And the answers, but we only did five years' worth so it's not many."

"And you remember the answers for this question? I might have changed some of the variables."

"You didn't."

Kieran reeled off the answers and the coordinator checked another sheet of paper.

"Extraordinary! Now, how would you tackle this problem?"

Kieran took the new sheet and read it through carefully. "This one's hard but I can do most of it. There's a part at the end I don't understand."

"Can you write the logical steps you would use?"

Five minutes later Kieran looked at Mr B.

"I'm still stuck on the last part. The answer is the area between the curve and the axis but I don't know how to calculate it."

Mr B looked at the coordinator.

"That is the integration section of Kieran's course which we haven't reached yet. It's also beyond the scope of the scholarship."

"It is. I included it because his scholarship answers showed a degree of proficiency I wanted to test. Let me look at that outline please, Kieran."

The formal tone from the start of the interview was suddenly gone.

"Yes, this *is* extraordinary. I devised this question to be more difficult than any on the scholarship and this outline shows an understanding of every concept needed.

"Kieran, I apologise for putting you through all this, but the combination of your unusual results and the allegations of cheating couldn't be overlooked. Your scholarship is confirmed, and I'm particularly impressed with your grace and cooperation through this whole unfortunate matter."

CHAPTER 3

Rhys was reading a novel outside and his face lit up at Kieran's happy expression.

"That wasn't long. You said you might be doing a whole new exam."

"They asked me about the methods I'd use instead. I could tell they were on my side almost straight away. Mr B must have told them about the study method we used because they got me to use it for only one problem."

"Just one? And they've given back your scholarship?"

"The coordinator was great. I was nervous about him at the start but as soon as I talked about the graphing stuff I could tell he was impressed."

"Well, Mr B said it would be okay."

"It's better than okay. As a kind of make-up for being called a cheat my scholarship starts as soon as I get back from Central Australia instead of two months later. Geston's practically done me a favour by starting it all because they're even offering me one of the private residences if I want it."

"Will you take it, or are you still going to look for a share house?"

"I don't know. The private residences are great because they're all on campus. I wouldn't have to worry about transport, but they're all one-bedroom setups and there wouldn't be room for anyone else."

"If you go to a share house there might be people you don't like."

"Not the way I'm thinking of doing it. I'd get a place under my own name and pick whoever I want."

"That would cost a lot. Rent's high for houses in this area."

"It's not too bad three suburbs away."

"That would mean travel time every day."

"I know, but the tram stops right at the college entrance so that's no big deal."

Rhys laughed. "Sounds like you've already made your mind up."

"Not really. It depends."

"It does? On what?"

"I have to find someone really friendly who likes to slave drive me at swimming."

"Me?"

The big smile that Kieran loved spread all over Rhys's face and Kieran knew it was going to happen.

"Of course, you."

"I hope you can cook, then."

"Cook?"

"I'm hopeless at it."

"Rhys. You're crazy."

"No, I'm not. I like eating. Have you seen any good places anywhere?"

"About four or five possibles, but we'd have to check them out to know what they're really like. Can you come with me for the next few weekends to have a look?"

Rhys nodded. "Wow! You getting your scholarship's great but I think a share house is even better. How big do you want it to be? If there were a few others it would be cheaper."

"I know, but they'd have to be people we both like."

"How about Tan? You could ask him. He's friendly. And he's got a car. That could help with transport."

"Hey, that's a great idea. We'll find out if he can cook first."

"Idiot."

*   *   *

The next few weeks were busy with looking for a share house and getting organised for the big expedition to Central Australia. Tan was enthusiastic about the idea of moving into a share house, especially as it would be cheaper than college accommodation prices, and he drove them to seventeen different places they wanted to check. It was his opinion which ended up deciding them on a big old four-bedroom place with a back and side verandah. At first glance they'd discarded it because it looked run down and didn't match the standards of all the other places, but then Tan pointed out that the enclosed storage area on the back verandah could be used as a study or an extra room for another person, and Rhys liked the idea that it was slightly cheaper.

"What do you think, Kieran? It's old. But it's got lots of room and it's the closest one to college too. I reckon we should snap it up."

Tan nodded his agreement as well. A drive to the estate agent made it a done deal, with a lease starting the week before the end of the semester break.

*   *   *

Kieran and Rhys had their places confirmed for the Alice Springs trip and in the two weeks before their departure there was an administration meeting about the itinerary and equipment, and then another very interesting session with Professor Miles who gave them a whole lot of background information.

There was no further trouble from Geston and his group, and Rhys laughed at the way they carefully avoided any contact. Kieran was pleased because the scary-look thing was on his mind, and with the other unusual occurrences lately he didn't want it to happen again.

Most days they spent some time at the college swimming pool because that was how Rhys kept fit. Mr B turned up a couple of times to coach Kieran. He'd promised a couple of sessions on the night he'd invited them round to celebrate Kieran's scholarship win, and Rhys kept complaining that wasn't fair because he was now being beaten in both backstroke and freestyle.

* * *

"I can't believe this is happening."

Kieran smiled because Rhys had said this three times so far. At the moment he was staring through the small window of the jet as the vast expanse of inland Australia passed steadily below. Technically, the window seat he was occupying was his, but because of the novelty of it all he'd been making swaps with Kieran so they could share the view. Without the college subsidy, Rhys wouldn't have been able to afford this expedition, and now that they were on their way excitement was bubbling through his normally quiet manner.

Kieran was just as excited and the thought that they'd be camping near the great monolith of Uluru that night was the biggest thing in his mind now that they were approaching Mparntwe. Everyone else called it Alice Springs, but after the talk with the Elder who'd given them the message stick, Mr B had got them into the habit of using the First Australian name. The message stick was stored safely in his pack for when they returned to Mparntwe in four days' time.

"Look! It's the airport."

* * *

"A barking frog?"

Rhys pressed the button to hear the recording of the Centralian tree frog again. The last three days exploring Uluru had been wonderful and today they were back in Mparntwe before heading off for two days at Kings Canyon. This morning they were at the nature park where many of the local birds and animals were on display. Kieran knew most of the birds because his competition with Mr B to get the biggest list was really going well and his tally was four ahead. The most impressive creature he'd seen was a giant perentie lizard which had sent Mr B and Rhys into a conversation about dragons. Their guide out at Uluru had told everyone to keep an eye out for the lizards but the only one they'd seen was a roadkill on the track between the camping ground and the Rock. The Rock had been amazing because, since the professor was with them, the whole group had been taken to a special place where ordinary tourists couldn't go, and they'd seen curious formations and listened to a Dreamtime explanation of how the Rock came to be.

"Make it bark, Kieran. It will listen to you."

That was a stir because two emus had followed Kieran for a quarter of an hour till he went through a gate to an enclosed section of the sanctuary. And then, ignoring everyone else, a big red kangaroo hopped close and stared at him.

"As if."

It was hard to ignore Rhys's theory about animals reacting to him though. Kieran moved his head close to the glass. Eyes blinked open, the frog's head turned towards him, and Rhys exclaimed with delight.

"See! It's watching you."

*   *   *

This centre was much bigger than the one at Gariwerd and there were people everywhere, marvelling at the murals, paintings and cultural artefacts on display. Professor Miles had arranged a private session for the tour group and Kieran was eager for it to get started. Because he was holding the message stick from Gariwerd, several First Australians had already checked him out, but he hadn't offered it to anyone because Mr B said whoever took the group presentation would be the best person. Professor Miles appeared from an office and Kieran's eagerness lifted because the dark-skinned person beside him was the Elder they'd met at Gariwerd. Kieran watched his eye traverse the twenty-one people of the group then light up with recognition.

"Welcome to Country."

He spoke to the general group, but then gave Kieran, Mr B, and Rhys a nod and a smile.

"Let's move to the auditorium. We have arranged a greeting ceremony and a special show to introduce you to some of our local traditions."

In the auditorium the lights were low. There was the rhythmic tapping of music sticks and, as the school group moved to find seats, two young people in ceremonial costumes painted everyone's forehead with an ochre stripe. Kieran's was a rich red.

The presentation went for half an hour, with a mixture of modern media and a group of First Australians dancing and acting while three Elders spoke. Mr B whispered that they were being given special treatment.

There was a time for questions at the end and then the Elder asked if anyone wanted to learn a ceremonial dance. Kieran couldn't resist because the rhythm of the background music had been getting to him throughout the whole presentation and he jumped to his feet along with four others. Rhys didn't move. He was too reserved. The five unsuspecting volunteers were taken to a side room where they were dressed in baggy loincloths and feathers were clipped to their hair. Back in the auditorium they lined up to face the dancers who'd performed during the presentation. Kieran peeked over and saw Rhys with the biggest grin ever.

The four dancers made a kind of stamping movement then waited. Kieran understood he was meant to copy so he did just that. There was laughter at the ragtag effort by the visitors but that died away and changed to a few claps over the next five minutes while a series of moves was demonstrated, copied and learnt.

Two of the dancers looked to be about twelve or thirteen years old. One was an adult. The leader—he must be because the others were taking their cues from him—was very striking in appearance and action and Kieran quickly stopped looking at the others. There was something unusual, though, and Kieran puzzled at it till he realised there was no eye contact. *Strange.* The adult gave the leader a guiding touch. *Oh my! He's blind!*

For the next five minutes, Kieran lost himself in the spirit of the dance, stamping and leaping in time with the blind leader, thrilled by the sound and movement. After a great aggressive bound they'd learnt, the dancers froze, the music stopped, and after lots of clapping, the audience gathered on the stage. Rhys rushed close.

"You looked amazing, Kieran. I didn't know you could dance so well."

Kieran was a bit surprised. He did love dancing but in his mind the blind guy who'd led them was the amazing one. He wanted to thank him but couldn't because he was being led through an exit by the older dancer. Kieran pointed.

"He's the amazing one, Rhys. He's blind and he showed us everything."

"Blind? Are you sure?"

"See, he's touching the other guy's arm so he knows where to go."

The door closed after the pair, and Rhys turned wondering eyes to Kieran. "Wow! It didn't look like it."

Mr B joined them.

"Another hidden talent, Kieran? You looked like a First Australian. We'll have to ask if you can keep your costume so you can put on shows for us round the campfire."

Kieran suddenly felt out of place and moved to the side room for his clothes. The blind boy was there, now wearing a raggedy pair of jeans and tying the laces of his runners, and by the time Kieran was dressed he was gone again. Mr B and Rhys weren't in the auditorium, which was weird because everyone else was, but Professor Miles saw him looking round and came straight over.

"Well done, Kieran. That was a great exhibition. Burrimul has taken Rhys and Mr B for a conference and they're waiting for you in the front office.

"A conference?"

"It's nothing to do with the tour so I have no idea. Burrimul said it was private business."

Kieran rushed to the office. He had no idea either, except maybe it could be something to do with the message stick which he was holding again. Mr B looked excited and Rhys was almost goggle-eyed. *Now what?*

Mr B spoke. "We're going to miss out on the open-air theatre, Kieran. Burrimul wants to welcome us to his family and we're going to be part of a proper corroboree."

Mr B looked to Burrimul.

"Yes, Kieran, while I was there the site at Gariwerd was visited three times by the local Elders and they all agreed it's a sacred place that had been lost to their knowledge. My people would like to thank you for restoring it to us. Would you accept our offer?"

Kieran wondered why Burrimul was asking him. It was Mr B who'd found the place. Mr B and Rhys were both nodding emphatically though, so maybe this was a formality which meant they had to agree independently. With sudden insight, Kieran realised this was an important moment. He straightened and instinctively assumed a mantle of dignity and courtesy.

"Burrimul, I deem it an honour. Your court is mine and my court is yours."

The moment passed and, as Kieran took in the three sets of wondering eyes, the words he'd just said replayed in his mind. Deem? Where did that come from? Rhys was sure going to stir him about it later.

* * *

The professor saw the three of them off when the crowded minivan collected them at the camping park. He must have been envious because his interests were much more with the corroboree than a movie show, but his duty of care meant he had to stay with the rest of the group. Kieran felt slightly guilty accepting one of the three available seats while others were standing, but they *were* the guests. *Oh my!* He was sitting next to the blind dancer. Kieran took stock as the minivan made its way along the busy highway. Apart from Burrimul, who was driving, there were twelve First Australians, all young looking. The blind boy said something that must have been about Kieran, in what must be their own language, and there were smiles all round and several responses.

"Sorry. I should speak English, shouldn't I? I wondered if you were nervous about being in a bus full of strangers. My name is Woorawa."

A hand extended and Kieran jumped to accept the proffered handshake.

"Hi, I'm Kieran. I was dancing with you at the Centre this afternoon."

The firm grip tightened a little but didn't let go and Kieran wondered if this was a blind person's way of assessing who they were with.

"Neat. We'll have lots of dancing tonight. Will you want to join in?"

Kieran nodded, then felt silly.

"Yes, we all will."

Rhys had an 'I'll get you' look at that but he didn't seem too worried. Mr B was smiling.

"Uncle thinks the spirits spoke to you at Gariwerd so we're taking you to our own sacred place … Do you know our Caterpillar Story?"

"Only what they explained at the Centre this afternoon. Our professor told us parts of it too."

"Uncle Burrimul, can I tell Kieran the Caterpillar Dream?"

Burrimul glanced back from his driving. "Yes, Woorawa, you can tell it to our guests while we get ready."

The streetlights ended as the minivan left the outskirts of the town and the only light to see anything by was a small courtesy lamp. Kieran glanced out the windows but everything was pitch black.

"Is your college a good place?"

Kieran wasn't quite sure what Woorawa wanted to hear. "I think it is. We have some good lecturers and there are lots of things to do."

"Do you have a hobby?"

"Not really, except for swimming. I use most of my time to study."

"Does that mean your college has its own pool?"

"Yes, and my slave driver makes me use it nearly every day."

"Slave driver?"

Kieran laughed. "Not really. He's my friend and he likes to train hard."

"Is he a good friend?"

Kieran was tempted to say something cheeky but he didn't. "He's the best. He's looking at us."

"Do you call him 'slave driver'?"

"Yes, I do, but if I say it now he'll kill me. His name is Rhys."

"Hello, Rhys. Are you really a slave driver?"

Woorawa's hand went out again and Rhys leaned across to take it.

"No, I'm not. He just says that."

"How do you kill him?"

"Easily. He's so weak and puny."

So much for Rhys's usual reserve. He was already comfortable with Woorawa.

"Are you strong?"

"Not really."

The extended handshake changed as Woorawa's grip tightened. Rhys responded in kind.

"Mr B is our friend too. He's sitting next to Rhys."

The battle of strength ended and Woorawa's hand reached again.

"Hello, Mr B. Is that your real name?"

"Hello, Woorawa. I try to get them to call me Peter but somehow I'm stuck with Mr B. We're having an interesting time in Mparntwe and listening to your Dreamtime story will be wonderful. Will you be dancing as well?"

There was a general laugh.

"Woorawa always dances. We couldn't stop him." This came from a guy sitting on the other side of Woorawa.

"We all dance, Mr B, unless we're making the music."

The van slowed and turned off the Ross Highway onto a gravel track.

"We're nearly there, and when the van stops there's a short walk to our meeting place. When we get there I'll show you the way to our Caterpillar paintings. Have you got a torch?"

"We've all got headlamps."

The minivan stopped and turned into a parking area where the sweep of its headlights showed a dozen other vehicles. There was a light touch on Kieran's arm and he understood he was being asked for help. After the bustle of leaving the minivan, Kieran took in the dark of the surrounding night and a red glow flickering in the distance.

"Can you see where we have to go?"

The light touch was there again and Kieran decided he liked the sense of trust that went with it.

"You mean the campfire?"

"That's it. Just follow the others. It's an easy track. It's all sandy."

Five or six of the others rushed ahead and Burrimul led the slower group.

*   *   *

"Can you see the caterpillars moving?"

For the last ten minutes, Kieran, Rhys, and Mr B had listened, first to a song which they didn't understand because it was in First Australian, and then to the Dreamtime story of how the fight between the three giant caterpillars and their enemies, the stinkbugs, had formed the mountain ranges and other local Mparntwe features.

They'd left the gathering near the big campfire and with Woorawa's guidance made their way to a cleared space near a rock face covered with sacred paintings. There, they started a little fire with the twigs and sticks they'd been prompted to collect. At that moment, they were using Kieran's headlamp for a close look at the striking caterpillar representations.

"In my mind I can. Why do they look so fresh? I thought they were hundreds of years old."

"They're much older than that. We have a repainting ceremony whenever they fade. Can you see the colours properly?"

Kieran switched his headlamp to high-strength and the rich red ochre stood out more.

"Yes, my torch is bright and the colours are strong. Woorawa, there are a lot more stripes than just three caterpillars."

"Can you see the red dots at the top?"

The red dots were obvious. Kieran suddenly wondered what red would mean to a blind person and went quiet.

"What's wrong? Can't you see them?"

"I can and they really stand out, but when you said red I started wondering what it meant to you."

"I could see till I was ten years old so I know all the colours. Blue is my favourite … Have you got blue eyes?"

"Rhys has. Mine are dark brown and Mr B's are green."

"Rhys has blue eyes? Does that mean his hair is blond?"

"A little bit, but mainly brown."

"Blue eyes, brown eyes, and green eyes. You are very interesting people. Would you be happy to let me see your faces? It might feel funny because I touch with my fingers and some people don't like that."

Rhys spoke up straight away. "Try me first, Woorawa. I've read about this in a novel. It means you'd like to know us better, doesn't it?"

"Yes, blue-eyed slave driver. It does."

Rhys took Woorawa's hand and guided it to his cheek. By the light of his headlamp Kieran watched the gentle fingers trace carefully across Rhys's features. When it was his turn Kieran got goosebumps. The almost feathery touch was nothing like the firm comfort of one of Rhys's massages.

"What happens, Woorawa? Do you make a picture in your mind?"

"For people who let me do this I usually already have one, Kieran. Sometimes it changes a lot and sometimes it hardly changes at all."

"Did Rhys's change?"

Woorawa's fingers left his face and Kieran guided them to Mr B.

"Yes, he changed a lot … And you didn't, Kieran! You got more definite."

"What do you think of Mr B?"

"You feel like you all fit together and he has a big smile."

Mr B's smile grew even bigger. The look that Kieran and Rhys were sharing was interrupted by the dramatic sound of a didgeridoo. A second one joined in, and then a third.

"Wow! That's unreal. Will we hear the didgeridoos playing much tonight?"

Woorawa laughed. "They won't stop till the night's over. Let's go. We have to get you ready."

"How much dancing will we be doing? Rhys is nervous about it."

That brought a hefty nudge in Kieran's side from Rhys's elbow.

"I'm not. I just don't know what to do."

"And I feel the same as Rhys," said Mr B.

Woorawa laughed. "A corroboree is exciting and you join in whenever you feel like it."

The didgeridoos got louder.

"How many are there?"

"About twenty, but they'll be playing at different times. Some people are learners and some are very clever."

"What about you? Can you play one?"

"A bit. I'll teach you how if you want to try."

Rhys was extra keen and asked questions about it while they made their way to the big campfire. People were in groups everywhere, the didgeridoo players sitting on a fallen tree while six young boys were close to the fire, stamping their feet in time to the music. Woorawa called out something and Burrimul answered. *Wow!* He looked spectacular in a big feathered cloak with lines of ochre on his face and arms. Woorawa had a rapid conversation with Burrimul, then a group of helpers gathered around to transform the three visitors. When they were dressed in the same saggy loincloths everyone else was wearing, the painters went to work. Mr B ended up looking distinguished with a cloak like Burrimul.

Kieran wished he had a mirror to see the effect of the red and white ochre being applied to his face. Rhys looked so wild that Kieran could hardly believe it. His chest and legs and back were covered with jagged lightning shapes. Not even one part of his face was left bare. According to Woorawa, Mr B was the Elder, Rhys was the warrior, and Kieran's designs meant he was a spirit man.

Burrimul raised two arms and everything came to a halt.

"The people of Mparntwe welcome you to Country. Tonight you share a place amongst us."

He called a phrase in his language and every person round the camp-fire repeated it. Woorawa moved towards the glowing bed of coals then dramatically started one of the stamping movement's Kieran had learned earlier in the day. The didgeridoos joined, growing louder and louder to match the motion with sound.

"Woorawa is stating your Welcome. He's dancing first because he feels he knows you better than the rest of us. Everyone else will soon join in."

Five guys who'd been in the minivan moved to join Woorawa. Another group started on the other side of the fire, and in moments the only people not dancing were Burrimul, the didgeridoo players and the visitors. Kieran's heart pounded with excitement. His eyes caught the different movement as three of the youngest boys darted aside then back to make a blaze of light with handfuls of dried leaves flaring brightly then dying away, complementing all the movement and sound.

"One of you might like to say something."

Mr B, looking resplendent in the long Elder's cloak, moved close to the fire and held up both arms. There were smiles at this direct copying of Burrimul, but it was most appropriate and Kieran was impressed.

"Thank you, people of Mparntwe. It is a wonderful honour to be with you tonight."

Instead of more words, Mr B made a copy of the stamping movement Woorawa had started with. It was a poor copy, without style and grace, but that didn't matter because after the smiles, cheers and clapping, the didgeridoos sounded and everyone joined in.

"Go on! Off you go!"

Kieran grabbed Rhys.

"Come on. We have to help Mr B."

Rhys had even less style but that changed as the spirit of the moment lifted him out of his awkwardness.

The next few hours passed with all sorts of dances, storytelling by Burrimul and another Elder which the visitors only understood because of Woorawa's running commentary, a steady supply of food, and the ever-present music.

Kieran was sitting with Woorawa, happily unwrapping the tinfoil from a couple of large potatoes which had been baking in the hot ashes, when a pressure behind his temples made him look at the campfire. *Oh no, not now.* Pain came from nowhere in a savage assault. In the moments before he closed his eyes the people around the campfire blurred to confusion. Another sharp stab of pain startled him so much he dropped the potatoes and clutched at his temples.

"Woorawa, can you see Rhys anywhere? I need him."

"What's happening, Kieran? Your voice tells me something is wrong."

"I get migraine headaches sometimes and this one is bad. Rhys knows how to help me."

Woorawa called out and after a moment the didgeridoos stopped. Woorawa called again and there were a number of responses.

"He's gone to the minivan with Mr B to collect my didgeridoo."

An even stronger stab of pain made Kieran groan and rock his head back and forth.

"Someone's running to the van and they'll be here in a few minutes. How does Rhys help you? Can we do something while we're waiting?"

"I'm sorry, Woorawa. It's usually not as bad as this. I just lie down and he massages my head."

There was a scurry of movement and Kieran felt himself tipped backwards. His head rested on the sand and his eyes opened long enough to register the shapes of a whole group of people round him. A hand rested on his forehead.

"Tell me what to do."

"Rub my temples. That feels best."

Firm hands rubbed at both temples and Kieran stayed quiet, accepting the help that he knew wouldn't work. He withdrew into himself. *Where are you, Rhys? I need you.* He sensed the continuing massages and the sudden movement of bodies against him but didn't open his eyes.

"What's happened? Is he unconscious?"

"I don't know. He said it was migraine and rubbing his temples might help till you got here."

"Hold his head up while I have a try."

After a few seconds Kieran felt the longed-for sensation of warmth. The pain was still there but he pushed it away and gratefully accepted the rising flush of heat. Rhys had done it again. A smile built. Kieran started to open his eyes but a great wash of sensation carried him away.

*   *   *

"He's still smiling."

Kieran blinked his eyes open.

"And he's awake. Kieran, do you feel all right?"

Mr B was looking down at him. Burrimul, without his cloak, was there too. The cloak was spread on top of Kieran and a whole ring of silent people were watching him.

"I feel good. Have I been asleep for long?"

"Fifteen minutes. We've all been waiting."

Mr B was speaking very softly. Kieran sat up and saw why. Also covered with cloaks, two other forms were lying on the ground beside him. Rhys and Woorawa. *Woorawa?*

"Lie down again and close your eyes, Kieran. They've both stirred in the last few minutes and we think they're close to waking."

Kieran closed his eyes, but only for a moment.

"Did I zap both of them?"

"You certainly did, and I'm not looking for a sensible explanation. Along with at least a dozen other witnesses I saw it with my own eyes."

Mr B touched a finger to his lips and Kieran looked at Rhys. Fifteen minutes. That was different. The other times it had only been a few minutes. Rhys's eyes blinked open and he turned straight to Kieran.

"You did it again. Are you all right?"

It was Kieran's turn to signal for quiet. Rhys gave a blank look then sat up and took in the circle of quiet watchers and the covered shape of Woorawa.

"Yes. We're waiting for him to wake."

"Why is everyone staring?"

Mr B answered. "Burrimul stopped the corroboree when I told him this had happened before and that you were just asleep and would wake in a few minutes."

Kieran realised the strangeness of all these people sitting quietly for so long. He started to say something but Woorawa moved and his arm appeared from under the cloak. Good. He was waking up. There would be a lot of explaining to do. Kieran started to smile. Rhys would be using his human battery idea and saying they'd been zapped. By the light of the little standing lamp someone had set up close by, Kieran watched Woorawa's face and wondered what it was like for a blind person to wake up. You'd have to get your bearings by feel, or maybe by listening for someone to tell you.

Woorawa's eyes opened, and Kieran's heart nearly stopped at the strange call of shock and the convulsive movement to roll to the side and cover his head. There was another indecipherable sound and Kieran's first weird thought was that maybe his migraine had somehow been transferred. On pure impulse, he moved right next to Woorawa and rested a hand on the broad shoulder presented to him. Lost for what to do he looked into the eyes of Burrimul who was now on his knees. Another hand joined his own on Woorawa's shoulder and for a puzzling few seconds they watched as Woorawa's hands moved back and forth from his face.

"The light is too bright."

During the few seconds it took for Kieran to take in the import, Burrimul shouted in his language and someone dived to turn off the standing torch. In the dim campfire light Kieran watched Woorawa's hands move tentatively to the side, as if ready to clap back into place. His head twisted up slowly.

"Uncle Burrimul. I can see you."

Half of Burrimul's face was in shadow, but the other half reflected a soft glow. For an utterly poignant moment Woorawa's palm rested against it. Kieran didn't say anything. With a feeling of wonder and unreality he listened to the murmur of voices spreading, watched Woorawa stare at his hands, then give attention to each of the people close to him.

"I can see! … I can see!"

There was an interchange of words between Woorawa and Burrimul which Kieran couldn't understand, but at the end of it Burrimul jumped to his feet and called with a loud cry which the whole gathering repeated. In the ensuing silence Woorawa said something else then covered his eyes while the little standing torch was switched on again. He carefully uncovered them and looked again at the much more brightly lit people around him.

"It's all right, Uncle Burrimul. The light frightened me the first time because it was such a shock."

Burrimul knelt again and, with a pause every time Woorawa stopped to stare at something new, the two spoke rapidly for several minutes in their First Australian language. Woorawa pointed to Rhys, spoke in a loud voice, then changed to English.

"I just told them that the hands of the Warrior let me see again. Thank you, Rhys!"

Rhys was stunned for a moment, then started shaking his head. "No!

No! Woorawa. It's not me. It's Kieran. When he gets his headaches he's like a battery. Didn't you feel the heat or whatever it is he gives off?"

"Heat? Yes, it was like that … But it only happened when you started your massages."

"I know. I don't understand that, but it definitely comes from Kieran. He's special. He can do things."

"Rhys, don't be silly."

"I'm not being silly, Kieran. You know it's true and so does Mr B. He can't understand how you can swim like you do and learn things so quickly. And there are all the other things. That's why it has to be you."

"Not now. Woorawa should be going to see an eye doctor."

That brought another several minutes of exchange between Burrimul and Woorawa. This time it was about his eyes because he closed them one at a time, followed his own moving finger with each of them, looked at things in the distance, and then things close to the standing lamp.

"Tomorrow, Uncle Burrimul. We'll see an eye doctor then, but I know I don't need to. Everything is all right. Tell everyone to start the corroboree again so I can watch."

Burrimul looked doubtful but he gave a nod and called out. A didgeridoo started and when Woorawa stood up he put the Elder's cloak across his shoulders.

"Uncle Burrimul tells me I have to wear this for the rest of the night. He says it's a spiritual thing, but I think it's so I won't start dancing. I want to see all my friends, so will you talk with him for a while?"

Kieran nodded then wondered about Woorawa's strange expression.

"I'm sorry, Kieran. I haven't seen a nod for such a long time I had to think about it."

He suddenly sobbed and, shaking with emotion, wrapped his arms round Burrimul for a huge hug. Kieran's throat tightened at the sight of the moisture glistening in Burrimul's eyes. The long embrace finished and Woorawa turned to one of the van travellers who was standing close by. Burrimul composed himself then turned to the three visitors and pointed at the ground. *What?* Rhys picked up the ground lantern and the pool of light followed as they moved away from the campfire.

"Did you light a fire at the Caterpillar place? My people will soon explode with excitement and we won't be able to hear ourselves speak."

The glowing coals were soon augmented with new twigs and sticks and when the flames started dancing they settled close. Burrimul chanted something in his language then sat in silence with a big smile.

"I just welcomed you to this sacred place again, but I don't know how to speak. My heart is filled with happiness and a great wonder for what you have done tonight."

He touched Rhys on the arm.

"Woorawa told me that as Elder for our people I must listen to your story. He thinks there is a great mystery surrounding you."

"Me? I haven't got a story."

"Yes, you have. You started to tell it when Woorawa thanked you and you said there was more."

"You mean about Kieran? That's not a story. It's real. Mr B tries to make explanations and Kieran says everything must be a fluke or coincidence or something, but it can't be."

Mr B responded. "After tonight I've changed my mind, Rhys. Faith healing is the only thing I know of that's anywhere near like what's happened. It's sometimes called the laying on of hands, and that part fits, but there are other things, Burrimul, and they don't."

Burrimul shifted his attention to Kieran. "Are you happy for us to talk about these things, Kieran?"

"We talk about them a lot, especially me and Rhys, so I don't mind at all. We can't make any sense of it. Well, I can't."

Mr B spoke up. "Kieran has a special mind. He understands things at an amazing speed and his memory seems to be almost photographic. That's the first thing I noticed … And his swimming and climbing ability."

"He swims like a fish and climbs like Spider-Man."

"I'm not Spider-Man. Rhys, you're a galah."

Mr B laughed. "Close, but not quite. Rhys, you tell the rest. You're close to Kieran and you've seen more."

"I *am* close to Kieran. And since I met him I've stopped being lonely. He helps me all the time, and does funny things to make me happy, and he's the most amazing person I've ever met. He's clever and complicated about ordinary life things, but as well as that he can do things that aren't ordinary." Rhys turned to Kieran. "Burrimul is a wise man, and I want him to understand you are much more special to me for things like friendship and kindness and trust than for the strange things."

Kieran gave a nod, because he couldn't speak.

Rhys turned back to Burrimul. "There's something amazing about Kieran and animals. When we were at Gariwerd an eagle nearly landed on his arm and then a wild honeyeater walked on his head. Today at the nature park, the emus followed him everywhere and when I told him to talk to a tree frog it reacted straight away."

"An eagle?"

"Yes, a big wedgetail."

Kieran watched Burrimul nodding as Rhys related the details of each incident. Nodding? Did it mean something to him?

"He can be scary too. There was a nasty group at our college who started picking on us and he stopped them just by looking at them."

"With the force of his personality?"

"Sort of, but it felt like more than that to me. One of them even fainted."

"You felt it yourself?"

"Not with the others. We did an experiment later when we were trying to make sense of it and it frightened the hell out of me."

Once again Burrimul wanted all the details and, as they poured out, Kieran saw Mr B's amazement.

"Kieran, I want you to try the same experiment on me right now."

"I don't like it, Burrimul. I'll have to make myself feel angry at you."

"You managed with Rhys, who loves you. So you can manage with me."

It was hard to reconstruct the right mood but eventually it worked and, when Burrimul leapt to his feet with both arms warding in front and chanting something, Kieran closed his eyes and let the induced emotions drain away. He opened them to see Rhys and Mr B standing as well, looking as amazed as Burrimul. Rhys broke the tableau.

"It's stopped now, Burrimul. See what I mean about scary?"

"This is a new thing for me, Kieran. We have old stories about songs or words of strength from Kadaitcha men which give fear, but you do this without words."

Rhys asked the question which Kieran was wondering. "What's a Kadaitcha man?"

"A man with knowledge and strength who can give justice. Some stories say his song can even make a person die."

At the sudden look and blossoming grin from Rhys, Kieran knew this was going to be a new nickname.

"So, a Kadaitcha man's very wise and clever, is he? Rhys is going to start calling me one."

"He might be right. I think ..."

Everyone turned to the approaching light.

"Uncle Burrimul, can I join in?"

Without waiting for an answer Woorawa grabbed a few sticks and added them to the little fire.

*   *   *

For the next two days the college group was exploring and camping at Kings Canyon so it wasn't till their return to Alice Springs that they caught up with Woorawa again. He stayed talking for almost an hour and his news was that the eye doctor had run a whole barrage of tests which all showed his eyes were in perfect condition, and that everything was organised for the special trip they'd planned in their talk at the corroboree. The original plan was for an evening meeting, but when Burrimul heard they had a free day for looking around the town he was keen to take them to a special place called the Valley of the Eagles. Getting there sounded like quite an adventure and Mr B and Rhys were as eager about it as Kieran.

*   *   *

"Wow! What a view. It's a wonder a lot more people don't come exploring here."

Kieran agreed with Rhys but was pleased they didn't. All the places they'd been were spectacular but there'd always been lots of tourists and to have just the five of them made this feel like a real adventure.

"It's a special place for our people, Rhys, and we leave the tracks rough to keep it that way."

Rough was right. When they first left the main road Kieran wondered why they needed the big four-wheel drive, but in the approach to the gorge itself they had to go into the lowest gear while the vehicle jolted and ground its way through the deep grooves and rocky crossings of a dry creek bed.

"Burrimul, will we have much time down there?"

They were way behind schedule because although the track through the gorge was only a couple of kilometres, there'd been delay after delay for all sorts of reasons. Mostly because Woorawa had to stare at every new rock or boulder or plant they came across, but also because Kieran had been urged to demonstrate his climbing ability. Not that he'd needed urging.

"That's up to Mr B. He's our timekeeper today."

"No, I'm not. The professor expects us back for the evening meal, but we can ring on the cell phone and tell him we're delayed if we want to."

"The cell phone probably won't work in the valley but it should up here. See if you've got a signal."

That only took a moment, and there was.

Burrimul pointed downwards. "See the two rock pools? We'll make them our base and explore from there." He lifted his hand and pointed again. "And see that craggy outcrop with the dark-coloured rock? There's a ledge to the left with an eyrie on it, and round the back there's a cleft where peregrine falcons' nest."

Woorawa pointed in a different direction. "Look, there's an eagle … and another one. Are they wedgetails?"

"Yes, those two are, and that one farther along is a black kite."

Kieran knew the kite because they were everywhere in the town, but the wedgetails held his interest now.

"Kieran, I want you to stand on top of that rock and call the eagles to you."

Kieran stared at Burrimul.

"Call them?"

"Not aloud. Hold your arm out the way Rhys said you did at Gariwerd and project an emotion of welcome. Your Medusa look and the animal responses might be two aspects of the same thing so I want you to build the same frame of mind but with friendly compulsion rather than aggression. Do you understand what I mean?"

"Yes, I think so."

"Good. We'll watch from farther down the track so our presence isn't a disturbance, and Kieran, if anything does happen, try to keep your cool and prolong it."

It dawned on Kieran that Burrimul's reason for bringing them here was to test this theory. Well, it wouldn't hurt to try. At worst he'd just look silly. Rhys was nodding his head with a look that said he was definitely expecting something.

"Don't rush it, Kieran. Put yourself in the falconer mood we acted out at Hollow Mountain and I reckon it'll work again."

After ten minutes Kieran was feeling silly. He'd surprised himself by bringing up the angry feelings that had worked on Burrimul two nights ago quite easily, but switching them to something positive and keeping the intensity Burrimul had mentioned took a great deal of concentration. He was so inwardly focused that the approach of the two eagles gave him such a surprise he lost it. The eagles swept up and away and he struggled to rebuild the aura. Yes, that was a good word, and thinking of it that way somehow helped lock it in place. *Whoo! They were coming again. Was this real?* He raised his arm. No, that was crazy. He lost it again and the eagles swerved away. He took a jacket from his daypack and slipped his arm in one of the sleeves, and then again through the other, before raising his arm. The aura came more easily this time and the eagles turned.

Keep calm. Hold the aura.

Another realisation came and he made his mind to choose the big one. It circled behind, then, with pinpoint control, settled in place.

Keep calm. Keep calm. Hold the aura.

The calmness came and with it a sense that the eagle was relaxed and happy. Kieran looked into the waiting eyes so close to his own. Yes, it really was waiting, but Kieran had no plan. Yes, he did. His wrist was straining, the weight hard to manage. Step-by-step the great talons shuffled to his shoulder and soft feathers touched his ear.

Thank you. You are free to go.

That was a feeling rather than spoken and on cue the eagle launched. The aura dispersed and, gathering his senses, Kieran waved to the four watchers and climbed down from the rock. Rhys came, racing like the wind, with the others close behind.

"I knew it. I knew it. What was it like? What did you do? Can you get them back again? Was it scary? I thought the claws might go into your arm."

"I think I could, Rhys. I wanted it to my move up my arm because it was too heavy and it knew. Its feathers were brushing against my ear and I could feel its claws, but they didn't hurt."

The others arrived, all with looks of wonder.

"The King of our Eagles came at your call, Kieran. That was no chance encounter. Rhys was right."

Rhys grabbed Kieran's arm. "What did you do? Did you start with the Medusa stare like Burrimul told you? What happened when it was on your neck?"

Mr B laughed. "Steady down, Rhys. Give Kieran a chance to explain."

"Yes, Kieran. And in great detail please. You appeared to have a degree of control."

Kieran glanced into the distance to the two eagles gliding over a ridge top.

"I really did, Burrimul. I told it to move up my arm and then, when I didn't have anything else to do, I said thank you and told it to leave."

"I didn't see your lips moving."

"No, and it wasn't words in my mind either. I tried that and nothing happened. It was sort of like I had to feel what I wanted and then it knew."

"Why did you tell it to leave? You could have found out more if it stayed."

"It didn't come for me to do experiments. I just knew it was time."

"Has it made you feel like going to sleep?"

Kieran looked at Burrimul and took stock of himself. "No. It's nothing like Rhys's hands."

"Good. When we get to the rock pools I want you to try again."

"On the eagles, Uncle? Kieran said he felt it was time to leave them alone."

"I was thinking more of other animals. Rhys mentioned some interesting reactions at the nature park." Burrimul nodded to Kieran. "I have high expectations, Kieran."

With much discussion and a barrage of questions the party made its way down the track to the largest rock pool where they relaxed and shared the lunches Woorawa had prepared.

"Did you make the sandwiches last night, Woorawa?"

"This morning. I was up early, Rhys. I wanted to see the sunrise, so I had plenty of time. Did I make enough?"

Rhys gave a distracted nod and Kieran knew he was wondering what it must be like to see your first sunrise in nine years.

"Did you see the sunset last night, then? It looked pretty good from our campground."

"Uncle Burrimul took me to the town lookout and I had a driving lesson on the way. I want to get my license as soon as I can. Have you got a car, Kieran?"

"No, we're just poor students but the public transport's good and a tram goes right past the college."

"He's not that poor, Woorawa. He's just won a scholarship for his mathematics."

"Maths, wow! I love maths but my teacher is boring. Have you got a good teacher?"

Kieran and Rhys burst into laughter.

"No, he's useless."

"I don't understand. What's so funny?"

Kieran pointed at Mr B, who was looking decidedly awkward.

"He's another slave driver. If it wasn't for him I wouldn't even have tried for the scholarship. He's the best teacher ever, Woorawa."

Mr B shook his head and pointed back. "Don't listen to him. He does all the work himself. I can hardly keep up and he's a teacher himself. He's been tutoring Rhys, and Rhys's levels have gone way up."

Now it was Rhys's turn to do the pointing. "And he calls me a slave driver. That's the biggest joke. When we have a half-hour session it goes for over an hour and he won't stop till I catch on."

"So you all help each other? It sounds like your college is a good place. Do they have any disadvantaged students?"

Kieran and Rhys looked to Mr B. He was the one to answer that. "There's a TAFE section that's good at that, Woorawa, but you must have TAFE here in Alice Springs?"

"Yes, we do. It's where I've been going but they've had lots of cutbacks in staff and it's not as good as it used to be."

"You're not disadvantaged, Woorawa. You can do anything."

"Yes I am, Uncle. I might have my eyes back but I'm still way behind with school stuff, and if I go to a good college I'll be able to catch up." Woorawa turned to Mr B. "Do they have any computer courses at your college?"

"You're interested in computers? Yes, there's a whole range, especially in the TAFE section, because they focus on jobs more than academic levels."

Kieran was as surprised as Mr B. His impression of Woorawa was of someone interested in his culture and this wild and ancient country. Burrimul started shaking his head.

"You couldn't go to Melbourne, Woorawa. It's too far away and it's probably too expensive."

"I don't see why not. The blind school in Adelaide would have been more expensive, and I'd be coming home just as much from Melbourne. I know some friendly people too."

He looked for a response and Kieran nodded enthusiastically. "Are you serious, Woorawa? Just because we like our college?"

"I'm very serious. My family and my people want me to get a good education and it was all arranged for me to live in Adelaide, to go to the special school for blind people there. Now that I don't need it I should go to a proper college instead. Are there any First Australians there?"

Kieran didn't know of any so he looked at Rhys and Mr B. Rhys looked excited and grabbed Kieran's arm.

"Kieran, Woorawa could stay at our house. It would be perfect. We've only got Tan at the moment and there're still two rooms free. We could help him catch up with all his subjects and we'd have four friendly people."

"Wow! You could, too, Woorawa. It would be great. Unless you want to live on campus? He'd be able to get a place at our college wouldn't he, Mr B?"

Mr B nodded but then turned serious. "Steady. Steady. I have a sense that Burrimul has taken on the responsibility for Woorawa's education and a big change like this might not be suitable or even feasible. Melbourne is a long way from here."

Burrimul sat quietly for a while before answering. "Woorawa is special for his family of course, and for all our people, and none of us want him to leave, but we all know his opportunities here are limited. He would have gone to Adelaide anyway but if he's happier in Melbourne then so are we. I'm worried, though, that he might not be qualified for a place at any college."

Everyone looked at Mr B.

"That's not a concern, Burrimul. TAFE's open to everyone and he'd fit in at whatever level is appropriate. The new semester starts in less than two weeks, though, so unless you want to wait till next year there would be a terrible rush."

"Next year is too long, Uncle. It would be six or seven months wasted."

"Yes, it would. Do you think we have enough time to arrange a long-distance enrolment, Mr B?"

Kieran smiled because Burrimul had caught the habit of saying Mr B instead of Peter.

"Talk it over first and let us know before we leave. The professor is on the college board and if you want to go ahead I'm sure he'll make it happen."

"Yay!"

Woorawa leapt to his feet and with the biggest grin Kieran had ever seen, danced his excitement with some of the wild steps they'd seen at the height of the corroboree. He pulled Kieran and Rhys up for a big hug then did the same for Mr B and Burrimul.

Mr B turned to Burrimul. "It looks like the conversation might be very one-sided."

The half-finished sandwiches were attacked again while Woorawa bombarded Kieran and Rhys with questions about college and the things that happened there. Burrimul passed a drink to Woorawa, told him to calm down, then pointed a few metres along the rock they were sitting on.

"Can you see the little skink peeking from that crevice, Kieran? We're all going to sit still and quiet while you call him to your hand. I've saved a tiny piece of meat from my sandwich and I want you to tell him where it's hidden."

The skink was a surprise. On the walk down the track, Burrimul had said they'd look for another eagle or the kite they'd seen earlier. It might work. Rhys had been convinced the lizard at the nature park had responded, so why not this one. Kieran nodded to Burrimul then stretched his arm and looked at the tiny eyes. It took a moment to push away the whirl of thoughts about Woorawa's eager questions and recall the aura that had worked with the eagles. Saying the word in his mind brought it back. *Come on, little lizard. Turn those wary eyes to me and feel like you want to investigate my fingers.*

No, don't mind-speak it. Send it as a feeling.

The little lizard made a sudden dart, then paused with its tongue flicking at the rock. Darted again, and again, till it was next to Kieran's pointer finger. *Come on, little fellow. Move onto my hand. I'm keen to say hello.* With one rapid sortie, the skink moved to Kieran's palm.

A moment later it darted to the morsel Burrimul had hidden behind a pebble then, with the meat dangling to one side of its mouth, moved back to the security of Kieran's palm. With a great gulp, which made Kieran smile and lose his concentration, the meat disappeared. Legs racing so fast they couldn't be seen, the skink scuttled for the safety of its crevice.

"Wow! Did you tell it to go?"

"No. Did you see the way it scoffed the meat? It made me smile and I lost concentration."

"But it did what you wanted and it happened in a much shorter time. Do you feel like you could try again?"

Kieran had a short think. "Yes, it's tricky keeping focused properly but it's not hard work. Have you got another piece of meat? He loved the last one."

Rhys's eyes widened. "Could you tell what he was thinking? Or was it just the way he gobbled it down?"

That startled Kieran and he had another think. "I don't know. That was the moment when I lost it."

"There are frogs in this pool, Kieran. See if you can call them to you."

"Frogs? I can't see them, Burrimul. I don't know how to start."

"Are you sure? Have a try anyway."

Kieran pictured a frog in his mind and tried the aura thing. He soon knew it wasn't going to work and shook his head at the quiet watchers. Burrimul stood up.

"Rhys, you go to the far side of the pool and look under those loose rocks. Woorawa, you try near the reeds and we'll look along this edge. When you find one bring it here and Kieran can have another try."

"A frog hunt. Neat! I haven't done this since I was a kid."

Rhys's yell alerted everyone to success and he rushed back with his prize cupped between his hands.

"Look at him. He's terrific."

Rhys moved his thumbs apart just enough to allow for a view of light green skin speckled with white spots.

"Hold still while Kieran tells him he's not going to be eaten by monsters. Can you do that while we're all crowded close, Kieran?"

"I think so."

"Great! When he's calm put him in the water and tell him to wait while you have another try at calling any others."

Kieran switched to the right frame of mind and, yes, seeing the frog made all the difference. After a few moments he gestured to Rhys to release the frog into the water then projected a welcome to any other frogs. The frog that Rhys had just released left the water and hopped close. Kieran saw the wonder in Woorawa's eyes and nearly lost his aura. Hmm, that would be an interesting test if he could manage it.

"Put your hand down, Woorawa. I'll tell him you're a friend."

Very tentatively Woorawa rested his hand in the shallow water at the edge of the pool. Kieran thought of Woorawa's hand as a friendly, safe refuge, and after a few moments the frog clambered awkwardly into place. Kieran suppressed a surge of excitement and his attention went to the reedy section as he returned to calling any other frogs. That felt like the right place somehow. Yes, a tiny ripple spread as a head popped to the surface. And another. And another. The heads disappeared and Kieran smiled. They were on their way. Burrimul pointed to a different part of the pool with a gentle gesture. Yes, again. There were two more frogs. A few minutes later eight little bodies were lined up at the edge of the pool near Kieran's foot, happy that their friend was there to protect them. Three were big, like the one still sitting in the palm of Woorawa's hand, and the other five were much smaller. Enough. Time to send them away.

"He came to my hand when you told him. He was beautiful, Kieran. Did you see his eyes? I could have watched him all day."

"Nine frogs, Kieran. I suspect you called the whole population for this pool. Could you call them again or would we have to catch another one first?"

"Um … It's sort of like I know them now. I think they'd come but I won't try because it's too soon."

"It's getting easier isn't it? You spoke to Woorawa this time without losing contact."

Kieran nodded to Burrimul. "Yes, much easier. We'll try something else?"

"We will, but not animals. I want you to confront Woorawa."

"Confront?"

"With your Medusa look. He's the only one of us who hasn't experienced it."

"What about Rhys and Mr B?"

"No, I want you to direct it just at Woorawa first."

Kieran looked at Woorawa and laughed. "I can't. My mind's in a happy mode from the lizard and the frogs."

"You can. You managed despite all the excitement on corroboree night. Force it. Woorawa's going to punch your nose in if you don't."

Woorawa looked so shocked that everyone, including Burrimul, had to laugh.

"I didn't mean literally, Woorawa."

"I know. I was listening with my eyes instead of my ears, and it's so different it mixes me up sometimes."

Kieran was intrigued, but Rhys asked the question first. "Listening with your eyes? That sounds weird."

"I mean paying attention, Rhys. Understanding what you say is different when I can see you."

Mr B interrupted. "Woorawa means facial expression and body language, Rhys. Nods and smiles and lifted eyebrows are all second nature for us but Woorawa is relearning them. Have you seen him nod to any of us today? I haven't, but I don't think it will take him long to start."

Everyone looked at Woorawa and, of course, he gave an exaggerated nod.

"In the bakery this morning when I went to get the fresh bread, the lady behind the counter was speaking quickly and I had to close my eyes to understand her. She went quiet and was staring at me when I opened them again."

"I haven't seen you close your eyes with us."

"It's easier when I know the person, Uncle Burrimul. What do I do about the Medusa look?"

He raised his eyebrows at Burrimul and the slightly exaggerated manner, showing it was a conscious action, made everyone smile.

"It's frightening. I want you to fight against it for as long as you can and when it gets to you too much, hold your hand up and Kieran will stop. The rest of us will try the same thing in a moment. Is everybody ready?"

There were nods all round, except for Woorawa who said yes. Kieran pushed away thoughts of Woorawa's nods and the frogs and filled his mind with aggression. No, that was no good. It had to be only Woorawa. How was that going to work? Make him the bad guy and everyone else the good guys? No, thinking of Woorawa like that was ridiculous. Maybe pretend the others didn't exist? Whoo! Woorawa had both hands up and Rhys and Mr B were backing away.

"Try again, Kieran. We all felt that. Woorawa, fight harder. You're going to last twice as long this time."

Kieran gestured everyone except Woorawa behind him and switched the aggression back in. Woorawa did last a bit longer but when he put his hands up he was quite shaken.

"Give someone else a turn, Uncle. I need a break."

"Mr B, you're next. You seem to handle this better than any of us. Kieran, can you keep going?"

"Yes, it's hard to feel angry without being angry, but I'm getting there."

Mr B did last longer, but then so did Rhys when it was his turn.

"Kieran, you went easy on Rhys. The effect wasn't as strong that time."

"I did?"

"I think so, unless you're getting tired."

Kieran thought about it and laughed. "I did too. I didn't realise at the time."

"That's wonderful, Kieran. It means you must have some control over the strength of your projection. It's my turn now, and when I give you the signal I want you to start lower than Rhys's level and gradually build up till I can't cope."

Burrimul moved in front of Kieran, composed himself, then chanted softly before opening his eyes for a go-ahead.

Switching the Medusa look on was getting easier for Kieran, but controlling its strength meant recalling his frame of mind with both Rhys and Mr B, picking out the difference, then focusing on Burrimul with a gentler version. Was it working? Burrimul was reacting. *Get more forceful.*

The soft chanting started again and Kieran lost his concentration. It quickly came back and he pushed harder. Yes, pushing was a good word for it.

Burrimul, still chanting, raised one hand just a little. Kieran eased his push then built it slowly till Burrimul once again signalled with his hand. Several minutes passed before Burrimul raised both hands and moved to sit on a nearby rock.

"Amazing! Let me gather my wits for a moment."

Kieran turned to the three silent watchers. "Do you know how to do the chanting, Woorawa? It really works."

"I understand the words but Uncle mightn't be able to teach me how to use them properly. I think it's Elder knowledge which helped him last so long."

Mr B passed a water canteen to Burrimul, who accepted it gratefully. "I'll teach you now, Woorawa, while Kieran practises his control with Rhys and Mr B."

Burrimul and Woorawa moved away and, till they returned, Mr B and Rhys copped continual doses of the Medusa look, sometimes together but mostly in turn. Curiously, it was hard work for both of them but easy for Kieran, who kept telling Rhys he was a wuss for having to sit down to recover each time.

"It's not fair. All you have to do is look at us and we feel like mental dishrags. It should make you tired or start your migraine or something. You'll be the wuss then."

Mr B laughed at them, but agreed with Rhys that it was time for a break. "There must be more to teaching Woorawa that chant than you'd think. They've been at it for nearly twenty minutes."

"Burrimul's amazing. He seems to know something about this stuff."

"I get the same feeling, though I think he's making up his ideas about how to teach you as he goes along."

"I wonder what else he wants us to do. He seemed very pleased when we rang the professor to say we wouldn't be back till after dark."

"I reckon he'll get you to talk to every animal or bird we see. I hope so. The frogs looked like a little fan club when they were all lined up at your feet. I hope we see a goanna … what about a snake? Would you be game to try it with a brown snake? On the way in Burrimul said the snakes like these rock pools for frogs and other animals. Hey! I bet he gets you to try two different kinds of animal at the same time. Do you reckon that would work?"

Kieran didn't answer any of Rhys's interesting questions because his attention was on Burrimul and Woorawa who were now approaching.

"I bet I'll be Medusa-ing while Woorawa does the chanting before we do anything else."

After a series of questions from Burrimul that was exactly what happened.

The afternoon passed with a mix of exploring the valley and breaks under Burrimul's guidance. Woorawa didn't stop smiling the whole time and posed a never-ending series of questions about life at the college, and Kieran's own excitement at the prospect of sharing the house with someone so interesting kept building. When Mr B grilled him about all his school results and his study habits, Rhys shook his head in disgust and complained he'd be surrounded by nerd-heads and wanted to know if Woorawa was interested in swimming or any other kind of sport.

"I like dancing, Rhys, and I want to go exploring. Uncle Burrimul was always talking about Gariwerd and he says there are lots of other good places in Victoria."

"Dancing? You mean your special kind or ordinary dancing?"

"All of it, Rhys. It's one of my best things."

"What about Irish dancing? Kieran goes crazy when he puts that on."

"Like this? This is what my friends taught me at the Centre."

He put his hands on his hips and did a quick step dance.

"What about the swimming? You haven't said whether you like that."

"I like it but I'm not very good. It was always a bit difficult. You said there was a pool at the college, right?"

"There's a great pool and Mr B coaches us. Kieran cheats because he's got fish blood."

"Kieran's got fish blood?"

Kieran grinned and shook his head. "Don't take any notice. He trains all the time and he could always beat me till Mr B showed me how to swim properly."

"That's why he cheats. He trains one quarter of the time I do and he's still faster. It's unnatural."

Burrimul chimed in. "It fits with his climbing ability, Rhys. I think his coordination and balance is probably way off the charts … Lift one foot off the ground, Kieran, and see how long you can keep your balance with your eyes closed."

Kieran tried and wondered why it was meant to be hard. Rhys and Woorawa lost their balance after five or six seconds. Mr B had a try and found it as easy as Kieran.

"How strong are you, Kieran? Can you beat Rhys in a wrestle?"

Rhys made a pose with his arm muscles. "He's as weak as water. He's sneaky, but once you get hold of him he's had it. When he gets *too* cheeky I squish him."

"Give him some cheek please, Kieran. I want to see how well he squishes you."

Momentarily startled by Burrimul's request, Kieran had to laugh. This would be fun.

"Rhys can't wrestle. He just squishes me like a big lump of blubber and I have to give in before he turns me into a pancake."

"Blubber? You've had it."

They did wrestle back at college in very much the manner they both described. Kieran dodged Rhys's lunge and sneaked a poke in his side. When he was caught, he copped it back tenfold but that was the fun of it, along with the friendly taunts about being bullied.

"See what I mean?" Rhys appealed to the watchers. "He's as sneaky as animated spaghetti."

"Spaghetti? At least I'm not a blubber mountain."

Kieran's attention wavered at the laugh from Woorawa and he was caught and dumped. A few minutes later he was helpless and complaining about death jabs to his stomach.

"I give up. Go and pick on Woorawa. He's the same size as you."

"No way. He's not cheeky."

From flat on his back Kieran peeked at Woorawa. Yes, he was definitely up for this.

"Wuss! You're scared the blubber mountain tactic won't work."

That prompted a parting death jab before Rhys stood up. A titanic struggle followed and only finished when Woorawa ran out of energy.

Rhys, looking very pleased with himself, turned to Kieran.

"Now you're in trouble, Kieran. You've got another blubber mountain to beat."

Woorawa was no blubber mountain, but Rhys was right. There was no way Kieran would be a match.

Burrimul picked up his backpack and pointed. "You can play after we've checked out the peregrine site."

Woorawa stopped dusting the sand from his shirt and shorts. "The peregrines? Are you going to get Kieran to call them?"

"Why not?"

* * *

Kieran watched the quivering flames of their little campfire and wondered what Burrimul was planning next. Probably more of the Medusa practice or animal connections he'd pushed at different stages throughout the whole afternoon. Rhys started calling him the Pied Piper after a flock of thirty or forty corellas followed them for ten minutes, happily perching on any offered arm and deafening the five with the concert of raucous calls he asked for. The pick of all the moments for Kieran though, was the whistle of air as the peregrine falcon stooped past.

Woorawa was feeding handfuls of dried gum leaves into the fire from the stock at his side and watching the increasingly effective flare of the flames and the play of the swirling sparks as the dusk deepened. Mr B and Burrimul were twenty metres away beside the rock pool, having an intense discussion about something, and Rhys was quietly entranced by Woorawa's fire activity. Another handful of leaves lit up Woorawa's features and, watching his rapt expression, Kieran wondered, as he'd done so many times since corroboree night, what it would be like to suddenly be able to see. It must be like living in a new world. Yes, and maybe it was even something like his own feelings about all the strange happenings.

On impulse he grabbed Woorawa's arm. "It feels like we're in the middle of a dream."

Woorawa gave him a searching look, then nodded. "I know what you mean, except it's like I just woke up and everything's better."

Rhys started a new train of thought. "What sort of dreams did you used to have, Woorawa? Could you see things? Blind people do have dreams, don't they?"

"I have normal dreams, Rhys, but I don't know what happens for people who are born blind. I think they dream with sound and touch and smell instead."

"Smell? I don't think I've ever had smell in any of my dreams."

"Are you sure, Rhys? I thought everyone did."

They both looked for Kieran's response.

"Not very often but I definitely remember smelling that jasmine bush near the college library in a dream."

"What's jasmine?"

"It's a creeper kind of plant with a strong smell. It's probably too hot for it to grow up here."

Woorawa tossed another handful of leaves on the fire.

"Does that hurt your eyes?" asked Rhys.

"Is it meant to?"

"No! No! I just can't help thinking they must be sensitive when they haven't worked for nine years … A bit like when someone switches a light on and you're not ready for it."

"I wonder what Mr B and Burrimul are talking about?"

"You, Kieran. What else? Yesterday, Burrimul called all our Elders together and they spent most of the day talking about what to do. We have to say thank you."

Kieran and Rhys were both startled by the intensity of Woorawa's statement.

"You don't have to, Woorawa. You brought us out here for the day and we've had all these amazing adventures when we didn't really do anything. And anyway, it all happened because you were helping me."

Kieran wanted to change the subject. "Have you ever lived away from home? Melbourne will be a big change."

"We used to go to Adelaide a lot when they were trying to work out what was wrong with my eyes, and then I stayed there for two weeks when I started to learn Braille. Burrimul came with me, thank goodness, because I got really homesick."

Rhys grabbed Woorawa's arm. "Lonely is awful. But it won't happen at college because you'll be with us and we'll show you everything."

"I don't think I'll be lonely. There'll be so many things to do I won't have time to think about home, except when I'm in bed."

"Well, you can sleep in my bedroom till you're settled in if you want to."

Typical Rhys. Kieran felt like giving him a hug then laughed when Woorawa did it for him.

"What's this Tan person like? Is he … ?"

Woorawa stopped because Burrimul came close to the fire and opened his carry pack.

"Take your shirts off boys. This is an important occasion and I want you to be properly involved in the ceremony. Woorawa, will you apply the white ochre please?"

Mr B sat beside Woorawa and set the example by pulling his shirt off. Fifteen minutes later the whole group was most definitely in a ceremonial mood, with their torsos and faces daubed in bi-colour patterns of red and white ochre while Burrimul kept up a soft, rhythmic chant.

"Our stories tell us that many lifetimes ago a powerful being passed through our lands and revealed many mysteries to our Elders. In some places he forced his will, with compulsion and unusual abilities our wise leaders struggled to resist. His way of ruling by strength clashed with the Councils of our people till a great gathering of healers worked to banish him from the land. Some of the Councils called him a Great One because he could speak with animals, grant healing with a touch, impose his will on those around, and appear and disappear at will."

Burrimul paused to throw a handful of gum leaves on the fire.

"Our Council considered the powerful magic of Woorawa's sight and the words of knowledge from Rhys, and we agree that Kieran is linked somehow with that being. After today's revelations, I believe we have a Great One in our Country once again."

By the light of the subsiding flare, Kieran took in the force of the stares directed at him.

"Me?" Kieran shook his head. "I'm not some kind of powerful being, Burrimul. I'm just an ordinary person with weird things happening. Why don't you say it's Rhys? It's his hands that did the magic."

"Yes, Rhys is part of the puzzle and so is Mr B, but you cannot consider yourself ordinary. Not after what we've discovered today."

"I can't appear and disappear."

"Maybe you just don't know how yet."

"What did the Great One look like, Uncle? Do our stories say anything about that?"

"Not really. There's a sense that they were human and very imposing in aspect. Evidently there is rock art in western Victoria which depicts them as tall, thin men with long ears."

"My ears are normal and I'm not tall."

"You are thin."

"One out of three, Rhys. And anyone can be thin."

"Not me. I'm thick."

"You said it, not me."

Rhys laughed and made a friendly fist at Kieran. "You don't look imposing either."

"Kieran does look imposing, Rhys. When he applies his will he's unforgettable."

"Hey, yes. The Medusa look. That makes it two out of three."

Burrimul reached into his daypack and, when he brought out a small woven bag, Woorawa drew in a breath.

"Is it a Churinga stone?"

"There is a Churinga stone in there, Woorawa, but you won't see it for many years. It's been guarding the artefact our Council wishes to present to Kieran."

Kieran had learnt something about artefacts a few days ago at the cultural Centre.

"You can't give me any of your artefacts, Burrimul, because I'm not a First Australian. It wouldn't be right."

"This artefact is yours to accept or refuse as you wish. It is *not* one of ours but it may be important for you."

"Take it, Kieran. I think you should."

Kieran was quite startled at Mr B's definite tone. Rhys was nodding strongly too, and Woorawa and Burrimul looked expectant.

"Thank you, Burrimul. Your Council honours me and I accept with gratitude."

Burrimul started a soft chant as he reached into the woven bag and Kieran watched curiously. The cupped hands emerged and opened to reveal a nondescript lump of orange-tinged rock. The chant stopped and Burrimul held his hand out.

"Take it, Kieran, and close your eyes while you hold it."

"Is something meant to happen?"

"I don't know. Our knowledge says the being used it against us till it was taken from him by the healers. I can sense nothing from it myself but if my suspicions are right it might be different for you."

Kieran took the roughly spherical chunk of rock, held it in his right hand and, wondering why it was necessary, closed his eyes.

"It's not very heavy."

"Shut everything else out and reach out like you do for the birds and animals."

Call to a stone as if it were alive? That was such an unexpected idea Kieran had to take it in for a while. Well, why not? So many of Burrimul's other exercises today had made things happen. With the mental switch that was now quite familiar, Kieran put himself into the calling mode that worked for the animals. Nothing happened. The coolness of the rock seeped into his fingers and gradually disappeared. Whatever Burrimul was expecting wasn't happening.

Come on rock. Talk to me.

The feeling of neutrality abruptly vanished, a strange sensation tickled his hand and Kieran opened his eyes in surprise.

"It's making my hand tingle."

Burrimul nodded. "Keep holding it, Kieran. Has the tingle stopped since you opened your eyes?"

"No, it's spreading."

"You haven't got pins and needles from holding it too tight, have you?"

"I'm not holding it tight at all, Rhys, and it definitely isn't pins and needles … It's nearly reached my elbow. Should I put it down?"

"Do you sense any danger?"

"No, it feels good."

"Keep holding it till there's no more change then."

The feeling spread, rapidly now, till Kieran gasped with pleasure and disbelief.

"I've got goosebumps except they're all over. My whole body's tingling."

"Keep holding. Can you feel anything else?"

Kieran laughed. "I don't want to let go. It makes me feel like … like when Rhys starts giving me a head massage."

The pleasant feeling made Kieran smile and everyone else one else caught it till Burrimul disrupted the moment by telling Kieran to pass the artefact to Rhys.

The artefact passed to everyone in turn with no effect, except for Mr B who thought it felt slightly warm. Burrimul directed Kieran to hold it again but, against expectation, nothing happened.

"Did you do something different the first time? I remember there was a bit of a wait."

Kieran remembered his light-hearted command for the artefact to talk to him. He tried it again … and the tingle started.

"Hey! I can feel it again."

CHAPTER 4

Kieran opened his eyes, immediately closed them because the light made his head hurt, and then when there was no let up with the ache, opened them again. Not another migraine. What was the time? Ten-thirty in the morning. WHAT? How could that be? He never slept in.

He sat up and put his hands to his temples. Rotten headaches, and the doctors were no help. Ten-thirty? Tan would be wondering where he was.

Twenty minutes later, and feeling quite a bit better, Kieran knocked on the door of Tan's room. It opened straight away.

"Morning, Kieran. I was about to come around and see what the holdup was."

"Sorry, I must've had a bad migraine last night, because I slept in and my head was all wonky. What do you want me to carry?"

"Anything you feel like. It's all ready."

Kieran grabbed a big cardboard box, Tan took a suitcase, and before long the car was loaded and ready for the first trip to their share house.

"Buckle up, Kieran. I don't feel comfortable if everyone hasn't got their seat belt on."

"Sorry, I don't know why I forgot. I've been feeling dopey ever since I woke up."

Tan laughed. "Dopey? I doubt that." He pointed to the clock on the car radio. "It's eleven-sixteen. How long do you reckon it'll take to get there?"

"Four minutes! But we have to get the keys from the estate agent first."

The agent had little to say, except that if anything broke down they should contact him and that he hoped they'd enjoy the house. It wasn't long before Kieran was unlocking the front door for the first time.

Everything was just as he remembered, and after a quick tour with Tan, they got the car unloaded and set off for college to get all of Kieran's belongings. That was a bit awkward, because they weren't all packed. He'd meant to do that last night, but the migraine must have put him in bed really early. Weird! He remembered turning some music on after tea and nothing else. He'd been fairly organised, though, and a final clean-up and loading everything into Tan's hatchback didn't take long.

"Hey, Tan, I saw you looking in the kitchen drawers. Was there anything there?"

"Not a thing. We'll have to get cutlery and cooking stuff this afternoon."

"Let's grab a roll or pie for lunch."

"Okay. It's your shout, because tonight I'll cook a nice meal to celebrate moving in. When you've finished unpacking we'll work out a list of things we need for the kitchen, then visit some thrift shops to get it all. They have lots of good things and it won't cost much."

Kieran was impressed. "That's a great idea. How do you know about thrift shops?"

"My cousin's in his second year at a different college and I helped him set up his unit. He got towels and sheets and kitchen stuff for hardly anything. There's even furniture at some of them and we can look for a kitchen table."

"Whoo! I wish I hadn't slept in. This'll be a busy day. Hey, you don't have to cook tonight. Mr B's coming to check the place out and we can just get a pizza or some fish and chips."

"We will *not* celebrate with a pizza, Kieran. That would be awful. Mr B can share the meal with us. You said he might be visiting us quite a lot, so we want to make him feel welcome."

"By cooking a meal? Well, it'll have to be you then, because I'm hopeless at cooking."

"Not for long. I'll show you how. Does the First Australian boy know how to cook?"

"His name's Woorawa. I don't know. I doubt it, because he was blind till a week ago."

"Blind people can cook."

"I suppose. It must be harder, though, and I think he's had too many other things happening in his life."

"I've never met a First Australian from the outback. Is he used to wearing clothes?"

Kieran stared in disbelief. "Tan, he's from Alice Springs. That's not the real outback and he wears the same kind of things we do."

"The other day you said he was a full blood. Doesn't that mean he has ancient cultural ideas?"

"He does a bit, but he knows ordinary things too. Tan, are you nervous about him? He's friendly as anything and clever too. He's mad about computer stuff and we're going to help him catch up with his Maths. You'll have to learn how to eat lizards and snakes if you want to share meals with him though. He likes raw frogs too."

Tan leaned back in surprise, then laughed. "And now you're tricking me. I suppose he doesn't carry a boomerang everywhere or blow the didgeridoo either. I'll make up my own mind when I meet him."

"I don't know about the boomerang, but he does blow the didgeridoo. I wonder if he'll bring it. Hey, do you know somewhere we can get keys cut? We need one for each of us and a few spares too."

"There's lots of places. We'll do that when we go to the op shops."

They set off and the rest of the afternoon was all activity. Tan was fun to be with and super organised as well, and by evening, the kitchen was set up with frying pans, saucepans, a couple of woks and enough plates and cutlery for half a dozen people. They'd transported an old kitchen table from the thrift shop on the car's roof rack, scrubbed it spick-and-span and covered it with a tablecloth. Meanwhile, the big old fridge that came with the house was now stocked with food.

*　*　*

"This is a surprise. I was expecting a pizza or takeaway of some kind and instead there's a delicious cooking smell."

Kieran and Tan exchanged smiles at the pizza comment.

"I was going to order pizzas, but Tan wouldn't let me. He's made a special meal instead. Do you want a quick look around while he finishes off the veal?"

"I'm not finishing it, Kieran. You are, so you'll learn what to do."

"He's bossy. I had to get all the roast vegetables ready and make the salad."

Mr B laughed. "This I have to see. We'll look around later."

Under Tan's supervision, Kieran finished the veal, transferred it to a platter, and helped put the roast vegetables and a tray of mushrooms with cheese on the table.

Kieran's teeth crunched through the crisp coating around the tender meat. Wow! This *was* delicious. He blew on a forkful of mushrooms to cool them. So good! And there weren't going to be enough roast vegetables.

"Tan, this is better than going to a posh restaurant. Where did you learn to cook?"

"My whole family is good at it, Mr B, and they've taught me how ever since I was little."

"Well, with food like this tempting me, Woorawa's going to get more help with his Maths than he expected. What other hidden talents have you got?"

"None really. I have to devote all my time for the next few years to my studies. I do like photography, but I haven't got a proper camera."

"That's neat. What sort of photography?"

"Any sort, but when I get the chance I'll specialise in macro."

"Do you like swimming, Tan? Mr B's going to coach Woorawa when he gets here and you could join in."

"I'm no good at it."

"You don't have to be good at it to like it. Do you ever go to the pool to muck around?"

"Not really, Kieran … Who wants the last piece of veal?"

Kieran was curious. It sounded like Tan didn't want to talk about swimming. "I do, but we'll go shares."

After the meal, Mr B helped wash the dishes and then they made the tour of both the inside and outside of the house.

"What are you going to do with the spare bedroom, Kieran, look for someone else to share, or make it a guest room?"

"We've talked it over and we'll wait till Woorawa gets here. Then, if we find someone we all like, we'll get them in. We'll use the enclosed part of the back verandah for visitors."

"And where are you going to work? You haven't got any study desks."

"Tomorrow's a big search day for furniture, because we saw some good things this afternoon at the thrift shops. We're going to get a desk for Woorawa, too, as well as a bed, because there's nothing in his room. He arrives in three days. Then we've got two days to show him round before semester starts, so we want to make sure everything's sorted out."

"Kieran, I'm impressed. You're really organised."

Kieran pointed at Tan. "Tan's the organiser, not me. He thinks of everything."

"And he cooks like a chef. Woorawa's going to love it here. Kieran, have you heard from him in the last few days?"

"There was an email yesterday asking about internet connections but I haven't answered it yet. I must have been completely out of it last night with one of my migraines."

"You too? Join the club. My head hurt so bad I went to bed early and I slept in for ages this morning."

*   *   *

"I am greatly reassured by the success of this new intervention, Uirebon, but where is Lord Maynor? I expected a firsthand report."

"His efforts were prolonged and considerable, my Lord, and when I saw the level of his exhaustion I advised an immediate restorative session with his healer. His determination to recover from the setback of the previous session stretched his abilities further than I thought possible ... Surely you were surprised by the amount of power he used?"

"Partially. He did warn that we must take account of Keryth's strengthening resistance and I gave him access to a modicum of Nexus energy."

"He used it all, my Lord, and it was barely enough. Manipulation of but a single mind in the Human World is difficult enough, but for this result he had to manage teachers and administrators as well as Keryth and all his associates."

"Why administrators?"

"Lord Maynor decided that, without complete separation, the young warrior would continually strain Keryth's conditioning or even block it. The administrators will facilitate his relocation."

"Good! No more rebound shock for Maynor and the triads from that healing touch. Apart from weariness, how have the triads performed?"

"Perfectly, my Lord. The melds are disbanded, and after an appropriate rest they will assist Maynor with clearing one final detail."

The High King regarded Uirebon with some surprise.

"While working with Keryth and Pethron's memories, Maynor discovered that the healing touch which rendered the triads unconscious also restored sight to a chance acquaintance who was subsequently invited to share Keryth's new living arrangement."

"Such an invitation implies more than mere acquaintanceship."

"Indeed. A bond of friendship developed, my Lord, and introduced a complication. The dark child has significant memories which need to be modified before he meets Keryth again."

Aglaron regarded Uirebon with more surprise. "Keryth has invited a child of that ancient culture into his home?"

"My Lord?"

"When Maynor recovers I must view the memories of these events and impress on him the need for caution. There are mysteries within that culture ... How significant are the memories?"

"Very. Along with his extraordinary healing, he observed Keryth communicating with various birds and animals, an ability which doesn't fit the normal human persona Maynor has just worked so hard to re-establish."

"I see, and what of my son's wellbeing? So much reworking of the persona would cause a strong reaction."

"Strong but fleeting. After one long sleep he will resume life, motivated in his human studies and happy in his home situation. Maynor's efforts now have the realignment proceeding as designed."

"… With the exception of one detail."

*   *   *

The next few days were busy, busy, busy, with getting the house cleaned and set up so they wouldn't have anything to worry about when the semester started, and Tan's hatchback made trip after trip. Kieran didn't feel guilty about it taking so much time when Tan obviously enjoyed it all.

On Saturday mid-morning they set out for the airport. Mr B couldn't go because of a staff function, and Kieran was relieved that Tan wanted to take his car. It was nearly an hour's trip, with part of it through busy traffic, but they timed it just right and Kieran yelled when he sighted Woorawa standing in the quick pickup area.

"There he is! There he is! Look, Tan, he did bring his didgeridoo."

Tan slowed and pulled to the curb. Kieran rushed out to give Woorawa a warm welcome and made a hasty introduction to Tan, who had opened the boot of his car. The big suitcase, a rucksack, a smaller daypack and the didgeridoo were quickly loaded and they set off again.

Woorawa had a smile about a mile wide and, feeling exactly the same, Kieran pointed at the didgeridoo.

"Play something for Tan. He thinks you can't speak English and he's wondering if you're going to wander around the house in a loincloth, or nothing."

"Total lies, Woorawa. He tells them sometimes. Did you have a good trip down? Kieran said you left Alice Springs at six o'clock this morning."

"There was a wait for an hour and a half at Adelaide, but it was my first time on a jumbo jet so it was really interesting. Do you really want to hear the didgeridoo while you're driving, or do you want to wait till I can do it properly with my ceremonial loincloth?"

Tan would be polite and say to wait, so Kieran pushed in. "Both. A quick song now, and again when we get a proper chance at home, and you can teach him some of your dances too. I've told him how good you are."

Woorawa rested the didgeridoo on top of Kieran's seat so the sound would spread through the front of the car, and spent four or five minutes playing a range of songs.

Tan was suitably impressed, and Kieran's excitement at having Woorawa live with them built to a new high.

"Where's Rhys? He was going to come to the airport."

"Rhys? No, he's gone. He moved to another college."

"What?" Kieran couldn't understand Woorawa's puzzled look.

"Kieran, what happened to him?"

"How would I know? Students change colleges all the time. He probably found a better course or something … Did you hear anything, Tan?"

"Not much. I think he got a literature scholarship. Some students swap to the city campus because of the advanced course there."

"You haven't even talked to him about it?"

"What do you mean? Why should I? It's none of my business."

"Did you have a fight?"

Kieran twisted in his seat to look at Woorawa. "A fight? Why would I? He was one of those quiet students and I saw him at the pool sometimes, but I hardly knew him."

"What? Your best friend? You even said he was your soulmate when we were at the Valley of the Eagles."

What on earth was Woorawa talking about?

"You're mixed up, Woorawa. Mr B and Tan are my friends, and you too, but not Rhys. I sort of remember him being there, but I think it was Mr B who invited him."

Kieran watched Woorawa's huge frown change to a big smile. "It's a joke! Rhys is waiting at the house with some sort of surprise for when I walk in."

This was getting weird, and Kieran turned to Tan for backup. Tan looked into his rear vision mirror to speak.

"It sounds as if you don't want to believe us. But he definitely isn't at the house. Why would he be? He didn't have much to do with either of us."

"But …"

After this puzzled exclamation there was an awkward silence which Kieran wanted to end.

"I told Tan how good you are at dancing and he wants to learn from you."

"I didn't say that, Woorawa. Now he *is* joking. I'm hopeless at dancing."

The rest of the trip was normal conversation, mostly about the house and its set up, and a constant barrage of questions and observations from Woorawa as they went through Melbourne city central and along the busy freeways.

At the house there was a quick tour, to show where everything was. Woorawa was obviously pleased with his room, and especially the big desk he'd be able to use for his study and his laptop computer, and while he packed his clothes into the small chest of drawers and cupboard, Kieran explained how the internet would be connected the next week, and their plans for the next day. Woorawa was interested about the internet, but then he kept looking at Kieran, and Kieran wondered why he seemed so distracted.

"Are you tired after your trip?"

"No, Kieran. Rhys isn't here and I don't understand it."

"Why do you keep talking about Rhys?"

Woorawa sat on the end of the bed and gestured for Kieran to do the same. "Do you remember Rhys at the Valley of the Eagles?"

"Yes, he was there because Mr B knew he liked exploring. I told you that."

"Do you remember his magic hands?"

"No. Did he know some magic tricks?"

"What about the eagle?"

"Which eagle? We saw lots of them. That's why we went to the valley."

"The one that sat on your arm."

"My arm? No way. Eagles are wild, Woorawa. That couldn't happen."

"I saw it. Try your Medusa look on me … but only gently."

Kieran felt uncomfortable. All these weird questions and Woorawa seemed to be completely serious. "I don't know what you mean. What's a Medusa look?"

"This is really off, Kieran. All sorts of things happened at Alice Springs and you don't seem to remember them. Do you remember the corroboree?"

"Of course I do. It was great. The dancing and singing, and you took Mr B and me to the rock paintings and told us the story about the Dreamtime Caterpillars."

"Who was sitting next to you?"

"You were."

"And where was Mr B?"

"On the other side of the campfire."

"What about your left-hand side?"

"That was Mr B. There were just the three of us."

"Rhys was there too."

"No he wasn't."

"Yes he was. You told me he had blue eyes and he let me see his face with my fingers."

Kieran put his hands to his temples.

"And then you teased him about dancing."

"I don't want to talk about this. It's giving me a headache. I think I'd better help Tan in the kitchen while you have your shower."

Woorawa gave him a measured look. "I'll ring Uncle first, to tell him I've arrived and to ask him some questions."

Kieran watched Woorawa take out his mobile phone, and then, wondering why the conversation had made him feel so uneasy, headed off to the kitchen.

*   *   *

"Is everything all right with Woorawa? He seemed to have something on his mind when we got home."

"I'm not sure, Tan. It's like he's got a fixation about that other student. I started to get a headache from all his questions."

"It's not one of your migraines, is it?"

"No, it's gone now, so it can't be. He's ringing his Uncle Burrimul to let him know he got here okay, and then he's having a shower. What do you want me to do to help?"

"Nothing really. Set the table if you like but we won't be eating for another hour and a half."

Kieran did that, then talked with Tan while he waited for Woorawa to start his shower. Three quarters of an hour later they could still hear the murmur of his voice through the door.

"It's nothing, Kieran. He must be one of those people who talk for ages on their phone and he's telling his uncle every detail about the trip."

"I suppose so. It's a long time when he's only just arrived though."

"Knock on his door. He won't mind. He's as friendly as anything."

Kieran knocked and when the door opened Woorawa had the phone to his ear.

"Kieran's here, Uncle. He must be wondering why I've been talking so long."

Woorawa listened for a moment then handed the phone over.

"Hi, Kieran. It was kind of you and Tan to drive all the way to the airport to pick up Woorawa. He says you gave him a great welcome and he loves the house and his room. Are you all ready for a busy semester?"

"Hi, Burrimul. He played his didgeridoo in the car for Tan and we're showing him around the college tomorrow. Did he tell you Mr B's going to introduce him to some of his lecturers?"

"He certainly did. He's told me all sorts of interesting things. Kieran, what have you done with the artefact I gave you?"

"The old stone? It's on my bookshelf at the moment, but Mr B says we shouldn't keep it."

"You mustn't think that. It's yours. It's a gift from my people and we'd be concerned if it didn't stay with you. Will you remember that?"

"If you say so, but we did think it would be better in a museum or somewhere like that."

"You mustn't. Speaking as an Elder, I tell you not to give it away … Kieran, will you do something for me? It's very important."

It must be something about helping Woorawa get settled in and Kieran rushed to assure Burrimul that he'd do whatever was needed.

"Of course I will. We're taking him to college tomorrow and Mr B's going to coach him once a week, and Tan and I will help him with his Maths and Science any time at all."

"That's wonderful, but it's not what I meant. There are some questions I want you to answer and some exercises I'd like you to do, and since I can't be there in person I've explained it all to Woorawa."

"What do you mean? My swimming keeps me fit."

"Not that kind of exercise. We did some at the Valley of Eagles but Woorawa tells me you don't remember, so I want to refresh them in your mind. Have you heard this sound?"

A rhythmic and deep chant came through the phone and Kieran listened, with goosebumps lifting on his neck till it finished.

"That's amazing, Burrimul, but if I ever heard that I'd remember, and I don't."

"It's connected with the exercises, Kieran, and Woorawa will use it when he works through them with you."

"Um, are they some kind of traditional thing?"

"Not quite, but they *are* very important and I want you to work through them this evening. Will you do that for me?"

Kieran was struck by Burrimul's forceful manner and he agreed straight away. He couldn't really refuse, and the whole business was intriguing. He said goodbye and returned the phone to Woorawa.

"Thanks, Uncle Burrimul. I'll ring you tonight to tell you how we went. I'm going to have a shower now and then enjoy the food that Tan's putting on to welcome me. Kieran's been raving about how well he can cook and I'm hungry as anything. Bye!"

Woorawa gave Kieran a thumbs up sign and pulled his shirt off.

"What do I do about towels, Kieran? Can I borrow one from you for a few days till I get my own?"

"There's one in the bathroom ready for you. I'll show you how the taps work, too, because the controls are tricky if you don't know them."

Woorawa blithely tossed his jeans on the bed and followed Kieran to the bathroom. Wow! He looked so fit.

*   *   *

"Hold it cupped in your hands, Kieran and don't let go. Uncle Burrimul says it's the first thing we should get working."

Tan's meal had been terrific and then the three of them had talked for over an hour about all sorts of things. Tan's questions about Alice Springs kept both Kieran and Woorawa smiling, and then his proposal to drive to Phillip Island to see the penguins one weekend had both Woorawa and Kieran really keen. Nothing was said about the exercises from Burrimul, but they were on Kieran's mind the whole time and he was pleased when Woorawa organised a move to the lounge to get started.

"It just looks like an old stone. Can it really do things?"

"I've seen it, Tan. Kieran doesn't remember and that's what my uncle wants to fix. It's not really stone. It's a protective layer of clay baked hard around a real artefact.

"Can I hold it?"

"Ask Kieran. It belongs to him. Uncle Burrimul gave it to him in a special ceremony."

"Of course you can, Tan. I remember Burrimul giving it to me, but not in a ceremony. We were sitting around a campfire."

Tan took the artefact, examined it closely, then held it cupped the way Woorawa had mentioned.

"Nothing's happening."

"No, it doesn't for me either. Give it back to Kieran."

Kieran took the artefact and, feeling slightly ridiculous, clasped it with both hands.

"How long do I have to do this?"

"Till we finish. Close your eyes and concentrate on it."

Kieran laughed. "How am I meant to concentrate on a stone?"

"Try. That's the first step.

Kieran waited for about twenty seconds then opened his eyes. "What's meant to happen?"

Woorawa nodded as if he was pleased. "That's exactly what you said last time. Close your eyes again and when you're properly focused tell it to talk to you."

Kieran stared. "That's bizarre, Woorawa. How could a rock possibly talk?"

"I know. I don't understand it either but you told us that's the way you got it to work when Uncle Burrimul gave it to you."

"This is freaky. I don't think I'd say something like that."

"Have a try."

Well, he'd made a promise, and since both Woorawa and Burrimul were making such a big deal about it, there was no real option for backing out without upsetting them.

Kieran closed his eyes then jerked them open again when Woorawa started the same chant Burrimul had used on the phone. So! He was building a ceremonial atmosphere. Kieran shut his eyes again and let the rhythmic sound fill his mind. It was great. Having Woorawa stay was sure going to be interesting if things like this kept happening. *No, don't think about things. Concentrate on the stone.*

The chanting went on and on and nothing happened. How could it? Kieran was about to give up when he remembered he was meant to talk to the stone. It felt slightly warm but that must be the heat transfer from his hands. A vague memory stirred and somehow his mindset changed. *Come on rock! Talk to me!* With a jolt of disbelief Kieran felt a tingle in his fingers. He opened his eyes and Woorawa stopped chanting.

"Are your fingers tingling?"

"Yes. How do you know that?"

"It's what happened last time. Keep holding and it should spread to the rest of your body."

It did, and as the sensation progressed Kieran explained how it felt to Woorawa and Tan.

"I've got goosebumps all over. Is the stone really doing this, Woorawa? Your chanting hasn't hypnotised me or something, has it?"

"No, Kieran. It was just a chant and I won't use it again unless you turn off the artefact and can't start it up again."

"I don't feel like turning it off."

"I know. That's exactly what you said last time, but I want you to keep practising."

"Okay, how do I stop it?"

Woorawa grinned. "You tell me. I reckon you know."

It must be the opposite of how it started, so, in his mind, Kieran told the stone to be quiet. The tingling continued so that was no good. What was the difference? Oh, yes, he'd been much more definite. *Rock, be quiet!* Every tingle stopped and Kieran opened his hands.

"This is unbelievable, Woorawa. It's just a piece of clay again. The feelings went away like I'd turned off a switch."

"Practise turning it on and off till you've got the technique fixed in your mind. Last time it only took a couple of tries."

"That's the third time you've said I've done this before. Why can't I remember?"

"I don't know. But that's a big change."

"What is?"

"You've started to believe me about your memory."

"Well … my mind tells me I've never used this artefact but everything else seems to prove that I have."

"Practise!"

Twice more Kieran turned the artefact on and off.

"It *has* got easier. Something's clicked and I don't even have to concentrate … well, not much."

"Good. Turn it on again and tell it to get stronger and weaker."

"Have I done that before?"

"No. Burrimul didn't think of it at the Valley of Eagles but he reckons it's likely to work."

Kieran closed his eyes. He'd discovered he didn't really need to with the switch-on, but it might help for something new. *Talk to me!* Immediately the pleasant tingle started, so, with the same kind of mode in his mind he tried the next step. *Stronger!*

The tingle intensified and Kieran opened his eyes in amazement. "It really works, Woorawa. I tell it to get stronger and it does."

"Uncle thought it might. Do you want to practise some more or are you ready for the next part?"

"What's the next part? Something else the artefact does?"

Woorawa looked surprised and didn't answer straight away. "I don't know if it does anything else. Do you think it might?"

It was Kieran's turn to think, but not for long. "I don't know why, but I feel like it does."

"When I ring Uncle Burrimul I'll ask him. Kieran, the next part might give you a headache. It did before so tell me straight away if you feel one starting."

Tan got very concerned. "I hope this doesn't start one of his migraines. The last one was so bad he had to go to bed straight after tea and he was still wrecked the next morning."

"That's because he didn't have Rhys's magic hands to fix it, Tan."

Kieran ignored that.

"I won't get a headache. The tingle feels really good."

"I'm going to ask you lots of question about Rhys and try to get you to remember him."

"Not more of this Rhys stuff? Skip that and do something else."

"Do you remember when Rhys told us he was your soulmate?"

"… No way."

"I heard him, Kieran. Who did you share your cabin with?"

"Mr B."

"No, it was Rhys. You told us the lecturers had their own cabins. Whose idea was it for me to live with you?"

"I'm not sure. Probably Mr B's."

"It was Rhys's, Kieran. He was really excited about us sharing this house."

"No, he wasn't. He has nothing to do with this place. Can we talk about something else?"

"We've only just started. Do you remember anything about a slave driver?"

"Um … Yes, I do. It was Mr B making me work hard at swimming."

"No, it wasn't. I heard you myself. You and Rhys used to say it to each other."

A pang of discomfort made Kieran hold his head. "This is crazy. Can we stop now?"

"Is your head aching?"

"Yes, these questions are getting to me."

"Tell the ache to go away."

"What?"

"When it hurts, push back against it and tell it to stop. Who's stronger out of you and Rhys when you wrestle?"

"He is … I mean … I don't know … Woorawa, this headache's getting worse."

"Fight it. Go on. Try … What's the name of the person who told me he was your soulmate?"

"No one … I mean, a minute ago you told me it was Rhys."

"Who?"

"Rhys!"

Each time he said "Rhys" Kieran's head throbbed. This was getting to be too much. "Woorawa, we'll have to stop. I'm getting a migraine."

"Fight it. You haven't really tried yet. Uncle Burrimul thinks you definitely can tell it to go away."

That was all very well. Woorawa's head wasn't so miserable he didn't want to think about anything.

"Say his name again, Kieran."

"No! This is crazy. I don't want to."

"Hey! Don't yell at me. Yell at the headache."

Frustration boiled over.

"Get out of my head! Go away!"

Woorawa and Tan jerked backwards in shock at the yell. Kieran's shock was the rush and tingle of warmth to his temples and neck and the relief that came with it. Yes, the ache was gone and the pleasant feeling from the artefact was back in full force.

Kieran laughed at Woorawa and Tan's expressions. "Sorry, I didn't mean to give you a fright. Woorawa, my head's clear. The throbbing's gone."

"Wow! That was dramatic. I nearly jumped out of my skin."

Tan was nodding his agreement. "Me too. I wanted to run out of the room."

"But, you *can* control it. Uncle Burrimul was right. What did you do? Was it just getting angry, or was it something else?"

Kieran replayed the moment in his mind. "I wasn't really angry. I got so frustrated I told it to go away and it did. I think the artefact helped, too, because I felt a rush of its warm tingly feeling."

"Do you think you can do it again if the headache comes back?"

"Um … probably. Yes, I think so."

"Think about Rhys then. That's what started it."

"I'll say his name first. That's what made it really bad. Rhys. Rhys. Rhys."

"Did you feel anything?"

"No."

"Try seeing his face in your mind. That might get a reaction."

Kieran stared at Woorawa. "I can't. I don't know what he looks like."

"Yes, you do. You've done everything together for months. Do you remember the Valley of the Eagles when he showed you the frog?"

"What frog? I remember seeing one at the nature park but nowhere else."

"Rhys caught one at the rock pool and brought it to you. You like frogs and you were really pleased."

"You know I like frogs? I don't even remember talking about them."

"You did, and a lot more, but we're getting off track. Make Rhys come into your mind."

"I can't. I told you."

Woorawa went quiet for a moment. "All right, we'll do it this way. Mr B sent me some good pictures of Rhys when I got my new mobile phone last Monday. You can look at those."

Woorawa held out his phone and Kieran and Tan leaned close to watch while he flicked through a few menus. An image appeared of Kieran and another person smiling at the camera. Kieran recognised the rock pool background at the Valley of Eagles but the two figures with their arms draped companionably over each other's shoulders made him frown.

"I don't remember this, and my mind's telling me it's a trick photo. Is that Rhys?"

Woorawa looked completely put out by the question. "You don't even know him when you see his picture? Kieran, look how happy you both are. You can tell you're best friends."

Kieran puzzled over the two happy smiles and shook his head in annoyance at the ache which had started again.

"You still don't believe it even when it's right in front of you?"

"I think I have to believe it, but I was shaking my head because the ache's come back."

"Well, make it go away."

Kieran recalled the moment of frustration and tried the command of dismissal. There was the same rush of tingly warmth and, instantly, his head cleared. "It worked again, Woorawa."

"I knew it would, and we just proved that thinking about Rhys starts it. Tell me something you remember about him."

"But I don't."

"Yes, you do. You told me you went swimming with him. Think about that."

Kieran tried. "Weird! I do remember the swimming but not much else … I think he wears blue bathers."

An image flashed in Kieran's mind of a strong body in light blue bathers and, despite the sudden return of the headache, he held it. "We used to say we were twins, because we had the same bathers … And the headache came at the same time I remembered."

"And what did you call him when he made you swim hard? You both joked about it to Uncle Burrimul and me."

Kieran stared at Woorawa and concentrated till an answer came. He quelled the accompanying throb of discomfort. "Slave drivers? Was that it?"

"That's what you said. And why did he call you the same?"

After a kind of mind push and another uncomfortable throb, Kieran had it. "We studied together, and it was Maths. He tried hard, and he got better and I loved helping him."

"Now tell me something about Rhys's magic hands. It's one of the big things."

"Big? Like important?"

"Yes, Kieran, unbelievably important. They worked magic when he put them on your temples."

Kieran imagined some hands touching him … and his head ached. That meant there was something to remember, so he reached for it. The ache flared but he dismissed it forcefully and reached again. The imagined hands became a memory which he knew was real.

"Oh my God! Rhys could stop my migraines. He gave me massages ... and we both got zapped. Woorawa, I can see him now."

"Do you remember when he saved you from the bullies?"

The process repeated. A push for memory, a throb of pain then, when the pain was dismissed, recall. The image of Rhys with a bleeding nose came with a flood of memories of how he'd got it. Kieran was horrified. How could he have forgotten this?

"I passed out and he fought the whole gang of them to protect me. Woorawa, what's making me forget something so ... so big?"

"What happened at the corroboree with you and me and Rhys? You remembered it a different way when I asked you before tea, and it's the biggest thing that's ever happened in my life."

Strain, a pain, and once again memory came. Astonishing memories which were hardly credible.

"You were still blind?"

"For years and years, Kieran, and you and Rhys fixed it, not some special treatment. It's why Uncle Burrimul and the Elders gave you the artefact, and why he trained your Medusa look at the Valley of Eagles."

"The way you said 'Medusa look' makes it sound like it's another big thing."

"It is, as well as talking to animals."

Kieran strangled his laugh when he saw Woorawa was completely serious.

"Think about the eagle and the frogs now, Kieran."

"You can't be saying I was talking to an eagle? That's impossible."

"Work at it in your mind before you say that. Think about the eagle, the frogs, the skinks, the corellas and the peregrine falcon."

One by one the memories returned, each requiring a mental reach and then dismissal of the insistent throb of discomfort. Wonder on wonder surfaced. The Medusa look followed, along with the memory of how to control it. Tan's panicked look as he scrambled to get away was tangible proof that it was real. Woorawa started a different chant and a sense of recognition led to the memory of Burrimul doing it as well, and then the recollection of how to control the strength of the look.

"Let's have a break and a drink before we go on. I want to ring Uncle to let him know what's happened and to ask what we should do next."

Tan jumped up because he liked being host and Woorawa reached for his phone. Kieran listened carefully to Woorawa's side of the phone conversation, thinking hard about his interpretation of what had happened. He agreed with almost everything, but when it was his turn he cleared up a few points before listening to what Burrimul thought they should do next.

"I know what to practise, Burrimul, but I'm worried about how to remember things when there's no one to prompt me. I don't trust my memories after I left Alice Springs because I know they must be wrong. Rhys and I both spoke to Woorawa on Mr B's phone when we were making arrangements for him and I only got that back because Woorawa knew about it. Tan was with me most of the time, well I think he was, but he remembers exactly what I do."

Burrimul took a moment before he replied. "Kieran, there might be other Great Ones involved. Everyone connected with you appears to have had memories altered to match yours. When was the last time you talked to Mr B?"

"He came for a meal when Tan and I moved in but he was only expecting it to be me and Tan, so Rhys must have been taken from his mind too. We'll all see him tomorrow at college."

"Tell him everything and make him hold the artefact. Do you remember that he was the only one besides you who could sense something from it?"

Kieran didn't, but a quick dig and dismissal of minor discomfort brought the moment back.

"Do you think it might help him?"

"I have no idea, but since it helped you it's worth a try. Kieran, I want you to break the protective clay and keep the artefact itself with you wherever you go."

"Break it open? I don't want to damage it. What's inside?"

"I don't know exactly, but the stories passed down speak of great beauty. Kieran, if you practise and experiment with it whenever you can I think you'll find a lot of the answers you're looking for. Can I speak to Woorawa again? We'll talk again tomorrow or whenever you want to."

Kieran said goodbye then handed the phone over and watched the surprise on Woorawa's features. Tan was back with three cans of apple cider, which he handed out once Woorawa put the phone down.

"Wow! Thanks! What's this for Tan?"

"A big occasion warrants a nice drink … and I have to keep Kieran happy or he'll give me nightmares with his Medusa look."

"Sure too! I've remembered how to control it now, so there's nothing to panic about. Hey, let's open the artefact first. Woorawa's uncle said it might be special."

Kieran put the artefact on the bench beside his chair and looked at it. The tingle lessened but, as they'd discovered earlier, it didn't disappear till he moved farther away.

"We need a hammer or a chisel but we haven't got either. How can we do this?"

"I know. I'll be back in a minute."

Tan jumped up and ran out.

"I like Tan, Kieran. He's taken all these strange things really well."

"I know. But what else can he do? The Medusa look worked so strongly on him he can't put it down to his own imagination. I'm worried about how to get his memory back."

Woorawa nodded, then laughed because Tan was back with two bricks, which he put on the floor in front of Kieran.

"I remembered they were outside near the back door. Do you think you can do this without wrecking whatever's inside, Kieran? I'm not touching it."

Kieran put the artefact on top of one brick and gave it a tap with the other.

"It's baked clay, Kieran, so it shouldn't need much."

Kieran carefully increased the strength of the tap, and when he did it again for a third try a small crack appeared along one side.

"Whoo! You're right, Woorawa. I hardly used any force at all. I'm not going to use this brick again. It's too unwieldy. Tan, can we use one of the kitchen knives? If I put the point in that crack, I might be able to lever it open."

Once again Tan ran, which added to the atmosphere of anticipation they were all feeling. Kieran carefully investigated the crack, inserted the knifepoint in the widest section, and then, holding the whole thing firmly with his left hand, carefully pushed the knife to one side. The crack lengthened and, after some careful manipulation, a whole section came off. Nestled within, like a yoke inside an egg, was an irregular-shaped black object.

"It's another stone?"

"Touch it, Kieran, and see if it's any different."

Kieran automatically controlled the warmth tingling through his fingers and pried off another piece of clay. "It comes off easily now that it's cracked."

Removing one more segment left the black stone free and, distracted by the novelty of goosebumps on the back of his wrist, Kieran lifted the kernel for a closer look. His hand twisted upward and an iridescent flash of blue stunned everyone into brief silence. Colour shone with every new move, all the colours of the rainbow really, but overwhelmingly a deep, fiery blue. Kieran stared at it in amazement.

Woorawa gawped with dawning comprehension. "Oh my God! Kieran, it's an opal. They're totally rare, and it's big. Does it feel different?"

"Yes, it's stronger. I had to calm it down. Do you want to hold it?"

Woorawa and Tan both took turns, twisting it in different directions and marvelling at the colours showing with every change of aspect.

Tan returned the gemstone and Kieran traced his finger across the surface.

A duo of gasps and incredulous looks from Woorawa and Tan interrupted Kieran's rapt attention.

"What? Did you feel something?"

"Kieran, you're glowing. Can't you see it?"

Kieran held his hand up. It was blue. A closer look showed his hand was quite normal. The blue was a thin layer surrounding it. He checked further. Unbelievable.

"Wow! It's all over me."

"It's the opal, Kieran. It must happen when you touch it directly."

Kieran put the artefact on the brick and the blue glow disappeared. A few experimental touches proved Woorawa's theory was right.

"Touch it, Tan, and see if you start glowing."

Tan and Woorawa both tried with no glow or any other effect occurring. Kieran laughed. "There goes Burrimul's rule about carrying it everywhere. I can't go to college if I'm glowing blue."

"Put it in your pocket. The material might be enough insulation."

Woorawa was right.

"Let's turn the lights off. It'll be spectacular in the dark."

Tan jumped up, and when he clicked the switch all three of them gasped again.

"That's unreal! Hey, I've had an idea. Hold my hand, Woorawa. I want to see if it spreads."

"Okay! Um, what if you zap me?"

"What do you mean by zap? Like an electric shock?"

"It was Rhys's description for when his magic hands worked. Remember it?"

A few seconds later Kieran had reclaimed another big memory.

"It wouldn't hurt, Woorawa, just put you to sleep for a few minutes."

"Okay. Try touching me with your left hand."

There was no zapping and for a moment nothing happened, but then the blue glow gradually built. Tan wasn't going to be left out and when he held Kieran's right wrist he also ended up glowing. This was exciting … and fun.

"Hey, Kieran. It's the artefact doing this, isn't it?"

Kieran was surprised by Woorawa's question. "What do you mean? It must be."

"You might be able to control it. Like you do with the tingle. Try telling it to get stronger."

What an interesting idea. Kieran switched in the command feeling and told the artefact to get stronger. The blue glow flared so bright he reflexively yelled at it to stop. The room was abruptly pitch black.

"Whoo! Specco! Why did you turn it off?"

"I tried too hard, Woorawa. I told it to get strong and it worked with the tingle as well. Turn the light on, Tan, so we know where we are while I have a think."

"Try again and practise first, Kieran. Get it set in your mind before you do anything else."

Woorawa was right and Kieran quickly discovered that as well as controlling the strength and colour of the glow he could also direct it to surround any object within the effective range of the artefact. At Tan's suggestion he managed to make a blue light float in midair and move at will.

"I wish Rhys was here to see this, Kieran. Remember how excited he was when you learned to talk to the animals?"

Kieran reached again and when the image of Rhys, eyes alight with wonder, filled his mind, he dwelled on it. The bond between them changed from Woorawa's second-hand description to full memory of the real thing. Loss welled and emotion took over. Woorawa and Tan sensed the change.

"What happened, Kieran? Are you all right?"

Kieran had to fight the lump is in his throat to get his answer out. "No, I'm not all right. Someone's taken Rhys away and I'm going to get him back."

Woorawa and Tan quietly watched the battle between emotion and concentration.

"Why would they do that? It's wrong. He's the best friend anyone could ever have and he's gentle and kind. He makes me happy and he stands up for me. You remember what he's really like don't you, Woorawa?"

Woorawa answered with a soft 'yes' and listened while more thoughts poured out.

"I wonder where he is. They must have made him forget everything, too, because he'd come straight back here otherwise. I hope they haven't been hurting him." A flash of anger surfaced. "They'd better not have hurt him. How are we going to find him?"

Tan answered. "We could ask tomorrow when we go to college? Administration must have a record if he's gone to the city campus."

"And if Tan will take us we can go and look for him."

Kieran wasn't listening. The flash of anger was now burning with an added mix of frustration and determination.

"I want to know where he is now!"

Woorawa and Tan jolted in alarm at the new imperative yell. The blue glow which had been momentarily forgotten flared brightly and darted to a point on the wall. Kieran pointed and yelled again.

"Yes!"

Woorawa and Tan jumped up and stared.

"He's that way."

"You can tell? Because of the blue?"

"Because I can. The artefact is helping."

Kieran closed his eyes and twisted his head in different directions then pointed again. "He's that way."

He opened his eyes and, sure enough, his arm was directed precisely at the glow.

"Can we go in your car, Tan? I have to see if he's all right."

Woorawa and Tan exchanged wondering looks and then scrambled after Kieran as he raced for the doorway. Twenty minutes later the car was parked, and the now-tiny blue globe and a very excited Kieran were both pointing at a four-storey block of apartments.

"He's up there."

The wonder was still with Woorawa and Tan but the doubt wasn't.

"You want us to come with you?"

"Of course I do, Tan. We're all in this together."

"How are we going to get in?"

Kieran led the way to the main entrance and Tan and Woorawa had to rush to keep up when he bounded up the stairwell.

"Come on!"

The blue spark led to a doorway on the third floor and Woorawa and Tan stood back while Kieran banged on the door. They all laughed about it later because under normal circumstances the insistent knocking would have been quite rude. The door opened and Rhys peered at them.

"Hello?"

Kieran wanted to grab him in a giant hug, but Rhys's querying look said exactly what they'd been expecting.

"Rhys, do you remember who we are?"

"You were in my class before I changed campus."

There was no hint of friendship or knowledge of shared dramatic events and the blandness of the answer set Kieran back for an instant. With his own memories now so strong, Rhys's whole manner was weird. This must be what Woorawa had felt after they met him at the airport.

"Can we come in? We need to talk to you."

Rhys was polite by nature so there was no doubt they'd be invited in, but even having to ask felt off.

"Um … yes. Is it something about last semester?"

He ushered them into a small sitting room and pointed to a sofa. When they were settled, he sat on a kind of padded footrest.

"Did I forget to do something before I moved?"

"Rhys, what do you know about me?"

Rhys hesitated, obviously puzzled about the point of the question. "Your name's Kieran, isn't it? You were good at Maths."

"Do you remember how you helped me with my migraines?"

Rhys looked blank. "What do you mean? I don't know anything about migraines."

"Who's your best friend?"

Rhys gave Kieran a look at the strange question. "That's a bit personal, isn't it? I've just changed campus so I don't know anyone yet."

Kieran turned to Woorawa and asked for his phone. "Find that first picture you showed me and let Rhys have a look at it. Rhys, this is a very important photo and I want you to tell us if it means anything to you."

Rhys moved beside Woorawa and glanced down. This was the photo where the two of them had their arms draped across each other's shoulders in a happy moment. He lifted Woorawa's hand for a closer look, stared for a while, dropped it, then held his head in his hands. Kieran knew exactly what was happening.

"What did you see, Rhys?"

"It doesn't make sense."

"And it gave you a headache and you don't want to look at it again."

"What did I forget to do before I moved?"

This was the same avoidance tactic Kieran had used with Woorawa.

"Why don't you want to look at the photo?"

"Which photo?"

Kieran could hardly believe it. The phone picture had gone from Rhys's mind after only a few seconds.

"The one on the phone. Show him again."

Rhys's reaction was a replay, except that when he lifted his head from his hands he was visibly distressed. "What happened? That felt awful!"

This time Rhys's answer was addressed to Woorawa, and Kieran's mind raced. Following Woorawa's tactic of concentration with memories that couldn't be denied would be too upsetting. What was different? The artefact? Yes, that was it. Whenever he'd felt headache pressure the arte-fact had helped him push it away. Could he use it somehow to help Rhys? An idea sparked. Maybe he could send the tingle effect outside himself the way he did with the glow? Kieran clicked his mind into gear, then stopped. This might freak Rhys out and it would be better to talk him through it first.

"I'm going to help you feel better. I had the same headaches and I know what to do."

Rhys kept looking at Woorawa, and Kieran, realising it was hard for Rhys to even look at him now, changed tactics.

"Woorawa, tell Rhys he's going to start tingling all over and his head's going to clear from all the pressure."

Woorawa already understood because he said a soft 'yes' before going on. "Rhys, don't get scared. We think you're going to feel strange all through your body. It will be good, though, because if it happens it will make you feel better."

"Is it like a reiki thing?"

"I don't know what reiki is. Does it make you feel tingly?"

The reiki word triggered something and after a quick push Kieran knew it was one of the things he and Rhys had researched after the Grampians trip. He was pleased, too, because it was a good lead-in for the physical contact between them that often made things happen.

"It's a bit like reiki. Woorawa, tell Rhys I'm going to massage his neck."

"Did you understand that, Rhys? Kieran wants to stop your headache."

Rhys twisted his head to look at Kieran, winced and quickly turned back to Woorawa. "What?"

The wince was too much for Kieran. He squeezed the opal, commanded it to help Rhys, and rested his hand on Rhys's neck. Rhys jolted in surprise and grabbed Kieran's hand.

*　*　*

Kieran felt someone adjust something soft under his head and opened his eyes. Tan smiled at him, then called over his shoulder, "Kieran's awake."

Kieran looked past Tan. Woorawa was moving towards him, and so was Rhys.

Wow! Rhys was glowing blue. Kieran's heart lurched. Rhys was looking straight at him … and he was smiling.

"You're hopeless, Kieran. You zap me and turn me blue then sleep for twenty minutes."

Kieran stared for a moment, not knowing whether to laugh or cry, then leapt up to give Rhys a giant hug, which was returned in spades.

"Did I really sleep for twenty minutes? How long did you sleep for? Have all your proper memories come back? Are your headaches gone? Are you coming back to the house with us?"

Rhys moved out of the hug and gave a look which sent a glow of happiness through Kieran. "Too many questions … and when are you going to turn this blue light off? Woorawa thinks it'll stay with me till you stop it."

Almost casually, Kieran dismissed the glow. He had too many other questions pressing on his mind. "You're all right? And you do remember everything?"

"You zapped me out for about five minutes, Kieran, and I've been talking to Woorawa and Tan ever since. I remembered who you were straight away but other things came back when Tan and Woorawa asked me questions or reminded me."

"Five minutes? Why didn't you wake me sooner?"

"We talked about it, and when Woorawa asked me if I remembered any other times you zapped me, I did, and we always woke up when we were ready. I knew it was best to leave you, so we did."

Kieran was puzzled. "You just remembered? Without having to fight against a headache?"

"No headache. Everything comes back easily as soon as I think about it. We reckon it was the blue glow protecting me."

"You've remembered everything? You're a double cheat, Rhys, because I still don't know lots of stuff and I still have to fight the headache to get it back."

Rhys liked this friendly pattern of stirring and he gave Kieran a happy nudge in the ribs, a familiar response which made Kieran happy all over again.

"How do you know I'm a cheat? The zapping might have fixed things like it always does. Try to remember something and see what happens."

"Give me an idea then. I need help to get started."

"What's my favourite book? We went and saw the movie."

"*The Mysts*! Hey, that was easy. I knew it straight away."

"What about when Tan took us looking for the share houses?"

"He wanted us to get the old one because it had so much potential. Rhys, all I have to do is think about it and it's there. Your magic hands have worked again."

"See if you can fix Tan. He still can't remember properly."

Rhys was right. Tan had now seen two people recover memories that didn't match with his own and Kieran wondered how much they'd talked about while he was zapped. It must have been a lot. He gripped the opal and, a little more gently this time, sent the tingle to Tan and commanded it to help him. The blue glow appeared. Tan jumped and grabbed Woorawa's arm for support then closed his eyes.

"Kieran, you're zapping him without even touching him."

Tan opened his eyes. "I'm not going to sleep, Rhys. I can't while I feel like this. It's awesome."

"Awesome? You mean the tingle?"

"That's for sure!"

"Has it brought your memory back?"

Tan's eyes scrunched as his thoughts turned inwards. "It has. Wow! I remember you with Kieran the day before you left, and you've stopped looking like a stranger."

Kieran firmed his grip on the artefact and, noticing how much easier it had become, sent the glow command to Rhys. It started and Kieran wondered why it was blue unless he expressly told it to be something else. It did look great though. Maybe it was because it was his favourite colour.

"Organise some of your things, Rhys. You're coming home with us right now."

Tan was right, and Kieran's thoughts focused on 'home'. It had always been called 'our house' till now and he decided to make the same change himself.

"Make us all glow, Kieran. You did before, so we know you can. Change colours too. Rhys hasn't seen that … or your built-in GPS."

"What's a built-in GPS?"

"A blue spark which tells you which way to go. We used one to find our way here. Can we try it on the way home, Kieran?"

Woorawa was saying 'home' too. Discussion and experimentation continued for over two hours, all the way home in Tan's car and on into the night, with the four of them gathered in the lounge, laughing, serious, curious and sorting through their memories. There was a great deal of planning too.

Tomorrow would be full on, with several car trips to move all of Rhys's belongings, Woorawa's introduction to college, and sorting things out with Mr B.

CHAPTER 5

Mr B was waiting near the entrance to the college car park and, after a wave, followed and caught up while Tan parked in a nearby vacant space. His reaction when Rhys got out of the car was expected but still confronting.

"Tan, it's kind of you to run Woorawa around like this. Are you and your friend coming with us while we introduce him to the college and his lecturers?"

Tan nodded, then looked to Kieran, who was meant to be doing all the talking.

"Um … Mr B, can we go to your office and talk there?"

"Of course. You've got me very intrigued by this mysterious topic you couldn't tell me about over the phone … But aren't you going to introduce Tan's friend?"

He didn't have a skerrick of recognition and Kieran wondered why. Tan and Rhys had both had a reaction.

"We'll introduce him when you're sitting down, Mr B. He's the reason we've come early."

"Curiouser and curiouser, as someone said. Is he new to college and wants to be part of today's little tour? … Sitting down? That almost sounds serious."

"It *is* serious, but it's good serious."

Mr B's gaze went from Kieran to Rhys and then quickly back again. "Serious business? All right, let's get on with it."

There were only three seats in the office so they went to the next-door classroom.

"This isn't a counselling matter is it, Kieran? One-on-one would be better for that."

"No, we're all involved … Mr B, who am I?"

"… I'm not sure how you want me to answer that, Kieran. It almost sounds philosophical."

"Just tell us some of the things you know about me."

"Just? That sounds like a command? Well, you *are* a top student with a good attitude and a special aptitude for maths. You're adventurous and you like helping people … Is this the kind of answer you are looking for?"

"Which people have I helped?"

"Woorawa. You've given him a place at your house and you're helping him with his move to college. And there's Tan, of course."

"Anyone else? With Maths coaching?"

"Yes, you'll be helping a selection of people when you start your tutoring this semester."

"What about last semester? Who did I tutor then?"

"I don't know, Kieran. Your scholarship hadn't started so anything you did then would have been a personal arrangement."

"It was, but it was you who arranged it."

"What gives you that idea. You must be confusing me with another lecturer … and what's the point of all this? I feel like I'm being interrogated."

"Sorry, Mr B, I didn't mean to come across like that. You're not going to believe me but your memory has definitely been changed and I'm trying to work out how much."

"… What a strange thing to say. There's nothing wrong with my memory."

"Tell us about the Medusa look, then. Three of us have seen how well you can fight against it."

Mr B took in the assenting looks from Woorawa and Rhys before shaking his head.

"You sounded serious when we spoke on the phone but this feels like some prank you've cooked up for the start of semester. I think we should take Woorawa to meet his IT lecturer."

"Mr B, look at me. I can prove we're not pranking. Face me for a few seconds then tell me what happens."

With a 'let's get this nonsense over with' air, Mr B looked and waited. Kieran sent a short, but very sharp, dose of the Medusa look. Mr B recoiled, horrified, and his hands reflexively warded the attack while he recovered his wits.

"What happened? I felt awful. How did you do that?"

"That's the Medusa look, Mr B. I can do it any time I want."

"Kieran, that's not possible."

"Yes it is. You want me to do it again?"

Mr B gestured strongly against that. "No thanks. I'll take your word, though I've never heard of anything like it. Is this the serious thing you want to talk about?"

"It's part of it. See what you think of this."

Kieran held out the opal and all four of them watched Mr B's astonishment. "It's beautiful, Kieran. Where did you get this?"

"It's the artefact from Alice Springs."

"No it's not. The artefact's an old stone we decided to give to the professor."

"It was baked clay really, and Burrimul told us to break it open last night. This was inside. It's the real artefact and it's amazing. Watch this. I'm going to use it to turn Woorawa's head blue."

Mr B didn't say anything till Woorawa's head had been glowing for about ten seconds, glowing brightly because Kieran had turned the strength up for effect.

"Now I know it's a prank. You've got laser lights set up somewhere."

"Okay, pick anything in the room and I'll make it glow."

Mr B looked round, searching for some unlikely object.

"Um … the inside of that rubbish bin."

Kieran gathered the glow from around Woorawa and, for a show, turned it purple then floated it across the room to the bin. He settled it inside and started it cycling through the colours of the rainbow.

"I can't believe what I'm seeing. How is that happening?"

"I don't know how. I just tell the glow to start and it does."

"How do you change the colours?"

"The same way. What colour do you want to see?"

"Turn the back wall blue."

"All of it?"

"If you can."

That was way more than Kieran had tried so far and he wondered what would happen. He floated the rainbow glow from the rubbish bin to the wall and told it to spread and turn blue. It worked, but the brightness level dimmed and by the time half the area was covered the glow could hardly be seen. Kieran squeezed the opal and told the glow to get stronger and cover the rest of the wall. It was spectacular but after about twenty seconds he turned it off.

"Leave it on. It looks unreal."

"I felt like it was time to stop, Rhys. I think I might need practice."

"Could you do two walls? Or even all of them?"

"I don't know."

"Try it, and tell the opal to help you."

"Not now, Woorawa. We're here to help Mr B, not to do experiments."

"Do you really believe a gemstone let you make that glow, Kieran? And what do you mean about helping me?"

"You already know the artefact can do things, because you've seen it yourself, but you've forgotten, and getting your memory back is how we want to help."

"Why do you keep insisting my memory isn't working?"

"Because it's not, and we can prove it. You don't even remember Rhys."

"Rhys? I do remember there was a Rhys at college last semester but I think he moved to the city campus."

"Mr B, Rhys is my best friend and he's here right now. We've done all sorts of things together and you don't even recognise him."

"Here? You mean Tan's friend?"

"He's your friend too. Look at these photos."

Woorawa held out his cell phone and started to flick through photos they'd chosen which showed both Rhys and Mr B. Mr B's puzzled frown lasted for three pictures then he shook his head and pushed the phone away.

"Not now, Kieran. I think we should take Woorawa on his tour."

"And you've suddenly got a headache."

"I *am* feeling a bit off, but that won't stop us from helping Woorawa."

"Mr B, your headache's going to get worse unless we get rid of it."

"It won't get worse. It's just a tension headache and it will go away when I relax."

"Remember at the Fortress when Rhys zapped me? What about the mummy curse and the green toothpaste? Think of the Valley of Eagles when Rhys wrestled with me and Woorawa."

"Stop! Stop!"

"Why?"

"Because …" Mr B went quiet and stared at Kieran. "How did you know that asking me strange questions would make my headache worse?"

"I know because the same thing happened to me. Every time you have to focus your mind on Rhys, you'll feel bad."

Mr B looked at Woorawa and Tan, then after a peripheral glance at Rhys, focused on Kieran again. "You had headaches?"

"Yes, and Woorawa helped me get rid of them. We can do the same for you."

Kieran's spirits lifted when the faintest of grins pushed its way through Mr B's frown. "Well, Dr Kieran. How do you think you can do that?"

"It's easy. All I need is a cooperative patient. Will you trust me?"

"Is the treatment painful?"

"Awful! It's my way of getting back at slave-driving lecturers. Do you think you can cope with a neck massage?"

"I've never had one, but I guess it makes sense for a tension headache."

"You'd better sit on the chair because it might send you to sleep."

Mr B looked dubious about that, but he complied because a chair was a sensible place to receive a neck massage anyway.

"Close your eyes and relax. Your whole body's going to tingle and you'll feel good all over."

Mr B closed his eyes then opened them again. "This sounds like a hypnotism routine."

"Close them … and see what happens."

Rhys moved behind Mr B and started the massage while Kieran used the opal the same way he'd used it to help Rhys and Tan.

Mr B started smiling and said, "Oh my, that *is* nice. I'll have—"

His head lolled forward and Kieran and Tan both leapt unsuccessfully to catch Rhys as he collapsed in a heap on the floor. Kieran's first thought was alarm, but that disappeared when Tan put a backpack under Rhys's head and arranged him more comfortably on the floor.

"This is exactly what happened with you and Rhys, Kieran. Watch Mr B to make sure he doesn't fall off the chair."

So this was what zapping looked like. Kieran steadied Mr B, who'd started a slow slump forward.

"Tan, do you think we should put him on the floor?"

"Just hold him. If he's like Rhys, he'll wake up in a few moments."

Kieran looked at Woorawa. Why was he smiling? "What?"

"You've done it again, Kieran. Mr B's going to remember everything."

Kieran thought so, too, but they'd know soon enough. "Did I look like that when I was zapped?"

It wasn't exactly a smile, but the expression from both Rhys and Mr B was close to it.

"Yes, the whole time you were asleep you looked kind of happy. We all wondered if you were dreaming."

"I don't think so, Tan. I usually …"

Rhys stirred and Kieran felt his brow. His eyes opened and his face lit up.

"Cheat, Kieran. You zapped me without even touching me. Is Mr B okay?"

"We think so. Why?"

"It's the first time he's been zapped. Have I been asleep for long?"

"Not even a minute."

Rhys got up and moved in front of Mr B. "Really? That's the shortest ever. I wonder if I'm getting used to it?"

Woorawa shook his head. "I don't think so. I think it mightn't have been as strong because you weren't touching Kieran. I think Mr B won't sleep long either. Why don't we try to wake him up with the opal, Kieran? It's the kind of thing that might work."

Kieran started to think about it but there was no chance because Mr B's head lifted, and when his eyes opened they immediately tracked to Rhys.

"Rhys!"

Everyone smiled at the tone of recognition.

"Mr B, you're back with us."

"I was asleep, wasn't I? What happened to you?"

"Ask Kieran. No, ask Woorawa, because he's the only one who didn't forget things."

Kieran watched Mr B gather his thoughts.

"This is very strange, Rhys. I had no idea who you were. I feel like I'm waking from a dream."

"It was the same for all of us. Tell him, Woorawa."

"When I arrived at the airport Rhys wasn't in the car, and Kieran hardly knew who he was and didn't remember what happened at the Valley of the Eagles. Then, when the opal fixed him, he knew where Rhys was. Tan drove us, and when we found Rhys he was so bad he couldn't even look at Kieran without getting a headache. The opal fixed that, too, so we took him back to the share house and talked everything over."

After a great deal of explanation and excited discussion, Mr B checked his watch and jumped to his feet.

"We'll talk later. The head of TAFE was expecting us ten minutes ago and he must be wondering where we are. The professor will be there, too, as he wants to welcome Woorawa and talk to him about a few things."

"The professor? I thought that wasn't till tomorrow afternoon."

"It still is. This is something else."

It was a pity they were now rushing, as Woorawa's head was turning in every direction to take in every room and feature they passed. Well, he'd know it all soon.

The TAFE section was in a different building but the hurry meant it only took a few minutes to get there.

"There you are. We thought you must have gone walkabout."

Kieran winced inwardly at the head of TAFE's comment and checked Woorawa's reactions. He just reached for the proffered hand and smiled as he repeated the action with the beaming professor.

"Welcome, Woorawa. You look like you've recovered from your long trip and I'm pleased to see you with such a capable group of friends. Kieran and Tan are your new housemates, aren't they?"

"And Rhys. There are four of us."

The professor's nod was accompanied by a rather blank look. Another altered memory? Kieran wondered how far it went.

"Very good. Well, before you meet your new teachers I want to let you know that the college has decided to provide you with a scholarship covering all your fees and materials. It's a mark of respect for the help your people gave our group in Alice Springs and the offer of an ongoing association with our college."

Woorawa was stunned. "All my fees! That's … that's wonderful. My uncle Burrimul will be amazed."

"I'm sure he'll be pleased, but he won't be amazed because I discussed it with him just before we left Alice Springs and he knew I was going to approach the college about it."

"What does materials mean, Professor? Does it cover textbooks?"

"It certainly does, Kieran, both digital and hardcopy, as well as a living allowance equivalent to the cost of staying in one of the residential units."

This was wonderful news. Kieran knew from Woorawa that supporting his college education was a big commitment for his people.

"It's not just the college being generous, Woorawa. Burrimul said I could ask for regular consultations with you, and he even suggested you'd be happy to give talks to my study groups."

Woorawa's teeth flashed with a big smile. "Uncle Burrimul has put me in for this without even telling me. Well, of course, I'll do what I can, but I'm only young and I'll have to talk with him about what to say."

"Excellent. Let's meet your teachers. I had a meeting with them this morning to explain your situation."

*   *   *

"I can definitely feel a tingle. It's not very strong but it's quite pleasant. I can't understand why it doesn't do something for you, Woorawa. It seems to me that it should if it's been a First Australian artefact for so long."

Mr B had been holding the opal for nearly five minutes now and all the group could see his growing fascination. After the talks with Woorawa's teachers they'd gone back to Mr B's office to discuss all the weird things and, at Mr B's prompting, everyone had taken a turn holding the opal to see if anyone apart from Kieran could sense any kind of reaction from it.

"I don't see why. It's warm but we've all been holding it so that's what you'd expect. I definitely didn't feel the tingle that Kieran passes on when he's holding it. Does the opal make a difference when you talk to animals, Kieran?"

"We haven't tried that yet. There've been too many other things happening."

"And the Medusa look? Does that get stronger?"

"I don't think so. I've only tried it once with Tan and once with you, and it felt the same as usual. Glowing's the only thing I've really practised with it."

"It helped you with the blue light to track Rhys, didn't it?"

"Um … it might have, but I think I can do that by myself."

"Have you tried tracking anyone else?"

"There wasn't any point. Rhys was the only one I needed to find."

"Are you sure? There could easily be gaps in your memory you don't know about."

Kieran thought for a moment, then turned to Woorawa. "Do you think there's someone else? You're the only one of us who hasn't lost memories, and if we did mention someone you'd be the only person who might know."

"No. There's no one. But how do you know my memory hasn't been affected?"

That was a startling idea and the whole group puzzled over it till Mr B spoke.

"I fairly sure we can count that out, Woorawa. It seems as if someone, or something, wanted to get rid of Rhys, and it would have worked perfectly if you hadn't turned up with all your memories intact. It wouldn't make sense to change some of your memories and not the ones that allow you to spoil everything else they've done."

"Why would anyone want to get rid of me. I'm no one."

Kieran looked at Rhys in disbelief. Woorawa and Tan stared, and Mr B laughed outright.

"Don't be silly, Rhys. How can you say that?"

"Um … I didn't mean just no one. I mean, I'm just an ordinary person, so what's the point?"

Kieran grabbed Rhys's shoulders and gave him a gentle, remonstrating shake. "That's not right, Rhys. You're not ordinary. You're our friend and you're special … and I think you're the best person in the world."

Woorawa joined in by grabbing Rhys's neck and giving it a squeeze. "If it wasn't for you and Kieran I'd still be blind, so you can't say you're not special."

Mr B and Tan were nodding their agreement and Rhys squirmed under the twin grip with slight embarrassment. His smile said it was important to him.

"Two things stand out as being special and unique about you, Rhys, and we've just mentioned both of them. The zapping thing that happens when you and Kieran are together and your bond with him. When you weren't there Kieran had his worst migraine ever and from what he's explained to us, that was when he lost his memories of you. That would be a logical reason to separate the two of you. He forgot about the special things he can do, too so that's another reason they might have wanted to stop your magic hands from working."

"It's more than that. Whoever they are, I think they don't want Kieran and Rhys to be friends."

Everyone's attention lifted a notch and they looked for Tan to continue.

"Well, why did they get Rhys moved so far away? He could have stayed here, and with their memories changed they'd never have had anything to do with each other anyway."

"Hey, that's right. Even if I looked straight at Rhys I wouldn't have noticed him. This is scary. You're right, Tan, and I think that means we should expect them to try and do it again. The more we talk about this the more I'm worried. Tan's right. They went to a lot of trouble to get Rhys moved and all our memories and the minds of staff and administration in both campuses must have been changed."

"Not necessarily, Kieran. We know *we've* been affected, but it would only need one person in authority here at college to arrange the move. The admin staff from both campuses would carry out whatever instructions they were given. It would have to be someone high up, though, at least a Head of Department. There'll be a record of who it was so I'll check tomorrow morning when Administration opens."

Mr B addressed Kieran directly. "You'll have at least one more person's memories to fix, Kieran. You'll need to be with me, too, because arranging for Rhys to return to this campus might be difficult. We'll need to meet at eight-thirty when Admin opens, and you might have to miss a lecture to make sure everything's done."

There was more silence as the significance of what Mr B was saying sank in. Kieran was first to understand. "What are you talking about? I can't help arrange anything. I'm not even sure I can help with someone's memory when I don't know them."

"I think there's a good chance you can. You put ideas into the animal's minds, like telling the little skink where the meat from Burrimul's sandwich was hidden, and this would be the same kind of thing."

"People's minds? That's pretty weird, like brainwashing."

Mr B nodded. "It's already been happening so that makes it even more likely that you can. Practise on Rhys when you get home."

Rhys's jaw dropped. "You want Kieran to try to brainwash me? That's not just a *bit* weird. It's *totally* weird."

"No, it's not. We already know he can fix you, and you're closer to him than anyone else, so you're the best one for him to experiment on."

After a moment's consideration, Rhys burst into laughter. "I don't trust him. If it works, he'll make me think I'm one of his frogs and I'll be eating flies all day."

Kieran nodded and bumped his shoulder against Rhys. "Sounds great! When do we start?"

Woorawa spoke up. "Right now! You'll be so busy tomorrow with Mr B and the start of semester, you won't have a chance till the afternoon when we all get home. You should spend the rest of today practising all the things they made you forget."

Tan added another thought. "And using the opal too. It's what fixed you when Rhys wasn't here."

"I agree with Tan and Woorawa, Kieran, and keep the opal with you wherever you go. Try the aura thing that you use with the animals on Rhys and see if you can get him to do something."

Kieran turned to Rhys who gave him a nod. So much for not trusting him.

"What sort of thing, Mr B?"

"I don't know. Make it easy. Something simple he's likely to do anyway. If that works you can try something harder."

"It feels strange to think of Rhys like an animal."

"We're all animals, Kieran."

"I suppose so."

Kieran pulled the memories back into his mind of the various animals and built up the aura he'd used with them. He hadn't done this since the big migraine but Mr B's use of the word 'aura' acted as another trigger and it clicked into place. *You're my friend, Rhys. You're with* me *now. What will we do?* No, don't mind-say it. That wasn't how it worked. Feel it and put it into the aura. Kieran started but lost all concentration and sense of the aura when Rhys suddenly grabbed him in a big hug. Kieran laughed and returned the hug.

"I was right in the middle of concentrating and you ..." Kieran stared in amazement as he realised what had happened.

"What?"

"Rhys, I didn't tell you to hug me but I was thinking you're my friend and it's so good you're back with me ... I think it worked."

"A hug? I didn't feel strange or anything."

Woorawa waved a hand for attention.

"I think it worked too. None of the animals acted as if they were upset or knew anything was strange. Try it again, Kieran, but use something more … more specific."

Kieran noted how quickly the aura returned this time and realised that the more he did this the easier it would be. What to do though? It should still be something easy, but more definite. Yes, that would do.

Rhys glanced at the office window then walked over and looked at the little courtyard outside. "Hey, Kieran, there's a magpie in the gum tree and some sparrows on the ground. Why don't you show Tan how the animals react with you? He hasn't seen it yet … Why are you looking at me like that? You need to practise this, you know."

"I wanted you to look out the window and you did. Mr B's right. I can give you ideas."

"You told me to? I don't believe you … Well, I do, but … You know what I mean. Did you tell me to look for the birds as well?"

"I didn't tell you anything, Rhys. I made it a kind of feeling about looking outside. The bird stuff was yours."

"It just felt natural. It could be a coincidence and we both thought about the window at the same time."

Kieran shook his head. "It was too definite, Rhys. I sort of know it was me."

"Get me to do something else then, but tell Mr B what it is first. I'll stand here without doing anything and try to stop you."

Kieran grinned. He had a great idea. "Good thinking! If you move you'll have to believe me." He went to Mr B and whispered that he was going to get Woorawa to ask for the opal and hold it up to the light then suggest he might drop it and Rhys would need to protect it. While Mr B started speaking Kieran set the aura going with Woorawa.

"That was very explicit, Rhys. See if you can fight against the impulse to move."

"Um … Can I hold the opal first, Kieran? I want to see if any changes happen while you're zapping Rhys."

"Interesting idea, Woorawa, but I don't think it will."

Woorawa took the opal and when he held it up to the light, Kieran redirected the aura. Nothing happened for a few seconds but then Rhys rushed from his position in a panic and closed his hand over the opal.

"Whoo! Careful, Woorawa. It's priceless and you nearly dropped it."

"No, I didn't. I was holding it firmly."

"Yes you …" Rhys's eyes widened and he turned to Mr B. "I moved."

"Yes, Rhys, and unless you, Woorawa and Kieran have worked some unbelievably elaborate trick on me I'm totally convinced. Kieran told me he was going to get Woorawa to take the opal and you'd have to protect it. You can let go now."

Rhys released Woorawa's hand as if it was on fire. Woorawa stared at the opal with a similar kind of disbelief then laughed as they both looked at Kieran.

"You're a cheat! You used me to get at Rhys."

"I know. It was easy, too, and kind of fun."

"Both of us at the same time? Was more than one hard? I suppose it wasn't, because you called all the frogs and that flock of corellas."

"I did you first, then when you had the opal I changed to Rhys."

"Try us all at the same time, Kieran. From what Woorawa just said you should be able to manage it."

For the next hour the group stayed together, their excitement and amazement mounting with every new mind-control experiment. Tan used that term for it after he found himself dancing his own interpretation of a sailor's hornpipe.

Eventually Mr B had work to do, and they left in Tan's car and drove to a shopping centre to get food supplies for the next week. At home they had sandwiches for lunch, then Tan and Woorawa sat down to check through Woorawa's Maths course and work out areas he needed to concentrate on. Kieran and Rhys went into Rhys's room and plopped down on the bed for a talk.

"Hey, Kieran, how are we going to fit our swimming in? We can't ask Tan to wait around for us five days a week."

"I know. It's a pity he doesn't like it. It'll work though. He enjoys studying in the library and we might be able to arrange a couple of afternoons when he goes there instead of here, and we can catch a tram when he doesn't."

"Why doesn't he like swimming?"

"I don't know. I asked him once and the way he dodged the question gave me the feeling he was scared."

"Scared? Maybe something happened when he was young and he's never got over it. That happened to me when I was in primary school and I didn't go in a pool for two years."

Kieran was amazed. "You? You're a swimming freak. What happened?"

"I used to get bullied and I got thrown in the deep end when I didn't know how to swim. I didn't get over it till I was at the beach one time and had so much fun in the waves I made up my mind to learn swimming properly so I could stop being scared. We'll take Tan to the beach when it's warmer and make sure he enjoys himself. That might help him."

"That's too long, Rhys. Summer's months away so we should try something else. I wonder if he'd try out a spa bath?"

"You can't swim in a spa bath, can you? I've never even been in one."

"Neither have I, but if we found one big enough for four of us we might be able to teach him to float. That would be a good start, and if he learnt that much we might be able to persuade him to try the college pool."

"Hey! You could persuade him with your mind. Except it doesn't feel right. I was thinking about it on the way here in the car and it's going to be weird. Not about Tan swimming … When you make us do things, I mean. How will we know if we're thinking for ourselves or if it's really you? Are you going to have any rules?"

"We'll have to. Tan and Woorawa said they're okay with it, but I'll only do things I know they'll be happy with … and the same for you of course. I was thinking about it too, and I'll only do it when we have special practice times or when you all know it's going to happen. It makes me angry that my own mind has been changed and it would be awful if any of you felt like that about me, even if it was only for a moment. Tan's the one I want to be most careful with because he keeps things to himself more than you or Woorawa."

"Woorawa will let you try anything. He's just about obsessed with how much he wants you to practise everything, and I'm pretty amazed he's not in here now telling you different things to try."

"I know, but Tan offering to help him with all the stuff the Maths lecturer was talking about made him really happy and the more help he gets the better."

"I can help him with English and Lit, but not Maths, and it sounds like he knows more computer stuff than any of us."

"I've got it all worked out. With me and Mr B and Tan he'll get at least an hour of Maths help every college night and then extra stuff on the weekends."

"I wonder how good he is at studying?"

"We'll soon find out."

"What are you going to make me do?"

"Five hundred hugs!"

"Idiot! You're going to use Woorawa's ideas, aren't you?"

"Of course, and our own ideas, too, and you have to fight against me as hard as you can. We've got to work out how the opal fits in as well."

A bit over an hour later Woorawa came rushing in, followed more sedately by Tan, and demanded to know what had been happening.

"Keep cool, Woorawa. Tell us what you did with Tan first and then we'll show you."

Rhys laughed. "Yeah, we'll show you all right. He'll have you sticking your finger up Tan's nose and sucking the boogers."

Tan looked concerned but Woorawa didn't.

"As if! We worked out a plan for some of the things I'm way behind in, and then he showed me the patterns he uses to solve equations. He's ten times better than my old teacher at explaining things, and he showed me where I was going wrong. Now, what have you been practising, and did you use the opal much? I'm going to ring Burrimul tonight to tell him everything."

Kieran spoke to Tan. "It's my turn for coaching Woorawa tomorrow night so what topic do you reckon we should work on?"

"He needs tons more work with equations, but I know where he's up to so I think I should stay with him for that. The only graphing work he's done has all been in his head, which seems just about impossible to me, and his class work for the next couple of weeks is about quadratics so he'll be left behind if he doesn't understand plotting."

Kieran thought back to Mr B's clever ideas for learning graphing. "What else? Mr B's brilliant at graphing so he should help him with that on Tuesday."

"Just about anything. Geometry and trig are his next big topics, or he could do a catch-up on surds and irrational numbers."

Rhys let out a big groan. It was false of course.

"The slave drivers are at it again, Woorawa. They'll strain your brain till you think you're on a different planet and you'll find yourself outside screaming at the sky. Then they'll give you two minutes to recover and start on another hour of torture. Come into my room whenever you feel like you're going crazy and we'll have some fun."

Kieran dived at Rhys and pushed him onto his back on the bed. "Torturers, hey? You'll get torture! Help me hold him down, guys. We'll make him show us what it's like to scream at the sky."

Woorawa didn't hesitate, and quiet, reserved Tan joined in when he saw how hard-pressed they were to contain Rhys's greater strength. Rhys did start screeching when the fingers dug into his stomach and vowed that Woorawa and Tan were both dead when he got them by themselves.

"That means we better make the most of it while we've got the chance, Woorawa. Take his runners off and tickle his feet then we'll really hear him screech."

"Don't you dare! If you do that you're mangled forever."

Woorawa hesitated. "Tickling's murder. If I don't tickle you will you promise not to tickle me?"

Rhys struggled even more to get free, then eventually subsided. "I promise! I promise!"

Conspiratorial grins passed between Kieran and Rhys and in seconds it was Woorawa who was restrained and helpless on his back. Tan just watched. The combined strength of Rhys and Kieran was too much and despite his desperate convulsions Woorawa's screeches filled the room.

"Stop! Stop! You're a cheat, Rhys. Stop. You promised."

"I'm not tickling, just holding. Get his shoes, Tan. That's what he was going to do to me."

Tan was quite gentle, but a light stroke on the arches of Woorawa's feet was the equivalent of starting an earthquake on the bed.

The struggles raged for ten minutes or so, with gales of laughter, dire threats of diabolical murder, and further torture and rapid and unpredictable changes in strategy and alliance, till Tan moved away to collapse in Rhys's chair. Everyone else paused to look at him. Rhys called him a wimp and when Tan happily agreed Woorawa wriggled out of Kieran's neck hold.

"We come in to find out what you've been doing and we get attacked. I'm going to report this to Mr B and Uncle so there's a rule about no more foot tickling."

There'd be no such rule because it was totally evident that he'd been loving every moment. A happy feeling crested in Kieran's mind. How lucky he was to have friends like this. Without him being conscious of starting it a soft glow covered the three of them. Kieran became the centre of attention when the three of them shared a very surprised look.

"Kieran! Control! You're projecting."

Whoops! How did that happen? Kieran quickly turned off the sensual bit and toned down the glow.

"Sorry, I didn't mean to. I'm feeling happy and I forgot to hold it back."

Woorawa laughed and turned to Tan. "How are we going to cope? Every time he feels happy?"

"I don't mind. It's better than him being unhappy."

Rhys thought that was funny. "Don't encourage him, Tan … I mean, encourage him to be happy, but controlled happy. We want him to be happy all the time but I don't think that would be physically possible for the rest of us. Is it just because we're friends, Kieran, or do you think we're all good-looking as well?"

Why was Rhys saying that? He knew very well what Kieran thought because they'd had a light-hearted comparison talk on the way back from Alice Springs. That was another memory he'd forgotten.

"Tan and Woorawa are good-looking. You're ugly!"

Rhys crowed with delight. "See, now we know why it happens. He's got lust in his mind for all of us."

Kieran nearly fell over with surprise. Woorawa and Tan just nodded as if that was a perfectly reasonable explanation.

"You lot, you're all as bad as each other. One little memory lapse, that's all it was. How come you're so strong, Woorawa? It takes two of us to hold you down."

"I'm not. That was because you were tickling me. I *have* done lots of dancing though, so I've got a bit of endurance."

"Is dancing very different now that you can see? I can't imagine what it would be like to dance in the dark."

"It wasn't dark for me, Rhys. I put a picture in my mind and watched it carefully while I moved. You can try for yourself anytime you like just by turning the lights off or closing your eyes."

"When are you going to dance for Tan? We're all expecting a full-on ceremony with music and costumes and everything."

"You'll have to join in then, Kieran, and let me paint you."

"Yeah! Rhys loves dancing and I can't wait to see Tan in a loincloth."

"Hey! What's that supposed to mean? I'm not dancing. I'll look silly."

"Good. You'll look silly and the paint will hide the ugly. You heard Woorawa. His rule is all of us or Tan will miss out, and you wouldn't do that, would you?"

"Cheat, Kieran. This is old-fashioned blackmail. Control without mind control … Hey! You can make me like the dancing till it's over."

"I could, but I won't. You wait and see, Tan. He'll like it anyway because he did at Alice Springs."

"And what *did* you practise, Kieran? Or have you got a conspiracy not to tell me?"

"I was going to tell you ages ago, Woorawa, but you all went crazy."

*   *   *

High King Aglaron studied the evidence of concern as Maynor approached, and immediately raised his privacy wards.

"Keryth?"

"Yes, my Lord. We don't understand how, but Keryth's new companion has somehow managed to reverse all the success of our recent effort."

"All? How can that be? Uirebon described the dark child's influence as a minor detail which you planned to clear."

"So I thought, but when I was recovered enough to try, all my efforts were confounded. The human's mind was hidden despite my possession of all the necessary recognition markers. Uirebon believes the Ancient People have unique protections."

"You attempted to reach him while he was with his people? I instructed Uirebon to warn you about that."

"He did, my Lord, but the action was necessary and I made the reach with great caution."

"Was there a reaction of any kind?"

"None at all, apart from the bewildering absence of the dark child's personality. Lord Uirebon counselled this new reach when the child travelled to join Keryth."

"Necessitating this latest call for power."

"Indeed, my Lord. I had no other option, but the enforced wait, short though it was while the triad recovered, was enough for him to re-establish Keryth's human memories and reconnect with the warrior."

Aglaron's frown started to match Maynor's. "The dark child did all that? What have you discovered, Maynor? I wouldn't have thought it possible."

"Very little, and Uirebon also finds it baffling. Without greater reserves of power my pathway to Keryth's mind was barred. The dark child also had a type of resistance. Pethron's memories were completely open but he was in his own dwelling and completely unaware of the changes."

"This venture with Keryth becomes increasingly difficult. Is there a way forward, or should we consider recalling Keryth and trying a new approach?"

"My Lord, look on this as a setback, not a difficulty. All we need do is regain control, and with the dark child separated from his people and amenable, we are, in fact, in a better position than last time. Keryth's growing resistance is the biggest factor for consideration, but with adequate power that will be overcome exactly as it always has been."

"Hmm! Yes, I see, and the procedure returns to its proper course. With several provisos, we will proceed."

"My Lord?"

"Our preparation, our coordination, and our resources must be the most comprehensive yet, and this time I will be present personally. How long to prepare three triads?"

"A third triad?"

"You asked for adequate power, Maynor, so a triad of triads will assist us."

"I will consult with Lord Uirebon but the principal triad, which bore the brunt of effort for this latest reach, will need at least two days for proper recovery."

"Two days here equates to almost ten days in the Human World. Inform Uirebon he should expedite the recovery."

*   *   *

Kieran and Tan met Woorawa at lunchtime the next day to see how his first classes had gone. Rhys couldn't be with them because Mr B had taken him to Administration to get all his courses re-established.

"How did it all go, Woorawa? Were there any hassles?"

"Everyone stared at me. Uncle Burrimul said they would but it didn't sink in till it happened. I think I must be the only First Australian a lot of them have seen in real life. It made me feel funny."

"Don't take any notice. They'll get used you in a couple of days. Were your teachers okay?"

"The Science one was great and the English one was ordinary. They both asked me all sorts of questions to find out what I know and that's when everyone stared at me."

"What did you do in your spare? Go to the library like you said you might?"

"No, I explored the college instead. Rhys told me about the swimming pool last night, so I went to check it out and I'm going to join up after we've had something to eat. Where *is* Rhys?"

"Mr B took him to the main office. Everything's all right but he has to be there for some of the paperwork. Let's go to the pool now because when he's finished he'll look for us in the dining room."

"I haven't got any bathers till we see Rhys. He said he'd bring some for me."

"I haven't either, so we'll just get you joined up for the semester. It'll only take a few minutes."

A short time later Tan was carrying on because Woorawa had paid for him to join as well, saying Rhys could teach them both to swim. Kieran kept out of it because Tan was obviously reluctant and only agreeing because Woorawa was so insistent.

"We'll have our first swim tomorrow afternoon, Tan, when lectures are finished."

"I won't be able to. I haven't got any bathers either."

"That won't stop us. We'll visit a shopping centre on the way home this afternoon and get some. I can't wait. Look how beautiful the water is."

Kieran used the pool so much he took what it looked like for granted. Woorawa was right. The water did look good.

"Let's go. Rhys might be at the dining room by now."

Walking into the dining room brought home to Kieran and Tan what Woorawa meant about being stared at. Right now was the busiest time, when everyone came for the good range of meals on offer, and as they joined the back end of the service queue the surrounding conversation stopped and heads turned from all directions to see why. Kieran spoke very softly.

"Do you want to stay here, Woorawa? We could go to the cafe instead, if you like."

"No, it's all right. I might as well get used to it, and Rhys wouldn't know where to find us. What are we going to get?"

Tan and Kieran both pointed to the big menu displayed on the wall behind the dining room staff.

"Whatever you like. I'm going to get a beef burger because they make good ones here."

"I'm having a chicken schnitzel. They're good too."

Woorawa was undecided till he nodded his head. "Can I have both. I didn't eat much breakfast this morning because I was nervous."

The hum of conversation had rebuilt to normal levels but Woorawa was still being watched.

"Of course you can."

A few minutes later they made their orders and found a spare table near the back of the room. Rhys arrived and Kieran gave him a wave when he saw him searching the room from the entrance. Rhys waved back, made his own order, then joined them at the table.

"What's happened? I thought you'd be halfway through your meal."

"Nothing happened. Woorawa signed up Tan and himself to be members at the pool and we just got here. Is everything sorted?"

"No problems. We had authorisation from the Head of Department. Mr B said you had to fix his mind."

"Yeah. He couldn't understand why you'd want to come back when you'd asked him if you could leave just last week."

"He thought I asked him?"

"He remembered it, till I used the opal, and then he knew you hadn't."

"Does he know you magicked him?"

"I don't think so. He looked funny then said his mind must be playing tricks and okayed everything."

"So, was he hard to fix when you didn't know him?"

Kieran shook his head. It had been no different to Rhys, Mr B or Tan. Easier really.

"Wow! And Tan's swimming with us? Did you zap him too?"

Tan jumped in his seat, and Kieran quickly shook his head again.

"No way, Rhys. Woorawa made a big deal about it and we're going to a shopping centre on the way home to get bathers for both of them."

"What for? I've got spare ones at home."

"They'd probably fall off, Rhys. You're bigger than both of us."

"I suppose. You could just tie the string tight but new ones would definitely be more comfortable ... The people at that table are rude. They're staring at us and it looks like they're talking about us too."

"You should have seen it when we first came in. You'd think they'd never seen a First Australian."

Tan replied, "I'm sure they haven't. Woorawa's the first one I've seen for real and he's the only one at college. He *is* very interesting to look at, too, so in a way you can't blame them."

"I'm interesting to look at? How come? No one says that at home."

Kieran, Rhys and Tan all laughed.

"Of course you are. Your skin looks unreal."

"And you're too good-looking."

Woorawa jabbed at Rhys's arm.

"And your hair's so curly."

"Lots of people have curly hair, Tan."

"Not that curly. And you smile all the time and that makes your teeth stand out."

Woorawa looked at Tan with surprise. "My teeth? What are you talking about? No one's ever said that either."

Kieran explained. "It's the contrast with your skin, Woorawa. Alice Springs people wouldn't notice because they're used to it but it makes your smile special here."

Rhys nodded towards the people he'd called rude. "Smile at them, Woorawa. They'll fall in love with you because you're so cute."

Woorawa clamped his lips shut, but had to laugh when Rhys went cross-eyed at him and made silly faces. "You're a wanker, Rhys."

Three sets of jaws dropped, and Woorawa's expression changed to puzzlement.

"What?"

Tan recovered from his startlement. "You just told Rhys he ... plays with his private bits."

"No, I didn't. That just means he's being silly."

"Not down here."

Kieran laughed, then stage-whispered, "Every night! If he doesn't shut his door you'll have to block your ears."

Tan nodded in emphatic agreement.

"As if! You wait till we get home, Kieran. You're dead … and you too, Tan."

Tan started to say something but Kieran interrupted.

"Hey! Order number seventy-four just showed on the board. That's your beef burger, Woorawa. Mine'll be ready in a second so let's go and get them."

*   *   *

Woorawa looked at the huge array of stock in the surf shop and turned to Rhys. "What sort of bathers do you wear? There's too many kinds here."

Rhys pointed to the speedo rack. "We use speed racers. You glide through the water easily with them and there's no drag."

"Okay, let's get them then. What colour do you want, Tan? I got you into this so I'm paying today."

"What? No … you don't have to do that. I mean … are you sure?"

"Of course. Why not?"

"Well, I like black."

Kieran shook his head. "Not black. It will look funny, Woorawa with black bathers, like he's got nothing on. Red would look terrific."

"What colours do you and Rhys wear, Kieran? It'll be fun if we all match up."

Kieran and Rhys shared a look then burst out laughing.

"What did I say now? Something else rude?"

"No, Woorawa, we've both got blue bathers and we call each other twins because of it."

"Quadruplets, Kieran. That would turn it into quadruplets."

"Quins when Mr B coaches us. His are light blue too."

"Really? That sounds great."

Woorawa's mind was made up, and in very short order two pairs of sleek, light blue racers were fitted and purchased.

*   *   *

"I can't fight you, Kieran, no matter what I do."

"I wonder why, Rhys. Mr B can hold off a bit, and so can Woorawa when he does his chant thing. We'll ask him to teach it to us after tea."

"Aren't you doing Maths coaching after tea?"

"Yes, but fifteen minutes before we start won't matter. I think Tan would like to learn the chant too. He's fascinated with everything about Woorawa."

"So am I. I can't wait for the ceremony on the weekend. He said if we do all the dancing and stories, it will go for over an hour."

"It'll be a lot longer than that with all the body-painting and getting ready. We'll get lots of photos of you dancing."

"As if! Hey, that's something we haven't tried. See if you can make me dance without even knowing I'm doing it."

Kieran had to think about that. "I don't know if I can. It's easy to make you dance and I can make you forget afterwards, but I don't know about while you're doing it."

"Why not? It would be like when people are hypnotised. Hey, you might be a super hypnotist."

"No way. The glow thing shows up on the photos on our phones."

"You could be hypnotising us to think that."

"No way, Rhys. I see the glow in the photos, too, so I'd have to be hypnotising myself."

"Self-hypnosis is real. Some people do it to stop themself smoking cigarettes."

Kieran shook his head because it just didn't feel right. Two minutes later, Rhys was happily dancing to the Irish music Kieran had started on his little sound system.

The door opened and Woorawa and Tan poked their heads in to see what was going on.

"I told him he likes it so much he can't stop. Will I make you join in too?"

Tan said Kieran could try but he wasn't going to, then immediately jigged from one foot to the other, copying Rhys and Woorawa's movements till the music finished and Rhys sat on the bed.

"How did I do that?" mused Tan. "I've never even danced to Irish music before."

Rhys looked puzzled. "What Irish music? We were talking about hypnotism."

Woorawa and Tan didn't understand till Kieran dramatically pointed at Rhys and told him to get his memory back.

Rhys jumped to his feet and very excitedly told Tan and Woorawa what had happened, before turning to Kieran.

"That was amazing. I never would have thought dancing could be so much fun. Can I borrow the music to try by myself? I want to see how different it is when I haven't been zapped. Wow! I wonder if you can make people like anything. Next time Tan cooks broccoli you can try and make me like it."

"That'll be easy. I'll make you eat everyone else's."

Rhys turned to Woorawa. "He's getting stronger at everything. Watch what he can do with the GPS glow."

In an instant the blue glow popped into view, hovered in mid-air, then formed into the shape of an arrow.

"Where's the college?"

The blue arrow swivelled through about 30°.

"Where's Mr B?"

There didn't seem to be any change, but that made sense because he should be at the college. Woorawa was totally impressed.

"The arrow shape's brilliant, Kieran. It's probably too far away but can you make it point to Uncle Burrimul?"

Nothing happened.

"He must be too far. I'll try again with the opal."

Kieran closed his eyes, built a mental image of Burrimul and strengthened the opal connection. Yes, that felt right. Now for a kind of push at the arrow. He opened his eyes and found himself the centre of attention.

"The arrow moved, Kieran. It's pointing in the right kind of direction, but do you think it can be correct? It's over two-thousand kilometres."

"It's right. I can tell."

"Where's Paris?"

"Paris? Why do you want to know where that is, Tan?"

"I don't. I just thought it might be a good test."

Kieran went through the process again. He opened his eyes and shook his head. "It won't work. I need something I know about for a focus."

"What about the Valley of Eagles? Have a try at that."

"What are you thinking now, Tan? From this far away it'll be the same as finding Burrimul."

"Not really. I'm wondering if finding people is easier than finding places."

"Hey, yeah. Try it, Kieran."

Kieran thought it was interesting, too, and using his connection with the opal, sent another push at the arrow. He didn't close his eyes this time because the finding process was now established and he wanted to watch. Yes, the arrow moved and it was right.

"How come you left your eyes open? Was it easier than finding Burrimul?"

"I had to push just as hard but I knew how to do it this time. The pattern kind of clicked into place like it did with the animals."

"Can you find specific animals? Ones you've talked to I mean. Like the sparrows at college."

"I think so."

The arrow moved.

"Yes, and I didn't need the opal to help me."

"Wow! Try the peregrine falcon in the Valley of the Eagles."

After a few seconds, the arrow moved again and Kieran grinned at the amazed looks. "I needed the opal that time but it definitely works."

Rhys laughed and put a hand on Woorawa's shoulder. "Next time you ring Burrimul tell him Kieran's mutated into a homing pigeon."

After a pause he surprised Woorawa and Tan by flapping both arms up and down and making a weird cooing sound.

"You cheat, Kieran. You didn't ask me first."

"Didn't have to. It's still practice time. As long as it's not embarrassing I can make you do anything."

"And flapping my arms and sounding like a bird isn't embarrassing? Make Tan and Woorawa do it too."

After that happened, Kieran was attacked by three vengeful foes and dumped on the bed. He could have made them stop or turn on each other, of course, but that wouldn't have been as much fun, so he started them taking turns at making animal noises instead. The attack dissolved into laughter at the expression on Rhys's face when he hooted like a monkey.

"This is cruelty. How long before practice time's over?"

"Just one more thing, Rhys. I think we'll have a fashion parade with the new bathers. What do you all think?"

Tan shook his head and Woorawa laughed. Rhys said he couldn't wait to see this, then had a sudden urge to join in. Ten minutes later, Tan was dressed again and asking questions.

"How hard is that, Kieran? I never would have posed like that if you hadn't made me."

"It's not hard at all, and it gets easier every time I try. Did I go too far?"

"No, but I've always been modest so I'm surprised I'm not embarrassed now that practice time's finished. I think it's because it was so funny watching Rhys flexing his muscles like a bodybuilder and me and Woorawa copying him, but I can't tell if you've changed something and it's stayed changed."

Kieran thought carefully about everything he'd done before answering. "I did make you think it would be fun, but I definitely turned that off when we finished. I know I'm not doing anything now because I have to kind of click things in to make them work."

"That's not what Tan means, Kieran. He's wondering if you might be making permanent changes without meaning to. That's a really serious question. What if you're practising and you tell him he doesn't like Maths anymore and it stays with him? It could wreck college for him."

Rhys was right and Kieran became very concerned. Could an easy thing like making Tan enjoy showing off his new bathers change him forever?

"What do you think, Tan? Does anything feel wrong?"

"No, I feel like we've been laughing and having a good time, and it's so exciting and unreal I can't wait to see what happens when we have more practices."

Woorawa interrupted. "Tan, this is what you should do. Put your new bathers on then walk along the street and make Rhys's muscle poses whenever you meet someone."

Tan looked horrified. "No way!"

Rhys joined in. "Go on! I dare you!"

"Get lost, Rhys. It was fun in here, but I wouldn't do it in public … unless Kieran made me, and I know he won't."

Rhys turned to Woorawa. "How about you, Woorawa? Would you do it?"

"Not here, but I would at home. People there would know it was mucking around."

"Woorawa was clever, Tan. He just proved you haven't really lost your modesty and Kieran didn't make a permanent change. I reckon you're just getting used to his warped sense of humour."

Practice time *was* over so Kieran made do with giving Rhys a jab in the ribs.

* * *

"Hey, Woorawa, Kieran wants to ask you something."

"I do? What?" said Kieran.

"About the chanting."

"Yes, when you do that special chant Burrimul taught you it's harder for me to get through to you with the Medusa look, so we wondered if you could teach it to all of us after tea?"

"Sure, it'll be fun. But it'll be hard, too, because you have to build the right frame of mind before any chants work properly."

Tan was immediately fascinated. "How many chants do you know, and what are they for?"

"All sorts of things, and I'll show you some of them when we do the ceremony."

"Are they words or just special sounds?"

"Both, so you'll have to learn some of my language as well."

"Really? I'll make tea a bit early then. Is that all right with everyone?"

*   *   *

The delicious smell brought everyone at a run when Tan called that the food was ready, and then everyone laughed because Woorawa was still wearing his new racing bathers.

"You should put something else on, Woorawa. You look so sexy we won't know if Kieran's drooling over you or the food."

"Ha! And you won't ever know, Rhys, because you'll be so busy looking yourself."

Woorawa didn't know what to make of it. "Do you really think I look … sexy?"

"Totally!"

Kieran and Rhys both nodded then looked for Tan's response.

"Yes, you do, Woorawa. Your skin's very striking against the light blue material and if there's anyone at the pool tomorrow afternoon, there'll be a lot more staring."

"Do you want me to put more clothes on? I like the way these feel."

Everyone shook their head and Kieran said he could wear whatever he liked. Eating took over and the food was so good that the murmurs of appreciation left little room for ordinary conversation.

*   *   *

Kieran, Rhys and Tan sat on the couch and Woorawa sat on a seat in front of them and, for a few minutes, there was laughter as they somewhat self-consciously copied Woorawa's rendition of the first part of the chant. The laughter subsided quickly, though, as Woorawa's strong atmosphere of purpose came through, and the three pupils applied themselves to the serious business of learning both sound and mindset. Half an hour later, Woorawa gave his approval and announced that it was time to see if chanting would help Rhys and Tan.

"Let's try it together first, Kieran. A group chant's more effective than a solo, and when I think we're ready I'll give you a sign to start the Medusa look. Do it very gently for a while, too, so we can get used to fighting against it."

His deep, rhythmic voice started and Rhys and Tan immediately joined in. Rhys watched Woorawa for a moment but all his focus was on Kieran. The strange quality of the sound dissipated and the mood clicked into place. A touch on Kieran's knee started the look with just a whisper of force. Nothing happened and, feeling quite excited, Kieran pushed a tiny bit harder. Yes, this was definitely working. He got through to Tan and Rhys, enough to sense a slight struggle. The chanting suddenly strengthened, and when the look stopped working, Kieran pushed just enough to make it start again. Twice more Rhys and Tan adapted, but then the push was too much. Tan faltered in his chanting and put his hand out in the warding sign and Rhys shook his head emphatically for Kieran to drop all the pressure. The chant stopped completely and when Woorawa saw the perspiration on Rhys's brow he was really pleased.

"Wow! That was strong medicine and it worked."

Rhys wiped his brow. "I don't know about medicine, but it was sure hard. What was it like for you, Kieran? Could you tell how much difference it made?"

"It really worked, Rhys. The amount of pressure I was using at the end would have had you running out of the room without the chant. I could feel it each time you built your barriers. Woorawa's right about doing it slowly."

"Slow! That wasn't slow."

"Yes it was, Rhys. You've been chanting and fighting me for nearly twenty minutes."

"Was it hard for you?"

Kieran shook his head. "Easy as anything, and I didn't even get close to needing the opal."

"Rhys, can you fight another Medusa look from Kieran? Just a quick one without the chant so we can work out whether your barriers are any better."

"Sure, but let's have a drink first. I feel like a break."

A few minutes later Rhys started a steady chant and Kieran pushed till Rhys couldn't cope.

"I didn't last very long. I think it works better when Woorawa's helping."

"I definitely have to push harder than before you learnt the chant, but your barrier was nearly as good when you stopped this time."

"That's what I thought. I bet it's the same if you try it with Tan."

Tan started chanting without being asked and the same thing happened.

"See, Woorawa's got a natural barrier and the chanting lets him share it. Could you tell how much you were getting through to him?"

"When he's chanting? I don't know. It worked back at the Valley of the Eagles but I can tell he's a lot stronger tonight."

Tan and Rhys looked at Woorawa with great interest.

"Really?"

"If I'm stronger it's because I practised the chant with Uncle Burrimul before I came down here, Rhys. He thought it was important."

"Wow! He knows a lot. What about a full-on battle with Kieran? You game for that?"

"Of course, and we should all try it every day because it will help Kieran with his practice."

"You're really keen for me to get lots of practice, aren't you?"

"It makes sense, Kieran, but I'm following Uncle's orders really. Every time I ring him, he insists that I push you as much as I can."

"Well, it makes sense to me, too, but I've done over an hour already today and we have to get to our college stuff."

Woorawa looked worried. "I'm taking too much of your time. We can skip our Maths coaching tonight, if you like, because Tan's already been helping and Mr B's coming tomorrow night."

"No way! I like coaching, and I promised, and I'm all organised, and I've been looking forward to it. As soon as we finish this battle we're into it."

Kieran was surprised and touched by the impulsive hug he received. Woorawa settled back on the couch and started his chant then, a moment later, signalled he was ready. Kieran started with a push that had first affected Rhys and Tan. Nothing happened, of course, so he lifted direct-ly to the level where they couldn't cope. Still nothing happened, so this time he gave quite a strong push. Woorawa stayed resolute and, amazed, Kieran steadily increased pressure then held it when he knew he couldn't go any further.

Woorawa's mind was a wall he couldn't pass. Maybe he could with the opal? Still keeping the pressure on, he made the familiar connection, felt the tingle that he now thought of as a kind of energy and directed it against the wall. The chant ceased. Woorawa gasped, slumped back against the couch and toppled sideways. Shocked, Kieran reflexively stopped all the pressure and, for a panicked moment, watched Woorawa's collapse. *No! No! No! He must be all right.* He reached forward to hold Woorawa's brow.

"Rhys! Magic hands. Quick!"

Tan looked in disbelief at Woorawa and Rhys asleep on the couch, with Kieran slumped awkwardly on the floor partly against Rhys's knees. With an awkward struggle Tan lifted Kieran to the couch then made sure all three were comfortable. The familiar half-smiles of a 'zap' eased his concern, though, and he sat on the chair watching and wondering exactly what had happened and who would wake first.

*   *   *

"Tan, stop looking so worried. We'll stay in the shallow end as long as you like and no one's going to force you to do anything you aren't happy with. Do you want to jump in or go down the steps?"

"Is it safe?"

Kieran was surprised by this response as the water here was not much more than waist deep. Tan's worry must be stronger than his usual calm and logical approach.

"Rhys, show him what it's like. What about you, Woorawa? Is jumping in new for you?"

"Kind of. It was always a bit scary and I only did it when I had someone with me I could trust."

Rhys closed his eyes then opened them again before jumping in and Kieran knew he'd been imagining what it would be like to commit to a jump when you couldn't see.

It was a very sedate jump and his head didn't go under the water.

"Come on, Woorawa, it's great. The water's terrific."

Woorawa laughed, spread his arms and legs wide in a kind of natural safety jump, then, after hitting the water, started splashing Rhys, who of course responded before turning to beckon Tan.

"Whenever you're ready, Tan. We'll make sure you're okay."

Tan moved to the edge then closed his eyes and made an awkward step forward, which resulted in an ungainly type of belly flop. Good grief! He really was frightened. Rhys caught his arms to steady him and told him to climb onto his back.

"Your back?"

"Yes, piggyback. We're going to walk across to the other side of the pool."

Kieran jumped in now, very carefully, and gestured for Woorawa to get on his back. Woorawa was so enthusiastic in his efforts he tipped them both over and when he stood up again, Kieran was pleased to see Tan smiling. After twenty minutes of activity, walking round, chasing in the shallow water and a couple of piggyback rides, Tan was relaxed enough to initiate a splash attack on Rhys and receive retaliation without flinching. More activity had him jumping in confidently, opening his eyes underwater, and trusting everyone to support him in an assisted float.

Mr B arrived, took over, and quickly showed Tan that floating was easy.

"See how long you can last without putting your feet down and then when I practise safety jumps and survival skills with Woorawa you can join in anything you feel like."

At one stage the pool attendant came over when all five of them were sitting at the pool edge and asked Mr B if he was starting a team for inter-college competitions.

"It wouldn't be fair, Mike. Kieran's a fish."

"What's with the uniform, then?"

"Looks like a uniform, but it's not. They're all copycats."

"What? All of them?"

Woorawa piped up. "I'm the copycat. I've never had racing bathers like these and when we got our club memberships I talked Tan into getting them too."

"Well, you look like you mean business. I've already had two enquiries asking if there's a new college team they can join."

Mr B shook his head. "No coaching, Mike. This is a friendship group. I think you'll be seeing a lot more of them but I'm too busy myself. I'll only be able to drop in occasionally."

Mike went off and Mr B showed Tan how to scull with his hands while he was floating.

*   *   *

"It's amazing, Woorawa. Your chant makes a huge difference in fighting off Kieran's look. Where did Burrimul learn it?"

"It's part of our people's old knowledge about the artefact, Mr B. He told me he learnt it soon after he became an Elder."

When the group had gathered for a practice session with Kieran, Mr B had joined in the chant with Rhys, Tan and Woorawa to battle against the Medusa look. He watched as Woorawa tested his limit against a much more carefully controlled opal push.

"Well, follow his advice and keep practising is all I can say. Have you learned anything new since we last talked?"

"Lots of things. Show us your muscle poses, Rhys."

Rhys raced out of the room and Mr B gave a puzzled look. "Where's he going?"

"I told him to put his bathers on, and when he gets back he's going to parade his bod for us."

"Told him to change? Without speaking?"

"It's the same as talking to the animals, except easier."

Rhys returned and put on his show. When that finished, Tan turned on some music and Mr B did his own version of the Irish jig. As the cheers and clapping finished, he turned, with building astonishment at the realisation that what had felt like a natural impulse was really a compulsion.

"I danced for you! You're modifying behaviour now as well as changing memories. It's hard to believe."

"We only thought of it last night. It's the same as working with the animals so I've probably been able to do it ever since the Valley of the Eagles. We're a bit worried about it, though, so I only do it in practice time with things we might do anyway."

"Worried? Well, of course. Kieran, you do need to be comfortable in your own mind about what you do to other people's. What was the bit that worried you?"

"For a while we thought I might have changed Tan permanently and stopped him being modest like he normally is. Woorawa worked out that it was just what we did last night and nothing else."

"Tan immodest? That *would* be a change. Did you make him do something rude?"

"It was what Rhys just did, Mr B. But before last night I never would have pranced around in front of people wearing such brief bathers."

Rhys laughed. "You wore them at the pool."

"The pool's different. It's okay there."

"What about Woorawa wearing his bathers to tea last night, Tan? Was that rude?"

"That's the whole point, Rhys. Before last night I would have thought it was, but now I think it's just fun and I like him wearing them."

Woorawa raced out of the room and was back in a few moments showing off his light blue bathers. Mr B wanted to know if Kieran had made him do it.

"Not this time. I did at last night's practice time when I made them all go through the poses, but then he told us he likes going around with hardly anything on."

"I do too. When I was little I didn't wear anything and my people gave me a nickname which means naked boy."

"What about you, Rhys? Would you have felt embarrassed about wearing your bathers around the house before last night?"

"Not me. I'm used to them because I wear them nearly every day for training."

Mr B gave Kieran a curious look. "Would you wear your bathers around the house, Kieran? You're the only one who hasn't had his mind fiddled with."

"If the others do, I will. I'm the same as Rhys."

"And he likes perving on us all."

Kieran gave Rhys a thump on the thigh and checked to see Mr B's reaction, but he was nodding as if that was what he expected.

"That all sounds normal to me. I've already advised you to think about this. Get together after a few more days of consideration and formalise your approach with rules you're all happy with. Are you ready for your coaching, Woorawa? I'm a bit nervous about our meal with Tan not doing the cooking and a bit of Maths will help get my mind off it."

The practice session wasn't officially finished so the next thing Mr B did was bow to both Kieran and Rhys and apologise profusely for doubting their cooking skills.

"Cheeky students!"

The meal turned out great because Kieran and Rhys, who'd decided to share whenever it was their turn for cooking, had chosen a dish they'd learned from Tan, and Mr B, now under no compulsion, was most impressed.

"Hmm! I think you'll need coaching for a long time, Woorawa, if all your meals are this nice."

Kieran jumped on that quickly. "Why don't we make it a regular thing, Mr B? For a couple of nights each week."

Mr B's eyes lit up, and when he agreed they worked out which nights would suit best.

"This is your fourth day here, Woorawa. Have you been missing home?"

"I've hardly had a chance to think about it, Mr B. I speak to Uncle every night but so much has been happening I feel like I'm in the middle of a storm."

"After the last few days I couldn't agree more. What about you, Tan? Do you think you'll cope with our two trouble magnets?"

"It's the most interesting time in all my life, Mr B. I was amazed when Kieran and Rhys even asked me to live here, and now I have three good friends. It's like someone made a magic spell and changed my life."

"Kieran's the trouble magnet, not me. I'm as quiet and sensible as Tan. All the weird stuff comes from him and the rest of us get dragged into it."

Mr B thought that was funny. "You poor, sad thing, Rhys, put upon by all these troubles which I sense you're enjoying more than any of us."

Kieran joined in. "Yes, you poor, sad thing. Blame it all on me when you're the one with magic hands that keep zapping everyone unconscious."

Rhys pushed his hands at Kieran in a threatening gesture, then helped himself to more ice cream.

"I *am so* put upon, and Woorawa's as bad as Kieran. Since he's been here I've had to learn weird chanting, and next weekend I have to get dressed up like a wild man and do even weirder dances."

"You don't have to."

"Don't take any notice of him, Woorawa. He's stirring because we called him a sad thing."

"What's this about dancing?"

"Woorawa's putting on a ceremony for Tan, except we all have to join in."

"Really? Rhys, that's special. You should make the most of it."

"I know. It'll be great—except when I'm dancing."

"Mr B, you should be part of this. Would you like to join in?"

"Woorawa, that's an honour. Of course I would. When do I turn up?"

"It's this coming Saturday evening but we need the afternoon to learn things to make it more interesting for Tan."

After a discussion about what that meant, Woorawa went with Mr B for another hour of coaching, and Kieran and Rhys helped Tan with cleaning up after the meal.

Chapter 6

"Let's move to the other side of the pool, Kieran. Those people who just came in are really unfriendly and they'll probably say something nasty to me."

Kieran swivelled in the direction of Woorawa's look and felt his hackles rise. What was Geston doing here? The pool wasn't one of his usual haunts.

"No way. We're not scared of him. He's useless. You watch. He'll go away as soon as he sees us … and if he doesn't I'll make him."

Woorawa looked uncomfortable. "Leave him alone, please. Uncle Burrimul says I should work out these problems for myself."

Kieran's hackles rose even further. "What problems, Woorawa? We all thought everything was going really well for you."

"It is, but there's always someone who doesn't like my people, and this group say things every time they see me."

Kieran wanted to know more but Geston had now stopped at the edge of the pool, looking at them.

"What's your wild friend doing in the pool? Doesn't he know he spoils it for everyone else?"

Kieran was so shocked he didn't say anything. Not because of the aggression and nasty nature of the comment—that was Geston's normal pattern for putting people down—but because for weeks now Geston had been no trouble at all and this sudden reversion somehow felt like a direct challenge.

Kieran checked to see if Woorawa was okay. His expression was unreadable but his body was stiff, upright and facing directly at Geston. Kieran gathered himself, then walked towards Geston.

"You're pig-ignorant, Geston! With that foul mouth you're the one who'd spoil the pool. Get out of here."

Surprise compounded when Geston's smirk indicated he was pleased to get this strong reaction. He'd wanted Kieran to get angry? That didn't make sense after what had happened last time. Well, if he thought he was going to win some sort of domination game he was in for a shock. Kieran smoothed his internal hackles and gave a very deliberate snort of laughter.

"You're a fool! Go away and stop wasting our time."

To reinforce this, he projected a short touch of the Medusa look at Geston and the four cronies with him. The four cronies reacted so strongly Kieran started to wonder if they were putting on an act. No, their horrified expressions were quickly lost to view as, without exception, they turned and ran. Kieran forgot about them, though, because Geston was still there, still smirking.

Weird!

Kieran reached again, with a little more strength, but again nothing happened. How could Gaston have this resistance? It hadn't been there on that first encounter. Kieran pushed harder, looking for a wall similar to the one he could sense in the practice battles with Woorawa, but there wasn't one. Geston looked to where his mates were disappearing through the pool entrance and then back at Kieran.

"I don't know what your freak tricks are but they won't work on everyone. You'd better watch it from now on."

He left then and Kieran and Woorawa watched silently till he was gone.

"You shouldn't have zapped them, Kieran. They'll probably be after me even more now."

"They're not after you, Woorawa. Geston made it look that way but it was me he really wanted. They never come to the pool so that means it was deliberate, and that's not his usual pattern."

"Why did you leave him out of the zap? So you could say something to him?"

"That's even weirder. I did zap him. It just didn't work, which I don't understand because the other time it hit him so hard he flaked out."

"He must have built up resistance then."

"No, it wasn't like that. I tried three different levels and he didn't notice. I couldn't even feel a wall like yours."

The battles between Kieran and Woorawa at practice for the last few days had been interesting every time, and the defensive structure they identified as a wall was settling into place more easily every day. Kieran couldn't get through it without help from the opal, but he was now better at control and had developed two ways that Woorawa couldn't resist. The best was to focus finely and kind of drill through. The other was to build enough pressure to make the whole wall give way. The second was very effective but needed instantaneous reining in to stop Woorawa losing consciousness.

"No wall, but you couldn't do anything? That doesn't make sense."

"I know, and he left before I could try something else. I wonder if Burrimul has any ideas."

"We'll ring him when we finish our swim."

"Woorawa, what sort of things has Geston been saying?"

"Geston? Is that his name? I've only seen him once before, and today was the first time he said anything. It's the others who are always rude."

*   *   *

Everyone laughed.

"You had a beef burger and a chicken schnitzel for lunch again, Woorawa. That's like two full meals, so are you going to do that every day?"

"Why not? I'm a growing boy and they're delicious."

Everyone laughed and watched Tan light a candle on their lounge room bench.

"You guts! You'll turn into a Fatty Boomba."

"What? I've never heard of that, Rhys."

Kieran gave Rhys a whack on the arm. "Don't take any notice of him, Woorawa. He just means you'll get fat from eating too much."

"Me? No, I won't. If I keep practising till I can swim thirty laps, then I won't get fat."

"Don't you mean forty?"

Rhys had been in a distance mood at the pool yesterday and totally amazed Woorawa and Tan by swimming forty non-stop laps.

"I only managed three without a rest so ten times that's good enough for my first target. Mr B thinks I can do it in three weeks."

"Three weeks will be hard work, Woorawa. Are you any good at running? That'll help you build up endurance."

"I don't know, Rhys. I haven't really done any running because I had to have someone next to me to stop me crashing into anything."

There was silence at this reminder of yet another everyday thing that had been a problem.

"Sorry! I wasn't thinking. Come for a few runs with me if you like. It'll help you get that first target."

"Really? That would be great, Rhys. When will we start?"

"Um … I don't know. It's going to be hard to fit in. How about just before tea?"

"After swimming? I'll already be worn out."

"We'll only go for a kilometre. That'll be enough, and we'll fit it in while Tan does the cooking. Kieran will come with us too."

Kieran nodded and looked to Tan. "How about you, Tan? Do you ever do any running?"

"No thanks. Swimming every night will be plenty for me."

Everybody was surprised. "Every night? Yesterday you said three."

"I know, but Mr B wants me to target for ten laps so I changed my mind."

Rhys got really excited. "Tan, you couldn't even swim a few days ago. That's terrific! Give yourself more than three weeks though. Mr B must be pushing Woorawa because he's fitter than you."

"I know. I'm not trying for any special time limit but I'll keep going till I make it. Ten laps is half a kilometre, and that's plenty for me." He grinned at Woorawa. "Woorawa's a cheat because he's naturally fit. Look at his muscles. He should be a photography model."

Woorawa stared at him in disbelief. "Muscles? Tan, what are you talking about? Rhys is the one with muscles."

"I know, but his are too big. You've got nursery rhyme muscles … not too big, not too small, just right."

Kieran couldn't resist. "Yeah, Rhys's a muscle-bound gorilla. That's why I made him act like one the other day … except he wasn't acting."

Rhys put on a puzzled look. "Which do you prefer, Kieran, cremation or burial?"

"What?"

"You know. What am I going to do with the dead bodies when I've finished with you? And you're first, Tan, because you started this."

Tan tried to escape but he was too slow, and a few seconds later was begging for mercy, then for help, and then for relief from the bodies wrestling on top of him. The happy scuffle reduced to a contest between Rhys and Woorawa, with Woorawa refusing to give in despite Rhys's greater strength. Wow! He really was stubborn, and Kieran and Tan exchanged glances of amazement at this unexpected show of willpower. Kieran fleetingly wondered if this might be part of the reason for his strong mind barrier. Rhys wouldn't stop either, that was a given. He turned to Tan.

"Get a bucket of water. That'll stop them."

They did stop, and when Rhys pointed at Tan and said, "Don't you dare", Woorawa laughed and relaxed.

"Let's save our energy for the run, Rhys. *You* mightn't need it, but I know I will."

"You definitely will because I'll be relaxing in my room while Kieran slave-drives you with Maths."

"Hey, Rhys, why don't you join in? It'll be good revision for you."

Rhys's surprise turned to instant agreement. "Is that okay, Woorawa? I don't want to hog any of your time."

Woorawa looked at him as if he was crazy and pointed at the folder waiting on the table. "There's tons of notepaper there for both of us. Do you want one of my pens?"

It was interesting coaching two people at the same time and Kieran was intrigued with their different approaches. Woorawa didn't know as much but he learnt so easily it wouldn't be long before he didn't need coaching. Rhys knew this basic equation stuff but he listened carefully and battled with every example, trying to finish before Woorawa.

They finished early, to fit the run in before tea, and Kieran went with them because he wanted to share the experience. By the time they got home, Rhys was declaring Woorawa a natural, and planning a timetable for regular runs.

"Four times a week's too much, Rhys. I think you should make it three max and limit each run to twenty minutes. Woorawa's got too many other things he has to do and he needs to concentrate most on college stuff … at least till he catches up a bit."

Woorawa reluctantly agreed. "Kieran's right, Rhys. Time's getting a bit scary with all my work and the extras for the professor. I've got a big talk in the library in two weeks and he's organised special sessions with all his classes too."

"All of them? How many's that?"

"I don't know, but it's once a week except if I've got exams or a big project to hand in."

"Wow! He's sure making you earn your scholarship."

"It was Uncle Burrimul's idea more than his. Uncle says it's fair because the professor helped me so much, and he's right."

"Yeah, I guess … What's this about projects, Woorawa? You don't really have them till next year."

"I talked with my IT lecturer and he's going to let me have a try at some of the Certificate Four projects in the last half of the semester, as long as I can show him I've learnt enough."

"You can't be serious. You'll go crazy with all this work."

"No, I won't, Rhys. It's what I want to do and it's going to be great."

"I mean everything. Not just IT."

"I won't. I can learn things easily now."

Tan's call from the kitchen that tea would be ready in ten minutes meant a rush to the bathroom for very quick showers.

*   *   *

"He's so happy and excited about college and learning everything, Kieran.

Is he going to see any eye specialists now he's here in Melbourne?"

"In a couple of weeks. He doesn't have to, but the professor organised it anyway."

Rhys nodded his approval.

"Hey! We'll have to make sure he knows how to use the trams and the trains. If Tan's tied up with classes he won't be able to take him."

"Good idea. We'll go on the tram tomorrow."

"In the morning? We'll have to get up early."

"So? We'll just set the alarm to give us an extra half an hour."

Rhys groaned because he liked his sleep. "Let's come home on the tram instead. Then we won't have to get up early."

"Not tomorrow. It's Mr B's day for coaching and Woorawa won't cut that short. And anyway, it's our turn to cook."

"I suppose. And if we have tea later that'll mess up the whole evening. I'd better go and tell them."

As Rhys left, Kieran gave his opal a squeeze and put the idea into Woorawa's head that he'd like to try the tram tomorrow. Yes, it *was* his opal now. He took his hand out of his pocket, opened it and idly started a glowing cycle of changing colours. Rhys would be back in a few minutes with his special smile, calling him a trickster as an excuse to wrestle him onto the bed. Yes … right about now. Kieran put the opal in his pocket as the door started opening.

"Cheat!"

*   *   *

Kieran watched Mr B powering down the pool and nudged Rhys's arm.

"Look how fast he is. He's like a dolphin or something."

"Yeah! He makes it look so easy, and you're the same. We reckon it must be because you learned everything from him. Woorawa says you've both got secret webbed hands and feet and they grow out as soon as you're in the water. Hey, what are those idiots doing?"

Idiots? Kieran followed the direction of Rhys's glance to the pool entrance where four of Geston's cronies were gathered. They'd been giving Woorawa a hard time for the last few days with put-down looks and blatantly obvious but unheard comments between them. Kieran wanted to front them but he didn't because Woorawa insisted he was going to work it out in his own way.

"If they come in here, they won't know what's hit them."

"They've seen you, Kieran. They'll run now, but they looked like they meant to do something."

There *was* an atmosphere about them. Maybe they'd come looking for Woorawa. Kieran glanced to where Woorawa was sitting on the side bench, unaware of what was happening as he tied his runners, then back to the entrance where all four were now in a rush to leave.

Rhys laughed. "I knew they wouldn't come in when they saw you."

"I don't think they meant to. It looked like they were checking up on us. I wonder if they saw Tan waiting in the car?"

"Could be. We'll ask him."

Woorawa was approaching and Kieran turned to wave goodbye to Mr B but he was swimming in the other direction.

"What are you cooking for tea tonight, Kieran?"

Rhys answered. "Witchetty grubs in garlic, and fried lizard legs."

Woorawa shoved him with his elbow. "As if. You wouldn't even know what a witchetty grub looked like, Rhys."

"Would so. There's a picture of them on the packet."

"What packet?"

"The packet from the supermarket. They're frozen ones we found the other day. Tan told us to get them for you while we eat our veal parmigianas."

"Parmigianas? Yum! I hope you got two each."

"Yeah! Six of them and a big packet of grubs. We're spoiling you because … Hey! Where *is* Tan? He's had plenty of time to bring the car over."

Rhys was right. Tan had left almost ten minutes before and collecting his car would only have taken half that. *Oh no!* Kieran squeezed his opal, reached, and turned to Rhys and Woorawa.

"Quick. Something's wrong. Tan's upset and he's not with the car."

Kieran broke into a run and Rhys and Woorawa chased after him.

"I bet it's those idiots."

Kieran agreed with Rhys but didn't answer because he was focused on running and pinpointing Tan's position. They reached the car but kept going.

"He's in the scrub."

The scrub was a large section at the back of the car park that had been left with natural vegetation to help local wildlife and give a bushy atmosphere. Kieran led the way in, past a big wattle tree and then some low shrubs. Tan was kneeling on the ground, apparently searching for something. He looked around, startled, then stood up.

"They stole the car keys and threw them in here."

"Are you all right? Did they hurt you?"

"No. I'm upset because it was such a shock. They followed me from near the pool entrance but I just thought they were going to their car. I was opening the door when three of them grabbed me and the other one took the keys. We have to find them, Kieran. They're my house key and locker key and we can't use the car till I get the spare from home."

Kieran gave Tan a quick hug. "Don't worry about the keys, Tan. Finding them's easy. They are … that way." Tan looked in the direction Kieran was pointing and realisation dawned. "Oh, sorry … I'm all flustered and I didn't think properly. I thought they were in here because that's what they said."

Rhys gave him a hug now. "Gods, Tan. Don't say sorry. It's not your fault. What happened? Did they just take the keys and that was all?"

"I couldn't see what was happening, because three of them were holding me while the other one went somewhere behind me. They said nasty stuff, that I had to get out of our house and not live with freaks and weirdos like Kieran and Woorawa. Then the fourth one came back and said the keys were in the scrub and they let me go. Are the keys very far away?"

"We'll get them now, so stop worrying."

Kieran decided on some dramatics to distract Tan and, pinpointing the keys with his mind, formed a brightly glowing blue symbol. "Follow that arrow!"

The dramatics worked, because Tan visibly relaxed and the hint of a smile appeared. "You're showing off for me, Kieran, and I know why. Thanks, but I'm all right now."

"Come on. We'll get the keys and go home."

As they headed off briskly, Rhys got mad. "They're maggots, Kieran. They did that on purpose so we'd waste ages and ages searching in the scrub. Let's front them after we get the keys. You can find them for us."

Kieran stopped in his tracks and recalled the image of the four they'd seen at the pool entrance, redirected the arrow and concentrated.

"There, on the third floor of the TAFE building, and they're watching us."

"You can tell that?"

"Sort of. Rhys and I saw them at the pool, Woorawa, so they're fresh in my mind."

"If they're watching that means they can see the blue arrow. You've got it really bright, Kieran. Aren't you worried they'll talk about it?"

They'd decided at one of their earlier discussions that it was important to keep Kieran's abilities secret because if people found out, their lives would become even crazier. Kieran was pleased because this comment meant Tan must have recovered from being upset.

"Good thinking. Hang on. It means I'll have to break one of our rules but I'm going to fix this."

Kieran closed his eyes and concentrated. It was easier than he'd expected, and a moment later he opened his eyes and grinned at the looks he was getting.

"I've sent them back to the residences so they don't watch us anymore, and they've forgotten about the keys. They think the arrow was a laser light. Come on, we'll get the keys now."

Woorawa didn't move. "You shouldn't have broken any rules, Kieran. Which one was it?"

Kieran shook his head and started walking. "I was going to make them friendly to you but that's one of the big changes we talked about so I just made them forget instead."

"Will they remember if someone talks to them about it? That's how we got our memories back."

"Who's going to talk to them, Rhys?"

"Geston. He's probably the one who put them up to it."

"I didn't think of that, but they won't remember. I'm sure of that. Damn!" Kieran sat on the bench they'd just approached and started taking off his shoes and socks.

Rhys spoke but the others were just as puzzled. "What are you doing?"

"Getting the keys. I turned the arrow off so any other people wouldn't see it, but they're in the fountain. See? Out near the pillar."

Sure enough, the keys were there, glinting in the shallow water.

"They *are* a pack of maggots! We'd never have found them there."

Kieran pulled the legs of his jeans up then yelled when he put his foot in. "It's freezing! I should have made them do this for us."

After a few moments of complaining about the cold Kieran was out again and drying his feet with his socks while Tan examined the keys. There was nothing to worry about, though, as water couldn't affect them, and soon they were on their way home.

*   *   *

When Tan and Woorawa finished cleaning up after the meal the group gathered in the lounge for their nightly practice session. Woorawa was the most insistent and would have liked more time but he had to be happy with the half-hour Kieran decided they could sensibly manage. When Tan started to light one of his candles Woorawa stopped him.

"See if Kieran can do it, Tan."

Tan paused and then caught on. "Without matches?"

Rhys liked it. "Hey, great idea, Woorawa. Like that spontaneous combustion they have in horror stories, or the wizard in *Mysts*."

"What's *Mysts*?"

Rhys looked horrified. "You haven't heard of *Mysts*? You must have. It's the best book ever written and they even made it into a movie."

"Oh yeah! Some of my friends were talking about it last year. The wizards say Latin words and fire zaps off the end of their wands."

Rhys grimaced as if in agony. "Not those movies. In *Mysts* the wizard uses his big walking staff."

"Same thing, just bigger. Do you really think you can light a candle, Kieran? It's different to everything else you can do."

Kieran looked at the candle, visualised a flame flaring up from the wick, then made it happen.

"Wow! Just like that. You didn't even have to concentrate."

Tan picked up the candle and laughed.

"What's funny, Tan. I think that's amazing."

Tan lowered the palm of his free hand carefully onto the flame and grinned at the collective gasp when he held it there.

"It's not real, Woorawa. It didn't flutter in the air when I moved it. It's the normal glow, except it's matched up to the candle."

Woorawa pushed his hand in. "I can't feel a thing. It looks real but there's no heat. Try it, Rhys."

Rhys moved closer then yelped, jerking his hand away in shock and shaking it in agony. "Are you mad? That hurts like blazes." When he brought his hand up to examine the damage his jaw dropped and he gave a cautious rub. "It's not even burnt? Did you make me imagine it?"

Kieran was feeling guilty because of Rhys's powerful reaction. "Sorry. I didn't mean for it to hurt so much. I was playing a trick but I overdid it. I knew it wasn't real and when Tan put his hand over it, I realised I could make you think it was. I'm annoyed with myself now because that's the second time today I rushed with this stuff."

"Second? What was the first? Those four with the car keys?"

"Yes. I'd part-way made them like Woorawa before I realised it was one of the big changes we'd talked about, and I had to reverse what I'd done. I need a new rule about not doing stuff till I've thought about it and I know I can control it properly."

Rhys was still rubbing his hand while he listened. "It sure felt real. Can you do it, so it just feels warm?"

"Course I can. Hold both your hands out and tell me when it starts."

This was totally fascinating and everyone watched eagerly. Instead of the impulsive idea of heat from a candle flare, Kieran made Rhys feel the tiniest amount of warmth in his other hand.

"Can you feel it?"

"No!"

Slowly and carefully, Kieran increased the strength of the idea in Rhys's mind till he suddenly shifted his focus. "Wow, you did it in my other hand. It's warm."

"Tell me when it gets uncomfortable."

Rhys looked back and forth between Kieran and his hand while the sensation built. "Whoa! Back a bit. That's enough. Weird. It's like the candle's almost touching me without it being there. Can you move it to my thumb?"

That was instantaneous because Kieran now knew exactly how to control what he was doing. Rhys experimented by moving the pointer finger of his other hand closer.

"That is so bizarre, Kieran. My thumb tells me there's a flame while my finger tells me there's not. Can you make them both feel it so my mind stops doing somersaults?"

That was easy till Rhys started swapping fingers. Okay. That was an unspoken challenge and Kieran tried to keep up but each swap meant sending a message to the new finger and Rhys was speeding up.

"Ha! Gotcha! I can tell it's not real because of the delay. Do it for Tan and Woorawa. They have to feel this too."

Tan put his hand out, but after a moment of careful calibration, Kieran made his left ear feel warm. Tan jerked sideways out of pure reflex at the sensation then steadied and put his hand up.

"Not near my ear, Kieran. It makes me nervous."

"Sorry. I didn't think again. Put your hand out and we'll do it that way."

Woorawa was far more adventurous. He made Kieran move the feeling all over and then he tried Rhys's finger swapping challenge.

"Can you get faster, so the flame doesn't feel like a match lighting up each time?"

"I can't tell the future, Woorawa. I'd have to know which finger you were going to move before you even moved it."

"I suppose. What if you made all of them think the flame was there? Would that work?"

Kieran laughed. "Of course it would. I got stuck in one pattern of thinking. Try it now."

"How did you know you could make us feel heat? You've never done anything like it before."

"Yes I have, Woorawa. Remember when Rhys thought he was a monkey and I made him have a banana taste in his mouth, and when Tan could smell rotten eggs in the fridge? It clicked in my mind that feeling heat was just another sensation."

"Really? Well, that means you should be able to do hearing and sight too. They're all senses."

Kieran started to think about that when Rhys added another idea. "So's touch and you've definitely never tried that on us."

Woorawa laughed. "I hope not. He could tickle us and we wouldn't be able to stop him." He turned to Kieran. "It *is* a nerve thing though, Kieran, just like the heat, so you should be able to. Have a go at it … but no tickles."

It *was* like the heat and Kieran knew straight away that he could work it, but Woorawa's suggestion about sight and hearing as well was intriguing.

"In a minute, Woorawa. What you said's got me thinking. The touch and sound feel right, but something tells me that vision's too hard."

"You know before you even try?"

"Sort of. It's almost the same as giving you a heat sensation."

"Try them both so you know for sure, then do the vision later."

"Okay. Rhys, you're the first guinea pig."

Rhys grimaced with fake nervousness. "Typical. What are you going to do? Give me a gut punch?"

"Hey! Good idea. I didn't think of that. Are you ready?"

Kieran sensed Rhys steel himself, just in case, but there was no way he'd try anything so forceful till he knew exactly what he was doing. With a minor variation of the heat technique he sent the sensation of a gentle touch to Rhys's ear. There was no reaction so he tried again with a smidgen more strength.

Rhys grabbed his ear and looked at Tan who was sitting next to him. "Wow. You tickled my ear, didn't you? I thought it was Tan but his hands didn't move."

"It was just a touch, Rhys, not a tickle, but I suppose it would feel the same."

"It feels weird. Do it again, but keep on touching."

Kieran did and Rhys got a funny look.

"That feels nice. Touch me somewhere else."

Woorawa and Tan exchanged knowing glances.

"No rude stuff, Kieran. You've got all night to experiment with that."

"All night? What's that supposed to mean?"

"We've seen Rhys coming out of your room for the last two mornings so we know he stays there."

After a moment's silence, all attention went to Rhys's face which had turned bright red. Kieran wanted to give him a comforting hug but he couldn't because Woorawa had beaten him to it. Tan joined the company with a friendly hand on Rhys's shoulder.

"It doesn't have to be a secret, Rhys. Woorawa and I are really pleased and we're going to get you a double bed so you're more comfy."

"Yep, and Tan's organised for someone else to rent your room in another two weeks, so you'll need it when you move in with Kieran."

"What? Where will I study? There's …"

The penny dropped and Rhys delivered a few friendly head bops while he dragged Woorawa around the room in a headlock.

Kieran watched happily while Rhys worked the embarrassment out of his system, then, when Tan told them to sit down so they could get on with the practice, Rhys asked him how long he'd known.

"Woorawa told me after we got our memories back. He knew from when you were at Alice Springs."

Rhys looked at Woorawa and shook his head. "You couldn't. We weren't even … together."

"Uncle Burrimul knew from watching you at the Valley of Eagles. He had a big talk with me about it because it might make life complicated, but I didn't care because I loved it."

Kieran thought that was a curious thing to say but he didn't get a chance to ask about it because Tan wanted to get on with the practice.

"Can you do the touch thing to all of us at the same time, Kieran? You should be able to."

Kieran's mind clicked into gear and they experimented with both touch and sound till Tan wanted to know if he could make it real.

"What sort of real? We can hear it, Tan, so it must be."

"No, it's not, Rhys. You heard an echo when Kieran called out but it was silent for Woorawa and me, so that means it's in your mind."

"That's how it works, Tan. It's real to our minds but not real real."

"What about the glow then? We know that's real because we took photos of it. If Kieran can make real light, he might be able to make real sound."

Everyone looked at Kieran for his thoughts, but he didn't answer. These practice sessions were unreal in a different way with all the unexpected things that kept turning up. Tan was right about the glow so there might be something in his argument.

"Kieran?"

"I'm thinking, Rhys. I know these sounds aren't real because I don't hear any of them. I just tell you what you're hearing and you do. I wouldn't have a clue about real sounds. That has to be totally different."

"You use your opal to help with the glow sometimes, Kieran. That might be what's different. Remember when we took it out of its clay shell and the glow started as soon as you touched it?"

Woorawa got excited at this. "That's clever, Tan. The glow is real and the opal is definitely connected to it."

Rhys wasn't so sure. "It seems to be connected with everything, if you ask me. Kieran uses it whenever he needs a boost."

"I suppose …" Woorawa turned to Kieran. "Have you been using it to help with the sound and touch, Kieran? You were concentrating really hard a few times."

Kieran had to think back before he answered. "I might have, but not on purpose. It's there all the time, so I think I call on it without even realising."

"All the time? Can you switch it off then, like when you want to concentrate on college work or relax or go to sleep?"

"No way, Woorawa. It feels like it should be there."

"Have a try. You should practise everything."

Kieran shook his head then had a rethink. Learning more about the opal must be a good thing but turning it off was something he'd never even contemplated. He started to push at the connected feeling and it was easy—the same as getting help but in reverse. As the connection steadily diminished, he grew more and more uneasy, and at the very point of losing the opal he reversed everything and brought it fully back.

"I'm never doing that again, Woorawa. I got scared I mightn't be able to reconnect."

"Scared?"

"Not frightened scared, more like worried scared. The more I turned it off the more it felt like I shouldn't."

"Wow! Has it ever made you feel bad before?"

"It wasn't the opal making me nervous, Woorawa. It was my own feeling. I can tell."

"I think that means it's important for you not to ever turn it off. We know you don't need it for everything because you could do the Medusa look and the animals before you even knew it existed. It's the glow that's different to everything else, so see if you can make do by yourself. You can tell when the opal's helping, can't you?"

Thinking hard about what he was doing, Kieran restarted the glow around the candlewick and had quite a surprise.

"Hey, I do use the opal. It's automatic. Hang on while I work out how to keep it separate."

Kieran held the little candle flame in his mind and reached to stop the flow of energy from the opal. A flush of sudden warmth was the sole warning that something wasn't right … He blinked his eyes open to the realisation that Rhys was massaging his temples.

"What happened? Did I fall asleep?"

"It wasn't sleep, Kieran. Just a mini flake out. It was like the other times when you overloaded yourself, so we knew my magic hands would bring you back. Woorawa thinks that making the glow without the opal must be too hard."

Kieran grabbed Rhys's hands and held them in place. "Keep massaging, Rhys. Your hands are still working."

"Really? Or do you just like getting a massage?"

Kieran smiled. "Both, Woorawa. It's the first time I've noticed it but I can tell that something's still happening. It's nearly gone now but I can feel it waking me up."

"Another new thing. We can hardly keep up. Can you remember what you did?"

Kieran thought back then grunted with self-annoyance. "Yeah, I'm an idiot! I rushed everything without thinking again. I should have gradually stopped the opal from helping me instead of all at once. You can take your hands away, Rhys, because they're just a massage now. I'll have another go."

Rhys let go but he looked concerned. "Straight away, Kieran? You've just woken up."

"I know what to do this time, and I won't flake out because your hands have made me feel better than I was before, so don't worry. Pass the candle over please, Tan. Distance matters for the glow so holding it should help."

Tan did that and Woorawa interrupted. "It might be even easier without the candle."

Kieran thought about the candle he was now holding and shook his head. "Making a candle glow feels more natural than a glow in midair, Woorawa. I'll turn it on the way I always do and then start a change."

A bright glow surrounded the candlewick in the same effortless way it always did and Kieran held it for a few seconds before making a tiny change to the help coming from the opal. Nothing seemed to happen so he made a slightly bigger change. Yes, the glow dimmed perceptibly.

"Hey! It flickered. Did you do that, Kieran?"

"Yeah. I need to practise a bit till I've got the control set in my mind. Watch this."

The glow brightened and dimmed with various patterns of experimental control and Woorawa wanted to know if it was hard to do.

"It's easy because the opal does all the work. It's exactly what I've been doing ever since the first glow. I just never thought of taking it lower than the basic level."

"It can't be easy if it overloaded you so much you flaked out. That doesn't make sense."

"Yes it does, Tan. The overload happened when I didn't use the opal at all. That's the big step I'm going to have a try at now."

"Make the glow really dim, Kieran. It should be easier for you then."

That was good thinking by Tan, so Kieran turned the glow into a tiny point of soft light before stopping the opal's help. The light disappeared so, consciously holding the aid from the opal at bay, he willed it back. Nothing happened so he tried harder, then harder again. There was a momentary flicker which was really exciting because it told him he could do this. *Whoo! So close! One more effort.*

Holding the tiny point of light aglow for five or six seconds was all he could manage before collapsing against the back of the sofa.

Why were the others looking at him like that?

"What?"

"Kieran, you're drenched with sweat. I thought we were going to lose you again."

"Did you see it? I couldn't hold it, but that light was all me."

"I stopped looking when you groaned. Are you sure you're all right?"

"Did I groan? Well, I'm not surprised. That was harder than fighting Woorawa's barriers without the opal. I can't believe that tiny light took so much effort. I'll have another go at it tomorrow to see if I can last any longer. Wow! This is unreal." Kieran took in the curious looks he was getting. "Now what?"

"You're a bit overexcited, aren't you? A little bit of light's nothing like talking to animals or putting thoughts into our minds."

"Yes, it is, Rhys. It doesn't seem like much because I've made it so many times we've got used to it, but it's a zillion times harder than anything else really, and without the opal we wouldn't even have found out about it. Think about it. Everything else is in your mind. What do you reckon, Woorawa?"

"I'll ask Uncle Burrimul, but if making a tiny, tiny light sends you unconscious it has to be different. I'll go and ring him now because you've done enough practice for one day."

Everyone agreed, and with a great deal to think about, particularly Kieran, they dispersed to their other evening activities.

*   *   *

"I ripped it down, Kieran. The professor can put another one up in the glass display case."

Kieran agreed, then changed his mind. "I don't know, Rhys. Woorawa might be annoyed if we do. He'll say it doesn't matter."

"And he'll tell us to put it back up so everyone knows what's going on. That's what he's doing about the comments on his folder."

An angry message from Rhys had sent Kieran and Tan rushing to the library entrance to see the nasty comments defacing a notice about the talk Woorawa was giving next week.

"What comments, Tan?"

"More stuff like this. He told me about it last night just before he went to bed."

Rhys reacted strongly. "And why didn't he tell us? Because it's no big deal and he has to work it out by himself?"

"Exactly, and we shouldn't really go against what he wants."

"How about talking to the professor and getting him to put up a new sign without even telling Woorawa?"

"No way, Rhys. That wouldn't be right."

"Yeah. I shouldn't have said that, but we can't just do nothing."

Kieran shared Rhys's feelings about doing something but he pushed them down and took charge. "Tan's right, Rhys. Put the notice back up. We won't have to tell the professor because he'll find out anyway, and so will Woorawa. Someone's sure to tell him about it."

"I suppose. I wonder what the professor will do. He'll be mad as anything."

Tan laughed, which surprised both Kieran and Rhys. "What?"

"If he finds out who did it he'll be so mad they'll probably get kicked out of college. The problem will go away then."

Rhys was halfway through replacing the notice when the nearby lift door opened and Woorawa came out.

"Is that the notice?"

Everyone nodded but, intent on watching his reaction, didn't say anything.

"Ha! That's pretty weak. Don't take it down, Rhys. I want to leave it there."

"I already did take it down but Kieran made me put it back. Aren't you angry?"

"What for? It's perfect. I hope they do the same to any other notices."

"You do? Woorawa, it's awful. They're like … barbarians or something."

"I know, but that's their problem. The professor will be really pleased at the meeting when the lecture hall fills up with all the people who come to find out what's going on."

After the collective silence while the listeners took this in, Kieran gave Woorawa's arm a friendly shake. "That's … that's brilliant, Woorawa, but the professor definitely won't let it stay up."

"I know but half the college has already heard about it."

That would be right. Stuff like this would spread like wildfire.

"Leave it, Rhys. Let's go to the canteen. I'm starving for my burger and schnitzel."

*   *   *

"Mr B's here."

Rhys called from the lounge where he could see their front drive through the old bay window, and a collective grin spread in anticipation of his reaction when he walked in. Apart from a big catch-up to talk about the happenings of the last two days, the reason for his visit was to practise for Woorawa's special ceremony and, to build the atmosphere, everyone was dressed in black T-shirts, red headbands and baggy loincloths made out of a sheet Woorawa had sacrificed to get suitable material. The plan was to tell Mr B he had to dress the same way, and though they all knew he'd happily join in, it was still going to be a good stir.

"Let him in, Rhys. You look wild."

With big white rings round his eyes and a dark red circle on each cheek, he certainly did look wild, and Kieran, Tan and Woorawa gathered behind him to watch. Mr B actually jumped backwards, which was great.

"Good grief! I've come to a house of cannibals. I hope I'm not on the menu."

"You will be if you don't get the same gear on. It's in Woorawa's bedroom and he'll tie your headband properly when you come out."

Mr B gave Rhys a more careful look-over. "Why are we dressing up now? The ceremony isn't till this evening."

"We have to be in the right mood to help us learn the chants and the dances. We're having our practice first because there's new stuff to show you, and then Woorawa's going to give you special coaching because you've got the most to learn."

Mr B moved past Rhys. "Hi, Woorawa. Is this mob looking after you properly? I hear there have been some negative events at college."

"Sort of. Rhys bosses me all the time. Tan stuffs so much food into me I'm well on the way to being the Fatty Boomba, whatever it is, and Kieran's coaching makes my brain hurt."

Mr B laughed. "Nothing's changed since I was here on Wednesday then."

"Nothing's changed with ordinary stuff but we can't keep up with everything else. We'll tell you everything as soon as you're ready."

"Really? Well, I'd better get moving then."

Mr B was back quickly, obviously intrigued, and after Woorawa had fastened the headband for him they moved to the lounge for a big discussion.

Tan told the story of the car keys first then Woorawa explained the developments that had followed in Kieran's practice session. Mr B experienced the new heat, sound and touch abilities, then, after Tan had pulled the blinds, watched the tiny little glow around the candlewick for the several seconds it lasted.

"What was the point of that, Kieran? You've been making glows ever since you opened the artefact."

"This is different because it's just me, Mr B. It's so hard I can only last for ten seconds. The first time I did it I had it at my normal brightness and I passed out. Rhys had to use his hands to wake me up."

"Ten seconds of that tiny light is enough to send you unconscious?"

"No, that was me not being careful. About six seconds was all I could last on Thursday, then it went up to ten seconds when we tried again last night so I'm going to practise every day."

"To the point of unconsciousness? Kieran, that can't be good for you."

"I know, but watch this. We had the best practice ever last night."

Mr B took in all the nods and smiles then watched with growing concern as perspiration appeared on Kieran's brow and the effort turned his skin pale. When the little glow disappeared, Kieran slumped back and looked to Tan who had his watch in front of his eyes.

"How many seconds? I could tell it was longer."

"At least twelve. You started before I had my watch up."

"How's that, Mr B? When I get to twenty seconds I'm going to try making the glow a bit brighter."

"I don't like it, Kieran. You look like you've just finished running a marathon."

Kieran glanced at the moisture on his hand from where he'd just wiped his brow. "It feels like it too, but watch what we figured out last night."

A light blue glow appeared around the hand that was still being held out, spread to cover the rest of Kieran's body, then suddenly intensified till it was quite spectacular.

"Do it, Rhys. I think that's enough."

Kieran swivelled sideways and Rhys, sitting next to him, lifted a hand to each temple. The blue glow dimmed and a flush of colour returned to his features. After about thirty seconds the glow disappeared and Kieran, radiating energy, grabbed Rhys in a happy headlock.

"How's that, Mr B. Do I look like I've run a marathon now?"

In fact, he looked more alive and fit than he had before he made the candle glow.

"What did you do, Kieran? You look like you could run two."

"When I flaked out on Thursday night and Rhys used his magic hands to wake me up, I noticed the opal was helping as well, so last night we experimented and found that his hands start working after I've called on the opal. It's like Rhys uses energy from it to make people better."

"People? You mean someone else too?"

"Yes. Tan's idea worked when we tried it on Woorawa. His muscles were sore after Rhys made him run too fast and they got better straight away."

"Try it, Mr B. It's unreal. My muscles all felt like I hadn't even been for a swim or a run, and Kieran and Rhys can do it whenever they want. They tried it on Tan and he felt so good he studied for an extra hour last night."

Mr B looked at Kieran and Rhys. "All right, but I haven't done any exercise since Thursday so I'm already feeling good."

Woorawa laughed. "Well, you'll feel even better."

Kieran went quiet for about ten seconds then said Mr B was ready.

"I am? I can't feel anything, and when do I start glowing?"

"We don't need the glow. That was just to show you something was happening. Go on, Rhys. Use your magic hands."

Rhys's hands made contact, and Mr B felt a sensation of wellbeing.

"Oh my! This is amazing. How long does it last? I don't want it to stop."

"The rush bit goes away as soon as my hand stops working and then you just feel better than usual."

The rush bit did go away and Rhys's hands felt pleasant in a normal kind of way. Mr B saw the enormous grin he could feel plastered across his face reflected in four sets of features.

"Have you been practising that between you very much? It feels so good it might be addictive."

"We all felt it for a few tries at last night's practice but then we talked about it and decided to only use it if we need it."

"Have you got any explanation for what you're actually doing, Kieran? It seems to need you and Rhys and the opal all at the same time."

"Yes, it's kind of clear in my mind. I tell the opal to put energy or whatever it is into the person, and when there's enough Rhys's hands will start to work."

"And what happens when you do it with Rhys? Does he have to hold his own head?"

"No, it's sort of automatic then."

Kieran and Rhys settled and waited for Mr B's next comment. He was looking thoughtful.

"This is puzzling because I'm wondering how it worked before you had the opal. If you need something from it, then where did that something come from with your migraines and Woorawa's eyes? Could the opal still have been involved before we even knew about it?"

"Maybe Kieran built the energy himself without knowing he was doing it, and when there was too much it gave him a migraine," Tan answered.

"Hey, that fits. That was the only time my hands worked back then."

"It could be, Rhys, but that doesn't explain the deliberate changing of all our memories. I think it must be someone else doing it."

"Someone else has got opal energy, Mr B?"

"It's the best explanation I can think of, Kieran."

There was all-round agreement with this and then Kieran brought up the same question they'd had on earlier occasions.

"I still can't understand why anyone would want to change my memories though. I'm just an ordinary college student."

That brought grins from everyone and outright laughter from Rhys.

"Get real, Kieran! Ordinary students don't talk to animals and set candles alight by thinking at them. Someone wants to stop you doing this kind of stuff because they made you forget when they sent me away."

"Hmm, could be. Except I was getting migraines before I could do anything at all."

"Hang on, Rhys. You just said Kieran was lighting candles? You meant making them glow, didn't you?"

There was a collective grin from the four housemates and Kieran answered. "That's the next thing we discovered last night. Hold the candle up, Tan."

There was a soft glow, a quick flare, then a steadily wavering flame with the first signs of melting wax at its base. Mr B stared, then carefully moved his pointer finger closer.

"It looks and feels real, Kieran. It's not a clever combination of both heat and light in my mind, is it?"

There were four heads shaking an emphatic no.

"But how? It doesn't seem possible when a tiny glow is so exhausting."

"Tan thought of this one too, Mr B. If I use the opal it's easy. It makes everything easy."

"Real fire! This is scary. Can you do it with anything … like a piece of wood or paper?"

"Anything, but when I want a flame I concentrate on one tiny spot."

"What about something big like the kitchen table? Warm it I mean, not burn it."

"I'm sure I could but I'm going to practise a lot more first. I've been rushing too much for some things."

Discussion and practice intermingled for almost an hour before it had to be put aside so Woorawa could start with the chants and dancing practice.

*   *   *

After the evening meal, everyone helped clear up then, one by one, had their faces painted. Woorawa was disappointed he couldn't do their torsos and legs as well, but with the small supply of red ochre and special clay he'd brought with him he barely had enough as it was. He also kept apologising because everything he was doing was from memories of descriptions his people had given him at other ceremonies, but no one took any notice because the results were still striking. Tan had the best reaction when he checked the bathroom mirror and saw the jagged lightning shapes on his cheeks and the white, symbolic eyes staring back at him from his forehead.

The next move was to the lounge room, which had earlier been cleared of most of its furniture, and Kieran lit six of Tan's candles set up in the centre of the room to represent a campfire. Rhys had suggested that Kieran could produce a realistic looking fire but without heat and it had been exciting to try, but then everyone agreed the ceremony should all come from Woorawa. For a moment Kieran thought the candles were going to be too dim but then his eyes adapted and the room took on real atmosphere.

"Are we all ready?"

Woorawa started a soft tap, tap, tap with his music sticks and everyone joined in with their improvised versions. Kieran was using the handle of a knife against a wooden ladle from the kitchen drawer. Then their first chant started, a new one they'd all learnt with Mr B, and built stronger and stronger for a few minutes till Woorawa stopped it with a gesture.

"Yeperenye! Iriperenye!"

Kieran's hair stood on end at the power in Woorawa's voice as he called aloud the First Australian names for the giant caterpillars and stink bugs of his home country.

"Back in the Dreamtime, three Yeperenyes came crawling to Mparntwe ..."

For the second time Kieran listened to the creation story of Alice Springs and, while the goosebumps stayed, his wonder grew as the strength and conviction of the story flowed over him.

"Yeperenye! Iriperenye!"

When the story ended with the repeated starting calls Woorawa leapt to his feet and began singing. The words were First Australian—they'd demand the meaning later—and marvelling at the distinctive tone and rhythmic stress patterns, Kieran vowed to learn at least part of this for himself. The song repeated and, using his music sticks, Woorawa danced as well, round and round the circle of enchanted watchers. The song changed to a chant and at Woorawa's signal everyone rose to join in with the steps they'd practised.

Woorawa grabbed his didgeridoo and Kieran was astonished how well it matched the chant. They should have been using it in their daily practice.

For the first short while Kieran wished Woorawa was dancing the lead for their movements, but he could hardly do that while playing the didgeridoo. The concentration required to keep in step with everyone else quickly took over and filled Kieran with the delight of rhythm and movement. A quick peek showed that Rhys was also completely involved, with none of the self-conscious awkwardness of their practices and—wow!— Mr B looked terrific, so light and nimble. The thrum of the didgeridoo stopped and for a minute Woorawa took the lead with the same skill and charisma that had amazed everyone so much at Alice Springs. He finished with a dramatic leap, sat everyone around the little circle of candles again, then stood behind Rhys and placed a hand on each shoulder.

"Brother! Welcome to my Country!"

A flood of First Australian words poured out and he moved behind Mr B, who was next in the circle.

"Brother! Welcome to my Country!"

The same flood of words followed and this time Kieran was caught by a strong sense of ceremony.

As Tan received his treatment Kieran thrilled with anticipation. They'd known about the Dreamtime story, the chants and dances, of course, but this call was a surprise, and from Woorawa's intensity, something very important.

"Brother! Welcome to my Country!"

The mellifluous declaration sounded out and Kieran's feeling of wonder was compounded by the awed look Tan was directing at Woorawa. Woorawa's hands dropped and his happy smile shone out as he resumed his sitting place.

"Uncle Burrimul sends a message of thanks for the great kindness you give me and welcomes you into our family. Those special words are his gift for our ceremony and he wishes he was here to say them himself."

"Can you translate them for us, Woorawa? You made them sound very official."

"I'll take you through them later, Rhys, but they're the words which make you my skin brother, if you want to be. All of you!"

Rhys stared in wonder. Well, they all did. Then he jumped to his feet to give Woorawa a powerful hug.

"Of course I do, Woorawa, but I don't know what to say. It makes me feel special."

One by one, everyone followed Rhys's lead and showed their agreement with a hug, which, by the time Kieran did it, felt ceremonial in itself. Woorawa explained what it meant, answered a few questions, then, with a big smile, started tapping his music sticks.

"This is an exciting dance, Rhys. Doing it means you agree to be my brother and the amount of energy you put into it shows how much you mean it."

"Which dance is it?"

Kieran guessed it would be the most lively of the dances they'd learnt, and one combination leap and arm movement by Woorawa proved he was right. Woorawa did another leap, started the chant that went with it, and in moments the lounge was bursting with movement and energy. Rhys suddenly let out a huge yell of exuberance, which spoiled everyone else's concentration. Not for long though, and everyone quickly followed Woorawa's lead again.

With his feet stomping in time with Woorawa and everyone else, Kieran took in Tan's rapt expression and was thinking how strange the whole scene would look to an outsider when there was a great crash of sound. Glass exploded everywhere as a large object came flying through the bay window. In the fraction of a second it took for the movement to register in Kieran's mind the missile dropped low and impacted against Tan's leg. Tan's cry of pain pulled Kieran from shocked disbelief and he started to move. *No. No. Wrong idea.*

"Don't move! Don't move! There's glass everywhere."

The room lit up in a bright blue glow of light and Kieran turned to Mr B, who at that moment was farthest from the window.

"Watch where you tread, Mr B, and turn the lights on. Tan, there's glass all around you so don't move till we can reach you."

The overhead light flicked on and Kieran cancelled his glow.

"Mr B and Rhys, find some shoes so you can carry Tan into the kitchen."

Through the gaping hole in the window sounded the loud engine revs of a car accelerating away.

Kieran looked back at Tan who was bent down, holding his left leg and examining his right foot which was turning red at the sides with smeared blood.

"There's glass under my foot, Kieran. I think I should move it."

"Try to wait, Tan. We won't be long."

Woorawa was making his way very carefully towards the kitchen and Mr B was back, with Rhys behind him rushing to catch up. There was a crunch of glass under their shoes as they approached Tan, and again when they carried him to the kitchen and sat him on one of the chairs. Woorawa appeared, carrying Kieran's shoes, and in moments the whole group was safely shod and gathered round Tan. Mr B staunched the slow trickle of blood, while Rhys rushed off to the bathroom to collect the first aid kit they'd bought, at Tan's urging, only a week ago.

"It's a long cut, Tan, but it will be okay. The bleeding stops when I keep the pressure on so a good clean and a proper bandage should be enough. Is it hurting?"

"I can hardly feel it. It's my leg that hurts. That lump is going to turn into an enormous bruise." He touched it very gingerly and winced.

"Ouch! That's bad. What was it, a brick or a lump of concrete?"

Tan looked up. "Woorawa, there's some ice in the fridge. That might help a bit."

Mr B gave a nod. "That's a good idea but we'll check your leg first. Wrap the ice in a tea towel, Woorawa, while I finish bandaging this cut."

While Woorawa went for the ice Rhys collected the heavy object from among the shards of broken glass. It was indeed a brick, wrapped in paper with the word 'FREAKS' showing clearly under the rubber bands holding the paper in place.

"Look at this! They're total mongrels."

Everyone looked, but not for long, because Tan's leg was a bigger priority. Mr B went to touch it but changed his mind.

"Test it very gently, Tan, but not that nasty-looking part in the middle. It's right on your shin and I think it needs an X-ray in case it's bruised the bone."

Tan looked worried. "Is a bruised bone bad?"

"You wouldn't need a plaster cast or crutches, but I think they take a long time to heal. Kieran, could you get Tan's ordinary clothes please. We'll all get changed and take him straight to emergency."

"You think it's an emergency?"

"No, Tan, but it's the only way you'll get an X-ray at this time of night."

"We'll try something else first, Mr B. Carry Tan to his bed and bring some chairs so we can all be comfortable."

Everyone paused.

"Comfortable?"

"Yes, in case we flake out. I am going to use the opal."

"With Rhys?"

"Yes, remember this afternoon when he called it healing?"

"This isn't just tired muscles, Kieran. It's major."

"I know, Mr B, but Rhys's hands worked for blind eyes and that's definitely major."

"Well … yes, you're right."

Mr B turned to Tan. "What do you think, Tan? Are you happy for Kieran and Rhys to try this?"

"Yes. It might stop the throbbing."

Kieran took in the range of looks he was getting. Mr B and Tan were somewhat dubious. Rhys looked surprised but hopeful, and Woorawa had a huge smile.

In short order, Tan was relaxed on his bed with Rhys beside him. Kieran sat comfortably in a chair next to the bed with Mr B ready to support him if he went to sleep, and Woorawa stood beside Rhys, ready to do the same. Very carefully, Kieran called on the opal and directed the energy or whatever it was into Tan's leg. It built and built till the understanding he'd gained from the previous practice told him there was enough for Rhys's hands to work.

"Okay, Rhys. Try your magic touch."

"Um. Right on the lump? I'll just touch without pressing."

Rhys's right hand made the lightest contact and Kieran felt the energy stuff disappear. When Rhys's eyes closed and Woorawa held his shoulders so he didn't flop on top of Tan, Kieran felt annoyed with himself and redirected the opal energy. Rhys's eyes flew open.

"Whoa! Thanks, Kieran. Something must've happened because I nearly lost it. Did you feel it, Tan?"

"It felt weird, all tingly and warm. My leg, I mean, and I feel sleepy."

Of course he did. Kieran started to direct the energy back to Tan then wondered if he could make it work for both of them at the same time. He could make three or four different objects glow so it should be similar to that. With a burst of concentration he filled both Tan and Rhys with energy. Yes. That worked well.

Rhys lit up with a rush of wellbeing and grinned at Kieran. "Whoo! What a boost!"

"Hold Tan's temples, Rhys, to do the same for him, and then we'll go back to his leg."

That worked. Tan's head came up and his quick laugh told Kieran he could concentrate on the injury again. Two general energy streams to keep Tan and Rhys awake, and a special stream to Tan's leg all at the same time would be best. How to manage it? It took a lot of concentration.

"Keep your hands touching the lump, Rhys. I've got everything balanced so neither of you will flake out."

Rhys placed his fingers gently on the swelling and gasped. So did Tan.

"I felt the tingle, Kieran, but it still hurts. Keep going, please."

Mr B interrupted. "I think you should stop working on his leg and try the cut first, Kieran. It's minor compared to that lump and it will be easier to show us if any healing is really happening."

Kieran agreed and concentrated on the cut. At his signal, Rhys rested two fingers alongside the bandage. Tan's foot jerked and he made a strange noise.

"Did it hurt?"

"No. It tickled too much and I wasn't ready for it. The biggest tickle feeling I've ever had. Take the bandage off, Rhys. My foot feels different, and I want to see."

"Are you sure? It might start the bleeding again."

"I don't think so. The stinging feeling isn't as strong."

Rhys nodded, carefully peeled the bandage away, then bent his head close to examine the cut. "The cut's still there but it's different. You dressed it Mr B. What do you think?"

Mr B bent close and after a few seconds lifted his head. "It's hard to tell, but Rhys is right. It hasn't got the same angry red look, and taking the bandage off so soon should have started the bleeding again. Can you keep the zap going for a while longer, Kieran?"

"Longer? I don't see why not, but we've never done it like that so we'll have to be careful. I'll have to use the opal a lot."

"Start slow and watch Rhys and Tan in case they pass out. And watch yourself, Kieran. If you're using the opal in a new way you might be affected too."

Woorawa was right and Kieran, annoyed with himself for not doing this all along, immediately loaded himself with energy in case he needed Rhys's hands.

"Ready, Rhys? Keep your fingers in place and we'll see what happens."

The first zap was normal but it taught Kieran that he had to send extra energy to both Tan and Rhys right when the zap happened to keep them both awake. It also taught him that a continuous zap of the kind Mr B wanted would need a scary amount of help from the opal. No way was he going to call that much in one go, so starting at his normal level and carefully monitoring what was happening with Tan, Rhys and himself, Kieran gradually increased his demand from the opal. Tan's foot started twitching. *What?* Oh, it was the tickle factor.

"Woorawa, hold Tan's foot steady so Rhys doesn't lose contact with it. It's tickling too much for him to control."

When that was sorted Kieran resumed his call on the opal and felt perspiration break out on his forehead. *Whoops!* Too much effort. How could he fix things? Easy. He reached out and one touch on Rhys's free hand made him feel better. Amazing! Tan's eyes were closed but he was smiling blissfully. Rhys was staring at the blue glow surrounding his hands. No, he wasn't. He was looking where they were touching. His mouth opened and he looked at Kieran with wonder in his eyes.

"That's enough, Kieran. Turn it all off and look at Tan's skin."

It took a couple of seconds and he sensed Rhys's hands turn a momentary burst of excess energy into life and wellbeing for each of them. Tan's eyes opened and he leaned forward.

"Unbelievable! The cut's gone. I can't even see where it was." He touched the area gently, then with more force. "It's like new. I can't even feel where it was."

Rhys laughed as three heads bumped together when they moved for a closer look.

"Are you okay, Kieran? You're sweating."

"Yes. I was concentrating so much on watching you and Tan I forgot about myself. I should've been touching your magic hands all the time. Are you tired? I want to get on with Tan's leg."

"Straight away? Well, I'm sure not tired. The rush thing at the end makes me feel like I could keep going for ever."

Mr B shook his head forcefully. "No! Not yet. Take a break for a while, especially you, Kieran. I've never seen you concentrating as hard, not even when you made the candle flame. Have a drink and something to eat while Woorawa and I clean up all that glass and do something about the window. Tan should relax too, because healing that injury's going to be a lot harder than fixing a simple cut. In fact, I want you all to relax on your beds for ten or fifteen minutes while Woorawa and I get busy."

Mr B was right. If it wasn't for the boost from Rhys's hands Kieran would have been completely wrecked right now. He made a little head movement telling Rhys to follow him and walked straight to the bedroom.

"What? Mr B said I should lie down."

"Yes, but lie down on my bed. Every time you use your magic hands I feel like I want to hug you or hold you or something."

"Hey! So do I. And it keeps getting stronger."

A moment later Kieran was relaxed with two strong arms around him and his headband resting on the towel he'd had the presence of mind to drape over the pillow.

Rhys gave a little laugh. "Two wild men in bed."

"Yes, and two skin brothers. Don't forget that."

"Hey, wow! We are too. Are you comfy? I think we should close our eyes and relax like Mr B wants us to."

"Mmm."

"Kieran?"

CHAPTER 7

"Time to get up you two. Mr B's just finished taping cardboard over the hole in the window and we've got drinks waiting for you. Unless you want me to bring them in here?"

Rhys's movement and Woorawa's voice brought Kieran fully awake and his opening eyes took in the very cheeky grin, which grew even more cheeky as Rhys disengaged himself.

"What's happened? Is Tan okay? Have we been asleep long?"

"Thirty minutes. Tan just woke up so we decided you could too. Mr B says we're having a big council of war."

"You're out of your costume. Aren't we going to finish the ceremony?"

"Yes, but not tonight. We don't know how well this healing thing with Tan's leg will work or how long it will take, and Mr B thinks you'll need an even bigger sleep after that."

"I bet I will. What about all the glass?"

"We've got most of it, but get dressed and keep your shoes on just in case. Your drinks are getting cold."

Kieran smiled at the hurry up then held his arm out so Woorawa could drag him to his feet. The drinks weren't cold and after changing quickly they took them to Tan's bedroom.

Whoo! Tan *was* smiling but his leg looked awful.

"Holy cow, Tan! Does that feel as bad as it looks? It's got twice as big."

"It's gone kind of tight and it's still throbbing but it doesn't hurt as much … unless I touch it."

"Are you ready for Rhys's magic hands? We'll start as soon as we finish our drinks. Hey, is your foot still all right?"

"My foot is perfect. Have a look."

Everyone had a quick, but cursory, look while Rhys made jokes about which other parts of Tan were perfect. The lump did indeed look awful but there was an excited sense of optimism as everyone took their place. Kieran took hold of Rhys's free hand and looked at all the expectant faces.

"Something tells me this is going to take a lot longer, but I really think the opal's going to make it happen."

He opened his free hand to show the beautiful gemstone and, on impulse, made it sparkle for a few seconds with a range of colours.

"Wow! What happened, Kieran. It looks like it's alive."

"That was me, Rhys. I'm getting a feel for its energy before I start."

Mr B squeezed Kieran's shoulder.

"Let Rhys's hands help you more often this time, Kieran. Do you think you can stop yourself from reaching that level where you perspire from so much effort?"

Kieran nodded. Of course he could. It just meant getting a regular boost from the opal rather than waiting till he felt he needed it.

After five minutes the swelling was half the size and Kieran knew they were going to be successful. The next five minutes was the most interesting for him as, besides taking all the swelling away, it taught him a huge amount about calling on the opal, and by the time he called a break he'd learnt how to build a kind of pool of energy that Rhys could draw on continually, how to manipulate different streams of energy at the same time, and how to control where they went.

"Why are we stopping? The lump's gone but there's still something wrong."

"I want a drink and a think for a few minutes, Rhys, then we'll get it finished. Put your hands on Rhys's head, Mr B and Woorawa, so we can all get an energy boost."

Mr B and Woorawa both looked surprised.

"What for? All we've done is watch and we said we'd only do this if we needed it … and doesn't it need to be from his hands?"

"It's a little experiment I want to try, Woorawa. You won't feel as much as usual and you can touch him anywhere."

A moment later everyone suddenly smiled.

"That felt good, but what was the point, Kieran?"

"How Rhys's healing works is a complete mystery to me, Mr B, but I've found out I've got some control over it and I wanted to see if I could reduce how much gets through."

"And that's related to the thinking you want to do?"

"Yes, if I can reduce it I should be able to invert the process and increase the effect. I've got enough to go over in my head while everyone gets another drink. What can you feel with your leg, Tan?"

"Nothing. There's no throb or anything."

"Test it with your fingers because Rhys and I both know it's still not right."

Tan experimented, then held his finger in one spot. "Yes. Right there, but I can only feel it when I press."

"And that's your shin. It fits with Mr B's idea about a bruised bone."

Everyone, including Tan, walked to the kitchen to make their drinks.

"I can't see any glass. How did you clean it up so well?"

"We swept and vacuumed, Rhys, but there'll still be tiny slivers we couldn't find. We'll have to go over it three or four more times before it's safe for bare feet."

Kieran put his drink down and turned toward the lounge. "No we won't! Watch this!"

The first thing everyone saw was a glow of light from all the kitchen windows and every glass object around them.

"Whoops! I didn't mean everything."

The glow stopped as abruptly as it had started, and Kieran pointed to the lounge where twenty or so bright little spots of light glittered from various positions all over the carpet.

"How did you do that?"

"Easy, Rhys. I did the search thing for any glass. When we finish Tan's leg, I'll make them shine again and it'll only take a few minutes to pick them all up with the vacuum cleaner."

"I can't keep up. It seems like you learn how to do something new every few minutes."

"Not really. I already knew how to search and how to make things glow. It clicked in my mind to put them together."

"I understand that, but every single glass thing glowed. A few days ago you had to struggle to make three of us glow at the same time, and just then you made far more things glow like it was nothing. I think fixing Tan's leg made you stronger."

"It's the opal, Rhys. I did figure out a lot of things with Tan's leg but I used it sort of automatically for all the glass."

"Make all of us glow then. I bet you can do it easily."

"After we've finished Tan's leg. That's what's important at the moment."

"Yeah, of course it is, but I still want to see you try, and if this next bit of healing's as hard as Mr B thinks it might be, you could end up even stronger. Hey! The best test will be making a light without the opal. I can't wait … no … I mean, yes, I can." Kieran turned to Tan. "Come on, Tan. We're going to make your leg as perfect as your foot."

Everyone was smiling. Rhys's excitement and eagerness to get going was catching. Back in Tan's bedroom the set up was the same except for Kieran's request that Mr B and Woorawa keep their hands resting on Rhys's head the whole time. That got some curious looks, but no comments.

"Are we all ready?"

Kieran surprised the group, including himself when, after only five or six minutes, he sent an invigorating burst of wellbeing and announced that Tan's leg was as good as new.

"Are you sure, Kieran? The cut took twice as long as that."

"Rhys's touch isn't doing anything in that area anymore, Woorawa, so it must be right."

"So you did something different? You thought it was going to take about twenty minutes when you started."

"Yes, I've worked out how to let Rhys use extra opal energy without getting overloaded. I think we could fix the cut in less than a minute now."

Everyone stared at him, except for Tan who was probing the area where his shin had been injured.

"This is hard to believe. The bad spot has definitely gone because it feels exactly the same as the rest of my shin. Maybe the bone wasn't bruised as much as we thought?"

"It would have been, Tan. Did you see how Rhys's hands kept glowing without a stop? Energy was pouring in and he used way more than he did for the cut and the lump put together."

In fact, Kieran could hardly believe how much. For the whole five minutes he'd worked a balancing act of steadily drawing more and more energy while at the same time giving Rhys just the right amount to cope with it. Tan jumped up from his bed, took a few steps to test his leg, then gave Kieran and Rhys a heartfelt thank you hug.

"It's like … like healing potions in a role-playing game except for real."

Rhys loved that and started gesturing toward everyone with his hands. "Like in *Mysts*! I'm the healer and Kieran's the great wizard. Turn Woorawa into a frog, Kieran, and when my hands touch him he'll be himself again."

Kieran was about to tell Rhys he was an idiot when he realised he could actually do this. Well, not a real frog, of course, but a false idea in their minds for a few moments would make them think that. This would be fun. Holding his hands out dramatically he formed a large blue globe of light and directed it to hover above Woorawa.

"Kieran, what are you doing?"

Kieran didn't answer, just clapped his hands together and instructed Rhys, Tan and Mr B's minds that the blue globe had enveloped Woorawa and in his place was a metre-high bullfrog. He exploded with laughter at the three sets of goggle-eyes, and then again when Woorawa asked why they were staring at him so weirdly.

Tan laughed first. "Use your healer hands, Rhys. That's what you're meant to do."

Rhys held his hands out then abruptly pulled them back. "Not yet. Woorawa's the best frog I've ever seen."

Totally bewildered, Woorawa looked at Rhys. "Why are you calling me a frog?"

Rhys's eyes goggled even more. "And you can talk to me."

Now even more confused, Woorawa looked to Kieran for an explanation.

"Rhys wanted you to be a frog so now you are. When he puts his hands on you, you'll turn human again."

Understanding dawned and Woorawa laughed and couldn't help checking himself. "I must be a pretty good one then."

"You are. You're as high as my waist and you even laugh."

"I'm giant? For Tan and Mr B too?"

Mr B answered. "You're a super-size version of the frogs we saw at the Valley of the Eagles, Woorawa, and Rhys is right about the talking and laughing. It gives an air of unreality that is beyond bizarre. Put your magic hands on him, please, Rhys. I'm finding this too weird."

Rhys moved closer but as he reached out Tan grabbed a hold of his hand.

"He'll feel froggy, Rhys, but healing him with your hands won't work."

Now it was Kieran's turn to be puzzled. "Why not, Tan? I was about to make it happen."

"It's a kiss that turns a frog into a handsome prince. Everyone knows that."

Kieran bubbled with enjoyment at this brilliant idea. "Hey, yes. Kiss him, Rhys. It's the only way."

There was a new explosion of laughter at Rhys's expression.

"Not yet. I like him like this. He's a nice frog."

"Pucker up. You have to do it now because Mr B's not comfortable with talking frogs."

"As if! He knows it's all in his mind."

There was a twinkle in Mr B's eye. "I'm still adapting to the idea, Rhys. Please kiss the frog."

"You just wait, Tan. I'm going to get you for this. Is he going to taste froggy?"

Kieran nodded. "Great idea, Rhys, now that you mention it."

"Ha, very ha!"

He puckered up, though, because he was enjoying this as much as everyone else really, and when his lips seemingly made contact Kieran covered Woorawa with a green glow for a few seconds and dismissed the frog image.

"Any more interesting ideas we can try, Rhys? That was fun."

"Lots of ideas, except I know you'll make them backfire on me. Anyway, now that Tan's leg's okay we have to stop mucking round and clean up those glass splinters so we can get serious about the brick attack."

Rhys was right, and the mood turned from frivolity to purpose.

*   *   *

Kieran returned the vacuum cleaner to its storage place near the laundry door then paused to listen to the muted sound of Woorawa's chanting. It was odd that he'd started by himself. Probably he wanted to teach Mr B something. Kieran headed for the lounge but once again paused. This time he cocked his head to listen more carefully. That was even odder. The chant was the one Woorawa used when they practised their mental barrier contest, not any of the ones they'd practised for the ceremony. Well, he must be reviewing it to Mr B.

Kieran sent a light touch to check and reeled in shock. Woorawa's barriers were straining at their limit from some kind of attack, and an instant of consideration showed they were wavering. After all their practice, Kieran understood exactly how Woorawa's barriers worked so another instant had them bolstered and rock-steady. Pressure built again in a way that Kieran didn't understand. Never mind, a burst from the opal would help and he could puzzle over this strange attack.

He reached for energy and reeled with shock again. It wasn't working and, worse still, there was no sense of connection. Automatically he grasped the gemstone dangling from the chain around his neck. Burrimul had insisted they see a jeweller as a way to keep it close when he was swimming. Using his direction sense he reached. Yes, there it was, but just a trace. With one great push of effort he rebuilt the connection to its normal level and directed a stream of energy to Woorawa.

At this stage, Kieran received his third shock. Those few short seconds had brought him to the lounge entrance where he could see Woorawa chanting with his eyes closed. The shock was the others, all slumped on the carpet, apparently asleep. Asleep? That couldn't be. A minute ago all of them had been brimming with life from the burst at the end of Tan's healing, excited by it, and curious about Mr B's 'council of war'.

The connection to the opal began to close again and with a touch of annoyance, Kieran locked it open and directed a surge of energy against whatever was affecting it. The pressure stopped abruptly and the opal was completely his again.

Woorawa's chanting stopped. *What was happening now?* Kieran checked, then rushed not only to reinforce the again-failing barrier but to add a barrier of his own against pressure now surging way beyond anything Woorawa could possibly manage. Kieran held it though, quite easily with help from the opal, and the strangeness quickly changed to partial understanding. His flicker of interest passed with the realisation that this was supposed to send Woorawa to sleep like all the others. Well, more help from the opal would stop that. Copying the style of pressure as best he could, Kieran called even more opal energy and pushed back powerfully.

Woorawa's eyes opened. "Why did you get so rough, Kieran? I thought …" His voice trailed off when he took in the three inert bodies. "What?"

"They're asleep, Woorawa, and something tried to do the same to you till I stopped it."

"That wasn't you? Are they all right?"

"I think so. It feels just like sleep but we'll know as soon as we wake them."

"It can't be ordinary sleep. We were too full of energy and excited. Wake Rhys first in case you need his hands. Kieran, I'm glad it wasn't you. It was scary."

"I know. Something tried to stop the opal working, too, and I only just got to you in time. I'll tell you about it as soon as we get everyone awake."

Kieran moved towards Rhys and felt a throb of migraine pain so powerful he nearly lost his balance. His eyes lost focus and the kaleidoscope of weird colours was so disorienting he dropped to his knees to stop himself from overbalancing.

"What are you doing?"

Kieran winced. The distorted tone of Woorawa's voice was an assault on his ears.

"Migraine! … Awful! … Help me reach Rhys … Make it go away."

"Fight it, Kieran. It's not a migraine. It's an attack to put you to sleep. Make a barrier against it till I get you to Rhys."

Kieran pulled meaning from the confusion of sound and sight and Woorawa's supporting grip on his arm was a life-saving reprieve from the pain and chaos battering his senses.

An attack? Of course. The supporting shield he'd given to Woorawa moments before now sprang into place for his own mind and the world steadied long enough to let him get to his feet. After a few assisted steps the assault renewed. Kieran leaned against Woorawa and built his mind barrier to a level where he could ignore all the pressure. Yes, it *was* pressure, directed pressure, not quite the same as the pressure against Woorawa, but very similar and that meant he knew how to counter it.

Defiance flared, along with a touch of anger, and with help from the opal, he reversed the pressure and flung it back to wherever it was coming from.

"Go away and don't try that again!"

Woorawa's supporting grip disappeared and Kieran blinked at his shocked expression. *What? Oh!*

"Did I say that out loud? It wasn't to you, Woorawa."

Woorawa visibly pulled himself together. "Thank goodness for that. My legs nearly started running. You fought off the attack, didn't you?"

"Only after you made me realise what it was. It was so bad I could hardly think."

"Are you all right? You did it without Rhys."

"Yes, I figured out how to push back with the opal. Hold Rhys's head while I help him."

Rhys recovered the instant the burst of opal energy reached him and, in short order, Tan and Mr B were also looking to Kieran for explanations.

*   *   *

Reeling with shock, High King Aglaron relaxed the group shield and directed attention to his stunned advisors. The automatic shield activation had snapped the intricate links between Maynor, Uirebon, and the Human World, and he watched with little understanding as first Uirebon and, a short moment later, Maynor, returned to local awareness.

Their very first step in reinstating Keryth's conditioning was now awry and understanding was imperative.

Uirebon rallied. "My Lord, you terminated the process?"

"Not at all, Uirebon. Our group shield acted to protect us from that unexpected but powerful response directed at Maynor, and severed the link to Keryth. When we return, our shields will be controlled rather than automatic."

"I failed, my Lord. The Dark Child was aware of my attempt at control and consciously resisted with a curious combination of mindset and a natural barrier which unaccountably firmed beyond my ability."

"We all failed, Uirebon. Keryth has somehow linked himself with an instrument of power and my attempt at examination was brushed aside, then completely blocked."

Maynor spoke. "I learnt many things from Pethron's mind before the links were broken. The instrument apparently augments his natural resistance and must be helping other abilities surface with his human persona. I counsel an immediate return before he grows even stronger. I was on the point of taking control when the link was broken."

"Are you sure of your control, Maynor? It was the response to your effort that triggered the shields."

"My personal effort alone was almost successful, my Lord. Against the combined power of three Realm Lords, a triad of triads, and an abundance of Nexus energy, he cannot stand. But we should return immediately. That young representative of the Ancient People has been helping Keryth to explore and develop both his abilities and the link to the instrument, which Pethron's mind sees as a gemstone called a black opal."

Aglaron raised a cautioning hand. "In essence I am in full agreement, Maynor, but rushing in without understanding could very well counter the value of speed. Enlighten us with the information you gained from Pethron first."

"Time is against us and there is much to consider, my Lord."

"Much? Explain."

"I learned that the human I shielded and guided to challenge Keryth responded far beyond expectation and caused an aggressive and dangerous physical action. A missile showered Keryth's group with glass and injured one of them. My poor judgement must be rectified."

"Physical violence! Show me."

A selection of Pethron's memories flowed and Aglaron, after a moment of review, spoke rather abruptly.

"The challenge against Keryth ceases, Maynor, and the artificial aggression must be removed from the young challenger's mind before it manifests with even greater severity."

Uirebon hastened to mediate. "My Lord, this relatively minor element of the situation will be quickly and easily rectified. We failed to take account of the propensity for some humans to express their aggression so physically."

"Not so minor for the challenger, Uirebon. His mind could well face turmoil as it attempts to understand actions beyond its norm ... but you are right. Information regarding Keryth is more pressing. Continue, Maynor."

"The Dark Child's urgings have somehow stimulated Keryth to develop surprising new abilities."

"New? That does require explanation."

"The first to appear was the ability to locate an object or person he has been associated with. He used it to find the warrior, and Pethron's mind has knowledge that Keryth was able to locate the opal giver from halfway across the dry continent."

"That is a useful ability, Maynor, but not uncommon."

"I agree. The next ability is really an expansion of his childhood affinity with animals to a broader level of conscious mental manipulation. Also, according to one of their discussions, he examined the changes we made to him and his companions' memories and partially copied our techniques."

"Conscious mental manipulation is fundamental to us. He may be accessing his previous training."

"That is not possible, my Lord, without breaking the underlying conditioning I gave him, and that hasn't happened. It's his degree of control that is so surprising. Just moments before we intervened, he turned the dark-skinned friend into a giant frog. The image was strong in Pethron's mind and functional for both touch and sight."

"Two senses at once is competent but not surprising."

"My Lord, he held the appearance with three onlookers simultaneously."

"That is surprising."

"Not as surprising as the light he can call into being—real light."

"The introductory skill for anyone training to use Nexus power. Keryth was so instructed some fifty years ago."

"Pethron watched him kindle the light *without* help from the instrument of power."

"Without help? How can that be? Real light requires energy which must come from somewhere. Do you have any explanation for this, Uirebon?"

"Keryth can only be using energy from the instrument of power in some way we don't understand ... or maybe he retains some of its energy without realising he is doing so? Otherwise, he has some other source of energy at his disposal."

"Such as?"

"Natural energy of the world around him, or maybe even his own life force, though I hope not, as that is fraught with danger."

"We can draw energy from our bodies? Why have I never heard of such an ability?"

"The knowledge is restricted."

"From me?"

"Of course not, my Lord."

"I see ... Well, under oath of secrecy, Maynor may also hear of it."

Maynor made the sign of committal and, with his liege, gave attention to Uirebon.

"My Lord, some eighteen centuries ago, one of the High Lords discovered he was able to augment personal strength with life force from his subjects, and attempted to take the Nexus from your father. Something went terribly wrong and all his court and two thirds of his subjects were drained of life in a matter of seconds."

"The Great Death and the foundation of Lady Narello's realm?"

"Indeed. Your father admired Narello's resourcefulness and gave her control of the almost-depopulated domain."

"What knowledge do you have regarding this life force?"

"None, apart from the frightening consequences of its use I just related."

"Search for understanding. Keryth may be in danger."

"There is nowhere to search, my Lord. After three centuries with no sign of the ability reappearing, your father agreed with me that it was lost with the death of his brother and all his line."

"My uncle was the High Lord you speak of? Brother contested with brother?"

"Times were stormy and your uncle had more ambition than wisdom. Ambition has ever been the bane of the Realms."

"You knew him, Uirebon? He was before my time and my father never spoke of him."

"His ambition and strength unnerved me and I inherit my reticence regarding him from your father. The Great Death was a dark time for all the Realms and when Keryth returns we must examine this use of life force, if that is what it is."

Maynor nodded worriedly. "My Lord, I fear that it is. Pethron's memory shows Keryth was reduced to exhaustion in a matter of seconds when he produced light. We must regain control and, for his own good, prevent any further experimentation. Without supervision he may be in great danger."

Alarm crossed the High King's countenance. "Uirebon, combine every flow of power and direct it to Maynor. We return to the Human World as soon as the triads can be made ready. Keryth must be protected."

*   *   *

Five friends gathered for explanation, before starting the now doubly pressing council of war Mr B had earlier called.

"Whatever it was, it nearly got us, Rhys, and we could have lost you again. You didn't feel anything, because you were asleep but Kieran saved me just in time, then frightened the life out of me when he collapsed on the floor with the migraine thing."

"Collapsed? It was that bad, Woorawa? How did he get better if I wasn't awake to help him?"

"I don't know. One second he was on his knees and about to fall on his side and the next he was on his feet looking so angry I nearly ran out of the room."

Kieran hastened to explain. "It was the strongest migraine I've ever had, Rhys. They usually build up slowly, but this time it happened so quickly I couldn't think. Woorawa snapped me out of it by telling me to fight and as soon as he yelled I knew he was right. I copied the barrier he uses for our mind fights."

"Wow! And it worked. Have you ever done that before?"

"Not for myself. I'd built an extra barrier for Woorawa a few seconds earlier, to protect him, and I used the same pattern for myself, so he kind of saved me twice. As soon as I made the barrier I got better."

"So our theories about some kind of attack are right?"

"Definitely, Mr B. First of all I nearly lost the opal. Then it was a fight to protect Woorawa, and then straight after that it was the migraine."

"How could you lose the opal? It's around your neck."

"Not the opal itself, Rhys. Something stopped it from helping me and I had to use the search thing to get back my proper connection."

"Why do you say separate fights, Kieran? Don't you think it was all part of one big effort to put us to sleep?"

"No. The first fight didn't have any effect on me. It was just about control of the opal." Kieran thought back. "The other fights were different too, Mr B. The more I go over it the more it feels like three separate attacks."

"We should be saying six attacks, Kieran. Three of us collapsed on the floor without warning and I don't know about Tan and Rhys, but I have absolutely no recollection of anything happening at all. One moment I was watching Tan light the candles and the next I was on the floor with Rhys touching my forehead."

"Me too. When I opened my eyes I thought Kieran must have tried some new trick because I couldn't remember lying down."

Tan nodded, and then Woorawa spoke up. "Check them all, Kieran. You might be able to tell if anything happened to their memories. And me too. I know I nearly lost it at one stage."

Woorawa was right and Kieran gave himself a mental kick for not doing that straight off.

"Everyone touch Rhys. We're all going to get an energy boost before I start."

Rhys smiled when Kieran and Tan held a hand each and Mr B and

Woorawa put their hands on his head and then there was a collective burst of assorted exclamations at the boost of wellbeing.

"Whoo! That was stronger than last time, Kieran."

"I know. I made it extra in case any of us needed it. Keep your hands in place while I concentrate."

A minute later Kieran opened his eyes to four sets of wondering looks.

"Something was different for Mr B and I don't know what it was, so I made it normal, a bit like I did with the professor and the administrator's memories. Everyone else is okay … as far as I can tell."

"How different, Kieran. You're making me feel uneasy."

"There was nothing bad, Mr B, just your memories seemed to be a lot more open than everyone else's so I sort of pushed them back where they should be. You're more complicated, too, but I think that's because you're an adult."

"You can move memories around to different parts of our heads? I thought you could only change them."

"It wasn't really moving and it wasn't really me doing it, Rhys. When I saw something odd I guided your healing energy the same way I did for Tan's leg and that's what made the change."

"That's another new thing, Kieran. When did you learn to do that?"

"It's not new, Rhys. I did tell you when we were fixing Tan's leg."

"That's different to fixing someone's mind."

"I haven't got a clue about fixing anything. That's all you. Without your touch nothing would even happen."

"We'll have to practise everything as much as we can. Every single day … and I don't think half an hour is enough."

"Are you changing the subject, Woorawa?"

"Talking is important, Mr B, but we'll understand the healing stuff better by doing it. The same as everything else."

"Doing it? That means someone has to get hurt."

Woorawa jumped up, went to the kitchen drawer, returned with a knife, and startled everyone by jabbing it into the palm of his hand.

"Holy cow! You're crazy, Woorawa!"

"No, I'm not. You and Kieran will fix it in less than a minute."

Woorawa pressed against the cut to staunch the bleeding then present-ed his hand to Rhys. He was right about the time because this was smaller than Tan's cut and Kieran *did* know exactly what to do. A moment later Woorawa rubbed where the knife point had gone in and brandished his hand for everyone to see.

"See. I'll jab it in deeper tomorrow. Anyone else going to have a try?"

After a wary pause Rhys took the lead. Kieran followed and by the time they'd all had a turn it was clear that without Rhys's touch nothing would heal.

"Why do you want so much extra practice, Woorawa? You reckon there'll be another attack?"

"Of course there will, Rhys. Whatever they were after tonight didn't happen, so they'll be back for sure. They want us all put to sleep so they can change our memories and get rid of you again. I think they don't like you being here because your magic hands keep stopping them from getting through to Kieran."

There was a general murmur of assent at this.

"I reckon that's right. Rhys was in the first group to collapse on the floor and that fits with the idea of stopping his healing. What do you think, Kieran?"

Kieran gave Rhys a very special look. "That means we'll protect him from now on. The migraine attack's the one that makes me forget things and I fought it off all by myself this time."

Woorawa interrupted, "Only just, Kieran. If you'd had the three attacks at the same time we'd all be asleep now. What if they all join together next time?"

That was a scary thought. "You're right about having lots of practice, Woorawa. I'll have to get stronger."

"The opal makes you strong enough."

"As long as I can last long enough to call on it, Tan. The energy only comes when I call it."

"Why don't you keep some with you all the time? You said you gave Rhys a big pool of it to make the healing go faster. Could you do that for yourself?"

"Well, I … Tan, that's brilliant. Hang on a second while I experiment."

Kieran opened his hand and made the opal sparkle as the indication for the others that he was using it. Yes, a store of energy for himself was even easier to control than the healing pool he'd placed with Rhys.

"Put the candles out, Tan, I've made a kind of reserve pool and I want to see if I can use it instead of my opal. I think I've called the right amount to light them all."

When Tan finished blowing out the candles, Kieran concentrated on the flame-starting technique but only managed to relight three out of the six.

"You can only do half of them?"

"Blow them out again and I'll have another try."

"So you did something wrong?"

"I wasted energy for the first three, Rhys. I'll do better this time."

When Tan's head was pulled back five candles lit up and Kieran laughed at all the querying looks.

"Bad judgement again. I didn't use enough for the fifth one and had to have a second go at it. It needs lots of practice."

"So, it's fairly hard?"

"Not really. I could have called a bigger bank of energy but that feels like I'm wasting it."

"How big can you make the bank? Enough for twenty candles?"

"Yes, but I won't do that straight away. I'll build up without rushing this time, Mr B."

"Another thing to practise. Kieran, I've been thinking about what you said you did to help Woorawa and it's given me an idea that might be a good help for all of us."

Kieran was surprised that Mr B seemed to be moving to something new before they'd talked out this energy pool thing. "What?"

"Well, the rest of us are all helpless against these attacks and I didn't think there was anything we could do about it. But then you said you gave Woorawa an extra barrier because his own wasn't strong enough. Can you do the same for Tan and Rhys and me?"

All thoughts about the energy bank disappeared from Kieran's mind. No wonder Mr B had been so insistent on this council of war.

"I think I can. Woorawa, fight me off as hard as you can so I remember what I did."

Woorawa's eyes closed and he started his chant. Kieran pushed till the chant hesitated, then reinstalled the extra barrier that had saved Woorawa. He dismantled it, then rebuilt it to establish the technique, pushed again and then again. With each careful push he added extra opal strength to the barrier and then a matching amount to himself. Woorawa stopped his chanting.

"Don't stop. I want you to keep fighting."

"What for? I can't feel you doing anything."

Kieran increased his pressure slightly, without a matching boost to the barrier, to show Woorawa that he was indeed being attacked. Woorawa took fright and backed away with his hands warding.

"Too much! Too much! Take it easy, Kieran."

Kieran instantly strengthened the barrier then wondered why the small increase had had such a strong effect.

"Whoo! Did you mean to do that, Kieran? It was bad."

"I've got the barrier working so well you can't feel how hard I'm attacking. When I let a bit of pressure through you weren't ready for it."

"That wasn't a bit. It was a lot. I would have flaked out if you'd kept going. Another thing to practise."

"I'm still going, Woorawa, but your barrier is stronger."

"You're attacking now … while I'm talking and not even concentrating?"

Kieran gave a nod and, with much finer control this time, allowed a few moments of pressure to get through. Woorawa closed his eyes with effort then opened them again when the pressure stopped.

"You're confusing me, Kieran. I don't know how to resist you when I can't feel anything."

"You will when we work on it, but you can relax now because I'm switching to Rhys."

Rhys looked worried and grabbed Kieran's hand. "Are you going to frighten me the way you just did to Woorawa? I can't stop you like he can."

"You won't have to, Rhys. Just fight against me the same as every other practice and that will show me how to make a barrier that suits you. I might frighten you once before I get tuned in properly."

"Tuned in? What does that mean?"

"Your levels will all be different to Woorawa's and I'll have to work out how much you can take."

"Still sounds scary!"

"You won't feel of thing … except for the mental torture."

"Ha very ha!"

After working out Rhys's barrier Kieran did the same for Tan, Mr B and himself, then practised till the pattern for each clicked nicely into place.

*   *   *

In short order, all three triads returned to full operation and with admiration High King Aglaron watched his Lore Master open nine separate paths of power, meld them to a single, stable focus, then transfer control to Maynor.

There would be no mistakes this time, no careless assumptions, no lack of power, and no automatic shielding cut-offs.

With only a minor change from Uirebon regarding the handling of the triad power and a commitment to extra Nexus energy on his own part, Aglaron could find no fault with the strategy Maynor had so hastily prepared and proposed. Interestingly, he'd insisted that Keryth's unusual method of shielding was a major factor of concern, and after urgent discussion it was agreed that the combined strength of three triads, three High Lords, and directed Nexus energy—all wielded as one—would be available if necessary.

There would also be no division of strength this time and, after the few seconds it would require to control the companions, all attention would focus on Keryth so Maynor's control pathways could be quickly re-established. When Uirebon added his personal resources, Maynor looked for the fourth and final supporting link from his liege. Aglaron constructed their four defensive mind shields, backed them with the Nexus and also added his own resources. The intricate web, designed by Uirebon and controlled by Maynor, locked into place. Maynor tested every link for stability then reached for the Human World.

With startling ease, contact was made and a quick burst of energy directed to the minor task of controlling the companions. Aglaron watched with surprise as the triad's defensive shield flared against a rebound of energy. How could that be? A second, more determined effort dissolved the resistance and four minds instantly moved to a state of deep sleep.

Success. There could now be no interference from the warrior's healing hands. That resistance *was* a surprise, though, and in the seconds while Maynor refocused the triad's power, Aglaron instinctively checked all four shields. Yes, Maynor also was a master in action.

He watched Maynor's exploratory push against his son with approval. Without precision, care and proper calibration, such overwhelming power was extremely dangerous.

A shield? Already in place?

The exploratory push increased in strength and again Aglaron admired Maynor's careful approach.

Pressure built and the shield wavered. Yes, with a little more strength it would crumble and Maynor would be able to take over. Aglaron took quick stock of Keryth's level of resistance. Extraordinary indeed, a match for the triads by themselves, but helpless against the overwhelming strength of three High Lords.

When the shield firmed, Aglaron briefly marvelled at his son's fortitude and for a fleeting moment felt a perverse inclination to give him aid. No, all this was for his own good and the good of the Realm. One more small increment of force would overcome this resistance and the plan would be back on course.

An inflow from Maynor's personal Nexus energy made the increment and Aglaron watched in anticipation for the success of their efforts. Keryth's shield held and Aglaron sensed the surprise from his two High

Lords. Maynor gathered more strength and tried again, but without success.

Surprise quickly gave way to shock, and then disbelief, as resource after resource was added to the pressure against this impossible shield. Maynor directed the total power of all three triads till finally there was an indication of progress.

The shield faltered, altered, then altered again in what appeared to be an effort to adapt.

Maynor called on the full potential of Uirebon's strength to take advantage before the shield steadied. Too late. An instant before Maynor applied what was now an unprecedented marshalling of power, Keryth's shield steadied and the onslaught raged, ineffective, while Maynor used every method at his disposal to probe and infiltrate this mysterious barrier.

With total disbelief Aglaron followed their agreed plan and ceded control of his own personal resources, resources almost matching those of Uirebon and Maynor combined, and watched the new level of power latch and hold.

How was this even possible?

A desperate call came from Maynor for direct access to Aglaron's link with the Nexus, the ultimate power source maintaining the very structure of the Realms. Yes, there was desperation in the call for this final contingency, but true to his word, Aglaron relinquished all control and watched Maynor wield the extra power with renewed confidence.

The pressure mounted then held,

and held,

and held.

Understanding came to Aglaron that instead of using a final hammer of brute force, Maynor was now waiting while Kieran expended his energy. Once again Aglaron approved. This new tactic eliminated the risk of any damage from overwhelming force. Nothing could hold against this amount of Nexus energy and when Keryth was finally drained, as he must be, his shield would falter.

Seconds passed and the combined power of three triads, three High Lords and direct Nexus energy raged against the strange shield till once again something wavered and changed.

Aglaron's new anticipation changed to shock when all four shields under his control flared to their full defensive strength.

Kieran could attack?

A rapid analysis revealed that all was secure and a second flare-up confirmed this. Amazement turned to satisfaction at the thought that the two attacks must be efforts of last resort.

Aglaron watched for any sign that he was right and he was rewarded, after several seconds, when the shield started to waver again. This must be the moment. The waver increased and the shield changed. It changed abruptly and Aglaron tried to understand why the pressure against it had suddenly fallen away. Why was Maynor retreating when they were so close to success?

A surge in demand from the Nexus, the only resource not outputting at full capacity, restored the pressure but at the same time started a tremor of apprehension in Aglaron's mind. The flow of energy under Maynor's control had increased to restore the right level of pressure?

That was wrong.

The feeling of wrongness flashed to certainty when the sense of pressure diminished again. Aglaron applied a tracing overlay to the converging streams of energy directed by Maynor and watched a significant portion vanish through his son's shield boundary. Keryth was taking it? Full realisation of where this could lead was instantaneous and Aglaron sent Maynor an imperative hold command. If Keryth was absorbing the energy being thrown at him, their whole strategy was futile … and even dangerous.

Aglaron reached for his last reserves of power just in time to bolster their four shields from a shockingly powerful attack.

Before responding to the bewilderment and dismay emanating from Maynor and Uirebon, Aglaron frantically sought for some response to this now-hopeless situation.

"Maynor, we cannot prevail. In the moments we have left to us direct all our resources to the construction of a portal to the High Realm. Our last hope is to take the warrior and use him as a lever for negotiation."

The four shields wavered. Maynor's response was almost instantaneous and the sleeping warrior's body disappeared. The shields crumbled and Aglaron wrenched control of his Nexus energy just in time to protect himself.

*   *   *

Kieran opened his eyes with a feeling of satisfaction that his last pushback had worked so well and looked to where he'd seen Rhys collapsed on the floor. A burst of opal energy combined with his healing hands would be a good start at recovery for everyone. Satisfaction changed to puzzlement when the rapid glance showed Tan, Woorawa and Mr B slumped exactly as he remembered in the moment before he nearly lost it himself, but no Rhys.

Maybe he'd healed himself and gone to get something? Kieran reached but his tracking sense didn't work. Was it damaged or shell-shocked or something? No, there was Woorawa, and … yes, there was Burrimul far away in Alice Springs. Rhys was gone.

"Rhys! Rhys! Rhys!"

Kieran reflexively squeezed his opal for help and called again. Worry receded with the wisp of contact that came to life. Wherever Rhys was, he would be found.

Kieran looked at Woorawa lying on his side, Tan slumped at the table and Mr B asleep on the sofa with his head leaning back and mouth slightly open, and decided to let them wake naturally while he had a good think. After putting a cushion under Woorawa's head he sat at the table and waited patiently. Woorawa was first and Kieran shushed him so as not to wake the others. That only worked for the few seconds before Woorawa realised Rhys wasn't there.

"Where's Rhys?" he whispered.

"I don't know unless I use the opal. We'll work out what to do when everyone else is awake."

The wait for Tan, and then Mr B, to wake was a long ten minutes and, for the whole time, Kieran's worry about Rhys built a reservoir of anger and defiance against whoever was doing all this. Twice he used the opal to reassure himself that the tenuous connection was still working, and just when Tan woke he thought to make a proper check of their memories.

"Where's Rhys?"

Mr B's first question when he woke was the same as Woorawa and Tan's, but this time Kieran was ready with a more detailed answer.

"Whoever did this has taken him somewhere, Mr B, and it must be a long way because I can't sense where he is without the opal."

"A long way? How long have I been asleep, Kieran?"

"It was the big attack you predicted, Mr B, and it was far worse than anything we talked about. The shields I gave you dissolved like tissue paper and all four of you crumpled so quickly I couldn't do anything. Then I nearly went with you. If we hadn't just done that practice I wouldn't have had a hope. We'll talk about it more when we get Rhys back."

Tan broke the silence that followed. "My watch says it's only fifteen minutes since we went to sleep, so he can't have gone far. We can use my car to find him again."

Kieran shook his head. "It's not like that, Tan, and I know the car won't help. Something really weird happened right when I worked out how to chase them away. Rhys just disappeared and I've played it over and over in my mind while I was waiting for you all to wake up."

"He couldn't just disappear. They must have made him walk out."

"He didn't walk, Tan. One second he was there and the next he wasn't. I'm really worried about him so we're going to help him."

"What do you mean, Kieran? It will have to be you, because we can't do that sort of thing."

"Doesn't matter, Mr B. We'll look for him together. If there was a way to make him disappear then there has to be a way to bring him back."

"You've got some kind of clue from your mind playback?"

Kieran nodded at Woorawa. "Yes. When I use the opal to find Rhys the playback thing comes to me as well."

"They're both about Rhys so that does make sense. What you want us to do?"

Not that he'd doubted their willingness to help for a moment, but the obvious eagerness buoyed Kieran's spirits.

"First of all you're getting a new shield each, but this time it'll be linked with mine so the only way you'll be overcome is if they get past me. When I connect to the opal I want you all to think about Rhys as hard as you can."

"How? Make a picture of him in our minds or something?"

"Exactly, Tan. I'm going to see his smile and his laugh."

In fact, Kieran had a far more personal memory.

"Anything else?"

"Yes, hold my hand so we're all in contact with the opal."

In Kieran's mind this was an extremely important moment and, holding out his hand, he surrounded the opal with a blue glow and made the colours sparkle. Woorawa reached through the glow, touched the beautiful gemstone, and then surprised Kieran by closing his eyes and starting a soft chant. Mr B covered Woorawa's hand, and then, with a decidedly awed look, so did Tan.

Energy flowed.

Kieran built the shields.

More energy flowed and the tenuous link with Rhys grew stronger.

"Come home! Come home!"

Kieran called, not aloud, but using more and more energy from the opal. Rhys was there now, in his mind, almost like normal but sound asleep. A pool of energy would trigger enough healing to wake him, so Kieran started sending some through the link. No, give him a shield and join it with the others first. The opal responded and a moment later Rhys's mind cleared.

"Rhys, come home!"

With the help of the opal, the call crossed the link and registered in Rhys's mind.

"Kieran?"

The question was immediately swamped with bewilderment and disorientation as Rhys's eyes took in his surroundings. Kieran felt the strangeness through the link and, along with another heartfelt call to come home, sent a feeling of reassurance and comfort. Something touched Rhys's shield.

"Kieran? I can feel you. Where am I?"

Kieran couldn't answer, which was a concern. More worrying was the second and stronger pressure against Rhys's shield which had just registered through the link, with the implication that someone had their attention on him and must be working to control him again.

"Come home, Rhys!"

The call strengthened, the opal responded, and the link between Rhys and his friends changed. Kieran recognised something of the pattern he'd seen when Rhys disappeared, seized it, added to the call and built on it.

Whoo! The structure of shields and connections faltered and Kieran, knowing he was about to lose everything, opened himself to the opal in a way he'd never done before. Energy came in a deluge. The strange pattern built to a crescendo and then flashed to completion.

For an indeterminate time reality dissolved and Kieran lost everything. Shields disappeared, links dissolved and his mind was battered by the deprivation of every sense.

Awareness returned with a confusion of weight and movement. *What?* Oh, someone was lying on top of him. No, two people. Awareness changed to partial understanding as Woorawa rolled to the side, Tan wriggled to a kneeling position, and Mr B cradled his head in his hands.

"KIERAN!"

The mighty shout came from behind and Kieran whirled to the familiar voice just in time to register Rhys's happy features in the dusk before being squished in a welcoming hug.

The hug ended and five sets of smiles quickly gave way to bewilderment.

"What did you do this time, and where are we?"

In the gloom of evening, Kieran looked from several impossibly massive tree trunks to rugged hills several kilometres away silhouetted against the darkening sky, then back at Rhys.

"I haven't got a clue, Rhys. We were trying to call you back but we must have come to you instead. You've been here longer than we have so you should be telling us."

"Ha, very ha! About a minute longer. And I'm not the one who does weird things all ..."

Rhys crumpled to the ground. Kieran groaned in annoyance at himself for not thinking properly and, reaching for opal energy, forcefully batted the interference from Rhys's mind. As he knelt beside Rhys he rebuilt all the shielding that had dissolved in the chaos of moving then constructed the pool of energy Rhys would access to heal himself. Everyone rushed to help and by the time Woorawa was reaching to support Rhys's head his eyes were fluttering open.

"They got me again?"

"Only for a couple of seconds, Rhys. I was so excited about seeing you and thinking about what happened, I forgot our shields. They won't get you again because this time I blasted them to oblivion."

Rhys bounced to his feet. "I hope not. I'm getting sick of waking up on the ground. Kieran, what happened? How did we get to this weird place? ... Those trees are too big!"

The whole group gathered together, looking to Kieran for whatever he could tell them.

"It was the worst attack ever, Rhys. The first shields stopped them for about a second but then they clobbered me so hard I nearly fainted. I fought them off but then you disappeared from the floor in the lounge. When Woorawa and Tan and Mr B woke up, we used the opal to track you. We tried to call you back but instead of that we came here. Someone really is after you because that was their third try since you got here."

"What will we do now? They might still be after me ... or all of us."

Mr B broke the silence of everyone considering what to do. "Can you use your tracking to tell us which direction home is, Kieran? If they brought Rhys to this place they must know where it is, and we should move."

Everyone agreed and Kieran made the blue arrow they were all used to, but when he thought of home nothing happened. A call on the opal still didn't give any result either.

"Look for a person, Kieran. Try the professor first, then Uncle Burrimul."

Looking for the professor didn't work but when Kieran thought of Burrimul there was a murmur of excitement when the arrow started spinning.

"What does that mean?"

"It's the same as it was for you, Rhys. There's a connection when I boost with the opal but direction isn't part of it."

"That doesn't make sense."

"It does to me," Tan said. "Earth doesn't have trees like that, so we must be somewhere else … like another world."

Everyone swivelled for another look at the two great trunks reaching to the sky.

"We might be in a forest no one's ever found before, Tan."

"Everywhere's been explored and trees like that would definitely show up on satellite scans. Look at them. They make the giant redwoods in America look like babies. That one on the left is wide as a house. Looking at it's giving me goosebumps."

Rhys made a strange kind of laugh. "We're in *Mysts* and they're the Emperor trees."

Rhys had given Kieran a beautiful illustrated edition of the book after they'd seen the movie together but he was only partway into it.

"I haven't read about them yet, Rhys. What are Emperor trees?"

"Two giant trees that rule all the forests around. They're so big that forest people have their town in them."

Heads lifted again.

"There's no town up there. Kieran, I think Mr B's right. We should move and find somewhere to hide and camp before it gets too dark. Those hills might have a cave or some sort of shelter." Rhys took a few steps, then stopped and looked back.

"And Tan's right too! This is another world."

* * *

GUARDIANS

CHAPTER 1

The shocking pressure on the shields vanished and, after making the imperative check that all flows of Nexus energy had regained their full function, Aglaron gathered himself and probed the wellbeing of the two High Lords slumped beside him. Maynor would require the attention of a healer adept. Uirebon, though stunned and exhausted, would have to cope with a short, assisted session of wakefulness, and Aglaron wearily directed his rudimentary healing skills to reviving him.

Uirebon's eyelids fluttered and he pulled himself erect. "My Lord?"

"Keryth destroyed our shields with so much force I had to break all our links. Your healer is approaching, but before he ministers I must have your knowledge of what happened after my son destroyed our linkage and your shielding. I was forced to abandon you before the warrior was taken but I detected traces of a portal to Maynor's Realm so I presume we might have at least one positive outcome for this fiasco?"

"Yes, my Lord, but the situation has become even more complicated. The construction of a portal was almost too much for Maynor and, lacking both time and strength, he drew on his personal reserves instead. The effort completely overwhelmed him but he did manage to transport the warrior to his Glade of Trees."

"It is inconvenient but hardly a complication. All we need do is collect him."

"In the instant before Maynor lost consciousness he passed me his link to the warrior's mind, and I acted to do just that. I dispatched mounted Fetches to the Glade and was keeping the warrior in a state of sleep when a new shield appeared in his mind and my control was brushed away."

"The warrior can shield himself against a High Lord?"

"No, my Lord. He was asleep. The shield must have come from Keryth in the Human World. The shield was suddenly dissolved, and through the eyes of the awakened warrior I saw Keryth gathered in the Glade with all his companions. An instant later I was swatted to oblivion like a gnat against a giant."

"Maynor must have moved the whole group to his Realm by mistake."

"He didn't. The warrior was by himself well after Maynor was overwhelmed. Keryth must have constructed his own portal."

"There has to be another explanation. Only High Lords have the required knowledge and training. Uirebon, when the healer has replenished your energy enough, you will give me the link to the Fetches. If Keryth continues to use these strange new shields it might be our only way of locating him, and we cannot leave him roaming Maynor's Realm in human persona while Maynor is out of action for, at least, the next twenty-four hours."

Uirebon closed his eyes and relaxed to the welcome touch of the now present healer.

*   *   *

"Come on. Let's move before it's too dark and someone comes to look for us."

They wouldn't be able to reach the hills unless this twilight lasted an unusually long time, but moving did seem to be the most sensible idea, so Kieran nodded to the others and stepped after Rhys.

"Everyone keep an eye out while it's still light. There might be clues about where we are. Woorawa, you can watch behind while Mr B and Tan take a side each. Rhys and I will pick the way forward."

"It won't be hard, Kieran. The big trees seem to be on the edge of a forest, but this way's nearly all open. I wonder if it gets cold at night. And what about food? We haven't got a thing."

"We'll just have to huddle together if it's too cold, and there's nothing we can do about food in the dark."

"Hey! There must be animals. We'd better listen carefully too."

Kieran wondered why Rhys sounded so definite and gave a querying look.

"Because we've hardly seen any long grass. Remember how short it was in the cleared area near the trees? And all these open patches are the same."

"That doesn't have to mean animals. The grass might be short naturally."

"There have to be animals of some kind."

"I suppose … We're not going to reach those hills. It'll take a while and it's already darker after just a few minutes."

After another five minutes, stars appeared and the hills became dark silhouettes, so Kieran stopped everyone and pointed to the left.

"Let's head for that clump of trees. If the moon doesn't come out it could get pitch black and we won't even be able to see the trail."

Tan made a curious snorting sound. "If there *is* a moon."

After a moment of speculative silence Mr B queried whether they really were on a trail.

"I don't know, Mr B. It's clear enough."

The trees were about a hundred metres to the side of their line to the hills and the group headed for them purposefully till Woorawa gave a soft call.

"Look. I can see lights."

Everyone froze on the spot and stared. Distinct in contrast against the darkness, five or six pinpoints of light glittered brightly in the distance.

"And they're at the base of the trees. They must be looking for us. You were right, Mr B ... It looks like five lights, but it's hard to tell because they keep moving. How many can you see, Woorawa? You've got the best eyes."

"I think it's six ... It's definitely six. Two of them just separated from the others ... and one of them's coming this way. Will we run for the trees or what?"

Kieran looked around then pointed to a dimly seen depression behind a slightly raised patch of ground. "Over there! We'll watch from the mound and hide in the dip if we need to."

Two other lights moved away from the trees in a different direction and disappeared from view. Attention snapped to the closest light which looked to be coming straight at them.

"Look how fast it is. It can't be walking."

Rhys was right, and the closer the light came the faster it looked.

"Shoosh! I can hear something ... It sounds like horse's feet."

Kieran beckoned everyone to crouch because the light, now obviously following the line from the trees to the hills, was approaching the point where they'd turned off.

"Sheba! It's stopped."

Rhys's muted warning was unnecessary and everyone dropped prone in the gully. Woorawa raised his head to look past a small plant and whispered to Kieran who was right next to him.

"It's coming towards us again. It's tracking somehow."

Kieran's heart started pounding as he lifted his own head just enough to see what he could. The light was low against the ground and sweeping back and forth with enough brightness to reveal the partial features of a horse. Kieran reached for a mind the way he did back home and encountered a weird nothingness. A boost of energy from the opal was having no effect and, with a shock, he understood that he couldn't get through. The horse was now only twenty metres away and, since it was inevitable they'd be found, he leapt to his feet.

"I can't stop it! Everyone get ready. It knows where we are."

Light flared brighter, bathing the five companions in strong relief, and

at the same time making it hard to distinguish the mounted figure looming above. Kieran took a step forward and held up his hand in a hold
gesture.

"Who are you and what do you want with us?"

"I seek the marked one. Submit to the sovereignty of the High Lord."

Puzzling over the terminology, Kieran was about to respond when
Woorawa ranged beside him.

"We are visitors, lost and looking for a way home. We hope you can help
us."

"Do you submit?"

Kieran felt a kind of outrage and took over. "Your lord is not our lord
and we will not submit. All we want is some help and guidance."

There was a flurry of movement and a rope lashed round Kieran's upper
body. In the instant before it tightened he thought it was a whip. It seemed to
constrict further, paralysing him and toppling him helpless to the ground.

"Submit!"

Kieran's outrage flared to a new level. His body might not be working but his mind was. In a flash he found the mind of the horse and sent
messages of fear and loathing for the frightening thing on its back that
wanted to hurt it in every possible way. Kieran couldn't see because he'd
fallen on his side and was unable to turn his head, but the result was spectacular. The horse panicked and, in a wild frenzy of bucking and contor-
tion, sent its rider crashing to the ground. The light extinguished.

"GET HIM! GET HIM"

Kieran heard the great yell from Rhys and sensed the movement as
his friends rushed forward. A strange cry sounded and then, even more
strangely, there was complete silence. Desperate to know what was
happening, Kieran jerked his head to see. It worked. Rhys and the others
were climbing to their feet. Within seconds Rhys was supporting his head
and Woorawa was pulling at the rope thing.

"Are you all right, Kieran?"

"Where is it? I couldn't see."

"It disappeared. When it attacked you the horse went crazy and it fell off.
I knew we had to get it while we had the chance."

"But where is it?"

"Who cares? Did he hurt you, Kieran? Do you need any healing?"

"That rope thing paralysed me. I couldn't even move my head."

"It was starting to stand up but when Rhys and Woorawa crashed into
it, it just disappeared."

Rhys's hand was now resting on Kieran's forehead, but a quick burst of energy from the opal showed he didn't need any healing. Kieran stood and looked towards the now barely discernible Emperor trees.

"All the lights have gone. I hope that means no one else is after us."

"Did this hurt when it went round you, Kieran? I thought it was whipping you."

Woorawa was holding the rope thing, though in the fading light it looked more like a strong cord.

"There was no pain, just instant helplessness. We'll have a good look at it later. Let's get to the trees before there's no light left."

"What about the horse?"

Tan pointed and, straight away, Kieran used steadying and friendly thoughts to dispel the horse's nervousness and bring it ambling to join them.

"Wow! It's big. Is it safe, Kieran?"

"It's as friendly as anything and it wants to stay with us. Climb up on that saddle thing and ride it, Rhys."

"No way. I've never even been on a horse, and it's dark. Hey look, there's another one of those rope things."

"Go on. Up you get. You can lead the way for us because it can see better in the dark than we can."

"You sure? What if it runs off with me? I'd have to dive off, because I wouldn't know how to stop it."

"Trust me, Rhys. It won't. But if you're too nervous Woorawa can ride it instead."

Rhys laughed, which was a relief after the dramatic encounter, then used the foothold thing to cautiously climb onto the saddle.

Rhys's interaction with the horse held everyone's attention as they moved towards the nearby clump of trees.

*   *   *

Uirebon, momentarily refreshed, thanked the healer and turned to the High King.

"You feel recovered, Uirebon?"

"Barely, my Lord, but enough to marshal the links and ready them for passing."

Uirebon concentrated, reached with his mind, and then looked to Aglaron with distress.

"My Lord, there are only five links. One Fetch is gone. Keryth must have overwhelmed it physically and dismissed it."

"Was it a full Fetch?"

"Indeed, my Lord, mounted for speed and strength, and equipped with restrainer cords. It was the only agent without susceptibility to the strength of Keryth's mind."

"I see. You should sleep now, Uirebon. We have no choice but to wait until morning, when Maynor will awaken and you will have regained a modicum of strength."

*   *   *

"What if it gets cold?"

"We'll just have to snuggle close to each other, Tan, or cover ourselves with leaves. We haven't got anything else."

"What about this blanket thing on George? If we take off his saddle it's big enough for a few of us."

"George? How did you come up with that, Rhys?"

"He has to have a name, Tan. We can't just call him 'horse'."

"Well, George doesn't make much sense. Use a name like Charger or Domino or Flash."

"Does so make sense … and he likes it too. I can tell."

"No, you can't. Kieran's the only one who can do that."

"Of course I can. You don't have to be able to read an animal's mind to know when it likes something."

"I suppose … George is still weird though."

The group was settling for the night. The clump of trees provided a degree of shelter as well as a sense of security, and after getting nowhere with lots of discussion they all agreed they probably weren't going to learn anything new while it was still dark. The consensus now was to set out for the target hills as soon as daylight arrived and hope the higher elevation would give some sort of clue about their situation. Woorawa was totally concerned that someone else would come after them and kept peering past the trees for any more lights or other signs. He then insisted they should keep a lookout through the night.

Rhys's diffidence about the horse creature had disappeared by the end of the short ride to the trees and quickly changed to companionship and even propriety. Kieran insisted they were made for each other. There was plenty of back and forth as to whether it was definitely a horse, as Tan and Woorawa reckoned it was too big and way too strong to be compared with ordinary horses. Rhys thought it might be more like a breed of graceful draft horse.

Kieran squeezed between Rhys and Mr B and, after pulling a whole stack of leafy ends of branches they'd collected over him, lay flat on a bed of even more leaves that Woorawa said would act like insulation from the bare ground.

"I feel like a kid playing cubbyhouses."

"Me too, but it can't hurt. Kieran, when you go to sleep will we lose the new mind-shields you gave us? The rest of us could be easily taken over without them."

"So could I, Rhys … That's scary."

It was so scary that Kieran, wishing someone had thought of this earlier, couldn't stop wondering what to do. Eventually, he sat up.

Rhys didn't stir.

"What's wrong, Kieran?" Mr B whispered.

Kieran whispered back, "I have to try something with Woorawa. I might be a while."

He climbed to his feet, checked where Woorawa was keeping watch, and very quietly walked to him.

"Are you testing me, Kieran? Or can't you sleep?"

"Testing you? For what?"

"To see how alert I am."

"I wouldn't even have thought of that, Woorawa. No, I need you to help me learn how to make our shields keep working while I'm asleep. If I don't the bad guys will be able to get at any of us."

"They seem to want Rhys the most, but you're the most important. What d'you want me to do?"

"We'll have a practice mind-battle, but I want you to push back at me instead of just defending yourself."

"Push back? … I wouldn't have a clue how."

"Yes, you do. Remember how you build up strength when I push at you. That's a kind of push back and if you do it before I even start then it's like an attack."

"Hmm! I suppose. It would be weak as anything though. Nothing like the real attacks."

"I know, but that's good. If a tiny attack registers with me that means it would be harder for them to make a sneak attack."

Woorawa thought for a moment.

"A sneak attack could be just as bad as a full on one, Kieran. Like you getting us to do things and we think it's our own idea. They could make Rhys think it was a good idea to ride off by himself on George to look for water or something. Or they could even sneak an idea into our minds about going in a direction that takes us straight towards them."

"And that's why we need to try this, Woorawa. It's very important."

"That's for sure, but I don't see how I can help if you're asleep."

"I've already worked out how to set up the shields with a store of energy from the opal and leave them there without having to monitor them all the time. If I increase the store of energy I think they'll stay in place, but the only way to be sure is for you to attack me when I'm asleep."

Woorawa started a soft chant and Kieran readied himself for any effect … *Yes, there it was.* Tiny and without the aggressive takeover feel of the external attacks, but definite. The chant stopped and the effect disappeared.

"Did it work, Kieran? I couldn't feel anything."

"It worked perfectly. Do it again and each time I give you a tiny mind nudge, do your pushback. You'll learn the feel of it that way and know exactly what to do when I'm asleep."

Woorawa's humming started. A few seconds later, when Kieran's shield reacted to a soft touch, he sent his first mental nudge. Five more times he signalled to Woorawa and five more times came the replying touch to the shield. A hand on Woorawa's shoulder let him know it was time to talk again.

"Well, that was different, but I think I've got the hang of it. How long you want me to wait before I try it?"

"We'll try it once more now, so I can work something out, and then again after half an hour. I'll definitely be asleep by then."

"How will we know if it's worked?"

"I'll wake up and tell you. If I don't then we're in trouble. Can you concentrate for long enough to make a series of attacks while I experiment?"

"Easily. With the chant I can do it lots of times."

"Okay, let's try."

By the sixth push Kieran had worked out a way to connect a small attack to a warning trigger that would wake him no matter how deeply he was asleep.

"Thanks, Woorawa. Just wait till I go to sleep then try again, so we know for sure it's working."

"I hope you don't get too tired with all these interruptions to your sleep, Kieran. We need you to be ready in case anything happens."

"It *is* nice to be sleeping, but with Rhys's healing we don't really need it … Have you seen or heard anything out there?"

"Not a thing … except for a weird crunching sound that gave me the heebie-jeebies till I worked out it was George munching grass."

They spoke quietly for a short while before Kieran went back to his position between Rhys and Mr B and closed his eyes. Almost straight away he leapt up with such a panicked yell he woke everyone else.

"What?"

"What?"

Kieran gathered his wits. *Oh no!*

"It's all right, Mr B. Go back to sleep. I was doing an experiment and it worked better than I expected. Rhys, come with me for a few minutes. I need your help with Woorawa."

"Why? What's happened to him?"

"I need your magic hands to wake him up. I clobbered him too hard and he's unconscious."

"What did you do that for?"

Rhys was only half awake, unlike Kieran, whose mind was racing from the adrenaline surge he'd just given himself.

"An experiment. He pushed against my shield and I reacted so strongly it knocked him out."

"How are we going to find him?"

"I know where he is."

"I mean us. You'll have to make a light or we'll bash into all the trees."

It *was* dark, but there was enough starlight filtering through to let them make their way carefully.

"Hold my hand and I'll lead, Rhys. I've got the way in my mind from a little while ago."

It was a nice feeling, edging through the dark like they were, but Woorawa needed attention so there was no dallying. A few moments later they were kneeling beside his inert form. Rhys's hands rested on his temples and after a burst from the opal Woorawa stirred and sat up.

"Gods, Kieran! It felt like a bolt of lightning hit me."

"Sorry. I overreacted, but at least we know the shields work when I'm asleep. Next time you do it you'll be protected."

"Next time? I don't know if I'm game."

"You'll be okay. I promise."

"Well … all right. How long do you want me to wait?"

"Um … How long before you finish your lookout time? I'll do the next one because I want to do some thinking and practising."

"Hey! That's meant to be me."

"I know, Rhys. How about we do it together?"

They only had Tan's watch to help them tell the time and Woorawa pressed the light button to read the display. "It's only forty-five minutes. I waited half an hour last time to make sure you were asleep."

"It's hardly worth us going back to sleep again, Kieran. Let's take over now so Woorawa can have a longer rest."

"I can't, Rhys. I have to make sure I've got the shields working properly, and that means Woorawa has to be awake while I'm asleep. Why don't you stay here and watch out for him when he attacks me?"

"An attack? A minute ago you said it was just a push. Is he learning how to do the same stuff as you?"

"You do the same each time you fight against the Medusa look when we're practising. He's just a lot better at it and his push is strong enough to make my shields work."

"Wow! All right. I'll stay here in case you knock him out again. I want to see this."

"He won't get knocked out."

"Something else you don't expect might happen though. I reckon … What's that noise? I heard something."

It was the soft crunch of George cropping a tuft of grass. Kieran nearly didn't say anything, then remembered how spooky it had been for Woorawa.

"It's your friend, Rhys. He makes that sound when he bites off some grass."

"George? Gods! That spook rider's got me thinking of night monsters sneaking up on us. I'm going to talk to him. Are you coming with me, Woorawa?"

Kieran made his way back to the resting place.

*   *   *

"I'm hungry. What are we going to do about food?"

"Keep your eyes on the lookout, Rhys. There's not going to be any shops, so we might have to catch an animal."

"What? A live one?"

"We don't want a dead one."

"I know that. I meant how. We haven't got anything to catch one with except Tan's pocketknife."

"We'll have to find it first. That'll be the hard part."

"Catching it will be easy. Kieran can tell it to stand still."

"What? Just tell an animal to stand still then we walk up and kill it? That's awful, Woorawa. Like we're cheating or something."

"I know, Rhys, but we might starve if we don't."

"I'm going to look out for fruit trees or wild berries. I'd rather eat them than kill an animal."

"Tan, you eat meat at home."

"Yes, but that's different because I don't have to kill it."

"Someone has to, and if you eat it it's just as much your responsibility."

"I know, I always think I should be a vegetarian, but I like the taste too much … What was happening last night, Kieran? I heard you getting up all the time."

"Woorawa helped me work out how to keep our shields going while I'm asleep and then I shared a look-out with Rhys."

"What about George? Have you got a shield for him too? They might be able to use him to work out where we are."

Kieran stopped in his tracks and everyone turned to look at him. "I wish we'd thought of that last night. Hang on while I have a try."

Kieran moved in front of George and rested a hand on his forehead. He didn't really need physical contact, but it felt right and after a few seconds everything clicked into place.

"There we are. We've now got six shields going. His mind's different to ours but not much. I had a quick look and he's cleverer than you are, Rhys."

"What? You can tell that? … You're an idiot, Kieran."

Kieran's grin had given him away.

"No, but I can tell that he likes you riding him, and he must be pretty smart to have worked out what you want him to do so quickly."

Mr B interrupted. "Let's talk while we're moving. I'm more worried about water than food. We haven't had any since the break for healing Tan's leg and we need it even more than we need food."

He was right about the water and everyone stepped out. The plan to get to the hills hadn't changed and after leaving the clump of trees they were now back on course. The surroundings were fairly open here but perhaps a kilometre ahead was a band of trees and Kieran wondered if the way might get trickier.

Woorawa suddenly laughed. "Well, we won't go hungry. The bird calls woke me up this morning and we've been seeing birds ever since. We know Kieran can call them up easily."

"We'll have to cook them. How are we going to start a fire?"

"I've learnt how to do that on our bushwalks at home, Rhys, but it's fiddly and a lot of effort when we've got Kieran. He'll just zap some dry grass like he does for the candles."

"Crikey! We'd be in a lot of trouble if Kieran couldn't do all these things. I hope we don't get separated … Look. There are two birds near that bush … I wonder what they taste like."

"What are they, Kieran or Mr B? They don't look like any birds we see at home."

Kieran looked to Mr B because he knew a lot more.

"They look like little magpies, Tan, but they're definitely not Australian."

"Will we catch them … in case there aren't any birds at the top of the hills?"

"Not yet. We need to find water before we stop for anything else. If we don't see a lake or a river from the top we might even have to think about going back to the giant trees and the forest. There has to be water there."

"And spook riders trying to get us. They didn't take long so they must have come from somewhere close."

When the group reached the tree line the theory that they were following a kind of trail became more definite when two tree stumps gave a clear indication of a narrow pathway heading up the slope. Woorawa led the way. He hadn't had firsthand experience of exploring new places himself, but he had a great deal of knowledge from listening to descriptions of ventures of his people into the bush and wild country near Alice Springs.

Rhys was next, looking very pleased to be riding George, and Kieran, Tan and Mr B followed in single file, except for the occasional stretch where the trail widened enough to let them bunch up. After steadily climbing for another half an hour the trees cleared and the top of the hill came into view. Everyone was eager to reach this target, so Kieran was surprised when Woorawa ran off the trail towards a small rocky outcrop.

"What's he doing?"

"He's seen something."

He certainly had. Woorawa was gesturing and pointing. Kieran shared the hush of amazement along with everyone else before rushing to Woorawa's vantage point.

Rising behind the forest near the two giant trees, and part of an extensive castle structure, were three tall spires. Surrounding them were quite a number of smaller spires.

"That's incredible! That must be where the lights and the scary thing on George came from."

"It's huge. Hundreds of people could live there."

"More than hundreds, Tan, and who says they're people? I couldn't find any trace of a mind with George's rider when it started giving us orders last night."

They'd already talked extensively about the nature of the disappearing rider.

"It must have had a mind, Kieran. How could it talk and control George otherwise?"

"I can't figure it out. Let's get to the top first and look from there. That castle's beautiful but it makes me nervous. If more of those riders come from there we'll be in big trouble. Can you see anything happening between here and the Emperor trees, Woorawa? Your eyes are better than anyone else's."

Woorawa raised one hand to shield his eyes from the brightness of the sky and stared for a while.

"It's too far to tell, Kieran. I might be able to pick up movement if I concentrate for a few minutes, but I'll wait till we get to the top before I try that."

They scrambled down from the rocky outcrop to where George was happily grazing on the grass beside the trail, then pushed on for another ten minutes with an unspoken sense of urgency. When they reached the top Woorawa ran to climb a rock for another good vantage point. Rhys dismounted from George with remonstrations that everybody was leaving him behind, then caught up and joined the perusal of the castle.

"Wow! It sure is big. That back part extends like a town … Hey look, there's a lake behind it." The mention of water prompted every head to turn from the castle and seek in other directions for any other lakes or signs of water.

"Gods! What's that?"

Kieran's mind reeled and he grabbed at Rhys for support. In the opposite direction to the castle a disturbing wall of shimmering light extended across the horizon. Looking at it was an assault on his senses and he had to close his eyes to regain equilibrium.

"Hey? What's happening?"

Rhys's grip firmed and when Kieran opened his eyes without looking at the bizarre wall, he saw that Woorawa was supporting a very woozy Mr B.

"Sit him down, Woorawa, in case he flakes out, and I'll do the same for Kieran. That wall's affecting them."

It certainly was. Kieran took another look and instantly turned his head away from the onslaught of sickening sensations and let Rhys lower him to a sitting position.

"I can't look at it at all, Rhys. It makes my head go weird."

Despite the concern on Rhys's face, a grin pushed itself to the surface. Kieran half smiled himself. Saying his head was weird was definitely going to be thrown back at him. Rhys checked Mr B before answering.

"I think we've got two weird heads here. I can look at it easily. It's like a giant aurora except it's white."

Kieran turned to Tan and Woorawa, who both nodded in agreement.

"An aurora is a good description, Kieran. It's bizarre, but I don't feel anything else."

Kieran took another quick peek. It was awful.

"Well, I definitely can't stand it."

Mr B agreed. "Neither can I. It feels like something's eating my brain and the longer I look the faster it eats."

Kieran was surprised at how close that was to his own feelings and he risked a slightly longer check. Yes, it really was like that.

"That's strange. I wonder why it affects you and Mr B and not the rest of us? What about a shield against it, Kieran? If we have to travel in that direction, it'll drive you crazy."

Kieran sent a burst of energy to his section of the group shield and peeked at the wall.

"Whoa! Our ordinary shield doesn't make any difference, Woorawa. I'll see if I can work something out after I've had a good look at everything in the castle direction."

"Give yourself and Mr B a healing burst from Rhys first. You both went wobbly for a moment. Hey! A healing pool thing like you did with Tan's leg might help."

"That's a good idea, Woorawa. We'll have a try at it, but it'll be awkward if we both have to be touching Rhys while we're on the move."

Woorawa laughed. "Rhys will have to walk so you and Mr B can hold his hands all the time. You'll be the triplets you call yourselves."

"Walk? What about George then?"

"Tan can ride him."

Rhys was dubious. "I don't know. He might fall off."

Now it was Kieran's turn to laugh. "What a traitor! You'd rather ride George than hold hands with me and Mr B?"

"Whoops! I was thinking George doesn't know Tan and it might be strange for him ... You're laughing?"

Kieran wondered why Rhys was asking. "Um, yes?"

"That means when you stop looking at the wall you recover quickly?"

"As long as I don't keep watching like the first time. I'm still a bit wobbly from that."

Rhys put his hand on Kieran's forehead and reached the other towards Mr B, who took it straight away and looked expectantly at Kieran. In a moment they were both fully recovered. Kieran turned his back on the wall and studied the view towards the castle and beyond.

"Is there a lake in the wall direction? We need to find water before anything else."

There was no answer till Tan spoke tentatively.

"I can't see a lake, but there's a run of darker trees and vegetation that might be a creek or a river. See down there on the right? What do you think, Woorawa?"

"Hey, yes. It is too. I can't see any water, so it can't be a river ... Yes, I can ... There's a tiny bit through the trees where I'm pointing."

Tan and Rhys moved to peer over Woorawa's shoulder for a more accurate line of direction but couldn't pick out any glint.

"Are you sure? It must be awfully small."

"It's hard to see but I'm fairly certain it's water ... It must be, because that line of trees is definitely taller than the surroundings and that would happen if there's a flow of water."

Kieran was quite frustrated with not being able to look for himself while Tan, Rhys and Woorawa discussed what they could see. He checked Mr B and saw that he was feeling the same.

"How far away is it, Woorawa?"

"If there was a trail going near, it would take us less than an hour, but it'll be longer if we have to find our own way. We mightn't have to go that far though because if it really is a creek we can search for it upstream."

"That sounds good. What else can you see?"

After another period of silence and searching, the answer came from all three that everything just looked like a lot of wild country and nothing else.

"It's just trees and open patches of ground all the way to the Wall, Kieran. The darker line goes there too, so if it's a creek we'll probably have to follow it."

"All right. We'll head for the water as soon as we can. Rhys, keep holding my hand while I try to figure out what to do about this Wall. Woorawa and Tan, I think you should keep looking for anything that might be interesting. It looks like there are farms and paddocks near the lake on the other side of the castle, so I think we're heading away from where anyone lives."

"You reckon? Maybe the Wall or whatever it is affects them too, and that's why there's no one out this way."

"That makes sense, Rhys, and this trail might even be here as a way to get to the Wall."

The group ended up sitting where they were for nearly twenty minutes. After the first five minutes of continued glancing at the Wall and calling on the opal and Rhys's healing to counteract the disorientation, Kieran had a partial success in blocking its effect. This convinced him there must be a way for a full block and filled him with determination to find it. Gradually, he extended the time he could look, trying variations of the shielding techniques he'd built up, till he could cope with ten or twelve seconds of direct viewing before needing a revival boost.

Woorawa kept a barrage of questions and suggestions flowing, which was distracting, but which also gave him helpful ideas. When he was just about to give up and rely on the holding hands plan while they walked, Woorawa put forward an idea that solved everything.

"Kieran, you're okay for the moment when you get a healing boost from Rhys, so can you sort of work out what's going on in your mind while that happens? I know healing isn't a shield, but it does stop the effect while you're doing it."

Kieran thought back to the last healing burst and looked at Woorawa in amazement.

"How could you tell that? I didn't even realise it was happening."

"I noticed a pattern that when you're being healed you look at the Wall and talk as if it's not doing anything to you."

"What? How can you know when I'm getting healed? Do I get a funny look or something, because that all happens in my head?"

"Your hands glow blue, Kieran. I think it's a habit. Try healing yourself really slowly and see if that lets you look at the Wall the whole time."

Kieran already knew it was going to work, but the slow-heal idea was interesting.

"Here we go with experiment number sixty."

Kieran placed a pool of energy with Rhys and then, using the opposite of the speed-up technique he'd worked out for Tan's healing, slowed the healing right down and gazed at the Wall.

"Wow! You're a genius, Woorawa. I've got the healing at about one quarter of normal and the Wall looks weird but that's all. I'm going to keep the healing trickling and look for how it blocks away the mind parasite."

"Mind parasite? That's a weird description. Does it feel like a live thing?"

"No, but I'm the same as Mr B with feeling like it's eating my mind."

No one spoke for the next few minutes because Kieran had the intense expression that appeared whenever he was concentrating fiercely on something. Mr B knew it from certain times in their tutoring sessions before the scholarship exams. Woorawa recognised it particularly from all the practice battles with their mind shields, and Rhys and Tan associated it especially with the time he'd healed the brick wound.

Six times Kieran stopped the healing process, each time trying to sense any internal change that was occurring in the moment when a restart meant the Wall stopped having an effect. The first three times he focused on his mind shield, thinking that something must be making it work better, but probing more and more delicately each time showed absolutely no change. The next three times he switched tactics and tried to follow where the healing energy was going … Amazing. A section of his brain linked with his eyes was kind of switching on and off according to whether the healing was coming through … and now that he'd seen the switch he should be able to replicate it. *Yes, that was it.* He stopped the healing, flicked "the switch" in place, looked directly at the white disturbance and startled everyone with his yell of excitement.

"Yay! I've worked it out. I can look and nothing happens."

"Can you keep looking?"

"For as long as I want to. It's like turning a switch on and off."

"What about Mr B? Can you switch it off for him?"

"Whoops! Sorry. Hold Rhys's hand, Mr B, and I'll see if I can make it work for you."

It only took one try. Kieran started the healing, followed it, and watched the switch happen. It was almost identical to his own and just as easy to operate.

"Let go of Rhys's hand, Mr B. You'll be okay from now on."

Mr B did so and straightaway looked towards the shimmering light. " Wonderful! Thank you, Kieran. It still makes me cringe in expectation, but then nothing happens. How on earth did you work out how to stop it so quickly?"

"That's his pattern, Mr B. Nothing seems to take long once he puts his mind to it."

"That just makes it all the more amazing, Rhys, and you're right about it being a pattern. It's exactly what he did with his Maths and swimming."

"Yeah, and when he learnt all those birds on the Grampians trip."

Kieran felt awkward and brought the conversation back on topic. "It wasn't that quick. I thought it must be part of our shields till I followed the healing energy and saw it changing a part of my brain that lets me see things. Then I just copied what was happening. It's no big deal, Rhys."

"It is to me … Let's get moving. We need to find water."

There was a chorus of agreement, but not from Kieran.

"Not yet, Rhys. Let Woorawa do his focus thing for any movement first. We're always rushing from one thing to the next and it'll only take a few extra minutes."

"Okay, but it doesn't seem like rushing to me. We do have to find water, and if that's a creek we'll end up following it. It's the only choice that makes any sense."

"Rhys is right, Kieran. I'm fairly sure it's a creek and that means it'll be the best place to find food too."

"Yeah, I suppose, Woorawa, but I still don't want to rush, and five minutes of checking won't hurt."

Woorawa swivelled 180° and settled to survey everything in the direction of the trees and the castle. Everyone did the same and sat quietly so as not to interrupt his concentration.

Despite the fact that it was too far away to see anything the size of a person or a horse, Kieran's attention kept returning to the castle, with the background thought that it had to be the most likely place for any activity. For a couple of minutes there was nothing, but then Tan pointed slightly upwards and everything changed.

"There are two big birds, Kieran. I think they might even be eagles, so why don't you get them looking at things for us? Birds of prey have unreal eyesight and they can see things from miles away."

Woorawa's quiet concentration broke, and he jumped eagerly to his feet. "Where are they, Tan? I've been focusing along the ground where we travelled … That's a brilliant idea."

With Tan's guidance the two birds were quickly pinpointed.

"Do you think you can control them, Kieran? They could check out the trail for us, or even the castle if they respond like any other birds."

"Not from that far. They're miles away."

"Use the opal then. That should help."

After a moment of startlement, Kieran laughed. "Of course it will … New idea number sixty-five. Hang on while I give it a try."

So far Kieran had been close enough to make out the features of any birds or animals before he identified and communicated with them, and the opal had never been part of it. If distance just needed more strength, then the opal would be perfect.

Looking at the birds from here gave no sense of connection at all. Focusing and kind of reaching still did nothing, so he called on the opal and tried again. Yes, there they were. The familiar connection started and then, abruptly, stopped. Weird. That had never happened before. Maybe it was because of the distance? Kieran carefully added more energy, tried again and was shocked to realise the barrier was really coming from an external source. Someone else had control … No way! He forced them out with a quick blast of energy, built shields of his own, then checked the wellbeing and awareness of the birds. His adrenaline surged and his mind started racing.

"Gods, Tan! Just as well you saw the birds when you did. They were searching for us."

"What do you mean?"

"Someone was controlling them the same way I do and making them look for us. I pushed whoever it was out, but if they'd been there for a few more minutes they'd have known exactly where we are."

Everyone gawked, then Woorawa scanned the sky.

"Can anyone see other birds flying? There could be more searchers … The top of this hill is too open, Kieran. I think rushing's exactly what we need to do right now."

"Can you tell what the birds are seeing, Kieran?"

"In a way. It's hard to explain, but I know that they're looking at the ground, and that one of them was interested in some small birds for food a moment ago, and now it's out of balance because it wanted to hunt and couldn't because my control wouldn't let it … There, I've made it forget the birds, and now I've sent them both lower to look for anything like a horse moving this way."

Woorawa led the way back to the trail, and Rhys went to climb on George but changed his mind.

"Kieran, you should ride for a while so it's easier to concentrate on the eagles and everything else. It's kind of relaxing sitting up there while George does all the work."

Woorawa and Mr B agreed. Kieran studied George dubiously then laughed because he'd stirred Rhys for having exactly the same feeling.

"Okay, I will. I'm bringing one of the eagles close so it can scout the water and they're not happy about being separated."

Kieran climbed into the saddle and enjoyed the feeling of pleasure that came from George.

"Are you using the opal much, Kieran? You've got an awful lot going on."

"A bit. The eagles are still too far away to control without its help, Woorawa, and keeping our shields going's a bit of a stretch too, since I've made the bird's shields as strong as ours."

Woorawa headed off smartly along the trail, which now had a downward slope, and Kieran twisted around for a last glimpse of the castle before it disappeared from view.

"Can you keep eight shields going indefinitely, Kieran?"

"Easily, Mr B. It's only complicated at the moment because I'm not used to the birds' minds. Once that settles in it'll be just as automatic as it is for George and the rest of us."

"And why do the birds need such full-on shields?"

"So that anything trying to get to them gets blasted. I'm sick of all these takeovers against us."

The vehement tone registered with everyone except Woorawa, who was far enough ahead not to be able to hear it.

"Can I sit behind you, Kieran? George can easily carry two at once."

Kieran nodded and took one foot out of the stirrup so Rhys could get mounted behind him. When two hands clasped round his middle, Kieran instantly decided that riding double was a very satisfactory way to travel. A few minutes later the fire in his voice was replaced with humour.

"Keep an eye out everyone. We've got a visitor."

Woorawa stopped dead in his tracks and searched to the sides instead of forward, while Tan and Mr B whirled to see who might be closing in from behind. Rhys was twisting in all directions except the relevant one. Whoops!

"Don't panic. Look up."

High above, a magnificent bird changed from glide to dive and plummeted at breathtaking speed towards the astonished group. Kieran shared the astonishment because, while he'd sensed power, this first sight of form and strength was as new for him as it was for everyone else.

"Stand still, Tan, and don't panic. She's friendly and I'm telling her to land on your shoulder."

Tan froze on the spot in complete disbelief.

With perfect control, the bird shed speed and alighted with widespread wings folding against its body.

Tan's worried expression lessened as the time of amazed group observation extended without any worrying moves from the bird perched, quite placidly, on his shoulder.

Kieran broke the silence.

"She's not going to bite or scratch, Tan, and she's happy to stay there till we give her a command to do something else. I'm sensing that she's used to it."

"Will she fall off or get upset if I move?"

"No. I can tell she's got really good balance. I'll leave her there for a few minutes while we get going again, so she gets used to us, and then I'll set her flying again."

"Gods, Kieran! That beak looks scary. I'd be nervous having it so close to my ear."

"I'm in full control, Rhys, but she wouldn't do anything anyway because she's worked out that Tan likes her."

"She has? George liked Rhys after only a couple of seconds too, so I wonder if that means something?"

Mr B's comment went unanswered because Kieran started George walking and everyone watched to see how Tan's new companion would react to movement.

For the next few minutes the fierce head, with an attitude that Kieran thought was definitely regal, shifted to take in the surroundings and everything happening. Kieran watched her carefully, normally as well as with his mind, and a few hundred metres down the track, where outliers of the tree line started, he gave Tan a warning and sent her aloft again.

"Wow, she's not as big as a wedgetail, Kieran, but she looks awfully strong. I wonder if they're the top bird of prey round here?"

"I wouldn't have a clue, Rhys. We've seen a few birds now, but none of them are like any of the ones at home. For all we know there could be birds twice as big."

"Is Tan going to be our bird person? He'll look specco with one on each shoulder … Is the other one the same size?"

"I don't think so. He feels smaller."

"He? Are they mates then?"

"Yes. There's a really strong bond between them and I have to keep making them happy to be separated."

"Neat. Where is he now? Will we see him soon?"

"No. He's close to the two tree stumps at the moment, but I'm sending him back towards the Emperor trees to check for anything new happening … Yay! There's definitely water close by."

Kieran's yell grabbed everyone's attention.

"Look for the eagle. She's found water and I'm sending her higher so we can see how close it is."

A few seconds later it was Woorawa making an excited yell and pointing.

"There she is … She's really close … Only three or four hundred metres, Kieran, and it looks pretty close to where the track's heading. Can you keep her circling where she is?"

Everyone could see the eagle now.

"We don't need to, Woorawa. We know where to look so I'm sending her after the other eagle. They're happier when they're working together."

The circling changed to a powerful burst of effort as Tan's new companion climbed for altitude and raced to rendezvous with her partner.

"What does it feel like when she's on your shoulder, Tan?"

"Unreal! Scary at first, and then I got goosebumps every time she moved or her feathers brushed against my ear. Now she's not here I've got a funny feeling that I'm dreaming while I'm awake."

Rhys had more questions but they went on hold because Woorawa was jogging away, and the group scurried till they rounded a bend and caught up. To the right, a secondary trail disappeared through the trees.

Woorawa was excited. "I bet this is the way to the water. It's right where the eagle was, so it must be close. D'you want to wait while I check it out?"

"Get real, Woorawa. We're not waiting here dying of thirst while you guzzle yourself full … and we shouldn't get separated anyway. What d'you reckon, Kieran?"

Kieran held a hand up.

"Shoosh. I heard a good sound."

The sound came again and the distinctive croak made everyone's eyes light up.

"Lead the way, Mr Super Scout. If there's a frog, there's water."

The super scout's eager smile disappeared in one second flat, not because it stopped, but because he was now ahead and already jogging. Forty metres farther on, they paused to take in the cleared area and the water bubbling over an artificial rock barrier from the little pool behind it. The surge forward stopped with Woorawa's forceful command.

"One at a time, and no guzzling or you might get sick. Kieran, you're first, and limit yourself to six good swallows. Rhys, follow where the water's trickling and see if there's a good place where George can drink without spoiling the water. Mr B, you're next, then Tan and me. Kieran, can we stop here? I want to follow the water for a while to look for pools where there might be fish. Now that we've got water we can concentrate on finding food, and fish would be much nicer for most of us than frogs."

Kieran nodded and looked at everyone else.

"Woorawa knows more than any of us about this kind of stuff so we'd be silly not to listen to him. What do you think, Mr B?"

"I agree absolutely. He's already stopped us getting stomach-aches, and without his ideas about leaves and shelter last night we'd have been miserable, so I vote we make him the boss of all food and camping."

There was rapid assent all round because, along with it being the default situation anyway, everyone was eager to get at the water.

Kieran dismounted, walked to the little rock wall and knelt for six swallows of beautifully refreshing clear water.

His throat wasn't parched, but all the activity since his last drink did mean his body was now greatly relieved. Conscious of everyone else's needs, he moved out of the way.

"It's beautiful water, Woorawa. How long before we have another drink?"

"Just a minute or two, Kieran, and if you're feeling okay you can drink as much as you like. I just thought it was a good idea to go easy for the first drink. It's a natural spring as far as I can see, so it'll be as clean as anything."

Kieran moved a couple of metres to the back of the pool and saw that Woorawa was right. There was no inflow, so the water must be welling straight out of the ground.

At the end of the clearing, where the watercourse went into the trees,

George had his head down at what must be another pool, with Rhys's hand resting on his flank. *Hmm! That was interesting.* There was a sense that he was familiar with this drinking spot.

Woorawa finished his drink and stood up. "Keep track, Kieran. I might be gone for ten or fifteen minutes."

"Not by yourself, Woorawa. Rhys is fitter than the rest of us so take him with you."

Woorawa hesitated, as if he was going to say it wasn't necessary, then jogged off to where Rhys was now kneeling not far from George. After a murmur of conversation they slipped out of sight into the tree line.

Tan looked anxious. "You can tell if they're all right can't you, Kieran? I don't like anyone being separated."

"Neither do I, Tan, but Woorawa's got it in his mind to find fish for our first food."

"Will we start a fire? I can collect some wood and leaves."

"Hmm. I don't know. Do you think we should, Mr B?"

Mr B shook his head. "Let's wait till we hear first. If Woorawa does find a deep enough pool, we'll have to go there anyway, because Kieran's the only one who can catch the fish."

"Shouldn't we all have gone with him then?"

"Probably, but it might be hard for George, and if there isn't anything we'll have to go back to the main trail."

Kieran had a second, and bigger, drink then sat quietly and concentrated on keeping track of the two eagles as well as Rhys and Woorawa, while Mr B and Tan explored along the watercourse for any sign of the frogs they'd heard.

After about ten minutes, Tan and Mr B returned to sit beside Kieran.

"Wow! George likes the grass in this clearing. He hasn't stopped eating except to have another drink. Have Rhys and Woorawa found anything yet, Kieran?"

"Yes, Tan. They're both feeling exc—Whoo! The eagles have just seen movement … They're near the Emperor trees and it's … three horses like George … with riders … and they're coming this way."

"Three? We'll have to hide, Kieran. Just one of them with that rope thing was almost too much. Are they moving very quickly?"

"Wait a moment while I send the eagles down for a closer look."

Mr B and Tan watched quietly while Kieran concentrated.

"Yes, really fast. The eagles' minds are comparing them with prey that's running to escape … No … They've stopped … And they're looking up … Ha!"

Kieran's commentary stopped and after a few seconds of fierce concentration he laughed. "They won't try that again."

"Try what? Kieran, tell us what's happening."

"Sorry. Something tried to break through the eagles' shields, but whoever it was got knocked silly."

"The three riders?"

"I don't think so, but the riders *have* started moving again so I'll keep the eagles watching them. Mr B, you can lead the way through the trees and Tan and I will follow. Woorawa and Rhys know we're coming and they say it's open enough for George to pick a way through, as long as we don't stay right next to the water."

"We're going off the trail so we can hide?"

"Yes, Tan, and to catch something to eat. Woorawa's seen ripples that must be fish."

With the need to pick a way for George it took nearly half an hour to cover the ground that Woorawa and Rhys had covered in ten minutes and most of the conversation centred on that. Their thoughts raced with other conjectures. Kieran suddenly let out a cooee and there was an exchange of grins when it was answered from not far ahead.

"They're only fifty metres past this pool with the two rocks in the middle, and Woorawa says we have to keep to the left because the trees are too thick from another watercourse joining in from the right."

The fifty metres turned into almost eighty because of a detour around a thick clump of trees but, with an exchange of *cooees* acting as a homing beacon, the smiling faces of Woorawa and Rhys were soon in front of them.

"Yay! You got here. This is a great spot to stop for food or even to camp, Kieran. Was it hard for George to get through? We've seen ripples six times so far in these pools and we can't wait for you to help us catch the fish. Woorawa got all the makings for a fire ready too, so we can start cooking straight away. We've ... What's happened? Tan looks worried."

"I'm not too worried, Rhys ... Well, I am really, because three of those spook riders are looking for us and someone tried to take the eagles away from Kieran."

Rhys's and Woorawa's eyes widened and they swivelled back to Kieran.

"Yes, the eagles are watching them and they're nearly at the two stumps at the other side of the hill. There's still a while before they get really close, and if they have to leave the track to follow us that will slow them down even more."

"You think the riders will know where we are, Kieran?"

"The one last night was definitely tracking us, Rhys, so we have to presume these can too."

Woorawa voiced his agreement. "And that was when it was dark enough to need a light, so they must be expert trackers when it's daylight. They *will* catch up sometime, Kieran, so what can we do to stop them?"

"As soon as I see them I'll make their horses buck them off like George did last night."

"Great idea! Let's hope they're not holding any of the rope things. If they've all got them, we've had it."

"Why don't you buck them all off now so they have to walk, Kieran? That would give us stacks more time."

"It's too far, Woorawa. I have to see them before I can take over."

"No, you don't. You can't see the eagles and you're still in control, and I remember at the Valley of the Eagles you called frogs you couldn't see once you knew the first one."

Rhys got quite excited with this idea. "And you've known George since last night, so won't the pattern be strong for these new horses?"

"Well, I suppose so … and if I can do it now it'll sure slow the riders down, which is totally important. Things are starting to get complicated, Rhys. Keeping our shields going is easy, but controlling two eagles and four horses at the same time might be too much."

"Your opal will get you through, Kieran."

"The first reach for the horses is the only time I'll need it. After that it's all about learning to juggle new things in my mind. Watch George while I concentrate, Rhys."

Kieran closed his eyes because there was an awful lot to focus on. The horse pattern was as clear as a bell in his mind, but taking it to new horses several kilometres away was beyond him. He reached out for extra energy in a similar way to that which he'd used for the eagles … *Nothing? Why not? What was different? Hmm. What if he did need eye contact?* Maybe pinpointing their position through the eagles' eyes would work?

Both eagles swooped low, and when they skimmed only metres above the riders' heads the three horses skittered sideways and came to a stop.

Kieran reached again and this time the finer focus let him link with … one … two … three horses. The hours of familiarity with George let the link change instantly to direct control and the three steeds erupted with an outburst of bucking, screaming, and violent twisting in their efforts to rid themselves of the vastly inimical creatures they'd suddenly sensed on their backs. In seconds they were free and bolting in panic along the track. After a few more seconds the panic vanished and their speed slowed to a steady and purposeful canter.

Kieran opened his eyes to a frightened *neigh* ringing loud in his ears and saw George, almost twenty metres away, with Rhys running after him. He steadied George and called to Rhys.

"It's all right now, Rhys. A little bit of what I sent the other horses leaked through and frightened him."

Rhys led George back, calming him all the way.

"If that was just a little bit it must've been awful for the other three. Are they all right now?"

"Happy as anything, Rhys. They've passed the two tree stumps and they know they have to follow the track till they catch up with us."

"What about the riders? Are they coming too?"

"I'll tell you in a minute when I'm properly settled in with the three horses and have their shields working. Where's a good place to see one of these fish, Woorawa? I'll have to do that before I can control them."

"You can control fish now, Kieran, as well as four horses and two eagles?"

"As long as it's not non-stop, Woorawa. I only have to be in control when I'm telling them what to do. The eagles can see the riders walking this way so I'll tell the male to keep watching while the female goes hunting … There, that's set in their minds till I make a change. And the three horses will follow the trail till I tell them to do something else … Hmm, they're hungry, so I'll let them stop when they reach the rock pool."

"Hey, if the three new horses are as friendly as George we won't have to walk anymore."

"As long as we're on a track or fairly open ground, Rhys."

Woorawa was now pointing to some bushes next to a wider section of the pool of water.

"You're hidden a bit just there, Kieran, and there were a few ripples near here when we first arrived. How are we going to catch them?"

"Um … Everyone stay still till I see one, and then, when I've called some others, we'll have to get in the water to pick them up."

It took a while for a fish to actually come into view, but once that happened Kieran was able to get his mind right, and a few minutes later there were six fish placidly waiting near the water's edge. Rhys did the honours and, following instructions, flicked them out of the water to Woorawa, who quickly dispatched and gutted them with Tan's pocketknife.

The next step after catching the fish was to get a cooking fire going and everyone gathered closely to watch Kieran make yet another call on the opal and ignite the handful of carefully chosen dry grass and leaves. Rhys cheered and Tan gave a whoop of delight when the first wisp of smoke changed to a healthy little flame. Woorawa took over and methodically added small twigs, then sticks, and then larger pieces of wood he'd previously gathered, till the fire was burning strongly.

"Are you going to cook for us, Tan? You've got the best touch."

"Not with an open fire, Kieran. Woorawa knows about this so I'll watch and learn from him."

Woorawa shook his head. "I know things from all the adventures of Uncle Burrimul and my friends, Tan, but I've never actually done it myself. I'd rather just explain how and let you be the cook."

"Okay. What do I do first?"

"How much time have we got before those spook riders get here, Kieran?"

"A while. It took us nearly two hours from the stumps, so even if they run all the way we still should have at least an hour."

"Well, the best way to cook is slowly in hot ashes, but we need the fire to be out by the time they reach the top, so we should skewer the fish with sharp sticks and hold them directly over the hot coals, with Tan telling us when they need turning."

He reached to a separate pile of sticks, quickly sharpened one, then forced it longways through the raw flesh of the largest fish and handed it to Tan.

"Start with this one, Tan, while I get the rest ready."

It took quite a while to finish because of all the experimenting with ways to best hold each fish secure. After the fish were almost cooked, there was a tendency for them to break apart. Rhys made everyone laugh with his carrying on when his fish fell into the fire and had to be rescued in pieces.

"That was delicious but I'm still hungry."

"We all are, Rhys, but more food will have to wait for later because the spook riders have nearly reached the top and the horses are already waiting for us at the clearing near the spring."

"Neat! Have they been there long?"

"About ten minutes, and they're as happy as George was with the grass there."

"I wonder if we'll ever be able to go home, Kieran?"

The silence that followed told Kieran this was a shared worry.

"I know, and it's scary, but something will turn up, Tan. If we really get lost or in too much trouble we can always go back to the Emperor trees and that castle. Someone there must know what's going on."

"No way, Kieran! Don't even think of it. That's where the spook riders come from. I vote we keep heading for the White Wall and look for someone friendly. We only have to see one ordinary person and Kieran can work out where we are from their mind."

Mr B spoke up. "I agree. I don't think we should even consider the castle, Kieran. That rider last night was extremely disturbing. In the few seconds before it paralysed you, it demonstrated complete arrogance and a single-minded determination to capture you."

Woorawa joined in. "I agree too. I reckon the castle's bad news. The riders frighten me too so we do need to get moving, but we also have to stay near this creek for food and water. My vote is to stick to our plan of checking out the Wall. What do you think, Tan?"

"The castle sounds awful to me and I don't want to change our plans. I was just thinking that home is so different to here. Where are the riders now, Kieran? If they've reached the top, then it's downhill and they might follow us a lot faster."

"Whoa! Good thinking, Tan … Quick, everyone. I just checked and they're closer than I expected."

Once again George was the hold-up, but not so much this time because retracing their steps meant they remembered many of the best ways.

Three horses' heads lifted from the grass when they re-entered the clearing and then gave some neighs and funny snorts at the sight of George.

"This is good. They know each other. Climb on, everybody. We'll walk till we get to the main trail so we get to know each other. I'll double up with Rhys because George is already used to both of us."

"Kieran, all these horses have two of those cords on their saddles."

"That's good, Woorawa. It means the riders can't use them."

Woorawa was mounted in a flash. Mr B and Tan were more cautious, but by the time the horses had walked to the main track they were all more relaxed. Gradually, as everyone adapted to this new way of travelling, the journey sped up and the concern about their steeds diminished. After about half an hour of downhill slope, the trail reached the extensive plain at the foot of the hills and widened, with thicker vegetation of the watercourse on the right and sparse vegetation ahead and to the left. Woorawa, who'd been leading the way, stopped, and everyone bunched close to find out why.

"This is looking good, Kieran. The trail's gone off course twice so far to link up with the creek and it looks like it stays with it ahead Are those things still following us? Because if they are, we could get the horses moving faster and build up a bigger lead on them."

Kieran had been checking regularly.

"I'm worried about them because I've had the eagles watching and so far they've never seen them stop. If they keep going like that we won't be able to camp for the night."

"Can we get the horses to walk in the bed of the creek? That's how people hide their tracks in all my books."

All eyes turned to Woorawa.

"We don't know enough about them, Rhys. If Spooks track by smell, like dogs, it could work, but if they track by looking then they'll easily see the disturbance made by four big horses like these. It's worth a try though."

"Not yet. We'll try for a bigger lead first."

With the trail more open, the horses could pick up speed, something that was quite uncomfortable till, once again, everyone got used to it. A bit over an hour later Kieran called to Woorawa to stop.

"Next time the trail meets with the creek we'll have to try Rhys's idea for hiding our tracks. Those Spooks have been jogging ever since they reached the flat and we haven't left them behind as much as I thought we would."

"How much of a lead have we built up, Kieran?"

"They're about halfway between here and where we stopped at the foot of the hills."

"They're travelling at about half our speed then … That means they'll reach here in an hour. Kieran, we can't keep going like this. The horses are okay but we're not. If I don't get off for a walk or a break I'll have blisters on my backside and cramps in my legs."

"Rhys can heal that for all of us, Woorawa, but we need more food and water too."

"Well, I vote we stop running. There are five of us, plus four horses and two eagles, and I reckon that's enough to face up to them."

Four mouths gaped.

"Are you serious, Tan? Just one of them was totally frightening last night, and now there are three."

"I know, and the one last night makes my stomach feel weird every time

I think about it. But Rhys and Woorawa did get rid of it. I reckon they give off scare vibes and stop us thinking properly."

"Scare vibes?"

"Yes, Mr B. All day the only thing I've been able to think about is how to escape, and a while ago I started to wonder why, when we actually know how to beat them."

Kieran blinked at Tan in amazement. "How are we meant to do that?"

"Rhys and Woorawa go for one, just like they did last night, and Mr B and I go for another, while you stay protected by all the horses and the eagles. The cord things are the biggest worry, but we don't think they've got them anymore."

Woorawa clasped his head with both hands then let it go and shook it. "Unbelievable! I mean, I believe you, Tan. All this time and I've never thought of anything else except how scary they are … Kieran, you could tell the horses to protect us, couldn't you? One kick from those hooves would mangle anyone."

Rhys spoke up next. "And if the first two do that disappearing act when we grab them, the third won't have a hope against four of us. We should have thought of this ages ago. Can the eagles tell if they're carrying anything like a weapon?"

Kieran concentrated. "I don't think so. It's hard to tell because the idea of weapons isn't part of their thinking. Rhys, I don't like the idea of attacking the Spooks directly. I'd rather send the horses charging at them."

"Hey, yeah! Like a cavalry charge. No. You're the centre for all of us, Kieran, so the horses are more important for keeping you protected. Woorawa, we need to find a good place to ambush them. Who's got any other ideas?"

"What about some strong sticks for weapons, Rhys? Like quarterstaffs."

Woorawa rubbed the side of his horse's neck. "We can talk while we're moving. Let's find a good place to make this happen."

Progress slowed for the next twenty minutes because talking as a group and riding didn't match. Ideas came thick and fast, particularly from Rhys, who kept quoting strategies from adventure novels he'd read, but then they came to one of the frequent sidetracks which turned off towards the creek.

"Let's check along here. The main trail's too open and with thicker vegetation and bigger trees near the water we'll have a better chance of finding a good ambush place. What does everyone think?"

Everyone agreed that was a good idea and a few minutes later they stopped again, next to a long pool of water.

"There must be fish in there. It looks deep and it goes a long way."

"Forget about the fish, Rhys. Look over there where that little bank goes up to the trees. It would be a good place to get the Spooks."

"In the water?"

"Why not? If we lead the horses through from this side and up that bank they'll follow all the tracks."

"And we hide and jump on them when we hear them splashing in the water?"

"I'll explore first, to make sure the horses can get through, and then we'll get organised."

As quick as a flash, Woorawa was off his horse. He waded for about eight metres through knee-deep water to the bank on the other side, where he paused to look back with a grin before scrambling up and disappearing. When he reappeared a short while later he made a thumbs-up sign with both hands.

"This is good, Kieran. There's thick vegetation for a while, but then it opens up to a clearing with big trees along the other side. Come and have a look while the horses have a drink and eat that grass."

Kieran led the way, stopping to stoop for a drink of the cool, clear water, then grabbing at some of the shrubs to help him climb to where Woorawa was waiting at the top of the embankment. Tan arrived next, after slipping a little and getting a backside boost of assistance from Rhys.

"See, Kieran. That's why I think it's a good place. They'll have to slow right down and we'll know exactly where they are. If we jump on them from up here we'll easily have enough momentum to knock them over."

Rhys and Mr B arrived and Woorawa and Kieran had to move to make room for them.

"It's crowded, Woorawa. You won't be able to have all of us jumping at the same time."

"That won't matter, Mr B. If I'd jumped on Tan just then, Rhys and Mr B would have ended up in the water with him and the next person could jump while everything was confused."

"I'm jumping first, Woorawa. I'm biggest and I'm the strongest, so it has to be me."

No one made a joke about Rhys being a poser. No one said anything for a moment and then Kieran grabbed him for a big hug.

"And we'll be one second behind you, Rhys. We'll all be on top of them before they even know what's happening."

"How long do you think it'll take them to get here, Kieran? We need to get organised and practise this a few times."

Kieran mentally linked with the eagles.

"They're still moving quickly, Woorawa. We slowed down when we started looking for an ambush site, but it'll still take them more than an hour."

"An hour's good. We'll let the horses eat the sweet grass they like for half an hour before we bring them across. The first thing is for everyone to find a good strong stick to make a quarterstaff … That would really help to bowl them over with your first leap, Rhys. You make one too, Kieran. If they get past us somehow and you can't reach their minds again it'll be a good defence for you."

"What about collecting rocks to throw at them?"

"Not from up here, Tan. We might hit them, but we're just as likely to miss, and I think we have to knock them down to make them disappear anyway … If we've got enough time we'll organise some rocks for where Kieran and the horses are. Mr B, could you make sure there's an open way from here to the clearing so we can reach Kieran quickly if we need to, and it'll be better for when we bring the horses through too."

"How about using my pocketknife to make sharp points on the ends of our quarterstaffs? They'd be double weapons then."

Woorawa made a grimace before answering. "You bloodthirsty thing, Tan … It's a good idea, but it might be dangerous for us too when we're so close to each other … You could sharpen one end of Kieran's quarterstaff if you get the chance."

"What about a fire? That could be a good defence."

"No fires, Tan. We're attacking, not defending, and smoke might act like a warning. The fire comes later … when we have our giant fish-feast. Let's move so we can get enough practice in to feel like we know what we are doing."

"I hope my stomach gets better."

Kieran was puzzled. Woorawa wasn't.

"Mine too, Tan. If we stay busy that'll help keep our minds from worrying too much. I thought of getting Kieran to make us all feel confident, but it doesn't feel right."

Mr B rested a hand on Tan's shoulder. "My stomach's doing somersaults too, Tan, but that's okay because there'd be something wrong with us if we didn't feel stressed. Let's look for some good quarterstaffs to dress with your pocketknife."

The time went way too quickly. At first the horses balked at the steepness of the embankment, but when George led the way they struggled valiantly up the rise and moved to the new clearing.

Kieran watched Tan and Mr B climb to their feet, unexpectedly drenched and surprised, when Rhys's first practice run went off kilter with a misjudgement of momentum and positioning and knocked them flying. Mr B threatened that Rhys and Woorawa were going to get the same treatment when it was their turn to be the dummy Spooks, then apologised profusely when a similar misjudgement made it really happen.

Eventually the eagles' eyes showed the Spooks approaching the turnoff from the main trail, and Kieran moved to be with the horses. He didn't like this separation but he'd been given no choice in the matter. He stood quietly at his designated place of safety and reached to bring the eagles circling low over the expanse of water. Yes, there were the Spooks, right at the edge of the clearing. Rhys would be seeing them now from his specially chosen position of concealment and making the first sighting signal to Woorawa, Tan, and Mr B, who couldn't see anything. There was a ready signal for when the Spooks reached the edge of the water, and then, when the time was right, a *go* signal.

There was hesitation from their foes. That was expected here, with the confusion of horse tracks all through the clearing to decipher. The forms separated, then quickly regrouped at the edge of the pool where the horses had entered the water. Kieran wasn't able to actually see through the eagles' eyes, but continuous access since he'd taken control meant he'd built an ability to interpret what their vision meant in the two predators' minds. And this gathering of the prey objects felt significant and somewhat threatening. To Kieran, it meant Woorawa's strategy was on track and the planned confrontation was about to happen.

The male eagle, coursing low for a better view, sent a warning shriek to his mate that the prey objects had erupted into escape mode. Kieran heard the shriek from above and instantly understood that what the eagles interpreted as escape mode was really the Spooks bursting into rapid movement.

Had they detected Rhys and the others and were rushing to engage them?

New knowledge from the eagles showed them racing upstream along the edge of the water. Where were they going? The eagles were having trouble following them now, because they'd left the clearing and were under the enclosing vegetation. A few moments later Kieran understood that the Spooks had reappeared briefly and were now positioned differently. He left the eagles' minds, whirled to look at the upstream end of his clearing, sent a distress call to the others, then took control of the four horses and readied them for a charge. The Spooks appeared, racing into view only forty metres away and rushing straight towards him.

Go! Go! Go!

The four horses, bunched as a unit, charged to intercept the three on-comers and Kieran felt a momentary satisfaction that the Spooks would have no hope against so much mass and momentum. Shockingly, his control slipped and he fought against the waves of fear overcoming the horses and making them veer to the side. Two Spooks were caught momentarily behind the milling horses, but the third headed unerringly through an opportune gap and came to an abrupt stop only metres from Kieran.

"Submit!"

No way. Kieran wrestled with flaring anger and a strange sense of indignation. What right did this creature have to command him. With fleeting puzzlement that his shields were ineffective, he gathered himself for whatever onslaught against his will was coming. The Spook raised a hand and a chill of fear crept into Kieran's awareness.

The Spook gestured again. **"Submit!"**

The fear intensified enough to hold Kieran frozen with the quarter-staff useless in his hands, a fear he recognised—the same fear that had unnerved the horses, a physical state of terror which his mind could not deny.

"Submit!"

Kieran's mind raged against the helplessness overcoming him, then reeled with the shock of release when a hurtling form knocked his adversary to the ground. Proper awareness returned to Kieran as a second form landed on the violently struggling Spook. With vast satisfaction, Kieran saw the impossible dissolution of his strange nemesis as Rhys and Woorawa leapt to their feet and raced towards the piercing and unsettling cry from Tan.

Gathering his scattered senses, Kieran rushed towards the frightening tableau of Tan, apparently unconscious on the ground, and Mr B standing motionless with both Spooks directing a raised arm at him. The tableau changed when one of the Spooks turned, too late, to direct the threatening arm at the two rapidly approaching forms. Rhys and Woorawa both wavered, but their speed and proximity knocked their target sideways, and then to the ground, where dissipation once again followed a violent struggle. The last Spook lowered its arm and, for a brief time, faced the three charging companions before venting a strange and despairing cry and dissolving to nothingness.

A soft curtain of threat lifted and Kieran, rushing to help, felt even more relief when Tan's stillness changed to movement. One glance at Mr

B's ashen features meant he was the first priority and Kieran rushed to give all the support and assurance he could.

"Help me hold him, Rhys, while we give him a burst of energy and hope it helps him recover."

In seconds, Mr B, still speechless, was supported with his arms across Kieran and Rhys's shoulders and held close. Woorawa was helping Tan disentangle one of the rope things and looking worriedly at Kieran.

"Is someone else attacking us?"

Kieran finished transferring energy to Mr B and hastily checked the group shields. "No, everything's okay, Woorawa. Help Tan stand up so we can get him better too."

Tan scrambled to his feet unaided and touched a hand to Rhys's shoulder. "I'm all right, Kieran. As soon as the Spook disappeared all my body started working properly. Why isn't Mr B saying anything?"

"They hit him with a kind of fear wave, Tan. He'll recover when he pushes it out of his mind."

Woorawa was staring at Mr B's drawn features. "You might have to help him, Kieran. Can you go into his mind to support him?"

"I had a quick look and he's going to fix himself. It's better that way."

Woorawa nodded and looked past Kieran's shoulder. "Help the horses. They're totally spooked."

Kieran twisted to look at the four horses bunched close to each other and cowering in fear.

Gods! Poor creatures! He quickly restored contact and sent messages of calm and forgetting. *Yes!* This grass was sweet and delicious, and definitely needed to assuage the hunger they were suddenly feeling. Kieran started to reach for the eagles but Mr B shuddered and his arm tightened around Kieran's neck, holding him close. Then, with a huge sigh, his body relaxed. He caught his breath.

"That was worse than the worst nightmare. Let me find somewhere to sit down and do nothing for a month. I know they've gone but all I can see in my mind is two arms pointing at me."

Kieran looked around and gestured to a suitable tree trunk about twenty metres away where the clearing ended. "Over there. We'll sit with you."

Mr B made a soft little laughing sound and disengaged himself from all the support.

"Don't worry, Kieran, all I need is some recovery time ... Rhys and Woorawa, you saved us all ... I thought we'd had it when Tan was paralysed and I was helpless. Why did the Spooks take that detour, Rhys? Do you think they worked out we were going to ambush them? What did the first Spook do to you, Kieran? We saw it point at you and then we had to go after the others. You look really good now, Tan. It was awful when I couldn't help you … Whoa! I'm waffling. Excuse me while I sit down and clear my head."

Mr B collapsed on the grass right there, so everyone sat with him in a little circle. Kieran quickly re-established contact with the eagles and sent them off to hunt for food, then refocused to listen when Rhys started speaking. "I don't know what happened, Mr B. They pointed to where the horses' tracks went into the water and then over to this side where they came out, then they took off like rockets upstream. I'm certain they didn't see me because they only seemed to react to the horse tracks."

"Did they go to the edge of the water?"

"No, Woorawa. It felt like once they saw where the tracks went, going upstream was their natural course of action."

"Weird! I wonder if they don't like going into water?"

"Could be, Tan. I was caught off guard and I waited a few seconds in case they came back. That's when we heard the horses and panicked because Kieran was by himself."

"You got my signal that they were in the clearing though. I know you did."

"We were already on the way, Kieran. Poor old Tan's had a rough time because I knocked him over when I pushed past him on the narrow track, and then he and Mr B had to go after two Spooks while we only had one."

Tan looked at Mr B. "Mr B had more trouble than me. The Spook we were after dodged away and then the other one used its rope thing on me and I crashed straight to the ground. I couldn't move a muscle but I landed facing towards them, and then when they both pointed and he stopped moving I thought it must be something like the Medusa look."

"It must be worse, Tan. I only had one doing it to me and I was so frightened I couldn't move. If Rhys and Woorawa hadn't clobbered it when they did, it would have got me."

Mr B shuddered and shook his head. "It's definitely worse. At least with the Medusa look you can run when it gets too strong. It's like fear oozing through every bone in your body … We didn't count on them having a cord though. I'm glad they didn't all have them."

Tan held up the cord in question then experimentally wrapped it round both his arms. "It's harmless now. It must get its strength from the Spook because as soon as the Spook disappears it stops doing anything … Hey! I'm bleeding. Look what you did to my arm, Rhys. You're a bully."

"Me? Why are you blaming me instead of the Spooks? I never even touched you."

"Yes, you did. You said so yourself. It must have happened when you knocked me into the shrubs. Get over here with Kieran and fix it please."

Kieran was impressed. Quiet Tan had just changed the charged atmosphere and made everyone smile. Even Mr B had a hint of a grin pushing through his still-strained features. Woorawa took over and examined Tan's arm.

"It's a baby scratch, Tan. The blood just looks dramatic. Take Rhys and Kieran to the creek with you so you can wash it clean before they heal it … And go downstream so we don't drink traces of your blood when we get thirsty."

"Yuck! I'm not drinking Tan's blood. I'd properly turn into a vampire with all the weird things that go on in this place."

"I don't know, Rhys. It might even suit you, being immortal and able to entice any human into your greedy clutches and have your way with them. Just think, Kieran would be number one in your harem of good-looking guys."

"Very funny, Woorawa. If you turned into a vampire you'd have a harem of kangaroos and wombats."

"That is so gross … Kieran, can you go in and clear out all the weird things in Rhys's mind?"

"It is not gross. What else would you expect to find when you go off in the middle of nowhere in Central Australia?"

Mr B covered his ears as if disgusted, then uncovered them again. "Go away, all of you, and don't come back without a dozen huge fish. Coping with Spooks is bad enough without the idea of Rhys drinking blood and Woorawa cohabiting with kangaroos. I'll collect all the materials we need for a campfire."

Woorawa started moving then paused and pointed to a spot a bit farther along at the edge of the clearing. "That's a good place over there, Mr B, but don't rush to get the firewood because we're not leaving here till tomorrow."

Mr B leaned back with his hands clasped behind his head and smiled at Rhys's parting comments.

"Cohabiting kangaroos, Woorawa. That's called alliteration, and we use it in literature to make a phrase stand out. Cohabiting with kangaroos, sounds good doesn't it, hey, Woorawa?"

"So does wanking with wombats, hey, Rhys?"

*   *   *

The High King sought a way through this inconvenient but concerning health report.

"Fragile? Maynor could never be described so. He has strength and resilience to match anyone in the Realms. All I seek is a moment of wakefulness. Surely with your support he could manage that?"

"Not under my watch, my Lord. I can assure you that, with adequate rest and constant supervision, he should make a full recovery, but not with another interruption to his healing. Look at him. My healing trance is barely adequate to sustain him."

Aglaron *was* looking, with a high degree of anxiety and a good deal of regret, and not liking what he was seeing.

"Would the backing of a triad help? There are matters of great concern which only Maynor can address."

The healer adept regarded his king with amazement. "Of course, my Lord. It would greatly strengthen my ability to support him and secure his recovery."

"A triad will arrive to assist you within the half-hour."

Aglaron surveyed Maynor's pallid and drawn features then departed to talk with Uirebon who—though not in the same dire condition—was, nevertheless, confined to his healing chamber for some time to come.

*   *   *

"My Lord, have you news regarding Maynor? My healer informs me there are complications with his recovery."

"Yes, Uirebon. My decision to wake him earlier was hasty and mistaken and my standing with his healer was low indeed till I arranged for a triad to give him assistance. His recovery is now assured, but provisional on him staying in the healing trance for at least another day."

"A full day? With a triad helping his healer? He was overtaxed more than we understood then."

"Much more. My precipitous withdrawal of the Nexus energy he was using for the portal meant an equivalent amount was drained from his already overloaded personal reserves."

"How was it possible to provide a triad? All three were rendered unworkable for days."

"At my personal request three junior courtiers volunteered to meld as a minor triad."

"Indeed? The High Court must be agog with your calls for ever more triad activity."

"They are, but they will adapt and accommodate. My calls will have to increase with our three major triads out of action."

Uirebon regarded his liege thoughtfully. "My Lord, I sense your disquiet. Has something gone awry with Keryth? My Coursers are well on their way and should be passing into Maynor's realm within the hour."

"We may have to withdraw them. In gaining momentary knowledge of Keryth's location, I have lost the three Fetches Maynor ceded control of to me. The risk I took in reviving him this morning was wasted and any proper actions in his Domain are now further delayed."

"Three Fetches? No entity in the Realms can easily face a Fetch. What has Keryth done? Has he developed yet another ability? Or is it related to the gemstone again?"

"Keryth was at the point of submission when the Warrior and the Dark Child released him by making a direct physical attack. In the chaos of the situation they were able to overwhelm a second Fetch and I had to relinquish control of the third."

"Chaos? With you controlling the Fetches, my Lord?"

"Yes, chaos. Somehow they overcame the Fetch-fear which had them fleeing and they orchestrated a fully planned encounter. Instead of overtaking a weary and dispirited group, the Fetches were suddenly faced with Keryth and four Chargers that he immediately sent to trample them. Fear overcame the Chargers, of course, but two Fetches were hindered and by the time they were able to pass, the four companions were all attacking with the aid of makeshift weapons."

"What sort of weapons, my Lord?"

"Staffs. Simple but sturdy, and well-suited for the task of unbalancing a Fetch. The one in Keryth's grasp was sharpened to a point at one end."

"That does indicate preparation. It also indicates cohesion and purpose as a group. How will we track them? Surely the powerful distance vision of my Coursers will be invaluable?"

"We will lose them, Uirebon. Kieran appropriated the most highly trained pair from Maynor's tower with enough force to put you in the hands of your healer. I have more than enough setbacks with the loss of Maynor's assistance."

"You know the location. Why not open your own portal and send more Fetches? No. That would require Maynor's consent and he is not able to give it."

"His assent can be regarded as a given. But while he recovers a portal is out of question. Any attempt to construct one to his Realm would interfere with his elaborate defensive network against Lady Narello's aggressions and result in a backlash which, though relatively minor, would be disastrous in his current condition."

"My Lord, our actions are grievously limited while we need to wait for Maynor's recovery, and our best course is to be prepared fully for when he is with us again. If it is still your intention to claim the Warrior and use him as your primary lever to force Keryth to accede to treatment, a larger group of Fetches should be assembled and readied for portal transport. It would be testing fealty, but sending a group of torced Power Masters is another option you could consider."

"A Power Master donning a torc? Uirebon, that is not an action I wish to contemplate. Ten mounted Fetches will be waiting for the moment when Maynor is released from his healer. A force of that size will overcome, and if we lose Keryth's location, such a group will also possess formidable tracking skills which the Power Masters lack."

"Ten Fetches is beyond your ability to control, my Lord. How will you manage so many?"

"With great difficulty and with your assistance. We will spend some time conditioning them prior to Maynor's awakening."

"As you wish, my Lord … What should I do with my Coursers? All four pairs are close to the border of Maynor's Realm."

"Let them continue their approach, but no closer than you feel is safe. When the time is right we will use them to survey the probable location of Keryth and his companions and hope for any information which helps with targeting a portal exit more accurately. At that stage I fully expect you will lose control to Keryth, but the loss will be well worth it for the knowledge it gives us."

"Hmm, yes. I see. Keryth must then be somewhere within a range similar to when he took Maynor's Coursers. I will position my own so that when the time comes they converge from the four points of the compass. Combining four sets of positioning at the moment of loss will be quite accurate. My Lord, this could save hours of tracking by the Fetches."

"Very clever indeed, Uirebon. If Keryth travels while we wait for Maynor, this strategy will likely save half a day or more, rather than hours. I will assemble the Fetches and build the foundation for a suitable portal while you make the most of your recovery time."

*   *   *

The plan to stay overnight was discarded with Woorawa's new suggestion that whoever controlled the Spooks was probably still after them, and that the first place they'd come looking would be where they were now, so it would be a good idea to get well away. The relief of having a break after the pursuit and the scare vibes holding them, combined with the eagerness for Mr B's fish feast, did mean a stay of over two hours though and, after a busy start, some time to relax and talk things over.

After Tan's 'baby scratch'—a long but shallow gash really—was cured, everyone except Mr B gathered to watch Kieran call for any fish that might be present. He already knew this pattern and it only took moments for three or four fish to arrive. By the time Tan and Rhys waded in there were even more, and when the process of flipping ten of the biggest ashore for Woorawa to dispatch with Tan's pocketknife finished, there were still about a dozen gathered close. Mr B, who had all the fire materials ready as well as some suitable skewer sticks, was most impressed by the bountiful catch and declared, almost ceremonially, that their fish-feast was well and truly underway.

For an hour the main focus was on food, with everyone discussing theories about why their own fish was cooked better than anyone else's, then sharing morsels by way of proof. A secondary focus was on getting runners and clothes comfortably dry.

There was an exciting break when Kieran called the two eagles down and had them rest, one on each of Tan's shoulders, while they walked back to the edge of the lagoon. Two more fish were called, then flipped, flapping onto the shore and everyone watched the drama as, with calls of satisfaction, the birds launched from their perch to grasp the wriggling fish in their talons and fly to a spot where they could devour this delicacy.

Back at the fire, everyone settled to talk and relax.

"How did you know the eagles would like the fish, Kieran?"

"They were watching when we took the first ones and their minds registered so much excitement and hunger I knew fish must be special prey. Letting them launch from your shoulders when the fish appeared, Tan, has linked you even more strongly in their minds as a source of rewards. When they finish eating they'll perch somewhere for a rest, but a bit later we'll teach them to come at your call."

"Are they tired from all the flying you've had them doing?"

"I don't think so. They perched quietly this morning after I sent them hunting, so I reckon that's their pattern. I had to send strong calming messages when I reconnected to them after the Spooks were gone. I think the scare vibes affected them too when they did that low-flying for us."

"You lost contact? It's a wonder they didn't fly off somewhere."

"I got back to them too quickly. I lost the horses too, and they were close to us and so panicked I knew I had to check all the animals."

Everyone turned towards where the four horses stood steadily grazing.

"They look as happy as anything. Are you making them like that, Kieran, or is it natural for them to get over things quickly?"

"Not too much. I only did the calming for a little while and when I started them eating they settled down almost as if nothing had happened. They think this grass is like going to Heaven and I know they're happy to be with us."

"Anyone would be happy to get away from those Spooks."

"Not really, Tan. They only freaked when the Spooks sent a fear wave at them. That's when I lost them."

"We're lucky they love this grass so much and we don't have to feed them anything else. Don't ordinary horses have to eat hay or oats to keep them healthy?"

"We're lucky the eagles can look after themselves too, Rhys. We've got enough problems finding our own food without having to worry about them as well. We can't just eat fish all the time."

"Wild birds are meant to be tasty. We can try them next."

Woorawa laughed. "I don't know about that, Rhys. There's a story at home about how to cook a galah. You boil it in a billy with a stone, and when the stone turns soft you throw the galah away and eat the stone."

"What? That's crazy. Have you ever eaten wild birds, Woorawa?"

"No, they're too hard to catch."

"Well, these fish are delicious, so I'm happy to keep eating them."

"That'll only work while we follow the creek, Tan. We'll probably have to leave it at some point."

"We can't. We need water."

"I've been thinking about that and I reckon Kieran should send the eagles to look for other water sources like lakes or dams."

"There won't be any dams. That means civilisation and we didn't see any, but water is a big thing for the eagles and that's a good idea, Mr B, so I'll get them to look when we set off again."

"You're our tactician, Woorawa. How much more travel do you think we should do today?"

Woorawa looked to Kieran. "Back on the main trail we thought the White Wall was still about half a day away, so I reckon if we ride for three hours that would be a good separation from here, as well as making tomorrow's travel not too far. What do you think, Kieran?"

"Three hours is as much as we've done since we got all the horses, so we'd have to use Rhys's energy boost a few times to keep going that long. Let's try two hours and then keep going till we find a good place to stop for the night."

Everyone agreed, then followed Woorawa's orders to lie down and relax or even sleep for the next half-hour while he kept a lookout.

Kieran thought it was a bit unfair if Woorawa was always going to be the first to do any lookout duty, but a rest was too sensible an idea to resist, and arguing with him wouldn't work anyway. The eagles were in a passive mode after eating, too, and since they'd soon be very busy, a quiet time was doubly called for. After a quick animal check, with the eagles asleep and the horses pleasantly satisfied and eating with less purpose, Kieran closed his eyes with his head resting on Rhys's chest and started thinking about how everyone was reacting to the unbelievable happenings since they'd reached this strange place.

Tan seemed the most shocked and had commented a number of times during the fish-feast that he kept wondering when he was going to wake up and be back in the real world. He wasn't freaking out though, and a few times he'd even lightened the atmosphere with his different way of looking at things.

Rhys was amazing, with all his energy and enthusiasm, and he was treating everything almost like an adventure from one of the books he was always talking about with Mr B.

Kieran thought back to the quiet, reserved student who'd needed coaxing to produce the special smile that so rarely lit up his face, and he felt a warm glow for the change to confidence, mischief and happiness which their closeness had released.

Woorawa was amazing, too, with all his practical ideas and matter-of-fact acceptance of every bizarre and unreal event. Kieran's own theory was that Woorawa's many years of blindness had made him live in a world of imagination connected with the Dreamtime stories that were so important to him.

Mr B was steady and thoughtful and full of good advice and support but the hardest to understand, probably because he was older. His mind was certainly more complicated and unusual. Another puzzle was the way he deferred to Kieran with any decisions.

Kieran smiled to himself as he thought about this. All four of them did the same really and he knew it was partly because of these strange abilities which made him so different, and partly because of several times when he'd taken over without thinking whether he should or not. It wasn't being bossy. Mr B would describe it as being a natural leader. Well, Woorawa had been the boss about having a rest, so now it was his turn to follow orders.

* * *

"Think of a command for landing on your shoulders and another one for flying to perch somewhere else, Tan, and we'll get the eagles to learn them."

"All right. I'll use 'shoulder' for me and 'perch' to perch somewhere else."

"Ha! Not very original but they do make sense. Now put an action with each command, so they've got a visual clue as well."

Tan thought for a second. "Right arm out sideways with a clenched fist means the female lands on my right shoulder, and left arm out means the male lands on my other shoulder. Pointing goes with 'perch' to rest somewhere in that direction."

"Okay, let's go. That'll be easy for them."

Ten minutes later the commands were locked in and Tan, bursting with excitement and pleasure, called 'perch' and pointed at a nearby branch with his left arm. The male eagle launched from his shoulder and flew almost exactly where indicated, while the female stayed in place on his other shoulder.

"How do they learn it so quickly, Kieran? Are you planting the ideas in their minds?"

"I am a bit, Rhys, but they're clever too, and there's a pattern in the way they react that tells me that they're used to following commands."

"George is really clever. He already knows to come when I call him without you putting it in his mind."

"He does now, but I did help a couple of times when you first tried it. We'll have a session like this with the horses next time we stop … Woorawa, go and stand by yourself so we can see if the female's happy with landing on your shoulder when Tan tells her to. Tan's shoulders are their home base, but I think they're familiar enough with the rest of us now not to get upset."

Woorawa rushed to comply. So far Tan was the only one to have this close encounter.

"Perch."

The big female spread her wings and gave a cry, which Kieran read as partial protest, before launching and traversing the short distance to Woorawa.

"Wow, Kieran! She didn't look too happy just then. Were you in her mind making sure she did what Tan wanted?"

"I was watching just in case, but I didn't need to. Tan's her boss now and he gave her a command."

"I wonder why these birds and animals make different choices?"

"What do you mean, Mr B?"

"The ones at home automatically chose Kieran to identify with, Rhys. Remember the eagle and the honeyeater at the Grampians? The rest of us didn't even register."

"Hey, yes! That doesn't make sense."

Rhys looked straight at Kieran. "Do you know what's going on, Kieran?"

Everyone was suddenly looking at him very pointedly and Kieran gave a semi-embarrassed little chuckle.

"Sprung! They're the same here, Rhys, but I decided to share them round and I transferred their focus to whoever matched with them the best. You were natural for the horses and the eagles were fascinated by Tan."

"George really likes me? ... Or did you tell him to?"

"He likes you naturally, and he likes you even more as time goes on. He loved it after he calmed down from the Spooks and you kept him company for a while."

Woorawa was too preoccupied with twisting his head to look at the eagle on his shoulder to take much notice of this conversation and Kieran waited for a few moments before interrupting. "Point straight up at the sky, Tan, and tell them to fly. It's time to get them working again and checking for any sign of Spooks or anything else coming after us."

Both birds launched and quickly rose above the trees at the side of the clearing with their new lookout commands while the companions mounted the horses and started to make their way back to the main trail.

*　*　*

Woorawa pulled to a halt at one of the sidetracks which they now knew would take them to the creek, and everyone joined him with a great deal of relief. They'd had one healing burst for their aching muscles and complaining joints about an hour ago and another was way overdue.

"Is this enough separation from the feast camp, Kieran? We've come a long way and there's been no sign of anyone coming after us."

Rhys leaned forward and rubbed the side of George's neck. "And the horses must be needing a rest after two hours without stopping. I vote we check out this track and camp if there's a clearing with grass for them."

The horses didn't need a rest. Kieran knew from his regular checks that they could go all day at that afternoon's pace and hardly notice it. He looked at the White Wall that had been looming more and more in his mind and toyed with the idea of continuing to one more turn-off. No, the defined side trails had been occurring at roughly half-hour intervals so far, and since the afternoon was drawing in it might be too close to dusk before they stopped.

"It's a pity not to keep going, because the Wall's further than we judged, but we don't want to travel in the dark either, so let's check this one out."

That got four very emphatic nods. Woorawa led the way and about two hundred metres later stopped his horse by a lazy-looking pool and declared this was a suitable place to stay for the night.

"It's not as good as the last camp and the clearing's not as big, but this does look like their favourite grass. There's a good spot down there for them to have a drink too … But first thing before we do anything else is to have a swim and a clean-up."

"A swim? Now?"

"Tan, I've got one pair of jocks and one pair of socks, and I'm going to wash them and let them dry near the fire so they feel clean when I put them on in the morning."

"Um … we haven't got any soap."

"We've got water and sand. That's better than nothing. Last one in is a wuss."

Rhys didn't join the rush. Instead, he disappeared behind some vegetation and shrubs for a while before returning with complaints about the discomfort and drawbacks of having to use grass and pieces of bark instead of toilet paper.

"What a pack of rudies. And I'm not a wuss, Woorawa. Some things take priority."

"Hurry up then and don't worry about frightening all the fish away when you strip off. Tan's already done that when he used mud instead of sand to wash his chest."

Instead of stripping bare like everyone else, Rhys raced into the water in his jocks and socks and started a great splashing war against anyone he could get close to before finally stripping to wash the way Woorawa demonstrated for him.

The laughter quickly finished and everyone got active with the various tasks involved in getting settled for the night. The horses were steadily munching and the eagles were perched, watching and waiting for the reward of a nice fish that Kieran had fixed in their minds. An hour later, with the bones and remnants of their third fish meal for the day tossed on the glowing coals, everyone settled around the campfire. Kieran's expectation for a big discussion about the day's events was put on hold when Tan collected one of the Spook ropes and handed it to Kieran.

"I've been thinking about the way it went completely useless without the

Spook, Kieran, like it needed power to make it work, and I wondered if you could use your opal energy with it."

Rhys got really excited. "That's an unreal idea, Tan. If we could make it work it might protect us from Spooks if more come after us."

"And it might not, Rhys. If the Spooks use them all the time they've probably got some sort of precaution against accidents."

"I suppose, Mr B … but they'd definitely work against wild animals."

"Kieran controls ordinary animals easily, Rhys."

"I know, Woorawa, but what about un-ordinary animals? See if you can make it active, Kieran."

Kieran trailed the intricately woven cord through his fingers then grabbed Rhys's hand and wound a short length around it.

Woorawa laughed. "Testing for wild animals and un-ordinary ones at the same time? Good thinking, Kieran."

Rhys's mouth opened for a comeback but then the consequence sank in. "You'll paralyse me!"

Kieran unwound the cord and changed his grip to the short handle part. "Only if I can make something happen."

Rhys waggled his little finger in front of Woorawa's face. "That's how we'll test it. We can't use your brain 'cause it's already paralysed."

Woorawa's eyes lit up. "Hey, wow! You really are volunteering?"

"Someone has to … and I'm only going to make a tiny touch with the back of my finger. Drape the end over these sticks while you experiment, Kieran."

Kieran called a trickle of energy and immediately the cord glowed blue.

"Does that mean it's live, Kieran?"

"I don't know, Rhys. It might, because the glow happened by itself. Give it a tiny touch and see … No! Woorawa can be the guinea pig and you can heal him if it works."

"What? Well, I suppose …"

Now Rhys was all concern and he insisted on demonstrating how to go ahead.

A light brush with the back of his finger was enough to make Woorawa gasp and he grabbed the finger and started working it back and forward.

"It's really strong, Kieran. Turn it down."

"I don't know how."

"Of course you do. Just take some of the energy away … like you do for glows or healing."

And it was as simple as that. If he called energy the cord seemed to automatically take it, so it was only a matter of controlling how much. The sense of achievement lasted till Rhys proclaimed it was useless. Everyone else had to be able to use one as well, and a solution only arrived with Tan's suggestion of a dedicated pool of energy, like the shield pools, and a lot of experimentation.

Woorawa insisted next on having a concentrated practice session involving all the abilities they could think of. There was a strong consensus that the complicated network of mind shields connecting everyone—including the horses and eagles—was the most important thing for their protection, and at least half the practice time involved ideas for testing and strengthening it.

Mr B was intrigued that the eagles were still protected when they were flying kilometres and kilometres away, and wanted to know if that needed extra help from the opal.

"Most of the time I hardly use the opal at all, Mr B. I needed it the first time I reached for the eagles, and when we started the fires, and the healing times of course, but that's about it."

"You used it when the Spooks attacked."

"No, I didn't. I might have tried making my shield stronger, but that was useless."

"Kieran, your whole body was glowing bright blue till after the third one disappeared. You must have been using it."

"He doesn't need the opal to make the glow, Rhys."

"Hmm. I suppose not, but it was awfully bright. Make all of us glow, Kieran."

"What colour?"

"Blue of course. That seems to come naturally."

In an instant all five companions were surrounded with a soft blue glow.

"That was quick. Did you need the opal?"

"Of course not, Rhys. The blue glow's just about the easiest thing I can do."

"All right. Add in the horses."

Everyone turned to look down the clearing where four shimmering blue shapes sprang into visibility.

"Wow! Ghost horses! Are you using the opal yet?"

"No."

"Okay, light up the eagles. Are they very far away?"

Kieran pointed even though he didn't need to.

"Any opal?"

"Not yet."

"I remember an extra big tree about twenty metres in that direction. Light that up as well."

"I can't see it, Rhys. It has to be in my mind before I can do anything to it."

"All right. Light up a pathway in the grass then. Can you do that for twenty metres without the opal?"

Kieran lit up the grass he could see by the light of the campfire, then progressively used each newly revealed section to extend a glowing ribbon towards where Rhys said the tree would be.

"Specco! Are you doing all this by yourself still?"

"Only just. I can't see the tree yet and my brain's straining."

"Try going to the left a bit … There it is. You can just make out the base of the trunk. Light it up."

Kieran couldn't. Five people, four horses, two eagles and a twenty-metre ribbon was his limit, so to go further he called on the opal. The strain completely disappeared and in a few moments the whole tree was growing brightly and outlined against the surrounding dark.

"Everything suddenly got brighter. You used the opal, didn't you?"

"I had to, Rhys. I'd reached my limit."

"Keep all the glow going, Kieran, and make us all see an elephant walking along the blue pathway."

That was a similar process to making someone look like a giant frog, but when Kieran started planting ideas in everyone's minds the blue glow of the pathway and the tree switched off.

"What happened, Kieran? I saw an elephant for half a second and now everything's gone normal."

"Doing the elephant's easy, and so is the path and the tree, but putting them all together at the same time isn't."

Woorawa laughed. "Well, we're not letting you stop till you've got it right."

When Kieran did get it right, after a few more tries, the practice finished and there was a general discussion about the various happenings. The White Wall—their target destination for tomorrow morning—quickly became the main topic though, with various theories about what it might be and what might happen when they reached it. Rhys had a theory that it could be like a rainbow and you'd never actually reach it, but no one else thought this was right.

It didn't take long to agree with Mr B that talking without any real information was interesting, but not going to get them anywhere. Eventually, when it was agreed that an early night and an early start in the morning made a lot of sense, Woorawa organised a roster for everyone to take a turn at lookout duty.

CHAPTER 3

The early start wasn't nearly as early as planned because Kieran slept in and only woke when Rhys sat on his stomach and told him he was a lazy slug. He didn't move because being sat on like this felt good and it took a few chest and stomach pokes, as well as the realisation that the other three were waiting and watching from beside the campfire, to make him sit up.

"Lazybones! Go and help Woorawa and Tan get some fish ready for our breakfast while Mr B and I look after George and the other horses."

"Everyone's up? Why didn't you wake me?"

Kieran dodged another chest poke.

"We all agreed you need more beauty sleep than the rest of us."

Feeling slightly guilty, but not really, Kieran got organised and only twenty minutes later their breakfast was cooking and the eagles were eagerly attacking the two small fish he'd given them.

"Why so small, Kieran? They can eat a lot more than that."

"And then they'd need recovery time to digest it all, Tan, and I want to send them up for a good look round before we set off."

"Of course."

"Did anyone hear anything while they were on watch?"

Woorawa answered that. "Nothing, Kieran. I checked that with every-one as soon we got up."

Mr B and Rhys finished putting all the saddle things on the horses and hurried to the campfire for their food, and after that it wasn't long before the freshly mounted expedition was underway.

*   *   *

Woorawa was stopped and waiting for Kieran to draw up next to him.

"Are you all right, Kieran?"

"Yes, of course. Why?"

"I'm starting to feel weird when I look at it, so I wondered if it's getting stronger and having an extra effect on you and Mr B."

Kieran looked at the strange barrier ahead with a mixture of unease and curiosity, while Tan and Mr B caught up and joined them.

"It's way stronger, Woorawa, but I've strengthened the sight switch thing for both of us and it can't get through. Is it starting to give you a mind-eating feeling?"

"No, I can put up with it, but it gives me a strange feeling that I need to focus on the trail or a tree or something close to make sure I'm not daydreaming."

Kieran looked for Tan's reaction.

"That's sort of what it's like for me too, Kieran, except that my brain keeps telling me it's not even there and I have to keep looking to prove that it is. What are we going to do now, go straight toward it or stay with the trail?"

Kieran's inclination was to leave the trail which was veering as if to follow parallel to the Wall, but he looked to Woorawa as the default leader while they travelled.

"I think we should keep to the track. It was obviously made to head for the Wall so there must be a reason for turning."

Tan interrupted.

"It's turning the wrong way, Woorawa. It's heading left, away from the water, and we shouldn't go much longer without a drink … especially the horses."

Woorawa shook his head in annoyance. "I'm glad we've got your common sense here, Tan. I should have thought of that. I wonder why there's no sidetrack branching off?"

Mr B turned his horse in the creek direction. "I think there is, Woorawa, but it's very faint."

Woorawa edged past the other horses so he could see properly.

"Hey, you're right … Let's water the horses and have a big drink for ourselves before we go on. We'd be silly not to, Kieran, and the creek won't be very far … Unless the eagles can see a different water source along the main track?"

Kieran was startled with the realisation that he'd left the eagles cruising at their own whim without checking on them.

"Whoa! I think you just snapped us out again, Tan. The Wall's giving us brain fog and you've seen through it the same way you did for the fear fog. Hang on while I bring the eagles for a closer look."

Kieran turned directly away from the wall to where he knew the eagles were circling and directed them to come close. *Hmm!* They were quite a way away.

"They're coming, but they'll take a few minutes because they've separated more from us than usual."

Woorawa swivelled to stare at the Wall. "Brain fog, hey? Well, that's my excuse for not noticing the faint trail or thinking about how important it is to keep hydrated. If we'd been thinking properly, we'd have had the eagles checking ahead like we did all yesterday."

"What?"

Everyone turned at this involuntary exclamation from Kieran that had nothing to do with Woorawa's observations, then looked to the sky where he was staring.

"They're coming, but they don't want to. I had to reinforce their commands."

"It's because of the Wall, isn't it, Kieran? They don't like it?"

"No, they don't, and now that I'm looking, I can see that it's in their subconscious to keep away."

"Why haven't the horses reacted then? It would make sense for them to keep away too."

Kieran shook his head in annoyance once again with the realisation that the horses also hadn't had a proper check for ages.

"They have reacted, Tan, but I've automatically been keeping them calm. The Wall's having subtle effects and the closer we get the worse they seem to be. Woorawa, lead the way to the creek, please. We're going to refresh ourselves then get properly prepared before we get close to this Wall."

Two piercing calls sounded and everyone raised their head to look at the approaching eagles.

"They're not happy at all. Tan, call them to land on your shoulders. They'll be calmer there than anywhere else till I work out what to do for them."

"While I'm sitting on my horse? We haven't done that before."

"Don't worry. They think of the horses as part of our group."

There was no time to worry anyway because the big female eagle was already landing, and as soon as her wings were folded, so did the male. Woorawa led the way again, and in only a few minutes the horses were drinking from a placid pool of water. The friends did the same then sat together for a break.

"We'll have a group refresh, please, before we do anything else. We don't want to be making decisions while we're affected by this Wall fog."

Rhys laughed when everyone automatically extended a hand to touch him, and then the smile expanded with the surging burst of wellbeing.

"Can you tell if the Wall is making you call on the opal more than you usually do, Kieran?"

The healing burst was now completely automatic for Kieran and he had to replay it in his mind to tell.

"I can't tell, Mr B. It *was* a bit extra, but that could be because we're all tired from two hours of travel."

"Are there any fish here, Kieran?"

"It's only just over two hours since we had breakfast, Woorawa."

"I know, but if we're going to head away from the creek we should fill up while we've got the chance."

Kieran looked to where the Wall rose in the sky.

"I've changed my mind about that and I want to head directly there from here. It's only about five hundred metres and there's no point in putting off finding out what it is."

Everyone joined in contemplating the incredible phenomenon.

"It gets spookier every time I look. Kieran, that's a double reason for stopping to eat then, because you said you wanted to be prepared. It'll only take us half an hour if we get straight into our routine."

Kieran cast his mind to the pool with the fish pattern and was quite surprised with the result. "That's weird. There aren't any fish."

Tan shook his head. "I don't think it's weird at all. The eagles and the horses don't like being here so it'll be the same for any other animals."

"And the horses haven't eaten any grass. They're just standing there looking at us. If there's nothing to eat, we should go now."

Woorawa was right and, as soon as everyone was remounted, he led the way through a gap in the creek-side vegetation. Kieran told Tan to keep the eagles on his shoulders where their sense of security would be strongest. The way got easier, with less and less vegetation till, eventually, with a growing sense of unease, the group stopped to survey the last desolate stretch of ground.

"This is scary, Kieran. Are we going right up to it?"

"Yes, look over there, Woorawa. The creek goes into it, so if we follow that we'll be staying with water and fish."

"No way would fish go through there, Kieran. I don't think I'm game to get much closer."

Kieran turned from the strange shimmering Wall to take in the worried looks of all his friends and realised there'd be no progress without some kind of special assistance. For some reason, he had a sense that this daunting barrier would provide information to help them understand their situation and lead them to a way home. *What to do?* Confidence was easy. That could happen with a switch in their minds, as long as he asked first, and staying close would help too.

"I really think we need to explore this, Tan. If you don't feel game enough I can keep you feeling calm like I do for the horses and the eagles.

Tan look shocked. "Control my mind? No way, Kieran. I'd feel weak every time I thought about it."

Kieran looked to Woorawa, Mr B and Rhys for their thoughts and received the same strong negation from each of them.

Woorawa spoke up firmly. "We have to keep together, Kieran, but I think it's important that we all stay independent in our minds, especially Tan, because his special way of looking at things has helped us get through two tricky situations already."

Kieran sat silently for a moment before nodding. "Well, I can still help. Bring the horses next to each other and we'll all link together by holding hands in a chain, and while we move forward I'll use the opal to make stronger protection for us."

Woorawa was puzzled. "What? Something different to our ordinary shields?"

"I'm not exactly sure, Woorawa, but remember how we all joined up just before we got transported to be with Rhys? I think it's because we were touching that no one got left behind."

They'd talked about this theory a number of times and were pretty much in full agreement with it.

"Makes a lot of sense to me, and with the ground clear of vegetation the horses can stay in formation all the way."

The horses were quickly manoeuvred next to each other and Kieran reached both arms out, to hold hands with Tan on one side and Woorawa on the other. Mr B joined with Woorawa and, after a pause while the eagles were calmed and reassured in their position on Tan's shoulders, the group started forward.

A blue glow crept through the linked hands and spread over everyone, and a smile sneaked through Tan's frown of concentration.

"Is this a dramatic show to help boost our confidence, Kieran? Coloured light won't really protect us from anything."

"It's not just coming from me. The opal's doing something extra."

"Extra?"

"I haven't got a clue, Tan, but it's way different to a normal glow."

At a steady pace the compact group approached the dizzying expanse of tortured nothingness. The distant impression of a White Wall was long gone and every set of eyes was wrenched between the need to pull meaning from the strangely hypnotic spectacle and the need to stay with reality by averting their gaze.

Rhys still thought of it as an aurora, but without any colour.

Woorawa thought of it as a kind of anti-glow, an expanse of vacuum that sucked in any colour instead of giving it out.

Tan had a strange feeling, more accurate than anyone else, that it was like an interface where everything that was real suddenly stopped.

Kieran and Mr B shared the impression, the moment they looked away, that the barrier wasn't even there, and then a powerful sense of wrongness when they returned their gaze.

The closer they got the harder it became to define an actual boundary, and by the time they were passing a small hump in the ground that had previously appeared to be quite separate to the Wall, the sense of distance was practically non-existent.

Kieran kept everyone moving despite seeing they all wanted to stop and, with each step forward, he sent more and more assurance and calm to the horses and the eagles. The complex network of protective mind shields started a strange reaction, and when he made a new call on the opal to strengthen them, the reaction increased and the blue glow surrounding them flared red and thickened.

Startled as he was by the dramatic nature of this unexpected effect, understanding that it was a help traced the compounding effect of holding everything together with an instant positivity. That was lost though, along with almost everything else, when, with piercing screams of pure fear, the two eagles launched and vanished from his mind. Reality dissolved and for an indeterminate period all he knew was a vast sense of pressure raging against the sea of fiery red glow being fed by a torrent of opal energy. Whether by their own unmindful movement or some function of the Wall, the pressure suddenly dissipated to comparative nothingness and Kieran battled his reeling senses to gain a semblance of recovery.

Fear filled his mind. Everyone was gone. *No!* That was just from his mind. The strength of Rhys's grip around his waist and the tight hold on his hands by Tan and Woorawa said otherwise. With a great rush of relief, he re-established their presence in his mind and rebuilt the network of mind shields. The four horses, bereft of any calming influence, plunged forward and broke the chain of physical contact linking their riders. Kieran instinctively pushed to keep the protective red glow in place then relaxed when it subsided and turned his mind to controlling the horses. He dispelled their panic, then, when their rush had built enough distance from the Wall, slowed them to a walk and brought them all together. The silent moment of shared disbelief at what had happened was broken when Woorawa patted his chest and legs.

"Am I still me? I got ripped apart then put together again. Kieran, that was even worse than when we got carried to Rhys. What did you do? Are you all right?"

"I don't know what I did, but it worked. It was mostly the opal."

Tan's twisting and turning to look in all directions made everyone else do the same.

"Gods, Kieran! Wherever we are now … it's awful … and the eagles are gone."

There was more silence while they took in the desolate terrain.

"It was bare like this on the other side, Rhys. When we get further away there'll be plants again."

"It's not the same, Kieran. That hill is at least four hundred metres away and there's not even one plant in sight."

"And we've lost the eagles, so we haven't got our lookouts anymore."

"I'm sorry, Tan. I couldn't keep hold when they panicked."

"Sorry? That's crazy, Kieran. You got the rest of us through whatever that was safely … Look over there. We've got a much bigger problem."

Kieran turned his gaze to where a very worried-looking Tan was pointing. It was just bare ground, no different to anywhere else around them.

"What?"

"We came through here to stay with the creek, but it's gone. There's no water."

There was no sign that a creek or even a watercourse had even existed, just open ground, gently sloping upwards towards the hill.

Tan's worried frown was now shared.

"Let's head to the top of that hill, Kieran. We can think better when we're further away from the Wall. I'm extra worried that there's no sign of any plants, because without them there can't be food and that's big trouble … Are all our shields working properly?"

"I lost them completely again, Woorawa, but I remembered this time and put them back first thing, even before I calmed the horses."

With a come-along sign to everyone, Kieran jigged George into motion and headed for the hilltop.

*   *   *

"This *is* a disaster, Kieran. What you want to do?"

With growing dismay, the whole group had examined the desolate plain ahead of them for any sign or feature of hope. The scene before them appeared devoid of life, extending way into the distance to where a dark range of mountains rose abruptly in stark contrast with the wide expanse of flatness, broken only by an occasional small, barren hill.

"We can't reach those mountains, Woorawa. Even with a proper trail for the horses they'd be days and days away, and there's no food or water. The whole place is dead. We'll have to go back through the Wall. There's no choice. We'll starve if we stay here."

"No, we won't. We'll die of thirst first. There's not even one plant out there."

"That's not funny, Rhys."

"I'm not being funny, Tan. I'm being serious. Staying here's not an option."

"There must be plants somewhere or there wouldn't be any air."

"Well, it might take weeks to get there. I hope you know how to make that red protection thing again, Kieran. Was it very hard to do?"

"I hope so too, Rhys. It really came from the opal when the Wall got dangerous. I'll have a few practice tries before we go."

"We'll have to go soon. George and the other horses don't like it here."

"I'm watching them, Rhys. They're okay. They're just standing close and watching us because there's no grass and they're expecting us to find some. We'll leave when I sort a few things out in my mind."

"What's that mean? Is there something you haven't told us?"

"No, Tan. I just want a break before I think about the Wall and getting through it again."

Woorawa was immediately concerned. "A recovery break or a thinking break, Kieran? You said you were all right when you stopped the horses."

"A quiet break while I think, and then some sort of practice in about ten or fifteen minutes. The Wall's kind of overwhelming and I want to psych myself up before we try it again."

"Kind of overwhelming! That's a total understatement if ever I heard one, Kieran. Take as long as you like. I could psych myself for a week and I'd still be too chicken."

"Don't talk about chickens, Tan. It makes me think how good a roast one would taste instead of more fish."

After fifteen minutes of quiet introspection, Kieran arranged everyone in a circle with their hands joined and practised calling the fiery red protection till he was confident he had it fixed properly in his mind. Woorawa, as usual, kept asking for the ins and outs of Kieran's thinking and making suggestions the way he did for ordinary practice sessions. Kieran liked this because quite often it worked as a type of foil to settle things more clearly in his mind.

"No, the colour's not coming from me. It's like the opal takes over or reacts on its own when I let myself sense the Wall."

"I wonder if colour means anything? Try turning it back to blue and see what happens."

"Um … that doesn't feel right, Woorawa, but I'll try it."

A minute later they knew it was bad news to interfere with the red.

"Okay, everyone, mount up. I think I'm ready for this."

"Yay! I hate going through that Wall, but it'll just about be worth it to get away from this dump."

Rhys calling it a dump was another understatement in everyone's mind, but it did tinge the apprehension for the coming ordeal with a trace of humour, and the group was quickly heading back down the hill. Rhys kept the atmosphere light for a while longer by raving about devouring roast chickens and eating fish and chips without the chips, but then the growing sense of oppression became too strong. The Wall was still about two hundred metres away when Kieran stopped George in his tracks and turned to face the other way. Everyone else stopped and Rhys tightened his hold around Kieran's waist.

"What is it?"

"The opal's giving me a weird sensation. I think there's something coming."

All the other horses were now turned in the same direction.

"From the top of the hill? There can't be, Kieran. We could see for miles and there was nothing alive."

Kieran didn't answer that. The weird sensation was stronger and compounding with alarm.

"I think we should …"

The four horses bolted, screaming with bloodcurdling calls of fear. Kieran, fighting to keep his balance, reacted with more strength than he'd ever needed to calm the panic and stay their movement.

George responded first, and then the others, and, turning to face the hill, Kieran had a few brief seconds to take in the monster coursing low towards them. Metre upon metre of widespread wings and huge talons grasped forward in hunting readiness registered with a mingle of shock, disbelief, fear, and almost panic in the brief time before Tan and his mount were struck a terrible blow and knocked fifteen metres to one side in a cartwheeling mass of newly screaming horseflesh and separated human.

With a thunder of wings the impossible creature descended on the horse as it struggled in agony. The petrified group watched talons take hold and impossibly huge fangs rip a hind leg free.

With a great wrench of purpose, Kieran overcame the paralysis of horror and fear and reached to control the lethal storm of anger tearing the poor horse apart. Nothing! Like the Spooks, except not. No mind at all. Just that weird sensation surging from the opal.

No! No! No! Kieran reached again, harder than he'd ever reached, but there was still nothing, and when the thing threw a great gobbet of flesh to one side and looked toward the inert form on the ground close by, a tide of despair started to flow. Horror and dread came with the understanding that the monster's attention was turning to Tan and there was nothing he could do to stop it. If they didn't run for the Wall while the beast was still rending the poor horse, they would all be prey. But how could they leave Tan?

The awful moment of hesitation while he faced this dilemma was disturbed when the tight grip around his waist vanished and Rhys slid to the ground. There was another moment—this time of utter disbelief—as Kieran took in the lithe form racing at top speed directly at the beast. He reached again, this time for the person who meant so much to him. The insane intention to attack a fierce creature ten times his size had to be stopped, even if it meant taking control without consent. Contact was instant, of course, and with it came a great flood of anger, fear for Tan and the rest of them, and purpose. Also with it came the knowledge of his intention and, frightened beyond belief for Rhys, Kieran knew he had to let this happen.

The great beast raised its head to watch the puny creature approach. In the last moment, as Rhys stopped his rush to prepare himself, the beast lashed almost carelessly with one fierce talon. With a continuation of fluid movement, Rhys leapt to one side and, with purpose, lashed his own weapon. His wrist flicked purposefully and the Spook cord whipped through the air and brushed for an instant against the retreating talon. Fearful in his mind that the delicate cord would have little effect on a creature with so much power, Kieran's hope for even a degree of paralysis was eclipsed by the explosion of light and sound that knocked Rhys flat on his back.

The beast was gone—completely gone—and when Rhys sat up shaking his head to clear it, Kieran released the clamps holding the horses in place and rushed them forward. While they covered the short distance, Rhys ran to kneel by Tan and start checking him.

"Use the opal, Kieran. I can't see anything wrong, but there must be something bad because he's completely unconscious, and when I straightened him out he felt awful. He's breathing but ..."

With a rush of thankfulness that the previous experience of healing Tan had taught him exactly what to do, Kieran built the special healing pool in Rhys's mind and as fast as he poured a torrent of energy into it, it drained through the contact against Tan's temples.

Rhys groaned and Kieran hurriedly built the little structure that would direct energy to let Rhys's body automatically work at its best. Rhys's eyes opened.

"Thanks, Kieran. Something must be happening because I suddenly felt like I was going to flake out."

"You were, but I've got you balanced now so you can keep going. You're draining energy like crazy, so it must be critical."

Rhys looked at Tan's blank face. "He hasn't changed. I hope he's all right, Kieran. We're not too late, are we?"

"Shush, Rhys! With someone like you protecting him, he won't dare not get better."

Rhys gave a smile which, if not for the demands of the moment, would have turned Kieran into a quivering lump of jelly. "I had to, Kieran. It seemed like the only hope we had."

Kieran couldn't speak, so he covered Rhys's hands where they were held against Tan's temple with his own hands and leaned forward so their foreheads were touching. After a moment another pair of hands rested on his shoulders. When Kieran looked up he received a gentle nod of approval and assurance from Mr B and another big smile, this time from Woorawa. Tan's body twitched and Rhys yelled.

"He's moving! He's moving!"

"His mind's coming back. He's waking up." Relief coursed through Kieran as the internal signs of awareness that only he could read flickered into existence. "I think he must have hit his head and got knocked unconscious when he came off the horse, because that's where most of the healing is happening."

Tan stirred again but his eyes didn't open. For the next few minutes Kieran's whole focus was on refining the technique of strengthening and speeding Rhys's healing ability that he'd learnt at home with the bruised bone. Tan's features contorted and, with eyes half open, he gave a soft, heart-wrenching moan of pain.

"Hold on, Tan. Rhys is healing you and you're getting better."

Tan didn't reply, but before he closed them again, his eyes registered awareness. At the same time Kieran was surprised to sense the healing energy transferring to the top of Tan's right shoulder. Did that mean his head was better? It must. Fascinated, he made an effort, beyond that of simply helping Rhys increase the healing, to watch how the energy was being distributed. Most of it was now focused in his shoulder area, but there was still a portion going to Tan's head and, as well, another portion centred low in the right side of his chest. Kieran increased the call of energy from the opal and watched the corresponding energy flow through Rhys's hands increase. Tan's eyes opened and flickered questioningly between Rhys and Kieran.

"Keep still, Tan. You need more healing."

"What happened? Am I all right? I remember a thing hitting me, but it must have been a nightmare. Did I fall off my horse?"

"It wasn't a nightmare. It was real, but it's gone now because Rhys killed it. You got knocked out when you hit the ground and there are a few other injuries too."

"My shoulder's hot and it hurts … Rhys killed the thing? It was too big."

"It's not your shoulder. It's your collarbone and I think it was broken. There's something wrong with your ribs and you had concussion, but Rhys has fixed that."

"Are Mr B and Woorawa okay? Did anyone else get hurt?"

Mr B spoke up. "We're right here, Tan, watching you get better. Rhys saved us all!"

"How do you know so much detail about Tan's injuries, Kieran? Resting my hands on him makes things happen but I haven't a clue what."

"What you do is beyond me, Rhys, but I've worked out how to follow the energy flow from the opal and to see where you're using it. At the moment most of it's going to Tan's collarbone."

Tan started to move his arm but stopped with a wince of pain.

"Don't move, Tan. It might interfere with Rhys's healing and it's bone again, so it's going to take a while … Woorawa, would you go and comfort the horses, please. They're all still trembling after what happened and some personal attention will be good for them."

Tan twisted his head a little, but it was held too firmly by Rhys. "Where's my horse? Did it get hurt?"

"Don't look, Tan. It saved your life by holding the monster's attention till Rhys dissolved it. You'll have to double up behind Woorawa when we leave."

"Double up? You mean …?"

"It was horrible, but it was all over in the first couple of seconds."

Tan just stared at Rhys for a moment then lifted his left hand across his body and rested it very tentatively on his shoulder.

"Not yet, Tan."

"I'm just checking. It's not hurting as much, but it's all hot, much hotter than at home when you fixed my shinbone."

Rhys looked for Kieran to give an explanation.

"That's all good, Tan. It means the healing's going faster. Rhys is using lots more energy this time."

"I am? How come I haven't flaked out then?"

"You nearly did at the start. I fixed it so you're healing yourself all the time."

Tan moved his hand again, this time to explore his rib cage. "Ouch! I just realised it's all warm there too."

"More healing, Tan. It's good. You'll have other bruises too, but they'll show up later. Rhys's healing seems to fix the critical things first."

"What was that thing? I remember giant wings and awful teeth, and then it hit me."

"I have no idea, Tan. It was a bit like the Spooks, because I couldn't find a mind to control, but at least the Spooks didn't want to hurt us. All that thing wanted to do was kill."

"Did you say Rhys dissolved it?"

"He used the Spook rope on it and it exploded."

Tan's eyes opened wider, which Kieran took as a really good sign.

Rhys laughed. "You should've seen it, Tan. When the rope touched it, it went BOOM and knocked me flat on my back like a tenpin skittle. All that was left was the rope handle. Hey, Mr B, can you go and look for the Spook ropes that were on Tan's saddle? We'll need them and I might be helping Tan for ages."

Tan moved his hand back to his shoulder. "I don't know, Rhys. I think it's healing way faster than the other time. If the heat is good then I think it must be. Feel what it, Kieran. It's like there's a radiator in there."

Kieran wanted to keep physical contact with Rhys because it made all his controlling techniques easier. He could manage that with one hand though, so he carefully rested his other hand where Tan was indicating. He took it away in surprise, then returned it. Tan was right. The area was so hot that in normal circumstances it would be described as burning with a fever.

"Wow, Tan! We could cook the fish on that. It's not painful, is it?"

Tan managed a smile. "Don't make me laugh; I think it would hurt. No, it's a weird feeling … It's too hot and kind of tingling, but at the same time it doesn't feel wrong."

Now Rhys was curious. "Can I use one hand to check it out, Kieran? That won't stop the healing if I keep the other one against Tan's skin will it?"

"Hmm! That's interesting. It might even work better with your hand close to the injured area. Keep one hand on his forehead, so there's no break in contact, and slip the other one under the collar of his shirt."

Rhys did that and was as startled as Kieran had been. "Holy cow! That's unbelievable … And my hands are doing that? How much are you calling on the opal, Kieran? Tan's shinbone didn't feel like it was cooking."

Kieran checked his mental gauge. "The opal's busy, but it's nothing compared to when we went through the wall … It's easier than when we worked with the bruised bone too. We're getting better at this, Rhys."

"Ha! You're getting better you mean. All I do is touch. Hey! What's happening? Either it doesn't feel as hot now, or am I just getting used to it?"

Tan laughed at this and immediately winced. "Ooh! Please don't make me laugh. My ribs don't like it, and now I can feel them starting to heat up."

He wriggled a bit then surprised Kieran and Rhys by yanking his T-shirt out of his jeans and pulling it up to his neck so his chest was bare. "Move your hands down to my ribs, Rhys. That's where they need to be now."

"One at a ti—"

Too late. Kieran strained to control the sudden build-up in Rhys's pool of healing energy for the few seconds while both hands weren't making contact.

"Ga! That was a shock. Don't break contact without warning me, Rhys. I have to keep the 'in' energy balanced with the 'out' energy."

Rhys gave one of his "whoops I made a boo-boo" grimaces mixed with an "I'm sorry" look. "Sorreee! I'll remember if we ever have to do this again. Does this mean Tan's shoulder's fixed already?"

"I don't know. I think the healing goes to where it's needed most … No, there's still energy going there, and a little bit to his head too."

Tan's left-hand explored his shoulder with gradually increasing pressure, then stopped in a spot about halfway along his collarbone. "There's a little bump just there that I don't remember having and it's a bit tender near it too, but not much. I'm going to try moving my shoulder."

He said this with a questioning look to Kieran, who nodded to go ahead.

"Carefully, Tan. Just stop if it doesn't feel right."

Tan concentrated while he moved his shoulder forward, then back, then in a big, slow circular movement. "It's stiff or different, but it doesn't hurt. Could it really have got fixed this quick if it was broken? The bruised bone took lots more time."

Kieran had absolutely no doubt at all, but his attention went to Mr B, who'd returned holding both of the Spook cords which had been clipped, one on each side, to the saddle on Tan's horse.

"One cord is clean, Kieran, but the other's a terrible mess. My hands feel awful after recovering it."

It did look awful, with clots of dark congealed blood all through the coil and smearing onto Mr B's right hand.

"As soon as we get back to the creek we'll get all cleaned up. Can you cope with looking after it till then?"

"Of course … Why is Rhys touching Tan's bare chest? It looks rather unusual."

Rhys really enjoyed that. "Because I'm copping a feel of his sexy body!"

"Idiot! Tan's ribs got cracked, Mr B, and we found out the healing works best when Rhys touches the place that's hurt."

"His ribs? What about his broken collarbone, Kieran? Isn't that a lot more debilitating than cracked ribs?"

"My collarbone seems to be a lot better."

Everyone grinned at Mr B's amazement and Tan reached up and grabbed his hand.

"Feel along my collarbone, Mr B. There's a lump that wasn't there before where it must have been broken."

Mr B started exploring, gently, where Tan was directing, but stopped in surprise—a surprise shared with Tan and Rhys—when Kieran suddenly stood and stared into the distance. The healing stopped, and when he let out a great yell to Woorawa, the three horses came charging towards them.

"Get on as quick as you can. We're heading for the Wall because I just got the sensation from the opal that there's another one of those things some-where. Rhys, take that Spook rope from Mr B and I'll charge you up for it."

Rhys was helping Tan to his feet, but when the horses and a worried-looking Woorawa arrived, he took the cord and turned to listen to Kieran.

"Help Tan onto the saddle first. Woorawa can support him from behind since Tan's ribs are still painful. We have to get moving because the sensa-tion's building and I think it's more than one monster."

Bending over slightly and holding his ribs, Tan shuffled hurriedly to the horse. Rhys and Woorawa boosted him into place then rapidly got mounted themselves. The horses, all under tight control, charged towards the Wall with their riders casting frequent worried looks behind for any signs of pursuit. Kieran's mind raced, figuring all the things he had to manage. First of all he charged up the pool of energy for Rhys's Spook rope then, as the Wall got closer, he called on the opal to help cope with the increasingly distressing disorientation. Kieran felt they were going to make it, despite the strengthening sensation now telling him there must be at least four pursuers.

Turning at Woorawa's great warning shout, Kieran saw three shapes flying low over their lookout hilltop, with another shape to the left, and, farther to the left, yet another two. With a great surge of power, Kieran called the red protection field. He linked even more strongly with the horses as he slowed and bunched them for the last twenty metres where everyone needed to be in physical contact.

Great screams of anger from close behind sent a rush of fear but, ready this time for their panic, Kieran held the horses' minds and muscles with a grip of iron till the last few metres of movement dissolved everything into weirdness.

Red! Red! Red! Kieran held everything together till they emerged and had covered the ten to twenty metres of distance it took for reality to re-establish and awareness of their surroundings and what was ahead to snap into focus. When the red faded to nothing and they no longer needed physical contact, Kieran stopped the horses and shared everyone's dismay at the sight ahead. The strong emotions and adrenaline rush from the narrow escape were now eclipsed by disbelief at what they were seeing.

"What happened, Kieran? Did we get turned around?"

Kieran shook his head and quickly turned to Tan, who he knew was in pain. "How bad is it, Tan?"

"It's not too bad while we're walking, but rushing made it stab with every bounce."

"We'll walk another few hundred metres till we're comfortably far enough from the Wall for another healing session and then Woorawa can scout out some water for us."

"Very funny, Kieran. We're back in the same dead place again. There's no water here, just flying nightmares."

The horses started walking again, slowly.

"It might be the same country, Rhys, but it's not the same place. There's no lookout hill."

Four heads searched then shared a look.

"I think it *is* the same country. There's no vegetation anywhere no matter how far you look … I reckon you're right, Mr B. And there's that big mountain range way off in the distance."

"Except it's not quite as far off this time."

And that made everyone look again in a more measured way.

"Sheba! It is too, Woorawa. Another impossible thing."

"Well, for once I'm glad for an impossible thing. If we'd been turned around and come out at the same place, all those monsters would have been waiting for us."

"Tan's right, Kieran, except if it is the same country we'll have to worry about monsters homing in on us again ... Can you make the opal pick them up from further away so we get more warning?"

After a couple of seconds of thinking, Kieran stopped the horses again. Woorawa was right, and while two hundred metres gave a comfortable respite from the Wall's effects, it would be critically dangerous time-wise if any warning they received was as scant as last time. He was conscious of Tan watching quietly, but this really was a priority.

"I wasn't making anything happen, Woorawa. The sensations came from the opal without my asking."

"Really? That's unusual, isn't it? Has it ever started anything by itself before?"

"Only that first time when we took it out of the clay protection and it made me tingle all over."

"What about the red protection for the Wall? You said that came from the opal."

"Sort of, but I was definitely asking for help when that happened. Ha! Screaming for help I should say."

"Have you got the monster pattern stored like you do with everything else, Kieran?"

Woorawa meant the "clicking into place" technique they'd talked about and practised in so many of their training sessions.

"I haven't exactly stored it, but it's sure burning bright in my memory."

"Well, store it properly, then keep it in your mind and call on the opal."

Rhys was really impressed. "How do you come up with all these ideas, Woorawa?"

"Tan has more ideas than me. This one comes from all the practice and talks I've had with Kieran for his abilities."

"Shush! He's got that look."

Kieran was indeed very much internalised because, once again, Woorawa had come up with a path of action which somehow had a feeling of rightness about it. The pattern storing was easy, and almost instanta-neous with the monster memory so strong from such a short time ago. Calling it back and setting it at the front of his thoughts was easy too, but making a link with the opal wasn't. He concentrated harder and the reflexive blue glow built around him as he willed for the result that felt close but wouldn't quite happen. *Think harder!* This was a bit like that complicated first search for the eagles when they were too far away for normal contact. That search pattern was definitely stored. Substitute the monster sensation for the eagle identity and try that. No ... but not a definite no, so try again with even more effort.

What a disaster!

Kieran switched the now-successful pattern off and on twice more to make this new technique part of his repertoire of instantly available actions, then focused on what was out there. Blinks of the sensation were everywhere, some stronger than others, which must be related to distance, and some with a vague impression of movement. *Gods!* It was the stronger signals that had the sensation of movement.

"They're everywhere! Dozens of monsters, and the closest ones are all moving towards us. Sorry, Tan, we can't stay here."

"You can see them? Will they take long to get here?"

"It's not exactly seeing, but they're definitely there, and I can't be exact about the time, but it might be five or ten minutes."

"We're going through the damn Wall again. Three times in less than an hour. Our brains will be like scrambled scrambled eggs."

"Scrambled scrambled, Rhys?"

"Yeah, technically it's scrambled scrambled scrambled, Mr B, but my brain's getting scrambled thinking about it."

"At least we've got more time, so Tan doesn't get bounced around ... except that means it takes longer before we're through."

The horses, at Kieran's prompt, turned and headed for the Wall at a gentle walking pace and, resigned to the necessity of the situation, the five companions rode in silent introspection till Kieran called for the physical contact he now looked on as a necessary part of the process.

Rhys gave a resigned grunt.

"I know what's going to happen. It'll be the same dead country again."

"As long as it's a different place, Rhys, without a dozen monsters flying at us."

"I know." His arms tightened round Kieran's waist. "Lead on, Macduff!"

The world dissolved into the weird loss of sense and sensibility till Kieran's will and the protection of the opal carried them far enough through to allow normal awareness to return. After a few more moments of progress came Rhys's carefully exaggerated groan of protest.

"I told you, didn't I? There's not one single plant anywhere. I'm going to call this place Dead World. I hope there aren't any monsters close this time because my brain wants to go on holiday."

No one acknowledged this brave attempt to lighten the situation because the Wall's effect was still dissipating. Even more, it was ignored because the sight ahead demanded full attention. Apart from his softly muttered exclamation of amazement, Rhys also lapsed into silence till they were far enough from the discomfort zone to stop and consider the situation. All eyes turned to Kieran, who'd been totally occupied with the business of disbanding the red protection, rebuilding all their shields, and managing the horses. After a glance to see how Tan was coping, he turned his mind to the top priority and called up the monster search technique, then shook his head negatively to the four watchers.

"No rest for the wicked, Rhys. There aren't as many, but they *are* here, spread out along those mountains, and the closest ones are already moving towards us."

"I don't believe this. They're moving already? We must give off bad vibrations or something. How long before they get here this time?"

Kieran had another look. "They're a bit further away than last time, but that's tricky because if they dived from so high they could build up incredible speed."

All eyes turned to the massive broken cliff face extending way into the distance, and to the rugged and spectacular mountains rising in the background.

"Yowies! If it's the same country then we must have zapped across more than a hundred k's. And look! There's snow on all those peaks, so there must be water here."

"With monsters everywhere, that won't help us, Rhys."

"I know, Tan, but it's interesting. Do you want us to help you get off the horse for a while?"

Tan put his hand against his chest then screwed up his face. "Ah! No thanks. Not if we're leaving in a few minutes."

"Just a couple more minutes, Tan. We should play safe and leave now, but I've never seen anything like this."

Kieran turned to drink in the snowy peaks and the great broken wall of nearby cliff face, till caution overcame awe and the group remounted to walk slowly and very reluctantly toward the Wall again. Rhys raised a smile with his quadruple scrambled comment, but the general concern, voiced by Woorawa, was rising.

"I know we don't have any choice, but it's starting to feel like we're stuck in a loop, like the Wall's fixed on taking us somewhere in Dead World."

Everyone had the same feeling, but the time to talk about it before they linked for the crossing passed with Rhys carrying on about his dream alternative.

"No more Dead World, thank you! This time I want trees and creeks and friendly animals and a campfire beside a beautiful pool."

Woorawa had to laugh. "Dream on, Rhys. Are you sure that's enough?"

"No! Fruit and a waterfall would be good too."

The Wall was imminent and all talk stopped.

*   *   *

The objective side of the High King of all elven realms' mind regarded the pique his subjective side was feeling with wry detachment. Twelve hundred years of unbroken rule had reinforced the understanding that even the most straightforward of plans could falter and crash with the vagaries of chance and surprise, and that the crisis of the moment always felt more frustrating than those of the past. That same long experience had also taught him that while maintaining a deep calm was critical, venting his surface tensions was a valuable form of relief. Privately, of course. Such behaviour before his Court would not only spread waves of doubt and dismay for his fitness to rule but further embolden Lady Narello in her recent futile and misguided ambitions. Ensconced with Uirebon behind the powerful privacy wards of this personal chamber was the perfect place to express this pique. Uirebon understood, thank goodness. Indeed, he had advised the value of this release on many occasions.

"Always when you least need them, Uirebon. Why do troubles compound at the very moment of least readiness?"

Uirebon nodded his agreement. Enough things had gone awry with his own part in this cascade of events to build a mutual understanding.

"Indeed, my Lord, frustration upon frustration, enough to make me ponder the possibility of an underlying cause."

Pique was momentarily replaced by curiosity.

"How so? I see nothing but chance in the spread of Chaos Incursions, the clash between Narello's forces and Maynor's Power Masters, and the baffling disappearance of Keryth. The setback with Maynor's recovery and the plethora of rumours and disquiet surfacing in three of our great Courts can hardly all be linked."

"Yes, my Lord. Incursions generally result from a temporary imbalance between Boundaries and the unpredictable forces of Outer Chaos. I know this is a long bow to pull, but we have suspected for some time now that disturbances in the Unordered Realm can match with an increase in Chaos Incursions elsewhere. Remember what happened six centuries ago when Ranevargar attempted to build a bastion of order in the Great Range with his Dragon Construct?"

"Yes, five years of turmoil before he stilled and abandoned the Dragon. We only connected the trouble with the Construct's activity when he offhandedly related a list of his failed animal experiments in a side conversation after one of our High Council meetings. Uirebon, do you think the Dragon may have been reawakened?"

"Not at all. Only Ranevargar could do that, and his distress at the likelihood his Construct might have caused so much destruction was so vast at the time that he'd never consider it."

"Something else then?"

"As I said, it *is* a long bow, but two things lead me to consider the improbability that Keryth might have taken his companions into the Unordered Realm."

"NO!"

Despite this being expressed in command mode, Uirebon continued, as he knew it was a rejection of the idea rather than an order.

"We know the unexpected energy drain that incapacitated the junior triad went mostly to bolster Lord Maynor's Power Masters, but a portion did flow to repair a breach in his Realm Boundary."

"And that repair was successful. I dealt with four other wearying breaches today, Uirebon, but all occurred in other locations." Aglaron stopped a moment as understanding renewed his concern. "You mean there was no Incursion related to Maynor's Realm Boundary because it was an outward breach?"

"The amount of energy involved makes it a possibility, a frightening possibility, which I have to inform you is increased by the knowledge I gleaned from Maynor's two Coursers."

"You surprise me, Uirebon. I judged Keryth's control unbreakable. How did you manage such a thing?"

"I didn't, my Lord. The birds returned to the Castle rookery by their own volition while you were resolving the Incursions to Narello's realm. It was fast fading, of course, but their strongest recent memory was of the fear and distress the Boundaries engender in all natural creatures."

"I see, and such an encounter would certainly dissolve any protective mind shield. Uirebon, what have we done? Keryth couldn't survive the Unordered Realm in full elven form, let alone as he is now. Help me prepare."

"Of course, my Lord, but not to make an entry of your own. Consider carefully."

"Our purpose is to cure Keryth, not kill him."

Uirebon spoke quickly and forcefully. "The glass is half full, my Lord, not half empty. Your paternal bond is intact, else you would be stricken with shock and sadness. Keryth is alive."

Aglaron did pause to consider, and eventually nodded his agreement.

"What would I do without your counsel, Uirebon? You are right, of course, but how could Keryth possibly survive in that place? On three occasions I have had cause to pass that Boundary, and every time I was forced to a hasty retreat."

"As, I believe, Keryth was also forced."

"There was only one energy event with Maynor's Boundary. A retreat would imply two."

"And there were four in total, though not all with Maynor's Boundary."

Aglaron stared at his advisor while he took that in. "You *do* make a link between Keryth and the Chaos Incursions? You think he is moving from Realm to Realm, hidden behind that wretched shield, and causing Incursions with each crossing?"

"I agree. It seems implausible, but there is the concurrence of events to consider. Our interpretations will change and become more accurate with further information."

"Advise me, Uirebon. How am I to find Keryth? Along with this ability to conceal himself, you now suggest he might be able to pass Boundaries without the consent of the relevant Realm Lord?"

"Till we learn otherwise we should entertain the possibility. My Lord, my strongest advice is to rest and restore yourself so you are properly prepared when Lord Maynor wakes. Tiredness is bringing your tendency for hasty action to the surface."

Aglaron gave his Lore Master a thoughtful look and then a nod of resigned agreement. "Yes, I see that it is, and to rest for the six remaining hours Maynor's healer has set would be a blessed relief."

"It is not just a relief. It is a necessity. This is your third day without proper rest."

"Three days? It feels like forever."

"Put Keryth out of your mind, my Lord. I begin to suspect that the gemstone is protecting him somehow. We won't find him directly, but when Maynor wakes we will have the resources of three Realms at our disposal."

"Hmm! Contact Ranevargar while I sleep. He will have no interest in any direct involvement, but he will advise us of any Incursion or interaction affecting his animals."

*   *   *

Reality returned and by the time their shields were rebuilt and the horses' fear reduced from sheer panic, the group had travelled far enough from the Wall to release their joined hands and take stock. The ground right here was bereft of life, but a hundred metres ahead a bank of shrubs and vegetation built quickly to a high forest wall and the excited yells from Woorawa and Rhys completely wrecked Kieran's first attempt at a monster search.

"Unbelievable! Look! The hills are all covered with trees and … and that's a flock of birds over there."

The monster search was put off while Kieran's eyes followed where Woorawa was pointing.

"Oh my God! We *have* escaped from Dead World."

Rhys gave Kieran's shoulders an excited shake before voicing the other possibility that had just occurred to him.

"Please don't tell us we'll have to move again, Kieran. If we're in a part of Dead World where water from the mountains lets plants grow that would be just too much."

The mixture of eagerness and apprehension being directed fourfold, in silence and with fierce attention, was a new distraction but not a total spoiler and when, after almost a full minute of concentration and searching, Kieran's features lit up, the yells of relief and excitement sounded for the second time.

"No monsters?"

"None at all, Mr B. I'll have to keep checking, of course, but we'll definitely have time to help Tan. Let's find a good place to stop."

Twenty minutes later, after a wondrous walk past lush green trees, with riotous bird-calls sounding at every new twist in the narrow trail they'd stumbled upon, they stopped in a forest clearing to a sight that started their senses reeling with even more wonder and disbelief. Not only was there a beautiful pool of crystal-clear water, with an outflowing creek following along one side of the grassy clearing, at the back of the pool a small waterfall tumbled happily down the ten-metre face of the rock wall behind it.

Tan said it first, and it became the topic of discussion till well into the night.

"You *have* made magic, Rhys. The only thing I don't see is the fruit trees."

As if to prove the point, a flock of about twenty cockatoo-sized birds settled noisily in the branches of the nearest tree to watch, with blatant curiosity, the new intruders to their domain.

While Woorawa and everyone else cast an eye over the varied possibilities, Kieran started his third check for signs of danger. He jumped in startlement when one of the noisy watchers landed on his head. Two more perched on his shoulders and he watched in amazement as the rest came close, some landing at his feet, and some making soft chirring noises from their mix of landing spots on his companions' heads or shoulders, or outstretched arms in the case of Rhys and Woorawa.

"You called them to us, didn't you, Kieran? This is too quick to be natural."

"Not this time, Rhys. I was still finishing my monster check when the first one landed on my head. I'm looking at their minds now and it's pure curiosity."

Mr B had one perched on the wrist he was holding close to his face.

"Look at the beautiful little crest. I'm always amazed at how brilliant the colours of bird feathers are when you see them up close."

Kieran stopped checking the birds' minds and let the enjoyment of the moment flow over him. The cheeky-looking crests, with their bright red colour contrasting strongly against the soft green body feathers, were indeed quite beautiful. More than that, each snappy display lift made you smile with the impression that mischief was about to be perpetrated. A few moments later the flock flew off and disappeared through the neighbouring trees.

"That was wonderful, Rhys. I kept thinking they were some kind of welcoming committee."

"Well, I like the way their little crests bob up and down … Are we going to stay here tonight, or do you want to keep moving?"

"We'll think about it while you finish healing Tan's ribs. That's our first priority."

Rhys grinned and pointed to the ground. "Make yourself comfortable, Tan, and show us your sexy chest again."

Tan started to kneel, but Mr B stopped him.

"Not here, Rhys. We'll make a bed of grass and leaves near the pool so Tan can sleep when you finish."

"Sleep? What for, Mr B? I want to look around with everyone else."

"Rhys's refresher boost makes us feel good, but this was a major trauma, Tan, and I think it makes sense to give your body a chance to recuperate."

"I don't think I'll be able to sleep in the daytime while other things are happening."

Mr B gave Kieran a look before answering.

"Yes, you will. With your permission, Kieran will make it happen while the rest of us organise a campfire and food. We'll wake you when there's something to eat."

Murmurs of assent from all round meant this was now the immediate course of action and everyone started the thirty-metre walk to the edge of the pool. Tan shuffled slowly, which brought the need to help him sharply back into everyone's mind, though he stubbornly refused the various offers of assistance. Woorawa rushed off to collect the makings for Tan's hospital bed, as he described it, and Mr B left in a slightly different direction for the same purpose.

Kieran, Rhys and Tan paused at the grassy verge to drink in the beauty of the pool, the waterfall and the lush green ferns growing along the base of the rock face. Some ordinary drinking took place next, with Kieran and Rhys relaying cupped double-handfuls of water to Tan. When the hospital bed was finished to Woorawa's satisfaction the interrupted healing session went ahead and, according to Tan's watch, lasted for 20 minutes.

"Are you ready to sleep, Tan?"

"No, I'm starving."

That was a reaction which surprised everyone.

"Well, too bad. When you wake we'll have that fixed."

At the agreed command from Kieran, Tan's eyes closed and he slept like a log for an hour and a half. Meanwhile the food routine swung into action and Kieran and Rhys went downstream with Woorawa to a section of the creek where he'd seen some promising ripples. The customary call didn't work and there was a delay till a dark black shape ventured closer and Kieran could make contact.

"It must be a completely different species to the ones we usually catch, Woorawa, but now that I know this one I can sense plenty more."

The dramatic moments of catch and dispatch were quickly over and they returned to the unlit campfire with six plump black specimens. Mr B had cooking sticks and a supply of wood for the campfire which was quickly started. The cooking was held off, though, because Tan was so deeply asleep that, despite the group's hunger pains, no one wanted to wake him. Instead, everyone sat quietly and started to discuss what they should do next.

Kieran did have an interest in moving on, as it was still early afternoon and, now that Tan was properly healed, they could easily manage about three hours of travel and progress towards more information. Everyone else was keen to stay for now and make an early start in the morning. Mr B clinched that by pointing out that, apart from Tan's obvious need for sleep, everyone would benefit by relaxing after the trauma of all the Wall crossings.

Kieran's part in the discussion didn't last. After the non-stop tension and pressure of the morning this quiet time was so different he couldn't resist the seduction of letting his mind slow down and relax. The quietness registered and he blinked lazily at Woorawa, who he thought had been saying something.

"What?"

"What nothing. You've been quiet for the last few minutes and your eyes just closed. Order your own mind to go to sleep, Kieran."

Kieran's shoulders were grabbed by strong arms that pulled him so he was lying flat with his head resting comfortably on Rhys's chest.

A delicious smell woke him and the dream about one of Tan's special meals became reality with the large piece of skewered fish Woorawa was waving under his nose.

"Try this, Kieran. You won't believe how good it is. Tan's cooked it just right and the other fish taste like cardboard in comparison."

Kieran's stomach gurgled so loudly it made the chest his head was resting on jerk with Rhys's laughter.

"Get up, slug. I'm starving too and I've had the torture of watching Woorawa and Tan gutsing themselves while I couldn't move."

Kieran's mind registered surprise that he'd slept longer than Tan, but the first bite of the fish on the cooking stick made him forget everything else.

Woorawa was right. Kieran couldn't believe how good this was, and under the indulgent grins of the onlookers he finished every skerrick of the large fillet … and looked for more.

"We kept the other fillet from your fish out of Tan's greedy clutches, Kieran, but if you're still hungry after that we'll need another food expedition. Tan gobbled down the whole extra fish we brought back like a vacuum cleaner going berserk."

Tan grimaced with embarrassment as he acknowledged this. "Sorry, Kieran. When I woke up I was so hungry I just couldn't stop. Mr B thinks it must be because of the healing and he made me eat it all."

Mr B was nodding quite forcefully. "It makes sense, Kieran. Rhys makes the healing happen but that must be using resources which Tan's body knows it needs to replace. I think he's going to feel like he's starving for the next couple of days."

Kieran didn't say much for a few moments. He was too busy devouring the second fillet and wondering if this hunger was connected to all his own efforts for the day.

"Has anything happened while I was asleep?"

"A big animal like a deer came in and ate grass with the horses for a while, and another flock of joker birds came and checked us out, and then Mr B and I explored a little bit. We didn't go far while you weren't awake, but there's an overhang behind the waterfall and we sat on that rock ledge watching everything for a few minutes. It's a good place to jump into the pool."

They'd done more than that because a bigger supply of wood was stacked to one side, as well as a pile of grass and leaves for the night's makeshift mattresses. *Trust Woorawa to get everything organised.* Kieran examined the waterfall and the ledge. They did look interesting, and the jumping comment meant there were plans for a swim at some stage. George and the other two horses were chomping steadily, and a quick check showed they were relaxed and content.

"Did you end up making any plans?"

Woorawa and Rhys nodded, almost conspiratorially, as Mr B answered.

"We had to, Kieran. You flaked out when we'd hardly started, so we worked the plans out anyway. First thing is a full-on training session with the Spook cords. They're the only protection the rest of us have from any nasties or things you can't control with your mind and we really need to get confident using them. Rhys and Woorawa have worked out some ideas to try on each other."

"Each other? No way. Those things are horrible when they touch you."

"Well, you can regulate the amount of energy more precisely so they only have a tiny effect while we're training."

"It's obvious when a rope touches anyone, Rhys. We don't need the effect as well."

"We talked about that and we reckon it'll make it a big deal in our minds and force us to concentrate much harder on what we're doing. As long as you make it just a partial effect while we train."

Even a partial effect would make for riveted attention, not just focused, and simply reducing the amount of energy in each special pool was easy.

"You said first thing, Mr B. That means you've got other things planned as well?"

"Lots, Kieran. Woorawa wants a big session to practise all your new things and we also reckon it would be a good idea to send an eagle or some other bird on a scouting expedition some time before it gets dark. There's plenty of time for that later though, because after we've had a workout with the Spook ropes we all want to relax and have some fun in Rhys's pool."

"Rhys's pool?"

"Absolutely! His dreaming about it must have something to do with why we came here, so we've told him we're calling it Rhys's Pool. The whole setting is Rhys Glade … and that's Rhys Falls."

Rhys shook his head to say they were crazy, at the same time sporting one of his special happy grins. "I tried to spread it around, Kieran, by saying that the yummy fish should be called Tan-fish, but Woorawa's got a fixation on word sounds from somewhere and reckons Rhys-fish sounds better. Then I tried their own logic and called the tree where they found the fruit a Mr-B-tree, but that wasn't good enough either."

Smiling and finishing a giant mouthful of fish didn't work together, so it took a few seconds for Kieran to respond.

"You found fruit?"

Rhys pointed to some dark brown objects next to Woorawa, who picked one up and passed it over.

"Mr B found them. There are a few trees down the creek a bit, but we're not game to eat them because none of them seem to have been touched by birds or any other animals."

"They look like figs, except round."

"They feel soft too, but they're different inside."

The specimen Kieran was holding was smaller and rounder than an apple and easily broke apart to reveal bright yellow flesh streaked with lines of small black seeds. He lifted it to his nose for a smell test.

"It's a new smell, that's for sure. Did anyone try tasting it?"

"You've got to be kidding, Kieran. If the birds don't touch it there must be a reason. We thought you could show it to the joker birds and learn from their reaction."

Of course. Kieran nodded his agreement then went back to the serious business of finishing his second big fish fillet.

*   *   *

"Try an underhand cast like this, Tan. It comes as more of a surprise and might suit you more than full overarm. Practise the wrist flick we showed you all the time too."

Kieran watched with total concentration and, along with Tan and Mr B, made his own effort at the underarm flick. Twice he'd been caught off guard, and three times there'd been no way to dodge the muscle-jarring Spook cords that Rhys and Woorawa were continually casting at them. Figuring how to reduce the paralysing effect to an unpleasant tingling sensation instead of instant helplessness had been as straightforward as Kieran had expected, and after a few minutes of very careful trial and error with Rhys and Woorawa, they'd agreed on the level Rhys wanted everyone to work with.

Tan's shoulder was quickly forgotten after a few minutes of activity showed it was working quite normally. Everyone's attention turned to Rhys's demands. They'd started, quite straightforwardly, by practising different types of casts and flicks, then added the element of accuracy by targeting pieces of wood Rhys had set out. Everyone got serious then, because he ranged Kieran, Tan and Mr B against himself and Woorawa, and instead of targeting lumps of wood they were now after each other. His instructions had become steadily more and more complex and the concentration involved in attacking, dodging and coordinating with everyone's own team was more than overwhelming.

This pause for Tan's personal coaching was a real relief for Kieran, because recharging the energy each time a cord touched someone meant squeezing in an extra bit of concentration every time it happened. Rhys demonstrated the underhand cast, got Woorawa to do the same, then watched carefully while Tan had a try.

"That's good, Tan. Flick your wrist even more strongly and you'll be perfect. Is everything okay? You're not as zippy as you were when we started."

"Yes, I just got lazy. Watch this."

The wrist flick was strong and the Spook rope snaked accurately towards a large piece of wood, but the watching didn't happen because everyone else was checking each other's reaction to what Tan had just said. As far as Kieran was concerned, 'lazy' and 'Tan' were mutually exclusive concepts. Mr B stepped in.

"It's time to coil up the ropes and relax. Kieran and Rhys, give Tan a healing check to make sure he really is okay and then our next hour is free time to do whatever we like. We'll have another practice later, Rhys, because it's so important, but we've been on the go and serious all day and it's only sensible to take a break while we have the opportunity."

Rhys dropped his Spook rope on the spot and rushed to Tan's side with a look of concern which didn't go away till the healing routine showed everything was good and all he'd needed was an energy boost. Mr B continued.

"Give Tan one of those boosts every half-hour. I suspect he's going to need them, and you'll need them too, Kieran. I can't imagine the pressure you've been under to do the things you've done today. Your long sleep tells me it's more than you realise yourself." A big smile appeared. "This is your teacher speaking. Follow orders! Wipe that cheeky grin off your face, Woorawa. I'm talking to you too. Rhys had a break while he looked after Kieran, but you explored and practised all the rope moves and gathered supplies without stopping, so you're going to take it easy too."

The cheeky grins were all round now, of course, but the seed of sense in Mr B's words was falling on very fertile ground.

The hour became two by unspoken consent. The first half-hour was an almost obligatory lazy time of dozing and quietly watching the play of water as it cascaded down the rock face then fell through the air and churned the pool with a mini maelstrom of bubbles and roiling surface. After Mr B's orders, what else? Half an hour was enough for Woorawa though, and he went to the side of the pool, stripped off, and leapt in. The yell of exhilaration at the shock of contact with the cool water disrupted the air of laziness in an instant.

"He's an idiot!"

"It's not that cold, is it?"

"What's he doing now?"

Dark buttocks swished sideways, back and forth, while the rest of Woorawa's body stayed underwater.

"He's mooning us, Tan."

"It looks rude—two little black hills poking out of the water."

Kieran burst out laughing, and this set everyone else off.

"It wasn't that funny."

"Black hills! It was the way you said it, Tan."

Woorawa surfaced for a breath, waved crazily with both hands and disappeared, now completely under the water.

"Now what?"

"He's heading for the waterfall. See, he's gliding like a giant Rhys-fish."

A dark-skinned face appeared through the shimmering curtain of the waterfall and a series of calls whooped loud and happy across the water.

"Oh my God! He's totally crazy."

This was the kind of craziness Rhys couldn't resist and, a few seconds later, Tan watched a second set of clothes get dumped in the pile beside Woorawa's. Kieran and Mr B watched too, and then laughter returned at the second great yell of immersion and the following copycat mooning.

"So, now we've got white hills. I think you should join them, Tan, so we end up with a multicoloured mountain range."

"Nude? You want me to go in there and put my end up without anything on?"

Mr B laughed. "I didn't say that on purpose, Tan, but it couldn't have been more appropriate. Of course you'll be swimming nude. It's the rule for the day."

Kieran was a bit surprised at this from Mr B, but quickly added his own encouragement. "Yes, it *is* the rule for the day and you have to do a stripper dance for us too."

Tan's dubious look was interrupted by the double barrel of yells coming from the pool where Woorawa and Rhys were having a great water fight. Tan's look instantly changed to calculation.

"If I do the striptease I get immunity from being splashed to death."

"You're a wuss, Tan."

"No, I'm not, Mr B. I'm sensible, and I'm waiting for Kieran to agree."

Kieran hadn't really expected Tan to do a muck-around striptease, but if a simple nod meant he'd go ahead, then a simple nod he'd get.

The act went ahead and was a total showstopper. The yells and activities in the pool paused, and Kieran and Mr B watched with delight and amazement. Rhys and Woorawa stirred for the rest of the day about hidden talents and kept asking Tan if he had any other secrets. There was a lot more merriment round the campfire later when Rhys proclaimed it wasn't all that unusual because *everyone* experimented with stuff like that in front of a mirror in the privacy of their bedroom.

The water was quite cool and Kieran gave his own yell when he surfaced from a "get it over with entry" rather than Tan's steady acclimatisation method.

The peaceful beauty of the setting was broken with happy sounds of laughter and activity till Tan announced that, besides feeling hungry again, he needed another rest. Mr B went with him, and Kieran followed, because having a rest was definitely a good idea.

Rhys and Woorawa happily taunted them that they'd won the wuss test with flying colours, and then proved their own rugged hardiness by staying in for all of five extra minutes.

Tan's eyes were well and truly closed by then and everyone else sat contemplating the rebuilt campfire with a soft murmur of conversation. Kieran was starting to drift off himself when Woorawa tapped him on the shoulder and pointed to the horses.

"Look, Kieran. Two of the big deer animals just came out of the trees. I wonder if they'll talk to the horses like the first one did?"

Kieran's drowsiness disappeared. He'd missed the earlier visitor because he'd been asleep and he'd been intrigued by the description of how tame it had been. He started to make a mind connection then decided to watch for a while first.

Sure enough, with heads raised alertly, both animals looked around the clearing as if making an inspection, then ambled towards the horses who also had their heads raised, watching these newcomers with interest. George nickered and nodded his head a few times—maybe it was tossing his mane—then stood nose to nose while a strange whiffling noise whispered across the clearing.

"Wow! You were right, Woorawa. It really does look like they're talking."

"Well, communicating, and they're just as relaxed as the first one was, even when Mr B and I were walking around."

"I don't think we've registered with them yet. Put another stick on the fire so they see the movement and know we're here."

Woorawa turned toward the woodpile, then stopped because the nose to nose act was interrupted as two heads lifted and stared.

"They've definitely seen us now, Kieran. Can you control them so they don't run away?"

"They're not going to run away. That's the same curious look the joker birds gave us."

As if to prove his point, both animals gave a parting whiffle and trotted quite confidently towards the campfire.

Kieran gasped with pleasure at the close-up whiffling sound as a moist nose nuzzled against his welcoming hand, then gasped again, with surprise and pure delight, as a long wet tongue rasped a friendly greeting across his cheek.

The process repeated with the second animal then, without a pause, they trotted back to the company of the horses and lowered their heads to munch grass.

Mr B, Woorawa and Rhys had huge grins.

"They did that all by themselves didn't they, Kieran? I mean, you didn't tell them to be friendly, did you?"

Kieran wiped the side of his face and looked at his hand before answering. "That was amazing. I didn't know a tongue could feel so nice."

Mr B spoke up with an undisguised twinkle in his eyes.

"I'm surprised, Kieran. You'll have to practise with Rhys tonight."

Rhys goggled at this and coloured up as his mouth opened to make a retort then closed again to hold his words in.

"It was nothing from me, Mr B. I held back from going into their minds because I wanted to see if they'd act the same as the one that came when I was asleep."

"King of the animals again, just like in the Grampians. And the joker birds came to you first too. You should make contact, Kieran, so you can call them if you ever need to. And you'll always know when any of them are near us too."

"Good thinking, Rhys."

Kieran looked across the clearing, did his mental reach, then grinned at Rhys. "All they're thinking about is how good the grass tastes, and … wow! Four more are coming from different directions."

Woorawa looked all around. "How far, Kieran? Can you tell, like with the eagles?"

Kieran concentrated and then answered. "I haven't worked with them enough. All I get is a sense that the grass is close."

"I bet they all come and lick you before they start eating. I can hear some joker birds over that way, Kieran. Can you call them and check the fruit?"

Kieran nodded and stood up. "Bring the fruit, Woorawa. The joker birds will be too noisy for Tan if I call them here."

The joker birds met them at a spot about fifty metres downstream from the pool and alighted on shoulders, heads and outstretched arms with their constant display of mischievous bobbing heads.

"Show them the fig things and I'll ask them if they want some food."

Every crest drew tightly in, and with squawks of outrage the little flock flew to the nearest tree.

"Oh boy! Just as well we didn't have a taste. Their minds all say danger and death. Your theory about why the fruit wasn't touched was exactly right."

"Why are you shaking your head, Woorawa?"

"They've just spoiled our theory that this place is Rhys's dream turned real. Everything else he wished for is here."

"So are the fruit trees." Kieran and Woorawa turned and went back to the pool.

"That fruit is definitely poisonous, so we can't rely on the wish theory. I was kind of hoping that if we thought strongly enough about going home the next time we go through the Wall it might take us there. What does everyone else think?"

Mr B replied first. "Our theory must have something to it, Woorawa. It certainly explains the times we returned to Dead World. It was definitely the strongest thing in our minds each time we entered the Wall till Rhys changed our thinking. The dream world part seems a bit much though. I don't think any of us imagined all these new animal and plants at the moment when we moved into the Wall. My own theory is that this place is real and the Wall sent us to the closest approximation of the ideas in our minds it could manage."

"That works even better … except it might be the ideas in Kieran's mind that count and not what the rest of us are thinking. Everything happens through him really."

Kieran laughed. "So all this is my fault, Woorawa?"

"No way! Mr B's right about it not being a dream world, because of all the things that happened before we got carried away from home. Someone started all this, so it's their fault, not yours."

Kieran laughed again. "Rhys is the one they keep going for, so it's his fault not mine."

Rhys put on a fake offended look. "Thanks very much. Monsters and walls and poisonous fruit, it's all my fault, except I feel like I'm in the middle of the most unbelievable dream ever. I can't make up my mind if I want to wake up or keep on dreaming to see what crazy thing's going to happen next."

Woorawa gave him a friendly whack on the arm. "Hey! This is my dream, not yours, and right now I'm dreaming that you are telling me I'm part of your dream."

Kieran was so taken with this that he couldn't resist extending it. "And my dream is that Woorawa's dreaming that Rhys is dreaming about him."

Mr B shook his head. "Stop! Stop! My brain's going in circles trying to follow that. I've heard of mass hallucinations but never of mass dreaming … What are we going to do tomorrow, Kieran, continue travelling in search of information or try Woorawa's suggestion of entering the Wall again while we think strong thoughts about going home?"

Without hesitation, Kieran pointed back to the campfire. "Tan's not ready for the Wall, so we'll keep to our exploring plan and see what happens with that before even thinking about facing the Wall again."

Everyone nodded. Kieran had just spoken with the command tone he sometimes used, and they all agreed anyway. Tan missed the Spook rope practice that followed, but he woke when Kieran, Rhys and Woorawa arrived at the campfire with a new supply of the delicious, fat Rhys-fish for their evening meal. He then wanted to know what had been happening and why he hadn't been roused.

"You're awake now, Tan, so you can make up for missing out on your practice with slave driver Rhys by cooking these fish to perfection. The only thing you really missed was seeing Kieran get his face licked six times."

Tan blinked a few times while he tried to figure what Woorawa might be talking about. "Licked? Was Rhys mucking around?"

Rhys grunted in protest and pointed to the three deer creatures still in the clearing. "Not me, Tan. Every time one of them arrived they came over to the campfire and licked Kieran's face. We think it's their way of greeting someone special."

This was Tan's first sighting of the visitors and he stared, intrigued, till Rhys started fussing about how hungry he was.

After they'd finished eating there was a general discussion for about half an hour, but then Woorawa took charge and made Kieran practise every ability he'd developed so far. This involved everyone with the usual effort of fighting against the Medusa look and then a great deal of discussion about what happened with the Wall crossings, the monsters and the healing effort. It was well over an hour of serious concentration before they finished and he asked for Tan's pocketknife. Rhys stoked the fire and everyone watched curiously while Woorawa experimentally tapped various pieces of wood together then broke them into suitable lengths and whittled the surfaces smooth.

"Sound sticks for our show, Mr B. They'll help us chant and sing while we dance."

"We're dancing?"

"You can just watch and enjoy if you're feeling tired, Tan, but you still have to help with your rhythm sticks."

Tan *was* tired, but he joined in anyway when Woorawa's lead became too exciting to resist.

The basic steps and chants they already knew built and built under Woorawa's guidance to an inspiring re-enactment of Rhys's epic battle with the monster.

Chapter 4

Kieran wondered why Woorawa and Tan wanted to stop again and leaned forward to rub George's neck while they caught up.

Their early start this morning had gone to schedule because an eager Woorawa had woken everyone and got things moving. Kieran and Tan had both complained that a couple more hours of sleep would be nice, but that had fallen on deaf ears and for half an hour now they'd been following the trail as it made its way through verdant trees and down the gentle slope of the beautiful valley they'd entered only a few minutes after setting off.

"What have you found this time?"

"Nothing really, Kieran. It's just that the track dips down into that stand of extra tall trees and I thought if we spent a quarter of an hour to climb up that rock face we might get a better idea of what's ahead."

Kieran considered for a moment then shook his head. "We'd better keep going, Woorawa. It looks too interesting and we'd end up staying longer than we mean to."

The trees closed in and for a while the overarching branches gave Kieran the feeling they were travelling through a living tunnel, and every now and again the group paused to drink in the atmosphere. Eventually the trees changed and the whole aspect opened when the trail entered a large clearing. Kieran's balance faltered when George's head went down to sniff at the grass, and that was a good signal for a short stop.

"Okay, we'll stretch our legs while the eating machines have a go at the grass."

Everyone dismounted and Woorawa looked across to the right. "Let's check the creek. I reckon it might have grown."

Kieran started walking and, almost as an afterthought, called on the opal to make a monster check. Regular checks ever since yesterday's Wall crossing had led them to believe the monsters were a Dead World phenomenon, so a purple flash registering in his mind was a terrible shock.

"THERE'S A MONSTER COMING!"

Four disbelieving looks changed instantly to the actions they'd planned as part of Rhys's whip practice and everyone rushed to collect their Spook ropes.

"How long, Kieran? Is there enough time to look for shelter or a hiding place?"

"No! Run for the trees. We can't stay here."

Kieran grabbed George and the other two horses and, with iron control, sent them racing to where the clearing ended while he ran with everyone else towards the limited protection the trees would provide.

They didn't make it.

A piercing, angry scream sounded overhead as the monster overshot their position then reversed direction with thundering wing beats. The five companions ranged fearfully towards it, holding their Spook ropes ready and staring in horror at the malevolent creature which was landing, surprisingly, some twenty metres in front of them. Jaws agape in a show of deadly intent, it stepped towards them and …

… unbelievably …

… stopped.

Kieran, reaching despairingly for some kind of contact, felt something. This was a different monster. It looked the same but it wasn't mindless. The moment of hope was dashed when the normal method of control worked… but was then brushed effortlessly aside by a surge of pure anger. In his peripheral vision, Kieran saw Rhys take a step forward and raise his arm in readiness to lash with his Spook rope.

The monster swivelled away and, with its wings beating so powerfully the blasts of air rocked the five companions, launched skyward with renewed screams of challenge and rage.

The friends shared this amazing reprieve with a moment of astonishment and disbelief before returning their gaze to the frightening sight of three more monsters plummeting from the sky. New screams of anger and rage clashed against old as the first new arrival collided in a mid-air maelstrom of lunging beaks, talons and gouging claws. In a cloud of feathers the first attacker dropped away and fell, screaming, almost twenty metres to the ground. The remaining newcomers now attacked with ferocity, one engaging from the front while the other attached its great claws and talons to the back, its beak ripping into the neck in front of it.

The initial monster's efforts to stay aloft were overborne by the weight on its back and the interference from in front, and the battle descended to the ground where, despite its raging resistance, death came relentlessly. Two powerful heads lifted to the sky to scream success. The third raised from the ground with a weakly echoed version.

The stunned onlookers watched with renewed trepidation as the victory call ceased and the triumphant monsters' attention turned. Kieran's despair that resistance to such power and purpose was beyond them changed to astonishment when the fierce aspect of two penetrating gazes was replaced with a bobbing-head motion of apparent recognition. Understanding exploded in his mind and he reached, not for the monster pattern but for the flesh-and-blood pattern of any normal bird or animal. The link flared into place and Kieran dropped his Spook rope and grabbed Rhys's arm in a hold of utter relief.

"They've come to protect us. They're as friendly as the joker birds and the deer creatures. They're … they're amazing."

The four wondering looks didn't last because the two great creatures bounded with ungainly leaps to their wounded companion. Two heads touched, preened against the bloodied neck, then were once again raised to the sky, this time with piercing calls of distress. Kieran reached again, this time to the wounded creature, and his grip on Rhys's arm tightened involuntarily as understanding, then sadness started tears welling from his eyes.

A strong shake brought him back to Rhys.

"What's happening, Kieran? You look awful."

Kieran wrenched his mind from the wave of emotion and his grip changed to a tug as he started running.

"He's the leader, Rhys, and his mind's giving us a welcome to this country at the same time he's saying goodbye. He's going to die unless we help him."

Rhys didn't say anything. Kieran was looking just as sad and determined as yesterday when Tan was hurt, so, despite the fearsome aspect of the creatures they were approaching, he ran faster. Two great heads, beaks open and keening, turned to watch the oncoming rush. The beaks closed and the sad keening stopped, as if in surprise, when, held by Kieran, Rhys's hands were pressed against the now inert head. Rhys watched Kieran's signature blue glow cover their hands and spread till all three of them were spectacularly enveloped. He saw tension and then perspiration appear on Kieran's face.

"Kieran, look after yourself! If you flake, we can't do anything."

Kieran looked at Rhys almost vaguely, he was concentrating so much, and the strained look reduced.

"Transfer one hand at a time to that chest wound. We have to stop any more blood from flowing out."

For a moment Rhys was shocked. Touching the horrible gash meant pushing his hands against either the mess of red saturated feathers or the torn and mutilated flesh of the open wound. Well, too bad. Blood would wash off and Kieran was asking. The reach from head to chest was a stretch but the transfer was made and, with red oozing between the fingers of one hand and the slippery feel of torn muscle under the other, Rhys marvelled as warmth built and the flesh quivered. Before his eyes, the wound changed, the welling blood stopped, and tissue started to knit. Kieran gave a grunt of sudden concentration.

"Press the sides of the wound together while they mend, Rhys. It has to be hands because we can't do stitches."

"Kieran, can you turn the blue off? It's so bright I can't see properly."

The light instantly disappeared and the first hint of a smile appeared.

"Sorry! The opal's working overtime and I always forget about it. You're amazing, Rhys. You've stopped the main blood loss and the biggest flow of healing at the moment is going to some sort of organ. When you've closed this gash we'll start on the talon wounds. I think he's going to be all right."

Rhys glanced at the great head resting limp on the ground and couldn't see any difference. He didn't dwell on it though, because holding the wound edges firm required a steady hand and lots of attention. The worst gash was longer than his own arm and half an hour later, when the wound was fully closed, Rhys asked for a break. Kieran shook his head.

"Not yet. He still needs us."

Rhys jolted when a burst of wellbeing filled every part of his body and he suddenly became aware of the surrounding situation. The other two creatures were crouched motionless, watching silently with their wings half spread, while Tan and Mr B were sitting a few metres away, also watching. Woorawa was in the distance with George and the other horses.

"Kieran, Tan woke up after only a few minutes. Are you sure everything's working all right?"

"Tan had concussion and some breaks. This was much worse and I'm keeping him in a kind of healing trance so he doesn't move and tear anything open again."

"Like an anaesthetic?"

"I guess … Put your hands on that talon wound. Once we've done those I think we can wake him up."

The talon wounds were everywhere, in sets of three or four and, under Kieran's guidance, Rhys held the sides of each gash or puncture for a few minutes while heat built and flesh quivered and renewed.

"Why's it so fast, Kieran?

"I don't know and it's puzzling me. The opal energy's transferring from you to the damaged places a lot faster than it did with Tan and it's more effective as well. We'll stop for a while, Rhys, when we've fixed that ripped place under his wing. I think …"

Kieran rested his head against the broad chest and said nothing else. Rhys stared in surprise then yelled for Mr B.

"Quick. I think he's flaked out. What will we do?"

Mr B checked. "He's not unconscious, Rhys. He's asleep. Rest your hands on his temples and see if that does anything, then I think we should just make him comfortable and leave him to wake up naturally. Remember how tired he was all yesterday after Tan was healed? This is the same except he's done a lot more."

Rhys looked at his messy red hands, gave them a quick wipe on his shirt, then rested them on Kieran's cheeks and forehead for a few seconds. He felt a fleeting tingle, then nothing except an impression that every-thing was all right. He lifted Kieran's head from its collapsed position and manoeuvred it to the comfortable support of his lap. Two majestic heads lowered. They still looked fearsome, but knowing their friendly intention changed that perception. They touched beaks against the head of their sleeping leader and then gently against Kieran. Four huge eyes regarded Rhys from disconcertingly close and, not knowing what else to do, he started talking.

"They're both asleep. They're all right but they both need to rest before we do anything else. Kieran will know what to do when he wakes up, but he's worn out. We'll have to wait. I hope you can be patient because he mightn't wake up for a long time."

The two heads lifted, as if in response, and with wings half open in what looked like a protective stance, settled to a quiet vigil. Mr B took over tending Kieran while Rhys went with Woorawa and Tan to clean up as best they could in the creek. The water bubbling merrily over its stony bed was just a minute's walk away.

"Strip off, Rhys. The blood's already dry so I hope it hasn't set too much to wash clean. Give Tan your shirt and I'll do your jeans while you clean your hands and face. We'll start a fire to dry everything out while we wait for Kieran to wake up."

Rhys paused from rubbing his hands in a sandy patch in the rocks. "How? We can't start a fire without him."

"Uncle Burrimul's told me what to do, so we'll try that. Wash your hair too, Rhys. There are patches where you rubbed it."

After the clean-up, Mr B insisted on staying with Kieran. Rhys sat next to the fire, which had taken a great deal of trial and effort to start. He wondered how long Kieran would stay asleep. The biggest drama was watching one of the Griffins, as he'd labelled them, launch into flight and leave soon after they got the fire going, and their following discussion about why it was leaving. Rhys's jeans were just reaching the stage of being dry enough to wear comfortably when Woorawa pointed to the sky.

"Wow! Look! It's back and it's carrying something."

Woorawa raced to where the Griffin landed, and a few minutes later he was back at the fire puzzling how to dress two rabbit-like creatures with Tan's pocketknife for cooking.

"I wish Kieran was awake to say thank you. They must be very intelligent to associate a fire with food. I wonder if it means they understand we might have to stay here for a while. Tan, the knife's getting blunt. Is it okay to sharpen it on a bit of rock? We'll have to be careful not to wear it down too quickly, but I need it sharp enough to skin these creatures properly."

Time passed and, just when Tan was sampling one of the creatures he'd been patiently rotating over the fire on a skewer stick, there was a soft call and a wave from Mr B which sent Rhys and Woorawa rushing over.

"He's been stirring and restless for the last few minutes. I think we can wake him up."

Mr B was whispering, unsure if he was right. Rhys went ahead anyway and grabbed Kieran's nose while poking him in the stomach.

"Slug! Wake up, slug!"

Kieran's eyes jerked open and his head twisted away from the grip on his nose. "What's happening?"

"You flaked out and Mr B made us let you sleep. You've been slacking for ages while we've done everything else. Tan's got some roast meat ready in case you're hungry."

"Hungry?"

Kieran sat up and took in the concerned looks. Full awareness returned and he instantly reached for the mind of the huge body beside of him

"Quick, Rhys. Healing hands on his head so I can work out what to do."

"What about you first, Kieran? You flaked out, so you mightn't be ready yet."

"Flaked out? Really?"

"Yes! Like a light switch turning off in the middle of a sentence."

Kieran paused, grabbed Rhys's hands, and pressed them to his temple. "I'm all right, just tired … and starving. Put your hands on Krol."

"He's got a name?"

"Of course, and the others are Kron and Kan."

Rhys's hands moved and Kieran concentrated. "He needs more healing, but not desperately. He needs food … and he needs water even more."

There was a call and one of the Griffins launched skyward.

"Kron's gone to hunt. Cooked meat's no good. How are we going to get water for him? We'll have to carry it from the creek in our mouths."

He looked across to where Tan was watching from beside the fire.

"Tan too. Our own cooking will have to wait—"

Woorawa interrupted. "Kieran, look at the size of him! We'll need about twenty mouthfuls each."

"It's the only way we can carry water, so what else can we do? He needs it right now, Woorawa. I think it's because of all the blood he lost before Rhys closed the wounds. Rhys, you'd better stay here while I wake him up. He might need some special healing."

Woorawa and Mr B collected Tan, who was a bit disconcerted about what to do with the almost cooked meat, and they rushed towards the creek while Kieran directed Rhys to rest his hands against the great head lying dormant on the ground.

"I want to give him an energy boost to help him wake up, Rhys."

"This could be dangerous. What if he panics and lashes out in a kind of reflex to defend himself before he knows what's happening?"

Kieran paused then turned to concentrate on the attendant Griffin. "Whoa! Kan says you're right and he's given me permission to take control of Krol's muscles while I explain what we've done. I'll have to wake him up very slowly and carefully."

"Permission?"

"Yes. Like I do with you. I'll explain later."

A quiver of movement started under Rhys's hands and continued for a long minute till two giant eyes snapped open. The look was so powerful Rhys couldn't help jerking nervously away.

Kieran laughed. "Don't worry, Rhys. Krol says he's hungry enough, but he won't eat one of his flock."

Rhys's expression made Kieran laugh again.

"I told him how your hands saved him. It's his way of saying thank you."

"I'm in his flock?"

Kieran concentrated before replying. "Only if you want to be. He hopes you'll accept and take a flight with him." Kieran laughed for the third time, then, turning at the sound of Woorawa, Mr B and Tan approaching, got his concentration look again. Krol's head twisted skyward and his beak gaped open to receive the first mouthful of water from Woorawa. Mr B and Tan followed and then the beak closed.

"Krol says thank you. Rhys, you can help collect water now. I'll help next time. We're still communicating."

Rhys jogged off with the others and paused at the campfire while Woorawa collected the skins he'd so painstakingly stripped from the two rabbit creatures.

"I knew we could use them somehow, though I was thinking more of moccasins than water carriers."

Quick experimentation at the creek showed the pliable skins could hold far more than a single mouthful. Thank goodness, because even with this greater efficiency the water-carrying exercise continued for almost a quarter of an hour, and there were interruptions every time Kron dropped another rabbit creature into the clearing, since they had to pause while Kan ripped the animal apart and dropped the pieces into Krol's voracious maw. Eventually, Kieran proclaimed that Krol's immediate needs had been met and he was going back into a healing sleep.

"Tan, is any of our cooked meat ready to eat? I'm so hungry I could almost eat the raw stuff that's been disappearing into Krol's mouth."

"Well, I hope you like it crispy, Kieran. It was ready ages ago. I'll see what I can do."

Krol was put back into the healing sleep and, after he'd eaten far more than his share of the well-cooked meat, Kieran did the same for himself. His half-hearted complaint two hours later that he'd asked to be woken after one hour was countered by Mr B who said that two hours actually *was* after one hour, and there was no point in complaining because he'd obviously needed it. Meanwhile, the clearing had been a hive of activity, and after devouring two more of the rabbit creatures Kron was continually stockpiling, the business of setting up for an overnight stay went ahead. Kan was crouched quietly beside Krol's sleeping form, watching alertly as the stock of firewood grew. The companions gathered fern and grass for bed material too, and then settled George and the other horses. Before he'd gone to sleep, Kieran had called the horses to meet Kan, and after a short skittish moment the group had been astonished at their seemingly instant and matter-of-fact acceptance of the situation.

Woorawa and Rhys spent a lot of time examining the remains of the dead monster with a mixture of wonder at the dimensions, which, by Woorawa's measurement of over five metres from head to tail, made it even bigger than the Griffins, and puzzlement at the strangely rapid decay of the wings and some other sections of the body.

"I wish Kieran was awake to have a look at this."

"He won't get much of a chance, Woorawa. If we have another healing session like he's planned he'll be so tired we'll hardly see him till tomorrow morning. Helping Tan really zonked him, so we might have to stay here all day tomorrow to make sure he's okay. I'm going to make him go to sleep as soon he's eaten."

"And we'll share our night watch without him. Rhys, help me move this leg. I've got Tan's pocketknife so I can cut some of the tendons off. I want to try joining the animal skins together to make carrying water for the Griffin easier."

"Yuck! I don't trust this thing, especially the strange way it's rotting. Use tendons from the rabbit creatures, Woorawa."

"Try using your Spook rope on it and see if that makes it dissolve like the one in Dead World did."

"Kieran's asleep and it won't be charged if anything else happens."

"We've still got seven others and the Griffin for protection. Kieran said Kan's not going anywhere."

"I suppose."

Rhys undid his belt to release the Spook rope he now always carried, rather than leaving it clicked in place on George's saddle, and flicked it to rest against the least grizzly part of the giant cadaver with the sense of command Kieran had taught them. Nothing happened.

"I think they only work on live things."

Everyone whirled to where Kron was landing with a rush of powerfully beating wings.

"Two more rabbit creatures? That's fourteen of them now. I wonder when he's going to stop?"

"Not yet, Rhys. We'll probably use three or four of them just for us and he needs enough for Kan and himself after Krol's eaten as much as he wants."

And, sure enough, after checking on Krol's sleeping form and communicating with a series of their strange keening calls, Kron launched into the air again.

"Come on! Help me skin two more of these things and we'll have a try at joining them together."

When Kieran woke and finished more complaining about sleeping for too long he was stuffed with helpings of delicious roast meat and taken to a suitable section of the creek to call up half a dozen big fat Rhys-fish to add some variety to their main meal, before being allowed to settle with Krol and Rhys for the planned healing session. Half an hour later, Rhys forced a stop by informing Kieran that he was going to remove his hands.

"You've done too much, Kieran. I know you want to keep going, but I'm not letting you. Krol's out of danger, and you're wrecked, so you'll have to wait till tomorrow morning. Tell him I'm sorry but we have to look after you too."

Kieran drew a breath to start arguing the point, but then a weary grin of agreement broke through. "Yes, boss! I think you're right. My head nearly flopped on Krol's neck a moment ago, and getting an energy boost isn't working properly. Hang on while I tell him we're stopping early."

Krol's head lifted then stretched to select from the conveniently placed pile of rabbit creatures. Rhys watched sixteen carcasses disappear into the lunging mouth and called for the two waterskins Woorawa had so pains-takingly devised by pushing tendons through carefully spaced puncture holes and then knotting them as tight as possible. Water dripped out, but with an estimated three litres arriving with each trip from the creek it was left for Mr B to tend to Krol's water needs while Woorawa, Rhys and Tan took Kieran on a quick trip to call yet another supply of fat Rhys-fish.

Back at the campfire everyone helped with the serious but enjoyable business of cooking, first for Kieran, who was weary enough to accept being waited on, and then for their own needs. Mr B joined them when Krol stopped drinking and, after eating a big chunk of the meat Tan had ready, started cooking his own fish fillet.

"He's only interested in eating the rabbit creatures now, Kieran. I made three water trips, so that means it's taken about ten litres to stop him feel-ing thirsty. Are you going to put him to sleep again?"

Three Griffin heads turned and Kieran's eyes widened.

"Yes, but not just yet. They seem to be saying they're going to shield us from getting wet. It must be going to rain."

"Rain? Well, I suppose it has to some time or everything wouldn't be so green. When we finish eating we'd better look for some bigger pieces of wood to make sure the fire keeps going. Are you sure they mean rain, Kieran? The sky's clear in every direction."

"It's not like talking, Woorawa. I have to work out what they are think-ing and feeling … Wow! They're going to completely cover us with their wings. I'm getting it from all of them … They really think rain's coming … Look for the big logs, Woorawa. While you do that we'll push all the bedding stuff into one pile."

Half an hour later, a bank of cloud, which was progressively blotting the surrounding hills from view, moved overhead and a soft misty rain started falling. As he drifted off to sleep, Kieran relaxed and smiled at the wonder in the eyes of his companions huddled close on top of their pile of fern and grass bedding with three outspread and overlapping Griffin wings making a completely rain-proof shelter.

*   *   *

A dig in the ribs woke Kieran and his eyes opened to Rhys's happy grin and the somewhat puzzling view of bright blue sky.

"Come on, slug! Everyone's finished breakfast and it's time to get moving. Kron's been hunting, and Kan and Krol went to the creek with us to have a drink."

Kieran jerked up to a sitting position. "It's morning?"

"It won't be if you go to sleep again. Everyone's been up for about three hours."

He gave Kieran a searching look and then a little nod. "You look good." A huge grin spread across his features. "Well, you always look good, but you know what I mean. We've got a special treat for your breakfast."

Kieran made a dash to the nearest clump of bushes and returned to the glowing campfire and lots of morning greetings.

"Where's Woorawa?"

Tan looked at his watch. "Exploring! He'll be back in ten or fifteen minutes. What do you want for breakfast, Kieran? Fish or grilled meat?"

Neither was being cooked, so Tan's slightly off-centre look meant it must be some kind of trick question.

"Make that bacon and eggs and a bowl of fruit, please. Did anything happen last night?"

Tan started scraping the coals and Mr B answered.

"Two hours of non-stop rain, Kieran, then it completely cleared and we were visited by lots of the deer creatures. The creek started rushing loudly and we wondered if the clearing would get flooded, but that's died down a lot now. Part of the fire survived all the wet somehow and Woorawa and Rhys built it up again, then we sat around it while Woorawa told us one of his Dreamtime stories."

Kieran sent a questioning thought to the Griffins and smiled with satisfaction when their heads turned. *Amazing!* Krol was vastly improved and just as alert as Kron and Kan. Tan had just scooped half a dozen blackened shapes from the coals though, so he returned his attention.

"What's this?"

"Breakfast. It's unreal. Kan fished a few out and showed us how to find them."

He transferred the shapes to a flat rock and bashed them one by one with another rock before peeling away bits of broken shell. "Suck the flesh out, Kieran, and see if you like them as much as the rest of us do. Be careful it's not too hot though."

Kieran lifted the shape close to his nose for a sample smell then blew a few times to cool it. He sucked the hot flesh into his mouth then promptly turned and finished off all the rest.

"New food! And they're delicious. Are they hard to find?"

The all-round grins meant they'd been expecting this response. Tan dug in a different area of the coals and scraped out more of the tasty shellfish.

"They wedge themselves between rocks in the creek bed and Kan probed them out with his talons so we'd know what they look like. I thought they were just rocks, but Woorawa looked closely and worked out they were alive."

Kieran looked over to the Griffins again. "What else have they been doing?"

"Kron was hunting while the others went to the creek and Krol's been stretching his wings and flapping a bit. He hasn't tried flying though, so we're not sure if he's just not ready or if he needs more healing … and he's been eating everything Kron brings him."

Kieran finished his second round of shellfish, but before starting on anything else he made another trip to the privacy of the brush at the opposite side of the clearing to the creek for a rather imperative call of nature, then a trip to the creek for a wash and a drink.

"Have you worked out any plans for today, Kieran?"

"Just that I hope we can get moving again, Mr B, but we can't leave till we know Krol's okay. It can't be too long, but I'll need Rhys's healing hands to work that out. Krol's waiting for us now."

Kieran was touched when one by one the three Griffins pressed their beaks against his chest and rubbed gently up and down in a way he understood was a gesture of recognition and preening. When they did the same gesture to a wide-eyed Rhys, Kieran explained what it meant.

"It's special, Rhys. They're saying we're part of their flock. Rest your hands on Krol's head so we can find out how he is."

Krol's head lowered, in anticipation, to a convenient position and the double contact with Rhys and Kieran went ahead. The blue glow spread till Kieran thought to switch it off, and a feeling of satisfaction and achievement filled his mind.

"He doesn't really need any healing, Rhys. All he needs is more recovery time, so I've told him to stuff himself full of food and then I'll put him into the same kind of healing sleep we used yesterday. After a couple of hours we'll wake him and he should be ready."

"He's eaten everything Kron's been bringing, Kieran. He must be fairly full already."

Kieran concentrated and then laughed. "He is, but he's going to force down two more rabbit creatures."

Three giant Griffin heads bobbed and keened with their sounds of communication and after taking a few clearing steps, Kron launched purposefully skyward.

"More hunting?"

Kieran watched as powerful flapping changed to the more skilful gliding mode of flight. "No, I don't think so. I got a sense that he had some other purpose."

Krol's head and neck convulsed with the now-familiar gulping motion as he swallowed the last half of a torn carcass and then squatted in his resting position.

Rhys was impressed. "You say it's not talking, Kieran, but he sure understands you well enough."

Kieran reached with his mind and implanted the deep sleep command. "And it gets easier every time I connect."

The next few hours were very relaxed as far as Kieran was concerned. He wandered to the creek to have a look at how much extra water was flowing after the rain and then, after being shown what to look for, found a few of the shellfish creatures and, prompted by Woorawa and Mr B, clicked their pattern into his mind. Next, he spent some time with the horses, encouraging them to eat their fill and relax in preparation for a long afternoon of travel. He relaxed himself too, then sat by the campfire talking with the others while they waited till it was time to rouse Krol. They were all very curious about what it was like to communicate with the Griffins, Rhys most of all, with the prospect of Krol taking him flying strong on his mind.

"Did he say when, Kieran? It sounds fantastic, but I don't see how I can stay on."

"I know. His neck's far too big to put your arms around and there's nothing to grip except feathers. I'd ask Kan about it, but he's kind of resting in tune with Krol."

"Could you go in and find out things like you do with the eagles and the horses?"

"I could, but it doesn't work that way with the Griffins, Mr B. I was going to explain it to Rhys last night but all I did was sleep. They've got strong rules about anyone going into their minds and they have to be happy with your reason why before they give permission. The same as you all do really."

"Amazing! They must be a lot cleverer than other animals then. They certainly seem like they are, but having concepts like privacy and morality is a huge difference."

Kieran was startled and then puzzled. "You're right, Mr B, and I don't understand. They *are* more clever than George, but they're definitely not like people. When I made contact yesterday, these rules were there as part of the getting-through process and I just accepted them without thinking about it. I had to."

Mr B nodded thoughtfully, paused, then took a big breath before speaking. "Well! That raises other issues, Kieran. Have the Griffins come into *your* mind after asking permission from you?"

"No, I don't think they can."

"What about with each other? It's my impression that they communicate mostly with those keening sounds."

"They do. What are you getting at, Mr B?"

"If they have a structure in place for mind communication but don't use it themselves then someone must be using it with them."

"We know that someone can do that. They've been getting into our minds, or trying to, ever since everything started."

"Indeed, but they've never asked permission and that's very different, Kieran. I think it might be of vital importance to try to find out from the Griffins who talks to them. We need to know what's been happening to us, and someone who works cooperatively with them could be quite reasonable."

Rhys thought that was funny. "No one's not going to cooperate with a five-metre Griffin who can snap them in half with one bite."

"If they can take control like Kieran does, then it doesn't matter how powerful or dangerous the creature is, Rhys."

"I suppose. How about asking if there are towns or people further down the trail? So far we've only seen animals and wilderness."

"It's beautiful wilderness, and I love the way the animals all seem to be friendly. There must be people somewhere though, Rhys, because the trail's too defined to be just an animal track."

"It could be animals, Kieran. There are a lot of the lickers around and if they keep moving between clearings to search for grass they'd easily make a trail as defined as this one."

"I'll ask Krol as soon as he wakes up. I wonder where the Griffins live?"

"It's probably somewhere close, Kieran. My imagination tells me it's a big cave high up in the hills where they can just jump off a ledge when they want to start flying."

"A cave? Well, they sure couldn't have big nests in the trees. The branches wouldn't hold their weight."

Kan woke when Krol stirred, then they both stood and stretched their wings. Kieran rushed over with Rhys and, while they were once again being given the touch to the chest and symbolic preening, he made full mental contact.

"Oh my God, Rhys! They're leaving, both of them, as soon they can. Krol says it's really important and they can't wait any longer. He says taking off will be a strain, but after that it's easy. Quick! Hold his head for an energy boost. That's all we'll be able to do for him."

Rhys's hands and Krol's head glowed bright blue for a few seconds and Krol gave a screech of what must be pleasure. His gaze stayed with Kieran for a few more seconds, then he walked a few steps, spread his wings, and launched skyward.

"He made it—and he looks good. He's bigger than the other two, Kieran."

Kieran was in communication and didn't speak till after Kan had joined Krol and both Griffins were shrinking into the distance. Everyone else had come rushing to find out about this unexpected development.

"They've gone and they're not coming back. Krol was in a terrible rush so I only had time to hear the biggest things in his mind. Someone's going to guide us along the trail and when we reach the trees we'll see Krol again. I got a sense that it's a long way for ground travellers and that we should get going straight away. I also got the idea that we'll be camping next to a big lake. I'll call the horses so we can get them saddled up."

Stunned looks and a quizzical silence was broken by Rhys's laugh. "Wow, Kieran. What happened just then? It feels like the Griffins just gave us our marching orders for the next few days."

Mr B, Woorawa, and Tan all nodded their agreement and Kieran steadied the rushing tangle of his thoughts before speaking.

"I didn't explain properly. They weren't orders at all, Rhys. Krol was especially excited about meeting up again and just seemed to expect it would happen. There's a person involved too, because I got a mental image of an old man from both of them."

"An old man? That must be who goes into their minds."

"Well, the Griffins have extra good feelings about the meeting and they wouldn't be liking him if he was bad news. I hope we'll be able to find out where we are."

"That's what we're looking for anyway, Rhys. I agree that this wilderness is beautiful, but I've been concerned that it's so vast we might have to travel for weeks and weeks before meeting anyone. Kieran's link with the Griffins tells us we'll have that meeting in a matter of days. It's great news."

"It could be even sooner, Mr B. Kieran said someone was going to guide us."

"Yes, I was going to ask. Who is it, and when are they going to turn up, Kieran? Do we start following the trail straight away and they'll meet with us somewhere along the way?"

"I have no idea. It was one of the last ideas to come through before we broke contact and it was more a general sense of assurance that we'd be helped on our way than anything specific."

"Does this mean we've got a long journey ahead of us for the rest of the day?"

"Yes, Tan, and tomorrow, and the day after."

"Well, we're going to eat something then. It'll only delay us half an hour if we cook now while we've already got a fire going and food we don't have to find. If we wait till later in the day we'll be held up at least twice as long."

"Good thinking, Tan! Rhys and I will get the horses saddled and ready while you're cooking."

Kieran was slightly puzzled. "There's no food here. Do you want me to call up some of the Rhys-fish?"

"The food's in the creek, Kieran. I've got two of the rabbit creatures held under water with rocks so they stay cool and fresh. I'll go and get them now."

Kieran went too, because he was feeling thirsty, and he laughed at Tan's reaction when they reached the creek.

"Just as well we came now or there mightn't have been anything left."

When Tan went to retrieve the carcasses, Kieran stopped him. "Wait a couple of minutes while I learn the new mind pattern, Tan. We'll take them back to the campfire and cook them."

"What are they?"

"Who knows! Woorawa would probably call them giant yabbies. Burrimul described something like them at the Valley of the Eagles when he was telling us about different kinds of bush tucker to look for in the creeks."

"How will we pick them up? Those claws look dangerous."

"Hang on. There, I'm holding them still. Pick them up like this."

Kieran grasped behind the horny head and weirdly protruding eyes, where the major claws joined the body, and lifted the creature out of the water.

"See, it's easy. I wish Woorawa was here to kill them so I don't have to. Grab a stone so I can make it quick."

Tan started to move, but then froze where he was. Preoccupied with the strange water creature he was holding, it took a few seconds for Kieran to register Tan's stillness. For an instant he thought Tan must be having some weird and unexpected reaction to the fierce pincers and spiny look of this water creature. When he lifted his head in query he saw total shock and fear in the eyes that were staring fixedly past his shoulder. *What?* Kieran whirled to follow the stare and froze with the same shock and fear.

Sitting on its haunches just a couple of metres away, a feline monster with huge fangs showing from its slightly open mouth was staring fixedly at him. Behind and to the side, another stood on all fours, also with fangs at the ready. Kieran's hair stood on end till, pushing through the fright, he reached with his mind in the hope he might have enough time to take control.

Amusement? Both minds were registering amusement at the reaction to their sudden appearance but, more importantly, there was no aggression, just a sense of greeting and pleasure to be meeting. With the pattern now clicked into place, Kieran felt three similar minds radiating the same message from somewhere in the distance. Intuition told him to play the game back at them, so he gathered his thoughts and, thanking Woorawa for pressing so much practice, he planted the image in both minds that they were suddenly facing a rampant Griffin with wings outspread in full aggressive display. Both monsters cowered and backed away for the short time before Kieran returned their perception to normal and projected his own amusement.

Whoops! Time to reassure Tan.

"Friends, Tan. They're the guides Krol was talking about. They think sneaking up like that's funny, so I paid them back. Hang on while I tell the others."

"Friends? I hope the payback was a good one. I think I got ten years older in ten seconds."

"Me too. Just stand still. They want to greet us properly and I'm not sure what that means."

It meant a degree of sniffing, then a lot of hand and face licking which was so obviously friendly Tan and Kieran both started laughing, and then some gentle headbutts to the chest and groin. Tan's look when this happened was priceless and had Kieran chuckling every time he thought of it for the rest of the day.

"Grab the carcasses, Tan, and we'll go see how the others are coping."

They'd all been traumatised by the initial sighting and Rhys was at the point of lashing out with his Spook rope when Kieran's reassurance came through. That reassurance was immediately backed for them by the horses who showed not a skerrick of fear at the proximity of tawny, panther-like creatures bigger than themselves, just the same kind of interest they showed to the deer creatures.

Back at the campfire, the five great felines squatted placidly while the sorry-looking carcasses were cooked and eaten. The interesting news that they now had a new food source was barely noted because Woorawa, Rhys, and Mr B were so conscious of the giant predators and their watchful eyes. Tan wasn't quite as wary, but as he said when Kieran told everyone to lighten up and relax, "It's hard not to be super-conscious when a huge panther with teeth and claws that could rip you to pieces in seconds is sitting just a few metres away looking at you like you might be a tasty snack. Kieran, you should get them to give Rhys and Woorawa and Mr B the same greeting we had."

Kieran laughed because that brought back the memory of Tan's expression at the groin bump.

"All right, but the Griffins are far more scary and no one was wary of them once we knew they were friendly."

"That's different, Kieran. The Griffins are impossible. These are huge versions of the top predators on earth that we associate with eating raw meat, and we haven't had the benefit of seeing the friendliness in their minds like you have."

"Okay, Mr B. You're first for a formal meeting with Gryl. He's the leader, and after he's sniffed you and licked you, you can rub your hands up and down the back of his neck. He loves that. I guarantee by the time Rhys and Woorawa have met him you'll all be relaxed.

"He told you he likes his neck rubbed?"

"No, but I found out lots of things I'll tell you after your proper hello."

"And which one's Gryl? This biggest and scariest looking one, I suppose."

"Of course, Mr B. Of course."

Being sniffed and nudged with great deliberation in private areas and having your face licked profusely with a long and powerful tongue leads to smiles and laughter and, in a few short minutes, Kieran's guarantee was well and truly successful.

"Gods, Kieran! I wonder if there's a reason why everything's so big? The horses, the deer and rabbit creatures, the Griffins and now these. What have you found out from them?"

"They've got the same rules built in about getting permission to go into their minds, Rhys, but they're a lot more open than the Griffins and sort of welcome it. They were sent here to guide us and protect us till we reach the big trees."

"Sent? Have they been in contact with the Griffins then?"

"No, it's that old man again. They've got the same important feeling about him that the Griffins had."

"What about … what's he doing?"

Gryl was on his feet and padding … towards George. Two heads approached each other and, after a sniff from Gryl and a noncommittal snort from George, George's head went down to continue his interrupted grazing.

"Wow! How was that? I almost expected George to get eaten. Gryl's back is higher above the ground than George's."

Rhys was right. This side-by-side comparison, well, nose to nose really, made Gryl's astonishing size really stand out. Woorawa was intrigued.

"The horses saddles wouldn't fit, but I wonder if you could ride them? Imagine how fast they'd be. Big cats on earth are built for speed. Ask them, Kieran. They might be friendly enough to let us."

The answer came back immediately.

"The answer is yes, Woorawa, but not here. I'm getting the idea they need a saddle that specially suits them."

"Unreal! Cheetahs can reach seventy miles an hour and Gryl has to be way faster with legs that long and strong."

Rhys chimed in. "We'll have a race, Woorawa, when I go flying on Krol."

"That's cheating. Flying's too easy."

"Too much talk. Finish your meat so we can get moving. The Panthers are all impatient to go."

"Why're we calling them Panthers? They're yonks bigger, their colour's different, and their heads look more like a lion without a mane—except their ears are longer."

"Don't ask me, Rhys. Tan started it."

"Their fur is sleek like a panther and there's something panther-ish about the shape of their body and the way they walk."

*   *   *

"Does anyone want me to cook this last piece of meat?"

"We've all stuffed ourselves, Tan. Throw it in the creek and let the crayfish things finish it off."

"What crayfish things?"

"We already told you about them, Woorawa."

"Um … I wasn't listening."

"They're big, like yabbies half as long as your arm. We'll look for some tonight when we camp."

The five Panthers stood up, trotted to the exit end of the clearing, then stopped and looked back impatiently.

"Boy, they don't like waiting."

"They saw that the food was gone and the horses were ready, so they headed off."

Everyone helped spread the coals and ashes so the fire would go out quickly, then mounted up and followed after the Panthers.

CHAPTER 5

For four hours, according to Tan's watch, they'd followed the gentle downward trail through stands of trees and frequent grassy clearings, and now they were walking around to loosen up their aching muscles. Every hour they'd had one of these short breaks, because Woorawa insisted it was the best way to cover long distances. No one disagreed. He'd called for this one a little early because the trail had just dipped steeply, and off to the right was the distinctive rush of a waterfall.

"I like waterfalls. I wish we could explore."

Kieran laughed. "No way, Rhys. Gryl's got a target he wants us to reach and he's impatient because we travel so slowly."

"Ha! He'll just have to put up with it. The horses are all doing the best they can and if we go fast on this steeper section it could be dangerous."

"I think it's going to be steep for a while, Rhys. I caught a glimpse of a big plain from back a bit."

"You did? Did you see a lake? That's the target Gryl's aiming for."

Woorawa stretched his arms wide and swivelled at the hips a few times to help loosen up. "No, it was just a quick glimpse. I hope there's another creek crossing the trail soon. I'm thirsty."

Everyone remounted and the steady descent continued. Occasionally, there were extra steep bits that had to be negotiated carefully while leaning way back to stay upright. Almost an hour later they came to a rocky section with much-reduced tree cover and the first little clearing since the track got steep. They *were* well overdue for a stop and there were smiles all round when Woorawa immediately rushed off to scramble up a rocky ridge.

"He's got explorer blood."

"Well, so have I, Tan, so I'm going too."

Woorawa's excited yell and dramatic arm gestures had everyone scrambling to join him.

"There's the lake, Kieran, and look how far to the other end. It's enormous."

Spread in magnificent panorama was the plain Woorawa had glimpsed earlier. Directly below them, where the steep became flat, their creek, looking more like a river, took a lazy path and snaked its way for kilometres to join the ribbon of lake water stretching into the distance. Silence reigned while everyone drank it in.

"Wow! We're going to travel through paradise. Look at all the islands, Kieran, and the other rivers flowing in."

Everyone nodded at Tan's unusual but apt description.

"I was thinking Garden of Eden, Tan. Look how green all the plains are. If that's grass, George will think he's in horse heaven."

On both sides of the lake, the plain was an expanse of green. Dark bands of vegetation, which Kieran presumed were rivers or watercourses, connected to the lake, and several small ranges or hills jutted as if to emphasise the surrounding flatness.

"Gods! That close island's white. I think it's crowded with birds. You've got the best eyes, Woorawa. Can you see?"

Rhys pointed to exactly where he meant and waited while Woorawa did his focus-and-concentrate act.

"You're right, Rhys. I can see some of them flying. I think it's a nesting ground. Thousands of them … Let's go!"

Woorawa might be the main explorer, but his sudden flare of anticipation lit strongly for everyone else too, and the scramble back to the horses was an eager rush. An hour later, the trail left the taller trees of the slopes and moved next to the flow of water. There were still trees, but the variety changed rapidly when the terrain flattened and the flow of the water slowed and deepened.

"Sheba! Look!"

The trail had left the band of trees and headed into a wide grassy area. A quarter of an hour later they realised it was a shortcut where the slowly flowing water wound its way in a big loop, but right now they were staring at a mob of animals watching from about fifty metres away. Kieran's first impression of the graceful, short-horned animals, was of antelopes, but as with every other animal they'd seen, a closer look showed they were different.

"They're not even scared of the Panthers, Kieran. Every animal we've seen so far seems to be tame."

Tan's fingers bobbed up and down in a little counting movement and everyone waited and watched till he finished.

"Nearly seventy, Kieran. I lost it when they started moving."

And indeed they were moving, all of them.

"Wow! Did you call them, Kieran?"

"No, I was about to, but now I'll see what happens first."

Sixty-eight graceful grazing animals, Tan's new count, trotted close and, with complete disregard for the formidable Panthers, proceeded to greet Kieran. For the next few minutes, the astonished companions watched as one by one they approached for a quick sniff or gentle touch to his leg for the first few and his extended hand for the rest when he gave his acknowledgement. Kieran watched, as dumbfounded as everyone else, when the whole mob then trotted matter-of-factly off and lowered their heads to the succulent-looking grass.

"You must be joking us, Kieran. Sixty-eight gazelle things wouldn't just come trotting up and act like you're their king or whatever."

"I can't believe it either, Rhys. I didn't even connect with them till after about a dozen had all done the same thing, so I could find out what was going on."

"And?"

"It was a pattern set in their minds. They all just followed it automatically."

"As if! They didn't do it to me, or Mr B. They picked you out and you can't tell me it's just because they like your BO."

"Idiot! I haven't got BO."

Mr B laughed and nodded his agreement. "Yes, you do. Everyone has BO, but Rhys is right. It's the King of the Animal syndrome kicking in. And the Panthers seemed to expect it too. They just moved aside and watched as if it was quite normal."

As if realising they were being talked about, the Panthers all rose from their haunches and trotted along the track.

The next hour was a series of encounters with bird and animal wonders as they made their way along the track, sometimes next to the shore of the lake and sometimes diverging past the endless series of shallow lagoons edged with tall reed-beds and teeming with all sorts of waterbirds. At one stage the track veered right away from the water and crossed the edge of one of the great grassy plains. For several kilometres they stared at mob after mob of the antelope creatures grazing on the grass, which George and the other horses also continuously paused to stop and sample. One mob, very close to the track, lifted their heads and started heading forward. Kieran, knowing their intent, was wondering how he should react when Gryl padded through the grass and, baring his fangs, gave out a low guttural snarl. The mob stopped in its tracks, watched the warning display for several seconds, turned and trotted fifty metres or so, then began to graze again.

"BO. again, Kieran. They must be downwind of us."

Kieran ignored him. "I'm glad Gryl stopped them. We would've been here for ages. How many do you reckon there are, Tan?"

"I didn't even try to count, but it's at least a couple of hundred. I can't imagine how many there are with all the other mobs we've been seeing."

Woorawa interrupted. "Looks like another river or creek ahead, Kieran. Time's getting on and if there's a good place on the other side we should stop and set up for the night."

Stopping was already on Kieran's mind. Today's six-hour stretch of travel was the longest so far and, despite everyone coping better than expected, they were all looking forward to calling a halt.

"Good thinking. I'll tell the Panthers as soon as we make the crossing."

When they reached the band of taller vegetation it did indeed turn out to be a river, almost forty metres across and the biggest so far. The Panthers plunged in without hesitation and, after pausing for a drink, easily made their way across.

"It's about a metre deep, Kieran. I keep expecting we'll come to a river where we have to swim."

Kieran pointed farther downstream. "The track always goes to a good place to cross. See how the current slows down? We'd probably be swimming there. I noticed how the track diverged a bit before two of the other rivers and I think that's why."

Woorawa and Tan led off, to follow the Panthers, and the group entered the water. The horses were far more careful in picking their way over the pebbly bottom than the Panthers, who were now watching from the other side. Fifty metres past the short incline of the riverbank, Woorawa stopped and pointed to a small clearing in the riverside vegetation.

"This looks good, Kieran. If we go any further we'll be too far away from the water."

"Let's keep this as a fallback and explore first. The lake's not far and I've got this idea of camping where the river flows in. It could be interesting."

"Neat! Have you told Gryl we're stopping?"

"Not yet. When we reach the grass again we'll turn off, and I'll tell him then."

The open grass was only a short distance and when Kieran sent the message that they were diverging to explore and stop for the night, Gryl and the other four Panther's minds filled with a burst of anticipation and their heads lifted alertly to scan the surroundings.

"Whoo, Kieran! What did you tell them? They all look excited."

Kieran was about to answer when Gryl and one other Panther took off at incredible speed.

"What?"

Rhys's surprise was shared by everyone except Kieran, who'd read the intention. In the distance, a mob of the antelope creatures registered the lightning-fast approach and scattered in panic with an explosion of movement. Fleeing was pointless though and the stunned companions watched two graceful creatures crash to the ground and die in a matter of seconds. The remaining three Panthers bounded to the kill location and settled to sate their hunger.

"Sheba, Woorawa! Cheetahs might be fast, but not like that. I've never seen anything like it."

"You mean speed? I think the Griffins are scarier, but not by much. Imagine if they weren't friendly. We wouldn't have a hope. What'll we do now, Kieran? Wait for them to finish eating?"

Kieran reached to read the Panthers' intentions. "No, we'll start exploring. They'll find us when they're ready and they're going to bring some of the meat for us to eat."

An hour later the camping spot was established, not where Kieran had envisaged on the edge of the lake, but back where the trees edged the grassy plain, and where the horses could graze close by and they wouldn't have to cart their wood supply too great a distance. Not far away was one of the shallow lagoons and, to supplement the haunch of meat Tan was preparing with his trusty pocketknife, Rhys and Woorawa collected a bunch of freshwater mussels which Kieran helped locate.

"Did you search for the big yabby things, Kieran? I'm interested to see what they look like."

"Woorawa wants to see them too, Mr B, but they're not in the lagoon. We'll try the river when we go for our next drink, but it's fairly deep and different to the shallow creek habitat where Tan found them this morning."

"Couldn't you just call them into a shallow place like you do with the fish?"

"I don't think they're there, Tan. I meant that the conditions are different. How are you going to cook this giant lump of meat? D'you want Rhys to sharpen the pocketknife so you can slice it into fillets?"

Rhys took a small stone from his pocket. He'd found it at the waterfall camp and claimed it was especially suited for the purpose.

"Thanks, Rhys, but I'm going to try cooking it in one piece, so all I need at the moment is a hole cut through for a big skewer stick. We'll need it nice and sharp to slice the cooked parts off though."

"Hey, neat! Cooking on a spit? We'll have to take turns rotating it slowly … I'll find some rocks or something to build a support for the other end of the skewer stick."

The experiment worked really well except that it took too long and needed constant attention. When Kieran went to the river for a drink, he searched for the yabby pattern but, as expected, there weren't any. When he got back Rhys was offering a chunk of cooked meat to one of the Panthers and laughing at the disdainful response. "He looks like he's disgusted … or is he just full from eating so much?"

Kieran checked. "Both, Rhys. He'd eat it if there was nothing else, but fresh is better."

The Panther in question bared his teeth in a lazy yawn of satisfaction and joined the other four in closing his eyes.

"They're all relaxing because their stomachs are full."

A bit later, after a good supply of grass for their bedding had been collected and the woodpile restocked for the night, the five friends were relaxing and talking quietly about what should be included in Kieran's mind training session when the peaceful atmosphere was broken by a deep throaty rumble. Gryl leapt to his feet and, with his tail twitching eagerly, stared upriver in the direction where they'd left the main track.

"Is it a warning, Kieran? Should we get the Spook ropes ready?"

"No. They're excited. Gryl heard something and it's—"

Five bellowing roars jarred everyone to their bones, then, as the shock of this new behaviour lessened, from the distance came a similar, much fainter, chorus of roars.

"Holy cow! I wish we'd had some warning. My stomach nearly turned inside out. It sounds like more Panthers, Kieran?"

Kieran was reading the state of things in the Panther's minds and everything was good. "It is, and Gryl's really pleased. They've known this was going to happen for hours and I didn't see it."

"Hours? You mean someone told them? At the speed Panthers move they couldn't have heard them or smelled them."

"Yes … I can see it now. The image of the old man is involved again."

"I wonder who he is? He was important for the Griffins too."

Tan's comment went unanswered because in the distance numerous forms could now be seen streaking across the grassy plain. Gryl and the other four Panthers ranged beside each other as if in challenge and Kieran, disconcerted by this, reached with the now very familiar Panther pattern to be assured there was no danger. There wasn't, but the pattern connected to mind after mind. His eyes caught up with his thoughts as the phalanx of rushing creatures flowed effortlessly closer.

"Sheba! How many are there?"

There were twelve, in fact, but the presence and power as the group slowed and stopped in front of Gryl was quite literally awesome, and any thought of counting was lost with the spectacle of one of the facing group leaping straight at Gryl with a rumbling roar and teeth bared in a savage display. Gryl leapt too, with his own rumble, and the companions watched the midair collision and writhing tangle of sprawling bodies in total disbelief till Kieran's laugh startled them yet again.

"It's Gryl's mate. They're just happy to see each other. They're playing."

Gryl rolled on his back and rumbled with pleasure when huge teeth closed gently on his throat.

"That's playing? Gods! I'll have a heart attack if they ever decide to play with me."

Gryl rose to his feet, nuzzled against his mate, then padded to sit, quite royally, next to Kieran, watching with an approving eye as, starting with his mate, each of the newcomers met Kieran, and then everyone else, with the same lick, sniff or nudge they'd received at the first meeting.

Their next surprise was watching all twelve of the Panthers, accompanied by Gryl, bound purposefully off across the plain.

"Now what's happening? They can't be leaving. They just got here."

"I was surprised too, Woorawa, but they're hungry and Gryl's gone to lead their hunt. They won't be long."

"Why has Gryl gone with them? He can't be hungry."

"He's their leader. I think it's just what he does."

"Seventeen Panthers is overwhelming, Kieran, so do you know why there are so many? They're not expecting any sort of trouble, are they?"

"I wondered that too, Mr B, but there's nothing in their minds except being pleased to escort us till we get to the trees, whatever that means, where that old man's waiting."

"Wow! It sure is an impressive escort. Let's get some of your practice done while they're away and then I reckon we should have an early night and get a good start in the morning."

"It's just turning dusk, Woorawa. We'll be awake for a couple of hours at least and Kieran can't practise all that time."

"He could if he really wanted to, but Tan's going to tell us a story about giant Panthers invading college."

"I am? Woorawa, I'm no good at stories."

"Yes, you are. You've got an hour to plan something, with us doing the parts you work out for us."

"Are you serious?"

"Of course I am. We're not going to sit around the campfire and do nothing except get hypnotised by the flames."

"Make Rhys go first. He knows about stories from all the books he talks about. Mr B too."

"They'll get their turn, and Kieran too, but you're tonight … Kieran, the first thing you should practise is putting all sorts of ideas into our minds. It might be really important for tomorrow when we meet the white-haired old man. Put something that happened at the Valley of Eagles into Tan's mind and he can describe it back to us to see how accurate it is."

"Why d'you think it might be more important than the other stuff?"

"Well, since we think we're on a whole different world somewhere, we can hardly expect anyone to speak English, Kieran. For all we know you might be better at understanding animals than people."

"Hey, that's right, and then the rest of us wouldn't have a clue what's going on till Kieran related it to us. How do you keep coming up with so many good ideas for these practices?"

There was a chorus of agreement with Rhys's observation. Woorawa laughed it off as nothing, but he couldn't hide his pleasure.

"Uncle Burrimul made it my job, Rhys, so I think about it all the time. If I could talk to him, I know we'd have even better ideas."

Everyone settled and, after a few quiet moments, Tan gave a reasonably accurate description of the frog encounter, then, at Woorawa's insistence, did it all over again with more detail. Twice more he repeated this, each time giving finer detail, till he finally refused when Woorawa wanted to know about the colours of different objects.

"I don't need to, Woorawa. I can see every bit of it now and it's so clear it makes me feel like I was actually there. Try something different, Kieran. If we can't understand this old man you'll probably have to get lots of big ideas across quickly, rather than worrying about details."

Twenty minutes later, the practice was cut off when the new Panthers returned and settled around the campfire in a great circle to recover from their hunt. Seventeen giant bodies lying in almost symmetrical order was distracting enough, but only for a short while. It was the antics of Gryl and the four Panthers as they now stalked, pounced and engaged in a series of play fights that were impossible not to watch.

"Gods! See that? He must've been two metres in the air and he wasn't even trying."

Gryl had just leapt completely over two other Panthers rumbling softly at each other in mock aggression. A rough-and-tumble followed with the others ganging up and holding Gryl pinned by the combined mass of their four carefully positioned bodies. After a few minutes a new victim was suddenly chosen and Gryl joined with the other three to keep him subdued.

"Look how they team up, Rhys. The one underneath hasn't got a hope of escaping. I think it's a kind of practice for real fighting."

Kieran watched with renewed interest, and Woorawa's theory seemed to be borne out when each of the remaining three Panthers took a turn at being the victim in what looked more and more like a practised, almost choreographed routine. When the last submission finished the five participants crouched on their haunches with tails twitching eagerly and looked to the watching humans with an air of anticipation.

"Now what, Kieran? They look like they're waiting for something."

Gryl's head cocked, one paw lifted slightly in a familiar request for contact, and a few seconds later Kieran relayed the startling invitation.

"You're our fight leader, Rhys. It's our turn to hold him down."

"Us? Against Gryl? You've got to be kidding. All five of us couldn't control even one of his paws."

"I know, but you saw how they did it. They think it's great fun and no one will get hurt. It's a pack ritual, so it's an honour really How're we going to do this?"

Rhys's grimace of disbelief changed into laughter. "Are there any rules?"

"No, except that no one gets hurt."

"All right. Put the Spook ropes on a gentle setting and when he thinks we haven't got a hope we'll hold him down for real."

"That's cheating! Gryl won't be expecting anything like that."

Rhys laughed even more. "I know, Tan, but how else are we meant to control a Panther who's nearly as tall as an elephant?"

Woorawa got all excited. "Brilliant idea, Rhys. Kieran can make him think you really *are* an elephant. When you put one foot on his neck, he'll be too scared to move in case he gets squished. It'll be good practice for Kieran too."

"An elephant?"

"Yes, a big male with gigantic tusks. If he's never seen one before he might be too petrified to even move."

"Gryl petrified? No way! He's a natural fighter. His first instinct is more likely to fight. I'll get chomped in half! Make him think we're all Griffins, Kieran. We know he wouldn't fight them … unless he really had to."

Mr B waved his hand in negation. "You're all getting carried away. I suggest we just attack Gryl as ourselves, without the tricks and surprises. We're going to win anyway unless we force him to change the pattern. Kieran said they think it's fun, so let's keep it that way."

Rhys reacted straight away. "Mr B's right. Tan, it's your job to hold his tail still. Kieran, you can hold his jaws closed, and the rest of us will dive on his body and hold his front paws down."

"Me? With his jaws? Get serious, Rhys. You're the fight leader. That's your job."

Rhys grinned. "This fight leader says Gryl thinks you're the king of all the animals, so he'll respect you more than the rest of us."

Kieran thought that Rhys was making a good point, but he'd save that for a later, personal time. "All right, but you're the leader, so start leading."

Beckoning everyone to follow, Rhys steadied his nerves and led the "heroic" assault against muscle, tooth and claw. Five human bodies piled onto Gryl in their allotted tasks and the initial sense of unreality and unavoidable misgiving quickly turned to enjoyment. Teeth were used to hold an arm or leg, but only with the gentlest of grips. Muscles were covered with a thick layer of glossy, luxurious fur, and claws were kept retracted.

Woorawa squawked and begged for help when the paw he was valiantly holding trapped against the ground with the weight of his whole body, casually lifted into the air, flipped him onto his back, then rested, immovable, on his stomach.

Tan ended up laughing when the constantly twitching tail muscles sent him waving helplessly back and forth.

Rhys was carrying on like an idiot, sitting on Gryl and pounding with clenched fists against the great rib cage with as much effect as a feather hitting a wall of steel.

Mr B's efforts to help by moving the restraining paw just made things worse when he was tumbled in place and held as an extra weight on top of Woorawa.

The task of holding such powerful jaws closed was more than impossible as, with sublime indifference to Kieran's efforts, Gryl continually opened them to companionably lick every bit of bare skin he could reach. Since this was mostly his face, Kieran was practically helpless with laughter.

This happy state of affairs continued till several of the resting Panthers roused and approached to watch with swishing, eager tails. Gryl, rising to his feet and shedding human bodies like water off a duck's back, pounced on the nearest onlooker. Kieran sat up from where he'd been dumped and watched the incredible sight of seventeen giant Panthers gambolling and wrestling in a happy confusion of bewildering motion.

"I wonder if it's an evening thing or an after-eating thing, Kieran?"

"More of an evening thing, Mr B. That's the pattern in their minds at any rate."

"Do you think Gryl will ask us to attack him again? That was unreal fun."

"I'm sure he would if we're still with them tomorrow night, Tan, but he thinks other things will be happening by then. They all do."

"What was it like holding his head? His teeth would have spooked me out of my brain."

Kieran shook his head. "No they wouldn't, Tan. You'd be too busy laughing from all the licking."

Ten minutes later the Panther-play finished and, when they settled in cosy groups at various distances from the campfire, Kieran did a quick connect with Gryl.

"We won't have to do any lookout duty, Woorawa. They're settling for the night, but a couple of them will be taking turns to keep guard. Gryl says nothing will happen, but they'll keep a watch on George and the other two horses while they graze and sleep out on the plain."

"It's still early, Kieran. I want to listen to Tan's stories."

Grins reflected in the glow from the campfire from everyone except Tan at Woorawa's statement.

"Give me a break. How can I think about stories when a giant Panther is waving me back and forth like a metronome."

"A what?"

Mr B held up an arm and waved it from side to side. "A metronome. It's a gadget for keeping time with music. Did you use one, Tan?"

"I started to learn the piano when I was little, but I stopped because I wasn't very good at it."

"As if! You're good at everything you try. And you're good at finding excuses too, so we'll let you off telling your story till tomorrow night."

It really was early but, since Gryl wanted a quick start in the morning, everyone was soon bedded down on the mattress of gathered grass.

*   *   *

"We'll start a fire here and cook some fish, Kieran. We've been travelling ever since we woke and it's time for a longer break. We can dry our clothes out too."

The five companions, clothes completely drenched, were standing by the horses and watching the rear contingent of Panthers make their way through the shallower edge-water and up the gently sloping bank of the biggest and deepest river they'd had to cross so far. Its crystal-clear water was hardly moving, and because the centre section had been deep enough to make the horses swim, everyone had slipped out of their saddle to swim beside them.

"Look out!"

Kieran started to duck behind George, but the spray from five Panthers vigorously shaking themselves caught all of them. Woorawa loved it and laughed at the final, curious whole-body quiver.

"They're watching us, Kieran. They came close on purpose because they thought it would be funny. Did you check for fish while you were crossing? Mr B and Tan can collect some firewood while Rhys and I help you catch some."

"Hang on. I'll tell Gryl that this is a big stop first, so they can do their own hunting if they want to. I did check for fish, because you've got me trained so well, and there are plenty. They're a new kind though, so I don't know what they'll taste like. We'd better take the saddles off the horses too, to dry them out."

The food routine was now quite practised, and after only half an hour Rhys was rubbing his stomach with satisfaction and eyeing the river.

"I'm going for a big swim. Who's coming with me?"

"How far?"

"Down to the lake, Tan. It's only about half a k and you swim farther than that when you practise your laps, so you'll do it easily. If we find a track, we'll walk back. There's a bit of current to help too."

A few minutes later, with their clothes left draped strategically to dry, the jock-clad friends swam off eagerly downriver, with Tan setting an easy pace. Rhys sent an occasional exuberant splash of water at whoever was close, then settled into the relaxed progress of Tan's speed. Every now and again Kieran followed him in a duck dive towards the changing features of the river bottom. When they reached the lake, Rhys scouted ahead and found the way to a break in the reeds where they could wade to a sandy little beach.

"I wonder how far it is across? You can't even see the other side."

No one answered because something had caught Woorawa's attention and he was in his concentration mode.

"Something's moving, Kieran. I thought it was an old piece of wood at first, but it's too regular and round. Can you see it? No, it's gone under now, but keep watching because it was coming this way."

Woorawa kept everyone watching and about thirty seconds later a flattened dome shape bobbed into view.

"See! It *is* moving closer, so it must be alive."

A reptilian head popped momentarily out of the water then the whole thing submerged again.

Tan spoke first. "It must be a turtle, and I've never seen one for real.

Kieran, can you bring it over for a look? As long as it doesn't get upset."

Mental contact was easy now that he'd seen it and the group watched its approach.

"It's freshwater, Tan, so it's probably a tortoise."

The slowly gliding shape reached the shallows and ponderously heaved itself towards Kieran.

"Tell it to stop where it is, Kieran. It's too awkward to be moving out of the water. And it's got flippers, so it must be a turtle."

"It could be a tortoise with flippers for all we know, Rhys. Is there any other difference between turtles and tortoises besides feet and flippers, Mr B?"

"I've no idea, Woorawa. Turtles are usually bigger, but I know there are giant tortoises too."

"Can we wade close or will that make it nervous, Kieran?"

"No. It's happy as anything, just like every other creature we've met."

The group waded closer and when a beaked head quested towards Kieran, stretching over half a metre from the creature's flatly domed shell, Kieran extended his hand and smiled at the nibble which he knew was a form of greeting.

"Careful. That beak looks strong enough to bite your whole finger off."

"He's not biting, Mr B. It's the way they say hello to each other."

Woorawa reached toward the placid creature with a querying look to Kieran, who sent a message of assurance.

"It's okay to touch. He'll hardly notice."

Woorawa gingerly traced his finger across the shell without getting any obvious reaction, then down the side and onto a flipper. "His shell's so hard. Are there many more of them, Kieran? You've got his pattern."

Kieran did the reach thing and, drawing a surprised breath, lifted his head to look at the surrounding water. "They're everywhere, Woorawa, hundreds of them. Hang on while I boost."

The hand that Kieran now rested automatically on the opal glowed softly blue for a moment and his features lit up with even more surprise. "Thousands! Way out into the lake and back all the way we've come from. They're ahead for a while too, but then all of a sudden they stop."

"Where the lake ends?"

"No. I can't tell properly. It could be a kilometre, or it could be four or five, but we know the lake goes on a lot further than that."

Woorawa got very interested. "Where's the next closest one, Kieran?"

"Um … that way. Why?"

"How far does it feel like?"

"It's close. It could be twenty metres I suppose."

"Make it pop up so we can see exactly."

Everyone was now wondering where Woorawa was going with this and looking to where Kieran had pointed. The shape, clearly bigger than their visitor, broached the surface at Kieran's suggestion then disappeared again.

"Neat. I reckon that's twenty-five metres, so you're out by about five. Do it again with another close turtle and see if you can get more accurate."

Kieran liked this sort of challenge and felt quietly pleased when the next turtle popped up very close to where he thought it would. He grinned at Woorawa.

"This is something else you'll have me practising. I can see the wheels turning in your mind." Kieran laughed at Woorawa's startled look. "I can see it on your face, Woorawa. I'm not peeking without permission."

"Well, it could be handy for pinpointing distances, and I think you wouldn't need much practice."

"Make them all surface, Kieran. I want to see where they are."

"All of them? No way, Rhys. That's major. I needed the opal just to see the distant ones. It would be a total brain strain."

"So? Your brain's good at straining. Have a go at it. It doesn't upset the turtles, does it?"

Everyone was looking expectantly at him, so Kieran gave a nod. "I'll see how many I can affect, but without the opal. That's the real brain strain."

Kieran closed his eyes to help concentrate, added the suggestion to surface to the pattern, and connected to about a dozen nearby turtles. *Easy.* With more effort another dozen or so connected and rose to the surface. *More? Yes*, but now this was hard to hold together and the impulse to ease the strain with the opal had to be held back. One more push added even more turtles and built a pressure in his mind that he could only just manage.

"Holy Moses! Look at them all."

With one last effort Kieran released the suggestion, broke the link, and opened his eyes to glimpse the shapes dotting the lake surface for hundreds of metres before they all submerged to proceed with their turtle concerns.

"There must have been at least a hundred, Kieran, and you controlled them all without the opal?"

"It wasn't really control, Rhys, more of a suggestion."

"That's still amazing. Are they easier than eagles or joker birds? Or are Woorawa's practices making you better?"

"It was more than a hundred. I can sort of tell, and it amazes me too, Rhys. I think it's both."

Kieran jumped in surprise at the tingle of touch to his leg. Oops! The turtle was still linked … No, it wasn't.

"It surprised me. I expected it to go when I stopped controlling it."

"You've got a new friend, Kieran. It'll probably keep following you."

Kieran said it wouldn't but, to everyone's amusement, it did and he had to put a suggestion in its mind that it was hungry for some delicious food that was close by.

"Have we got time to swim back up the river? Coming down was too easy."

Kieran was tempted, because he felt the same as Rhys. Mr B would too, while Woorawa and Tan could walk together. He reached to check.

"Gryl's wishing we could get moving, Rhys. We'd better hurry."

Hurrying was awkward with bare feet till Woorawa found a narrow animal track that skirted past the lagoon and then followed where the grassy plain met the river vegetation.

Gryl and several other Panthers greeted them with a chest bump and a friendly lick then watched, slightly impatiently, while everyone got dressed and then saddled the horses.

For the next hour the track gradually moved farther and farther away from the lake as the interlocking lagoons and shallow waterways steadily widened. The group stared with wonder as the flocks of waterbirds grew in size and variety to match the larger expanses of reedy areas and open surfaces. On the right-hand side the grassy open plains stretched lush and green to the distance, broken only by two more major rivers and the occasional small watercourse, and always dotted with mobs of grazing animals.

"Look ahead, Kieran. For a while I thought it was a hill on the horizon, but now I think it's the giant trees from Gryl's mind."

The track here was at the top of an anomalous rise and the group had stopped for one of Woorawa's hourly breaks. Their first interest after not being able to see it for so long had been the view of the main lake, about two kilometres away according to Woorawa, but then they'd focused in the direction of travel.

"It *is* a hill, Woorawa. Trees don't grow that big. Your eyes must be playing tricks."

"Emperor trees might."

Kieran called up the memory of the two giant trees they'd seen and shook his head. "Not the ones we saw. At that distance they'd be dwarfs."

"I suppose so, except you said Gryl felt like we'd get where we're going in two or three hours and that's about where that hill is."

Kieran looked as hard as he could. "The trees must be on the other side then."

Half an hour later Woorawa was grinning like a Cheshire cat. "It's definitely trees. Can't you tell? I can see at least three and maybe four crowns."

No one else could quite pick out such detail but, despite the impossibility, now agreed that the hill was indeed a group of trees.

"It's still a long way. Do you think two hours will get us there?"

Woorawa looked back to the pimple of the small rise where they'd stopped to help judge. "Close, maybe even a bit less, Tan. Gryl's picked up the pace slightly since we stopped. Trees as big as a hill? I wanted to have a closer look at those Emperor trees when we were escaping, but this will be even better. There are unbelievable things everywhere we go and I'm starting to feel like it's Rhys's dream world turned into reality again."

He considered a mob of mini horse-like creatures watching from the grassy plain on one side, and a wading flock of tall, dark-blue waterbirds with long, sharp bills in the swampy area on the other.

"And it's unbelievable that we've travelled all the way from the waterfall without seeing a single person. There are so many birds and animals it makes me wonder if we're in some kind of sanctuary where people aren't allowed to go."

Mr B nodded his agreement. "I've been thinking something like that too, Woorawa. Everything here is optimal for animals."

"Optimal?"

"Yes, Rhys. There are huge swamps and lagoons for wading birds, the lake is vast and must be full of underwater plants and food to sustain all those turtles and who knows how many fish, and look how much grass there is for land animals."

"So you think we're passing through a giant open zoo, Mr B?"

"It's just a theory, Kieran. I suspect everything will change when we meet this mysterious old man, and then we'll have a whole new range of theories … What's happening with the Panthers? They don't usually stop unless we do."

Gryl and all the other Panthers were not only stopped but sitting on their haunches and facing the companions. The three horses, already bunched close because of their riders' conversations, now came to a stop because the way was blocked. Gryl was looking directly at him with one paw raised, so Kieran reached.

"Someone's coming. The Panthers are going to leave us … but they'll see us later."

"They can't be leaving us now. After all this time? Kieran, can we ask them to stay? It's only for another hour or so."

"They're all excited and they're going to run."

A deep rumble sounded from Gryl and every single Panther took off at high speed. The contingent from the rear passed the stunned group with a blur of effort to help catch the rapidly moving main group.

"Who's coming then? Do we wait here in case they're behind us, or do we keep going till we meet them?"

"I don't know, but they must be somewhere close because Gryl didn't think he was abandoning us."

Woorawa focused on the track where the Panthers were now almost out of sight. "There's nothing ahead of us."

He turned to survey in other directions, then jumped when Tan gripped his shoulder and yelled, "Look! Up there!"

Ahead, and high in the sky, five shapes were gliding towards them. Four heads turned to Kieran with a shared tingle of apprehension till he finished reaching and his face lit up with pleasure.

"It's Krol, not the bad monsters. He's seen us and they're on their way down."

Five sets of widespread wings folded in and the Griffins plummeted in an amazing display of speed and purpose. Tan's comment about reaching terminal velocity went unnoticed when, with a great flare of scooping wings, speed was lost and all five Griffins landed with an impressive show of grace and precision. Kieran wondered briefly if such a show involved much practice, then forgot everything as he joined the rush to dismount and run to greet Krol. When the fierce beak touched gently against his chest, he reached to acknowledge the welcome with his mind and his pleasure was instantly overlaid with wonder. Rhys was going to be out of his brain with excitement. Well, they all were.

"Rhys, look at their backs! They're going to carry us the rest of the way."

They took in the beautifully crafted harness strapped to Krol's back, and the harnesses on the other four.

"Carry? Flying? Unreal!" A frown appeared as Rhys thought ahead. "But what do we do about George? We can't abandon the horses."

Communication flowed between Kieran and Krol.

"I just have to tell them to keep following the track to the trees and they'll be looked after when they get there. Climb onto Krol and I'll show you how the belt thing works."

"Belt?"

"It's in Krol's mind. We have to use them so we don't fall off."

The reality of what was about to happen really hit home then, and the wave of apprehension didn't recede till Rhys was securely in place atop Krol, with a belt buckled around his waist and the straps connecting it to the harness tightened to the degree Kieran had taken from all the other instructive mind images.

"Those two handle things on the saddle are security to hang onto if you're nervous or they do any wild manoeuvres, and the goggles are for eye protection when they build up speed. Are you ready, Tan? You're next."

Kan and the other three Griffins crouched, and Kieran supervised, with help from Krol, till everyone was securely in place. He went to the horses next and, with lots of assurances, started them on the way then, with a distinctly increased heart rate, climbed onto Kron.

Kieran hung on grimly while the powerful beat of Kron's wings worked to gain lift. He marvelled at the strength and was thankful for the straps holding him in place. Without the straps he'd have been thrown upward in reaction to every single wing beat. He knew that his extra weight was making the difficult take-off from the flat ground even harder.

In a matter of seconds the buffeting and frantic effort changed to a steady beat, then, just when Kieran had centred himself enough to start checking surroundings rather than adapting to all the movement, the beat of the wings stopped altogether as Kron went into glide mode. Krol was in the lead, and on his back Rhys was twisting to look for everyone else. Kieran lifted and waved his arms, caught the joy being expressed. Rhys twisted the other way and repeated the gesture, and Kieran laughed his happiness into the rushing air at the sight of Tan also waving.

Whoa! Keeping in sync with Krol, Kron had just banked the slightest amount and a strange stomach sensation—like feeling a lift ascend—told Kieran that without beating their wings the Griffins were gaining height. He'd seen the wedgetails do this way back at the Grampians and understood they must be riding a thermal.

Kieran's mind thrilled for the next few minutes while the Griffins banked and circled as a unit, keeping with the thermal while they spiralled higher and higher. The excitement of the climb changed when they bunched closer in formation and started a directed and purposeful glide, and Kieran's attention turned downwards. The green and silver of water and plain spread below in splendid contrast, and for the first time the full extent of the lake and the parallel landscape of lagoons and swamps was briefly in full view. A change in Kron's motion snapped Kieran's attention back to the Griffins. Krol was suddenly below rather than level, with his wings slightly retracted, and a glance showed the same variation with Kan.

The press of air built, and built, and Kieran's grip tightened on the handle gadgets. The speed increased till the air, trying to brush him from Kron's back, felt like a living, palpable force. *How fast was this?* The flesh of his lips and cheeks was moving in a strange, involuntary way and without the slitted leather goggles he wouldn't have dared open his eyes. The flight levelled, slowed and veered, then changed to another upward spiral as the formation rode a new thermal. Kieran had the strange sensation that the ground below was reeling in great circles rather than themselves. A new, high-speed glide started and, loosening his grip, Kieran focused ahead. His stomach churned when Kron followed Krol in a sudden, mind-blowing dive, and just as collision with the spread of foliage seemed inevitable, wings flared and beat powerfully to make a landing.

Kron folded his wings and, gathering his wits, Kieran slipped the goggles off to get a proper look at their surroundings. The first thing he saw was Rhys, his own goggles in hand, looking across and waving. He returned the wave, smiled when he saw Woorawa, Tan and Mr B doing the same thing, then tried to make sense of the wider view. The Griffins had landed in a grassy clearing, enclosed on three sides by the foliage he'd glimpsed in the final seconds at the end of the dive. Behind them though, the clearing ended with what looked like a sudden drop-off.

That was a puzzle for later, because three curiously dressed people were approaching.

People? Excitement mixed with trepidation built in Kieran's mind and he carefully reached, as he knew he must, to check their intentions. His mind shield flared—in fact, all the mind shields flared—when something pried, quite gently, looking for a way through. *No way!*

His own reach met no surface resistance though, and in a completely new experience, Kieran discovered that the white-haired old man in the centre of the three did have a barrier at a deeper level. Pleasure and friendliness radiated clearly from all three, and a huge sense of relief spread through Kieran's mind.

The gentle pry came again, this time with a questioning air, as if asking permission for entry. His instincts said everything was good. His caution was saying to *take care.*

Kieran hesitated, then decided to lower his own barrier while keeping everyone else's in place. No, even better would be to copy the old man's pattern of an open surface with the deeper levels still closed. *How was he doing it?* Kieran probed the barrier till he understood its structure and was surprised at how straightforward it was compared with his own. Conscious that everyone from both groups was waiting for him, Kieran quickly restructured his shield and opened it to the questing probe.

"Welcome, young traveller! All is well and the Realm greets you with gratitude and wonder."

Kieran staggered with shock as the words sounded, clear as a bell, in his mind. Another new experience. He examined the texture of the thoughts and tried, unsuccessfully, to reply. He projected a feeling of thanks, as well as a sense of apology that he didn't know how to reply in kind.

"It matters not at all. Let us make greeting and speak aloud for everyone to hear."

Kieran nodded and, taking the lead, unbuckled and clambered from Kron's back. Everyone rushed to follow suit and then joined him in approaching the quietly waiting trio. The old man took a step forward and extended both arms.

"Greetings, young travellers. My name is Ranevargar. All my Realm welcomes you with gratitude and wonder."

Kieran wasn't sure how to respond till a helpful image formed in his mind and he reached his own arms forward for a mutual wrist grasp.

"Kieran is my name and thank you for your greeting."

Kieran stepped back and indicated to Mr B to follow suit, with the sudden knowledge that this was a simple but very significant formality for Ranevargar. One by one, Rhys, Woorawa and Tan did the double wrist clasp, and when that was finished Ranevargar took a container from the person next to him, lifted it to his lips, then passed it to Kieran. Two mouthfuls was the right amount, then, savouring the wonderful, sweet taste, Kieran passed the container on.

"Why do you visit my Realm, Kieran? Do you seek my counsel?"

"Yes, please, and any help you can manage. Someone kidnapped Rhys, and when we tried to rescue him we ended up here. We came through the White Wall to get away from monsters and we have no idea where we are, or why so many strange things are happening to us."

"The White Wall?"

Kieran called the image into his mind and Ranevargar reacted with surprise.

"You came not by portal? That is a Boundary to my Realm and increases my confusion and wonder."

Rhys's laugh broke the formality. "Confusion and wonder are our invisible friends. They must be, because they follow us wherever we go and moving through the White Wall was so confusing it nearly sent us crazy."

Ranevargar took in the smiles and nods of agreement and turned to Kieran.

"You have the power to pass a Boundary without knowledge of what it is. Kieran, your strange manner of dress suggests you come from beyond the Realms. Are you a mystical Great One from the Human World?"

That set Kieran back completely and Woorawa eagerly took over. "The Elders of my people call Kieran their friend and they used the same words to describe him. He brought us here from our world when Rhys was stolen from us."

Ranevargar gave a look that conveyed great respect for Woorawa's forceful declaration and spoke with renewed formality.

"I honour the wisdom of your Elders, young Woorawa, and I look forward to learning more of them. You have the appearance of the people of the dry continent on the Human World and you stand with Ranevargar, ruler of one of the Realms in this place that you sometimes call Faerie."

Everyone stared in disbelief till Rhys broke the silence.

"You're saying you're … an elf?"

"Yes. I am an elven lord, a Realm Ruler, and subject only to the High King. My greeting ceremony has bound me to welcome you all with my friendship and protection. My heart flows with gratitude for the wondrous gift of Krol's life."

"You don't … you don't look like an elf! All our stories say elves have pointy ears."

"A seeming only, and a discussion we will share, along with many others. Kieran, let us all take counsel after Pelnor guides you for a refreshing break."

Kieran got the message and beckoned everyone to follow and find out what was used here as a toilet. Behind them, Ranevargar and the other person—or apparently elf—moved closer to the Griffins.

A short while later the companions followed Pelnor to where Ranevargar was waiting at the open end of the clearing. As they approached, the grass underfoot stopped and the layer of soil supporting its growth gave way to solid wood. Wood? Kieran's puzzlement switched to astonishment when Ranevargar gestured them to a kind of balustrade, again made, apparently, of solid wood, with an outlook showing the great open plains stretching way into the distance and a vertical drop which he figured must be at least several hundred metres. To one side, and not far below, a number of giant branches jutted horizontally for about forty metres. Understanding crystallised and Kieran whirled to take in the vegetation reaching high into the sky around the clearing. Now that he was looking for them, he could make out three massive tree crowns with a tangle of interlocking branches.

"Rhys, these are the trees Woorawa could see. They've built a giant platform way up here for the Griffins to land on."

All heads switched upward from looking out and down, and then turned to Ranevargar for confirmation.

"Yes, Kieran, this is a grove of my Realm Trees. The platform is fully alive and was grown rather than built, as is this small safety barrier. In a while you will see more, when the Guardians take us to join Gryl and your steeds."

Wonder at trees 400 metres tall was shunted aside by the implication that the clearing was grown by design, and that in turn was displaced by Rhys's question.

"What are the Guardians?"

"You saved the life of the greatest of all Guardians, Rhys. Krol has served to protect my domain and helped vanquish every Chaos Creature and Incursion from the Unordered Realm for over seven hundred years. Replacing him is a work now beyond me."

So many things to understand. Every sentence from Ranevargar contained some new puzzle. Kieran voiced their primary concern.

"Can you send us home, Ranevargar, or help us find the way?"

"The only way I know to reach your world is to portal through the Gateway Realm with the aid of the High King. My power is limited and very much restricted to happenings within this Realm, but I will do what I can. It is my right to seek such aid from the High King, Kieran, but without more knowledge I hesitate to do that, since you can't have been brought here without his involvement."

"A High King? Does that mean there are other kings and he rules over them?"

"Yes, Rhys. I am one of four Realm Lords. The High King controls the Nexus energy which sustains our Realms and is responsible for ensuring their continued existence and wellbeing."

"Is he a good king or a bad king? I don't like him if he kidnaps innocent people."

"I have always had respect for him, Woorawa. The Realms have long been managed with a mix of impartiality and independence and his underlying integrity has always had my support. Kidnapping a human is so far from my understanding of his nature that I suspect there must be matters involving the Realms. Relate every detail of what has happened, Kieran, and we will seek to make sense of it."

"Well, our troubles really started when Woorawa came to Melbourne and discovered that Rhys had been moved away from our college and wiped out of our memories. We—"

Rhys spluttered, almost with indignation, and looked at Kieran as if he was crazy. "You've got to be kidding, Kieran. Funny things were happening way before that. The first weird thing I knew about was the way you swim and your migraines. And then at the Grampians the birds came to you and you zapped me."

Mr B added to that. "Don't forget how fast he learns things, Rhys. That started even before you helped each other and became friends."

Kieran looked to Ranevargar for guidance. "There are too many minor details, Ranevargar. We'll be talking for hours if we tell you everything."

"One minor detail, which seems insignificant now, might be a pathway to greater understanding, Kieran, so the more description I hear the better. We have time before we meet Gryl and your steeds. After eating we can talk well into the night … Start by telling me of these migraines, Rhys, and what he does with them, and then we will hear how everyone else perceives them."

Ranevargar heard Rhys and Kieran's version, then listened to Mr B give his explanation of the zap event in the tent on the first trip to the Grampians, and called a halt.

"Kieran, with your mind protection so strongly in place, I am missing details and associated thoughts about these interesting events. If your friends are happy for me to access their thoughts while they speak I can build a far better understanding."

Kieran hesitated a moment then nodded his agreement. *"I can't take the protections away, Ranevargar, that would be too dangerous for us, but I can let you through to anyone who's okay with it."*

"You can safely release the protections while in my Realm. Nothing will harm you here."

Kieran shook his head. This was the first time since they'd arrived that he knew he understood something better than Ranevargar. *"No, someone knows our patterns so well they attacked us at home and then straight after we arrived. If I release the barrier they'll know where we are and send the Spook things to get us."*

"What are Spook things?"

When Kieran built an image of the Spooks attacking, Ranevargar registered surprise and then thoughtfulness.

"They are a construct called a Fetch and controlled only by Realm Lords and the High King. Keep your astonishing shields in place at all times, Kieran, and continue with your stories."

Kieran turned to everyone else. "Are you happy to let Ranevargar see your thoughts? He's been seeing mine ever since we met and it helps with understanding. He won't look at anything private unless you ask him to."

"Does it hurt?"

Typical Rhys. That brought a surprised look from Ranevargar and smiles from everyone else.

"Idiot! If he looks in your mind he'll be the one suffering, not you … It's the same as when you let me in for our practices, except he's a lot better at it than I am."

"Will he make me think I'm a giant bullfrog?"

Kieran gave Rhys an elbow in the ribs and told him to get serious. "That means it's okay, Ranevargar. He just likes saying weird things."

Following Kieran's obvious trust, everyone was completely okay with Ranevargar seeing their thoughts and the discourse continued with Rhys describing how the Medusa look got started.

After another half an hour they'd reached the trip to Alice Springs but, after hearing Rhys and Woorawa describe their experience of the camp-fire healing, Ranevargar reluctantly called a halt and said it was time to meet Gryl. Kieran knew Ranevargar was particularly interested to see this meeting because he'd been invited to follow the questioning as best he could and watch not only what information was received but also the reaction to it.

"Our transport is about to arrive, Rhys, and since you arrived in such a precipitous rush, Krol is eager to give you a more relaxed view of my Realm Trees."

Kieran was curious. He hadn't seen any contact with Krol in Ranevargar's mind and, since there was no sign of him anywhere in the sky, he wondered how Ranevargar knew he was close. Instantly the link became obvious, and so strong Kieran took a more careful look at its structure. *Amazing!* Somehow it was a natural part of Ranevargar's mind.

Krol and five other Griffins appeared from behind the wall of tree foliage, gliding effortlessly closer and then landing one by one. The spectacle pushed all other thoughts from Kieran's mind till, following Ranevargar's mindlink to the Griffins, he sensed a whole bunch of communication between them. Ranevargar turned to Rhys and gestured towards Krol.

"Lead the way, Rhys. Krol was torn between his loyalty to me and his new life bond with you, and I've just told him it honours me to cede you right of position as his rider."

Rhys surprised everyone by giving Ranevargar a little bow of respect before moving to Krol and receiving the usual chest nudge.

The launch into flight was very different this time as, in turn, the Griffins moved to the drop-off and, with outspread wings, fell into a glide. Kieran's stomach rose for an instant then settled as Kron steadied and moved to keep close behind Krol as they left the trees and cruised toward the lake. When Mr B, on the sixth Griffin, caught up, they flew higher and wheeled in leisurely circles above the grove of Emperor trees.

Kieran smiled at himself. They'd called them Emperor trees so much

it was stuck in his mind. From this changing viewpoint there were clearly four: three formed a surprisingly symmetrical triangle, the fourth, a
significantly higher tree, grew right in the centre of the triangle. Kieran's
mathematical bent found the regularity intriguing and he sent a query to
ask Ranevargar if it was natural or by design.

Ranevargar explained that it *was* by design and they'd all see more for
themselves when they landed.

The Griffins lost height now, gliding beside the trees for a closer look,
and as they neared the ground the perspective changed. The real size
sent a surge of awe through Kieran and the excitement of landing was
completely overshadowed when the Griffins touched down in the lee of a
gigantic wooden buttress, angling upward to the closest tree.

Gryl was waiting, though, and ranged behind him were all the other
Panthers. When everyone was dismounted, Gryl approached Ranevargar
and received a lingering touch to his head. Kieran watched, because
Ranevargar had sent a message he should, as Gryl's mind and body quivered with achingly beautiful joy. Gryl moved to stand proudly beside
Ranevargar while his mate, and then all the others, approached. With
each touch to a proud head, Kieran's understanding of the bond between
Ranevargar and the animals of this Realm built till the wonder of it sent
his body into goosebumps.

Rhys bumped against him and spoke softly in his ear. "Are you all right,
Kieran? You've got a funny look."

"Ranevargar's letting me share his meeting with the Panthers and it's
too amazing. It's so beautiful I've gone shaky at the knees. It's hard to
believe, but I think that he looks after every animal in the whole Realm …
I'll tell you more later."

Any discussion would *have* to be later, because the reception was
finished and Gryl's attention had turned. Kieran started with surprise
at the request that Ranevargar had just placed in his mind then reached
with his own hand to touch the top of Gryl's head. Something sparkled
through his mind at the moment of physical contact, not the all-encompassing joy of a moment ago but definitely a hint of it, and extra to the
usual link. Gryl swung his head in a big arc and his amusement flared as a
playful chest bump knocked an unsuspecting Rhys to the ground.

"You great lump. You could at least have warned me."

A paw the size of an elephant's foot very carefully massaged Rhys's
chest, and Kieran watched a muscle twitch in response when Rhys tried
bending one of Gryl's retracted claws.

"Help! Help! Grab his tail, Tan. Pull his ears off, Woorawa, and you can make him think he's turned into a mouse, Kieran."

A quick check showed that Ranevargar was curious about all this, so Kieran "led the attack". It only lasted a short while though, because George and the other two horses were watching from behind the rest of the Panthers and also eager for attention. Ranevargar watched everything and Kieran could see his huge interest in each interaction.

"Food is prepared, Kieran. We can rejoin Gryl and your steeds when that is finished."

Kieran sent assurances to the horses and discovered they'd already received them. The group now walked towards the great pillar of the closest Realm Tree, following beside the buttress and staring up about seventy metres to where it's top joined the main body of the tree.

"The outer layer of trees help the stability of the Grove with a living anchor, Kieran. The inner layers all join by growing their branches together."

Mr B was extra curious. "What do you mean by inner layers, Ranevargar? There's only one inner tree."

"Two of my groves are bigger, Mr B."

Kieran smiled because Ranevargar was using the group's name.

"And my Central Grove spreads far with many, many trees ... Here we are. These chambers have been established for our comfort."

Kieran, along with everyone else, stared around with interest and took everything in. He'd expected the trunk to be enormous, but standing here was like standing next to a curving wall. On the left was the triangular structure of the great buttress but, dwarfing that, the main trunk rose to where the lowest branches hid the upper reaches from view. On the right, the trunk itself curved slowly away.

"How far round is it?"

"I'm not familiar with your terms for distance, Woorawa, but I think one hundred good strides would be close. Follow that path around and tell us your finding. I see your companions share your curiosity."

"Around? To the buttress and then back again you mean?"

"No, the Managers have provided a walkthrough."

Another puzzle. Woorawa looked to see who else would make this interesting side-trip, then moved off with everyone except Mr B, who only had to wait a couple of minutes to learn that it had taken 108 steady strides for Rhys and 115 for Woorawa.

"What's your estimate for the actual circumference, Kieran?"

"At least ninety metres, Mr B, which means its diameter's about thirty metres straight through."

Ranevargar pulled aside a curtain of leafy vines hanging just where he was standing and gestured for everyone to enter. Kieran studied a narrow room where four people were sitting at a long table laden with food and drink. His eyes lingered a moment then turned to check the clusters of large glowing flowers lighting the room.

Rhys, too, seemed captivated by the sight. "Wow! Fruit! I can't believe how much I'm looking forward to … Double wow! Are those plants glowing by themself, Kieran? Or is it like the glow you make?"

As far as Kieran could tell it was natural, but he waited for Ranevargar to explain.

"Many plants and animals can make light, Rhys. We use the effect in some of our living spaces."

"We call it bioluminescence at home."

"Life light. Yes, Tan. That is a precise description. The Tree Managers have enhanced these flowers to make our life more comfortable."

"Tree Managers? The same ones who cut the tunnel all the way through the buttress?"

"Yes, the same ones, Rhys, but it wasn't cut. It was grown."

Ranevargar introduced Deltar and Tenlon who, along with Pelnor and Manen, had evidently gathered the food, and everyone tucked in eagerly. Big platters of what looked like earthenware were loaded with all sorts of food, and the companions followed the example of their hosts in choosing what and how to eat.

Manen took what looked like a golden, cooked potato, and Rhys, sitting opposite, was surprised to hear a distinct crunch when about a third of the almost-spherical food was bitten off.

"What's that, Manen? It looks like a potato."

"It is rumin, the kernel of a large pod from a plant which we grow in symbiosis with the Trees, and one of our staple foods. It is particularly nutritious and very tasty. Try one."

Rhys's first bite was cautious, but then his face lit up and there were smiles all round at the eager crunching sound after a much more enthusiastic bite. "Man, this is unbelievable. I could live off these."

That led to quite a chorus of crunches as everyone else tried one, and pleased smiles from the five hosts.

Ranevargar pointed to a platter with hand-sized slices, about a finger thick, of dark brown material edged with white.

"This is even tastier, Rhys, and our main substitute for meat."

"You don't eat meat?"

"It's unnecessary with the bounty of the Realm Trees, and rarely practised in this Realm."

Rhys bit into a slice and once again his eyes lit up. "Weird! It's not meat, but at the same time it sort of is. Chew a piece, Kieran, you're going to love this."

"Chew? Is it tough?"

"No, but you can't just bite and swallow. It's kind of heavy, but when you finish you'll want another slice. What's the story with this stuff, Ranevargar?"

Ranevargar waited till four more mouths were happily chewing before answering. "It's a special fungus we grow in plant material which collects where large branches spread from the main trunk."

"Fungus! You're kidding!"

"You're bonkers, Rhys. Mushrooms are fungus and you always tell me I should have cooked more when we have them at home."

"Well, I suppose! Tan's the best cook ever, Ranevargar. Is there some reason why that food has brighter colours?" He pointed to a big platter near the end of the table.

"It is a selection chosen for soft texture and sweeter taste. The brightness of the colours is a signal of readiness for eating."

Pelnor filled their mugs—again earthenware and rather large—with a delicious, tingly liquid that tasted strongly of honey. Questions flowed and the group learned that everything they were eating and drinking came from the Realm Trees and that the four hosts lived here permanently and represented Ranevargar, who had arrived from what he called his Central Grove.

For a while, Woorawa was very much the centre of attention when he described some of the Central Australian wildlife. Manen was particularly fascinated to hear about rock wallabies and was amazed when Ranevargar relayed Kieran's mental image of the pair at the Nature Park.

"They carry their young in a special pocket of skin? What a wonderful idea."

"Lots of our animals have pouches. All the kangaroos and wallabies and possums and even some of the little native mice."

"Don't forget the koalas and wombats, Rhys. They have pouches too, but the opening faces their back legs."

"What? Are you sure, Mr B? The babies would fall out."

"I'm sure, Rhys. I went on a trip to a special sanctuary and the keepers explained it all. The wombats dig burrows with their powerful front claws and the pouch has to face backwards so the dirt doesn't get in with the young."

When Ranevargar relayed Mr B's memories of these animals to the four hosts, Kieran jolted with disbelief at the question which resulted.

"No, Manen. That is beyond our resources."

Mr B and the others weren't part of this mind-talk, so Kieran explained.

"Manen asked Ranevargar if he could make some animals like koalas and wombats for this Realm, but he hasn't got enough energy."

"Make them? You mean bring them, don't you?"

This was for Ranevargar to explain. "Kieran has it right, Rhys. Watch my hands."

He touched his fingers and thumbs together, rested them on the wooden bench next to a platter of purple and orange fruit, then closed his eyes till a soft green glow filled the enclosure of his hands. A small bud appeared then opened and grew a slender shoot with two tiny green leaves.

"Life, and the nurture of living things, is my special gift, Rhys, and this Realm is my sanctuary for all the creatures you will see here."

Ranevargar closed his eyes again and the little shoot shrank back into the surface of the table.

"Was that a real plant? Kieran shows us things like that, but we know he's putting them into our minds. He turned Woorawa into a giant bull-frog once and it was so real we could feel the moisture and softness, like the frogs we told you about."

"Yes, the plant was real, Rhys, but I returned it to the living structure of the table because without a lot more effort it would have quickly withered."

"And you can make animals the same way?"

"I have that knowledge, Woorawa, though it would be more accurate to say I change the form of a life that already exists. The shoot you just saw was adapted from the structure of the Realm Tree."

"You mean this table is alive and it's part of the tree?"

"Yes. As I mentioned, these shelters are the work of the Tree Managers. Under the guidance of our hosts, they keep the Realm Trees healthy and functional."

Tan regarded Ranevargar with renewed awe. "Krol and the Panthers came from you?"

"Yes. I had great vigour in earlier times, Tan. Krol leads my Air Guardians and Gryl oversees creatures of the land."

"What about water creatures then? Krol and Gryl can't watch over them."

"A perceptive thought. Yes, I do indeed have Water Guardians, and if the opportunity presents itself you will meet them."

The two sets of images appearing in everyone's minds lit up Tan's face. "Dolphins? They're sort of like dolphins, and the big ones are something like killer whales with different colour patterns. I love dolphins, but I've never seen a real one, so I hope we do get a chance to meet them."

The information coming with the images showed the bigger Guardians protecting the sea and the smaller Guardians looking after the freshwater lakes.

"Tell me what happened when you reached Kieran's home with intact memories, Woorawa. I suspect your Elders must have given you some manner of protection."

"My uncle did teach me special chants, and they help when Kieran and I have mind-battles. It was really strange when I arrived, because no one even knew Rhys except as a vague memory, and Kieran went all weird when I showed him Rhys's picture."

The conversation continued with descriptions of everything that had happened till their arrival at the waterfall, and Ranevargar very politely asked if it was possible to experience what happened with Woorawa's campfire ceremonies. That meant leaving the tree shelter and gathering several hundred metres away where someone had collected a pile of dry timber.

It was quite a gathering: with the Griffins, all the Panthers who'd travelled with them, along with their four hosts and Ranevargar—all watching while Woorawa put his energy and spirit into a dance showing the bravery of the three Griffins, the sadness when Krol was wounded, and the joy when he first stretched his wings after Rhys and Kieran's healing.

When the dance ended, Ranevargar surprised Woorawa with the same apparently formal touch of recognition he'd used with the Panthers and everyone else jolted with the shock of ten powerful Griffin voices piercing the night with a chorus of acclamation.

Ranevargar spread his hands toward the campfire and Kieran couldn't help backing away when flames leapt higher in a great whoosh and formed into a giant glowing Griffin with showers of sparks cascading spectacularly and incandescent red eyes tracking Rhys's scramble for safety. The fiery head inclined to Rhys, and then to Kieran, and the whole thing collapsed to nothing.

Rhys looked wonderingly at Ranevargar. "Did you really shape the flames, or was it one of Kieran's mind tricks?"

"A memory for you, Rhys, lacking the genius of Woorawa's motion and spirit, but adding to his tribute."

Ranevargar left Rhys's question unanswered and sat cross-legged with a nod indicating everyone should join him. Rhys dropped to the ground, then laughed when Gryl crouched near and butted his head against his side.

"Can you make up a dance for Gryl and the Panthers, Woorawa? I think he's feeling left out."

Gryl wasn't but, now that he'd been challenged, Woorawa would come up with something.

For the next while Ranevargar watched the group involve themselves in a run-through of the mental exercises Woorawa had built into a routine. It wasn't just watching though, because as soon as he understood a purpose he would join in or show a more effective technique. Everyone had happily agreed for both Kieran and Ranevargar to mentally watch their efforts, and Kieran was astonished at the deft way Ranevargar was putting images in his friends' minds and nudging their efforts to more effectiveness. He was learning far more for himself though, and when he wondered how Ranevargar could do so many things with so little effort, the clear mind-voice of their first meeting sounded with a touch of amusement in his head.

"These skills should be easy for me, Kieran. I have had millennia of practice. Follow my pattern and speak directly to Tan. When you succeed with him the others will follow easily."

Tan's face lit up, and then again when Kieran followed Ranevargar's message with one of his own.

"That feels unreal, Kieran. Are the others hearing it too?"

Rhys, Mr B and Woorawa looked at him curiously then, one by one, registered their own surprise as Kieran practised this new way of communication. Rhys loved it and, thinking it was completely private, made a very personal suggestion that sent the blood rushing to Kieran's face.

"Rhys, Ranevargar's teaching me how to do this and he can hear everything."

Rhys wasn't one bit embarrassed, though he did look for Ranevargar's reaction. Kieran's own check found a matter-of-fact acceptance and a hint of approval. *Approval?*

"Of course, Kieran. It is an expression of the powerful bond you share."

Rhys spoke up. "You're talking about me, aren't you?"

Ranevargar nodded and, when Rhys turned to him with his special smile, Kieran realised there'd been a private communication he hadn't heard. There was still a lot more to learn about this mind-speaking.

"Show Ranevargar how you make a flame without the opal, Kieran. That's one of the hardest things and he might be able to see if you're doing something wrong, or if there's a better technique."

"Without an energy source, Woorawa? That can't be right."

"He can, but it's so hard we make him practise."

Woorawa passed a twig across. Kieran focused to build a hotspot and jumped with surprise at the cry of alarm as a wave of negation flooded his mind.

"Kieran, that process is extremely dangerous. Eighteen centuries ago its misuse caused the death of a Realm Lord and most of his subjects."

"Dangerous?"

"Energy must come from somewhere and you are drawing on the life force of your own body. A continued drain could leave you insensible and even incapacitated. I don't understand how you can do this."

"Rhys just gives me a booster zap and I'm okay again … You think we should stop practising this?"

Kieran watched a great swirl of thought mixed with astonishment and concern.

"I advise you so, but I really don't know. At the least you should make sure Rhys is always present and ready to help. Show me how you order the flow of energy from your artefact. I wonder if it might be protecting you without your knowledge."

Rhys grabbed Kieran's bare arm: the boost happened, and then Kieran switched the opal energy in and out several times for Ranevargar.

"Extraordinary! Would you be happy for me to examine your artefact, Kieran? It is very much a puzzle."

Without hesitation, Kieran unclasped the chain, handed the opal over and watched Ranevargar close his eyes. Seeing this concentration, everyone sat quietly for several minutes. Kieran, with his unique access to Ranevargar's mind, tried, with little understanding, to follow what was happening. There was a sense of probing, a small flow of energy from the opal glowed blue around Ranevargar's hands, then a larger flow of energy when the blue brightened and extended to envelop Kieran. Most surprising of all for Kieran, just before Ranevargar opened his eyes, was the impression of a link between the opal and something else. While Kieran reclasped the chain, he watched Ranevargar's unfathomable thoughts change to a far more comfortable state of puzzlement overlaid with wonder.

"Your artefact is a new thing for me, Kieran. It has the appearance and all the qualities of what we call a Stone of Power, but it is far more than that and I sensed strength at a level beyond my reach. I suspect it will outrank even the High King's great Amethyst, and I advise you to regard with renewed respect." Ranevargar smiled and reached inside his tunic. "Yes, Tan. I can explain a Stone of Power and, indeed, show you mine."

Ranevargar undid the lacing of a little pouch and extended his hand so everyone could view the beautiful white sphere glistening in his palm.

"And yes, it *is* a pearl—a beautiful pearl which came from the Human World at the time of separation."

"You used to live with humans before you came here?"

"Not personally, Tan. The separation happened thousands of years before my time, but we did live on Earth till our ways clashed with the rest of humanity and we had to leave."

"Elves are really humans? That doesn't make sense to me. We don't live for a thousand years or build plants with our bare hands … though there *was* a guy called Methuselah who was meant to live for ages."

"That was exactly the problem, Rhys. When our people developed new knowledge of the human mind and started unlocking some of its deep abilities, ordinary people were taught to fear the difference and a great persecution forced our adepts to build a refuge. The six Realms of Faerie are the result."

"Six? We've seen the Spook place and Dead World and yours, so what are the others?"

"Your memories tell me you arrived in the Realm of Maynor, a lord of great power. We call your Dead World the Unordered or Lost Realm. Lady Narello has closed the borders to her Realm and in recent times directed her subjects to study the arts of Chaos. Lord Uirebon's Realm is a peaceful and pleasantly structured place, mostly dedicated to learning and the recovery of old knowledge. The Gateway Realm is the pinnacle of elven achievement, the only passageway to your world, and controlled by the High King because of its importance."

Ranevargar reached his open hand to Kieran. "A Stone of Power is linked to the structure of each Realm and the High King entrusts an elven lord of suitable strength and standing with its use. Examine mine, Kieran. You will find it enlightening."

Kieran stared at the glistening orb resting in his palm and gently tested its surface with the pointer finger of his other hand. "It's so smooth and beautiful, Ranevargar, and the colour is really interesting. At first it was pure white, but when I look closely there's a tinge of green."

Rhys leaned his head closer. "No there's not. You're seeing things, Kieran. There's a reddish colour reflecting on the side near the campfire, but there's no … Hey! There *is* green. I can see it now."

Kieran didn't answer because his fingers tingled and a soft green glow followed the spread of a familiar sensation through his arm. "Why is it green, Ranevargar? This is exactly what happened the first time I held my … Opal, except it was blue."

"Green manifests naturally when energy is drawn from my Pearl. I

believed you would sense the power within, but somehow you have started an activation as well. Pass it around to see any other reactions."

Kieran gave the Pearl to Rhys, quickly, because a sense of unease was
rising in Ranevargar's mind. *Unease?* Understanding flashed when he
remembered his own violent reaction when the outsider was accessing his
Opal and trying to take it away.

"Sorry, Ranevargar. I didn't realise what I was doing."

"Nothing happens for me. I feel like I'm holding something precious,
but there's no green."

*"I don't know how that was possible for you, Kieran, but my shocked sense
of propriety is now controlled. We should study this further at some stage."*

"You mean Kieran might be able to get energy from this Pearl the same
way he does from his Opal?"

"There is no might about it, Mr B. We saw it start to happen. He somehow established a connection despite my Pearl being uniquely aligned to
me. If he put his mind to it, he would be able to call on the limited energy
it has available."

Woorawa was holding the Pearl now, but he stopped examining it while
he asked his own question. "That's a big difference then, because Kieran's
Opal gives him whatever he needs. It seems like the more he uses it the
more he can get out of it."

"Yes, Woorawa, and even the properties I do recognise and understand
add to its mysterious nature. The energy stored in a Stone of Power comes
from the one source of energy, the source that powers the very existence
of the Realms. We call it the Nexus, and without it the Realms would
dissolve into the Chaos they hold at bay."

"Chaos? The way you say it makes it sound like a real thing instead of a
mix-up."

"It's very real, Rhys. You felt its touch each time you entered one of the
Boundaries."

"Chaos is a good name then. The Wall makes us feel like we're going
crazy."

Tan was holding the Pearl now. "How does the energy get into it,
Ranevargar?"

"I put it there, Tan, but it is more complicated than that. The basic structure and maintenance of a Realm is an automatic function of the Nexus,
but the overlay of purpose and design comes from excess energy that the
High King controls and directs. The demands for that energy are in cease-
less contention and my Realm has little importance in the concerns of the
High Court. I am limited with how much I can store for personal use."

"That's unfair. Why don't you build your own Nexus gadget and have as much energy as you like?"

Kieran watched the flow of surprise in Ranevargar's mind as, quite taken aback, he considered this idea of Tan's.

"What an extraordinary idea, Tan … The possibilities would be endless … Tempting, and at the same time fraught with complication and difficulty. It would completely change the working of all Faerie. It can't happen though. The knowledge of how to construct a Nexus passed with the adepts at the time of separation."

"Tan always has good ideas, but if you really need more energy, this one seems like common sense to me."

"Common sense would be of little concern to the Realm Lords, Rhys. The struggle between them for power and influence is never-ending and only controlled by their reliance on the Nexus energy the High King distributes. A new source of power would disrupt the balance of all Faerie."

"Are they all bad?"

"Not bad, Rhys. Highly ambitious is a more accurate way to describe them, especially Lady Narello and Lord Maynor. Lord Uirebon holds his Realm by virtue of knowledge and the friendship of the High King."

"What about the High King then? Is he ambitious too?"

"Very much so, Rhys. The position of High King is one of strength and it can be challenged for at any time. Aglaron has held his position for twelve hundred years and held off two such attempts with relative ease. His ambition is tempered by long experience and the integrity I have already mentioned."

"Would you ever think of being High King, if you had the extra power?"

Ranevargar gave Woorawa a penetrating look before answering. "That is a deep question, young Woorawa. Through the experiences and considerations of my long life I have learnt that my deepest fulfilment comes when I use my special gift for guarding and guiding the life in my care. The mantle of a High King is broad but, while bestowing great power and opportunity, it also demands endless attention to management of the ambition and will of others. Good kingship is a wonderful achievement but not, in the long term, suited to the outlook and abilities that make me who I am."

"I think you'd be a wonderful High King."

"My nature would have to change and I would lose my independence, Rhys."

In the silence that followed, Tan returned the Pearl and Ranevargar replaced it in its pouch. Woorawa put a few more sticks of wood on the campfire and Rhys unconsciously rubbed the fur on Gryl's neck. Kieran tried to follow the contemplation of Ranevargar's mind, but it was too rapid and complicated. Ranevargar's moment of introspection ended.

"Kieran, before I share my thoughts on your situation, I would like to help Tan and Woorawa overcome their sadness and concern for the worries of their people at home."

Kieran jolted with surprise. He'd comforted Tan as best he could. They all had.

"How can you do that? I told Tan I could make him forget, but that would be awful."

"Of course, but you found Rhys across the Boundaries between your home and the Realms, so you should be able to do the same with Tan's people."

"I don't know them. I can't locate anyone unless I know them in my mind."

"They are so strong in Tan's mind that you can use him as a pathway to send a message of wellbeing. We will practise with Rhys and Krol, so the process is clear in your mind before you try the distant reach. Their bond is strong and immediate and will help you see the pattern."

With Ranevargar's help, Kieran was soon able to make indirect contact with Krol. It needed Rhys's cooperation by putting Krol at the forefront of his thoughts, but that was easy and Kieran quickly grew confident with the process.

"Are you ready to try, Tan?"

"What do I have to do?"

"Exactly what you just saw Rhys do. Concentrate on your family as hard as you can and tell them you're alive and well."

"Will you put my voice in their minds? That would be very strange or even frightening."

Kieran had a quick back-and-forth with Ranevargar before answering. "No voices, Tan. Ranevargar says they'll just suddenly know with great certainty that you're alive and well, but out of touch. Is that all right?"

It was more than all right and when Tan's thoughts abruptly overflowed with powerful memories of his family, Kieran linked to follow them. There was nothing … No, that wasn't right. There was something, but following it was blocked.

"Help! What do I do, Ranevargar? It's too hard. I can't get through."

"You needed your Opal to reach Rhys. Recall how you did that and apply it again."

Kieran felt like kicking himself for not thinking properly. He moved beside Tan and held his hands for the physical contact that he now remembered helped when he needed to reach Rhys. Yes, the tiny trace of a link strengthened and he called on the Opal. It was still too hard.

"Rhys, help me please. I need your touch to keep us going."

Rhys rushed to make a three-way hand contact. Kieran called the Opal once again then, after a few seconds, gasped with relief.

"It worked, Tan. Could you tell?"

Tan nodded with a smile of gratitude that touched everyone.

"Astonishing! Now you should do the same for Woorawa and his uncle."

Kieran nodded, so Woorawa knew it would happen. "When I've recovered, Ranevargar. That was really hard … What do you have to tell us?"

"I have no explanation for much of what has happened, Kieran, but what I do see gives me great concern for your wellbeing. Rhys's portage to the realms can only have occurred with the express consent of Aglaron, the High King, and your arrival at his two Realm Trees implies the involvement of Lord Maynor as well. The persistent pursuit indicates that Rhys, at the very least, is wanted for some matter involving the two most powerful individuals in all of Faerie. Never let your shields down, Kieran, especially that unique function which hides your existence. I received news earlier that a number of Coursers crossed our Boundaries late this afternoon and flew as if guided in search."

"What are Coursers like? Not flying Spooks, I hope."

"What a thought! No, Rhys. You befriended two till your first encounter with a Boundary frightened them away."

"They've sent eagles to look for us? Can you stop them? It's your Realm."

"I could, Rhys, but that would be a poor strategy. If I thwart the High King's will, he'll want to know why, and if he questions me formally I will be bound to reveal your presence."

"What? Why? You said you'd protect us."

"And I'll do my best, Rhys, but if your presence here is a matter concerning the High Court, I will be bound by my oath of fealty to accede to his will."

"Wow! That makes things complicated for you."

"Complication is a game I am very good at, Rhys, and tomorrow we will play it to the full."

There was silence at this surprising statement till Rhys laughed. "Against the High King?"

"Yes, Rhys, unless he formally demands my assistance. I don't have enough strength to send you home, but I do know I can show Kieran many things which might help you on your way."

Kieran saw an associated image of the Realm Trees and asked aloud for everyone else's benefit. "The Realm Trees might help us? How could that be?"

"I developed them as a means of instant transport, Kieran, and tomorrow I will show you how to use them."

"Instant?"

"Yes, Rhys, like the portal which brought you, but limited to the locations of the groves."

"You mean people can simply jump from one set of Realm Trees to another?"

"It's not at all simple, Rhys. Before Kieran arrived I'd have said only a Realm Lord would be able to access the energy and knowledge required."

"You mean Kieran's as strong as one of these Realm Lords?"

"Strange question, Tan. Of course he is. His Opal was involved, but he forced at least two of them from his mind and carried you all through a portal."

"I really meant that your comparison sort of feels like you think he might be one himself."

"He can't be a Realm Lord. All five positions have been stable for centuries, but many of his abilities do seem to suggest a connection with Faerie, and even the possibility that he comes from one of the Realms."

"What? That's crazy. Kieran could be an elf? I don't believe it."

"There is enough mystery about Kieran to make it unlikely, Rhys, but I don't discount the possibility."

"Wow, Kieran! We all know you're a weirdo, and now you're a mystery too. What are the mystery bits, Ranevargar?"

Ranevargar watched Kieran give Rhys a whack in the ribs before answering.

"Well, the friendly way he puts up with being called a 'weirdo' could be classed as a mystery. Otherwise, I'd point to his astonishing affinity with animals, the ability to draw on his own life force—apparently without any lasting ill effect—and his mastery with mind shields."

"But Rhys is a mystery too, isn't he, with his magic hands?"

"Yes, Kieran. Healing is a highly respected art through all the Realms, but Rhys's touch is beyond anything I have ever encountered."

Woorawa laughed. "So now we've got two weirdos. Does that mean Rhys might be an elf too?"

"All five of you are unusual in some way, Woorawa, but I see Rhys as the least likely to have any connection with the Realms. Apart from his mighty spirit, he has almost no resistance to an elf probe."

Kieran smiled at Rhys's awkward look and felt especially happy to see the others doing the same and nodding in agreement.

"The rest of us aren't really unusual, Ranevargar. Why did you say that?"

Ranevargar gestured to the campfire again. The flames rose and for a few seconds formed a life-sized image of Woorawa dramatically posed as he'd been at the end of his Krol dance.

"There is mystery and the power to touch the soul in the story of your movement, Woorawa. It can only be classed as unusual, and apart from that there is a sense of ancient otherness overlaying the thoughts you have shared with me. Tan appears normal till he speaks or thinks, and unique perceptions are presented. Mr B is a puzzle too. The structures of his mind closely match those I see in Kieran, but he has no unusual abilities."

"Another difference you all share, Kieran, is the attraction of like-for-like. I say this in private because Woorawa and Tan have not quite acknowledged this for themselves."

"Everyone? Mr B too?"

A touch of amusement entered this very private conversation.

"As you very well know, Kieran. Your study sessions were partially motivated by the mutual attraction you feel."

"I'm with Rhys now."

"Of course, but your bond with Mr B is powerful. I advise you to consider whether exclusivity is the wisest course."

That was too big an idea and Kieran switched thoughts. *"Are you sure about Woorawa and Tan? The likelihood that all of us are the same must be very, very low."*

"I am sure, Kieran. I suspect a subconscious recognition of Widderkin is a big part of why you drew them into your circle."

"Widderkin?"

"The term used in the Realms … More later, Kieran. Woorawa has an interesting comment."

After the pause while Kieran and Ranevargar looked fixedly at each other, Woorawa agreed.

"That makes sense too, because when we first saw the White Wall, Mr B and Kieran couldn't look at it till Kieran worked out how. It didn't affect the rest of us till we got close. Mr B's unreal at swimming too, just like Kieran, but that probably doesn't mean anything."

Ranevargar hesitated and Kieran watched his churning thoughts. "It possibly could, Woorawa, but I'd have to access the deeper levels of their minds for more certainty."

"Go ahead, Ranevargar. If it might help then we should."

Rhys laughed and gave Kieran a cheeky arm bump. "If you go deep into Kieran's mind, you'll probably never get over it."

Kieran bumped him back. "Look who's talking."

"Kieran has already invited me deeper into his mind than any of you, Rhys, and it certainly is very unusual, especially when he's thinking about you."

Rhys didn't know what to make of that and then was more puzzled when Kieran grabbed his hand. "What? Do you want me to be part of it?"

"No, Rhys. I want you to help us contact Burrimul. I've had enough of a break and that should happen before we do anything else."

Woorawa scrambled eagerly to get between Kieran and Rhys so they could all be in physical contact. After some drama when the blue glow surrounded all three of them, Kieran collapsed sideways against Woorawa.

"Quick, hands on his temples, Rhys. He's tried too hard."

Kieran lifted his head. "It won't make any difference, Woorawa. My mind needs a rest, not my body. That was way harder than it was with Tan and we nearly didn't make it. You did feel it work though, didn't you?"

"Yes. It's kind of amazing."

"What happened, Ranevargar? Could you see why it was different?"

"I don't know how you managed that last push, Kieran. But it appears that Woorawa's uncle must have an even greater natural resistance to intrusion than Woorawa does. My counsel now is for immediate sleep and recovery."

"What about the mind stuff with Kieran and Mr B? You were going to do that next."

"It's not a passive process, Rhys, and Kieran's resources are momentarily too low. Take him to the shelter and make sure he gets to sleep without delay. I will work with Mr B who has decided to stay."

There had been more to the private contact, but the idea of sleep was suddenly so attractive Kieran wondered if it was Ranevargar's doing.

"Maybe. Rest well!"

*   *   *

Kieran reluctantly opened an eye and took in the glowing green where bright light from outside was making the plants hanging across the shelter entrance translucent. *Neat!* What was the time? He twisted sideways beneath the luxurious softness of his cover for a better look, then sat up to centre his thoughts. What *was* the time? And where was everyone? He scrambled to the little alcove to relieve himself, slipped into his clothes, then pulled the entrance vines to one side.

"Good morning, Master Kieran. When you have had food and drink I will take you to Ranevargar."

"Where's everyone else?"

"They were very busy familiarising themselves with their new travel supplies, and then Gryl took them exploring when it became clear you needed a longer rest."

Kieran switched the background connection he always kept with Rhys to the foreground and surprised Penron with his exclamation.

"Sorry, Penron. I had to laugh because Rhys's excitement is so contagious. Can I carry some breakfast with me, so I don't keep Ranevargar waiting?"

"Break … fast? Yes, of course."

Ten minutes later Kieran was sitting with Ranevargar and wishing he'd brought more of the honey-bread with him.

"Ah! You are well rested I see, Kieran. The others will be with us shortly, but in the meantime I have a great deal to show you."

"What about the deep look into my mind you were going to do last night? I feel like it's important."

"So do I, but let us try a few exercises first. That will enlighten and help us. Link with me as closely as you can."

Linking was easy, but Kieran wasn't exactly sure what "closely" meant.

"You are already close, Kieran, but practice will bring you even closer. Follow and watch while I make a familiar link."

Kieran followed and automatically looked to a distant branch where the small flock of joker birds must be.

"Use your mind rather than your physical eyes to gather information, Kieran, and study the way I focus on an individual."

That was a much-practised skill which Kieran already knew.

"Yes, but you only use it at an elementary level and you can do far more. Learn my patterns, as you call them, and try them for yourself."

An actual image of several small flowers nestled between green leaves appeared in Ranevargar's mind and Kieran, understanding this was a joker bird's real-life view, eagerly watched and stored the variation to his own pattern.

"Good. Now try it without my help."

After a moment of blurriness, the head of another joker bird appeared and Kieran felt like yelling with delight.

"Wonderful, Kieran. You're grasping the pattern for sight. Now watch and learn the patterns for taste and smell."

Five minutes later, Ranevargar switched the target animal.

"Something new now. Ride my mind, Kieran."

After a breathtaking reach, which Kieran had no hope of copying, a new image showed clear in Ranevargar's mind. Grass? Gods! This was one of the deer creatures. Instructions passed from Ranevargar and the creature's head lifted to gaze at a grassy clearing and a beautiful little waterfall.

"The pattern for sight, Kieran. Try it for yourself."

That was no problem, and Kieran even sent an instruction to look towards the remnants of their old campfire.

"Well done! Now can you manage completely on your own?"

The link snapped abruptly, but Kieran didn't even try to make a reconnection.

"No way, Ranevargar! It's so far away I couldn't manage it without an enormous call on my Opal."

"Interesting. Ride with me again and watch closely, but on no account make any attempt at control. There is information you should have."

Ranevargar made another breathtaking reach which told Kieran they'd covered a great distance again. An image of startling clarity showed the view of a lake far below, through the familiar pattern of an eagle, or Courser, as he was now finding them named. The image became secondary and a sense of purpose primary. This Courser had powerful instructions to search for any sign of a group of ground travellers. In rapid succession, Ranevargar switched seven more times to new Coursers, each with the same overriding purpose.

"Early this morning Lord Uirebon made contact with a forceful request to pass on any information I might have about travellers or unusual occurrences within my Realm. I told him, with great concern, that my Guardians had been hard pressed recently to manage a surge of Chaos Incursions, as well as a fearsome beast from the Unordered Realm, and I gave notice that if the rate of incursion continues I will need an infusion of Nexus energy from the High King."

"Lord Uirebon is the one who rules the study Realm, isn't he?"

"Yes, and this means yet another Realm Lord is actively involved in the matter of you and your companions. The orders for the Coursers all carry his signature."

"Are any of the Coursers close enough to see Rhys and everyone else? No, I know they're not, but they travel very quickly, and I don't know the distances."

"One is tracking this way, but it won't arrive for more than an hour. When it does arrive it won't see anything unusual."

"Three rulers of Realms are after us? It's crazy. I wish we knew why."

"I very much agree, Kieran. I made my puzzlement very clear, but Uirebon offered no explanation and kept his thoughts behind a powerful shield."

Kieran made a kind of mental snort. "He wouldn't keep me out … unless he's different."

"Maybe, but that would be most unwise. Your strength and technique would be sufficient, but a Realm Lord has centuries of experience to call on."

"I know. It aggravates me, that's all. They'd probably figure out where we are and send more of those Spook things after us. Do you know how to control them, Ranevargar? They don't seem to have minds."

"Physical dissolution is the only way, Kieran. They are constructs formed without an independent mind, so the purpose of the maker cannot be changed."

"You said *construct* with the same kind of feeling you use for the Realm Trees. Is that how you talk about unusual creatures?"

"The Fetches are an inferior class of construct. Find your companions and sneak into their minds."

"Without their permission? That's not our rule."

"They gave it when I explained this exercise to them earlier and alerted them to be wary for any sign of intrusion."

"It's hardly an exercise, Ranevargar. I know them all so well it's not even an effort."

"Practise with your newly improved patterns to show me what they are experiencing, and at the same time influence their behaviour without their knowledge."

Kieran reached and was instantly flooded with Rhys's excitement. That wasn't what Ranevargar wanted though, so he built a similar pattern to the ones that had given direct sight access with the joker bird and the deer. *Wow!* The surroundings, visible past Gryl's head, were racing by at an unbelievable speed.

"Relay to me, Kieran. That's better. Now make Rhys look at your other companions."

Kieran started a bit of a push for Rhys to look behind, but immediately stopped because the speed was so great, and Rhys was focused so strongly with holding on during this high-speed burst.

"Not at the moment. It's too dangerous for him."

"Yes, I see. Add another sense and relay that to me as well."

Motion added to the mix, along with the rush of air making moisture stream from Rhys's eyes.

"Can you feel all that, Ranevargar?"

"Yes, Kieran. So much exhilaration and excitement is captivating. Switch to Gryl's mind before he finishes his dash and taste the same experience from another viewpoint."

For the next while Kieran followed Ranevargar's directions in switching through all his companions' minds, relaying everything, and sneakily controlling some of their actions.

"Enough, Kieran. I've just told Gryl it is time to return. Can you see how the steady relay process has opened your mind to me? Watch as closely as you can while I probe more deeply."

Kieran did watch, but the process was very complicated and more than he could properly follow. Eventually he sensed Ranevargar's withdrawal and return to ordinary surface thoughts.

"Did you find anything important, Ranevargar?"

"I'm not sure. I get the impression that there are barriers in your mind beyond my ability to find. There is also a strange uniformity to your older memories which puzzles me."

"Uniform memories? What does that mean?"

"Memories range in strength according to importance, your frame of mind, their association with other memories and many other factors. Your recent memories vary with your older ones."

"How long ago? My memories did get changed once, but I fixed that."

"The difference is subtle, but your college memories show a more natural variance."

Movement distracted Kieran when the Griffins sailed into view, and then again as the great mob of Panthers, four of them mounted, bounded from behind the Realm Trees.

"More later, Kieran."

The excitement and eagerness to share their adventure radiated from all four companions and Rhys could hardly contain himself while he unclipped and slid recklessly from Gryl's back.

"Yo! Slugsy! Wait till we tell you what you missed. Riding Gryl's as exciting as flying with Krol and we saw where the Realm Trees drink water from the lake ... Have you been awake long? We saw a flock of birds bigger than a cloud fly out of the Realm Trees and Krol did acrobatics right through the middle of them. You won't believe what it feels like when the Panthers start to race."

"I know some of it, Rhys. Ranevargar taught me how to piggyback your mind and I watched the bit when you were racing."

"Watched? What does that mean?"

"I'll tell you later."

"Okay. Hang on while I take Gryl's saddle off. He can't do it by himself."

Penron and the other three hosts appeared and, in a very short time, everyone was gathered around Ranevargar with the thrill of their adventure pushed aside by an overriding curiosity about what they saw as a far more important event. Kieran wondered about that, then saw how much they'd discussed the Realm Trees' portal function while he was asleep.

"Are you ready, everyone? Kieran, Krol, and I will disappear for a while, then reappear, depending on how quickly I can marshal my resources. Kieran, the pattern I use is much simpler than the one you tapped into when you brought everyone to the Realms and I'm hopeful that after several trials you will master it for yourself."

Kieran was totally taken aback. "Um … aren't we all going? We made a big decision that it's important never to get separated."

Kieran sent the image of the campfire discussion which showed how strong this had been for all of them.

"Hmm! I don't see how we can manage this. I have a similar need to keep at least one Guardian with me at all times and such a portal would exhaust me. My energy is limited."

Woorawa had an instant answer. "Hey! Energy's nothing. Kieran can give you some from his Opal. That's easy isn't it, Kieran?"

"Yes! I can easily make a mind pool like I do for Rhys's healing or the Spook ropes … or I could help you transfer some to your Pearl if that would help."

"There are still problems, Kieran. My recovery from such an extensive portal would be slow."

Rhys started waving his hands like a crazy man. "No it won't. We'll zap you and you'll feel good as new straight away."

Kieran was completely puzzled by the great wash of uncertainty flooding Ranevargar's mind. He'd seen, almost first-hand, what Rhys's healing had done for Krol, so there was something slightly off about this reaction. Pulling some recollection from their recent session he probed past Ranevargar's surface thoughts and saw reluctance to even accept the possibility of help.

"Ranevargar, hold still while we show you how good a boost feels. Rhys, rest your hands on Ranevargar's temples. We know that works best."

This was Kieran using his command voice.

Ranevargar froze. Rhys leapt to comply, and everyone else stared in startlement.

Kieran pooled the normal amount of energy they used for a boost and reached to cover Rhys's hands with his own. The energy disappeared, drained to nothing when Rhys's healing gift took every possible skerrick of resource for its own purpose. Totally unprepared, Kieran sent a call for Opal help in the moment before the overwhelming demand from Rhys washed his consciousness away.

What? A gentle hand caressed his forehead and he opened his eyes at Mr B's touch.

"Just relax and wake yourself up properly when you're ready, Kieran. Rhys and Ranevargar are still asleep, but they must be nearly awake because they've both got that relaxed kind of smile that happens when Rhys's zap fixes something."

Kieran sat up, then blinked with the surprise of seeing Krol's fierce features staring at him with an unreadable look. Pressed close and sitting motionless, every Griffin and Panther also stared at him with a disconcerting quietness.

"They all went into shock and nearly frightened us to death till Krol saw that Ranevargar wasn't hurt."

Kieran's gathering wits wondered at that, but checking Rhys and Ranevargar was first priority, particularly Ranevargar, who'd somehow made a routine energy boost turn into a full zap event.

"Was I asleep for very long, Mr B?"

"About five minutes, but you started stirring almost straight away."

Kieran had a fleeting thought, as he reached for Ranevargar's mind, that the energy pool must have buffered him against the full effect. *Whoa!* Ranevargar's sleeping mind, without the complexity and strain of consciousness, was curiously different. It was a good difference too, more relaxed but at the same time humming with life. Was the zap causing that, or was it the normal restoration process of a sleep state? Whatever it was, it looked good, so Kieran grabbed Rhys's hand, called enough energy to help him wake up, and smiled when his eyes twitched open.

"Sheba, Kieran! That was … Gods! They're all staring."

"Help me wake Ranevargar. I don't know why but you zapped us all. Just a little boost because he's almost awake anyway."

Rhys sat up and took in all the surrounding watchers before reaching to Ranevargar. "Another boost? We might get zapped again."

"We won't. I'm ready this time."

And indeed, the patterns Kieran had learned with the two big healings were now well and truly in place, but covering Rhys's hand with his own showed they weren't necessary. A smaller than usual—but quite normal—energy boost flowed and Ranevargar woke.

Kieran, connected to Ranevargar's mind as a kind of precaution, watched the relaxation of a moment ago explode into a kaleidoscope of mental activity. He recognised introspection but then, beyond his comprehension, a multitude of links reached in every direction.

"What have you done?"

The words, spoken softly but sounding like a great shout in Kieran's mind, were rhetorical and quite unanswerable.

"You're all right, Ranevargar. You just got zapped."

Ranevargar removed his hands from the double grip holding them and, with a gesture that looked like a kind of blessing, rested his fingertips on Rhys's head. Stunned and speechless, Rhys peered through the soft green glow which appeared. Ranevargar turned and transferred the touch and, for the few seconds, while the glow tinged everything he saw with green, Kieran's mind and body tingled with the happiness and gratitude he was receiving.

A request for assistance shone clear in Kieran's mind and, seeing the need and yearning behind it, he impulsively opened a channel to his Opal and let the energy flow. The green glow spread and with it went an overwhelming feeling of joy. Kieran's senses reeled. His voice joined his companions and hosts in a shout of sheer exhilaration. Griffin heads lifted, Panther roars joined in a thunderous chorus, and a myriad of birds burst from the Realm Trees to fill the air above with a wondrous, high-pitched skirl of sound.

Ranevargar's hands lifted from Kieran into a wide gesture and with them went a call for calm. All the sound and motion quietened and, over his steadying emotions, Kieran saw the brightness of Ranevargar's vast network of links subdue and recede. Ranevargar's arms relaxed to his sides and his smile further calmed the hushed gathering.

"Peace follows joy and I am restored. The Realm is renewed with your gift, Rhys."

All eyes turned to Rhys.

"Um! What *have* I done?"

Ranevargar chuckled and the air of high drama disappeared. "A healing, Rhys. I will explain later, but you have also made our group portal possible. Ready yourself to depart."

"Ready? Now? All the animals just went crazy and you'll leave them? And how do we get ready?"

Kieran wondered why Ranevargar wasn't explaining more, then saw that that would happen while he was recovering after the portal.

"The animals are happy and quite used to my departure."

Kieran took over because he saw that Ranevargar was just making an announcement rather than asking for some sort of preparation.

"We'll join up like we do for the Wall crossings, Rhys. I don't think it matters, but it'll be a good backup."

There was a scramble of movement and Kieran laughed as eight hands latched firmly on.

"This is going to be like moving through the Wall. I can just tell. Ranevargar, where are we going?"

"Kieran will choose our destination, Rhys."

"I will?"

"Yes, concentrate, Kieran. Watch carefully while I show you the identity of the first grove. When you have that fixed in your mind we will learn all the rest."

A new pattern appeared in Ranevargar's mind. No, not quite new. There was a strangely familiar feel about it. Approval washed to Kieran.

"This is our current grove, Kieran. Without this pattern we cannot return."

"I've got it."

"Show me."

One by one Ranevargar cycled through ten other location patterns, insisting each time that Kieran show he could make it himself.

"They're harder to hold in my mind than the one for here."

"Only till you make a visit."

"What's the hold-up? We've been standing like this for nearly five minutes."

"We are almost ready, Rhys. Kieran is learning the locations of all the groves in my Realm."

"All? How many's that?"

"We are about to leave, so I will let you discover that for yourself."

"Which one, Ranevargar? How do I choose?"

"We can reach them all, Kieran, but I suggest the Central Grove with its stronger support structure for a start."

"Okay. Which one is it?"

"The strongest pattern, Kieran. You tell me."

That was easy.

"Good. Now I'm going to show you the connection between this grove and our destination. Watch carefully because it's almost undetectable while it's passive. I'll have to activate it and hold it steady while you take it in. Ready?"

"Yes."

Something happened, but Kieran couldn't figure it.

"It's tricky till you know it. Look more outward, rather than deeply into my mind, this time."

An external pattern? Well, if it was between two groves it must be. Instead of looking for the pattern itself, Kieran decided to track the signal Ranevargar was using to switch its active/passive condition. Yes, there was the "off" signal, a tiny current of mind energy. A second tiny current flared out and this time Kieran was watching the right place.

"Wow! That's beautiful, Ranevargar. It looks like silvery green spider-silk stretching all the way between the two locations."

"Excellent, Kieran, and interesting too, because my mind interprets it as a current of green energy, like a river flowing Now, it's time to go. Take in as much as you can."

Reality blurred, much as it had with the Wall crossings, but without the disturbing sensations of nausea and disorientation.

Kieran's senses blinked off then came straight on again and he was looking at the Realm Tree platform. No, he wasn't. This platform was bigger with a different-shaped edge.

Everyone's hands dropped as they stared around. Off to one side, Krol stretched and then folded his wings.

"**I**s that it? One big blip and we're here without getting turned inside out?"

Ranevargar didn't answer Rhys straight away, because he was silently communicating with Kieran.

"How much did you understand, Kieran? It was a faultless transition for this size group."

"A lot of it, I think. I want to watch how you used your energy again though. It was much less than I have to call when we go through your Boundaries."

"The Boundaries are a different process."

"Where are we, Ranevargar?"

"This is my Central Grove, Rhys. My home base, and if you want our next portal to be more dramatic I can easily arrange it. What would you like? Headaches, blurry vision, stomach nausea? It would be a pity to spoil the pleasure of our refreshments though."

"Ha! None of them, thanks. The zap must've made you cheeky. Or you're learning from Kieran."

Ranevargar smiled. "Your zap has indeed changed my outlook, Rhys, but we have a while to wait while I recover, so what would you like to do? There is much to discuss, or you can venture out with Krol for a view of this grove."

"Just me? Are there any more Griffins so we can all go?"

"I can call more, but by the time they arrive and are prepared with saddles we will be ready for our next transition."

"Is there much to see?"

"More than you can imagine. This grove is not like all the others. It extends far."

"Realm Trees? All the way?"

Kieran turned to look, Yes, he could see at least eight or nine treetops towering around them.

"I'll stay here, so I know what's going on. What did you find out, Kieran?"

"Ranevargar's still showing me what to do, but it should only take a few more runs before I can try by myself."

"Without us?"

"No way, Tan. I mean me making it happen instead of Ranevargar."

"So, it's going to work? Unreal. What about another energy boost, Ranevargar? Will that speed up your recovery?"

"Definitely, Rhys. We won't be able to proceed without it."

Rhys jumped to grab Ranevargar's hands and gave Kieran a get-with-it look that set Ranevargar smiling.

"Patience, Rhys. Even with your bonus energy I need time to recover from a translation. I am also adjusting to the healing you have given me."

Kieran completed the physical contact and, watching carefully while the boost took place, was surprised at the spread of energy through Ranevargar and its instant absorption.

"Yes, Kieran. I know how to use it."

"Why was the zap such a big deal, Ranevargar? You said you'd tell us."

"I have lived long for an elf, Woorawa, and sometimes the ability to maintain full health starts to slowly decline. The condition was irreversible till now, and meant my time was limited and the stewardship of this Realm would falter. Now, beyond all possibility, the condition is healed and I am renewed."

"Um! I don't like to say it, but you might be jumping to conclusions. Rhys's touch could be temporary and wear off after a while."

"That was my first thought in the moment of realisation, Tan, but my deepest search shows every marker restored to full health and vigour. I have a whole new life ahead of me."

Kieran wondered exactly what that meant. "More vigour, Ranevargar? Your mind's so complicated and capable I can't see how."

"If you should stay in my Realm, as my heart desires, Kieran, you would see the ravages of decline reversing and the steady restoration of my physical and mental vigour."

There was silence while everyone looked for Kieran's reaction. "We want to stay, but we can't. I know you understand."

"Of course I do. Your welcome is not limited."

"How sick were you? You said it happened slowly, but do you know how long it was going to be before it got really bad?"

Ranevargar rested his hand companionably on Woorawa's shoulder. "My death, Woorawa! The thought is clear in all your minds. Yes, and the end would have arrived in less than four hundred years."

"Four ... hundred ... years!"

"Not much time for a life in Faerie, Rhys. It takes over two hundred years for an elf child to reach maturity."

"Gods! You did say that the High King has been ruling for twelve hundred years, but I thought he must be special. Is he the oldest elf of all?"

"Not quite. Lord Uirebon, the Lore Master, worked with Aglaron's father and is widely regarded as being the eldest."

Tan spoke up. "Does Rhys's healing mean you'll live longer than any other elf?"

"Very much so, Tan, unless Rhys's healing gets applied in a similar situation."

Tan grabbed Rhys's arm in total excitement. "That could be why they're after you, Rhys. They found out about your healing and they want it. That High King might have worked out he could keep ruling for another thousand years if he gets control of it. You did say he was extra ambitious, didn't you, Ranevargar?"

"I did, Tan, and Aglaron would definitely seize such an opportunity if he thought it available. He is at the height of his power and health though, so I doubt Rhys's gift would affect him very much. It *is* reason enough to explain the involvement of three Realm Lords, but there are still inconsistencies."

Kieran was totally impressed. This was the first explanation of what had been happening that made any sense. "That's brilliant, Tan, but Ranevargar's right. All they did with Rhys at the start was move him away and make us forget about him."

"I suppose. And you were at the centre of everything till Woorawa arrived."

Tan brightened after a moment. "Well, what if they only found out about his gift when you figured it out yourself? It was just after you healed my leg when they grabbed him."

"Hmm! That sort of fits, but it means they were already watching us. Wouldn't that be hard, Ranevargar, to watch all the way from the Realms to our college?"

"Yes, Kieran, an extraordinary effort. You know how difficult it was to reach Tan's folk and Burrimul with messages of reassurance. Such surveillance and manipulation would be a major undertaking and implies a very strong purpose was already in place well before Rhys was taken."

Rhys was glad for Ranevargar's ideas and couldn't fault this logic.

"Learning of Rhys's gift could very well have changed that purpose … or even added to it."

Mr B spoke up. "I don't see how they can know anything about Rhys's healing except for what he did with Tan's leg. Kieran has had us all shielded since then, and he's certain they can't get through."

Ranevargar gave a definite nod. "I agree, Mr B. Kieran's shields astonish me."

"You tested them, Ranevargar?"

"Yes, Kieran. When we first met, and again when I looked deeply."

Mr B continued. "So unless they're watching some other way they can't know he can give certain elves a whole new life. That only happened half an hour ago. Can they see into your mind, Ranevargar?"

"Only with my permission, Mr B. Lord Uirebon did make contact, but he saw only the surface thoughts I provided. He wasn't even aware of Kieran's shielding."

"Kieran's got you shielded the same way as us?"

"Yes, Woorawa, we agreed on it soon after you arrived."

"You say lots of things to each other without talking out loud, don't you?"

"We do, and for much the same reason you push him to practise his other abilities."

Ranevargar surprised everyone by reaching for Rhys's hand. "It's time for our next translation. Where would you like to go this time, Rhys?"

"How would I know?"

A series of images flashed through everyone's minds.

"Wow! How about the place near the ocean?"

Woorawa eagerly grabbed Rhys's hand. "I've never seen an ocean, Ranevargar. Can we please go there?"

While Ranevargar was nodding, he communicated with Kieran. *"I recovered in less time than I expected, Kieran, but another energy boost would be a help. This time, along with everything else, I want you to take particular note of how I bind everyone to the pattern between the two groves. You were watching too many other things last time."*

"Whoa! And that is so important."

"All of it is. Are you ready?"

Everyone was holding Rhys's hands by now, except Krol, of course, and Kieran carefully directed the energy boost just to Ranevargar, who was the only one who could use it anyway.

"Here we go. Do you want me to add the disorientation and funny stomach you were asking about, Rhys?"

"No way!"

Kieran concentrated and very carefully watched how everyone, and Kron in particular, was held together in a strong group-link. The spider-silk connection between the two groves glowed beautifully for Kieran again, and this time he took in how Ranevargar made the group react with it. Reality blurred again, then returned, and because he was watching for it, Kieran saw the group freed and each individual made independent again.

"You saw my connections, Kieran?"

"Yes, and I saw how you released them too. I missed that last time."

"You can make them next time and then I will take over to check they are right."

"Oh man! Look at that!"

Kieran's attention turned outwards and he shared the outlook from the new tree platform. The open ocean was there, but it wasn't till after the group rushed to the lookout at the edge that the shoreline and a small estuary below came into view. Including the river mouth, and sweeping into the distance on the right, a sandy beach stretched till a rocky promontory blocked further view. On the left the land rose high in a line of what must be cliff tops. Scattered offshore from the promontory, a group of islands made for even more interest.

"Well, Rhys, are you going to take a tour with Krol? Or are you going to make way for Woorawa's first ocean experience?"

Rhys just laughed. "That's not playing fair. Of course Woorawa can go. Has he got enough time to see much? The last stop was pretty short."

"Time enough to fly to the rookery islands and back without lingering … if he hurries."

Woorawa rushed to Krol who was settling in the crouch which allowed a rider to climb on and get harnessed.

"You wait, Woorawa. You owe me big time for pinching my turn."

A quick grin was all the acknowledgement Rhys got. Woorawa was too focused on clipping himself secure while Krol moved to the Griffin take-off point. With almost ten metres of wings spread wide, Krol dropped into an effortless glide and then a speed dive.

"Lucky thing. Those islands look really interesting."

"Woorawa will tell you all about it when he gets a chance, Rhys."

Ranevargar received his needed energy boost then sat while he answered a new barrage of questions.

"Can we go to the grove in the mountains next? I can see four Realm Trees here. Are all the outpost groves the same size?"

"All except the grove next to my biggest lake, Tan. It's a four-layer grove with thirteen trees."

"I would've put the Realm Trees on top of the cliffs to look straight down on the ocean."

"No, you wouldn't, Rhys. The trees need an abundant water supply and must be near a river or lake."

"Your groves have at least four Realm Trees and they're all bigger than the trees we saw in the other Realm."

"Yes, Tan. They are inferior and grown solely for their portal function. There are only four pairs of trees outside this Realm and they require far more energy to use. Kieran, Woorawa is almost overcome with his experience. I suggest you practise linking with him."

Kieran hurriedly made the link and only vaguely took in Ranevargar's comment about the Tree Managers making these Realm Trees so different. Woorawa's mind was practically sparkling with wonder as the ocean slid past close beneath and a group of giant porpoise-like creatures leapt skyward and crashed back to the surface. Krol made a lazy circle while they broached again, then straightened and started flying with purpose.

What? He was returning already?

"Yes, Kieran. We should proceed with the next translation. Call up the pattern for the mountain destination while we wait, and see if you can build the link then make the connector for me to check."

The spidery network glimmered into Kieran's mind-view, faded, then brightened and steadied when he adjusted his energy usage.

Next he started to make the group-link, but stopped because it needed Woorawa and Krol.

"Finish, Kieran, and give it into my control. You were faster than I expected, so you will get an extra practice ... and here they are. Start again while Woorawa is still mounted."

The link between the two groves faded, but after a brief moment Kieran, feeling quite pleased with himself, had it rebuilt.

"Very good. Now! Do you want to wait till Woorawa can join hands with everyone else or will we surprise him and go ahead?"

That was interesting. The group-link thing Ranevargar used had almost the same effect as physical contact and Ranevargar had gently pointed out that he'd forgotten to get everyone to join hands.

"You didn't really forget it, Kieran. Your subconscious registered that you didn't need the touching in this situation. I would continue the practice though, as it is definitely your best form of backup."

Reality blipped and the startled looks from his companions registered briefly as he went into assessment mode with Ranevargar.

"Another seamless translation, Kieran ... and I see that you marked the trigger. I will use it myself once more but let you hold the spider-link. You are almost ready to try this."

"No, I'm not. I still can't see how you do this with so little energy."

"Little? I am drained, Kieran. Without Rhys's boost we would be waiting for the rest of the day."

"But the amount you use isn't enough for the result it gets."

"I see your problem. You are looking in the wrong place again. When I send the activation trigger the grove supplies most of the energy for the transfer, so watch there."

Kieran was so surprised he spoke aloud. "The trees store energy? That's amazing, Ranevargar."

"Not really. Every living plant and animal has a certain amount of energy, the life force you have been tapping, and my Realm Trees have been purposefully designed to keep an amount in reserve. Without them my access to the different sectors of the Realm would be much reduced … Rhys, we will relax for a while longer this time, so Krol can show you his mountain home."

Rhys, and everyone else, turned from taking in their surroundings. "His mountain home? Is it a cave? That's what I liked to think till we decided that if he's your Guardian he must live in the groves with you."

"Krol will take great pleasure in showing you, Rhys, and my reliance on his aid does indeed keep him away most of the time. He would like to take you to several of his flying and hunting haunts as well, so make haste to take Woorawa's place."

Rhys made haste, great haste, and his eagerness set everyone smiling and wishing they were going too.

"We will make it your turn next, Tan, so start deciding whether you would like to explore a jungle location or a desert oasis."

Krol launched from the platform edge with Rhys smiling and waving like crazy till the sudden drop had him grabbing for the handgrips. They dwindled rapidly into the distance, leaving everyone gawking at the sheer rock face they were heading for and the giant buttresses off to one side.

"Walk with me, everyone, and we will meet a mystery … And to help with the curiosity you all share, we are heading for an encounter with a Tree Manager, one of my earliest constructs, and the reason for the success of my Realm Trees."

"You told us they made the shelter where we slept and the table and benches for our meal. Are they like expert carpenters who know how to cut the wood without hurting the tree?"

"No, Tan. As with the buttress passages, there is no cutting involved. The Managers work in harmony with the trees and modify and enhance the way they grow in accordance with our wishes."

"Like you did when you made the little shoot?"

"Yes, Woorawa, though on a slower but grander scale. They have access to every root, branch and stem, and the major part of their work is ensuring their Tree stays completely healthy. Only a relative few are involved with modifications for host and visitor comforts."

Ranevargar held aside the vines hanging in front of the entrance to a shelter identical to the one they'd had their meal in last night. "Here we are. Who's going in first?"

That made everyone look, and then look at Kieran with the message that he was the leader. Kieran had the advantage of knowing that Ranevargar was just being dramatic for Woorawa's benefit, and stepped forward.

"It won't mistake me for a tree and make flowers grow in my hair, will it?"

"I hope not, Kieran, but send Woorawa in first just in case."

Woorawa, knowing very well that this was a put-on, linked elbows with Kieran and grinned at Ranevargar. "Send Tan in first then. He'll look great with yellow flowers all over his head."

Tan didn't rise to this, but Kieran could see that he was quite enjoying the attention. The inside also appeared almost identical to the one the previous night. On the table there were two platters, one with fruit, the other piled high with the honey-bread they all liked so much, and several jugs—presumably drink. Next to the table a beautiful host elf was smiling in welcome, and along the wall the bioluminous flowers were glowing softly. The only different element was a large hanging plant of some kind on the wall and Kieran presumed they must be going to see the Tree Manager after they'd had a snack.

"Welcome, my Lord. You have surprised us with this unexpected visit. The others are still on their way."

"Thank you, Melnaria. The visit is short, and after meeting the Tree Manager my new friends and I will be departing."

Ranevargar made the introductions and everyone eagerly tucked into the honey-bread. There were more greetings when a second host arrived, and Kieran was starting to wonder why Ranevargar wasn't moving things on when Woorawa gave him a sudden attention-grabbing nudge and stared at the wall.

"Kieran, that plant moved. One of the vines just touched the light flower and it got brighter."

He was looking at the hanging plant. Kieran didn't see any movement, but some of the flowers close to it did look brighter.

"Well spotted, Woorawa. This is one of my Tree Managers."

The honey-bread stopped being the focus of attention.

"A plant? But I definitely saw the vine end move."

"Not exactly a plant, Woorawa. It is a combination of both plant and animal, though plants and animals all move to different degrees. Kieran, this first direct communication with the Tree Manager since my healing will be an experience I'd like everyone to share."

"Um! What do you want me to do?"

"Rest your hand on mine while I make contact, and link with Mr B, Tan and Woorawa, so they feel your reaction."

There were fascinated nods of anticipation when Kieran placed his palm on the back of Ranevargar's hand and moved to the plant mass attached to the wall. With touch came the recognition of intelligence, but then the link with Ranevargar flared to brilliance as something passed between them.

Kieran tried to hang on, but the life and joy filling the Tree Manager was an overload of wonder that held him helpless till Ranevargar intervened. Woorawa and Tan had both collapsed to the bench seat and Mr B was clutching Melnaria for support. Ranevargar had passed the joy of his healing to the Tree Manager, and Kieran's wits were now gathered enough to understand it was being passed, in turn, to the rest of the Grove and … other Tree Managers.

The great wash of feeling appeared to subside, but Kieran's access to Ranevargar's mind showed it was still there and spreading.

"Hold still while the Tree Manager learns who you are. I think that, given enough time and effort, you might begin to understand our unique and quite special method of communication. I have instructed the Manager to accept you as a friend. The contact will surprise you, but try not to move till it finishes."

Surprise was an understatement when the movement Woorawa had glimpsed became general. Four viny tendrils crept slowly away from the wall and coiled round Kieran's wrists. There was pressure, but not uncomfortable, and a strange probing sensation tingled where his flesh was being touched. *Probing?* Oh … Ranevargar was showing him the Tree Manager's intention and telling him this would take several minutes.

"Can you see my link with its intelligence, Kieran? The pattern for the animal parts should be available to you."

Kieran tried, saw something, but it was too difficult to hold.

"I think so, but I can tell I'd have to work to know it properly. It's not a natural pattern."

Woorawa had moved close and was staring goggle-eyed at the proceedings. "What's it doing? Is it talking to you, Kieran?"

"Just what Ranevargar said. It'll take a few minutes to get to know me."

"So what does that mean? Is it like the way you connect with ordinary animals?"

Ranevargar answered, "It's more complicated than that, Woorawa, but I'm setting things up in the hope that Kieran might eventually be able to pass on instructions of his own."

"You're kidding! Like you did to make the shoot grow out of the table?"

"Not exactly like that, Woorawa. That is a different skill but, through the Tree Manager, yes. I'll show you an example in a moment when the Manager finishes learning Kieran."

"Learning him? That sounds funny."

"Yes, knowing would be a better description."

"What would happen if I touched it? Would it do the same to me?"

"Do you want to see?"

Woorawa looked for Kieran's response and got a definite go-ahead. "All right. Will I feel anything? Kieran had a funny look for a while."

"Just the normal sensation of touch while it holds you."

Woorawa looked now to Mr B and Tan, and Ranevargar gave a soft chuckle.

"Yes, you are all welcome to an encounter with the Tree Manager, but we will do it simultaneously to save time. Tree Managers have their own rate of doing things."

Kieran's wrists were released and after a moment of communication between Ranevargar and the Manager, Mr B, Woorawa and Tan reached forward then watched quietly till their hands were released.

Ranevargar rested his palm on the Manager again and Kieran marvelled at the pleasure building through them both.

"Watch carefully, Kieran, while we demonstrate to Tan how the tree is shaped without cutting. Our time is limited, so revealing a secure storage place should be enough to help your understanding."

The Tree Manager moved slowly to a position farther along the wall and slightly higher. Kieran wondered briefly how it was holding on, but then four of the vines settled with obvious purpose in one place and a tiny hollow appeared and steadily deepened and widened.

"Unreal! It's like watching a time-lapse video."

Ranevargar was too preoccupied to query what time lapse might be, and so was everyone else, because the four active vines had just stilled. Ranevargar reached, almost full elbow length, into the now well-formed hollow and withdrew a misshapen woody lump which he handed to Woorawa. Woorawa turned it this way and that but couldn't figure anything. Neither could Kieran, but he saw the intention in Ranevargar's mind.

"It is yours to keep, Woorawa."

"Thank you very much, Ranevargar … What is it?"

"A Realm Tree. A treasure for your elders and a replacement for their gift to Kieran."

Woorawa stared at the seed pod in his hand and amazement, awe and puzzlement moved across his features. "For me?"

"Yes, Woorawa. Part of what your friends say tells me that your intervention and pushing for Kieran to improve his abilities has helped him face the troubles and confrontations your group has met. You also gave a part of yourself and your people to me."

Woorawa made a nod of acknowledgement, then followed it with a short, soft chant. Kieran was impressed because Woorawa had recognised the partly ritual nature of Ranevargar's action and responded appropriately with a simple thank you ritual of his own.

Ranevargar turned back to the Tree Manager for one more touch. When the hollow started to narrow, he indicated it was time to leave.

"Krol and Rhys are on their way, so let us move. I need to prepare Kieran for our next portal."

Woorawa was bursting with questions about the seed pod and, while they walked, Kieran watched silent communication flow between him and Ranevargar.

Everything stopped for the spectacular sight of Krol's landing and Rhys's exuberant waving, but as with Woorawa, hearing about his adventures would have to wait.

"Tan has chosen the Desert Grove, Kieran, so build the connection and link everyone to that while I watch. This time *you* will use the grove to grove channel and *you* can trigger the jump while I manage the group."

Whoa! That was a bit nerve-wracking ... but not really. The spider-link part was well and truly locked in after their practice so far, and the trigger part was quite straightforward.

Rhys came racing close after practically diving from Krol's back, but Ranevargar's hand waiting for a boost left no time for any talk.

The spider-link was built and approved. Six people and a Griffin were grouped then passed to Ranevargar. Somewhat tentatively, Kieran called up the trigger pattern and waited for the go-ahead.

"More energy, Kieran. The grove will supply what's needed for the translation, but the trigger energy has to come from you. You will pass out if you are not ready."

The Opal glowed from Kieran's rushed call and then Ranevargar's surprise registered. "*So much and so easily. That's far more than you will need.*"

Half wondering if he might pass out anyway, Kieran set the trigger going ... and everything blurred.

"Well done, Kieran. How do you feel? That was a very strong trigger you sent to the grove."

Apart from a peculiar emptiness from the sudden disappearance of the energy he'd called, Kieran hardly felt any different.

"Well, I know I've been busy, but I'm not exhausted or anything."

"The resilience of youth, or natural ability, but probably both. When Tan returns from his tour with Krol, the next jump is all yours."

Kieran started to wonder why this translation had brought them to the base of the trees, rather than a platform, but Ranevargar talking to Tan about their new surroundings was too distracting.

"There are two oases, Tan. Krol will take you to both of them while Rhys demonstrates his swimming skills."

"You know I like swimming?"

"It is laced though all the memories you have shared with me, Rhys, but just now it was your first thought when you saw the combination of sand and water. Woorawa almost had the same reaction and Mr B does too."

Rhys looked to Kieran then back again. "What about Kieran? He loves swimming."

"Maybe later, Rhys. There are many matters I must discuss with him … We will extend our stay. The prospect of the experience is quite infectious."

And indeed, the sparkling water surrounded by a broken ring of shrubs and other low vegetation looked very inviting. Kieran glanced to the Realm Trees then back again and made a non-descriptive little sound of surprise.

"What's funny, Kieran?"

"Just me, Rhys. The Realm Trees are so big I thought these other ones were shrubs till their proper size clicked in."

Tan climbed onto Krol and everyone's attention was taken while they made the more difficult launch from flat ground.

"What are you and Kieran going to talk about? We might be able to contribute some helpful ideas."

"I wish to explore Kieran's ability to connect with both Opal and Pearl, Mr B. Much of what we do will be silent, but you are certainly welcome to stay if you wish."

"Come to the oasis, Mr B. Kieran can tell us all about it later when they're not sitting like a couple of stone Buddhas. Ranevargar's too polite to say we'll be sitting here clueless while they practise mind stuff."

Ranevargar laughed in a way that meant Rhys was right.

"Rhys is refreshingly frank."

"Yes, and it's all new. He hardly even used to speak to people when I first met him."

"Your friendship and love have released his true nature, Kieran."

"Um! What are we doing with the Opal?"

Ranevargar laughed yet again. This time because Rhys had Woorawa in a headlock and was dragging him towards the oasis.

"I have been puzzling about how it was possible for you to access my Pearl. Can you show me how you did it?"

"Yes, of course, but tell me to stop if you don't like it. It made me really angry when my Opal was accessed."

"I'm ready this time, so I don't expect we will need to stop."

He reached inside his tunic for the little leather pouch then opened it and took out the Pearl.

"Can you sense its presence without physical contact? The reaction last time happened when you took it into your hand."

"Not at the moment, but I kind of shut it out when you got upset. I remember starting to feel connected, like I did the first time I touched my Opal, so I'm fairly certain the same thing will happen if I hold it again."

"I think so too."

Ranevargar offered his Pearl, but before taking it Kieran unclasped his neck chain.

"If you hold my Opal again, we might learn extra things."

Ranevargar's pleasure at this exchange, overlaid with a tinge of awe, came clearly through their wide-open channel of communication, then changed to deep concentration when the green glow appeared, and the tingle of sensation spread from Kieran's hands to the rest of his body.

A quick probe showed no hint of diffidence and a strong sense of curiosity from Ranevargar, so Kieran welcomed the reaction and added strength to it.

"Can you see how I'm connected, Ranevargar? It's nearly the same as my Opal."

"Amazing! Can you draw power?"

Kieran used his normal call pattern and a tiny trickle of energy made its way into the pool he automatically constructed to receive it. *A trickle?* He stopped abruptly.

"Ranevargar, there's hardly anything there. I know how, but I'm not going to take it."

"Once again you surprise me with the amount of energy you are accustomed to. Yes, my reserves are very small."

"Watch this. I know it will work."

The call went to the Opal this time. A strong call which, compared to the trickle from the Pearl, brought a torrent flooding into the storage pool and then out again through his link to the Pearl. Ranevargar's surprise and gratitude made Kieran feel very pleased.

"Stop! Stop! You mustn't deplete your own reserves, Kieran. That's too much."

"No, it's not. There's plenty more. I can tell, and there's enough there now to test your Pearl properly."

Kieran stopped the flow from the Opal, called on the Pearl for what he considered to be a normal flow, then reversed the direction to replenish the Pearl.

"Wonderful, Kieran, now let us explore. Is my own connection to the Pearl obvious to you?"

"Yes. At first I saw it through you, but now I can see it my own way."

"Try to break my connection."

"No way! That would be awful."

"It would. Try anyway, but stop if you have any success."

Kieran increased the strength of his own connection to the Pearl, thinking it might be a way to take over. *Wow!* It showed some interesting things, but it didn't change Ranevargar's link. *Hmm!* What else could he try? Memory of the attack at home flooded back. His pattern of defence was there too—very strongly there—and if he could combine them it might work.

He reached to Ranevargar's connection. A great wave of shock shook both of them for the instant before he cut his effort.

"Sorry, Ranevargar! Sorry! Sorry! Sorry! It worked way better than I thought it would."

There was a long moment while Ranevargar did something that Kieran couldn't understand.

"All is now well, Kieran. I was expecting trial and error. Rather than an instant attack of such strength."

"I don't know why I can't learn to be more careful and not rush things."

"How did you do that? I was too shocked to watch properly."

"I copied the way I was attacked at home."

"And is it an all-or-nothing technique?"

Kieran had to think before, with some relief and a kind of mental smile, he answered. "No. I can be gentle … or rough."

"Good. Try again, but gently, very gently."

"Are you sure? Something bad nearly happened. I don't know what it was, but I don't want to frighten you like that again."

"I'm sure, Kieran, because you *must* develop more control."

This time the touch was so light Ranevargar didn't know it was happening. Kieran increased its strength in tiny increments till its effect registered.

"That's uncomfortable, Kieran. Keep your pressure at that level while I figure a way to counter it."

For the next few minutes, Ranevargar battled each new attempt to wrest control of his Pearl.

"Enough. I've reached my limit and it's your turn to be on the defence. I will start very gently. The rule is to counter without fighting back."

Ranevargar tried, tried harder, then even harder before laughing aloud.

"The Opal is yours and yours alone. No one in the Realms could possibly break that bond."

"But I *could* take your Pearl if I really tried. It doesn't seem fair."

"You have taught me a new method of defence, Kieran. You have mastered a much finer degree of control for yourself as well, so we have both benefited a great deal. I am still completely at a loss to understand where the energy you call comes from though, and you don't appear to have studied your Opal in any detail."

"I've practised different ways of calling its energy. Rhys's healing takes a lot more than making things glow or finding animal minds when they're a long way away."

"What about its protective function? You describe that as something it initiated without input on your part."

"I'd have to go back to Dead World with all those monsters, but that's too dangerous."

"Not necessarily. I can help you with that, but first I want to show you other possible functions for your Opal. Close your connection to my Pearl and follow mine. I want to show you what you interrupted when you disturbed my linkage."

Kieran did what he was told and followed Ranevargar's pathway to the Pearl, wondering what could be ahead, because so far it was no different to the pathway he'd just switched off.

"Follow my link to Krol first. It's the most powerful and easiest to see."

"What do you mean? You're not linked to him."

"Yes I am. Always, but not in my conscious mind. Follow the highlighted connection."

And there it was, a trace of linkage leading to a tiny spark of identity located deep in the Pearl.

"I can see it, Ranevargar. It's like you have a special place for him."

"Good. Now, let us add in Kan and Kron."

"Wow! The Pearl keeps you permanently linked to them."

"Yes, and here are the rest of my Griffin constructs."

Kieran could hardly believe it. Fifty-seven tiny sparks all linked through the Pearl to a part of Ranevargar's mind he'd never seen.

"And here are the Panther constructs."

Kieran was suddenly aware of 276 Panther sparks, all tracing through the Pearl pathway to Ranevargar.

"How do you do that?"

"That's what I hope to teach you, Kieran, but prepare yourself first, while I reveal some of the greater potential in my Pearl."

Tiny sparks, the impression of them really, appeared for the dolphin constructs, the Tree Managers, and then an avalanche of what Kieran knew must be all the living things in the Realm. His mind overflowed with wonder and all he could do for a long time was watch and try to build his understanding.

"Thank you, Kieran. Your appreciation is another gift."

"It's like your Pearl is alive."

"It's not alive in itself, but as you can now see, it connects me to the life all around. Are you ready to try with your Opal?"

Kieran couldn't understand what Ranevargar meant.

"I don't have a Realm full of animals and other life, Ranevargar. Do you mean we can share all this through my Opal?"

Ranevargar was startled. "I have no idea if that is even possible, but you do have lives, Kieran. Precious lives which are perfectly suited. We will start with Krol first though."

"Krol?"

"Yes, he is strong in your mind and we can use his pattern to get you started. Watch carefully while I make a copy of his link, and anchor it to a new location in my Pearl."

A second link for Krol appeared.

"Your turn, Kieran. Duplicate that link and anchor it in the same place."

Kieran was tricked by the anchoring part and had to be guided by Ranevargar who was totally delighted when it finally worked.

"Wonderful, Kieran. The location part is the key to the whole network and I wasn't sure if it would be possible for you. Make a new copy, but this time anchor it in your Opal."

Kieran had more trouble but, after referencing Ranevargar's network several times, he finally had Krol anchored.

"What have I done wrong, Ranevargar? The link's there, but it doesn't feel right."

"It should. You did everything correctly as far as I could see."

"It *is* Krol, but there's something different about him."

"Oh my! Now I see what we've done. You are seeing my view of him. Build your own link instead of using a copy of mine."

A couple of minutes later, Kieran's Opal had its own mini-network with seven special lives connected.

"There we are, Kieran. A whole new function for your Opal and another indication of its similarity to our Stones of Power. Now, I have one more exercise for you before we join the swimmers."

Kieran swivelled to look at the oasis where the calls and yells suggested Rhys was happily fending off some sort of double attack from Mr B and Woorawa.

"Let's get started then. This heat is making me want to join them."

"I think this will be easy for you, Kieran. Look into my Pearl and tell me what energy flows you can see."

Kieran was immediately very confident. He'd had lots of experience at energy flows with his practices, and especially when Tan and Krol had been healed, so he went straight in to look.

"Wow! Your Pearl's busy, Ranevargar. There's a big inflow from somewhere which goes out again all over the Realm, and a small flow going into your reserve pool from the Realm Trees."

"The large flow comes in constantly from the Nexus I told you of and is constantly monitored by the High King, who is responsible for maintaining its stability. The Realm Trees provide a trickle of energy, but only when they haven't been depleted by a recent translation."

Kieran turned his attention to another supply of energy, which looked almost identical to the main inflow.

"What about that third stream? It looks like more of that Nexus energy."

"It is, Kieran. It's the portion set aside for my personal use."

"Where's it all going then? It follows a very strange link ... Wow! That's Dead World. Why are you sending energy there?"

"You can see that link?"

"Only because the power flow goes through the Boundary. Is it meant to be secret?"

"Not particularly, but it is meant to be inaccessible."

"Oops! Sorry! I'll leave it alone then."

"Yes, for the moment at least. If you did manage to follow it, it could give you a great deal of trouble. We will join your companions now and I will explain more after our next translation."

Kieran was totally intrigued, but he'd have to be patient, because Krol was gliding out of the sky on a path that looked set to land right in the oasis.

"What's he doing?"

"He wants to join in, partly to refresh himself, but mostly for enjoyment. Go ahead, Kieran. I'll be with you all in a while."

Kieran rushed off, completely eager for action and laughter after the heavy concentration demanded by Ranevargar's mind work. He paused to watch the unusual sight of Krol landing in the water, and then paused again at the edge where three piles of clothes had been dumped.

Rhys came splashing towards him. "Yay, Kieran! We should stay here all day. What's Ranevargar doing?"

"Catching up with his Realm stuff. He won't be long … Watch out!"

Too late. Krol's great beak sneaked between Rhys's legs from behind and lifted till, startled and unbalanced, he fell sideways into the waist-deep water. He came up splattering with mock outrage and splashed scoops of water at Krol's face.

"Great overgrown chook! You've had it … Help me get him, Kieran."

Getting Krol was pointless, but fun. Scoops of water either rolled off his feathers or, if better targeted, caused an eye to blink as Kieran joined Rhys in a double splash-attack.

Woorawa arrived to help, and promptly disappeared when an outspread wing landed on his head and pushed him under.

Krol's head came close again, trying for some sort of mischief. Rhys dodged, but when he dived and wrapped both arms tight around the probing beak he was lifted, yelling, into the air and tossed, with a quick sideways flick, to splash down some five or six metres away. When two fierce eyes focused on Kieran, he mentally reached to see what was coming. Nothing for him, but Tan, watching from his apparently safe position, was surely going to be surprised.

Krol's head and neck dipped suddenly under, then lifted so a surge of water rolled backwards to drench his rider. Tan's total surprise was compounded when widespread wings also dipped then rose in a V shape. More water cascaded and a bedraggled-looking Tan made the wise decision that, despite being fully clothed, he'd be better off in the oasis. Everyone else was practically helpless with laughter.

*   *   *

"Build each step carefully and only trigger the translation after I have checked everything, Kieran."

The whole group was dressed and full of expectation for Kieran to take them to their next location: a small grove surrounded by rainforest at the base of a low mountain range. The laughter and happy excitement of their antics in the oasis were now subdued by Kieran's change to quiet preoccupation with making sure he was ready for this first independent portal, and everyone was waiting with hands touching in the physical contact he'd asked for.

"Do you need an energy boost, Kieran? You did all that stuff with Ranevargar and the mucking round with Krol was full on."

"I feel good, Rhys. I'm relaxed and ready, but I'll have it anyway. We'll all have it, so we're ready for anything."

Whoops! That last comment brought questioning looks.

"That came out wrong. Ranevargar's watching and he won't let me mess up."

"Stop talking and get on with the jump, Kieran."

Spider-link! Group-link! Trigger! Blur!

Hands dropped and all heads turned to take in the new clearing with a Realm Tree base at one end and a wall of dark green vegetation at the other. Kieran turned too, but then grabbed Rhys for support.

"Whoa. That was harder than I expected. Give me another boost, then let me sit down for a moment, Rhys."

The surroundings were forgotten and Kieran became the centre of concerned attention.

"What did I miss, Ranevargar? You said the Realm Trees would do all the work."

"You missed nothing, Kieran. It was a perfect jump."

"Why was it so hard then? You don't collapse when you do it."

"Hmm. It wasn't the jump process, so it was something of your own doing ... Yes, I see. You were hugely overprotective and drained yourself by holding the group connected too strongly, many times more strongly than necessary."

Rhys was gently massaging Kieran's temples and looking very worried.

"It's all right, Rhys. We've worked out what I did and it won't happen next time."

"What won't happen? It's scary when you collapse in a heap on the ground."

"I used way too much energy holding us together and it's easy to fix. How long do we stay here, Ranevargar?"

Ranevargar had a big smile. "I would suggest at least half an hour for recovery this time, but that's up to you from now on and we can leave whenever you feel ready. We also need to continue our private discussion, so your companions might like to explore the surroundings for a while."

"You're getting rid of us again? Kieran hasn't seen anything at any of the groves, Ranevargar."

"You're welcome to stay, Rhys, but our communication will be non-verbal and I do believe you would be quite taken by a walk through the moss forest."

"Taken?"

"Delighted. Enraptured. Impressed. All should apply for someone with your high level of curiosity."

Rhys laughed. "All right. Woorawa will drag us away anyhow after that description."

Woorawa jumped eagerly to his feet and Rhys laughed again.

"See what I mean. We'll be back before half an hour … if he doesn't drag us too far."

Woorawa hadn't waited to listen to any of this, so Rhys, Tan and Mr B jogged after him.

"Rhys is right, Ranevargar. I've missed out on all their exploring trips."

"I know, Kieran. I regret the persistent way I have dominated your time, but with three Realm Lords actively seeking you, I am very concerned for your continued independence."

"Actively? The Coursers are still searching then?"

"Yes, but far more significantly, a powerful probe of far-seeing has been directed at my Central Grove and two of the other groves we activated."

"You mean they look through the Coursers' eyes the way you taught me with the joker birds?"

"No, a craftsman, gifted and trained in the ability, looks directly with the aid of a mirror or water surface. To do so across my Realm Boundary means either direct aid from the High King or the use of a triad of power."

A burst of information from Ranevargar showed Kieran how a triad worked.

"Wow! That is interesting. Can you tell which it is?"

"Aglaron has only a moderate ability for far-seeing, so it will certainly be a triad."

"What if they look at this grove? Can you stop them?"

"Yes, but that would immediately make this location the centre of even greater attention."

"I suppose so, and if they see us we'll have to run again."

Ranevargar said nothing and instead instructed Kieran to watch carefully. Through the network in his Pearl he linked to one of the hosts at the Seaside Grove and immediately become aware of the far-seeing probe.

"They are systematically looking at groves that have been activated, Kieran, which is a puzzle, because activation implies someone has left."

"Yes, but they will find us if they keep changing like that. Why don't we make our next portal to one of the places they've already been?"

"*Hmm! That is a good idea, but it won't work ... My new theory is that they are choosing locations where a Courser is ready to keep watch when they move on. If I'm right they will far-see my Central Lakes Grove next, because a Courser has just arrived there.*"

"*Have they sent even more Coursers? There were eight the last time we looked, so that leaves three groves they can't cover.*"

"*They can far-see them, Kieran, so that still leaves us with a likelihood of being discovered.*"

"*What if we move away from any of the groves and wait till they've stopped their far-seeing? We can go wherever we like then, because the Coursers are easy to trick. I already knew how to send false memories before you taught me to be even better at it.*"

"*Time is important, so let us move now. In this rainforest, the thick canopy will hide us even from a Courser's keen eyes if they direct one here.*"

"*Why not hide inside a shelter? The Coursers can't see inside a Realm Tree.*"

"*With far-seeing they can. Let us move.*"

Kieran's earlier impression of Ranevargar as a fragile old man faded even more as they trotted at a good pace across the clearing and into the rainforest.

"*Yes, Kieran. Without Rhys's healing I would most definitely be walking ... but here is Krol to help me.*"

The great Griffin joined them, and in an instant Ranevargar was mounted and Kieran was running to keep up. At least the track was wide enough and suitable for Krol's large strides. Ten minutes later they caught up with the rest of the group, wide-eyed and wondering, where they'd stopped at Ranevargar's mental prompting.

"What are we hiding from, Kieran? Have Spooks arrived at the Realm Trees?"

"Not Spooks, Rhys. Eyes. Invisible ones from another Realm, that can see through the trees and inside the shelters, so we need to get out of their range."

"From another Realm? Why can't they see us here then? The Realm Trees would be more cover than this."

"They could see us anywhere if they knew where to look, but the effort involved in searching without a focus like the grove is too much, and this canopy will hide us from the prying eyes of any Courser they might send."

"How can they see from another Realm? Do they look into birds or animals like you and Ranevargar do?"

"No, Woorawa, they use mirrors, but I don't know how. Ranevargar hasn't had a chance to tell me."

"Mirrors to see from a long way away? That's called scrying in my novels."

"We call it far-seeing, Rhys. Scrying is when it is local."

"They're still after us. I wish they'd give up and leave us alone."

Ranevargar nodded seriously. "Far from giving up, Woorawa, their efforts are escalating and, if the High King decides to become directly involved, your whereabouts will inevitably be revealed."

"What's the point of hiding out here then?"

"Time, Rhys. The longer we have, the more I can help Kieran prepare for confrontation, or for further flight, if you think that necessary."

"Confrontation's not going to help. They're after us and they'll do anything to get us, Ranevargar. We don't trust them one little bit."

"I tend to agree with you, Kieran, but what if I were to intercede on your behalf, while you remain hidden and free?"

"And try to find out what's going on? No, that's not going to help us get home."

As soon as he said this everyone gave him a questioning look.

"You explained that the High King's the only one who can send us back, so that means he's the one who took Rhys in the first place. I know you think he's got integrity, but the actions against us have all been ruthless and we're not going to trust any of them. Somehow my Opal helped me bring the rest of us here, so that means we can get back by ourselves when I find out how. I love learning from you, with all your help and trust, Ranevargar, and that's the right way for me. High Lords or High Kings who paralyse us with Spooks and kidnap Rhys and break into our minds are the wrong way. I don't want anything to do with them."

There was silence while everyone reacted to the power behind Kieran's words and then Mr B spoke up. "We're completely behind Kieran when he makes important decisions like this, Ranevargar."

"So be it. We will attempt our own path to knowledge and understanding. Kieran, to translate beyond the Realms you must form powerful focus patterns for your departure and destination locations, construct a unique spider-link—as you term it—between them, and then use your power to access the great portal structure that services all of Faerie."

"My Opal will give me the power. It did to get here, and going through the Boundaries took even more, so I know it can do it again. I've sort of got the spider-link between home and where we first arrived, too, so I might be able to figure out how to use that."

"You can't use that spider-link, Kieran. It will only take you in one direction."

"So, have we got any hope of getting home? You make it sound a lot harder than jumping from grove to grove."

"Vastly harder, Mr B, but don't lose hope, because Kieran has already shown extraordinary capability. His startling performance today has taken him well on the way to where he needs to be."

Rhys linked his arm through Kieran's and pulled him close in a happy expression of pride. "See, Kieran! You're a startling performer and we're all part of your circus … How close are we to the big act, Ranevargar?"

Kieran smiled outwardly because Rhys was a twit, a happy twit, who kept them all grounded and close with his own performances. And he smiled inwardly at Ranevargar's efforts to understand the circus imagery.

"I see Mr B thinks of it as a finale, Rhys, but there will have to be a number of smaller acts before Kieran is ready for a big one."

"Okay, Mr Ringmaster, what are they then?"

Kieran was as curious as everyone else about that, but he had to wait while Ranevargar figured out ringmaster.

"Well, Ringmaster for the moment, Rhys. Kieran's next act must be to master the skill of focusing his own unique settings for departure and destination locations."

Rhys swivelled Kieran so that they were face on. "Can you do that, Kieran?"

"I hope so. As soon as Ranevargar shows me."

"You learnt the eleven grove locations with little effort, Kieran, so I want you to apply a similar structure to this place."

Kieran went quiet while he started to think, then couldn't help laughing at all the expectant faces. "You're not going to see anything. I have to do it in my mind."

"We *will* see if you nod or shake your head."

Kieran nearly nodded in reply to Tan, but stopped in case it mixed the message, then looked carefully at the surrounding trees and vegetation. It was easy to fix the images in his mind—that was straight-out memory— but calling up the location pattern for the Realm Trees they'd just left showed a big difference to just plain memory … Yes, Ranevargar had called it a structure, and that was a helpful word for it. Each Realm Tree had an overlay of connection to its neighbour, which built a unique identity for the group as a whole. He'd have to do the same for this collection of tree trunks, ferny growths and traceries of hanging moss. Startled, he realised this was easy.

"Wow, Ranevargar. This is a bit like using my GPS … I mean my direction sense."

"And it is looking good. Finish up, lock it in your mind and you can use it to take us to another grove."

"What?"

Krol's head lifted high and the four companions jolted with surprise at Kieran's exclamation.

"Sorry, Ranevargar just told me we're going to portal from here instead of back at the Grove."

"Yes, Kieran. Your Opal will have to help, because there's no grove to provide energy, but that shouldn't be a problem."

"Now? You said we rushed out here to stay hidden for a while?"

"Rhys is right, Kieran. When the far-seeing ceases we can choose any grove without a Courser, and in the meantime we can work through those other matters."

"Which matters, Ranevargar? Are we part of them or are they just for Kieran?"

"They are special things for Kieran, Rhys, but we will explain them as we go, because my concern is growing and I think we should stay close together."

"Till the far-seeing stops?"

"Yes, Woorawa. It is an exhausting process and the elves involved must be tired already."

Rhys pointed to a fallen tree trunk at the side of the track. After a few moments Ranevargar, Kieran and Mr B were sitting on the tree trunk, facing Rhys, Woorawa and Tan, who were on the track itself with their backs propped against Krol's body.

Woorawa spoke up first. "What sort of things have you been talking to Kieran about, Ranevargar? Apart from learning the grove portals, I mean. You've been working together after every move so far and we haven't heard about any of it."

"We have been refining some of his skills, Woorawa, as well as sharing knowledge about my Pearl and his Opal. Right now, I am hoping to learn something of the special shields he uses to keep us hidden and protected. Without them, my whereabouts are open to the other Realm Lords and especially to the High King. If we are separated I will be besieged with demands for explanation and information, but if Kieran can teach me his shields I will be able to choose my own time to open myself to all the demands directed at me."

"You think we're going to be separated?"

"Yes, Mr B, at some stage, and probably sooner than we would like."

"We should stop talking then, so you can work with Kieran."

Rhys grinned, made the zip movement to close his mouth, then looked to Woorawa and Tan to join him.

"You've been looking at my shields ever since we met, Ranevargar. Can't you just copy them?"

"The pattern is too complicated, Kieran, and beyond that I don't have a constant flow of energy to maintain them."

"Energy? It doesn't need much. Make a special pool in your mind and I'll fill it for you."

"I store excess energy in my Pearl."

"Okay, but check how we all keep a pool ready for the Spook ropes. I think that might be better."

"Ranevargar paused while he examined the pools. "Yes, you are right, but there is much I don't understand here, Kieran. Somehow you have passed a degree of control to non-power users. Can you do the same for me?"

"Of course."

The wide open connection between Kieran and Ranevargar made this easy and an elegant self-contained pool structure formed, then absorbed a flow of energy from the Opal.

"That is extraordinary, Kieran, but how do I use it?"

Kieran, surprised, watched Ranevargar's attempts at access.

"Sorry, I made an automatic access key to use with the Spook ropes. How about I do the same for you, except linking it to your shields?"

Ranevargar nodded, then explained what was going on to everyone else.

"Kieran just gave me a reservoir of energy in a way so different to anything I've seen I couldn't use it till he showed me how. Now that I have it, I hope to use it with his special shield patterns."

"There's always something different when Kieran's involved. That's something you have to get used to, Ranevargar."

Silence followed while Ranevargar watched Kieran build copies of mind shields and tried, with very limited success, to follow what he was doing. Eventually he put a hand to his forehead and spoke his resignation.

"Part of what you do requires strength I don't have, and part is beyond my comprehension. Constant training sessions might help me make progress, Kieran, but for now I must accept my limitations."

"Yes, you have got better, but you wouldn't be able to fight off a big attack like the one they tried against me … Is anything changing with the far-seeing?"

"Come with me while I check my theory. This ability is one I have mastered, but I suspect you might be able to learn the technique for yourself."

Kieran studied everything as a link was made to a host elf at the Central

Lakes Grove. Through her, a subtle trace enveloped the whole Grove and brought instant awareness of watching eyes. A shift in perception also showed a Courser wheeling in a great circle above.

"Lord Uirebon controls the Courser, Kieran. Can you see the pattern of his identity?"

"Sort of. It's not very clear though."

"Something else for you to practise. Let us return to our companions."

Kieran turned the following off and focused on his friends.

"Ranevargar's idea about the far-seeing seems to be right, because they're looking at the Central Lakes Grove and a Courser has just arrived there."

"Does that mean you can tell where they're going next?"

Kieran followed again while Ranevargar made the long distance reach to all eight Coursers.

"One is approaching the Oasis Grove, Woorawa, and another is … ten or twelve minutes away from the Mountain Base Grove. If the pattern follows, the far-seeing will move to the Oasis next."

Woorawa spoke again.

"And did Kieran learn how to tell when the far-seeing is happening?"

Kieran answered, "Yes, Woorawa, but I'll need lots more practice with Ranevargar before I'm good enough to do it by myself."

"Yes and no at the same time? How does that work?"

"I can do it, but I'm so clumsy they'd know I was checking on them. Ranevargar really is a master and they haven't got a clue when he's watching."

"Is that what you're going to practise now?"

This time Ranevargar answered, "There are several other matters with a higher priority, Woorawa. I want to show Kieran how to fight with Krol." Kieran had no inkling of this and his astonishment was as great as everyone else's.

Ranevargar laughed. "With him, Kieran, not against him. If you'd known how to help him at the time, he'd have vanquished the Unordered Monster with little or no harm to himself."

"You mean with the Spook ropes? There was nothing else I could do. I did sense its mind a bit, but it was too different and there wasn't time anyway to do anything about controlling it."

"No, not with the Spook ropes, though whatever you've done to them does seem to have made them more effective. I shudder at the thought of any encounter with such a flimsy means of defence. My Griffins are unique in the Realms and grow with a combination of power and normal flesh, Kieran. You noticed this when you healed Krol, but till now we've been too busy with other things for any elaboration."

"Power? So that was why he healed so quickly? We thought it must have been because Rhys and I were getting better at it, but now that I think about it, he did soak it up like crazy."

"I'm sure you were, but his affinity with power was helping. Watch while I activate his special defence mechanism."

Everyone looked to Krol and watched his head lift and the feathers of his neck and crown ruffle in display.

"That display is Krol's acknowledgement, Rhys. Kieran is the only one who can see the real change."

Rhys turned to Kieran for more explanation.

"Ranevargar's sending a tiny trickle of power to Krol and something is all around him, a bit like the glows I make, except it's different as well as being invisible. What does it do, Ranevargar?"

"It's an aura of dissolution and a shield of revulsion."

Rhys turned from Kieran to Ranevargar. "Good grief! That sounds scary. What's it mean in ordinary words?"

Ranevargar laughed and the trickle of energy faltered. "Exactly what it says, Rhys. A physical touch from Krol will affect the body of the Unordered Monster. At the same time, Krol's flesh will feel repulsive if it gets touched."

"Wow! Except it's not working. Woorawa, Mr B and Tan are all leaning against him and they're not dissoluting."

Ranevargar laughed again and once more the energy flow faltered. "Dissolving is the word you mean, Rhys. The aura is specific and will only affect Dead World Monsters."

Woorawa moved his hand amongst the ruffled neck feathers. "And he doesn't feel repulsive either, Rhys."

Rhys told Woorawa he was the repulsive one, then asked how well the aura worked.

"That depends on how much energy I can provide. When Krol, Kan and Kron faced the Unordered Monster which was about to attack you, I was exhausted from the effort of making a portal to the Grove with them then speeding them to the confrontation, and they had no assistance at all."

"How did you know where we were? Kieran had us all hidden behind his shields."

"I didn't know, Woorawa. Any Incursion must be dealt with as rapidly as possible, as the Monster will detect and destroy any life it can find. My first knowledge of your existence was through Kieran's approach to

Kron and Kan, and then your care for Krol made all other Realm matters secondary."

"So, if Krol had had this aura thing working, he wouldn't have been hurt?"

"Not mortally, Rhys, but he still would have been hurt. My energy resources are limited, especially over such a distance."

"Kieran will give you some … Do the Monsters come very often?"

"Kieran has already given me a large reserve through our shield practice. There are two types of Incursion, Rhys, and there is no way to predict either."

"Two? I hope the other ones aren't as bad."

Kieran spoke up. "We already know they aren't, Rhys. The Monster you killed wasn't as bad as the one Krol fought."

"It wasn't? I thought they were the same. They looked the same."

"No, they weren't. Remember how your Spook rope worked differently on them?"

"Kieran is right, Rhys, but that first Monster you encountered is unable to leave the Unordered Realm. Most attacks are of a type we call Chaos Incursions and their strength and form constantly changes. They are dangerous and destructive but usually within my ability to banish."

"Usually? What happens when they aren't? Does Krol help you?"

"No, Rhys. My Griffins would be destroyed. It is the High King's responsibility to keep all Realms free of Chaos Incursions. He has the resources as well as surpassing ability, so I call on him in extreme cases."

"If it's his job, then he should do it all, and you could keep your energy for other things."

"Aglaron is often too busy to respond quickly, Rhys, and I don't have to use my own reserves. Kieran have you figured the aura pattern yet?"

"Hang on. We've been talking about too many interesting things … There's nothing to learn really. It's built-in to the Griffins and all they need is a flow of energy."

Ranevargar raised an eyebrow. "You think so? Have a try then."

Kieran tried. Energy flowed but no aura appeared. *Weird.*

"It's similar to the Realm Trees, Kieran, where nothing happens without you sending the right trigger. I thought you missed it, so watch again."

And there it was, a simple trigger pattern with the very first trickle of energy.

"I've got it. Let me have another go."

"Good, but start very gently till you understand the process properly."

Ranevargar switched off and Kieran used the trigger with a matching energy flow. Krol's eyes focused on him and his feathers ruffled. A quick check showed his surprise as well as recognition that his aura was working.

"Excellent, Kieran. Feel your way carefully and see what you can do."

That meant increasing the energy flows slightly. *Aha!* That was okay as long as there was no spill-over effect. This was interesting.

"Watch this, Ranevargar. I'm going to show everyone else."

"??"

With a small extra call on his Opal, Kieran chose the colour purple and made the part of the aura outside Krol's body glow.

"Whoo! That looks unreal. What does the colour do, Kieran?"

"Nothing. I just added it so you could see the aura."

Woorawa, Rhys and Tan all moved their fingers experimentally through the glow, while Krol lifted one taloned foot to check this surprising development.

"Impressive indeed, Kieran. Is the strength of that glow linked to the strength of the aura?"

"Um … it is now. Watch this."

Very carefully, because Ranevargar's concern for Krol's wellbeing was very clear, Kieran gradually increased the flow till the aura was much more powerful. The correspondingly bright glow was uncomfortable to look at and a big handspan in depth.

"Stop! Stop!"

Kieran did, of course, while Ranevargar checked carefully for any ill effects.

"You have so much natural strength, Kieran. I would never have been able to approach anywhere near that level. I see how your slight change to hold the energy more steadily in the aura protects Krol too, and I will apply it to all the other Griffins."

Kieran was really pleased that he'd learnt this so well and impressed Ranevargar so much. He wanted Ranevargar to feel good too, so he switched the aura off.

"It's your turn now, Ranevargar. Build Krol's defence to the same level."

"I can't do that, Kieran. You know very well how limited I am for energy use."

"Yes, you can. We'll just make another special pool for you with plenty of reserves. How often do you get attacked by Unordered Monsters, and how many Griffins is best to fight them off?"

"There is never more than one and they are quite rare. Kieran, with an aura of that strength a single Griffin would easily overcome an Unordered Monster, but Griffins, by nature, are group fighters and I would never send less than three."

"Well, that's no problem, except it'll be a lot of energy to store. I think we should use your Pearl this time. Can we set aside a place separate to your ordinary storage, so the energy doesn't get frittered away on other things?"

"Another new way of doing things for me to get used to, Kieran. Of course we can, but I'm finding it increasingly hard to understand where all your energy comes from. At some stage we must spend time looking into it more thoroughly."

"I suppose, except every time we do something it leads to so many other new things to think about. I can't keep up ... Here comes your energy."

Five minutes later Ranevargar was in a state of disbelief. Kieran took no notice though and didn't stop till there was enough energy reserved to cope with three more Unordered Monsters and Ranevargar had practised making the full-strength aura.

"Why don't you use the glow as a weapon?"

Everyone turned to Tan.

"What do you mean? A bit of purple light won't make a scrap of differ-ence to an Unordered Monster. I only put it there so everyone could see what Ranevargar and I were working with."

"I know it wouldn't hurt physically, Kieran, but it got so bright I had to squint to keep looking at it. If you made it white instead of purple it could dazzle the Monster for a few critical seconds, and if you only turned it on when Krol was about to attack it would be even more effective."

Rhys expressed his approval of the idea by giving Tan a friendly whack in the chest and a hug before turning to Kieran and Ranevargar. "He *is* brilliant! Kieran, who'd ever think of using a glow for a weapon? It doesn't take much energy either, does it?"

Kieran shared some quick thoughts with Ranevargar before answering.

"You've done it again, Tan, and Ranevargar's really impressed. Shield your eyes, everyone, while we experiment."

"Hang on! What about Krol's eyes? You'll have to do something to stop him getting dazzled too."

"Hmm! Yes, Mr B, that's a problem."

Kieran wondered if there was any such thing as a light shield or filter, or some way to adapt Griffin eyes to bright light. Ranevargar shook his head.

"There is no need for complication, Kieran. We will just activate Krol's blink reflex while the light flashes ... Cover your eyes, everyone."

Four times Ranevargar warned everyone while he experimented with Krol's blink reflex and the duration and intensity of the light flash.

"Wonderful, Tan. I have spent six centuries confronting Unordered Monsters, but in a matter of minutes you have lightened my burden with this new tactic. I hardly know how to express my thanks."

Woorawa flashed a brilliant smile as he gave Tan a big hug. Then he turned to Ranevargar. "There! I've given him a thank you hug from all of us … Ranevargar, there's something puzzling me. You use the Griffins against the Unordered Monsters, but the other Realms don't have any Griffins, so what do they do instead? That High King must be really strong if he does it for them."

"Aglaron has never faced an Unordered Monster, Woorawa. He *would* be sorely tested, but his strength and access to Nexus power would ultimately allow him to prevail."

"Never? That's not fair. How come he leaves it to you when it's his responsibility?"

"It *is* fair, Woorawa. All High Kings have steadfastly faced Chaos Incursions since the very founding of Faerie, and Aglaron is no exception. The Unordered Monster manifests solely in this Realm and is a burden for which I alone am responsible."

The friends all waited in silence and watched deep emotion play across Ranevargar's suddenly aged-looking features. Kieran, with his special access, saw sadness, regret, tiredness and a deep sense of loss that shocked him so much he reached impulsively to offer both mental and physical support. Ranevargar accepted both and, over a long moment, rallied.

"My apologies, everyone, for my lapse of control. Once again I express my gratitude. Yes, Woorawa, six centuries ago I made a mistake that I was only able to contain with a great sacrifice of power and ability, and the attacks by the Unordered Monsters are an ongoing side effect."

Rhys couldn't contain his amazement. "That terrible Monster's just a side effect? Ranevargar, the real thing must be awful."

"In a sense you are right, Rhys. I built a construct which would definitely have you full of awe. In the hubris of my burgeoning abilities and ambition, I believed I could infuse a whole Realm with the profusion of life, a Realm which for thousands of years has been barren and unassailable."

"Dead World!"

"Indeed, Rhys, and I almost succeeded in making it a living world."

"What's hubris?"

That brought a hint of amusement.

"Pride, Woorawa. My knowledge and ability with living things became so great I was able to form new creatures, create special guardians, and even grow Realm Trees with the power to make portals. I poured all my resources and energy into making a creature with the ability to master the Nexus energy which, in that Realm, had been wild and uncontrollable for millennia. I *did* believe I could rejuvenate the Unordered Realm, but my understanding of the structural forces and energy flows wasn't complete, and my construct was pitted against forces it could contend with but never quite master. That contention spread havoc through all of Faerie, with constant destructive Incursions that had to be stopped."

Ranevargar paused and Rhys spoke up.

"You created it, so you must have been able to control it."

"That was one of my mistakes, Rhys. Cooperation *is* there, but I also instilled an overriding independence which I believed would enable the construct to manage the Realm without constant oversight on my part. That independence, combined with an imperative to improve the Realm, overrode my strongest efforts for direct control. For months, I despaired that my well-intentioned efforts had impacted all of Faerie with dangerous forces which could only be resolved by sacrificing my life."

Ranevargar paused again and Kieran went with him while he checked what was happening with the far-seeing and the Coursers. Rhys thought he was remembering, or being dramatic, or looking for a response.

"Well, we're glad you worked out something else. Did you unmake the construct?"

"Listen harder, Rhys. Ranevargar said cooperation "is" there, not "was" there, so the construct must still exist and he's got it under control."

"Sorry! I didn't pick that up, Mr B … But why did you think you'd have to sacrifice your life, Ranevargar?"

"We stopped while we checked the far-seeing, and they are currently examining the Oasis Grove … Mr B is correct, Rhys. The construct is alive and well, but your thoughts about unmaking are exactly the reason why I thought I might have to end my life. There is so much of myself invested in the construct that any involuntary unmaking would take me with it, and this Realm would pass to someone of the High King's choosing. The end of my stewardship would have meant a loss far greater, with a diminishment and change in the nature and purpose of the whole Realm. Eventually, I solved the problem by keeping the construct in a state of permanent hibernation. It takes a great deal of effort though, and while it is in effect I have no access to the special abilities and knowledge I poured so freely into it."

Kieran suddenly understood. "That's what drains all that energy through your Pearl?"

"Yes, Kieran. The energy must flow to sustain its life and keep it in a sleep state. If it doesn't, the construct will reawaken and, instead of an occasional attack against this Realm, all of Faerie will be faced with constant incursions of Unordered Monsters."

Kieran was horrified. "You've been draining all that energy for six hundred years? Ranevargar, that's beyond belief. There must be some other way to control the construct?"

"I developed the knowledge for amicable control, Kieran, but I've never had the resources, and won't for another three hundred years, when my Central Grove becomes large enough to provide them."

"Realm Trees? How will they help?"

"My Realm Trees produce energy, Woorawa. That's the reason we can portal from one grove to another without using our own power. The energy generation is a slow process, though, and a small grove takes a day to recover enough power for a new translation."

"The Central Grove's already enormous. How much bigger will it have to be?"

"As I said, Rhys, it will require at least another three hundred years of natural growth and storage before I would be confident enough to visit the construct, restore its mobility, and control it while I bring it home."

Tan spoke up. "I'm liking this High King less and less the more I hear. He's left you without a proper amount of energy for six hundred years without offering you any help?"

"That's not really a fair assessment, Tan. The amount of Nexus energy required would disrupt the rest of Faerie."

"Not if he'd made it a steady, small flow over a long time."

"That may be, but he has no real understanding of what happened, and the problem was of my own making. I've always considered it my responsibility to overcome."

Ranevargar held up a hand to pause any conversation, and Kieran went with him while he made another check on the far-seeing.

"Hmm. The triad must finally be exhausted, because the only watching now is through the Coursers. Kieran, it's time to get yourself ready to take us to a new grove."

Without being asked, everyone moved to make the physical contact Kieran liked.

"Which grove, Ranevargar? One of the six without Coursers obviously."

"Yes. Let's aim for the Grove at the other end of the lake system. It's well away from any Courser and it should give us a good respite from interference."

Kieran worked everything quickly and skilfully till he tried to build the one-way spider-link to the destination. He checked the last spider-link pattern he'd used and tried to adapt the parts that might apply, but got nowhere.

"You'll have to show me what I'm missing, Ranevargar. Building a new spider-link's different to using one that already exists."

"Have another try, Kieran."

Kieran tried, but after nearly five minutes of intense concentration and no helpful nudge in the right direction, he knew that he was lacking something fundamental. Ranevargar must be testing him somehow.

"I'm sorry, but I just can't figure it. You'll have to show me."

"I can't, Kieran. It's one of many advanced techniques I lost when I invested so much of myself in the construct. I let you keep trying in the hope you just might be able to figure it out for yourself. Without waking the construct, I'm afraid the only way forward for you is through the High King or one of the other Realm Lords."

This was a real shock, but Kieran considered only briefly before shaking his head in determination and looking for support from all his companions. "No way, Ranevargar. We've already said they can take a running jump … If waking the construct's a way to get the knowledge, then that's what we'll do."

The astonishment and disbelief flooding Ranevargar's mind played powerfully across his features as well, and Kieran rushed to forestall the refusal he could see building.

"And it will save you three hundred years of waiting. It's the best way for all of us, Ranevargar. It's a double-banger reason to go ahead, so you mustn't say no. My Opal will do it—I know it will—and we'll all get what we need."

"You can't, Kieran. It's far too much. You don't understand what you are offering."

Ranevargar's protestation masked the yearning and hope Kieran could see rising in the background of his mind.

"We will when you explain it to us."

Rhys grabbed Ranevargar's arms and whirled him in a couple of impetuous circles. "You'd better say yes … or … or … We'll sic Krol onto you … Or get Gryl to tongue-lick you till you do."

A guttural sound startled everyone as Woorawa broke away and executed a few dance steps, accompanied by lots of dramatic pointing and continued deep chanting.

"The spirits say they will haunt you if you don't work with Kieran."

Mr B and Tan, catching on, whispered to each other, then, as if they'd rehearsed somewhere, performed a slow and very courtly bow towards Ranevargar.

"High Lord of this great Realm, we humbly beseech thee to assist us in this great and noble venture."

Ranevargar, unable to hold back a smile in the face of these antics, replied in kind to Mr B's request. "Companions of the quest, visitors to the Realm, and bearers of hope, your exhortations leave me no choice but to accept the unacceptable and accede in joining this … noble venture."

"Yay!" Rhys cheered and, full of exuberance but no style, copied Woorawa's little dance.

Ranevargar continued to smile, but his mind was now a maelstrom of anticipation, consideration and compounding preparations that Kieran couldn't keep up with. The smile became subdued and Ranevargar finally nodded to the whole group.

Chapter 8

"Kieran, to prepare for a journey to the heart of the Unordered Realm we must return to the Central Grove. I have sent word for provisions and a cohort of Griffins to be readied and told all my Guardians of my coming absence."

Krol's head lifted in distress.

"Not you, Krol. We need you with us for protection and transport."

Ruffled feathers flattened and Kieran sensed the flash of fierce pride and pleasure at his inclusion.

"Are we going to fly into Dead World on the backs of the Griffins?"

"Yes, Rhys. The Griffins will shorten days of travel to a matter of hours. Kieran, can you concentrate while we walk? There are many things I must now share with you."

"I can try, and if there are extra hard bits we can stop while I learn them."

"Good … Lead the way, Woorawa. Kieran and I will be silent but very busy while we walk."

"Access my Pearl, Kieran, while I unlock the energy stored by my Central Grove over the last six hundred years. I will share every process with you, so that if I falter or fail at any time you can give your support, or even take over, if that should be necessary."

"Of course, but how could I? I'm not built into the construct like you are."

"You couldn't by yourself, I'm fairly certain, but if I falter we will still be linked, and you will be able to channel anything unique to my identity."

"I will?"

"Yes. We will work through every necessary step till you have complete mastery. It is a daunting task, but mostly in terms of understanding, rather than memory of detail."

That remained to be seen. Right now Kieran was watching as Ranevargar revealed a new structure deep within the Pearl and proceeded to unravel a complicated barrier.

"Lend me some energy, Kieran. This final lock can only be passed at a time when I have an abundance of power."

Kieran called on his Opal, watched how Ranevargar used his power to dissolve the lock, watched a strange link reach way into the distance, then followed as Ranevargar raced along it. Kieran stopped in his tracks with astonishment while his mind stretched to take in the huge reservoir of Realm Tree energy pulsing gently through the link to the Pearl.

"It's real, Kieran, and seeing it inspires me. I knew by computation how much would be there, but the reality is breathtaking."

"What's wrong, Kieran? Are we stopped so you can think harder?"

"We just linked to all the energy the Realm Trees have stored, Rhys, and it makes our healing pools look like a dewdrop beside a river ... We really need all this, Ranevargar? The construct must be unbelievably powerful."

"Yes, Kieran, and more than as much again, but the call on it won't be instant. It will spread from the time we take control till we return to the safety of this Realm."

"What is this construct? Is it like a big version of Krol?"

"No, Rhys. Krol would have as much effect against it as a joker bird attacking Gryl."

Rhys, and everyone else, stared at the five metres of contained ferocity trailing close behind, then, wide-eyed, back at Ranevargar.

"I don't believe you! It's not possible!"

They all knew it was, but at the same time everyone shared Rhys's incredulity.

"Is there some reason we shouldn't know more about it, Ranevargar? We'll have to see it eventually."

"No good reason, Kieran, apart from worrying about the fear it might induce. Even the image is startling, so prepare yourself."

Kieran held his hand out and everyone grasped it for the support and wellbeing of one of Rhys's energy zaps.

Ranevargar nodded his approval, then sent an image of his special construct to all five friends. Kieran hardly noticed when the hands gripping his own tightened like some sort of multi-vice. He was too startled and shocked to think of anything else while he struggled to force some sort of reality onto what he was seeing.

"Holy dragon balls! I take it all back, Ranevargar. Krol's a cuddly puppy compared to that thing."

Rhys's bizarre, but apt, exclamation, and the unlikely comparison of Krol with a puppy, broke the group's attention and set off Ranevargar's smile. Mr B broke it further.

"We call that a dragon, Ranevargar. Did you have a reason for using that form?"

"We share the same heritage, Mr B. I chose the Dragon form because it signifies the power and wisdom needed for managing an unruly Realm."

"I'm glad you showed us with a mind picture. If I'd seen it for real, I think I would have fainted."

Woorawa gave Rhys a disbelieving whack. "No, you wouldn't. You'd probably go for it with your Spook rope."

Ranevargar was saying nothing, and Kieran could see that it was to let everyone adjust.

Mr B asked another question. "What's the scale of … Sorry, that was an unintentional pun. What size is it, Ranevargar? Its eyes unnerved me so much I didn't take the rest of it in properly."

"It is large, Mr B. Except for some of my whales it is the largest creature in all Faerie. I will show you again, but for a little longer now you are all ready."

The image formed again, so clear that, when he thought about it later, Kieran knew he needed either more learning or an awful lot of practice before he'd be able to match it. This time a Griffin was there as well, standing next to a foreleg with its head just reaching the level of the scaly underbelly. At least ten metres of head and body dwarfed the Griffin, and the ridged tail doubled that. *Good grief! It was enormous!* Kieran started to wonder about the wings, but the eyes grabbed and held him till the image ended.

There was another silence, broken this time by Woorawa.

"It's so big it can't possibly fly. Has it got hollow bones, like birds, or something?"

"Something, Woorawa, not hollow bones. Power assists its take-off … But we must move on while Kieran becomes adept at controlling grove energy."

Woorawa wasn't quite ready to move. "Power can help things fly? Would that work for Kieran then? He's got lots."

"Most likely, Woorawa, but it requires a profligate use of energy for very little effect. I can't show him how either, because that knowledge is lodged in the construct. Lord Uirebon would have the technique somewhere in one of his study centres, but you are avoiding him, so if Kieran is really interested in something so esoteric, he will have to wait."

"It can't be that … esoteric? You used it with the Dragon."

"To help with the launch into flight, Woorawa. The construct is a natural flyer and once airborne needs no assistance."

Rhys was staring at Kieran with one of his big grins plastered widely across his face. "So, now he can leap buildings in a single bound."

Oh! Kryptonite jokes were going to be a new feature from now on.

"We're going to keep finding new things he can do with the power, aren't we?"

"Of course, Rhys. I sense a strong affinity in Kieran for the ways of my Realm. Given the time and opportunity, I would show him much, but there are a multitude of other paths for power as well. There are arts of the mind, techniques and schools of conflict and domination, ways of using the structured energy of the Nexus and the wild energy from beyond the outer Boundaries. Rhys, we are being distracted. It is time to proceed."

Kieran wanted to talk, like everyone else, about the Dragon construct, and particularly its eyes, but that would have to wait.

"Create a reservoir and make a five-second transfer of energy from the Central Grove, Kieran."

"That's easy. I don't see the point."

"You will, but go ahead now, and then return the energy without any loss."

No loss? Kieran paused, because so far he'd just called for energy and used it without any thought about wastage. *Hmm!* He'd need a technique for accurate measurement.

"Show me how you measure, Ranevargar, and save us time. You've probably been doing this for a thousand years."

Ranevargar drew a little energy from the Grove, then returned it, and Kieran watched how he measured the amount for both ways. *Neat.* He made his own two-way transfer—wasn't pleased—so tightened everything and did again.

"That's better. Now, take double the energy in the same time."

That was easy, but after doubling four more times it wasn't.

"You must figure a way to cope, Kieran, because we still need at least two more doublings."

Two more? That wasn't possible … well … maybe.

"Ranevargar, I can only move that amount by using a part of it to keep it contained … or by using my Opal."

"Both ways will work, but use your Opal, Kieran. You will need to call on it just as heavily when the grove energy fails."

Kieran concentrated on this new task so much that he had no awareness of how startled his companions were by the brilliant blue glow now enveloping him.

"Excellent, Kieran. Now, instead of five seconds, try for a sixty-second transfer."

Kieran hesitated because something wasn't right. *"That's too much, Ranevargar. Is there another way of storing so much energy in my mind?"*

"You know more about mind pools than I do … but the pool is not important. Making sure you can manage that rate of flow without letup is."

Without let-up? Whoa! That was so much. Kieran reeled with new understanding of the commitment he'd made.

"Your Central Grove can hold far more than sixty-seconds worth, Ranevargar. What about transferring in from my Opal and just leaving it there?"

"Of course. So sensible. Your young mind and fresh approach humble me."

When the blue glow intensified yet again, Krol's squawk of concern penetrated Kieran's concentration enough to make him check its purpose, realise that everyone was squinting, and reduce the level.

"Sorry. Ranevargar's being a slave driver."

Ranevargar didn't understand Rhys's laugh.

"Have I been unreasonable in my expectations, Kieran? If I'd sensed any real discomfort, I would have moderated our efforts."

"Don't take any notice of Rhys. He was laughing at a joke we have between us when we push each other to work at something. I'll start the energy transfer again, because I lost concentration."

Sixty seconds later Kieran was really pleased. He'd managed the flow with increasing ease, and figured how to make the whole process run automatically, much like his shields.

"Your mastery continues to astonish me, Kieran. Your talent with energy seems to be natural, but the speed at which you learn new things has a sense of training. Have you always been able to learn this way?"

Kieran, full of his accomplishment with the energy flow, was surprised at this digression. No, not really. It was another wake-up to how carefully Ranevargar was watching.

"Um, no. I first remember it after the migraines, when Mr B started coaching me."

"Yet another aspect to consider if only we had the time … Kieran, the moment has come to take you to a part of my mind that can only be reached by accessing my Pearl and then knowing how to unlock the pathway to the Dragon-construct knowledge I have hidden there."

Kieran went into Ranevargar's Pearl and, with great wonderment, followed the pathway being revealed to him.

"Learn this key, Kieran, and hide it somewhere in your Opal where only you can find it."

A six-pointed star projected into Kieran's mind, glowing green, with a Guardian shape in each outer section and a stylised dragon in the centre.

"I've got it, Ranevargar. I'll hide it in my Opal with a lock of my own."

"In a moment, Kieran, when you have seen the full complexity of the lock. The key has to be applied three times, thus."

Kieran watched as, first green, then blue, and then red, the symbol was applied and yet another pathway appeared.

"Wow! What a brilliant idea. Hang on till I catch up."

That took a few seconds while Kieran copied a similar structure into the Opal and used an image of Rhys as the key.

"I'm with you now, Ranevargar. My Opal's getting a lot more complicated than I ever imagined though."

"Yes ... follow the link and I'll take you through the construct controls. I think we should stop walking till we finish, because this will take some effort and the Grove is only a few minutes away."

Kieran would have stopped anyway, because when he surfaced from his deep concentration he found himself sitting on the ground with his back against Krol and everyone else watching quietly.

"Oh boy! That really was close to slave driving, Ranevargar. I got most of it, but there are a few parts that don't make much sense."

"And they won't till you see them actually applied. Relax now, till we reach the Grove."

Kieran's grunt of amusement changed the group's looks from quiet to quizzical.

"Ranevargar's just given me a whole two minutes for relaxing before we reach the Realm Trees and do another portal."

"What were you doing, Kieran? You looked like a bomb could have gone off and you wouldn't even have noticed."

"Mind locks and secrets and new things with Ranevargar's Pearl and my Opal, Woorawa. Learning about the Dragon and how to move lots of energy around."

"What secrets?"

Kieran looked to Ranevargar to answer that.

"Secrets between Kieran and me, Rhys. We'd tell you if it was safe, but you don't have the privacy protections that we do."

Kieran touched his Opal briefly and Rhys understood. "Wow! Heavy stuff, Kieran. Have you really learnt how to help Ranevargar control the Dragon in just ten minutes?"

"Ten minutes?"

"While you've been sitting there against Krol."

"I was slave driving him so much he wasn't aware of the time passing, Rhys, and, yes, I'm confident he can help, or even take over if need be."

"Take over? You seriously mean he'll be able to control that thing all by himself?"

"In practical terms, yes, Rhys. It can't happen without my involvement, but after one more run through, and enough practice, he will be able to get that far even if I'm exhausted or unconscious."

"I suppose it must be something like how he can make us do things or give commands to other animals, but you gave us the feeling your Dragon's way different. Could you teach Mr B or one of us how to control it?"

"The control process for my Dragon does require the ability of elementary mind manipulation, Rhys, but other unique abilities are so important it stretches my own credulity that Kieran can possess them all."

Rhys, who'd fallen in beside Kieran, gave one of the friendly whacks which usually accompanied a stir. "Yeah! He stretches us too. You take one look at him and you know there's something weird going on."

The whack was immediately followed by a companionable arm draped across his shoulder, and the pleasure from this instinctive support did more for Kieran than any relaxing walk ever could.

"Your warrior is a princely friend, Kieran."

"None of you could learn to control my construct, Rhys. Kieran shares my gift of life affinity. He has extraordinarily abilities with the control of power, and he has a consummate skill for the recognition of new patterns. All of these are needed, and he is the only individual I have encountered in over eleven centuries with an adequate level of the life gift."

"Gods! This life thing must be awfully rare then?"

"Not at all. The ability is quite common, Rhys. You have it yourself to a degree."

"Go away!"

"Go away?"

Kieran joined the group smile, then watched Ranevargar make a quick check of Rhys's thoughts.

"I see. An expression of disbelief. Yes, Rhys. Since your arrival in the Realms you have established your own bonds with George, Krol and Gryl. For you, it needs the effort of interaction, open concern and a degree of proximity. Kieran does all that and more with no effort at all."

"Ha! That's why we call him King of the Animals. What would happen if he did make an effort?"

"Give me a month with him, Rhys, and we could start to find out."

"You've got to be kidding? He's learnt how to portal with the groves, control a Dragon, and who knows what else in just today. You say you can keep showing him new stuff for all that time?"

Kieran was hanging out for Ranevargar's reply as much as everyone else.

"As I said, that would be just the beginning. This is my special gift, Rhys, studied and used for the stewardship of my Realm ever since I received my Pearl of power. More and more I am starting to suspect that Kieran could follow the same path, if he so wished."

There was silence till the group reached the Grove clearing.

"Where are we going now, Ranevargar? Straight to the Central Grove?"

"Not directly, Mr B. Kieran wants to practise another translation first, so we will visit the Plains Grove. Join hands, everyone."

"Don't we have to worry about a Courser seeing us?"

"Not this time, Tan, because it is one of the three groves currently without a Courser."

"So what happens when we get to the Central Grove then?"

"It's not too big a problem. I will intervene directly and manipulate the Courser's minds to send false messages indicating nothing unusual is happening. It will require concentration on my part, but only for the five or ten minutes before we leave again. Kieran, I'll watch and warn if necessary, but this translation is completely yours."

Kieran was surprised at this extra jump, because he could see a shimmer of urgency and vague unease taking root in Ranevargar's mind.

He was also pleased that, despite seeing it as unnecessary, Ranevargar was giving him this confidence-booster jump.

"Yay! Plains Grove here we come!"

Rhys's outburst was good, because it told Kieran that the earlier association between a grove portal and a Wall crossing was completely gone.

* * *

Ranevargar's confidence was completely well-placed because the blip of translation went so smoothly Kieran was almost surprised by the realisation that he was looking at new Realm Trees. A turn of his head revealed a great grassy plain and the vegetation of what must be a river course.

"Neat! Look at all the animals. Is there time for Mr B to have a turn at checking things out with Krol?"

"It would be better if we all stay together this time, Rhys. After Kieran consolidates his understanding of how we wake my Dragon I think it would be wise for us all to take some precautions before we go any further."

Mr B cut off whatever Rhys was going to ask. "I'm going to sit here quietly till Ranevargar's ready, Rhys. He knows far more than we do, and his advice is the same as a command as far as I'm concerned … But do we have time for a snack of honey-bread, Ranevargar?"

"Some time, Mr B, because I want another deep session with Kieran, much like the last one, and then a session involving all of us. The honey-bread is an excellent idea though, and we can eat while we walk."

A while later Kieran peeked into his companions' minds to see why Rhys was shaking his head in mock disgust, while everyone else was happily agreeing with him. His own grin registered in answering why, and he quickly scoffed the rest of his honey-bread.

"Two bites, Kieran, then you went off to weird world while the juicy stuff kept dribbling on the ground. Mr B wouldn't even let us hold it for you, in case we disturbed your thinking."

Despite his mouth now being chock-full, Kieran managed to put the blame on Ranevargar's slave driving again.

"When you've finished that mouthful, we will work on some group precautions, Kieran."

Kieran chewed faster, till he saw Ranevargar had a distinct twinkle in his eye. He was definitely catching on to the dynamic Rhys added to the group.

"You wait, Rhys. I gobbled my mouthful because you taught Ranevargar about slave driving. When I get a chance I'm going to stuff your face till your cheeks look like balloons."

"As if! You and what army?"

Ranevargar watched, with slight bemusement, as his planned precautions were put on hold while Woorawa and Tan joined Kieran in a rough-and-tumble to hold Rhys down and manoeuvre a large piece of honey-bread into the mouth he was holding open in a kind of reverse defiance. It was over quickly though.

"Amazing! Such antics make me feel I am old."

"Careful, Ranevargar. If Rhys sees that hint of approval he might even do the same to you."

"And I'd be too startled to stop him. I am used to Gryl licking me, but I can't imagine him sitting on my stomach and shoving food into me."

"Cease, children. It's time to be serious."

Woorawa and Tan jumped to serious. Rhys, somehow sensing Ranevargar's hidden amusement, sat up and gave him a salute.

"Kieran, you built me a pool of energy that can maintain your special mind shields independently. Can you do the same for everyone else?"

"I don't see why not. They've already got a pool for the Spook ropes, so I'll adapt that."

"More than one pool would be better, to keep their purposes separate."

"That's easy! Rhys already has a different one for healing. How big will I make them?"

Ranevargar hesitated before answering. "Well, the more the better, Kieran. Slightly smaller than the one you built for our energy transfer exercise would be ideal."

"Why smaller?"

"You said the levels didn't feel right."

"I fixed that when I figured out how to cope with the last two doublings."

"Not really. You had to use extra energy for full containment, Kieran. These pools shouldn't need any maintenance on your part."

"Hmm. That's a lot harder. Let me think."

Rhys turned to Woorawa. "Are you following this?"

"Only the main idea, Rhys. It's stuff from their last think-session. We'll hear about it all eventually."

There was quiet till Kieran finished thinking.

"I can see how to make a pool that big, Ranevargar, but I can't stop a tiny trickle from eventually degrading it. It might lose about a quarter after three or four weeks, so that's pretty good ... I think. Watch while I work it with Rhys."

"What? I'm the guinea pig again?"

"Yep! If it backfires your brain will melt."

"Thanks a lot ... and why is everyone grinning? ... Don't answer that."

Ranevargar watched very carefully while Kieran constructed a new energy pool for Rhys and filled it with energy from the Opal.

"Wonderful! But it's beyond me, Kieran. I can see how you make it, but I couldn't match that fine control."

"Is it finished?"

"Yes, Rhys."

Rhys immediately pressed his hands against his temples, looked horrified, then dropped to the ground and started twitching. Krol's neck feathers ruffed, and Tan, frightened and worried, knelt beside Rhys and reached to help him.

"Kick his butt, Tan, then sit on his stomach. That'll cure him quick enough."

Rhys's eyes opened and he grinned at Tan. "Kieran's a cheat. How am I meant to trick him when he's reading my mind?"

"You tricked me, and probably Mr B and Woorawa too."

"No, he didn't. The twitches were too dramatic, and Kieran laughed before he even fell down."

A giant claw descended and pinned Rhys in place till a message passed from Ranevargar that it was time to release him. Rhys jumped to his feet and leaned against Krol.

"Overgrown chook! What happened to that bond we're meant to have?"

"Chook? I see. A domesticated bird designed for eating and profuse egg laying. Should I pass that meaning on to Krol?"

"Um! Better not. I might get squished again."

The nonsense finished and Kieran went ahead with giving everyone an independent pool, like Ranevargar's, for their mind shields, as well as a top-up for the Spook ropes.

"Are we ready to jump to the Central Grove now?"

"Not yet, Rhys. I want Kieran to learn how to make long-distance mind-links. It's well within his ability and it will let him make contact with anyone he knows."

"He's already tried that and he needs lots of help from the Opal, especially when it's more than about a kilometre."

"That is correct, Woorawa, when he is reaching for new minds, but the network he has built within his Opal allows a far more effective connection."

"What network? More new stuff?"

"Yes, Rhys, and I'll explain it all when we get a chance. Ranevargar's Pearl has a network connected to just about everything in the Realm. Mine has only got seven—us, and Ranevargar and Krol. I don't know much yet, but it tells me where you are all the time."

"Like your GPS thing?"

"Sort of. I can tell it's better, but I don't know why yet."

Ranevargar nodded. "It's a tiny part of that month I'd like with Kieran, Rhys, and it will help us keep in touch wherever we are."

"In Faerie you mean, or even back at college?"

"Outside of Faerie would require a lot more energy, but still small compared with what he used to reach Tan's family."

"Rhys, shush! We're interrupting too much."

Ranevargar reassured Mr B. "Yes, you are, but it works well for us. The discussion helps Kieran refine his understanding. At the moment he has his little network at the forefront of his mind, exactly where it needs to be."

"Kieran, follow my link to Krol."

Kieran blinked at Ranevargar with puzzlement. *"How can I? You're not linked."*

"Ah! But I am. It's not the link I use with close proximity, but it's there and I know you can see it."

It had to be through Ranevargar's network and, since he'd been invited, Kieran mentally entered the Pearl and then the network. Yes. There it was: a link highlighted by Ranevargar with a kind of mental glow to make it stand out.

"Good. Watch how I use it instead of a direct link."

Kieran watched and couldn't find any difference. *"It's the same pattern, Ranevargar, just complicated by having to go into your Pearl and then your network."*

"Yes, and pointless when Krol is close, but come with me now while I connect with Gryl."

A new link glowed faintly and, riding along with Ranevargar, Kieran was presented with the grisly sight of a newly killed plains animal and Gryl's pleasure with the bone he was crunching.

"Whoa! Feeding time. I haven't seen it from Gryl's point of view before. Everything's still the same, except for using Gryl's pattern instead of Krol's. What are you showing me?"

"Reach for Gryl directly, Kieran. Your direction sense will tell you his location."

A moment of consideration showed Kieran the point that Ranevargar was making. *"Unreal! Reaching directly would need a whole torrent of energy and the network doesn't need any."*

Kieran got the mental equivalent of a snort of disbelief.

"I wish I could afford your cavalier approach to energy use, Kieran. Of course it uses energy. Look closely and tell me how much."

That was a not-too-subtle hint, and Kieran used the measurement technique he'd learnt at the last grove.

"That's better. It doesn't seem like much, Kieran, but if you need to contact every water creature in the lakes, or all the plains grazers, it becomes significant … Now, make Gryl part of your Opal network and show me how you link to him."

After a moment of recall, Kieran's network expanded and he was sharing Gryl's contentment with Ranevargar.

"That's brilliant, Ranevargar. I never would have worked out how to use my Opal like that."

"What's brilliant?"

"I just linked to Gryl without using Opal energy, Rhys, and we watched him chomping his food way back at the Lake Grove."

"From here? Wow! What about George and the other horses? Can you check if they're okay?"

"Ah! They're not from this Realm. Can I put them in my Opal network, Ranevargar?"

"You know their minds, and they developed a bond with you, Kieran, so I'm sure you can. Try it and see."

Kieran's Opal network grew by three more and he was immediately relating that George was thinking of nothing except the delicious grass he was munching.

Ranevargar nodded his approval. "You know the rest of Gryl's cohort well, Kieran, so show me how quickly you can link to each of them."

Kieran wondered why Ranevargar wanted speed, then marvelled when making sixteen new links under the pressure of haste ended with an almost instantaneous process.

"You have it. Now, come with me while I falsify the memories of the Courser before we move to the Central Grove."

"We're ready to jump?"

"Yes, Rhys. As soon as we fix the Courser."

"I like these jumps. They're exciting."

Kieran piggybacked in Ranevargar's mind and tried to follow what he was doing to manipulate the Courser's memories. It was very delicate though, and happening much too rapidly.

"You know the basics for implanting false memories, Kieran, but bypassing Lord Uirebon's safeguards is extremely tricky and not something you can learn quickly."

"One of your month-long things?"

"And more … There we are … The Courser will see an empty clearing while I keep a link with it."

"That's not difficult, is it?"

"No, but time is important, because if Lord Uirebon focuses on this Courser directly he will sense my interference."

Ranevargar's final check showed five Griffins hidden from the Courser's view under a section of heavy canopy, with five grove hosts tending to them.

"It all looks good, Ranevargar. Will I make the jump?"

"Yes, one of the grove hosts has some sort of apprehension, probably about the Courser, but I have that under control. Go ahead."

Kieran opened his eyes and grinned at all the expectant looks.

"Join hands, everyone. It's time!"

"Yay! The Dragon Quest starts."

Ranevargar smiled at Rhys's anticipation and excitement, smiled at the rapid jump to make group contact, then watched Kieran's meticulous preparations with pleasure and a touch of pride.

"Go ahead, Kieran. The portal will be faultless."

Kieran initiated his trigger and reality blurred.

The transition was smooth.

The reception wasn't, and, in the seconds before his body succumbed to paralysis, Kieran took in the strange and daunting company arrayed around the Grove clearing.

"*Rhys! Rhys! Where are you?*"

REALM LORD

CHAPTER 1

Kieran toppled, along with everyone else, and his mind registered a snapshot of countless Spooks and people with strange golden heads. A jolt of pain when his face slammed against the grass passed and was forgotten as his mind raced with shock and attempts at understanding. A terrifying scream of defiance and rage paralysed his thoughts till the sudden cut-off of the noise built an extra thread of fear that Krol had been wounded or disabled. Helplessness surged. His body was useless. There was no sense of Rhys's presence or any other mind anywhere. *The Opal ... call on the Opal.*

"Steady, Kieran. We are outmatched but not overcome. Our attackers are completely unaware of your network linkage, so use it to contact your friends while I try to gather information."

Ranevargar's calm voice in his mind was hugely relieving, and Kieran did steady. He made a network link to Rhys first and a new emotion eclipsed everything else when he saw that, despite being paralysed, flat on his back and unable to see anything but sky and a section of Realm Tree, Rhys's only concern was that Kieran might be hurt or in trouble.

"We're all paralysed, Rhys, but Ranevargar is trying to work out what to do."

"Are you hurt?"

"Not really. I have to check everyone else is okay and work with Ranevargar for a while. Okay?"

"Go for it, Kieran. You'll get us out of this."

Kieran had no idea if that was possible, but Rhys's blatant confidence sparked a fire of determination. He rapidly contacted Mr B, Woorawa and Tan, then left them when Ranevargar's voice returned to his mind.

"Link to Krol, Kieran. He is restrained but not paralysed. You will be able to see through his eyes."

"What did they do to him?"

"Nothing. I stopped his attack myself. There is such a massive concentration of power around us, I believe he would have been brushed aside."

The first thing Kieran saw when he leapt into Krol's mind was the quelling of the great rage evoked by the sight of Ranevargar's sprawled body, and the order calming his need to take action. Ranevargar had that in hand though, so Kieran accessed a clear view through the powerful Griffin eyes. Spooks! So many? And ranged behind them on tall horses were uniformed riders wearing strange golden helmets and pointing black rods at Krol. Farther away, three white-cloaked elves sat with eyes closed and knees touching knees.

Two other figures demanded far more attention.

One, dressed in a long yellow cloak, was standing farther back, with a look of intense concentration and both hands moving before him with a strange rhythm.

The other, shockingly impressive and garbed magnificently in dark red leather, was striding toward Ranevargar accompanied by one of the golden-helmeted elves. A surge of pressure whirled against Kieran's mind shields and with it came recognition.

"Ranevargar, this is the mind that attacked me and took Rhys. He'll reach you in a few more seconds, but I can fight him off."

Ranevargar's response was almost a yell in Kieran's mind. *"No! No! He is ready for that, Kieran. Do not use power against him, especially not power from your Opal. Lord Uirebon is maintaining a field of diversion which will transfer any power you call to Lord Maynor's control."*

"I can't use my Opal? I don't believe this Maynor. What if I use my reserve energy instead? There should be enough."

"No, that would still leave us to contend with Uirebon, the Fetches, and all these Power Masters while we're paralysed."

Kieran suddenly felt excited. *"I can portal us all to another grove."*

"The triad is blocking any portal attempt, Kieran. This whole confrontation has been meticulously planned. Make yourself ready, though, and hope the triad falters. It's our only way out ... Now, I must concentrate."

The red-clothed figure was beside Ranevargar now, waiting while the accompanying Power Master rolled his helpless body onto his back for eye contact. Krol's view was clear but from behind, and since Kieran needed to know everything, he switched to Ranevargar's mind instead.

"End your foolish resistance, Ranevargar. Lower your shields and submit to the will of the High King."

"My title is Lord Ranevargar. My shields remain, and you and your company should leave this Realm forthwith. There is no submission between Realm Lords, as you well know. Submission to the High King is given only to the High King in person, and only for matters concerning the wellbeing of all Faerie."

"Hear my second call for submission. Refuse and the consequences will be dire."

"The call of three does not apply to a Realm Lord in his own domain. Lord Maynor, I formally refuse."

"My third call demands your submission and assistance in the matter of these visitors."

"I have no choice but to refuse. These five have been formally given the full protection of my Realm."

The awkward viewpoint of looking from the ground to the face above did nothing to mask the flash of anger now directed at Ranevargar. Lord Maynor pointed a glowing red finger and Kieran shared the strange sensation enveloping Ranevargar. After a few seconds it dissolved to nothing.

Maynor looked even fiercer. "The geas fails, Ranevargar, but the consequences I promised now follow ... He is no help to us at this time. Bind him utterly."

Kieran wondered what that could mean, because Ranevargar was already completely paralysed.

"A golden helmet will keep me fettered to Maynor or the Power Master who fits it, and it will contain my mental abilities. Ready yourself, Kieran. I believe he intends to penetrate your mind shields with a massive application of the Nexus energy he commands."

"He won't get me, Ranevargar. He's angry because he couldn't get you."

"Not so. The anger was feigned and covered a deep feeling of satisfaction which worries me."

"I didn't see that. Here's the helmet. Will we lose contact once it's on?"

"No ... Don't react to Maynor without thought, Kieran."

Maynor was blocked from view while the Power Master leaned over to put the helmet on. Kieran jumped to all his friends' minds for a moment, then switched to Krol's view and watched Maynor start walking.

"He is marshalling energy, Kieran. You might have to use some of your reserve as a bolster, but don't waste it on attack."

"He's glowing red again?"

"Through his Stone of Power, the ring he wears on his right hand ... Kieran, you accessed my Pearl. If you can do the same with his Ruby you can stop all this."

The hope showing in Ranevargar's mind was restrained, but Kieran jumped at the straw. *Yes!* Like Ranevargar's Pearl, but different too. He sensed it glowing with power just a few metres away.

Disappointment banished hope when Kieran's cautious reach for contact wavered and disappeared.

"I can sense the Ruby, Ranevargar, but when I make a reach it's taken away from me."

Ranevargar's reply didn't register because danger alerts were flashing in Kieran's mind as his shields reacted to a mounting onslaught. The grass in front of his eyes turned red and through Krol's vision came a striking view of his whole body englobed with a pulsing red light. The generalised pressure abruptly changed to the equivalent of a mental lance, stabbing repeatedly in search of any chink it might penetrate. Kieran modulated the structure of his shield accordingly and sent a burst of gratitude to Ranevargar.

"He can't get through, Ranevargar. He's using that spear attack you showed me when we practised with our shields. I only need a tiny trickle of extra energy to stop him."

"Hold tight, Kieran. He has planned for this."

When the lance attack built, and built again, Kieran increased his supporting flow of energy. He was starting to wonder about its purpose though, as he'd had time now to realise that this attack was nothing like the mighty onslaught he'd rebuffed at home.

"Support him while we speak."

Through Krol's eyes, Kieran watched the Power Master reach through the red glow, grasp his body under the armpits, then lift till he was held sitting with his back resting against a pair of knees. Maynor, now seen directly, gestured and the paralysis dissolved from Kieran's head and neck. Instinctively, he looked to his friends, sprawled where chance had left Tan the only one facing this way. Kieran sent Tan a quick reassurance while he looked at Maynor through the red glow.

"Lower your shields and submit to my will."

"And let you mess with my mind? Get lost!"

Maynor extended the hand with the red Ruby and a change came into the nimbus surrounding Kieran.

"I make my second call for submission. Refuse and the consequences will be dire."

This was, word for word, the geas thing Maynor had just tried on Ranevargar. Kieran's automatic response surprised even himself.

"The call of three does not apply to protectees of this Realm. I formally refuse."

Kieran was grateful to see Maynor's startlement.

"My third call demands your submission and the cooperation of all your party."

"I have no choice but to refuse. I and my friends have the protection of Lord Ranevargar and all his Realm."

"Ranevargar appears to have taught you much, but your resistance will be heavy in your heart if you choose it over the disposition of your companions."

"You're a kidnapper, and now you're a blackmailer as well. No one could ever trust you."

"I will have your cooperation, if not by negotiation, then by force … Power Master, bring me the energy source resting against his chest. Without it, his defences will crumble."

A gloved hand reached under Kieran's shirt, hesitated, then withdrew.

"My Lord, it is beyond me. The power unnerves my fingers."

Kieran tilted his head in defiance. "You can take it, Realm Lord, but it won't help you. It is always mine."

"Tell him nothing about your Opal, Kieran. I think he seeks to control its power."

Maynor gestured again and the glow brightened around the hand he moved to touch the Opal.

"Yes! So much power … Now I understand how you can resist even a Realm Lord."

He slipped the silver necklace over Kieran's head and enclosed the Opal itself in his hand. The pleased look of acquisition and anticipation now evident on his features aggravated Kieran and indignation surged. Kieran knew very well that physical separation meant nothing to the bond that had never stopped strengthening since the very first touch, but this was still like having part of himself taken, and by instinct he resisted. The bond, always deep and strong, surfaced in his mind with an affirmation of identity and belonging.

Maynor straightened and, stepping back a few paces, opened his fingers and stared so fixedly at the Opal Kieran suspected he must be probing and testing, much the same as Ranevargar had done previously.

Kieran puzzled when something stirred, then jolted with surprise when, with no effort on his part, his shields suddenly strengthened and tightened.

"As with his mind shield, this stone resists examination. We need another helmet to break the connection."

Maynor, or the Power Master, must have sent a signal because another Power Master dismounted and started forward. Maynor's attention abruptly seemed to turn inward, in what looked like introspection, and Kieran called urgently to Ranevargar. *"Can a golden helmet do what he says?"*

"Of course not … But, Kieran, why are you using your precious reserve energy to strengthen my mind shields?"

"What? Yours too? I'm not doing that."

Kieran used his secret links to make a rush-check and saw everyone's mind shield radiating unexpected strength. *"Yes, I am, Ranevargar, but it's not from my reserve."*

"Your Opal must be bypassing Uirebon's diversion field. I wouldn't have thought it possible, but this can only be good."

Maynor stirred from his introspection or whatever it was and turned to the approaching Power Master.

"Quickly. Bind him while I ready them all for transport. This grove has an aspect that disturbs me."

Transport them all? Kieran didn't like that one bit, but then the Power Master knelt beside him and his mind welled with apprehension about the strange golden helmet being lifted toward him.

Kieran's bond with the Opal magnified, dazzling his uncomprehending mind, and became the conduit for a blast of physical and mental power.

Every mind in the clearing—save the seven behind their flaring protective shields—lost cohesion or consciousness.

Every body, save those already sprawled in the grove clearing, was hurled to the ground by a concussive blow of physical pressure.

The support behind Kieran disappeared and the image of a Power Master flying unaccountably away whirled to a view of sky and Realm Tree as his body collapsed backwards. Startled and bewildered, Kieran's instinctive head twist in search of information showed Rhys close by and apparently unaffected. He needed to know more and was about to switch to Krol's eyes when wonder and elation, together with an imperative call for action, powered into his mind.

"Jump, Kieran. Jump! The High Lords are recovering and will quickly re-establish control. Lord Maynor is already on his feet. Now, Kieran! It must be now."

Kieran acted, with huge gratitude that Ranevargar's foresight had made him ready, and everything came together instantly. No, not everything.

"I can't, Ranevargar. Something won't let me link you to the group."

"Leave! You can help from afar."

The force in Ranevargar's thoughts snapped Kieran from the thrall of indecision and Kieran reached for the beautiful glow of a spider-link. Yes, there it was, ready and available. Reserve energy sent the trigger. More reserve energy joined the energy of the partially recovered Central Grove and five paralysed friends and a very groggy Griffin disappeared from the clearing.

*   *   *

The High King turned from consideration of the troubles looming at Lady Narello's border and, resigned to the prospect of further delay and lack of progress, opened the channels of communication Maynor and Uirebon were finally requesting.

"News, Maynor?"

"Yes, my Lord. Your understanding of Ranevargar, and the tactics you suggested, have given us vital information and the means to ensure Keryth's full cooperation."

Relief, combined with anticipation, coursed through the High King. *"You know his whereabouts?"*

"Not at the moment, my Lord, but the memories I have gathered show him healthy and being chaperoned by Ranevargar. Protection has been conferred and the old lord appears to be conducting the whole group on a whirlwind tour of his Realm."

"Protection? Is there any indication that Ranevargar wishes to interfere with our purposes?"

"That is puzzling, my Lord. I have taken control of every close elven mind and they all see Keryth's group as visitors from the Human World."

"A whirlwind tour would explain the failure of the triads far-seeing ... You are in control of elven minds?"

"Yes, my Lord, of necessity. Your understanding of Ranevargar's propensity for using his Central Grove for his undertakings has rewarded us with this breakthrough. The moment Lord Uirebon and I arrived, I took control of the local wardens and, through them, five of Ranevargar's flying Guardians. From them I learned that when Keryth arrived yesterday he was given a ceremonial welcome and that Ranevargar has hosted him personally ever since."

"A ceremonial welcome for a band of humans? I wonder what motivated such an unusual reception? In centuries past his mind was a force of significance, but with the ravages of age and waning strength, he has increasingly withdrawn from wider concerns and devoted his declining power to maintaining his Realm and nurturing the animals he regards so highly. Maybe Keryth's own empathy with animals has struck a chord with him?"

Maynor's focus was more immediate. *"My Lord, we must prepare. Before Lord Uirebon and I arrived, these wardens were gathering provisions for an extended expedition of some kind, with the expectation that Keryth would arrive soon to collect them."*

"Excellent! Do you need my assistance yet?"

"Soon, my Lord. I'm about to portal our support forces, and Uirebon is confident that the preparations we planned will be successful."

"He has established a barrier against the strange gemstone?"

"I have never seen anything like it. He describes it as an energy trap rather than a barrier, and it diverts any flow of power to my control ... I do have

a concern that Ranevargar's grant of protection might give him cause to interfere."

Aglaron considered, briefly. *"Yes, with the granting of protection he must. Invoke a call to fealty, and if he refuses, render him temporarily helpless before confronting Keryth."*

"I must make haste. Ranevargar is now interrogating his warden's minds for signs of anything unusual—his arrival may be imminent ... Stay in contact, my Lord."

Aglaron watched the play of concentration in Maynor's mind as he marshalled energy for this major portal event. Fetches, Power Masters and a junior triad, all gathered in an unusually large meld and translated with a surprising application of power. Curious. Maynor had unexpected reserves.

Aglaron watched Uirebon guide the triad in its precautionary task against Ranevargar's Tree portal, build a paralysing network through the assembled Fetches, then construct a protective field for the Power Masters and energise their rods with force carefully structured to control any fierce flying Guardian.

Aglaron watched Maynor call on his Stone of Power for recovery and the construction of the new and powerful mind shield designed with the help of Uirebon's researchers.

Yes, this time success was certain. Aglaron overlaid his link to Uirebon with satisfaction and appreciation, then tapped the Nexus for the overarching strength they all knew Maynor must carefully wield against Keryth's baffling shield. Uirebon's belief that the mysterious gemstone needed to be isolated had resulted, after calls to many of his learning centres, in the energy trap now covering the clearing. Aglaron marvelled at the form and function while holding some reservation that it would be enough. A moment of fierce concentration reduced Nexus flow to the Realms, freeing a major portion as a safeguard against Maynor becoming over-extended yet again.

Time passed. Aglaron followed Maynor's control links to the grove wardens and examined their expectations. Yes, Ranevargar's instructions intimated both haste and imminence ... And their memories showed Keryth looking very strange in his human garb, slightly strained but well ... Energy stirred and registered.

"Maynor! Uirebon! A portal has been initialised."

Energy flared from the fetch field, power surged through the energy trap, and the interference from the triad peaked as six bodies materialised then crumpled to the ground. A fierce scream of defiance and rage erupted and a great flying Guardian lunged toward Maynor, then abruptly stopped, held by the Power Master's rods.

Maynor moved to deal with Ranevargar who, as expected, refused the demand for submission and had to be helmet-bound as a precaution.

Aglaron, considering the exchange carefully, was surprised by Ranevargar's dignified acceptance of this treatment and felt a twinge of respect for the solitary old Lord.

Maynor now moved to Keryth, and Aglaron's attention focused for this confrontation. All the energy pulsing so strongly through Maynor's Ruby pressed futilely against that strange shield.

"As you suspected, my Lord. This is beyond me. Is Uirebon's energy trap functioning?"

"Perfectly, Maynor. Hold that pressure while we implement his plan."

Not surprisingly, Maynor faltered. As Uirebon had predicted, Maynor was not able to maintain the level of unrelenting pressure that would eventually break through Keryth's degrading shields. Aglaron hurriedly transferred control of the Nexus power and watched with relief as Maynor steadied, then rebuilt the pressure.

"And let you mess with my mind? Get lost!"

Tied to the High Court by the need to be near the Nexus, a smile of pride at his son's strength played briefly across the High King's features while his mind watched from the distance.

"... the consequences will be dire."

The geas of submission, augmented by Maynor's Stone of Power, settled then faded to nothing when Keryth voiced a legitimate formula of rejection. The likelihood of an early takeover was now gone and Aglaron watched Maynor's assault on Keryth's shields reach a new level.

This was the beginning of the prolonged stage of Uirebon's strategy, where isolation from the mysterious stone should separate Keryth from his energy source and eventually drain his reserves to normal levels.

"The power unnerves my fingers."

The gemstone was acting against the Power Master? That shouldn't be possible. Aglaron rushed to check the energy trap, and then to question Uirebon.

"Your structure appears to be functioning, Uirebon. How can the gemstone repel a Power Master?"

Uirebon was struggling to hold his concentration on so many things that he couldn't manage further focus. *"Later, my Lord."*

Aglaron forgot Uirebon, because Maynor flexed his newly acquired Nexus power then directed it to his Ruby. *"I must, my Lord, the gemstone has a natural resistance."*

This was a departure from Uirebon's carefully considered strategy ... but it was working. When Maynor's hand made successful contact, Aglaron saw his amazed realisation at the sense of vast latent power.

His son's shield flared against a gigantic new thrust of finely concentrated pressure.

"What are you doing, Maynor?"

There was no answer. Another frightening thrust preceded a deep probe of the stone ... and then access to Maynor's mind was unaccountably gone.

Aglaron's first thought was of interference from the gemstone ... No, the link with Uirebon was intact ... and showing his stirrings of puzzlement, first with Maynor's use of brutish and concentrated force against Keryth's shields instead of the steady wearing-down process they'd carefully planned, and now with the suddenly severed link. The need for information sent Aglaron through Uirebon's link to the Power Master supporting Keryth.

"Aglaron, cede control of the High Court, offer me your fealty, and Keryth will be returned to your keeping."

This order, clear and demanding through a guarded link, so shocked Aglaron he had no response while implication and possibilities raced through his mind.

"Impossible, Maynor. You propose both treason and treachery with this unconscionable demand. The High Court and convocation of Realm Lords would revoke any such action."

"For treason, yes, but not for the formally expressed Challenge of a Realm Lord with the strength and ability to take the position."

"Strength? Pure folly."

"I control all free Nexus energy, the resources of three Realms, and now the vast store of power contained in this gemstone. You will inevitably succumb."

"Then why resort to this cowardly act of holding Keryth. Release him and make Challenge in a manner befitting a Realm Lord."

"Keryth is now a pawn in the game of power and there is much I will learn from him."

The guarded link severed abruptly and, while gathering the strength he'd need to regain control of the Nexus power he'd so freely offered, Aglaron watched through the Power Master's eyes as Maynor confronted Keryth again.

A new lance of energy rebounded ineffectively from Keryth's mind shield. Rebounded? That was new.

"We need another helmet to break the connection."

Aglaron watched the second Power Master approach and, worried about the effect it might have on Keryth's shields, but not yet ready for his own attack on Maynor, he strengthened his link to Uirebon and saw, with cautious relief, the growing bewilderment and outrage filling Uirebon's mind.

"You have no part in this treachery, Uirebon?"

"Only through misplaced trust and years of deceit, my Lord. Use me as a conduit for your actions while I redirect my energies to support you."

Uirebon's offer was invaluable. The advantage gained by contending directly with Maynor, rather than from afar and across the Realm Boundary, could be critical.

The few short moments needed to make ready weren't granted.

Through Uirebon's vision, Aglaron saw the red glow of Maynor's Realm Stone flare to brilliance then disappear in a chaotic maelstrom.

Uirebon's own mind, reeling on the verge of consciousness, struggled to recover, and Aglaron, protected by distance, saw the whirl of sky and Realm Trees as his host's body lifted into the air then sprawled backward on the ground.

After a few seconds though, Uirebon struggled to his feet and took in the incredible scene of all the Fetches, Power Masters and their steeds, as well as the triad members, lying unconscious on the ground metres from their previous positions.

Keryth, his companions, and the huge flying Guardian vanished through a beautifully ordered portal structure. Maynor, the only other conscious being, turned from the still-paralysed body of Ranevargar to regard Uirebon.

*   *   *

Sky! That was all Kieran could see till he turned his head to the side where Rhys was looking at him with teary eyes.

Crying? That wasn't like him. Kieran linked instantly, and smiled at the mix of relief and excitement. A rapid check revealed the tears were simply his eyes' response to being unable to close or blink. Kieran expanded the link to include everyone.

"We're all okay, except I had to leave Ranevargar behind."

"Can you move, Kieran? All I can see is a Realm Tree bole."

"We're all paralysed, Woorawa, except for Krol. I can move my head because that Realm Lord wanted me to speak."

"Can Rhys heal us?"

"No, I ..."

A familiar flow of energy sought to replenish Rhys's healing pool then rebounded to Kieran's own pool when there was no room for it.

"What did you do?"

"I can't believe it. My Opal's here. That Maynor had it, but it must be linked so strongly it portalled with the rest of us."

"Kieran, can Krol move enough to push you in contact with Rhys?"

"Good thinking, Mr B. Hang on while I make it happen."

There was a happy scrawk from Krol when Kieran linked, reassured him, then asked for his help. After a cautious and wobbly approach, Krol's giant talons closed carefully around Kieran and gently moved to dump him on top of Rhys. Kieran had just enough flexibility of his own to move his cheek against the warm flesh of Rhys's neck.

Zap!

Kieran scrambled to his knees and lifted Rhys's lifeless hand to touch his own temple.

Zap!

Rhys galvanised to life, wiped his blurry eyes clear, and wrapped Kieran in an irresistible hug. It had to stop though, and in short order, Krol, who was closest, and then the others were zapped, stretching, laughing and gathered round Kieran.

"Damn Spooks! What did you do to them all, Kieran? The whole clearing exploded without touching us."

"I didn't do anything. The Opal didn't like that High Lord taking it, so it blasted them all. Ranevargar snapped me out of my shock and made me use the portal while we had the chance."

"Can they follow us?"

"I don't know. Probably. They must have got there by portalling, so I guess they can go to any of the groves."

Tan, looking very serious, interrupted. "Kieran, there are a thousand questions, but don't we need to be doing something, and why couldn't you bring Ranevargar? All the supplies and Griffin mounts he organised are back at Central Grove and we've hardly got anything in our packs."

"Everything happened too quickly, Tan. I couldn't bring him because they put a gold helmet on his head and I think it blocked him from the portal. He made me leave, because those Realm Lords were recovering and we couldn't help him if we stayed."

"We can't be any help from here either, can we?"

Kieran jolted with guilt. "Gods, Rhys! We're all free, and the Opal's not blocked, and I haven't checked in with Ranevargar yet. Hang on!"

The only access to Ranevargar was by the secret pathway through his Pearl or the Opal network. That had been broken by the jump and Kieran reached to reconnect and was surprised that a small burst of Pearl energy kicked in.

"Wonderful, Kieran ... I see that everyone is safe for the moment."

Kieran looked through Ranevargar's eyes at a bewildering view of moving ground, part of a horse's side, and hooves stepping forward.

"Sorry I took so long to reconnect. We had to get everyone healed from the paralysis. Where are you? This link was an extra long reach."

"Yes, a great deal happened, very little of which I understand. Lord Maynor and Lord Uirebon were barely recovered from your astonishing assault when a great contention of force raged between them. Bound with the helmet, and my body still helpless, I am taken from my Realm and captive to Lord Maynor."

"It wasn't my assault, Ranevargar. My Opal did it all by itself. I think it got angry when that Maynor took it away from me."

Kieran saw knowledge of the Opal's presence burst into Ranevargar's mind

"Kieran, I saw Lord Maynor using his Realm Stone to contain your Opal. Did you call it after you made your portal?"

"Call it? No, it did that by itself too. Can I send you some energy? I can feel him pushing against your shields."

"No, Kieran. These marvellous shields will hold for weeks, and much as I would appreciate it, there is a strong likelihood of detection. If Lord Maynor learns of any connection between us he will take steps to cut it off ... Our best course is to free the Dragon."

"Okay. But do you think it will be safe to portal to the Central Grove for the supplies and the Griffins?"

"It should be safe, but check the Courser and the grove hosts first. Kieran, apart from Krol, who is committed to you, I must assign the Griffin Guardians to the protection and maintenance of the Realm. My absence and reduced function make that imperative. Collect your supplies, then portal to the Lake Grove, where Gryl and four other Panthers will help you reach the Boundary Wall."

Kieran took more advice and ideas from Ranevargar then made the link fade gently away and refocused on the five sets of waiting eyes. He relayed the reassurance and new instructions from Ranevargar to Krol, then voiced some of his aggravation.

"That Maynor's a total mongrel. He's kidnapped Ranevargar and kept him paralysed and helpless while he takes him to that Castle we saw. I'll tell you more when we get a chance, but we have to rush for the supplies at the Central Grove and then jump to the Lake Grove and meet Gryl."

Woorawa surprised everyone with his big snort of wry amusement.

"What? None of that's funny."

"Yes, it is, Kieran. We've said we're going to talk everything out when we get the chance so many times now it'll take a whole day — except something else will happen and you'll be 'saying next time we get a chance' again."

Three other heads nodded in strong agreement.

"Yes. I suppose, but we need to get moving."

"Back to the Central Grove? Right now? Won't they just grab us again?"

Kieran felt a mini stab of guilt. "I think they all went when they took Ranevargar, Rhys. But I'm about to check anyway."

"Checking didn't work when we left the Rainforest Grove. How do you know it'll work this time?"

Tan's question set Kieran back.

"You're right, Tan, but I think an ordinary check will be good enough, because the Realm Lord isn't there anymore."

Kieran made a little hand movement which signified his attention would be elsewhere and reached for any Courser pattern near the Central Grove, and then for the hosts.

"The hosts are gathered on the edge of the clearing and the Courser is miles away ... Whoa! All the Coursers have left the groves and they're racing at top speed towards the Realm Boundary ... Join hands for the jump."

This was Kieran speaking with authority and four hands snapped instantly into place. The grove had no transfer energy at all now but, with the Opal free to provide that, it didn't matter. Reality blurred and everyone turned as four saddled Griffins screeched a welcoming cry to Krol. While the group moved to join them, Kieran reached for the host elves to relay Ranevargar's set of instructions, and was surprised to see that their only memory of events in the clearing was a sudden and mystifying appearance of an elf glowing yellow with the discharge of great power. That appearance was brief, and before any approach could be made the elf collapsed on the ground and vanished. Kieran remembered from Ranevargar's discussion about the Realm Lords that yellow was the signature colour for Lord Uirebon's Stone of Power, so he stored the scene to share with Ranevargar the next time they linked.

There was huge consternation when Kieran informed the hosts that Ranevargar was a captive and currently being carried sideways and bound facedown across the back of a horse in another Realm, then rapid acceptance and calming when Ranevargar's plans gave them purpose and understanding. The next step was to link with Kron, Kan and the other Griffins, and pass on Ranevargar's instructions about their vital new guardianship role. A concert of enraged Griffin screams sounded at the understanding of Ranevargar's capture, then cut off when all four glowed with the power flaring from the Opal.

"What the blazes are you doing, Kieran? For a moment I thought they were burning."

"Krol won't be here to protect the Realm when a Dead World Monster arrives, so I've activated auras for Kron and Kan and given them enough energy to fight off at least two attacks. Kron's in charge now, and he knows what he has to do while Ranevargar's not here."

"You said 'when'. Ranevargar told us those Monsters only come rarely."

"Except when someone disturbs things in Dead World, Woorawa, and going through the Boundary's a big disturbance, and then Krol protecting us against all the internal Monsters will make it even bigger ... Swap packs everyone. The hosts have rushed to set up the new ones with water and supplies for at least a couple of weeks."

"Sheba! This pack weighs a ton. It's going to be hard work without the Griffins."

Kieran hefted the new pack and shared a disconcerted look with everyone.

"We'll get used to them, Rhys. We'll have to, and they'll get lighter every day." Mr B was right and, because he'd seen Ranevargar's instructions to the hosts, Kieran knew exactly why.

"You know what Dead World's like, Rhys. Water's the biggest problem and we have to carry enough to get us to that snow we saw. When we reach our waterfall, Krol's going to load up with as many water skins as he can."

Woorawa and Rhys preferred their first packs, but Kieran vetoed swapping the contents and hurried everyone to get ready for the next jump.

"What's changed, Kieran? Ranevargar said the groves needed a day of build-up before they were ready for a new jump, and we've always needed recovery time."

"Nothing really, Mr B. Ranevargar had to wait for the groves to recover, but I just top them up with the Opal. I had to figure out how, to save us from the Realm Lords."

"I can hardly believe it, but these portals are starting to feel like a normal way of travelling."

"Not the one after we were paralysed, Mr B. That was the best portal ever."

"Hands gripped, everyone. It's time to see George and Gryl again."

Wishing he'd had more time for better explanations, Kieran sent a message of thanks and farewell to the watching host elves then gathered Krol and his friends for another journey across the shimmering spider-link.

*   *   *

"Quickly, my Lord. Attack before Maynor recovers. You must regain control of your Nexus energy."

Aglaron was way ahead of Uirebon, marshalling every readily available resource of power for a strike against Maynor's battered shields before they could be rebuilt. Precious seconds passed. The clearing shuddered with new contention, but despite the welcome flood of assistance from Uirebon, Maynor's newly structured shields held. Maynor, sheathed with the glow from his Ruby, pointed angrily toward Uirebon, then, along with all the support forces, portalled out of the clearing.

"Build new locks for the Nexus power you still control, my Lord — his first effort will be directed there — then rouse the Court and strengthen the High Castle."

Aglaron was already doing this, but making new locks was pointless. *"New locks, Uirebon? We worked just recently to improve them."*

"And that is why you must change them now. I suspect that Maynor has been manipulating my mind."

"Can I trust any of your advice then?"

"I believe so. Manipulation is not control, and I share your rage at this deceit."

This was an imperative and for the next few seconds Aglaron turned his attention to the Nexus. Building new locks would take minutes — far too long if Uirebon was right — whereas accessing a protected area of memory for previous locks would be instantaneous. Done. A surge of energy distracted his mind. The Boundary to Lady Narello's Realm was flaring with disruption? Later. The High Castle wards faltered and a force of carefully directed energy reached into the Nexus, probed momentarily against the changed locks, then disappeared.

"Uirebon, Maynor penetrated my wards and tried to access the Nexus with the keys we had in place."

"We have a serious problem, my Lord. Alter the structure of any wards

we built jointly and set a triad to watching the forces Maynor has arrayed against Lady Narello."

"Why?"

"Consider his claim of having control of three Realms. One must be through Ranevargar, taken against his will. The other must be through Lady Narello or myself."

"You think Maynor can force you to fight against me? He and Lady Narello have been bitter enemies for decades."

"Access through manipulation is not control, my Lord. Look for conflict between Maynor and Narello."

"Narello's Boundary is already registering high levels of activity. Uirebon, do you have reserves enough to portal here? Your insight will be invaluable."

"I have the reserves, but first give me time to analyse my mind and make certain my thoughts are my own. I have a protected sanctum designed for such a purpose. Activate every triad at your disposal and accumulate power."

That was already happening, along with a multitude of other strategies available to a High King.

"Build defence, not offence, my Lord. To take the throne, Maynor must gather enough strength to take the High Castle first, and given enough time I believe I can negate his use of the purloined Nexus energy against you."

"Time?"

"Yes, use it effectively. Maynor won't act against you until he is Warded in his Castle, and his mistakes give you an advantage."

"What mistakes? I have been too active for an analysis."

"Until a formal Challenge comes to the High Court, my feasance remains with the High King and, unless he has little regard for any effect my assistance might have, he has acted rashly. Any chance he had of using your concern for your son against you has disappeared, along with Keryth, and Ranevargar's submission is by no means certain."

"He has Keryth's stone. That could well be the deciding factor."

"Physical possession only, my Lord. Keryth's act of reprisal bypassed our elegant structures of isolation as if they didn't exist. I suspect that stone will reject Maynor's efforts to control it."

Aglaron recalled the shocking rebuttal of his own attempt.

"As always you speak sense, Uirebon, and what do you make of that reprisal? I have never seen anything like it."

"Neither have I, my Lord, but later ..."

Uirebon staggered under a new blast of Maynor's stolen Nexus energy. His body collapsed, but his mind held while he firmed his shields and used his last vestige power to portal to the protection of his own Realm.

Uirebon's sanctum wards cut their link, and Aglaron turned his mind to the babble of question and uncertainty rising among the gathering elven lords of the High Court.

*   *   *

Seventeen proud Panthers, their minds awash with the elevated guardianship responsibilities relayed from Ranevargar, stood guard while Pelnor and the other Lake Grove hosts rushed to ready everything for the race to the Realm Boundary. Rhys had his arms wrapped rather awkwardly around George's neck for a fond farewell, and Kieran watched Manon and Deltor clip the last of the extra water skins to Krol's harness.

"Our thoughts are with you for this strange journey, Kieran. Krol has communicated his qualms for the dangers ahead and his joy in your company. Our Lord's instructions include the blessing of the Realm before you depart."

Pelnor's hand, glowing softly green, made a formal touch to five foreheads and a Griffin beak, and Kieran, watching as none of the others could, saw a strange gentle flow passing from the Realm Trees. Rhys responded with a thank you hug which lifted Pelnor from his feet, then scrambled to pride of place on Gryl's saddled back.

"Hold tight, Kieran. You're going to love this."

Kieran, mounted on Gryl's mate, was astonished at the sensation of speed and controlled strength and purpose as the group moved along the trail at double the speed the horses could ever have managed. The feeling of excitement and progress steadily waned though, as muscles and minds worked to keep balance and readiness for every direction change dictated by the trail, and after half an hour Kieran called for a halt.

"We're okay, Kieran."

"Yes, but our muscles aren't used to this. We'll have an energy boost every time we stop to contact Ranevargar."

"Can't you do that while we're moving? Night's coming."

"I have to concentrate too much, Woorawa."

"Fair enough. Have we got time to stretch our legs while you're thinking?"

Kieran gave a nod and dismounted. He walked a few wobbly steps before reaching afar. As agreed previously, Kieran activated the link to the Pearl slowly, gently seeping into Ranevargar's consciousness without any blatant energy changes Maynor might detect.

"*Ranevargar?*"

"*Welcome, Kieran. This isolation is trying. Tell me how things stand in my Realm.*"

Kieran passed on the success of their interactions at the two groves, and at the same time looked for signs of how Ranevargar himself was coping.

"*I appreciate your concern, Kieran. I'm doing as well as this paralysed body can expect. Cut off from everything, all I can do is think ... Replay those memories you gathered of Uirebon's last moments in the grove, please. They don't fit my expectations. Hmm! That was a fierce assault. He was in contention, either with the High King or with Maynor. Are his Coursers still watching my groves?*"

"*No, when I looked they were all racing home.*"

"*Good. Your journey to the Boundary should be unhindered, but keep your own watch and pass these new instructions to all the Guardians and hosts you have links with ... And, no, nothing has changed here. Maynor is unlikely to pay me serious attention till he has the assistance and security of his Castle.*"

Kieran showed the memories from the very first Courser.

"*Yes, that is his Seat of Power and presumably where I am being taken. Resume your journey, Kieran. I hope I will have new information when you next make contact.*"

Kieran opened his eyes and couldn't help smiling at all the serious looks.

"That was longer than we expected, Kieran. What's happened?"

"Nothing really, Rhys. Ranevargar says it's important for me to be sneaky when I'm using the link, and that slows me down. He's still paralysed on the back of that horse, and he doesn't think much will happen till he gets to Maynor's Castle."

"The one near the Emperor trees?"

"Yep. We think he's about halfway. I'm contacting all the hosts and Guardians for him, so give me a moment before we get moving again."

The race resumed. Not really a race, except against time, but the rapidly changing landmarks and the unexpected alteration from their fast trot to this new and much faster bounding gait gave a strong feeling of urgency.

"Whoa! Gryl wants to keep up this speed till it's too dark to see. Just as well we had the energy boost."

The sky above the plain turned an astonishingly brilliant red with the approach of evening, bathing riders and mounts in a light reminiscent of Maynor's Ruby, a thought which Kieran kept very much to himself. Wheeling above and ahead, the light changes on Krol's wings were even more spectacular, till the red morphed to purple and then darker still. After a river crossing, Kieran called a halt.

"Grab your honey-bread snacks and loosen up while I check with Ranevargar. We'll have to wait for a while before we can travel again."

"Long enough for a little campfire, Kieran? We could make a hot drink with the herbs Manon gave us."

"No, Woorawa, fire stands out like crazy if anyone's looking for us ... He did say it's better hot though, so put some water in the billy gadget and I'll use the Opal to heat it."

"Hey! Neat idea, Kieran. You're more than just a pretty face."

Kieran could just make out the smiles and he took a few seconds to grab a hug before settling to check, first with Krol, who'd decided it was easier and safer to stay aloft rather than land in the uncertain light, and then with the hosts and Guardians at the different groves. After walking back and forth for a minute, he chose a spot where he could sit and close his eyes against the distraction of the dimly seen movement around him.

Tan took his billy gadget to the water's edge, smiled at the lapping sounds of five Panthers busily slaking their thirst, then found a spot slightly upstream to dip enough water for human drinks. One of the Panthers grunted softly, the lapping noises stopped and the five great shapes drifted silently away. Tan looked at the water, inky black and spooky in the dimness, and was pleased he'd been on a Panther's back for the crossing. The soft murmur of voices and movement silenced so abruptly he stood and turned to stare at the black shadows outlined against the light shining around Kieran. Billy in hand, he made his way carefully back.

The light brightened and Tan's scalp prickled when Kieran uttered a small cry. He left the billy and, taking a few more steps, linked arms with Woorawa to watch Kieran's changing play of concentration.

And watched.

And watched.

The light softened then faded to nothing, and Woorawa's occasional arm squeeze felt extra reassuring. Everyone was silent and still, five Panthers and four friends, watching and worrying why Kieran's communication was extending so long. A glow through the riverside vegetation startled Tan with the thought that it was on fire until a proper look showed it was moonrise, and the light that Penron had explained would be enough to allow a night journey was on its way. More startling was the call breaking the silence.

"Come close and listen everyone. Everything's changed and we're going to race through the night."

"Kieran, tell us what's going on. We've been scared out of our brains with your glowing and calling out, and you've been twice as long as you said."

"They've got Ranevargar in that Castle and the Realm Lord wants to take his Pearl and use it against the High King. If we don't stop him it will be terrible for Ranevargar and all his Realm."

"We're going to stop a Realm Lord? You've got to be kidding!"

"Not by fighting, Rhys. We wouldn't have a hope. Ranevargar wants *me* to take it instead, so all the Guardians and Realm Trees don't fade back to ordinary animals and plants."

"You?"

"When we get to the Boundary Wall, we're going to Maynor's Realm instead of Dead World. Krol will carry me to the Castle."

"No way, Kieran. We won't let you. Those Power Masters will use the rod things against Krol and you'll get captured again."

"Rhys! Rhys! Listen to our plan first, then tell us your ideas. Ranevargar reckons if I take over his Pearl firmly enough, it will come to me like the Opal did. I already tried from here, but the Realm Boundaries interfere and I can't make it completely mine without hurting Ranevargar ... Where's that water? I'll heat it for our drink while I explain some more. Ranevargar's been faced by that Maynor again and there are a few things that really scare him. The worst would be losing his Pearl, but he also thinks Maynor might be able to sneak into his mind and control him."

"Through the shields? Ranevargar told us no one in all Faerie could do that."

"No, the shields will hold for ages. Ranevargar's worried he might be tricked into taking them down himself. Evidently Maynor knows more about manipulating people's thoughts than anyone. We got caught in the Central Grove because he made all the hosts think there was no one there."

"Wow! Can Ranevargar do anything against it?"

"He thinks he's safe for a while, Rhys, because Maynor's got too many other things happening to get at him straightaway, but he's worked out an amazing plan to protect us."

"Us?"

"Yes, Maynor's angry because we got away, and he's still after us. That's a big reason why he wants to get into Ranevargar's mind, so he can know everything about us and what we're doing."

"He's mad!"

"No, he's not. He thinks if he gets me he gets a super mind shield as well as power from my Opal to use against the High King."

"He *is* mad. You'd never give them to him."

"Yes, I would, Woorawa."

Rhys broke the startled silence. "How come? We know you can't stand him and your mind's too strong anyway."

"He told Ranevargar about a horrible place where he'd keep you all, so I wouldn't have a choice. I don't really understand how, but Ranevargar says anyone who stays there ends up losing their mind."

"More blackmail. This Maynor sounds worse every time we hear about him."

The billy of water in front of Kieran started bubbling, and when Tan added some of Manon's crumbled herbs an interesting aroma wafted upwards.

"That just makes it extra dangerous to go into his Realm, Kieran. What if it's another trap?"

"It can't be, Mr B. He doesn't know we're coming, and even if he did he wouldn't know where from."

"If you take Ranevargar's Pearl, won't that make him weaker against Maynor?"

Tan tested, but the drink was still too hot. Kieran looked to where the moon was now rising just above the vegetation and saw that very soon there would be enough light for the Panthers to see by.

"It would, Mr B, but if the Pearl's there physically, Maynor can do stuff to affect it. If I've got it, Ranevargar's basic links can still keep working and his Realm stays free from danger."

"I see. Ranevargar's making a sacrifice to protect his Realm. That's no surprise ... It *is* more danger for us though."

"It's not, Mr B. Ranevargar's plan protects us even if Maynor gets into his mind. I think he's way too clever for Maynor anyway, but he doesn't want to take the chance."

"Kieran, what *is* this plan?"

"It's like what happened to us at college, but even stronger. He's going to wipe all the memories about us from his mind and give them to me to keep. After he transfers them to me, he won't even know we exist."

"He will when Maynor talks to him."

"Yes, Mr B, and he'll also be puzzled because he's got special shields. Maynor could even show him memory images of us all together at the Central Grove. He'll understand something's happened to his memories, but Maynor can't get any information about us because it's not there."

"Our own memories weren't really gone. They were there when we looked for them."

"That's the spooky part, Woorawa. If I don't put them back they'll be gone forever. Ranevargar says there's knowledge from when I let him examine my Opal that Maynor mustn't get, and it's even more important for him not to find out about the Dragon Quest."

"Kieran, it makes me feel awful. He's choosing to be imprisoned there, paralysed and helpless, so he can protect us, without knowing that help might be coming."

Mr B grabbed Kieran's shoulders. "Tan's right, Kieran. That's a horrible place to be. He's there with no hope in his mind to help him through. We can't leave him like that."

"I don't like it either, Mr B, but he's certain it's the best way, and we couldn't think of anything else. He's already started the process."

The seed of an idea was planted.

Tan gulped his share of herbal drink and passed the billy to Woorawa. "Can the Panthers see better in the dark than we can, Kieran? The trail's almost clear enough even for me."

"And what about Krol? Has he been gliding all this time?"

The billy went on a pass-around.

"He landed where he wouldn't crash into trees, Rhys, when he found out how long I was taking. I've been keeping a kind of background link with him ... Man! That was a lot better than drinking plain water ... Rhys, when you've had your share we'll give the Panthers an energy boost. It's a race to Woorawa's waterfall from now on ... And you're right about their eyes too, Tan. I didn't think of that."

A few moments later five sets of paws were padding the trail, softly and quietly till they left the band of river vegetation, then with the great loping bounds of Panthers determined to travel far and fast. The first hour was an exciting and unforgettable mixture of speed and purpose. The terrain, brightened by silver moonlight, switched rapidly between open plains and bordering wetlands with glimpses of dark, glistening water. Occasionally a clump of trees would slow the tempo, and the drop to walking pace for two shallow river crossings heightened the sense of speed each time the run restarted.

Choosing a stretch of open plain so Krol could land safely, Kieran signalled for their first stop, then gathered everyone together.

"It depends on Ranevargar how long we'll be here, so after we've given the Panthers their next energy boost, I want to put everyone to sleep till we're ready to move again."

"Give us a couple of minutes to walk around and loosen up first, Kieran. I need to get rid of that last drink."

"Yeah! Me too, Mr B."

That worked well, because Kieran needed to check with the hosts and other Guardians before linking with Ranevargar. Krol moved close and watched Panthers and companions, refreshed by Rhys's touch, slump together in an induced sleep.

"Keep watch, please, Krol. I have to talk to Ranevargar."

A sense of pleasure about Ranevargar and a comforting reassurance came back while Kieran made this link.

"Kieran?"

"It's me, Ranevargar. What's happened now?" Kieran asked this because an element of uncertainty was coming from Ranevargar.

"A serious development! Maynor has taken my Pearl and threatened harm to my Realm if I don't help him use it against the High King. He pitted his Ruby against it to such a level I was worried it might have affected our link."

"It feels perfect to me. Tell me what to look for and I'll check."

Information flowed and was applied.

"There's no change or damage, Ranevargar ... What sort of threats is he making?"

"Destruction of one of my groves as a first step, but isolation from my Pearl is far more serious."

"How long can you hold out? The Panthers are racing, but we won't reach the Realm Boundary till the morning ... Unless Krol carries me?"

Alarm flared strongly in Ranevargar's mind. *"On no account become separated from your companions, Kieran. The process of fully isolating an unwilling Realm Lord from a Stone of Power is a difficult and drawn-out process even for the High King. Maynor has far more pressing challenges, so we'll keep to our plan."*

"Mr B made me think, Ranevargar, and I'm going to keep helping you after you forget everything. You won't know I'm doing it, so Maynor can't find out either."

"??"

"I can sneak a feeling of confidence through the link."

"Show me! Yes! Tighten the way you send it ... like this ... and it will be a wonderful support . Watch through my eyes frequently. This secret link should provide vital information for all of us ... Now, no farewells, Kieran ... I won't be aware of it, but I know you are with me through the trial ahead."

The parcel of Realm Lord memories passed far more quickly through their secret link than Kieran expected, and he returned to watch the nearby sleeping shapes till his sense of loss passed and he could shake himself into action again.

"He's amazing, Krol! We'll see him again as soon as we can."

A quick command brought everyone out of their sleep and grouping together. Kieran's report was very brief and, understanding he was in no mood for questions, everyone mounted quickly and quietly.

The race was on again.

Stars wheeled, too slow to see, the silver moonlight bathed the Realm with a steadily changing aspect, and Panther muscles pushed ceaselessly to force three days of travel into one long night. Not quite ceaselessly, because roughly every hour the group stopped to revitalise weary muscles and loosen up while Kieran checked for anything happening with the now-sleeping Ranevargar. The stops were only a brief interruption to the pattern though, and the gradual rise of the foothills was just starting when an extended break was needed to heal the cramps which Tan had been quietly suffering, and to watch Ranevargar being fed.

"Tan's been walking and stretching his muscles and he feels okay now. What's happened with Ranevargar?"

"Not much, Rhys. They've woken him, and if they're feeding him so early it must mean Maynor's coming again. I'll have to keep checking."

"I reckon we'll reach the waterfall in about three hours, but you need to have some sleep."

"The energy boosts will keep me going till after we get the Pearl, Rhys. We'll all have a sleep then."

The trail, now climbing through forested land, slowed their passage till the light of the dawning day brightened enough to dispel the moon shadows and let the Panthers hit full stride. Two short stops showed Ranevargar's physical needs being attended to and a quiet time. A third stop, in a vaguely remembered clearing, extended to nearly thirty minutes while Kieran watched Maynor realise that his captive's memories of the last few days were gone.

"You're smiling, Kieran. What did you see?"

"Maynor just discovered that Ranevargar hasn't got a clue about who we are, or how he has mind shields he doesn't know how to turn off. He asked a few questions then did something with his Ruby while he stared at Ranevargar. Whatever it was didn't work and he went off in a rush. I'm smiling because Tan's idea for Ranevargar to have no control over his shields worked so well, and because Ranevargar was telling Maynor off for being an ambitious fool."

"Wow! Did that make Maynor angry?"

"No, he just ignored it ... But I think it puzzled him. Ranevargar thought so and he was pleased that he'd made Maynor rethink something."

"Do you see everything Ranevargar's thinking, Kieran?"

"Just his surface thoughts, Mr B, and anything through his senses. He's hoping the High King knows he's been captured and will work out some way to free him."

A burst of joker bird song carolling from the edge of the clearing turned every head to the glow of early sunlight catching the tops of the trees.

"Crazy birds! I wish Ranevargar could hear them."

There was another chorus, of deep rumbles this time, as Gryl led the Panthers through a short readying routine of stretching and tensing every muscle. Time to move.

* * *

"Wear your packs through the Wall, everyone."

"We're coming straight back, Woorawa. We don't need to."

"I hope not, Rhys, but it's a sensible precaution."

Kieran agreed with Woorawa and reached to undo the double lashings holding his pack securely to the Panther saddle. It took a bit of effort, but soon he was waiting, pack on his back and shocked at the weight, for Mr B and Tan to catch up.

"What about the Panthers, Kieran? Do you want them to wait here while we go through the Wall? They'd be a lot more comfortable back at the pool and it's only five minutes away at Panther speed."

"They deserve every bit of comfort they can get, Rhys, but I'm hoping we'll be gone such a short while they might as well stay close. They're going to stop just far enough away for the Boundary effect not to make them uncomfortable while they rest."

Woorawa turned from his Panther, shrugged his pack into place, then moved to help Tan. "Is the Wall going to be as bad as usual, or did Ranevargar show you some way to make it better?"

"Just as bad, Woorawa. There were too many other things to learn."

"Will you have to calm Krol, like you do for the horses?"

"No, just the same protection we all get."

"Will he be hard to bring? He's a lot bigger than a horse."

"I'll use whatever energy I need, Woorawa. It's no big deal."

"I knew that. It's the Wall getting to my nerves."

"Yeah. Me too. Let's go!"

"All right. Get the picture of where we're going in your mind and hang on to it."

"What about Krol? He hasn't been there."

"He's seeing what I'm seeing, Tan. I've locked it in till we're through."

The approach to the Wall, out of their minds with the passage of time and so many other events, threatened more with every step. Kieran's glow of protection turned red for the transition, then faded away as more movement gave blessed relief. Rhys stopped and turned to look at the strange shimmer.

"What happened, Kieran? That was worse than the other times."

Kieran didn't think it was and cast his mind back.

Mr B also disagreed. "No it wasn't, Rhys. It feels like it was because it's immediate in our minds and we're still reacting, but I remember thinking exactly the same after every other crossing ... and we've been spoiled because all the Tree Portals have been exciting and pleasant."

"I suppose, but Tree Portals are totally different ... aren't they?"

"Well, it acts like a portal, except it's horrible. Did Ranevargar tell you anything about how the Boundary works, Kieran?"

"Only about concentrating on the destination. He was amazed we could come through at all till I showed him how the Opal protects us. There are billions of things we didn't have time to talk about. Let's hurry."

The walk out of the dead zone resumed.

"Hey! Here's the pool where there weren't any fish. This is exactly where we're meant to be."

"We'd be in big trouble if it wasn't, Rhys. Sit down and rest and I'll check for any danger before I try for the reach."

Krol surprised everyone by stalking to the pool and settling in the metre-deep water for a drink and a clean. Kieran shifted his attention and closed his eyes to reach for any signs of danger or activity that might be of concern. First he looked for energy signatures. Ranevargar said he had a natural flair for this and had shown him the rudiments of looking externally. *Wow!* There was something powerful and close ... It was fading? Of course. Their passage through the Wall needed help from the Opal, so no wonder there were signs.

That wasn't a concern, so he looked further afield ... *Good grief!* Massive pulses of energy registered, but they were so far off they weren't any immediate worry. Nothing local. Kieran looked for any familiar mind patterns next. There were no horses close enough to reach without help from the Opal, so no Spooks or other riders to threaten the group. There was the tickle of a Courser pattern, but that was also too far away to worry about. Good. The coast was clear.

The secret link to the Pearl was always there — permanent till Ranevargar no longer needed assistance — open and ready for the tendril of possession Kieran now sent through it. The pleasant tingle of connection and ownership, almost the same as he felt with the Opal, once again spread through his body, building and building as the Pearl responded to his will, till it approached the threshold Ranevargar had showed him, oh-so-carefully, where any further takeover would break the Realm Lord's vital connections and result in exclusive possession. The Pearl should now answer his call. Kieran sent the signal, but felt resistance and knew that, as Ranevargar had predicted, distance was still the enemy. He quickly reduced the level of possession and opened his eyes.

"Ranevargar was right. The Wall's not interfering anymore, but there's not enough strength in the Pearl. I have to get closer."

"What about using your Opal to help?"

"It doesn't work that way, Rhys. If the Pearl was one hundred percent mine there would be enough strength to call it from here, but the whole point of this is to protect Ranevargar's links. He warned me against using any Opal power here in Maynor's Realm too, because it would stand out like a beacon and give him a position to portal to."

"They'll try something if they see you. You might have to use it then."

"I hope not, Woorawa, but there *are* Coursers out there, and if we have to get close to the Castle anyone who looks up will see us."

"If you fly at treetop level and come from behind the Emperor trees, you'll only be in view for that last little bit."

"It's good advice, Woorawa, but Krol thinks it'll be better to go extra high and have the option for a power dive and greater speed."

"Whoo! Griffin speed is unreal ... How long before you get back?"

"I'm not sure. I'll contact you as soon as I know."

Kieran climbed onto Krol's back and, monitored by four sets of watchful eyes, fastened all the safety harness straps firmly and securely. Those eyes looked anxious too, worried about the prospect of separation.

"Put your helmet on now, Kieran, ready for fast flying."

"Krol's a danger machine, Rhys. No one will hurt me."

Krol lifted from his crouch, trotted to position himself, then spread his wings and powered forward. The ungainly take-off motion morphed to the grace and control of flight, and a scream of Griffin accomplishment sounded for the ground huggers. Kieran felt Krol's determination for success in the striving for ever more height with every powerful wing beat. The ground below spread in a growing panorama, and the widened view gave Kieran a startling realisation of their height — at least a kilometre and still climbing — along with a new understanding of the strength and determination inherent in Ranevargar's primary Guardian.

The flight levelled and, despite the helmet's protection, Kieran's eyes watered when the energy directed for altitude changed its purpose to horizontal speed. He marvelled. The sensations from the minds of the first Coursers paled to insignificance compared with this height and speed. His own eyes, watering from the air forced through his goggles' vision slits, were practically useless, so he switched to Krol's. The superior vision brought details of the ground, so far below, into startling clarity. Yes, there were the hills they'd traversed with George, and far ahead the Emperor trees were two tiny spires. A quick message diverted Krol to look beyond them to the castle, then Kieran turned his mind inward and followed the secret link to check that all was well with Ranevargar.

Whoa! His shields were reacting.

Maynor was standing in front of him with a red glow surrounding his hand and the object in it. The glow looked like a replay of the time when Maynor had taken the Opal. Yes, the object *was* the Pearl and the red glow must be the outward sign of an attempt to bind it. Ranevargar's shields were holding easily though, and the man himself was defiant but quite okay, so Kieran strengthened his awareness of the Pearl through the link and, pushing through a strange, clingy resistance, started the possession process. *Hmm!* Just as well. The interference gave a sticky sensation, slowing progress, but not seriously. Kieran stopped well before the critical threshold, held the final call in readiness, and passed a command to his steed.

"Speed, Krol! Dive then disperse as fast as you can ... but warn me when it's final approach time."

Kieran almost lost his concentration with the combination of stomach lurch and buffeting air pressure as Griffin and rider plummeted.

The connection to the Pearl built to the critical level then held till the right moment. The special call Kieran had practiced with Ranevargar pierced the tacky red binding of Maynor's Ruby and, strengthened by proximity, the Pearl responded. Elation and excitement rushed through Kieran with the awareness that nestled beneath his shirt, and close to his Opal was a new Stone of Power. He shared the joy of success with Krol and, emphasising the need for speed, switched his attention to watch their passage through eyes built to cope with the rush of air. The view frightened the life out of him. Hurtling so close to the ground with the speed built by a vertical stoop of more than a kilometre was a shocking contrast to the majestic progress of their previous lofty flight.

Krol banked slightly to avoid the Emperor trees and, wings beating with the greatest power and speed yet, changed his flight path to regain some elevation. Pushing aside the exhilaration of speed and success, Kieran checked his link with Ranevargar. *Whoops!'* The Pearl responded so strongly he was in Ranevargar's mind before he had time to adjust to the subtle approach.

"Where is it?" Maynor was leaning close and, through Ranevargar's eyes, Kieran saw the storm of anger clouding his features.

"I told you, I don't know. Your unlawful meddling must have activated a protective response, or maybe the High King is acting to defend me."

"Call it back, old fool, or face losing it completely when the High Court is mine."

"Fool I might be, Maynor, but while I am bound by this helmet and the Wards of this place, you know full well that is beyond me. Remove these restraints and return me to my Realm and I will honour the convention of neutrality while you make your Challenge."

"Lower those shields and I will consider it."

Ranevargar had absolutely no trust in Maynor's words. "My mind is my own, Maynor, and you seek to violate my privacy. The shields remain."

Maynor gestured angrily and Ranevargar examined the shields with puzzlement and wonder while thrusts of Nexus energy lashed uselessly against them.

That was interesting. Ranevargar was mystified by their presence but fully confident he could trust their effectiveness for the long-term.

Maynor turned and walked away, and Kieran, feeling pleased, returned to his own situation. Krol was past the hills now and racing in a slightly downward trajectory. *Good grief!* They were only minutes away from rejoining the group.

"Grab your packs everyone. We're nearly there."

Kieran smiled inside at the wave of excitement and relief that came back at him ... And there they were, clearly seen through Krol's superior vision, two figures pointing their arms and two helping each other with packs. Krol's wings stopped beating for the power glide of the last few kilometres, then changed attitude to catch air and reduce their incredible speed. With a flare of wings and action, he landed and squatted to let Kieran scramble off. When his helmet and straps were released, Kieran retrieved the Pearl from inside his shirt and made a triumphant little display for everyone before slipping it into the fob pocket of his jeans.

"Head for the Wall, everyone. The sooner we're out of here the better."

They didn't. Instead, as soon as his feet touched the ground, he was swamped with enough hugs and smiles to make an army happy.

"Yikes! This is embarrassing. You should be thanking Krol. He did all the work."

Krol gave a happy *scrark* when his neck was wrapped with Rhys's impulsive hug, and ruffled his neck feathers with pleasure at the attention from everyone else, including Kieran.

The walk to the Wall followed quickly though, because everyone was as keen as Kieran to get back to the relative safety of Ranevargar's Realm.

"Did they try anything against you, Kieran?"

"Nothing! Krol's tactics were so good I don't think we were there long enough to even register. He did an unreal power dive from more than a kilometre high and we went past the Castle so fast I was frightened out of my brain when I got around to looking at what was happening. I watched Maynor through the link and he thinks Ranevargar made the Pearl disappear."

"Did Ranevargar get upset?"

"No, he was really puzzled, but Maynor was in the middle of trying something against the Pearl and he thinks some kind of safety mechanism has taken it back to his Realm. He was strong against Maynor too, telling him off for breaking the rules about the Pearl, and when Maynor got aggro and crashed against his shields, Ranevargar watched how it had no effect and decided he'd be able to hold out for ages."

"How long is ages? We still have to rush to get Maurice, don't we?"

Kieran turned to Mr B. "Maurice?"

Mr B shook his head in puzzlement. "Don't ask me. It's another Rhys mystery."

"Dorks! Maurice is the Dragon."

Kieran gawped at him, well, so did the others.

"Maurice? Rhys, you're joking us. We can't call a Dragon, Maurice."

"Why not? I'm sick of saying the Dragon or the Dragon construct or the Ultimate Guardian or whatever other names we've been calling him so far."

"Maurice makes him sound like someone's twin brother ... or a lawyer."

"Does not! Maurice came into my head straight away."

Woorawa started laughing. "I can't wait to see this. You walk up to a gigantic dragon and say, 'Hi Maurice, old buddy. I hope you like your name and please don't incinerate me if you don't.'"

"As if. He's a Guardian, so he'll be friendly as anything, just like Krol."

"Rhys, the first time we saw Krol we thought we were going to die, and Ranevargar said Krol was like a chicken compared to ... to Maurice."

Rhys laughed, because with Mr B using the name he knew it was going to stick. "Did you really dive from a kilometre in one big stoop, Kieran?"

"At least. It might even have been one and a half. Why?"

"It must have been specco. When something falls through the air it reaches about two hundred kilometres per hour."

Mr B knew about this. "Completely spectacular, Rhys, but with Krol's mass and flying skill it would have been much faster. I know a peregrine falcon can reach about three hundred kilometres per hour in a controlled dive, and Krol would be faster still."

"Heebie-jeebs! Over three hundred! What did it look like, Kieran?"

"I don't know. I was totally concentrated on the Pearl till after we levelled out ... Join up, everyone. It's protection time."

The curious little procession of five friends with linked arms, and a giant Griffin resting his beak carefully on Kieran's shoulder, made its way forward with the destination image fixed firmly in their minds until the Opal flared into protective life and everything dissolved into a morass of disturbed reality.

Kieran checked how everyone had coped while they trudged quietly towards the verdant growth where the Panthers were now on their feet waiting, and felt proud at the way they all fought to dispel the disorientation and misery.

"Oh boy! That's the most fun I've had since last time. How soon can we do it again?"

"As soon as we stock up with water and get organised, Rhys. We've got a long way to go once we're in Dead World."

"We're not going anywhere for at least another three hours. I don't care what you say. Kieran, you didn't have one bit of sleep last night and you can't keep yourself going with energy boosts. Well, you can, I suppose, but Ranevargar said not to. How long will his shields last?"

"I can't be exact, Woorawa, because it depends how strongly Maynor keeps attacking them, but the energy pool I gave him should last for twelve or thirteen days."

"And how long to get to ... Maurice?"

"I tried to work that out while we were racing on the Panthers and I reckon it'll be five days if we stop to camp each night."

"That gives us six days up our sleeve at least, Kieran ... Of course we're going to camp at night."

"I suppose we can. I don't like Ranevargar being a prisoner for all that time though."

"Of course not, but these packs are heavy and we won't make it if we're not sensible. If Ranevargar was here I am sure he'd tell us to have long days of hiking but then a proper rest every night."

Kieran had to smile. "Yeah. He did, and he said six days, but that's too long."

Woorawa nodded thoughtfully. "I've got it planned in my mind. We'll start every morning as soon as it's light enough to see and try for at least twelve hours of walking."

Mr B interrupted. "Wait till we get there before we plan too much, Woorawa. There won't be any convenient animal tracks to follow this time."

"And there's no vegetation either. It's like a moonscape."

Talk stopped because they'd reached the Panthers. Ten minutes later, they were deep, deep, deeply asleep.

CHAPTER 2

Kieran opened his eyes reluctantly, resisting the demand from his body that the three hours of sleep Mr B had insisted on hadn't been enough, and saw the slight head movement as one pair of watchful eyes reacted.

"Yes, Krol, it's time to wake everyone and get organised."

Krol's neck feathers lifted, and his strong rush of anticipation and excitement washed away Kieran's lethargy. Kieran sat up and couldn't help smiling at the curious sight of every other form deeply asleep, despite the bright sunshine, the soft background rush of the waterfall, and the cheeky calls from a group of joker birds in a nearby tree.

A dig at Rhys's side got absolutely no response. A second dig, with just as little effect, brought realisation and, wondering how long it might stay in effect, he cancelled the sleep command. This time the dig brought a funny little grunt of complaint before Rhys's eyes blinked open.

"Go to sleep, Kieran. You need to rest."

"Our sleep's over, Rhys. It's time to go."

"No, it isn't. I just closed my eyes." He woke now though and sat up. "Gods! It looks like they're all drugged or something. Did you put the Panthers to sleep as well as us?"

"No, that's from their giant effort. They'll wake up on their own."

And, indeed, the soft talk had already set Panther ears twitching.

Krol stretched his wings and gave a demanding wake-up screech that startled everyone to wakefulness. After a short while the serious business of preparing for the transition to Dead World began in earnest. Mr B set Rhys and Woorawa refastening all the water skins and another pack of supplies to Krol's harness, while Kieran and Tan joined him in making a considered inventory of their own packs. Curious fascination with the special cloaks Kieran knew nothing about was interrupted when Rhys and Tan came rushing over with concerned expressions.

"Kieran, there's no food for Krol ... except for a few biscuit things which won't be enough for even one day. The hosts must have forgotten him, and there's nothing in Dead World except monsters."

"They haven't forgotten. Feeding him is my job."

Tan and Mr B joined in with Rhys and Woorawa's blank stares.

"You? What? Kieran, they ate fourteen of those rabbit things in one go."

Tan grabbed Kieran's arm. "What don't we know this time?"

"You half know, Tan. Ranevargar told me Krol can last for two weeks without ordinary food, so long as I feed him power and he gets a basic amount of water."

"He eats power? That's unbelievable."

"No, it's not, Rhys. Remember how Ranevargar explained the Griffins are partly ordinary bodies and partly power, so they can match the Dead World Monsters? If I give him energy, the power side will keep him going."

"Eating energy is a totally weird idea."

"Not really. Well, I suppose it is, but he absorbs it ... like you do when you heal things."

Woorawa gave Rhys a cheeky shove. "Hey, energy gobbler, how about a power munch for lunch?"

Rhys didn't respond. He was still intent on the idea that he himself was an energy eater.

"How long have you known this, Kieran?"

"Ranevargar explained it, Woorawa, when I saw how much energy he sends to keep Maurice alive. Maurice is all power and doesn't eat any food ... There's lots more to tell you when we get a chance."

"I know. We're too busy just now. It's one of the rules."

Kieran could only laugh at the concert of nods. "Once we're through the Boundary, Woorawa. We can catch up all the time when we're walking. Packs on, everyone. Time to go.

It wasn't. There was a short but heartfelt delay for goodbyes to Gryl and the other Panthers before the short trek to another ordeal of passing through the White Wall.

∗   ∗   ∗

Kieran took in the awful, bleak and familiar scene, reached to tally the number of Monsters in the vicinity, and motioned everyone to keep moving.

"There are six close Monsters and lots more further away. What do you want us to do, Rhys?"

Rhys pointed to a small outcrop of rock a couple of hundred metres away. "We'll dump our packs there. I've just realised we'll have to unhitch all those water skins, because they'll slow Krol down, and we can't let them get damaged either. Does coming through the Wall spoil our Spook rope charges, Kieran, in case we have to use them?"

"We're all ready, Rhys. I have a routine to rebuild everything every time we come through."

A busy moment later the packs were stowed and the twelve precious water skins unclipped from Krol's saddle. Krol himself was bristling with fierce energy and searching the sky. His aura was activated and ready, of course, and, if all went according to Ranevargar's expectations, after the improvements it would make the success of his efforts against any Dead World Monsters a foregone conclusion. The biggest concern was a group attack, but luckily that was not the case this time.

Kieran pointed and Krol took to the air. "A couple of minutes, everyone."

"How do they know where we are, Kieran? Your mind shields are so good they can hide us from the Realm Lords and even the High King."

"I don't think they do know, Tan. They must home in on the energy disturbance we make when we come through the Boundary and then simply attack anything they see."

"Gods! That'll be Krol for sure. Look at him."

Rhys was right. Krol, wheeling in fierce anticipation, was a total magnet of attention. Kieran linked with him and, through his keen vision, instantly saw the shape winging close. When Krol launched forward, screams of defiance and answering rage shook the watching companions. The combatants closed, then disappeared in a dazzling burst of light. Kieran, linked to Krol's view, and protected from the flash by the special blink reflex, saw Krol's talons rip into the disoriented Monster. A weird cry was cut off when the physical contact unleashed the power of the aura and melted flesh. A rapidly dissolving skeleton plunged earthward, disappearing altogether before any part reached the ground.

"How was that? Gods! The aura works like a hundred Spook ropes at once. We—"

Waves of distress reached Kieran, through the Opal network interestingly, and he turned to where Rhys had both hands over his eyes and Tan was groping blindly for support with outstretched hands. Krol's scream of success went unnoticed. Kieran's hands touched Rhys's temple for a healing zap, then the two of them moved in quick succession to Woorawa, Tan and Mr B.

"Flaming hell, Kieran! Is that going to happen with every Monster? All I could see was an afterimage of Krol till we fixed it. He went off like a supernova."

"Rhys is right, Kieran. We'll need a warning signal of some kind or we'll be useless if we need to protect ourselves."

Krol's screech of defiance warned that another Monster was racing closer.

"Close your eyes and look the other way. When this one's gone we'll figure out what to do."

Four bodies swivelled and Kieran switched to Krol's view till a second Monster, so deadly and frightening in their memories, dissolved with a single touch of the aura and Krol's victory scream sounded again. Why were his own eyes protected? He'd been looking directly at Krol like everyone else. Yes, the blink reflex Ranevargar had developed for Krol had acted to close his own eyes. If he hadn't been linked he would have suffered like everyone else.

"Can we look yet?"

"Yes. When you hear that victory call it's all over."

Four sets of eyes lifted to Krol's triumphant wheeling flight.

"How do they disappear so quickly?"

"Like the one you got with the Spook rope, Rhys, except the aura around Krol is way stronger. You'll see for yourself next time 'cause I'll relay Krol's special blink reflex to all of us from now on."

"Relay? Won't that mean a delay?"

"There wasn't any for me, Mr B, but we'll test it with a softer flash to make sure."

Woorawa was amazed. "You know how to connect our minds to Krol's blink?"

"Ranevargar did it with the first tests and I remember his pattern."

"Is there enough time for a test? How far away are the rest of them?"

"A few minutes at least, Mr B. Plenty of time."

Plenty of time it was and, after three tests with increasing brightness, everyone was able to watch the incredible sight of two Monsters dispatched and dissolved in a matter of seconds by two efficient talon gouges. Kieran laughed when Rhys and Woorawa echoed Krol's victory call with their own, then shared the rush of group excitement and renewed confidence.

"Krol's magnificent, Kieran. The monsters haven't got a hope against that light flash and the aura."

"Tan's the hero, Rhys. His light flash idea protects Krol and gives him a huge first strike advantage. It's made this expedition a lot safer for all of us."

Tan blushed and looked quite disconcerted at all the smiles and Rhys's impulsive bear-hug.

"Um ... Krol's used his aura three times now, Kieran. Won't he need a recharge?"

"It's already done, Tan. I'm topping him up straight after every fight, so he'll always be ready."

"Are we going to wait here for the next two, Kieran? Krol's so strong we might as well start walking."

"He is, except for all the water skins, Rhys. He shouldn't have anything slowing him down when he's fighting."

Rhys whacked his head in a gesture of annoyance. "Sorry. I didn't think ... We should figure out some sort of quick release, so we don't have twelve skins to unbuckle every time a Monster gets close."

Woorawa was impressed with this idea and moved to examine the pile of water skins.

Mr B disagreed. "Each skin is secured with its own buckle and they're too important to try anything fancy. We're better off if we have two of us working on each side of Krol, and three skins each won't take long."

Everyone turned to Kieran for a decision. "Mr B's right. Our water *is* precious, and unless there's something wrong with me we'll always have plenty of warning. How long would it take you to unbuckle three water skins, Rhys?"

"What? Less than a minute, I suppose."

Kieran nodded and pointed. "We have to work our way to the end of that cliff wall, then get close to that first mountain before there's any chance of finding water."

"You haven't told us how you know where to go, Kieran. Did Ranevargar give you a mental map?"

"It's kind of straightforward till we get past that second mountain, Woorawa. There's a valley to cross and then a third mountain we can't see from here. We have to climb part way up that to a ruined old structure."

Rhys's jaw dropped. "Sheba! Look how dead everything is. Will we be able to make it, Woorawa?"

Mr B and Tan had made the best stocktake of all their supplies, but Woorawa looked at the first mountain, way in the distance, and grinned.

"Mr B told me there's enough water for three days if we limit ourselves to two litres a day. We'll have to be careful though, because Krol needs more than we do ... Kieran, all these boulders and rough stuff at the base of the cliff are going to slow us down. We'd be much better off if we diverge and stay where it's more open."

That was a no-brainer and everyone instantly agreed.

"Where are the other two Monsters, Kieran? The sooner we get going the better."

"Not too long, Rhys. I'm going to check on Ranevargar's link while we wait."

The last check had been back at the waterfall clearing. This check was the first from Dead World and Kieran was relieved that the link was functioning as securely and as well as it always had. Ranevargar was frustrated by the constant helplessness of his paralysis, but his mind was full of confidence and plans and speculation.

Five minutes and two spectacular flashes of dissolving Monsters later, Krol was standing very proudly while the twelve vital water skins were buckled securely in place.

An hour later Woorawa called a halt for their first ten-minute break and the loaded packs were shed with huge relief. Tan was finding the hike particularly tough going, but he hadn't made a single complaint, and Kieran, who was monitoring everyone's wellbeing, was particularly impressed. There'd been a few brief stops to adjust and readjust the way their packs sat for the most comfort, but otherwise they'd trudged steadily along behind Woorawa, the trailblazer.

"This place freaks me out. All this walking and we still haven't seen one living thing."

"We've seen Monsters, Rhys. There's been enough of them."

"They don't count, Tan. Ranevargar said they're different, like the Spooks. I wonder how there's proper air when there aren't any trees or plants?"

Mr B finished a carefully calculated sip from his water skin. "I've been wondering about that too, Rhys, and I've decided it must be getting refreshed all the time from the other Realms. There has to be water coming in from somewhere too, to keep the air breathable."

"Breathable?"

"Air needs a certain amount of moisture, Rhys."

"Yeah, I knew that. Remember the creek that disappeared the first time we went through the Wall? That fits into your theory ... What's your Monster-radar saying, Kieran?"

"I can sense eight at the moment, Rhys, but they're a long way away and I don't think any of them are coming for us."

"Why aren't you sure? You can sense the movement."

"They're all moving, and three of them are sort of heading this way, but it's probably just random. Bring your foot here, Tan, so Rhys can fix the uncomfortable part on your heel before it turns into a blister."

"Are you checking our feet?"

"No way, Rhys. Yours probably smell too much. Tan's been thinking about the rubbing on his heel."

Rhys pulled his runners off, then his socks, which he gleefully waved in everyone's face.

"Shouldn't we all air our feet while we have our breaks? Oh boy! What are we going to feel like now that we can't wash anything?"

Mr B laughed. "We'll have to sit five metres apart in a few more days, going by those socks, Rhys."

The trek continued through the afternoon with a ten-minute break every hour, then stopped at the first sign of dusk. This was earlier than the plan, but Woorawa was adamant a catch-up on proper sleep was absolutely necessary to get through the next long, long day. No one argued. Five hours of hiking with packs so heavy made the thought of the thirteen hours Woorawa was planning for the next day totally daunting. It also worked well to familiarise everyone with the contents of their packs; Kieran in particular, because this was his first chance for a leisurely look. After ten minutes of forced inaction, Woorawa allowed Tan to organise the evening meal. This involved collecting half a litre of water from everyone, plus a matching amount from one of Krol's water skins, and putting half in one billy for the herbal drink and the rest in the other two, mixed with five heavy biscuit things.

"What are they, Tan?"

"I'm not exactly sure, except that one biscuit mixed with water and heated is meant to be a whole day's worth of energy and nourishment. The host elves explained them to us the very first day when you were asleep and we got the smaller backpacks ... Kieran, we can't make a fire without wood, so you'll have to heat everything for us."

Rhys interrupted. "Not yet. Krol's not eating anything, so we'll give him his water before we do anything for ourselves. Can you tell him the right angle to hold his head, Kieran, so I can pour the water into his mouth without wasting any?"

A whole water skin was carefully given to Krol, and by the time it was empty Rhys had learned just how much to pour for a comfortable swallow.

"Is he still thirsty, Kieran?"

"Yes, he is, but he understands that's his ration. Watching him drink has made me extra thirsty."

Everyone watched eagerly while Kieran called on the Opal, and soon the steadily warming contents of the billy gave off their herbal aroma.

Rhys groaned. "That stuff shouldn't smell so good. It means I'll want twice as much as soon as I finish."

"Sip it, Rhys, and make it last. That's what I'm going to do. There's no more water till the morning."

Woorawa wasn't right, because a matching amount was soaking into the biscuit things in the other billies.

"Hey! I wish we had a campfire. When you watch coals glowing you can kind of relax your mind every now and again."

"Yes, Rhys. We didn't think it at the time, but we were completely spoiled with the friendly fires and delicious fresh food at our other camps."

Mr B's comments prompted Kieran to jump up and move off, casting his eyes at the ground in the gathering dusk.

"What are you doing?"

"Help me gather some rocks and you'll see."

"Gather rocks? He's done too much today, Mr B, and gone loopy."

Everyone left their drinks to help collect a small pile of rocks.

"Are we making a signature cairn?"

"That's a great idea, Woorawa, but no. Let me warm the drinks again and then watch."

A blue glow, hastily adjusted to a more appropriate mix of red and orange, covered the rocks and spread a circle of friendly light for the companions. Rhys reached to tentatively touch one of the stones.

"That's brilliant, Kieran. It looks so real it's weird when the stones aren't hot."

"I could do that too, I suppose, but it would waste energy."

Five bodies and a great Guardian settled in a circle around the artificial campfire and the glow of appreciation in their thoughts was reflected in their smiles.

"What's happening with Ranevargar, Kieran? You haven't said anything about him for ages."

"That's because nothing's really happened. Just before we stopped a couple of attendants were feeding him, but Maynor hasn't been back since this morning. Ranevargar asks the attendants questions all the time, but they must have orders to be quiet, because they never answer."

Tan placed the next billy in front of Kieran, then, while it was heating, stirred the contents with a wooden spoon from his pack.

Kieran leaned closer. "It smells good to me."

Tan, testing to make sure the top of the billy wasn't too hot, tilted it to let the campfire glow shine in.

"Can you keep it simmering for a few more minutes till the biscuits finish dissolving, Kieran? There are still lumpy bits I can see."

"Yeah!" Rhys said. "If there's any lumps in my food Tan gets the sack and I'll be the new cook."

Woorawa grabbed his throat and made horrible choking sounds.

"Idiot! I know how to cook."

Tan and Mr B made the choking sounds now, and Rhys shook his head in happy disgust. After a few more stirs with the spoon, Tan was satisfied the food was ready. Rhys took a tentative mouthful, then another.

"Not bad for dissolved biscuits, Tan. I'll see what you do tomorrow night before I take over."

"I've already thought of a way to make it taste better, Rhys."

"What? Cook it for so long it gets a burnt taste? There's nothing else you can do with biscuits and water."

That made everyone curious. Kieran liked the surprisingly rich taste anyway and ate his share slowly, though he smiled at Tan's way of making sure he stayed in charge of the cooking.

"Are we going to sleep straightaway, Kieran, or do you need to practice anything?"

"Ranevargar told me to practice calling lots of Opal energy, Woorawa. But it's time to send another reassurance message to Burrimul and Tan's family, so we'll do that first. That's all though, and then we'll get a proper catch-up for our sleep."

"Proper? As if! Woorawa wants us to wake before it's even sunrise."

"Yep! And you're the first, so you can get breakfast ready for everyone."

"Torture! What are we having? I'll get it organised now. Hey, how do we clean everything without wasting water?"

"There's plenty of sand, Rhys, and we need to do that now."

Kieran supplied a new glow of light for Woorawa's scouring process, then everyone gathered around the rock fire.

"Are we going to do the connection for Tan and Woorawa every couple of days, Kieran?"

"Ranevargar told me time's different here, Mr B. Two days in the Realms is about a week at home."

"That's ... impossible!"

"No, it's not, Tan. Lots of stories about people going into Faerie talk about it. Some of them even have a couple of days being years when people return."

"I hope not, Rhys. Ranevargar's version's bad enough. Half the semester could be gone before we get home ... Hold my hand, Tan."

Woorawa followed Tan with a reassurance call, then, with an enormous surge, Kieran transferred Opal power to the great reservoir of the Realm Trees. He opened his eyes to darkness. *Whoops!*

"Sorry, everyone. I was concentrating so hard I forgot the rock fire."

The cheery light reappeared while everyone got ready for the night's rest. Mr B came back from relieving himself with an idea that so much moisture was being wasted there should be a way to recycle their urine.

"You mean drink it? You've got to be kidding."

"There *is* a way to distil it with a plastic sheet and a container for collection, Rhys."

"Oh yeah! I've read about that, but no thanks. I'd rather wait till we reach the snow."

Krol crouched comfortably on the ground and Woorawa, first to be ready, sat with his back resting against his flank.

"Come on, everyone. Cuddle up close to keep warm, but no mucking round, because we need our sleep."

"Ha! Speak for yourself, Woorawa. We'll put Tan next to you and see what happens."

Tan *did* cuddle up and it *was* with Woorawa. Kieran knew keeping warm wasn't going to be a problem though, because he could see Krol's intention to cover them all with his wing, but snuggling close to Rhys was going to happen anyway. There were *good-night* murmurs all around and, enjoying the comfort of Rhys's arm draped across his chest, Kieran decided to make a last routine check before telling Krol they were ready for sleep.

Ranevargar was okay, puzzling why Maynor had left him alone all day.

Gryl was half asleep somewhere, sprawled amongst the other four Panthers.

Kan was ... *Wow!* Kan was at the Lake Grove, full of Griffin success against an Unordered Monster incursion. That was a big achievement and good news to tell everyone in the morning. Now for a local Monster check.

SHEBA!

Kieran yelled and jumped to his feet.

"Monsters, Krol! Three of them are nearly here. Can you take off in the dark?"

With his signature scream of challenge, Krol launched skyward with wing beats so powerful Kieran had to crouch to keep steady. Four bewildered friends picked themselves up.

"Get your Spook ropes ready. Three Monsters are about sixty seconds away."

"What? Where? Which direction, Kieran?"

Kieran started to point, but that was useless ... and even more of a problem for Krol.

What to do? Krol's aura, now glowing eerily in the sky, was drawing the invisible Monsters to an ever-so-dangerous attack from the dark. *Bad.* How could he help Krol beat this huge disadvantage? *Yes ... and it would be easy too.*

A tiny touch of Opal power made the rapidly closing Monsters light up with a white glow.

"Holy cow! Three at once, Kieran. Will his aura cope with that many?"

"Only just, Rhys, but I'm ready to top it up each time he strikes."

With the three Monsters lit up like fireflies, the fear and uncertainty of an attack from the dark by an unseen foe became confidence that Krol would win as easily as he had all day.

"I can't believe how dangerous Krol looks. Have you made his aura more spectacular on purpose, Kieran?"

"It's the night making it stand out, Rhys."

"We won't need the Spook ropes. They're zooming straight at Krol and they won't get a chance to look for anything else."

Kieran didn't answer because the aerial display disappeared for the length of a long blink, then returned just as Krol lunged at the single remaining Monster. Talons raked across the back of the obviously dazzled foe and for a few seconds the five companions gawped as a glowing skeleton dissolved to nothing.

"Gods, Kieran! And I thought it looked unreal in the daylight ... Is Krol okay?"

Kieran wasn't sure why Rhys might be wondering, but he made a check as a matter of course anyway. "He's very pleased with himself, Rhys, and I've told him he might as well keep flying till the rest get here."

"More? How many?"

"Another three, but this time they won't arrive together."

"Six of them practically at the same time is the biggest concentration yet, Kieran. Do you think they might keep arriving like this all night?"

"If they do we won't get any sleep."

"I'm the only one who can sense them, Mr B, but you'd still get woken anyway if Krol has to take off. You could sleep separate from him, I suppose, but then you won't have his wing to keep you warm."

"Can you see any more after these three, Kieran?"

"Lots of them, Woorawa. There always are, but I thought we'd be okay because they all stopped moving when it got dark."

"I think you might have called up these close ones yourself, Kieran, when you used your Opal. That was a lot of power you used, and Ranevargar told you they're attracted by energy disturbances."

"What would we do without your common sense, Tan? Of course that's why they came."

"Can you tell if topping up Krol's aura started any new ones moving?"

"More good thinking, Tan ... No, there are only the close ones, and that makes sense, because refuelling Krol's aura is tiny compared to contacting your family."

Rhys was still concerned. "It's still a bit scary if something draws them while you're asleep, Kieran. We'd be okay, but Krol might get hurt if he hasn't had any warning. Can you have automatic Monster sensing like you do with our mind shields?"

Kieran laughed. "Everyone except me is having good ideas. I can use a pattern like the one I worked out for our night watches. Hang on. The next Monster's close enough to light up for Krol."

Krol's challenge sounded and he headed on a collision course with the glowing object arrowing toward him.

"Hey, turn my blink reflex off, Kieran, so I can see them light up. It shouldn't hurt my eyes from that distance."

"Are you sure, Rhys? It'll look extra bright in the dark."

"Quick! They're about to meet."

"All right, but I'm keeping mine."

The purple and white lights converged and Kieran, watching through Krol's vision, saw only a moment's worth of dissolving skeleton.

"Holy hell! Why did you let me do that? Now I can't see."

Kieran checked and laughed. "What did you expect? You'll adjust in a few minutes."

"I won't be able to see Krol fight the other two. Give me your hand so I can zap myself."

Woorawa yelled, "No! No! If they're this close they might sense the power use and head for us instead of Krol."

"A little zap won't matter ... will it, Kieran?"

"I haven't got a clue, Rhys, but we'd better not take the chance."

"I suppose so. And we'd be in Krol's way when he chased them too. Quick! Connect me back to the blink reflex."

That took only an instant. The last two Monsters clashed with Krol and dissolved. The triumphant Griffin wheeled in the night sky to return to the companions.

"How's he going to land in the dark? The ground's pretty uneven and I remember seeing a few boulders."

"... I just checked and he can see well enough to be safe, Rhys. His eyes are a lot better than ours."

Krol landed without trouble and the five companions settled against his flank again.

"Wow! Feel his heart beating. It's like a giant engine inside. Are there Monsters moving anywhere, Kieran?"

"There are Monsters, Rhys, but they're all a long way away and they're all still. I reckon they won't move again till the morning."

"Krol must be super fit. His heart's almost back to normal."

"Stop talking, Rhys. I want to go to sleep."

"Whoops! Sorry, Mr B."

Rhys wasn't really very sorry, and seeing all the questions and thoughts pushing for expression, Kieran worked a now-familiar mind pattern to quieten everything and put him to sleep. Then he did the same for everyone else, including himself.

*   *   *

Aglaron, High King of all the Realms, considered the belated but insistent request for communication from the Lore Master with puzzlement and a sense of loss, and, pointless as it must be, accepted out of courtesy and the strength of their long and close association.

"Lord Uirebon? Do you seek a formal audience with me?"

"No, my Lord. I seek permission to join you in person."

"For what purpose? To observe the overthrow of the High Castle and the collapse of balance throughout the Realms?"

"Indeed not, my Lord. My intention is to help fight this illegal Challenge with every resource at my disposal."

Aglaron's reply was tinged with a degree of bitter regret. *"You were in your sanctum too long, my friend. A formal Challenge was presented to the High Court three hours ago, and as Lore Master you are now bound to neutrality. The time for your assistance has passed. Your offer moves me, but the honour of your position demands I refuse it."*

"Not so, my Lord. The Challenge might now be formal, but the broken conventions of its implementation render it illegal. My honour, as both friend and Lore Master, binds my loyalty to you and your position."

"A Challenge can be illegal? Are you certain? That will mean little if it succeeds. Maynor, as new High King, will just proclaim it legal."

"Completely certain, my Lord. I have conferred with the full Court of my Realm and every adviser agrees. The independence of a Realm Lord is sacrosanct, and Lord Maynor has torn Ranevargar from his Realm and holds him bound and helpless."

"Maynor still holds Ranevargar helpless? You've seen this somehow?"

"My Realm has resources for knowledge unknown to Lord Maynor ... My Lord, we should speak behind the security of your Wards. Permit me to make portal."

"Certainly, Uirebon, but think of your position first. I can hold the High Castle for a time, but Maynor's control of the free Nexus energy must eventually allow him to prevail. For the good of your Realm you should consider a position of neutrality."

"And lose my self-respect? There is nothing to consider."

With vast relief, Aglaron cleared the way for Uirebon's portal, then welcomed the reality of his physical presence with the double wrist clasp of mutual respect and acceptance.

"Your silence was greatly extended, Uirebon."

"I am sorry for that, my Lord, but Lord Maynor's influence was subtle and hard to clear. I discovered that for at least two centuries he has had quiet dealings with study centres all across my Realm."

"I've been deceived for two centuries? His advice through all that time has been faultless and invaluable."

"Indeed, my Lord, and I suspect that your clearly expressed appreciation of its worth may have been a continuing reinforcement of his ambition."

"I always understood his ambition. His strength was the reason I gave him Stewardship of his own Realm ... Uirebon, how do his dealings with your centres concern us?"

"More recently, as we now know, his recognised natural ability for mind manipulation has been given all the time and effort needed to become a master. Beyond his collaboration with me to develop Keryth's treatment, I discovered seven study centres across my Realm where he learnt other aspects of control."

"You think Keryth's treatment was a strategy to help with this Challenge?"

"Not directly, my Lord. From my advisers I also learned that for that same time Lord Maynor has also been studying the control and storage of power. Keryth's treatment was most likely a means for access to your Nexus energy. Three times you allowed him to wield unprecedented power, and each time he learned more of its control. I believe even more strongly that this Challenge was a mistake, decided in haste when Keryth and the mysterious gemstone were apparently his to wield."

"Interesting. He certainly knew how to bind the Nexus energy with his own locks. Uirebon, if Maynor is in collusion with Narello, their constant clashes may have been an excuse to practice the use and control of power."

"Narello is definitely in collusion with Maynor, but I begin to suspect that she might not be aware of it."

"Her mind is controlled?"

"I believe so, my Lord. It also explains why Lord Maynor has taken Ranevargar."

"Yes, it does, and Ranevargar's waning strength makes him quite vulnerable ... Do you have a way of watching his Realm for any contrary signs?"

"I have good news. One of my centres has been tasked to do just that and I can report that a cohort of Maynor's Coursers fled in disarray from a group of the Flying Guardians."

"Aggression against the Coursers? Normally Ranevargar would ignore them, so that is good news indeed. Quite inexplicable though, because Guardian aggression suggests direction from their completely isolated Lord."

"Yet another mystery, my Lord."

"And why would Maynor dispatch Coursers?"

"It must be to find Keryth, which is a puzzle since Maynor already possesses Keryth's gemstone. Maybe the stone confounds him and he needs Keryth present to make use of it."

"Maynor must fail then. Has your centre noticed any sign of Keryth in Ranevargar's Realm? Those shields are beyond me."

"A localised energy flare indicated an incursion by something like a very powerful Chaos Creature, but by the time they focused their attention they could only find three of the Flying Guardians."

"That is not a Chaos Creature. It is an incursion unique to Ranevargar's Realm, requiring the special ability of his Guardians to overcome."

"Another mystery?"

"Not really. That incursion comes from the Unordered Realm and Ranevargar has always taken the responsibility for action to dispel it. It's puzzling that the Guardians could be effective without his presence though, and curious also that a similar incursion happened only days ago when the normal interval is decades long ... Uirebon, why do you consider Maynor's interest in energy storage important? Individuals can have limited and temporary reserves, and Ranevargar's Realm Trees even less, but the only place for significant storage resides within a Realm Lord's Stone of Power."

"There are other storage methods, my Lord. The Fetch constructs exist only while they can draw from the pool of energy we give them, and the rods wielded by Power Masters also store energy."

"Yes, but in small amounts compared to Nexus energy."

"A hundred and fifty years ago, Lord Maynor spent almost two decades working with one of my centres to develop a way of storing power in lesser gemstones. The study was successful, but then discontinued on his suggestion, so it only came to light when I asked my Council of advisers to recall interactions they might have had with him over the years."

"Your Council has been very busy, Uirebon, but why is this significant?"

"With my Council, I sought an explanation for the power flows you sensed near Narello's boundary, and we suspect Lord Maynor has been stealing energy and storing it in the gemstones of his famous ruby collection."

"I have controlled the distribution of all free Nexus energy very carefully, Uirebon. I don't see how that would be possible."

"Lady Narello has Chaos Masters, my Lord. They draw from the energy of Chaos for their own use, while leaving you to clear the resulting imbalance. Every Chaos Incursion is most likely the result of a deliberate action which forces you to use power which is then not available for general distribution."

Aglaron stared, aghast. "Every Chaos Incursion for all that time? Uirebon, that is a vast amount of energy. The High Castle will fall."

"Maybe, my Lord, but we can give ourselves time to prepare. Lord Maynor cannot wield the power directly and must bring the Power Masters or other holders to his presence. If you deny him the ability to make portals we will have days to prepare while they make the journey."

"Hmm! Yes, I can do that, but only by expending energy I can't really afford. It will only delay the inevitable."

"Delay can only work for us, and we will develop other ways to hinder Lord Maynor's assaults. My Lord, can you confine the disruption of portals to Lord Maynor and Lady Narello's Realms? I have advisers and triads willing to help defend the High Castle."

Aglaron paused. "Wonderful! But bring them quickly, Uirebon. A general disruption is far easier to manage. How many triads?"

"Three, my Lord. A triad of triads will be far more effective."

"Indeed. We will use them to help sustain the Castle Wards. Are they ready for transport? Negating Maynor's ability to portal is an inspired strategy and the sooner implemented the better."

"They are ready."

The way through the Castle Wards was cleared again, and Aglaron watched three triads and eighteen advisers arrive in a large chamber adjacent to the Great Hall.

"Uirebon, I recognise many of these advisers and their presence here weakens your Realm. Are you sure about this?"

"Lord Maynor will only make demands on me and my Realm if he becomes High King."

"He lashed at you in Ranevargar's Grove, and when he learns you have decided against neutrality he will lash again."

"I have considered that, my Lord. The High Castle is my best defence, and if he directs power against my Realm he detracts from his critical assault here."

Aglaron showed his appreciation. "And your advisers agreed?"

"Every one of them."

Aglaron and Uirebon were both distracted when a flow of power from a newly active triad strengthened the Castle Wards.

"This level of assault is manageable my Lord. Has Maynor made any serious attempt to overcome your Wards?"

"Just the once when he couldn't use the old pass keys. I believe it was a test to gauge and compare his own strength."

"Have you sensed him using Nexus energy for any other purpose?"

"See for yourself. I think something is happening in his Castle, but unless I waste energy his Wards are impenetrable."

Aglaron's special sense of energy showed the constant flow of power being directed against the High Castle and, both shocking and puzzling, almost twice as much disappearing into Maynor's own Castle. Uirebon quailed at the magnitude of what they were facing.

"So much power, my Lord."

"Yes. We can only be thankful it's not all directed here."

Uirebon considered a moment. "Ranevargar's mind shield and Keryth's gemstone! They are key to Lord Maynor's plans. Only they would warrant so much effort."

"That could well be, Uirebon. Let us hope the effort continues without success for a long time. Come with me to the Great Hall. Knowledge that the Lore Master is here and providing assistance will be a great relief to the Court."

*　*　*

Kieran finished all his important inner checks and, by the soft glow he was providing against the pre-dawn dark, took in everyone gathered close and waiting.

"Are any Monsters on the move, Kieran?"

Kieran adjusted the position of his pack straps slightly while he rechecked and started moving. "Not yet, Woorawa. Why do you want to know?"

"Well, it's too late now, but if we could rely on them only being active in the daylight, Krol could leapfrog us forward one at a time and save a lot of walking."

"We'd be separated then and that's too risky. Without Krol to protect us we're dead meat. And they do move in the night if they sense anything."

"Dead meat? Thanks for the graphically depressing description, Rhys, but I think you're right. The logistics mean that even with only a five-minute return trip for Krol we'd be separated for twenty-five minutes. I'm really tempted, but the gain doesn't justify the risk."

Mr B, along with everyone else, turned to Woorawa. "It's a great idea, but we won't try it. We made it our rule to never get separated unless it's absolutely necessary, and Ranevargar emphasised that it's especially important here in the Unordered Realm."

"Yeah. I suppose. And it would be hard on Krol too ... You were in a specially deep concentration mode for a while, Kieran. What have you found out?"

"A few things, Rhys. Ranevargar's still asleep, so it's all quiet there, but the Griffins got really active yesterday afternoon when the hosts sent them to chase off a new lot of Coursers."

"Coursers back in the Realm? That means they're still after us, Kieran."

"I don't know about the High King, but that Maynor definitely is. He asks about us every time he talks to Ranevargar, then gets annoyed because Ranevargar hasn't got a clue what he's talking about."

"It sounds like he gets annoyed fairly easily," said Tan.

"Yes, he wants to take over as High King, and Ranevargar thinks his irritation is because his plans aren't going the way he wants them to."

"Well, if we're part of his plans he'll have to come to Dead World to get us. Do you think he'd be able to get past all the Monsters, Kieran?"

"I really don't know, Tan. He might, because Realm Lords are very powerful, and I've seen from Ranevargar's mind that, except for the High King, Maynor's the strongest of them all. I'm not worried about him coming here though, because you need Griffins for protection and he hasn't got any."

A soft glow of light was starting to contrast the horizon line of the dark and desolate plain against the sky, and Kieran made another quick check to see if any Monsters were stirring.

"You told us he controlled the hosts and all the Griffins when he tried to capture us, Kieran. If he did that again he could *make* them protect him. He could come after us then."

Kieran stopped in his tracks. "Good thinking, Woorawa ... I should've been shielding the hosts and Griffins ever since the Central Grove. If he took control of even one of them he'd learn way too much."

"You can shield them from here? You've got to be kidding."

"I've got control through Ranevargar's Pearl, Woorawa. I'll have to call on my Opal, so it might bring a few Monsters, but I do need to protect them."

"Well, you'll have to add in Gryl and all the Panthers who've helped us too. They all know we're in Dead World. Can you keep that many shields going?"

Woorawa was right. Eleven hosts and five Griffins from the Central Grove, plus four more hosts and five Panthers was way too many without making a constant call on the Opal.

"I can because Ranevargar's network makes it possible, but I'll have to work out something different or Krol will have non-stop Monster fights. Hang on while I think."

The party trudged quietly for another five minutes.

"I've got it. It'll take a big burst of energy to set up, but then I can forget them."

"Forget them? You mean with independent shields like you gave Ranevargar?"

"Almost independent, Mr B, but they're really different to Ranevargar's. They'll hardly use any energy because they'll only spring into full life if something tries to get through, and they'll have a trigger to warn me if that happens."

"I don't understand. How will they work if you're not using the Opal?"

"The same as yours, Mr B. They'll all have a pool of energy to draw on, small compared to yours, but big enough to last for about five days."

"This is mind-boggling, Kieran. You can make shields and put pools of energy in all those minds from across the Boundary Wall?"

"Only because I have control of Ranevargar's Pearl, Woorawa. It lets me do things through his special network."

"Unbelievable! Why don't you use it to send energy to Ranevargar then? It might help him break away from that helmet thing."

"I wanted to, Rhys, but before he erased all his memories about us Ranevargar warned me not to. He said new energy would alert Maynor that we were tricking him. I'm ready though, because if his reserve gets low I won't have any choice. He's got about eight days at the moment."

"What? You said it was twelve or thirteen."

"Yeah. But Maynor's been attacking Ranevargar's shields with huge amounts of energy lately. He must think he's going to wear them down."

"He's right then, Kieran. Ranevargar will only last a bit over two days at that rate and we'll still be hiking towards ... Maurice."

The morning light was now bright enough to reveal Rhys's approving smile.

"I'm watching, Mr B, but I'll keep to Ranevargar's strategy as closely as I can ... Hang on while I make these new shields."

The patterns that Kieran had been rehearsing during the conversation came to the front of his mind and, reaching through Ranevargar's link, he called on the Opal for the energy to set everything working.

Hmm! Woorawa was right. The Boundary Wall was interfering and he had to make an extra Opal call to push past it.

"Hey! What happened, Kieran? You'd better check for Monsters, because you lit up like a torch."

"I strained my brain, Rhys. I had to make the Pearl and the Opal work together and the Boundary was a big barrier ... Whoa! Packs off, everyone. It did wake the Monsters and we've got four incoming."

Krol was completely practised with their defence, but Rhys still insisted on the group routine of being ready for unencumbered action with the Spook ropes.

*   *   *

"This flaming pack is breaking all the laws of physics!"

"How come?"

"I've emptied my first water skin and eaten food out of it, but it's heavier now than it was yesterday. Isn't it time for our break, Woorawa? We've been walking for hours."

Rhys's complaint was more of a group expression than a real grievance and received four varying responses of agreement.

"Another ten minutes, Rhys, and then we'll stop for half an hour instead of ten minutes ... Look at that valley, Kieran. Do you know where it goes?"

"I haven't got a clue, Woorawa. Ranevargar only gave me images of the actual course. The rest of Dead World's a mystery."

"It looks interesting. If there were trees and water and food and no Dragon Quest it would be good to explore."

"Ha! And no lumping great pack to carry. I think you forgot that bit, Woorawa."

"Rhys, you won't even notice your pack by tomorrow. You'll be so used to it."

"As if!"

The valley did look interesting. The long cliff wall they'd been following all this time made an almost right-angle turn along one side of the valley in question, and in the distance closed in to form a kind of pass with the mountain flank.

"I reckon there must have been a river flowing through there. You can see where the bed might have been."

"You've got a good imagination, Woorawa. If it's a river it must have been dry for the last million years. How are your feet, Tan? Will they last another ten minutes?"

"Eight minutes, Rhys, and they're okay, just aching and tired."

"Mine too."

* * *

Woorawa's soft but deep chant pulled their attention from their silent contemplation of the flickering rock fire and, following his nod of invitation, everyone joined in. Without stopping, he reached into the rock fire for two stones.

Click! Click! The sound complimented the chant, and when he stood and commenced an easy, rhythmic stomp, three more sets of feet automatically joined in.

Deep weariness passed from Kieran as he drank in the astonishing presence of Woorawa pouring himself into the movement. The spirit took him and he rose to join the rest of the group.

Five or ten minutes later — Kieran was too immersed to have a proper sense of time — Woorawa made a dramatic leap over the rock fire and the shared moment came to an end.

"It's sleep time, Kieran. Tomorrow's an even bigger day than today."

* * *

Kieran kept watch as the first rays of sunlight caught the snow-covered mountain tops and worked their way steadily lower in a breathtaking contrast against the darkness of all the lower reaches, and wondered why Woorawa hadn't yet called for a stop. Their extra early wake-up had given them at least an hour of walking without Monster attacks and a good start to the trek around the flank of the closest mountain.

"Are the Monsters on the move yet, Kieran? I thought we might keep going till the first attack, but it's getting a bit too long."

"Not yet, but we'll see the sun in the next few minutes and that's when they got active yesterday."

"How far's the closest one?"

"About ten minutes away. We'll stop then."

Rhys laughed. "We'll get them later, Tan. They're making us walk because they love being slave drivers."

"It's not a problem, Rhys. I haven't even noticed my feet since it got light enough to watch the mountains. I can't believe I'm saying this, but that light on the snow makes Dead World look completely beautiful."

Woorawa pointed to the second mountain. "It does looks unreal, Tan, but we'll run out of water today and you can see how far it is to that snowline."

Tan looked back to where the long line of the cliff wall now looked low and less significant. "It's not as far as we travelled yesterday."

Woorawa made his own comparison. "No, but the terrain will change because of the pass thing Kieran told us about, and then we have to find our way far enough up the side to be in reach of the snow."

"We stop in five minutes, everyone. The first Monster's on its way."

*   *   *

After the first delayed stop, Woorawa went back to the usual regime of carefully timed hourly rest breaks and the group made its way with a sense of progress lifting their spirits. In the late morning, the steady trudge slowed when the change of direction as they skirted the mountain took them through a jumble of rocks and boulders. Woorawa was a marvel though, clambering up to the highest vantage points to scout for the best path forward for more than an hour till the raggedy way cleared to open plain again and they finally stopped for a meal break.

"It's another old river flat, Kieran, much wider than the last one. You can even see the depression where the river bed was."

"Ha! I wish we had a bed instead of sleeping on solid rock every night."

No one took any notice. They were all looking into the distance where the plain narrowed and disappeared.

"Is it the pass Ranevargar showed you, Kieran?"

"It must be, Woorawa. It's right where his mind map tells me to go ... How long to get there?"

"Not even three hours. Our packs are lighter, we're all walking better, and it looks like open-going all the way. When we finish our snack you should put us all to sleep for thirty minutes."

Kieran focused his Monster sense. "We won't get that much time unless we leave it all to Krol. There are three fairly close Monsters."

"Use some power to draw them in, Kieran. You've got it worked out well and we've been on the go for seven hours, so real sleep will be the best pick up."

Kieran did have it worked out well, after all the aggravation yesterday of having to stop five times for attacks just ten minutes apart had prompted him to experiment with the knowledge that his Opal power acted like a beacon.

"Yes, that's a good idea, because that way I can put Krol to sleep too, after he clobbers them. Get the food and drink ready and I'll charge up his aura."

"And heat the water at the same time, please."

"This is quite amazing."

"What do you mean, Mr B?"

"Three Monsters, so powerful each of them could rip us all to shreds with hardly any effort, are about to attack and we're more interested in the food and drink Tan's getting ready. Krol's a complete wonder."

Krol, who had landed when the group stopped to take off their packs, gave a querying *scrark* when he saw five sets of eyes regarding him.

"Three Monsters arriving in a while, Krol. Mr B says thank you for being a wonderful protector and we're all agreeing with him."

Krol's head lifted proudly; then he scanned the sky.

* * *

"What happened, Kieran? Is Ranevargar okay?"

Kieran pulled his mind back to the here and now.

"He *is* okay, Rhys, but puzzled about how his mind shields are surviving. Maynor just bashed them with the biggest amount of power yet and tried to persuade him it was time to give in and tell him where his Pearl is."

"Persuade? You said that in a funny way."

"Yes, it was weird, sort of like a Medusa look except charming instead of scary. Ranevargar knew what it was though, and told Maynor that glamours were kid's stuff."

"Wow! Kid's stuff?"

"Not in those words, but that's what he meant. Maynor was surprised, but then he got annoyed, which was exactly what Ranevargar wanted."

"You see Maynor clearly enough to read his expressions?"

"Ranevargar taught me that the first day we met him, Mr B, but his thoughts tell me more, so I rely on them the most."

"Two viewpoints coming in at the same time. That could be confusing, Kieran. Would it be possible to work through Ranevargar to control the attendants when Maynor's not there and make them take that golden helmet off?"

"I wouldn't have a clue. I can work with the hosts and the Guardians because of the Pearl network, but I wouldn't even try with Maynor's attendants, because all I'm meant to do is watch."

"How are his shields holding up? This big attack must have drained extra energy."

"It did, but not too much, because it only lasted for ten minutes."

"Did you learn anything new about what's going on?"

"No. He wasn't happy about his Coursers getting chased off, but the rest of it was just trying to charm Ranevargar and asking about the Pearl."

"Is he still looking for us in Ranevargar's Realm?"

"This was the first session with Ranevargar where he didn't even mention us, so who knows what that means. He's no danger to us, Rhys. He won't believe anyone's crazy enough to come to Dead World with all these Monsters."

"How's Ranevargar coping with being paralysed all this time, Kieran? It's been four days and all he can do is think."

"The confidence boost we worked out won't stop till he's himself again, Tan, but I can hardly believe how active his mind is."

"What about his body? So much time without moving is really bad."

"The attendants look after him really well with massages and body rubs, Rhys, and they're keeping him clean too. That's one good thing about Maynor."

"That *is* amazing. I've kind of been expecting Ranevargar might get tortured to make him give in."

"I don't think they do that, Rhys."

"Like it's a taboo?"

"Yes, even the Spooks only wanted us helpless."

"Something doesn't fit, Kieran. Ranevargar told us about that other Realm Lord studying the arts of conflict and it would have to be a weird war if no one gets hurt."

"Hmm! You're right, Rhys, but weird's normal here."

Woorawa laughed, then pointed to the cliff walls on one side of the pass they were approaching.

"On! On! On, everyone. That pass looks weird and we can talk while we walk."

*   *   *

Uirebon watched as Aglaron's brow furrowed with intense concentration.

"Trouble, my Lord?"

"Indeed, Uirebon. Maynor seeks to have me drain our resources and hasten the fall of the High Castle. Do you have knowledge of how many trained Chaos Masters Narello can command?"

"I know she has a major Centre dedicated to the study and use of Chaos energy, but little more."

"We currently have seven Chaos Incursions, four close to the High Castle, two in your Realm and one in Ranevargar's domain."

Uirebon was shocked. "Simultaneous? My Lord, every one of them will wreak endless destruction until it is stopped. How can we possibly cope?"

Aglaron took an aspect of power and determination Uirebon had rarely seen. "If I must, I will cope, Uirebon. The cost will be great and might hasten the downfall of the High Castle, but ..." The grim look now softened with the hint of a smile. "... my Lore Master's forewarning has allowed me to prepare a suitable response."

"Against seven Chaos Incursions?"

"The number now stands at nine and precludes any possibility other than direction and purpose. Show me the location of Narello's Centre for Chaos study."

Uirebon came to the wrong conclusion. "You wish to attack the Chaos Masters before they direct more incursions against us? The state of our resources doesn't justify such a course of action, my Lord. I advise you to reconsider."

"Good advice, Uirebon, but you misunderstand. Watch with me while Maynor discovers what Chaos Incursions can do."

Uirebon watched. Aglaron's stricture against portals collapsed, power transferred from their defences and focused on every incursion, peaked for transmissions to two separate locations, then returned to the High Castle Wards. With a nod of satisfaction, Aglaron restored the portal ban and turned to Uirebon.

"Do you approve, Uirebon? The incursions are no longer my problem."

"More than approve, my Lord, I ..."

Uirebon's expression of admiration was forgotten, because the assault against the High Castle defences stopped — the first moment of relief since the Challenge was made.

Uirebon watched quietly while Aglaron used the bonus flow of free energy for renewal and greater defensive strength. He observed as Aglaron reached to sense the great flows of power surrounding Maynor's Castle and the Chaos Master's centre.

"Will he cope, my Lord? He has no experience."

"He will cope. He controls all the free Nexus energy and he has observed the banishment methods on several occasions."

"Against a single incursion, yes, but you transferred five incursions to his Castle and five to Lady Narello's Realm."

"And I did it without compunction, Uirebon. He faces only what he himself unleashed, and in doing so he has gifted us with a time of respite. We will make the most of it."

*   *   *

"We're going up there?"

Ahead was a huge rock face, an unexpected barrier which, according to Kieran's scan through Krol's eyes, was the easiest way to reach their target plateau.

"We have to, Tan. It looks bad because it's so far, but it's all scrambling rather than real climbing and we'll only take you where it's safe."

Tan grimaced. The rock face might only have an incline of about 40° but it would be a first time experience and very different to the steady trudge of the last three days. Woorawa was looking apprehensive too, which was kind of reassuring. Rhys put a comforting arm across Tan's shoulder for a moment.

"You'll be okay, Tan. Kieran's brilliant at finding the easiest way, and you can follow right behind him so you know exactly where to put your feet. Mr B's nearly as good, so Woorawa can follow him and I'll be last."

"What happens when a Monster comes? We'll be helpless."

"No, we won't. Krol's ready and he'll protect us the same as always. It was good thinking to mention it though, so we're all ready to react properly."

"Properly? What does that mean, Rhys?"

"Well, we'll have warning from Kieran, so there'll be time to make sure we're standing or sitting securely, and then we don't move, not for one step, till we know the Monster's been clobbered. Until then, we lock ourselves in place like we're part of the rock."

"I agree, Rhys. Any movement that might attract a Monster could be very dangerous. Maybe Kieran could even lock our muscles, in case we panic."

"I won't need to do that, Mr B. We're all experienced enough with the Monsters to hold a 'keep still' command in our minds."

Rhys gave one of his snorts. "Ha! If one's only a few metres away and coming straight at me I won't be."

"That's not going to happen, Rhys ... Tighten your pack's straps while we do this and let's go.

When Kieran moved a few steps sideways and clambered for about five metres up a natural staircase, Tan followed close behind, concentrating intensely to match the guiding footsteps. Kieran paused to give Tan a smile for this achievement.

"You did that easily, Tan, and the next bit's even simpler."

It was too. This time they climbed at least twice as far, and when Kieran stopped to check everyone and survey the next section, Tan realised he'd been so focused he'd forgotten to be nervous. He looked past Mr B to see how Woorawa was going and the pair shared an understanding smile.

Mr B saw the look. "Is the adrenaline rush subsiding, Tan? It must be if you can manage a smile."

Tan relaxed even more.

"Okay, Tan. This next bit's slightly tricky, but then it's an easy walk along that ledge. Watch where I hold with my hands as well as where I put my feet."

Tan's steadily increasing confidence took a blow when, about ten minutes later, Kieran gave warning of two approaching Monsters and made sure everyone was in a secure position.

"Hold still! Krol's taking off and we'll have a spectacular view."

Every view of Krol fighting Monsters was spectacular as far as Tan was concerned, but he decided that one episode of watching from an exposed perch on a rock face while holding every muscle locked rigid was more than enough.

Krol's victory call sounded and he soared to his waiting spot above.

"No more for a while. Let's move."

Kieran was right, and the zigzag path went all the way to the top with only one strange moment when everything stopped for a few minutes.

"What's the hold up?"

Tan answered Rhys's call. "It's his concentration look, Rhys. He's not here. We'll just have to wait."

When Kieran stirred, he laughed at everyone's concerned looks. "Whoa! That was major, but I think it must be good. I'll tell you when we stop at the top."

On! On! Up! Up!

The group clambered their way till the rock face levelled to a platform where they dumped their packs for a well-earned break. Tan stood for a moment, looking down with amazement and pleasure at what he'd just achieved; then he moved quickly to join the others and hear what Kieran was saying.

"I'm not sure why, but I had a strange feeling, and when I checked on

Ranevargar his mind was racing with ideas about why all the pressure against his mind shields was gone. His strongest idea was that the High King and Maynor might be having another Challenge against each other, and Maynor's using all his power for that."

"Could it give Ranevargar a chance to escape?"

"No, that damn helmet stops everything, and Maynor's done something so he's the only one who can take it off. Ranevargar's enjoying not having the mental storm raging against his shield and he's expecting other things might start happening."

"Can you tell where the energy is going, Kieran?"

"I'd need to be there to do that, Mr B."

"As you did when you took the Pearl, I suppose. How long will Ranevargar's shields last if they're not being attacked? You might be able to postpone renewing his reserves."

"I hope so. We'll just have to see." Kieran turned to look across the plateau. "The mental map says we'll find traces of an ancient road we can follow all the way up to the caverns."

"How can there be a road in Dead World?"

"It wasn't always dead, Rhys. The road might be hard to see, because it's wrecked in Ranevargar's memories and they're from six hundred years ago. Who knows how much it's broken down since then."

*   *   *

Trudge! Trudge!

Two more hours and seven more Monster attacks took them across the plateau, but also brought the concern of approaching dusk and the much bigger worry of finding a safe place to shelter.

Apart from one emergency water skin, all the water would be finished that night and the plan was for Kieran to fly with Krol to the closest snow-field. A big worry was that getting the snow into the water skins meant the power used to melt it would draw Monsters from everywhere. In all probability, Kieran and Krol would be the focus for every attack, but Kieran didn't want to risk being wrong on that front. Woorawa's solution was for Kieran to use Krol's superior vision to scan for something like a cave or some other suitable shelter. This turned out to be a double bonus when the view from aloft revealed a long section of raised rock which was clearly too ordered to be natural, as well as a promising cleft between some fluted columns which might suit as a temporary haven.

"I hope this works, Kieran. It'll be awfully scary if anything happens while you and Krol are away. I wish we'd had more practice with the Spook ropes."

Woorawa looked back. "Don't be a pessimist, Rhys. Think of a nice big cave with a little spring of water trickling into a pool big enough to wash ourselves, as well as beautiful soft moss to sleep on even if a hoard of Monsters is waiting outside."

"Dream on, Woorawa."

Mr B added his bit. "Woorawa's got a point, Rhys. A negative attitude gave us Dead World every time and a positive attitude gave us good things."

"We need the Wall for that, Mr B. There's no Wall here."

"Anything could happen, Rhys. We're in the Realms now, not back at home."

Rhys laughed. "No way! We've been walking since before the sun came up and all we've seen is rock and dirt."

"Oh yes? How many Monsters have we seen? Twenty? Thirty?"

"They don't count. You know what I mean."

Now it was Mr B who laughed. "I do, Rhys, but four or five metres of fury and destruction dissolving to nothing at the touch of a mysterious purple aura counts as unusual in my view."

"Well ..."

"Give up, Rhys. Mr B got you this time."

Rhys nodded, as if agreeing, then grinned cheekily at everyone. "Open sesame!"

"What?"

"I'm being an optimist, Woorawa. When we get to those rock columns I'll say that and a cave will appear with all the good stuff, plus piles of trea-sure and a helicopter to carry us the rest of the way to Maurice."

Four heads shook in mock disgust.

"That's a curious expression of optimism, Rhys. I hope it doesn't mean we also get captured by forty angry thieves."

Rhys yelled in delight and raised his arms in a victory gesture. "Be posi-tive, Mr B! Be positive!"

Fifteen minutes of smiling and chuckling later the packs were shucked and everyone followed Woorawa to the opening between the columns of rock.

"It *is* perfect, Kieran. It goes for at least ten metres before it gets narrow. Even Krol couldn't get at us in there ... Hey, wow! There's even a sign at the end which says 'magic door'. Rhys has done it again."

"You're a total dork, Woorawa."

Woorawa made a rude sign at Rhys — one he'd learned from him — and moved aside. "Head off while there's still enough time to see, Kieran. The earlier you get back the sooner we can get settled for the night."

"Hey, I just realised. Without Kieran we won't have any warning if a Monster finds us. Should we stay in that gap till he gets back?"

Woorawa looked around. "I'll find a good place to keep watch from, Rhys, and we'll be all right for another fifteen or twenty minutes. It won't hurt us to do nothing for a while, and it's also good because it means one less thing for Kieran to worry about."

Rhys nodded and turned to watch while Kieran put on his cloak. "I wish I was going with you."

Kieran leaned close to give him a shoulder bump, then climbed onto Krol's back and attached the harness. "So do I, Rhys. Look after everyone."

Krol rose from his crouch, spread his wings for the takeoff, and with a switch of focus, Kieran was in his mind and using superior eyes to scan the way.

"Head for the top of that big spur, Krol. Do you think we'll get there before it's fully dark?"

The destination registered, Krol's wing beats strengthened with purpose, and in just over ten minutes they were coursing above an extensive snowfield.

"Look for somewhere with an easy takeoff. There might be lots of fighting for you."

Anticipation thrilled and, after an automatic terrain scan, Krol veered, then landed beside an island of rock protruding from the surrounding sea of snow. In a great rush, Kieran unclipped six water skins, scooped the billy full of snow, heightened his Monster awareness, and called on the Opal to charge Krol's aura to the maximum.

Hmm! Five Monsters in close proximity and another eight likely to be drawn by the amount of power he was about to use. *Why so many?* Well, Krol could cope with up to three at once and their single-minded aggression would almost always mean a staggered arrival.

"Incomings, Krol. Wait till I'm about to light the first one up before you take off ... and stay close, please."

Kieran was using his own eyes now and he could just make out the fierce ruffle of Krol's neck feathers. A straightforward glow lit up the immediate surroundings and with a burst of concentration Kieran directed heat into the snow-filled billy. *Whoa!* A full billy of snow became less than half a billy of water. *Top it up?* No, the snow was too hard and too cold for bare hands. Warning flared.

"Go, Krol! I'll light up the first one as soon as you're in the air."

As quickly as he could, Kieran poured the melted snow into the first water skin, scooped up the next billy full, then paused to watch Krol make his first aerial encounter and veer towards the next glowing Monster.

Scoop! Melt! Pour! Scoop! Melt! Pour!

Opal power surged with every burst of heat and with every recharge of Krol's aura. It also flowed steadily to light up every incoming Monster. When three water skins were full, Kieran stopped to make a complete situation check. Krol's mind was raging with triumph, aggression, and an almost overpowering urge to fly in search of more encounters, so, along with a message of praise and admiration, Kieran sent a calming command.

"Marvellous work, Krol! Can you keep going? There are more Monsters on the way."

Gods! The flares of power were reaching farther than expected and the eight-count had now become eleven. Kieran made a new, very quick reach.

"Yo, Rhys! We're crazy busy, but okay. Krol's unreal and I've got half the water skins filled. See you soon!"

"KIERAN!"

Kieran winced at Rhys's happy mental shout, sent a burst of reassurance, cut the contact and melted a new billy of snow. Ten minutes, later the sixth water skin was full, and after an aura top-up the power flares were all finished. After another five minutes, Krol had vanquished the final two Monsters and was able to rejoin Kieran.

The first wake-up call brought a mumbled chorus of groans and a reluctant stirring which then subsided to motionless denial of the need to do anything. Woorawa's second call, more insistent, brought a strongly expressed imitation of a very vulgar sound then some muted snorts of amusement. Rhys was awake and, obviously, so were at least two others. How did Woorawa always manage this, like he had a built-in alarm clock? Kieran stretched, muscles complaining, and sighed inwardly at the prospect of leaving this cosy warmth. Ranevargar's advice that an energy boost from Rhys was no substitute for proper rest had proved oh-so-right and was most evident during get-up. Someone's scramble allowed a waft of cold air in.

"Cloaks, everyone. It's cold. I'll get the breakfast food for you, Tan."

"I want mine here, Woorawa."

Three other voices joined Rhys.

"Me too!"

"Weak efforts! All of you!"

Woorawa lifted the covering section of wing high and, with a reflex to compose himself, Krol stood and ruffled all his feathers. Woorawa's laugh indicated his satisfaction that the day was now started.

Food was the first group priority and then preparations for the long day's trek ahead. The packs were all sorted, but their start was delayed when Kieran's important routine of checks revealed startling information in the Central Grove hosts' minds of a brief but fierce confrontation between the Griffins and some weird kind of Monster. A closer look showed the Griffins were hurt enough to warrant assistance with a supply of extra energy, and that meant an explanation for everyone else.

Woorawa was keen to know how it might affect their prospects for progress.

"Will you be using enough power to attract long-distance Monsters, Kieran?"

"Definitely. Some energy will help them heal, but I have to recharge all their auras as well. The power I use to push all that through the Wall will probably register out to about thirty minutes' distance."

"How many?"

"None for about twenty minutes, because Krol cleared out all the close ones last night. After that I don't know, because I need to use the Opal to find out."

"Have you told Krol that Kan and four other Griffins got hurt?"

"I'm not going to, Rhys. They're not serious wounds and I don't want him worrying about anything except protecting us."

"How come they got hurt? Krol's fought zillions of times and never even been touched."

"It wasn't anything like our Monsters and the auras hardly helped at all. I think it's what Ranevargar called a Chaos Incursion. Have a look, because if we ever see one the only thing to do is run."

Kieran shared the shocking images of crazy destruction he'd gleaned from the hosts' memories.

"Gods, Kieran! It's like a weird sort of Monster with bits of the Wall shining out of it. The Griffins' attack didn't seem to have any effect on it."

"I could tell that the auras had some sort of effect, Rhys, but if that thing hadn't disappeared when it did, the Griffins would have all ended up dead. I wish I could search Ranevargar's mind to find out more."

"Do you think it died?"

"No, I think it went through a portal."

"Fix the Griffins, Kieran. We need to get moving."

Kieran agreed. Power flowed from the Opal into Ranevargar's Pearl network, linked to the specific Griffin pathways, and forced its way through the resistance of the Realm Boundary. Five Griffins roused from recovery sleep with the stimulating sensation of inflowing energy, then relaxed with Kieran's message of reassurance.

Woorawa expressed his concern. "You were glowing really bright, Kieran. Every Monster for yonks must have felt that."

Kieran pointed to the remnant trace of roadway ahead and grabbed his pack. With the concentration of the past few minutes over, they could talk while they walked.

"Is it possible to find out anything from Ranevargar's mind while he's still asleep?"

"Hardly anything, Mr B, just a kind of background hum while I'm limited to his surface thoughts. He'll be awake soon though, either by himself or from the attendants bringing his breakfast."

"How are his shields holding up?"

"They'll be all right till tonight, Rhys. The six hours of peace yesterday made a big difference."

"How strong's the attack on them now?"

"That's back to usual, so Maynor still wants the Pearl. Ranevargar was expecting him today, because he hadn't been since the glamour session."

Woorawa fell back from his lead position and grabbed Kieran's arm quite urgently. "Use your radar to tell us the Monster situation, Kieran. If there's any spare time I want Krol to scout ahead for us. I could kick myself for not thinking properly."

Rhys offered to do the kicking while Kieran used a smidgeon of Opal power for a longer reach.

"It's just like I said, Woorawa. We've got at least twenty minutes free, but then there are lots of them. What's the problem?"

"Quick! Send Krol ahead, Kieran, and use his eyes to look for another safe place where we can shelter. If he finds one we might be able to reach Maurice today."

Krol responded instantly.

"How?"

"We *can* use the shuttle strategy up here, Kieran. It's so rough there must be lots of caves or shelters where we can stay safe while Krol moves us one at a time."

"We've got ten minutes before I have to bring him back. Let me concentrate."

"We want to find a cave or shelter, Krol. Help me look."

Caves were naturally strong in Krol's mind, but Kieran quickly modified the standard pattern to something smaller. The keen eyes scanned and very quickly registered five possible positions.

"Check that dark opening in the small cliff, Krol."

Krol swerved and swooped with a great rush of speed, then veered away in disappointment. Kieran's laugh surprised everyone.

"Krol's disappointed because the cave we're looking at is too small, but he's thinking in Griffin terms. It'll take us about half an hour to trek there, but I think it's just what we want."

Twenty minutes later Woorawa was balanced on a low ledge and peering into a narrow opening.

"We can all fit and it's wider inside. Pass the packs up, Mr B, and I'll ride with Krol."

"Ride? Won't it be better if Krol's by himself to clear out all the Monsters? There'll be zillions if he flies for half an hour."

Half an hour forward was the time they'd all agreed was the best for a shuttle option.

"It's one less trip for him, Rhys, and I won't get hurt. Krol's never even lost a feather."

"He might if he's slowed down by the extra weight of a person. What do you think, Kieran?"

"I don't know. Hang on."

Krol's head lifted proudly as communication passed rapidly with Kieran.

"He's completely confident ... But *I'm* going first, Woorawa, so I don't have to recharge his aura from here."

Woorawa considered.

"That makes sense I suppose. Especially for the first trip ... Kieran, it might be the scariest thing you've ever done. Tan's the only one of us who's been that close to a Monster."

"I know. I think I'll look through Krol's mind instead of my own if we get attacked."

"If? There's no if about it, Kieran. You'll be clearing out Monsters all the way."

"Yes, Mr B, and I'm going to turn the dazzle level up even higher, so they're blind for longer."

"Hey, neat idea! That'll make it a lot safer. This is going to work."

Tan cut through Rhys's excitement. "We're breaking our rule about being separated."

After an awkward silence and an exchange of slightly guilty looks, Kieran attempted an explanation.

"It'll be worth it, Tan. Even if a Monster finds this place there's no way it could get in, and I'll make sure the shelter at the other end is just as good."

"I think it's worth it too, Kieran. It's just that I'm remembering how strongly Ranevargar emphasised we should stay together ... especially in Dead World."

That brought another round of concerned looks.

"Tan's right, Kieran. I remember wondering what Ranevargar knew about Dead World that he wasn't telling us. Maybe the mountains have some new kind of danger?"

Kieran held up one hand while he recalled all Ranevargar's special instructions and advice.

"Ranevargar's big worries about Dead World were Monsters, water and time, Mr B. There's not even a hint of anything else. I'm fairly certain he meant interference from the High King or Maynor or something else from outside."

"Like that thing in the Central Grove?"

Kieran grimaced. "Could be, Rhys, but if one of those turns up we'd be better off separated. There's nothing I can do to stop it."

"Sheba! The more we talk about this the scarier it's getting. Maybe we shouldn't try this shuttle?"

Mr B held a hand up, an intentional copy of Kieran's gesture, and got the smiles he was seeking.

"Steady everyone. This is our fourth day in Dead World and the likelihood of anything new happening won't change till we get close to Maurice. Kieran's said several times that Maynor or the High King aren't a worry while we're here. Since one of Ranevargar's concerns was time, I think this shuttle will actually be worth it."

Every head turned. Kieran laughed and ran to Krol. "Have a good rest and I'll let you know what's happening."

By the time he was properly harnessed, Woorawa and Mr B were inside the opening and Tan and Rhys were watching from the ledge.

"Go, Krol! As fast as you can for twenty minutes, then we'll look for another shelter."

Krol's flying *was* fast, but the progress wasn't. Greater speed meant more frequent Monster encounters and a dozen times the journey paused, a dozen times the angry approacher disappeared for the blink of two pairs of eyes, and a dozen times Krol's aura-clad talons triumphantly reached to dissolve a blinded and disoriented attacker.

Almost five hours later, Mr B made the last shuttle trip and the group once again shouldered their packs. Another leg of shuttling was very tempting, but Krol was weary and Kieran vetoed the idea completely.

"I'm not sure we *will* make it tonight, Kieran. Walking on this snow's hard work and much slower than we're used to."

"It certainly is, Woorawa, and there's a section ahead where the road zigzags up a really steep part, so that'll be another slow down. We can't complain though, because we're still way ahead of where we expected."

*   *   *

The shuffle of weary footsteps behind ceased and Woorawa turned to see why.

"We shouldn't stop here, Kieran. It's not far to—"

The light was fading, but there was still enough to reveal the familiar withdrawal of intense concentration. Woorawa retraced a few steps and spoke softly to Rhys.

"I wonder what it is this time?"

"It's Ranevargar. Kieran said something was coming through the Pearl link, then he stopped dead in his tracks."

"Whoa! It must be big deal then. He usually keeps walking."

"Well, we'll just have to— Sheba! He's using the Opal."

Curiosity became concern and the four friends closed in to watch and wait.

Kieran, observing a new assault on Ranevargar, had his own concerns. The shields would hold, that wasn't a problem, but the reserve of power maintaining them most definitely was, and at this rate it would be completely depleted in ... less than an hour.

What to do? There was no choice really and, conscious that he was going against Ranevargar's advice, Kieran initiated the process of sending Opal energy through the Pearl link and into Ranevargar's shield reserve. With careful control, he gradually increased the flow and watched for any sign of discovery. Nothing. Maynor's new assault was like a deafening roar covering the whisper of input, and with great satisfaction Kieran cut the flow when Ranevargar's small reserve had doubled in size. Wondering where Maynor was accessing so much power, Kieran started his normal pattern of checking Ranevargar's wellbeing and state of mind.

So confident! If Maynor knew how unconcerned Ranevargar was by this new level of attack he'd certainly be puzzled. With a mental smile and a decision to return for a far more detailed observation, Kieran was about to leave the Pearl link when Maynor himself entered the room and approached Ranevargar's supine form.

"Time and opportunity are at an end, Ranevargar. Join me willingly and I will allow you to remain in control of your Realm."

Ranevargar's head turned slightly, still the only movement allowed to him, to consider Maynor's confident expression before answering. "Time and opportunity are not always what they seem, Lord Maynor, and there must be just cause for replacement of any Realm Lord. You have neither the authority nor the cause to treat me so. Release me or face the judgement of the High King."

Through Ranevargar's eyes, Kieran noted Maynor's dismissive smile.

"Your trust in the old ways is foolishly misplaced, Ranevargar. My strength is almost gathered and tomorrow, when the High Castle falls, the Realms will all be mine, the Nexus will be mine, and the Realm Stones mine to bestow as I choose."

"No Realm Lord has the strength to take the High Castle. You pit yourself against the source of your own power."

"And you lack knowledge, Ranevargar. The free Nexus energy I already control will be augmented with enough power to overwhelm defences far greater than any Aglaron can possibly present."

"Maybe, Lord Maynor, but knowledge can be a two-edged sword and I suspect you haven't taken full account of Aglaron's centuries of experience and the value of Lord Uirebon's assistance."

Maynor laughed. "You stubborn old fool. Your time is well and truly passed. Knowledge will mean nothing against the power I have gathered. Give me the use of your Pearl or tomorrow night I will divest your every connection to it."

"I may be foolish, Lord Maynor, but I have wit enough to recognise that the power in which you place so much trust bounces inconsequentially from the strange wards around my mind. If Aglaron deploys similar wards to protect the High Castle your power will mean nothing."

Maynor said nothing for a moment, then laughed in what both Kieran and Ranevargar interpreted as derision. "Your efforts to goad and discomfort are pitiful, Ranevargar. Aglaron knows less of Keryth's shields than I do, and when you reveal his hiding place the warding will be mine."

"Keryth, the High King's son? I do lack knowledge, with my mind bound and body restrained how could I be otherwise after all this time, but I don't need much wit to recognise an obvious deceit. Aglaron's son is barely of age and this shield could only come from an adept with centuries of application. To suggest a youngster could construct such a thing is absurd."

Maynor studied Ranevargar thoughtfully. "You claim you don't recall being in Keryth's company? Your conviction is so persuasive it indicates some sort of memory manipulation. When your shield falls, a recall trigger will reveal everything you know of Keryth and his power stone."

Kieran missed the next short while. His astonished mind was reeling and racing. Maynor thought he was an elf called Keryth? No, he didn't just think it. He'd stated it as a fact. An elf? The son of the High King? The High King who, according to Ranevargar, must have been part of all the attacks? Impossible! But ... being an elf was one of Ranevargar's explanations for all these things he could do.

He couldn't be. All his memories were of growing up in Melbourne ... But then Ranevargar had also said there was something not quite right about them, and memories could be changed. A whole lifetime though? Kieran's whirl of thought was interrupted when a new surge of power raged against Ranevargar's shields. In quick response, he used this cover to push more energy into Ranevargar's reserve.

"You try my patience, Ranevargar, but I have other pressing concerns. You should consider that this is but a portion of the power tomorrow will bring."

With a gesture of dismissal Maynor strode from the room.

Ranevargar's surface thoughts were rushing too and very interesting, with a degree of amazement about his mind shield, and puzzlement over where Maynor could be accessing this unaccountable new power from. Why did Maynor hold the High Castle's defences in so little regard?

Concern for what was to happen on the morrow grew strong, so Kieran decided to reinforce Ranevargar's level of confidence through the Pearl link. Ranevargar felt the change and identified its external nature. How did he do that? He himself had shown Kieran how to make it undetectable as part of their planning. Yet another puzzle. As abruptly as it had commenced, the storm against the shields dropped to almost nothing and it was time to leave the kaleidoscope of Ranevargar's mind.

"That must have been major, Kieran?"

Kieran took in all the curiosity and concern.

"Unbelievable, Rhys. Maynor lashed at the shield with the most power ever and told Ranevargar this was his last chance to be sensible. He says he'll be the High King tomorrow and that he'll take Ranevargar's Pearl away from him."

"Tomorrow? Ranevargar hasn't even got the Pearl, so that doesn't make sense."

"Yes, it does, Woorawa. He doesn't mean physically. He means to break all Ranevargar's links. It sounds like it's something the High King has the power to do."

"So that first time when you nearly lost the Opal it must have been the High King?"

"It must have been, Tan, and it would be like death to Ranevargar if it happens, so we have to stop it."

"We don't have the time, Kieran."

"We'll reach Maurice in the morning, Rhys, and Maynor said he wouldn't see Ranevargar again till the evening."

"Whoa! So tomorrow we have to reach Maurice and then save Ranevargar. What else happened? You were using the Opal."

"I sneaked some energy into Ranevargar's reserve and I found out that Maynor's biggest attack against the High King starts in the morning."

"That's good then. They won't be thinking about us."

"Could be, Rhys. If Maynor does win he's going to come looking for us, so it would probably be best if there's a stand-off. I'm going to spend more time with Ranevargar once we're set up for the night."

Woorawa pointed along the road remnant.

"Walk and talk, Kieran. Time's getting more and more important, and if we're going to camp at the top we'll need your glow to show the way."

"That's no good, Woorawa. If Kieran makes a glow it will keep the Monsters awake."

"No, it won't, unless Kieran makes it strong enough to need the Opal."

"Rhys is right, Woorawa, but three close ones did react when I sent power to Ranevargar."

"Three's nothing. Krol will get rid of them easily."

Their target of reaching the top of this climbing section took another hour of steady but slow progress up the old road. For some reason it was improving in condition and that was a complete bonus. When they passed the crest, Rhys rushed past Kieran and Woorawa and happily wrapped his arms around Krol's neck.

"Tell him he's the best, Kieran. We'd be dead without him, and I can't wait to get warm under his wing."

"What about food?"

"I can't make up my mind which I want most, Mr B."

"You don't have a choice, Rhys. If you don't eat you'll feel the cold even more."

"Food is Tan's job. I'm going to cozy up to Krol till it's ready."

"Tan's job? You're a lazy grub, Rhys."

"I know. I'm going to poke my head out and watch while everyone else does all the work."

"Suffer then. When Kieran heats the water, Krol will have to leave ... unless we have cold food."

"Cold? Yuck! What's the Monster situation, Kieran? Are there many close ones?"

"... That *is* weird. There aren't *any*."

A distance reach, with a touch of Opal power, revealed a different story.

"Gods! Tomorrow's going to be scary. Close by is all clear, but then there are ... about twenty of them all grouped together."

"Together? That's new."

"And bad news, Rhys, when it's that many. How far are they, Kieran?"

"That's another interesting thing, Mr B. They're all gathered round about where Maurice should be."

"Monsters and a Dragon at the same time? Definitely scary!"

"You're right, Woorawa. We'll have to separate them somehow, because Maurice will need my total concentration."

"Using your Opal will attract them ... but we don't want twenty at once, so is there any way to focus on a few at a time?"

"Brilliant, Tan. I already do that when I light them up for Krol. I'll just change the directed glow to straight out power. Problem solved."

"Hey! Still too much talk. We can make plans after we eat."

Woorawa turned towards Rhys. "It was your question got us talking. Blame yourself."

"Minor detail, Woorawa, and anyway I only started it. It was you lot who kept it going."

"Give him last serve, Tan. He's a nutter!"

Kieran heated their food and drink with a reduced flow of energy. It took longer but meant no Monster worries.

As quickly as was practical, Kieran had the group set for the night, snug against Krol, wrapped in their cloaks and covered with the wonderful insulation of his great wing.

"Controlled sleep tonight, everyone. I'm making it deep all night, so you're as fit and ready as possible for tomorrow."

"Sounds great to me, Kieran, but you didn't include yourself."

"As soon as I can I will, Mr B. I've got stuff I have to do first."

"No way. You need to be refreshed more than any of us."

"About an hour, Rhys. I need to run through the instructions for waking Maurice and check Ranevargar's situation."

"Ranevargar? Won't he be asleep?"

"Probably, but that won't matter. I can check his reserve any time. ... Now, go to sleep!"

The full-on command put the four friends, plus Krol, instantly into the deepest level of sleep.

Making sure the construct-awakening procedure was clear and practised was the biggest imperative of all. At least once every day he'd made the time to practice the technique, and every time had improved his confidence. Tomorrow was the real thing and one last run through could only help.

The Rhys key unlocked the special area of his Opal network and, with the thought that he really should change it to something less obvious, he brought the complex set of instructions to the front of his mind and concentrated on the patterns of their application ... So much power was hard to envisage ... Yes, the link to the Central Grove was clear and strong. After only ten minutes he was satisfied this revision had locked the procedure as securely in place as it would ever be, and the special knowledge was returned to its hiding place.

Now for Ranevargar. The Pearl network activated and, with his usual careful reach, Kieran mentally left Dead World, crossed the Boundary Wall, bypassed the powerful wards surrounding Maynor's Castle, and slipped into Ranevargar's consciousness. Well, the background hum of sleep rather than his stronger buzz of consciousness was a help for his current purpose.

Shields first. Yes, they were functioning exactly as they were meant to, with no sign of degradation, drawing just the right amount of energy to foil the constant pressure from Maynor and keep Ranevargar's mind free from the influence he'd been worried about.

Reserves next. Not so good. That earlier onslaught with the extra power had seriously depleted them, and without the two undercover bursts the shields would have collapsed by now.

The constant pressure from Maynor would drain them in ... approximately four hours ... and there was no storm of assault to hide another burst from the Opal. What to do? Well, there was no choice. Ranevargar was reliant on the shields, so if a burst wouldn't work it would have to be a trickle so small it wouldn't be noticed. The session where Ranevargar had made him practice the control of energy flows sprang to mind and, calling a tiny tendril from the Opal, he carefully, ever so carefully, directed it through the Pearl link and into the reserve.

Yes! This would work ... The pressure against Ranevargar's shields was enough cover, but the tendril was so small its supply would have to be continuous. Not good enough. Make it an automatic process or stay awake all night .... Done ... But the number of triggers and automatic happenings was becoming a complicated structure to maintain ... How did Ranevargar manage the vast complexity of his Realm? Through his Pearl, of course. It took a search of the Pearl and some fierce concentration, but a new structure formed in his Opal network and kind of took charge.

Wow! That was neat, like a delegation of control that would unclutter his conscious mind. Yet again Kieran marvelled at the possibilities Ranevargar was opening for him. If only he had the time, there must be zillions of great things to learn from the Pearl.

With great satisfaction Kieran watched the tiny trickle of energy now flowing from the Opal to Ranevargar's shield reserve without any effort on his part. Hmm! If Maynor's pressure stopped, the trickle would become obvious. A new trigger to cover that went into the command structure.

Kieran switched his attention to the third puzzling reason for this extended visit with Ranevargar. Something was different and he'd noticed it strongly during Ranevargar's last confrontation. Yes, even though Ranevargar was asleep it was still there, and even more pronounced. The background hum of his thoughts was changed, stronger and definitely more complicated, and despite the constant paralysis, Kieran sensed that life and vigour brimmed more strongly through Ranevargar's body than it had just a few days ago. Yes, there was definitely a change and it was definitely good. Another puzzle but, for once, a positive one.

Confident that Ranevargar was secure, at least until Maynor's promised attack tomorrow night, Kieran withdrew to focus on his own concerns. Was he ready? Only time would tell, and he'd certainly followed Ranevargar's advice and guidance as best he could. The strange grouping of Monsters would be a major worry if their numbers couldn't be reduced before he called the great power flows from the Central Grove and the Opal. The intensity would send them crazy ... and attract others from a huge distance.

Hmm! That energy control technique for tiny amounts had worked well. Reviewing the techniques for the other end of the scale might also be a help ... Tomorrow though.

Now, the revelation from Maynor. So puzzling! The High King? Why would a father be part of such awful attacks? It didn't make sense. If only he could talk to Ranevargar he'd have good advice. Come to think of it though, he'd already said way back that there were too many puzzling things to allow for any certain conclusion. Yes, he was right. Puzzling it out without proper information would get him nowhere and use valuable time. It would have to be put on hold.

Kieran made a final check of Krol and his amazing companions, then relaxed into the comfort of resting his head against Rhys's chest and the secure warmth of Krol's covering wing.

*   *   *

"Ten more Power Masters will reach Maynor's Castle within the next two hours, my Lord. He discarded every measure against blocking our observations a short while ago and it is now clear that each party consists of one Power Master and an escort."

"He flaunts them, Uirebon, and seeks to daunt my resolve with the knowledge that each arriving Power Master will augment his strength. The onslaught last night, with the aid of the two early arrivals, was designed to instil despair. He believes I will quail before his power and surrender, but with all my strength I must hold the keys of control."

"He *will* take them, my Lord. We held the High Castle last night, but at great cost. His full strength will overwhelm all our defences."

"It will, Uirebon, but fourteen hundred years of just rule will only end when it is torn from my mind."

Uirebon regarded his liege with dismay. "My Lord, what of your Realm? His terms allow you to hold it."

"Never, Uirebon. Without power purloined from its proper use Maynor is no match for me. He will not leave a Stone of Power with a mind stronger and more capable than his own. That would be folly. No, he will make the Gateway Realm his own."

"He will bind your mind, my Lord."

"So be it. I will resist, and in the meantime I wish you to seek some way of wresting the free Nexus power from him. You know more of its function than anyone."

"I don't hold much hope for any success with but two hours left to us."

"Hope is all we can hold, Uirebon. Gather your helpers for the task."

*   *   *

"What is it, Woorawa? You've got the best eyes."

"No, I haven't, Rhys. Krol's are better."

"I think it might be the ruins of a castle or some big building. Check through Krol, Kieran."

"Maybe in another ten minutes, when the light's a bit stronger, Rhys. The Monsters are stirring and I'm more concerned about them."

"When are you going to start drawing them away? We'll be there in about an hour."

Woorawa paused in his lead position to stare at the features appearing ahead. "Rhys is right, Kieran. Did Ranevargar say anything about a structure close to Maurice?"

Kieran called up Ranevargar's mind map. "It might be, Woorawa. Maurice is inside a sort of big cavern and some of the piles of rock near it could be fallen down walls. It's definitely the right place ... and I'm going to wait till we're a lot closer for the Monsters, Rhys. I don't want to use any power just yet."

"Has anything new happened with Ranevargar?"

"It's just turning daylight, Mr B. The usual pattern is for at least another half an hour before he wakes up. He's safe though, because I've been sneaking power into his reserve all night."

"What? You said that was too dangerous."

"It was, but I figured out how to send a non-stop trickle that's too small for Maynor to notice."

The old road was no longer looking so old and for almost an hour they'd been tramping their way along a pavement of white stone which was in relatively good condition.

"How long will it take to wake Maurice once we reach him?"

"It'll be a while, Mr B, because of the different stages and all the energy transfers. Ranevargar didn't give me a time frame."

"Can you start now, to save time? Maurice must have a link to the Pearl network like all of Ranevargar's creatures."

"I wish! Then I could have woken him as soon as we came through the Boundary Wall. This link only activates when I'm physically there with him. It's a kind of precaution, I think."

The high ground behind their destination lit up with the first rays of sunlight.

"Hey! You don't need to look through Krol's eyes. I can see the castle shape myself now."

"It makes sense when you think about it, Rhys. No one's going to build a road to nowhere."

Tan spoke up. "I think it's the other way round, Mr B. The road starts there and goes away. The structure must have been a really important place and that's why the road's better close-up."

"That makes complete sense, Tan. I wonder if it was a castle like Maynor's or the High Castle Ranevargar told us about? It's extra proof that Dead World wasn't always dead too."

The burst of conversation stopped and for the next half hour everyone pretty much kept their thoughts to themselves. This was really in response to Kieran's concentration, and the quietness only ended when Kieran himself spoke up.

"It's action time, everyone. Form up and get your Spook ropes ready. I'm about to start using power."

"Do you think we'll need them, Kieran?"

"Not really, Rhys. I'm going to select groups of two every few minutes, because Krol can handle that with hardly any effort."

"Have you noticed they're not acting normal, Kieran? They've been awake for over half an hour now and not a single one has come this way."

"Hey, Woorawa's right. What's their movement pattern, Kieran?"

"They haven't really got one ... but that's about to change."

Two Monsters lit up with power instead of light — directed power so they'd be instantly aware of the source and know exactly where to go. With his senses alert, Kieran watched them rise above the others, head this way then, inexplicably, turn and retrace their course.

"That's weird! They started towards us then headed back."

"Did you use enough power?"

"Tons, Mr B, but I'll try again with more."

Changing the power and then the target Monsters made no difference. Kieran stopped in his tracks and everyone gathered close.

"What are we going to do? We can't survive twenty Monsters in one go."

"We can't give up, Rhys. Kieran will think of something. He always does."

Tan broke the protracted silence. "Make Krol's aura a lot stronger and we can walk underneath his wings. You already know how because you made it three times as big when Ranevargar first showed you."

Everyone stared at him ... then at Kieran.

"Would that work?"

"The aura part's just lots more power, Woorawa. Making sure Krol can cope with the extra is the tricky part."

"Work it out now, Kieran. You need to have it properly set up so you get a clear go if something else goes weird."

Kieran was already in communication with Krol and gathering energy from the Opal.

"A big change, Krol. I want to turn your aura into a fire of death in case the Monsters all attack at the same time."

The great head lifted in anticipation and, along with unquestioning acceptance for whatever Kieran wanted to do, Krol sent a query about what 'all' represented.

"It's why I have to make you stronger, Krol. There are twenty of them and they might all attack at the same time."

Krol's wings spread wide and every one of his body feathers lifted in a strange display.

"What did you say to him?"

"I'm calming him down, Rhys. He'll never give up, but his mind's telling him twenty Monsters is too much for any Griffin."

"You mean ...?"

With a great yell, Rhys leapt to comfort his special friend and companion. The fierce beak stooped to rest for a tender moment against Rhys's back and Kieran stared in wonder as the feathers all sleeked and Krol's head lifted proudly.

"Stand back, Rhys. He's ready for this experiment now."

"No way! He's too proud to let you know, but he likes me here. I can tell ... and ... if we're going to walk under his wings we have to know the aura won't hurt us."

Kieran had been surrounded by the aura without harm when Krol fought Monsters on the way to collect water, so he wasn't really concerned ... except this would be an extreme aura.

"Okay, guinea pig. Tell us when your skin starts sizzling."

Rhys's eyes widened momentarily and then the smile appeared. "Make some crackling for Tan, barbecue master."

Power surged and Krol's aura gradually extended for an extra half a metre while Kieran strengthened the interface between natural flesh and the power structures of his body. Good for a start, but the end result had to provide certainty, so try again.

The power flow built and Kieran managed almost another half-metre extension before pausing to watch Rhys pretending he was breast stroking through the aura.

"What are you doing?"

"I'm a guinea fish, not a guinea pig."

Mr B shook his head. Woorawa rolled his eyes and laughed along with everyone else.

"Why have you stopped, Kieran? Is that enough?"

"Not really, but if I make it any stronger it will damage Krol's flesh. I've reached a limit I can't change, Rhys."

Rhys moved away from Krol. "Well, it must be enough. I've never seen anything so unbelievable. He could already dissolve two or three Monsters before you even started, and now look at him. If they don't fly off in terror they're crazy."

"That's the trouble, Rhys. They *are* crazy, and I'm worried we might get buried under a mountain of dissolving bodies. I don't know what will happen if that flesh stuff touches us."

"Will it hurt Krol?"

"No, he's partly like them."

"As long as we're underneath him we'll be all right then."

Woorawa interrupted. "We'd better get moving, Kieran. You used so much power you've probably attracted other Monsters."

Kieran checked, then rechecked.

"You're right, Woorawa. There are seven, but we won't have to worry about them because the area is clear for a long way."

"They're attracted to Maurice. That's my theory."

The next twenty minutes of progress was spooky because the closer they got to the ruined structure the more agitated the Monsters became.

"It's like they're all tethered with giant rubber bands which pull them back whenever they try to leave."

"I've been thinking about Krol's aura, Kieran. How much stronger do you want to make it?"

"It'll be okay, Tan, as long as we keep close and underneath, so none of that dissolving flesh falls on us. Any extra strength would hurt Krol."

"What if Rhys was healing him all the time? Could you make that work?"

Rhys's face lit up with excitement and he grabbed Kieran's arm. "He's being brilliant again. Try it, Kieran. It's an extra safety margin if it works."

Kieran considered for all of two seconds before alerting Krol. "Hold his leg, Rhys. I've told him it might be uncomfortable, but he doesn't care a scrap as long as it helps."

Krol spread his wings in the protective stance Kieran put into his mind and, when everyone was positioned to Kieran's satisfaction, started a slow walk forward. Energy flowed, and when the death aura reached its safe limit Kieran started monitoring Rhys's healing reserve.

"Here we go, Rhys. Very slow at first while I watch the effect."

Krol *scrark*ed in surprise at the warm sensation spreading through every part of his body but continued walking. Healing flowed. The aura increased. Healing flowed and the aura increased yet again.

Whoops! He'd better keep Rhys's healing reserve properly balanced or he'd flake out.

Hmm ... Time to back off.

The aura subsided and Rhys's eyes opened and looked for information.

"It's all good, everyone. I can hold the new level for about ten seconds. Tan's idea has made us safer."

"Except that power burst sent them berserk, Kieran. Look."

Woorawa was right. Every one of the Monsters ahead was flying and wheeling in a frenzy of chaotic motion. Kieran marshalled his resolve, checked everyone's state of mind and marvelled that their concern was overlaid with confidence that he'd get them all through this.

"Move just a bit further apart, Mr B, Woorawa and Tan, so you can use the Spook ropes if you need to. Everything's about to happen."

It didn't, not for another five minutes, and Kieran switched to Krol's vision for a closer view. Interesting. Why was there a clear space of several hundred metres between the Monsters and the cavern entrance that was their goal? The five closest Monsters started toward them and Kieran readied himself. Would the rubber band effect turn them back when they were this close?

No!

Krol screamed his defiance and, instantly shining with purple brilliance, held position.

The blink reflex activated and five enraged attackers plunged blindly downwards. Still present in Krol's mind, Kieran felt four distinct impacts. Against the moment of his own dazzle, Krol pushed to recover his sight.

"Hold still, Krol, till your wings are clear."

The weight dissolved in seconds and Krol, now able to see properly, took two steps and reached his beak for contact with the thrashing and completely blinded fifth Monster.

"Holy hell, Kieran. My eyes blinked shut but I'm still dazzled."

"My mistake everyone. Touch Rhys for a healing burst, then take your positions again."

This was command mode and, with no choice in the matter, everyone leapt to comply.

"Sorry. I've fixed the amount of dazzle. *Krol, don't move again till this is over.* Rhys, I'm going to use the full ten seconds of healing time. Grip tight to Krol's leg."

Every remaining Monster was racing frenziedly toward them, stimulated by the blaze of power and, after another adjustment of the dazzle factor, Kieran waited till the very last second before raising Krol's aura.

Rhys's healing flowed, the deadly shield of purple radiance spread upwards and outwards and the first Monster to arrive became an inanimate blob of dissolving matter. Momentum lasted long enough for a remnant to penetrate and crash against Krol's right wing. Kieran, watching through Krol's eyes, monitoring Rhys's healing reserve, replenishing the aura, and controlling the powerful Griffin instinct to rise to the attack, barely noticed as three more disoriented Monsters flashed against the aura.

Krol reacted, as new remnants touched him, with a kind of full body shiver then, helped by a command from Kieran, steeled every part of his body for the coming onslaught.

He screamed his rage, blinked with the dazzle effect yet again, then shuddered and strained against the weight of seven amorphous death plunges impacting against him. His left wing sagged and there was a mental cry of shock when Tan was knocked flat and momentarily squished. Kieran couldn't help him. He was too busy managing Krol, Rhys's healing, and the flow of Opal energy. A massive lump of matter spilled from Krol's back and Kieran, carefully reducing the aura to the level where it didn't need Rhys's healing, took in the image of Woorawa's Spook rope speeding its dissolution.

Krol blinked, two more dazzled Monsters flared and dissolved. Krol blinked again, and called his triumph as the death of the last two Monsters cleared the sky.

Kieran, caught by the strength of Krol's exultation, staggered with the sudden shock of a new onslaught. Rhys's victory hug squeezed the breath from his lungs and a jubilant shout nearly deafened him. Three more sets of hugs joined the chorus, then stopped as suddenly as they'd started.

"Unreal, Kieran!"

Rhys's beaming face turned to Krol and, in a striking gesture, he held his arm extended with an open palm. "Champion of the Realms!"

Where did that come from? It felt completely appropriate though, and four more arms joined for a moment of honour.

Kieran felt the pride and joy coursing through Krol as he lowered his head to touch his beak against each palm.

Woorawa swivelled to survey the sky. "We'd better move, Kieran. Every other Monster in Dead World must be heading this way."

"I'll check, but I want everyone to get a healing burst first. We all used a day's worth of adrenaline just then, and Tan got knocked over."

"What? Again? How come? I didn't see that."

"You were focused on helping Krol, Rhys. Just as well, too, or we wouldn't have got through that."

Tan joined the group grip in the little ritual with the casualness of familiarity.

"It wasn't the Monsters, Rhys. Not directly anyway. Krol's wing sagged and surprised me. I was too busy hoping I wouldn't need to use the Spook rope to think properly. I didn't get hurt."

Kieran pointed and started walking. "We'll reach that entrance in a few minutes, so I'm going to start calling on the big energy flows. It might get interesting."

"Big? Wasn't that ten-second flow for Krol's aura big?"

"Not really, Rhys. It was baby stuff compared to waking Maurice."

"Sheba! You've got to be kidding! ... Except I know you're not. How do you know you can handle it? You haven't done any practice."

"Ranevargar showed me way back, but I couldn't practice in Dead World without attracting Monsters."

"How long before we have to start worrying about them again?"

Kieran reached—a giant reach as a kind of preliminary to the coming power calls. "Whoa! Woorawa was right. Every Monster I can sense is heading this way ... but some of them are so far they'll take a couple of hours. We've got about twenty minutes clear before the first arrivals, so I'll set Krol to guard the entrance and keep us safe inside."

Kieran opened the special Pearl link to the Central Grove, started the energy flow, then stopped when he bumped into Woorawa. "What?"

"Something's weird, Kieran. We have to stop."

"No, we have to keep going. Follow me!"

Kieran took the lead, advanced two steps and then hesitated. One more determined step was, unbelievably, too much, and he hurriedly backed up.

Rhys, puzzled, stepped past them, then retreated so hastily he almost fell over backwards.

"Gods! It's like an invisible White Wall. Can you call up the red protection from your Opal, Kieran?"

While Kieran did that, Mr B and Tan experienced the irresistible urge to turn back for themselves. Kieran dismissed the red glow after a single, futile step.

"It's completely different to a Boundary Wall. Try and push me through."

That didn't work. As soon his body passed the invisible boundary, Kieran frantically scrambled to get back.

"Something's taking control the same way you can, Kieran. Can you sense it or block it?"

"No! I can't sense anything."

"Can Krol fly over the top?"

"Don't bother sending him, Kieran. He won't be able to."

"He won't?"

"The Monsters can't, so it'll be the same for him."

"What about asking Ranevargar? He might know."

"No, Tan, there's no way he wouldn't have told me about a barrier like this."

"It's a mind thing, isn't it? There must be something you can do, Kieran."

Kieran hadn't stopped probing and he shook his head. "It is, Mr B, but whatever it is, it's new to me."

Rhys made everyone jump with his yell of frustration. "All this way! What are we going to do?"

A tinge of despair pushed into existence when nobody had an answer. Rhys moved back about ten metres, took off with a power run, and flung himself across the line with a great burst of speed, only to frantically reverse. He gave a great gasp of disgust, then straightened and stared.

Woorawa was standing motionless with his eyes closed. Rhys started to say something but was nudged to silence by Kieran.

Woorawa's features had the distinctive aspect of one of his campfire performances. No, more the air of their mind battles. A soft sound started deep in his throat, welled in volume and surrounded everyone with a fierce but familiar chant. In another familiar routine, the pattern strengthened and set. With eyes still closed he moved slowly forward. One step, two steps, three steps, a pause while the volume increased, then step after step till, ten metres ahead, the sound stopped, his eyes opened and a huge smile appeared.

"I'm through! I'm through! And I can't feel a thing. I'm coming back to help you all."

His walk was normal for a few steps and then he raced.

"That's unreal. Okay, everyone, get in the mood and start chanting. Keep close and start walking when I do."

The chant rose, louder and louder, till the frame of mind took hold and Woorawa started moving forward. Two steps into the zone he slowed and increased the intensity of the chant. To no avail. First Mr B and Kieran, then Rhys and Tan, faltered, panicked and raced back. Woorawa followed them.

"It's too powerful for the rest of us, Woorawa. It overrides the chant straightaway."

Tan spoke up. "It's all right, Rhys. Woorawa can pull us through with the Spook ropes."

"That won't work. We'll fight against him like crazy."

Tan clicked his wrists and ankles together. "Not if we're tied up enough. Try me first, Rhys."

"No way. It should be me."

Kieran overrode them both. "I'll be first, Rhys. I need to get through more than anyone."

"No, you're wrong, Kieran. I should go before you, so we know if it has any bad effects, and I'm going before Rhys because I'm a lot lighter. What do you think, Mr B?"

"I agree with you, Tan. I can't fault your logic, and if it works okay then Rhys should be next."

"What about Krol? Can five of us drag him through?"

"He'll have to wait here, Rhys. Using the spook ropes against those muscles would be like trying to hold him with spaghetti."

"Whoa! He won't be happy."

"I don't like it either. We'll just have to hope we don't need him for the last few hundred metres."

"Will he be okay by himself? You said more Monsters were on the way."

Kieran made a quick check. "About ten minutes now, Woorawa, but they're not in groups, so he'll cope easily. Start your chant, please."

The chant started. Mr B joined three Spook ropes in a long chain and, while Woorawa made his way through the barrier, Tan was trussed securely. Woorawa reached safety, turned and pulled the trailing Spook ropes taut.

"Ready, Kieran?"

Kieran waved for action and, ankles and wrists bound, Tan started his uncomfortable crossing. Straightaway he started threshing. Kieran reached to control his movement and calm his mind. Weird! The calming worked, but not the muscle control. He yelled.

"Get him through as quick as you can, Woorawa."

Woorawa gave a nod and, slinging the end of the ropes over his shoulder, strained forward till Tan's body suddenly relaxed.

"How was it?"

"Awful, but then it's all gone. Tell Kieran I'm okay and get me untied."

Kieran already knew and was busy helping Mr B get Rhys ready. Ten minutes later, just when Woorawa was trussing Mr B, Krol launched against the first of the arriving Monsters. Kieran, Rhys and Tan started dragging and, while Woorawa was slinging the last of the packs on his back, the sky flared and a Monster dissolved.

Rhys yelled in concert with Krol, then laughed at Mr B's expression

"Leave him tied up, Kieran. Look how much fun he's having."

Kieran was too preoccupied with watching Woorawa's progress to answer.

As quickly as possible the group passed the ruin of some large structure, headed for the cavern entrance, and glanced back at another flare of Monster-death.

"How many more?"

Kieran kept to himself that there were more than fifty.

"Um, ten in the next twenty minutes, Rhys, but never more than two at once. And don't worry—his aura gets renewed automatically from now on, even if I'm too busy to think about it."

For almost a minute the final approach held everyone in a contemplative silence.

"It's big!"

And indeed it was: at least twenty metres high and nearly as wide.

"It's dark too. I can't see anything."

Kieran was puzzled that all he could see through the dimness ahead was a blank wall.

"It looks empty. Make it glow."

That was easy and resulted in excited yells.

"Round to the left! Keep the glow going, Kieran. It goes further in."

After another ten metres they rounded the bend and Kieran's heart stopped. Well, not really, but his body did surge with adrenaline.

"Holy hell! It's a statue. Kieran, they've built a gigantic statue of him."

Kieran gathered his own startled wits, brightened the inner chamber even more, and reached according to the first of Ranevargar's instructions.

"Look again, Rhys. It's Maurice."

"No way! Ranevargar put Maurice in our minds and that thing's twice as big. It's solid rock, and half of it's locked in ice."

"It *is* him, Rhys. The cavern ends back there."

"But ..." Rhys's splutter of disbelief changed to silence while he shared the group's awe and struggled to acceptance. He was first to speak again.

"He must've kept growing. What do you want us to do while you're waking him?"

Kieran indicated the monstrous head locked partially in ice and resting on the cavern floor.

"I'll climb up there for a while, because I have to be in physical contact to get everything started, but when I get back we'll group like we do for going through a Boundary."

Rhys nodded, then turned in surprise. Woorawa stopped his new chant to explain.

"We all know this one, Rhys. It is a friendly message which might be a support for Kieran."

"Thanks, Woorawa! You're a wonder kid."

Kieran moved, then puzzled how to reach the giant forehead which he knew, with certainty, was the best place to make contact. Rhys understood, rushed close and cupped his hands for a bunk up.

"Stand on my shoulders, Kieran. That'll make it easy. Hang on while I get a better footing. This ice is slippery."

One foot went on Rhys's hands, the next on his shoulder and, after a few seconds, Kieran was standing secure with his body leaning against the giant snout and both hands pressed against the scaly forehead. Ranevargar's Pearl came to life, and calling power from the Realm Trees, Kieran sent a tendril of thought with the special key that was the only possible way into the mind of this huge construct ... Yes! There it was. Energy flowed, the lock opened, and the Pearl network completed a connection unused for six hundred years.

Kieran followed the connection exactly according to instructions, paused in amazement at the complex but dormant mental structure, then searched for the spark of partial awareness he must find and revitalise. Nothing? It must be there or the Pearl would not have connected ... Follow that. Yes, there it was, deep, deep, not a spark, hardly even a glow. Grove energy transferred through the Opal and disappeared. Disappeared? Or maybe that little glow was stronger? Kieran increased the flow and made it last longer. Yes! This was exactly according to plan, except for the excess of power. A wisp of puzzlement appeared and, elated, Kieran watched a new flow of Grove energy turn the spark of awareness into a tiny, spreading fire.

"Cold! Terrible cold!"

The deep distress communicated so powerfully Kieran shivered, then shook so violently he nearly lost balance. He blocked the communication. Good grief! That was so awful it would be cruel to let it continue. Well, as long as he was careful he could change that. A great flow of Opal power enveloped the construct and converted to warmth. With careful control, Kieran warmed flesh and heated the surrounding ice till water flowed and pooled in a low part of the cavern. Rhys made strange noises of disbelief when the ice melted beneath his feet. The awful distress lessened and Kieran returned to Ranevargar's procedure. Grove energy fed the awareness in steadily increasing amounts for the next twenty minutes.

"Go away!"

The command was expected and Kieran replied with Ranevargar's signature and a brief revelation of the Pearl network. *"No! You must awaken."*

A vast mental rumble of discontent dissipated as the signature did its job and Kieran sensed muted acceptance. Five hundred years of accumulated energy drained from the Central Grove. Too soon. Maurice still wasn't properly awake. Well, he'd have to use Opal energy.

"??" Maurice sensed the changed source and instantly accepted it. *"Who are you?"*

"I am Ranevargar's friend. He has given me authority to awaken and restore you."

"Authority is mine."

"No, authority is Ranevargar's, and through him, mine." When Kieran's mind shield quivered he projected amusement. *"Behave yourself, Maurice, and delay your challenge while I restore you."*

Kieran's mind shield reacted again, though this time it was a probe rather than an assault. *"Who are you?"*

"My name is Kieran, and when your challenge is finished we will be friends."

"Never!"

"Don't shout."

There was a thoughtful silence, tinged with surprise. *"You will provide enough power for a fair challenge?"*

"That's better ... But of course. And when your imperatives have been honoured I will restore your body as well."

"Curious indeed. I perceive a stripling wielding strange power and ability.

Whence came you?"

"Time passes, Maurice. Make your challenge when you feel ready ... and then we will talk."

In full accord with Ranevargar's procedure, Maurice built a great reserve of Kieran's Opal power before announcing his challenge. The challenge he must make before accepting authority from anyone except Ranevargar.

Two golden orbs appeared with the slow parting of scaly eyelids just a metre from Kieran's glowing hands and Kieran hastily summoned the defences laid out in Ranevargar's instructions as he jumped to the ground.

"Join the others, Rhys, and tell them not to look for a while. He's focused on me but the side effects might suck you in."

"I can stay here in case you need healing, Kieran."

"I have to do this on my own or it doesn't count. Don't worry, Ranevargar made sure I was ready."

Kieran turned from Rhys and smiled into the piercing stare. *"Beware the eyes of a Dragon, Maurice ... unless the master who taught the trick has passed knowledge of a counter."*

The hypnotic gaze intensified. *"Relax, Kieran. I mean you no harm."* Maurice added a blue beam, which did absolutely nothing, and Kieran laughed and intensified his own gaze.

"Relax yourself, Maurice, and enter the world of dreams."

Eyes as big as bowling balls blinked, disconcerted, and looked with a normal gaze. *"Danger, Kieran. Your mind and soul are in peril and your body faces destruction. Open yourself to my protection."*

Kieran steeled himself. Maurice had mastery of illusion and was about to call into apparent reality creatures of nightmare and fear from the depths of his mind. Without Ranevargar's guidance he would never have coped.

The bogeyman lurched forward, a shapeless monster from dreams where his feet were glued to the ground. *Click.* Ranevargar's counter illusion switched the bogey to a miniature, rainbow-coloured version of Maurice.

Mr B appeared, draped in funereal shrouds and laid on a bier with leaping flames consuming his body. *Click.* A miniature, rainbow version of Maurice gambolled playfully atop the bier.

Rhys appeared, dangling from a monster's mouth with entrails spilling free, a dismembered leg on the ground below, and moans of agony issuing from his mouth. *Click!* A miniature rainbow-coloured dragon gleefully punched the monster in the eye.

Kieran made a desist gesture. *"Turn for turn, Maurice. I haven't the knowledge to conjure fanciful phantoms of light, but consider this image."*

For a long moment Maurice saw a mind picture of himself re-encased in a prison of ice, and the implication of return to dormancy.

"Enough games, young stranger. You have had guidance in the rituals of challenge. Yield to my will and bow."

Kieran staggered. The compulsion to submit held every muscle in thrall ... almost. Behind and to the side the thrum of the group chant stopped and, from the corner of his eye, Kieran saw the movement of his four companions dropping to their knees.

Almost, but not completely, and Maurice's demand faltered because, as part of preparing him, Ranevargar's guidance had also shown Kieran the way to negate the Construct's will. Steadying himself against the battering waves of compulsion, Kieran stood tall. He recalled occasions when he'd had the need to press his own will and raised an arm to point at Maurice.

"ENOUGH!"

The compulsion vanished and astonishment echoed from Maurice's mind.

"Yes, my will is strong, Maurice, as you see, but I also stand in Ranevargar's stead. Observe the embodiment of your master's authority." Kieran held Ranevargar's Pearl, glowing with a beautiful green haze, for Maurice to see, and watched astonishment replaced by puzzlement. *"It is not mine. I wield it by request."*

"I recognise your authority, Kieran, but I am bound by the rules of challenge."

The change was fast. Maurice now wanted this finished.

"Of course. Would you like more power? The test of strength will only be validated by your utmost effort."

"More? I am bound to accept, but what of your companions? There will be spill from our contest."

"They have my protection."

Power flowed and Kieran could only smile at Maurice's growing puzzlement.

"Enough, Kieran! Build your own protections. Our contest starts."

Kieran brought his Opal into view and redirected the powerful flow to his own use. His shields would hold, he had no doubt of that, but Ranevargar had warned that this final test, a test against a creature expressly built to wield power, would appear to be irresistible and shake his confidence to the core. Thankful for the techniques he'd been pushed to develop, Kieran watched energy compact and coalesce to a dense, lance like structure, shining with fierce brightness and deadly appearance. Good grief! Quivers of lightning! He was going to throw lightning bolts.

Woorawa's chant faltered. Kieran raced to complete the group physical contact, englobed them with a mirror-surfaced shield, and sent assurance that everything would be okay. A dozen bolts flashed down, struck, and reflected. Light flashed, sound crashed as volley after volley was hurled with increasing tempo till Kieran laughed and called aloud.

"It's a great show, Maurice. What's next?" In the sudden silence four sets of eyes regarded him with disbelief. "It's real power, everyone, but it's not real lightning. I'm making a shield that acts like a mirror."

"It's real, Kieran. The ground's trembling."

Rhys was right, but how? Maurice's bolts were stopped and he was preparing the next test. Light flickered momentarily beyond the bend in the cavern and a new crash of sound followed. Real sound? Kieran reached for an instant of Krol's perception and, while passing a message of admiration and support for his efforts against continuing Monster attacks, directed Krol to look upwards. The unchanging clear blue sky was changed, replaced with massive banks of angry black cloud.

Shock from his companions demanded attention when the cavern walls started collapsing and a great boulder toppled to rest beside them. For a brief moment Kieran shared the shock, but understanding came, and with a pointed laugh he stopped the group impulse to run. The mirror shield changed its seeming to a protective buttress of solid steel girders. More rock tumbled and masses of dirt piled higher and higher.

"It looks like dirt, but it's Maurice power again. He's going to crush us. Start chanting again, Woorawa. It's good for everyone's nerves."

The ceiling fell with a rumble and crash, completely burying their protected space and cutting off every bit of light. It would have been very effective if Kieran hadn't been glowing with Opal power.

"I don't like this, Kieran. We'll run out of air."

"Watch this, Rhys. I can match his show easily."

Limning the virtual steel girders with his signature glow, Kieran gestured dramatically and with a double-palmed pressing motion extended the corresponding portion of their shielded enclosure.

"Whoo! That's better. How long is he going to keep us trapped?"

Opal energy surged, overpowering Maurice's effort and revealing the cavern as it really was. Woorawa's chant stopped, and after looking at the intact walls and the giant immobile form, attention centred on Kieran.

"It was all imaginary?"

"Yes and no, Mr B. He used a huge amount of energy and made it act like dirt, so in a strange way it really was there. I used even more energy when I got rid of it and somehow it's turned into a storm outside."

As if confirming this, brilliant light flashed from beyond the bend, followed by three great thunderclaps.

"Is Krol ... Gods, Kieran! Look at the walls. That better not be real water."

Water gushed from three locations, pooling deeper and deeper and washing around their ankles. Kieran laughed again when the entrance way became solid rock.

"Maurice is being dramatic. He's going to fill the cavern with thousands of litres of water and drown us."

Tan wasn't reassured and he looked with dismay at the water now surging forcefully against his thighs. "Stop it, please, Kieran. It's scaring me."

With a twist of thought the steel girders took on the aspect of a half-dome, and through the transparent walls they watched the flood rise higher and higher. Woorawa draped his free arm across Tan's shoulders.

"There's too much drama, Kieran. Too many things are happening."

Kieran didn't answer while he called the power necessary to counter this water challenge.

"He's only going to try one more thing, Woorawa. We've had fire and earth and now water. Next will be air."

Kieran unleashed his gathered power and the pseudo-water vanished. Rhys's excited cheer stopped when the loudest crash of thunder yet followed the light flash from around the bend.

"Holy hell! It sounds even worse out there. Is Krol all right?"

For a brief moment while Maurice was rebuilding his strength, Kieran reached, reached and took in the Griffin form crouched on the ground in stoic defence against the wild weather.

"He's not happy, Rhys. It's storming like crazy. But he'll be okay as long as lightning doesn't hit him ... and every Monster within about half an hour has stopped moving."

"Stopped?"

"I think the storm's too powerful for them."

A strong gust of wind swayed the group off balance.

"Whoa! It must be wild outside if it can reach us here."

"It's not the storm, Rhys. This is the air test. Hang on while I adapt the shields."

Another buffet of air rocked the group, and four grips tightened instinctively. Woorawa restarted his chant, then stopped when the weird howl of rushing air over-matched it. Normal speech was pointless against the sound and fury rising all around.

"Enjoy the ride, everyone. I've made our position the eye of the storm so nothing can touch us."

The howl rose in pitch, the whirling air opaqued with water blasted from the cavern floor. Rhys, confident of Kieran's protection, reached his hand tentatively towards the edge of their safety zone.

"Don't touch, Rhys! You'll be mentally taking yourself outside the shields and you'll feel like you're being sucked into a tornado."

Rhys snatched his arm back.

The cacophony built with the greatest aggregation of power yet, and Maurice, bound by his challenge, pressed with all his effort. The Opal responded instantly, and between one breath and the next the whirl of air and misted water vanished.

"My challenge is discharged, Kieran, and I recognise both your authority and the authority of the Pearl. What news of the Maker?"

"We need your help to free him from Maynor's Castle."

"Maynor?"

"The Realm Lord who took him prisoner."

Images of Ranevargar, paralysed and helpless, passed to Maurice's mind.

"Maurice, we have to hurry. Activate your body with the power I send you."

"Of course, but the mobility you imply will be hard won. My long dormancy will only be overcome with careful healing and renewal."

"Ranevargar needs us today."

"Not today, Kieran. A call of that magnitude is more than the Realms can provide."

"I will provide, just tell me if the flow becomes too great."

"How long have I slept, Kieran? You access power in ways new to me."

"It's been over six hundred years according to Ranevargar, and the power you need will come from my Opal."

"A Realm Stone?"

"My Opal is a gift from Woorawa's people. Ranevargar looked at it closely and he says it's partly like a Realm Stone but a whole lot of mystery."

"Woorawa's people?"

When images of the gifting ceremony at the Valley of the Eagles transferred, Maurice's realisation that this was outside the Realms prompted a series of questions that had to be cut off.

"Tell me about your other companions."

"We'll talk later. We need to wake your body."

Kieran laughed and enveloped Maurice with a spectacular field of glowing Opal energy. He watched Maurice's first tendrils of control reach eagerly to channel every last portion internally ... and more questions rising. Kieran laughed again and made the Opal flow constant.

"What's funny, Kieran? Is Maurice making you laugh?"

It was definitely time to update everyone.

"He likes talking even more than Ranevargar, Rhys, but it's mostly relief that the challenge is all over, and he's friendly and curious."

Rhys's glance went to the nearby gigantic claws.

"Friendly? He gives me the heebie-jeebies and he's still frozen. I nearly wet myself when he made me bow."

Kieran paused to increase the energy flow.

"He's as friendly as Krol, Rhys. He's concentrating like crazy while he wakes his body, but he'll talk to everyone when he's ready."

"He can talk?"

"Greetings, Rhys."

Rhys jumped with surprise, then recovered enough to reply. "Greetings, Maurice."

Kieran laughed again and increased the energy flow. Rhys turned to everyone.

"He spoke in my head just like Ranevargar does ... Kieran, I'm worried about Krol. It sounds like it's getting worse out there."

"Krol?"

"Krol is Ranevargar's Guardian. He's blocked from being with us by a barrier and stuck in the storm."

Maurice examined Kieran's mental image and his energy uptake paused for all of ten seconds. *"Call him to shelter, Kieran. My barrier held the annoying plague of pests at bay."*

Kieran sent his thanks, called Krol, and once again increased the flow of energy. "The barrier's gone. Let's go to the entrance to meet Krol."

"Don't you have to be here with Maurice?"

"It's just around the corner, Woorawa, and we'll be back in a few minutes."

Rhys charged off with Woorawa just behind him, rounded the bend and halted abruptly when a startling flash of light was followed by a nerve-freezing thunderclap. Twenty metres ahead the cavern entrance was a curtain of water flickering in and out of view with each random lightning flash. Everyone caught up and stared.

"Can he find the way, Kieran? It must be like walking through a waterfall."

Kieran reached, fixed Krol's slight confusion with a touch of direction sense, then quickly moved the group to one side.

"Stand back! He's coming with a rush."

Coinciding with a blast of light, Krol's form bounded from the downpour, halted with a scrawk of relief, then sprayed everyone with a prolonged effort to shake his drenched body free of water. When the startled yells of protest and amusement ended, Rhys rushed to reassure Krol and Woorawa moved to the very entrance.

"When the storm stops the monsters will be a problem again, Kieran."

"That's not for a while, Tan, and they'll have to come through the entrance, so Krol will manage easily."

Tan nodded and brushed a smear of water from his hair. "It's real water this time, isn't it?"

"Yes. Ranevargar didn't mention it, but Maurice kind of said the storm's a side effect of us using so much power."

Another flash of light silhouetted Woorawa against the silver curtain of rain, and Mr B winced at the following crack of thunder.

"He calls that a side effect?"

Maurice suddenly drained every bit of power being fed to him.

"Something's happened, Mr B. Maurice wants more energy."

"A lot more, Kieran. A prolonged flow, if you can manage it."

Kieran was already close to the limits Ranevargar had thought he'd need, so more was going to be interesting. He grasped the Opal for the extra feeling of connection physical contact always gave and examined the existing flow.

Whoa! It was at a total maximum, surpassing the earlier flow from the Grove and straining his controls to the limit. Any more and the control would shatter, releasing wild energy. Too dangerous. Maurice would have to accept the current level.

Hmm! Interesting. A trickle was reaching him through the channel from the Grove ... Good grief! Make a new channel. Such a simple solution.

A second channel, complete and independent, formed and Kieran, very pleased with this simple but effective achievement, made a new call for power.

The Opal responded with a call of its own, a call unavailable and unused for a long, long time.

*   *   *

Beyond the Realm Boundary, beneath the structure of the attendant High Castle, the engine of power sustaining the Faerie Realms recognised a signature missing for millennia. Power flows adjusted automatically and the Nexus hummed with the restoration of proper balance and harmony.

The High Castle defences wavered, dissolved momentarily to nothing, then rebuilt.

Lord Maynor watched, unbelieving, as a significant portion of the free Nexus energy was wrenched from his iron control.

Dangerous monsters, a symptom of a Realm in disorder, dissolved to nothing as order returned.

*   *   *

Energy flowed abundantly through the newly formed channel, so abundantly it outpaced the ability of the great Construct to take it in.

"Kieran, what have you done?"

"I made a new power channel, Maurice. The first one couldn't carry any more ... What do you mean?"

Maurice's great puzzlement registered. *"Examine your Opal and the Realm around us. I sense enormous change."*

"My Opal? It's working flat out, Maurice, sending you twice as much energy."

"Examine the new flow, Kieran."

*   *   *

Uirebon abandoned his activities in the Great Hall, rushed worriedly to Aglaron's sanctum, then, recognising the withdrawal of deep concentration, held his pressing concerns and tried to assess the High King's well-being. A long minute passed before Aglaron stirred and focused on his immediate surroundings.

"Uirebon, ease the furrow on your brow. We still stand."

"My Lord, what was your purpose? When the Wards fell we feared that Maynor would take control, but then you raised them again."

"The purpose was not mine and the control was beyond anything Maynor could manage."

Uirebon strained for understanding. "... Narello then? Surely that is not possible?"

"Forget Lady Narello. She is Maynor's pawn. Uirebon, my friend, the Realms are changed. Our Wards wavered while the Nexus restructured itself. Maynor's control of the free energy has been reduced, giving us a temporary respite while he tries to assess what happened."

"The Nexus? Restructured? I don't understand."

"Neither do I, Uirebon, but something in the Unordered Realm has changed the power balances flowing from the Nexus. Observe."

Without hesitation Uirebon accepted this invitation to see, from the unique perspective of the only mind directly linked to them, the patterns of energy flowing throughout the Realms. Awestruck, he took in the Nexus, its close proximity a looming presence.

"... My Lord. The pattern is beautiful beyond belief."

"Indeed, Uirebon, balanced and splendid as we have never seen, but look to the Lost Realm. Order has returned."

Awe vanished and Uirebon's mind struggled to even accept what was being presented. "Is it Maynor redirecting all his stored Ruby power?"

"Look closely, Uirebon. There are two distinct channels of power, one flowing cleanly from the Nexus and the other sourced at the very centre of that power sink."

The close look pushed Uirebon's incredulity to a new level. By virtue of Aglaron's perception the channels of power were clear to see, but what were they doing?

"I have never seen or heard of power produced like that, my Lord, but it all disappears. Can you see where it goes?"

"Not at all, and I sense it would be unwise to intrude."

"A far-seeing?"

"Into that vortex of power? No, Uirebon, the seeker's mind could be torn apart, and we must conserve all our resources for defence."

Uirebon returned to immediate concerns. "You think Maynor will resume his assault?"

"We must assume so, because when the last three War Masters arrive his power will reach its peak. Are all our triads ready?"

"Yes, gathered in the Great Hall along with all the High Court."

Aglaron showed his appreciation then turned to access his Gateway Realm for power sources of last resort.

*   *   *

Kieran looked closely, Maurice's exhortation was practically a command, and saw straightaway that his Opal was sourcing the new channel of power from elsewhere then, according to his will, directing it to Maurice.

"It's not Opal power, Maurice. It's from somewhere else."

"Trace it, Kieran. You have the skill."

Only because Ranevargar had pushed him. Wow! This was a beautiful, clean flow reaching from a long way away.

"It's coming from way past the Boundary. Something else has changed,

because that used to block my viewing."

New surprise blossomed in Kieran's mind with the realisation that the flow pattern was somehow familiar ... Where ... Oh my!

"This is too weird. It's like the pattern of permanent power that Ranevargar distributes through his Pearl."

"Yes, you appear to be receiving energy from the Nexus itself, Kieran. Did Ranevargar instruct you in the technique to manage that?"

"He mentioned the Nexus, but that's all. There were too many other things to do."

"This Realm is no longer dead. The pests have disappeared and the land cries for recovery."

Kieran had no idea what Maurice was talking about. The pests? That had been his earlier term for the Monsters, so Kieran switched attention, reached, and turned to his companions with an excited yell.

"The Monsters are gone!"

"What do you mean? Has the storm frightened them so much they've gone somewhere else?"

"No, Rhys, I mean really gone. Maurice just told me and I can't see a single one."

Kieran laughed, because all four weren't quite believing him, thinking the Monsters must be hiding or have flown too far to sense.

"You'll see for yourselves when we go outside."

Woorawa gestured at the constant flicker and rumble. "We can't go out there, Kieran, not till all that stops."

Kieran made a quick communication with Maurice before replying. "I'm giving Maurice twice as much power as Ranevargar suggested and his body will be awake in about twenty minutes. After that the storm will start to die down."

"Double? Wouldn't it be wiser to keep to Ranevargar's plan?"

"It worried me too, Tan, but Maurice was desperate for the extra. It has to be because he's had six hundred years of growing that Ranevargar didn't count on."

Rhys moved and pressed experimentally against Maurice's front leg. "He still feels like solid rock. Does he come to life gradually or what?"

A sense of amusement, along with a message, came from Maurice.

"Maurice says you should stand right in front of him, Rhys."

"No way! What if his first reflex is for food? He hasn't eaten anything for six hundred years."

"He eats power, not food, and he likes you ... He likes all of us."

"All right, but I bet he opens his mouth and breathes fire over my head or something."

Maurice's plan had been to turn on a Dragon stare of friendship, but Rhys's idea now took his fancy. Nothing happened for a few minutes, well nothing as far as Rhys was concerned. Kieran watched the two huge energy flows seized and directed through the great network of tissue, watched every tiny structure absorb the energy thirstily, and sensed the fire of life build in strength and meld with the still-growing fire of mind. Rhys, emboldened by the lack of anything happening, moved to the end of Maurice's forepaw and, with a, 'hey-look-at-this', expression, circled his hands around one of the shining black talons. The talon twitched.

"Holy hell!"

Rhys whirled but forgot whatever it was he meant to say. Along with the already spectacular blue glow of Kieran's energy, Maurice's head was now quivering and twitching in an eerie transition from dormancy to function. Everyone stared, mesmerised, until the tremor quietened. Maurice's first movement, somewhat unnatural-looking because the rest of his body wasn't yet awake, was to incline his head towards Rhys. The mighty jaws parted, exactly as Rhys had suggested, and a fiery glow started deep in his throat. Kieran was as shocked as everyone, then, seeing the reality, he sent a group assurance and a memory of Ranevargar's phantom fireside Griffin.

"It's not real. It won't hurt. He's just being dramatic."

A roaring gout of flame enveloped Rhys, swirled impossibly, then leapt in four streams to surround the disbelieving onlookers. The flame stopped and billows of imaginary smoke curled upwards.

Rhys involuntarily checked that his flesh hadn't been roasted and recovered his wits at a request for permission to come into his mind.

"Welcome, Rhys. I enjoyed your suggestion for an introduction."

"Welcome, yourself, you great lump! I didn't suggest making us all into roast dinners."

"Lump!"

Amusement loomed in Maurice's mind and was communicated so strongly that the roast dinners all had to smile.

"Steady, Rhys."

Dragon eyes turned. *"Greetings, Mr B. I see you are a thoughtful balance for the unit. Have no concern. Greetings, Tan. I look forward to many interesting conversations with you. Greetings, Woorawa. The mysterious power of your song helped dispel my stupor."*

A new burst of quivering, major this time, started in the rest of Maurice's body.

"Move in front of me, everyone. There will be some reflexive wing movement while my body returns to full life."

Woorawa led the quick change of position and Rhys made a comment about swapping the frying pan for the fire.

The trembling increased and became alarming till, slowly and unsteadily, both wings stretched as far as the cavern walls allowed. At the same time, the rest of Maurice's body gradually became mobile. The great shoulders arched upwards then relaxed. One massive foreleg, and then the other, lifted, extended shakily toward the companions, then returned to the cavern floor.

"Are you all right, Maurice? That looks painful."

"Thank you, Rhys, but I don't feel anything. The involuntary muscle movements cause slight damage, so I'm waiting for the process to settle before I restore feeling."

"You can control whether your nerves work?"

"To a degree, Rhys. The recovery is inevitable, but the process lets me make a delay."

Faster than they extended, the wings retracted, and both front legs moved rather awkwardly from their resting position to become vertical pillars, lifting Maurice's head and neck almost to the ceiling.

"Gods, Kieran! Is he too big to fit through the entrance?"

That was a startling thought, but once again amusement entered everyone's minds.

"That is no problem, Rhys. When I am ready to move, my talons will easily claw a way if need be."

"Through rock?"

"Yes, Mr B, as long as I have power to assist me."

Rhys examined the talons with renewed interest. "They must be harder than diamonds."

The whole length of Maurice's back arched with a mind-blowing wave action, his tail made a slow motion swish, and attention switched.

*   *   *

"Tell me, Ranevargar, do you know of any way to alter the Nexus?"

"That knowledge was lost with the adepts, and I warn you to curb your ambition, Maynor. Any attempt at such an interference would endanger the Realms."

"The High King has lessened the flow of free energy and reduced my Realm's allowance."

"I don't believe you. This is another deceit. As well as being beyond his ability it would dishonour his integrity as steward of the Nexus."

"It is no deceit. I would have agreed with you, but those changes happened, as I describe, just half an hour ago. When I become High King all such knowledge and secrets of the position will be mine. When the last two Power Masters arrive the High Castle defences will crumble and my attention will turn to you. Work with me now. Spare your Grove, keep your Realm and your Pearl, and hold an important place in the new order."

"You bind my body without compunction, Maynor, and I sense you will do the same with my mind if it furthers your purposes. I may be helpless, but while these shields protect me I will remain myself and wait for the High King's intervention."

Maynor shrugged dismissively. "Wait in vain, Ranevargar. Aglaron's last resources are almost consumed and the High Castle defences have no chance against my accumulated ruby power."

"Maybe not, but consider your position, Lord Maynor. If, as you believe, the High King can alter the Nexus then he can divert the very power that sustains your Realm to defence of the High Castle. A full assault could well lead to the desolation of your Realm."

Maynor stiffened with the shock of understanding. "Never! A High King is bound to care for the Realms."

Ranevargar couldn't help but laugh. "Threatening to destroy my Central Grove and diminishing my Realm by taking my Pearl can hardly be termed as care."

"In the long-term, yes, it can. My chosen replacements will restore and reinvigorate every Realm."

"Precisely the logic the High King can use for his own defence."

Maynor was silent for a moment while he considered this. "You have a devious and complicated mind, Ranevargar. Our next confrontation will be lengthy and interesting."

Ranevargar, pleased that he'd disconcerted his captor, couldn't resist a parting shot. "Maybe more interesting than you count on, Lord Maynor. There are forces in play you haven't considered properly."

Maynor hesitated, then hurried to depart. Ranevargar extended his puzzling to this news of a change to the Nexus. If true, as Maynor appeared to believe, it couldn't be the High King. So who could it be?

*   *   *

Understanding what was meant to happen wasn't a preparation for the actuality of Maurice's awakening and everyone watched, incredulous, while the torrents of power from Kieran invested his body with life. The last few minutes, when he'd restored feeling to his nerves, had been frightening. The unfettered dragon-roars of pain, amplified by the confines of the cavern, had held the group huddled reassuringly close through every excruciating blast of sound.

"My apologies, everyone, but expression is more helpful than repression. The storm of pain has passed and I am fully awake."

"Thank God! That was the scariest sound I ever heard."

"I am thankful too, Rhys. My enlarged throat can produce more volume than I care to hear."

"You can say that again!"

"?? … For what purpose?"

"Rhys is just agreeing with you, Maurice. How long before we can leave to rescue Ranevargar?"

"My body is awake, Kieran, but it will be several days before I am able to fly."

"Days? We have to leave now. As soon as the storm dies down. Ranevargar is worried there's big trouble looming."

"You speak with him?"

"Not exactly. He trusted me with his memories so Maynor wouldn't be able to find us and stop us from waking you up, but I have a link to him through his Pearl which lets me see what he sees and know his thoughts."

"Who is Maynor?"

"I told you. He's a Realm Lord who's keeping Ranevargar paralysed in his Castle."

A wash of Maurice's anger jolted everyone.

"I recall your image of the Maker bound and helpless, Kieran. Explain, please."

Kieran did so mind to mind, for greater speed and nuance of detail.

"Kieran, I am not yet able to take you to Ranevargar, but haste is definitely needed. Can you take me through your secret link?"

Kieran was completely startled and he turned to Mr B.

"Maurice wants me to take him through the link to Ranevargar, but that might warn Maynor."

Mr B nodded. "I'm hearing Maurice's questions, Kieran. I think we all are. Take him. If he can't fly at present, he might be able to help Ranevargar in some other way for now."

"I am certain I can help, Kieran."

Mr B continued. "We know Maynor can't get through the shields, and the persuasion techniques Ranevargar was so worried about haven't worked either. It's too late for Maynor to stop Maurice being awoken, so I think it's time to give Ranevargar back his memories."

"I'm not so sure, Mr B. If Maynor finds out where we are and comes for us, we won't be able to stop him."

"You must be kidding, Kieran. If he comes here, Maurice can eat him."

This typical Rhys comment made Woorawa and Tan splutter with laughter.

"Ranevargar couldn't stop him, Rhys."

"The Maker was unprepared, Kieran, and the paralysis you all experienced would have no effect on my body. An ordinary Realm Lord is of little concern to me. I am equipped to rule and, if necessary, defend this Realm."

"Can you protect someone else from the paralysis? If Ranevargar was free he could take off that helmet thing and look after himself."

Tan spoke up. "When Maynor's not watching, give Ranevargar his memories back and ask *him* what to do. He knows more than everyone, even Maurice I suppose, and if it's too dangerous to keep his memories, he'll tell you to look after them again."

"Hey! You're a brainiac, Tan."

Kieran agreed along with everyone else and Tan became the centre of approval and admiration.

"It will be a big relief to talk to Ranevargar, rather than just watch and listen. *Maurice, I think I know how to take you through the link, but I'll see what Ranevargar says first.*"

"Certainly, Kieran, mind riding is not a skill I have practised ... You can close one of the power channels, if it suits."

"No, I'll keep it going, in case Ranevargar wants it."

"You'll have to ask him first, Kieran. You've been worried about tiny trickles of power and that's an unbelievable amount. When can we expect you back?"

Kieran gave Rhys a curious look. "What do you mean?"

"You'll be concentrating so hard you wouldn't even notice if Maurice laid an egg."

"??"

"Oh! Yes. The memory bit's just a few minutes, but then there'll be a lot to talk about ... and then I expect I'll be taking Maurice through the link."

Kieran carefully reached through the subtle pathway of the Pearl to the buzzing surface thoughts of Maynor's immobile captive and sent a gentle recognition signal.

"Ranevargar?"

Shock jarred every train of racing thought. *"Who speaks through these impossible shields? Do I know you? A friend?"*

"Yes, a friend. You can't remember our strategy, but here is the special mind-key you gave me. Use it to recover your lost memories."

"Lost memories? So Maynor's nonsensical questions were legitimate ... That is my key, but where do I use it?"

"Follow your Pearl link into my mind."

Excitement, exhilaration even, flared. *"My Pearl? You have it safe?"*

"Exactly as we planned, Ranevargar. Use the key because I need your advice."

The wave of questions was overridden as he rushed to comply, and Kieran watched Ranevargar's wonder at the link, the key activating, and memories flooding back.

"KIERAN!"

The excited mental shout cut abruptly when Ranevargar almost frantically started accessing information.

"... You are all safe ... The Construct is awake ... Maurice?? Krol is proud and happy."

Kieran smiled inside with each mental exclamation of realisation, then wondered at the puzzled pause.

"Kieran, what have you done?"

Kieran noticed with interest that the manner and tone of Ranevargar's question was almost identical to Maurice's.

"Not yet, Ranevargar. You come first. We decided it should be safe to give you back your memories, because Maynor's manipulations don't seem to work on you."

"They do work, Kieran. Just a short while ago I started to think he was almost reasonable, but when he rushed off I quickly came to my senses."

"Tan thought I might need to look after your memories again when we

finish talking since we've had a big setback. We can't come to help you for a few days, because Maurice says it will take that long before his wings are ready."

"Days? I don't understand that."

Kieran projected a strong image of the cavern and its occupants. *"Look at him. The stasis didn't stop him growing and he's much bigger than you showed us. His size meant the waking was really hard on his body."*

"Yes, I see that now, but Kieran, that means our power calculations were completely inadequate. However did you manage?"

"The Opal gave me everything. The Grove energy wasn't nearly enough, and then Maurice needed far more for the challenge as well."

Kieran watched with growing bewilderment while Ranevargar reviewed the power usage for Maurice's awakening, scanned the memories of everything Maurice had said, accessed all his interactions with Maynor, then rode through the Pearl link to check on his Guardians and Hosts.

"I am confident in my ability to withstand Maynor's manipulations, Kieran. Along with your amazing shields I have a secret weapon."

"How did you do that?"

"??"

"The thinking, Ranevargar. So many things almost at the same time?"

"Thinking? I have done nothing else since Maynor bound me ... Oh, I see. This new vigour is Rhys's gift, and beneath the cloak of paralysis my physical form is also invigorated."

"What's the secret weapon that protects you?"

"Your constant supply of extra confidence is the element which gives me the edge. Whenever I waver, the first indication of Maynor's effectiveness, it kicks in and restores my mind to independence."

"Will it keep helping now that you know it's happening?"

"Even more, Kieran. Please keep it going. It will be a critical help for me during the coming extremity."

"What extremity?"

Once again Kieran watched Ranevargar study the memories of Maurice's awakening.

"You were occupied with ... Maurice ... and didn't observe my most recent visit. Maynor is about to unleash power beyond anything the High Castle can stand and make himself High King."

"Using the ruby Power? I know about that from earlier when he bragged about it. Ranevargar, I don't care what happens to the High Castle. You said yourself it was involved in taking Rhys away. It's you I want to protect."

"I must confront Maynor, Kieran. He threatens to destroy my Central Grove, take my Pearl, and give Stewardship of my Realm to a new Lord. The current High King would never contemplate such a dishonourable action."

Kieran remembered how convinced Ranevargar was about the High King's integrity and didn't know what to think.

"Kieran, sometime later today Maynor intends to use every resource he can command to penetrate these shields. If, as High King, he takes full control of the Nexus, I am not sure they will hold."

So, that was the extremity? Kieran thought the shields would be strong enough but was uncertain enough to be worried.

"You're our first priority, Ranevargar, and we can't do anything about the High King from here anyway. Maurice says he can do things for you, but I wasn't game to bring him through the link. I have to sneak in carefully myself, and Maurice's mind has so much power there's no way Maynor would miss him."

"Well considered, Kieran. His mental presence behind Maynor's defences would start a great turmoil of alarm and reaction. If you can take me through your link to meet him, Maynor will have no knowledge of the meeting."

Once again Kieran was puzzled. *"Of course, but why ask me? It's your Pearl and your link."*

"Not quite, Kieran. Your elusive technique has partially hidden it from me."

"It has? Oh, I see ... Is that better?"

"Yes ... That is interesting ... but time passes. Let us make haste."

In an instant Kieran's attention was back in the cavern and turning to Maurice.

"It's not safe for you to go to Ranevargar, so I've brought him here where your mind can be as open and active as you like."

"MAKER!"

"Well met, my pompatus Guardian. My heart rejoices with your safe recovery."

Joy radiated to all the companions and Krol—almost the same joy the Realm Guardians experienced when Ranevargar woke from the healing zap—and the shared wonder stretched till, through Kieran, Ranevargar addressed everyone.

"The Dragon Quest is successful beyond expectation, my friends, and the gratitude of two Realms rests with all of you. Now, pardon my haste, but as Kieran will explain, time is valuable and I must speak with our curiously named Maurice."

Kieran, present by invitation, watched with little understanding as Ranevargar's mental touch activated a dormant area in Maurice's mind. A second area blossomed into life, then another, and another. Kieran, confounded by the new complexity, stirred uncomfortably when the Pearl link lit up with the amount of information Ranevargar was calling through it.

"Careful, Ranevargar. You'll trigger Maynor's alarms."

"All is well, Kieran. My lost abilities have taken the first step to recovery and I can now protect myself."

"What's happening, Kieran? Ranevargar said you'd explain."

"I can't keep up, Rhys. Ranevargar did something to make Maurice's mind work better, then collected a whole lot of memories from him, except it's more complicated than that."

"Why did he say two Realms?"

"He means this one, Mr B, as well as his own. He says the Opal has stopped it being Unordered."

"Your Opal? Godfather, Kieran. It keeps doing new things. But what about Ranevargar? He sounded all excited, and I thought he'd be disappointed we can't get to him for so long."

"He's just told me he can protect himself from Maynor. He's learning stuff from Maurice."

Kieran jumped when Woorawa grabbed his arm forcefully and urgently. "What sort of stuff, Kieran? Has he found out how to do the big portal?"

Four sets of eyes were now riveted on Kieran.

"I don't know. When their minds stop breaking speed limits, I'll find out."

"Can't you see? You've been watching what Ranevargar's thinking for days."

"I can, but at the moment there's too much. It's like they're swapping whole libraries of information and I haven't got a catalogue."

Tan turned to look at Maurice. "He's closed his eyes. I suppose that means they're still transferring?"

Kieran nodded and silence stretched till Ranevargar's attention shifted to them.

"I am sorry, final recovery of my knowledge and abilities can only occur when Maurice and I make physical contact, but that needn't be delayed. If Rhys is willing to offer his healing touch, along with your careful application of power, Kieran, Maurice could be ready to fly in a very short time."

"Offer? Of course I'll offer."

Mr B shook his head. "We all know that, Rhys, Ranevargar included. It's just his polite way."

"Wonderful, Rhys. It will be quite a task, but if you start promptly Maurice could well be ready to fly by the time your storm subsides."

Rhys grabbed Kieran's arm. "Have you got much more mind stuff, Kieran?" He gave Kieran a look of anticipation. "Helping a Dragon's a bit mind-boggling and so is seeing him fly."

"Seeing will come later, Rhys. Your first experience of Dragon-flight will be from Maurice's back."

"Won't he need a practice by himself? I mean, he's been asleep for six hundred years and he's twice as big."

"I know first-hand the astonishing effectiveness of your healing, Rhys, and the race to this Castle will be more than enough for Maurice to acquaint himself with his new flying abilities."

"New abilities?"

"Changed is a better description, Kieran. Some loss of manoeuvrability will be offset by a greater capability for speed."

Kieran smiled as new anticipation welled in Rhys's mind.

"Unreal! ... How will we stay on? We haven't got saddles ... And will he carry all of us?"

"Yes, Rhys, including Krol, who mustn't be left behind."

Carry Krol? Kieran wondered how that would work. Well, they'd find out soon enough.

"One more thing, Kieran. Can I make a request for increased access to my Pearl and a store of power? My current personal resources won't cope with the coming confrontation with Lord Maynor."

Kieran now understood that this was the extremity Ranevargar had referred to, but he also saw an overtone implying it would be Ranevargar's confrontation.

"How much power, Ranevargar? I've kept it going in case we need it. It's still all pouring into Maurice, but I can swap it to your Pearl for as long as you like."

"Not all, Kieran. You haven't been watching how Maurice is using it."

"??"

Kieran hastily checked. Wow! The first channel was building a reserve to help Maurice with his flying. Of course. Ranevargar had said way back that Maurice's take off needed power assistance. The new channel, though, was dispersing all through the Realm.

"What's he doing with it?"

"Using it for its intended purpose, Kieran, and eagerly exercising his primary function of nurturing the life of this Realm."

Kieran had a closer look at the busy complex of activities humming through Maurice's mind.

"Amazing! I was going to direct both channels of energy to your Central Grove, but it'll have to be just the first one now. It feels like he really needs that second channel ... Ranevargar, there's a big problem ahead. He's going to be totally upset when I stop calling power through the second channel."

"There is no problem, Kieran. That channel is the greatest wonder for Faerie in over ninety centuries and you won't stop because if you do the Realm will die again."

"But ..."

Kieran looked at the power flow more closely and Ranevargar, watching from afar, shared some of his understanding.

"Your Opal is now aligned with the Lost Realm, Kieran, and the power you direct to Maurice is bringing it to life."

Kieran saw and shared Ranevargar's wonder, but along with that came a troubling realisation.

"Does that mean my Opal has to stay here? We need it to get back to College."

"Don't feel trapped, Kieran. Your bond with the Opal will make it possible. We will find a way."

Kieran, conflicted by the thought that returning to College might mean this Realm dying again, took heart from Ranevargar's optimism.

"Stop all that thinking, Kieran. We need to heal Maurice so we can get to Ranevargar."

Rhys's grip on his arm refocused Kieran's attention.

"Just a couple of seconds, Rhys. Ranevargar's about to leave the link and there's stuff we have to do."

Rhys grinned. "There's always stuff."

What an understatement. Kieran redirected the flow from the first energy channel and sent it flooding through the Pearl and into the Central Grove, released the amount of Pearl control that Ranevargar felt was safe. Then he told Maurice to ready himself for healing and reluctantly bade farewell to Ranevargar.

"Thank you, Kieran. I need a time of deep meditation and assimilation now, but my confidence is higher than ever and I will make contact as soon as I am ready."

"Will I keep watch, in case you need me or Maurice?"

"Only if you sense me using power from the Central Grove. Give your full attention to Maurice and your companions for the next while."

Ranevargar's connection died and Kieran's attention swapped yet again.

"Yay! Finally! That couple of seconds lasted about a minute."

Maurice's head moved to rest on the cavern floor.

"Hands on his snout, Rhys. Your Dragon-healing is starting."

Rhys eagerly complied and Kieran finished the flow to the Grove, checked Rhys's healing reserve as well is his own, then watched the Rhys-effect work its way through Maurice's body. Whoo! All his body, not just his wings.

"Heat, Kieran. Should I feel so much heat?"

"That's good, Maurice. It means the healing is working."

Rhys and Kieran shared a puzzled look as to why Maurice was suddenly projecting amusement.

"What? Is it like you're being tickled or something? Krol and Tan never thought it was funny."

"No, Rhys. I am reflecting on the unexpectedness of your ability to return my greeting ... I feel just like a roast dinner."

Proper control of the healing collapsed when Kieran's own amusement joined the feeling already resonating from Maurice, then wavered again when he saw Rhys's huge grin.

The healing resumed with new pleasure and achievement for Kieran and Rhys, and a quick check showed Maurice monitoring the progress with amazement and vast gratitude.

"Yes, Kieran. Days of healing accomplished in minutes is just one of so many things to take in."

"I know. I'm talking to a Dragon ... Maurice, can Woorawa, Tan and Mr B do anything to get ready for flying? We haven't got any harnesses to keep us safe."

"Your safety is assured, Kieran, as you will see. I do suggest you all get accustomed to climbing into place though, by carefully negotiating my back ridge."

"Not yet. We'll all do that together, so Rhys can lead the way. We decided it's his privilege to be the first Dragon-rider."

"He will be second, Kieran. The Maker came on the flight from his Realm to help me become established."

That brought a whole flood of questions to Kieran's mind.

"Did you get upset about being put to sleep, Maurice?"

"Very much, Kieran. It clashed with my primary drive to actively manage the Realm, but it was also a relief to know that the dangerous results of my inability to counter disorder would end ... My body has a sudden urge to move. Will that interfere with the healing process?"

"Whatever you like as long as you don't move your head and lose contact with Rhys's hands."

Maurice's wings stretched, his body arched and his tail lashed in slow motion.

"How's our healing going, Kieran? You haven't said anything."

"Sorry, Rhys. I've been talking to Maurice and watching where the healing's happening. It's almost finished for his main body and the energy's mostly working on his wings. We'll be finished in about five minutes."

"You're joking? Ranevargar said it would be a big task."

"I know. He probably thought that because Maurice is so big, but we're handling way more power than we did for Krol."

"We are? It doesn't feel any different to me."

"Yes, it does. There's that tingle in your hands where they touch Maurice's skin. I can see it in your mind."

"Hey, it is too. How did you notice that?"

"It's part of how I make sure you don't flake out."

Woorawa moved closer. "How much more power, Kieran? Is it from the control exercises Ranevargar got you started on?"

Kieran laughed. "So you can add it to my practice routine? A bit, but more because I had to figure out how to cope with two big channels to wake Maurice. He's like a bottomless pit for energy."

"Is he getting much now? The blue round his head's stopped, but your Opal's still glowing. For the healing, I suppose?"

"Gods! Woorawa, I can't believe how much power he's using. He's using one channel to build a reserve, so he can fly, and the other channel's healing the Realm."

The great golden eyes, so close with the contact of the healing process, blinked with deliberation.

"*Not so, Kieran. The flying reserve is complete and every bit of energy you send is helping the Realm ... The heat in my wings is receding?*"

Kieran checked and gave Rhys a big smile. "Thirty seconds, Rhys, and Maurice will be ready to fly."

Rhys grin returned. "The roast dinner is ready for action?"

"*Very much so, Rhys. The touch of your hands is a mysterious gift.*"

"How come I can look at your eyes now without getting hypnotised?"

"*??Only when Kieran commands it, Rhys.*"

"What?"

Kieran nodded. "Yep! When I'm getting squished by a blubber mountain you'll be hypnotised into surrendering."

"Ha! More cheating."

"Grab your rucksack, Rhys. You're leading the way up Maurice's back."

Maurice's head lifted almost to the top of the cavern, and Kieran watched, fascinated, as different groups of muscle and flesh tensed and relaxed. Rhys took no notice. He was in a rush to get his rucksack on.

Maurice moved toward the bend in the cavern.

"Hey! Wait for us."

"Rhys, he hasn't moved for six hundred years."

"I know. I'm impatient too."

He wasn't really, just excited at the extraordinary prospect of riding a Dragon and eager for action. Everyone followed around the bend, then stopped to watch the meeting between Griffin and Dragon. Kieran had seen with an earlier mind check how Maurice's greeting protocol included both physical and mental contact.

Krol's head lifted proudly. Maurice's head lowered, quite sedately, and there was a moment of distinctly formal contact.

"Greetings, brave Guardian. I give you my thanks and a message of appreciation from our Maker for protecting your companions."

Krol didn't answer with words of course, but Kieran watched joy and achievement flood towards Maurice.

"Well! Look at that. Krol's not one bit nervous. He even looks happy as anything."

"Maurice just gave him a thank you message from Ranevargar, Rhys, and he thinks about Maurice the same way he does any other Guardians or animals in Ranevargar's Realm. They're being quiet while Maurice looks through his memories."

Rhys clipped his already-shouldered rucksack and grinned at everyone. "Who's coming?"

The healing was well and truly finished, but everyone looked to Kieran, who nodded and gave his own grin.

"Go on, Dragon-rider. We'll watch till we know it's safe."

Rhys gave an 'I know you're joking me' look, then hesitated till Kieran pointed to Maurice's tail with a go motion.

Tan asked the question. "It *is* safe, isn't it, Kieran? Does he have to be careful of sharp scales or the ridge of spikes?"

"Maurice said it was completely safe, Tan. We just have to get up there, and we're all good scramblers now."

Tans eyes widened at that. "Mountains don't move while you're climbing them, Kieran. I hope he stays still."

Kieran, along with everyone else, jolted with the surprise of a particularly brilliant lightning flash and the accompanying crash of sound.

"Gods, Kieran! That was close. The storm seems as strong as ever."

Maurice, looking to the entrance, answered. *"Without further stimulus the storm will dissipate quickly, Woorawa, and we will be able to leave."*

"Stimulus? You mean you can keep it going if you want to?"

"If we didn't have to leave, I would keep it going for hours, Rhys. Water is the essence of life, Woorawa, and the Realm thirsts for every drop that falls."

Kieran saw Maurice's strong yearning to do just that, but attention shifted back to Rhys who was now standing where Maurice's tail rested on the ground.

He grasped the prominent ridge, pulled himself up, then promptly fell on his back. He flipped to a kneeling position, then stood up with a highly indignant expression. "That wasn't me. He twitched."

Warily he picked his way, holding one side of the double ridge in case of any more twitches, till he reached a broad area between Maurice's wings.

"Come on, everyone! His back's so lumpy it's easy ... if he doesn't play tricks."

And easy it was, with parallel ridges for handholds and curious corrugations providing plenty of secure footholds.

Woorawa led, with Mr B following and Kieran escorting Tan. He didn't really need assistance though and soon everyone was standing with Rhys on a kind of platform area of smoother skin.

"Unreal, Kieran! We're boss of the world up here, but flying's definitely going to be scary."

Kieran agreed, quite puzzled how Maurice could think this was safe. The only handholds were the big ridge protrusions at the sides. What? Humour reached everyone as the whole flat area they were standing on began to twitch.

"Move back while I raise your protection."

Everyone, receiving Maurice's image, scrambled back and watched the great flap of skin they'd been standing on rise from his back.

"Sheba! That's brilliant, Maurice."

"Thank my Maker, Rhys. He needed security while flying, and protection from wind and cold."

Rhys and Woorawa moved to explore the sheltered space and excitedly yelled for everyone to join them.

"Come and feel, Kieran. It's like fur. The thickest I've ever seen, with kind of straps for holding on."

"And others for your feet, Rhys. Try them now to get used to them."

Kieran found a position, sank into the luxurious layer of fur, slipped his hands and feet into the strange restraint growths, and marvelled at how comfortable and secure he felt.

"Maurice, what happens if you forget we're here and lower the shield? Will we get squished?"

"Not at all, Woorawa. Observe."

The great plate of skin lowered, cutting off the light, but at the same time the bed of fur lowered as well, leaving a gap above their heads.

"There is plenty of air, Tan. In this configuration you will be completely protected whatever my speed or contortions."

"What about Krol, Maurice? He won't be shielded like we are."

"There is great power in his claws and beak, Rhys. Enough to hold him in place at any speed. For any major contortions he will simply detach."

"How fast do you travel? We've flown with the Griffins at astonishing speed."

"I don't know the answer to that myself, Mr B. I am greatly increased in strength, and Kieran provides me with energy at rates I have never contemplated. It will be fast."

"What's happening with the storm? Is there any change?"

"Patience, Rhys ... fifteen minutes or maybe more for safety. Emerge from your cocoon to watch with me."

The barrier above their heads lifted and returned to being an observation platform.

"The lightning and the deluge of water is specco, Maurice, but are we watching for anything else?"

"It is enough for me, Rhys. Apart from barely formed dream visions, I have seen nothing for six hundred years."

Four sets of eyes turned to see Woorawa's reaction.

"They're looking at me because I was blind for eight years before Rhys and Kieran healed me, Maurice, but that's nothing compared to six hundred."

"Not so, Woorawa. You were aware of your loss."

The silence of contemplation broke with a new question from Rhys. "Your eyes are huge, Maurice. Does that mean you can see better than Krol?"

"I believe so, Rhys, but you will be able to make your own comparison when we fly."

"What? How?"

Kieran saw the expectation. "You're going to love it, Rhys. Maurice will send what he's seeing, or what Krol's seeing, whichever you choose ... It's the way Ranevargar saw everything when they flew here."

"Wow! Unreal."

Out of curiosity, Kieran accessed Maurice's vision and had an inward smile because, along with extra clarity of all his features, Krol was suddenly looking tiny. Well, of course he would, from a mighty Dragon's perspective.

"Mighty, Kieran? Not really, just fit for purpose."

"You were fit for purpose before all this growing. I think mighty works ... What are you doing with all my first-channel energy? I tried following your path for it and it disappears into thin air."

"Quite an apt description, Kieran. I am using every bit you give me to generate another storm."

"Another one?"

"If I had enough energy I would start many more. As I informed Woorawa, water is the key to begin restoring the Realm, and the right kind of storm will fill the rivers and flood the plains."

Kieran looked at the water sheeting down at the cavern entrance. *"We'll be confined here for ages."*

"Kieran, you have the skill. Search the Realm for a manifestation of energy."

Whoops! Slightly embarrassed, Kieran reached, observed, then made a comparison.

"It's a long way from here and it's big, much bigger than this storm."

"Big enough to feed the four nearby river systems, Kieran. The run-off will be the kernel for new life."

"Kernel? How much water do you need?"

"There is plenty of water, Kieran, centuries of accumulation as snow and ice. Gathering energy to transform it to liquid form will be the greatest difficulty."

Kieran looked with new care at both energy channels. The new one, according to Ranevargar, was all accounted for, but the first was his to use however he wished.

"We'll keep the energy coming as long as you like, Maurice, and you can make a new storm each time you are ready."

Gratitude flowed in a great flood, along with a tinge of regret.

"What's wrong?"

"We will manage one further storm, Kieran, but when we pass the Realm Boundary I will lose control."

That *was* a big problem. Maurice understood there was uncertainty about Kieran's return to Dead World. Maybe? Why not? Yes, it was worth a try, and with the technique so new and strong in his mind, Kieran formed the structure for a third power channel and sent a new call to the Opal.

"What are you doing, Kieran?"

"Experimenting. I'm trying to get extra energy for you, but it doesn't seem to be working."

Indeed, for the first time ever the Opal wasn't responding to his call. Maybe the torrent raging through the normal channel was the maximum it could provide? Kieran was about to dismantle the containment structure for the channel when he had another thought ... Maybe the two channels already operating were masking his call?

Kieran made the call again, not quite a demand, because that wasn't how it worked, increasing its strength and, for emphasis, holding it longer ... Yes, something was definitely different ... A strange tension built, snapped then disappeared. The new channel flooded to the maximum so rapidly Kieran almost lost control. Shock and alarm thrilled through Maurice's mind as a glowing reserve of unexpected energy enveloped his body, expanding towards the ceiling, surrounding all five companions with a glowing, white nimbus, then stretching to the cavern bend.

"Sheba, Maurice! Send it to the storm. Quick, before it gets too big and I have to cut it off."

The new reserve connected and Kieran watched Maurice struggle to cope. *"There is too much, Kieran. Far too much. You will have to slow it down before my pathways burn out."*

"No, they won't. See how the structure of the channel holds it? Build that same pattern into all your pathways."

"??Help me!"

The glowing white reserve slowed its expansion as Kieran and Maurice cooperated in tracing and strengthening the overloaded energy pathways.

"See how the pathways grab passing energy to strengthen themselves? That's what I had to figure out for the first two channels."

"Yes, a new thing. Extraordinary ... but what have you done this time?"

"This time? I've made an extra channel to help with your storms."

"That I understand ... It is the new energy that confounds me. Where does it come from?"

Since that seemed to be blatantly obvious it was Kieran's turn to be confounded.

"Kieran, the first channel has your blue signature. The second channel has the rainbow signature of Nexus energy. This new energy is pure white, powerful beyond my understanding. Look at it."

It *was* different, but the closer look was interrupted by insistent tugging on his arm.

"Kieran, what the blazes is happening? When this white glow came Maurice quivered like a jelly till it started to shrink, and now we look like a pack of angels. Is it another emergency?"

Four very worried sets of features relaxed with a message of reassurance.

"Sorry, everyone. It was my fault this time. I wanted to help Maurice make new storms and lots of stuff happened all at once."

"Storms? What was the quivering, Kieran? It was so weird we all freaked."

"So did Maurice. I gave him extra energy without enough warning."

"To use your term, Rhys, it frightened the hell out of me. I faced the prospect of becoming a roast dinner again."

"Um ... you mean for real?"

"I do, Rhys. This new energy was more than I could cope with till Kieran showed me how. The quivering you experienced was a physical reaction to an unexpected threat."

Woorawa surprised everyone with his laugh. "Don't mess with Kieran, Rhys. He hands out halos and makes Dragons quiver in their boots ... Was all that glow the new energy, Kieran?" He turned to look at the diminished reserve near Maurice's head.

"Yes, it came in a rush."

"Why are you making it white?"

"I'm not. That's one of the things we don't understand. We haven't looked properly yet, but Maurice is really puzzled."

"Ask Ranevargar. He'll know. But I think it might be time to move, Kieran. The lightning's stopped."

With Tan's comment, the focus of attention changed yet again and Kieran followed Maurice's tendril of perception.

"Tan is right. The rain will persist, but the danger from a lightning strike has passed. Move beneath the shield and we will proceed."

The lightning returned, well, a shared burst of excitement with the same shock of impact, as everyone scrambled into place.

*   *   *

The furrows marring Uirebon's brow reflected his own sense of impending doom as he watched relentless strain diminish the High King of all Faerie. The light of fourteen centuries of just rule dimmed with every flicker of the inner sanctum's deep purple wards.

In the time, less than an hour, while Maynor's massed strength battered for ascendancy, the High King had sacrificed resource after resource to fight the inevitable.

Centuries-old structures throughout his Gateway Realm crumbled to ruin as the power behind their strength and beauty withdrew.

Nexus energy allotted to the maintenance of every Realm flowed perilously low till the outer defences of the High Castle collapsed.

The path to the Human World disintegrated, along with a vast accumulation of power supporting the Faerie-wide portal structure, a sacrifice helping to maintain the Outer Wards till a short time ago.

In the Great Hall, Uirebon's own contribution, an unprecedented triad of a triad of triads, was on the verge of collapse.

"My Lord, we cannot hold. It is time to concede."

"I will hold to the last, Uirebon."

Sadness welled in Uirebon. If the High King committed himself to stand against such power when all else had failed, his mind would inevitably be damaged beyond repair.

"I *will* hold, Uirebon. There is a factor which I do not understand and which Maynor cannot see. Ride my view of energy flows while I still have the strength."

For the second time that morning Uirebon accessed the High King's unique ability, as Steward of the Nexus, to view energy flows anywhere in Faerie, and for a brief moment the collapse of a Kingdom went from his mind. Manifesting in three distinct torrents, power was flooding to the Lost Realm. One flow, coming from the Nexus, looked almost identical in nature to the basic maintenance flow for his own Realm, but the other two shouldn't be possible.

"What does it mean? Where is the hope in this, my Lord? Can you gain access?"

"If only I could, Uirebon. Even a portion would render Maynor's offence pointless, but I daren't. Look at the focus directing the energy. A short time ago it began to speed towards the Realm Boundary."

Focus? Uirebon followed where Aglaron directed and took in enough to recognise yet another puzzle. "I don't understand the apparent speed. Even one of Ranevargar's flying Guardians couldn't come close to matching that rate."

"Neither do I, Uirebon, but the rate does suggest purpose."

Uirebon's heart sank at this vain hope. High King Aglaron's defences were at an end. "My Lord, any such purpose could well be directed against us."

"Indeed, Uirebon, but hope will sustain longer than despair."

A purple glow surrounded the Stone of Power Aglaron now raised and Uirebon fleetingly wondered if some final unknown resource was being summoned. Fleeting because at that moment the great offence battering the Inner Wards disappeared.

Uirebon stared uncomprehendingly at his liege. "What did you do?"

The purple glow faded, vast strain smoothed from the High King's features and the Stone of Power returned to rest against his chest. "Nothing,

Uirebon. I did nothing except prepare for the end. Unaccountably, Maynor has redirected his power. Look!"

For the third time, Uirebon joined the High King's view of energy flow and once again found it hard to understand.

"Against his own Castle?"

"No, against one specific location in his Castle. He has turned everything against Ranevargar."

*   *   *

Ranevargar, his thoughts racing close to overload, closed the monumental link with Kieran and Maurice and constructed a deep and secret compartment in his mind where he could consider the range of actions now open to him.

The absolute priority was information, reliable, first-hand information to inform and rank every action so, calling on knowledge and ability unavailable for six hundred years, he bypassed the restraints of the golden helmet, quested for Maynor, then studied the links directing power against the High Castle.

So much! Thirteen lines from the Power Masters, all Maynor's personal resources, and an inordinate amount of Nexus energy. How was it possible for Aglaron to resist? A new questing brought understanding and dismay: the Gateway Realm so drained of resources it faced centuries of recovery, and the High Realm itself on the verge of ruin.

Vastly grateful for Kieran's latest gift of energy waiting within his Realm Trees, Ranevargar strengthened the link with his Pearl and made an overt and clumsy attempt at influencing the mind of one of the attendants currently bathing his leg. A damp cloth dropped to the floor, hesitant hands moved to fumble with the helmet fastenings and a startled cry rang out as the second attendant leapt to interfere.

When external power flowed to strengthen the attendant's mind, Ranevargar reached to make another interference. This time to the nearest Power Master, and with enough strength to wrench at the energy flowing from his ruby. His own shields flared while the two attendants ran from the room. Yes, he had Maynor's attention and a personal and private confrontation would now occur. Skills lost for six hundred years stirred, flexed, and with a touch of energy called from the Grove, Ranevargar interrupted Maynor's control of the free Nexus energy. The response was instantaneous and Ranevargar watched the amazing shield he'd been gifted firm, and hold, as every resource under Maynor's control lashed against it. Bolstering energy flowed through the Pearl link with enough in reserve to last for ... weeks?

Maynor arrived, his anger and disbelief an almost physical force radiating through the room while he examined the function of the golden helmet, the helmet which should prevent the projection of any power or ability.

"Where is your Stone of Power, Ranevargar? Somehow you are calling on it with this attempt to interfere, and if you don't give me immediate access my every effort will stay directed to crush that infernal shield and take it by force."

"My Pearl is not here, Lord Maynor. Its proper wielding is beyond you, and this malignant challenge for the High Throne is finished."

Maynor's anger lifted to a new level and scorn was clear in his short laugh. "The High Castle falls as soon as I finish with you here, Ranevargar. With your body paralysed, your mind bound and all but helpless, how can you refuse to see?"

"What we see is not always what is, Lord Maynor."

This brought an even more scornful laugh, followed momentarily by a measured look. "Why waste time with foolish riddles, Ranevargar? I am the uncrowned High King and I see with a Realm Lord's vision."

"Show me everything you know of the visitors from the Human World."

Taken aback by both the irrelevance and the authoritative tone of address, Maynor regarded the strange old elf Lord, who was surely losing his touch with reality.

"Show? Ranevargar, you—"

Ranevargar sat up, and through his shock and confusion, Maynor realised the significance of the intricate hand gestures now directed at him. His Ruby flared red with warding ... then unaccountably quietened.

"Hold still while you pass the information I seek."

Maynor stood quietly for several minutes and information flowed till a new set of instructions settled in place.

* * *

Determination surged anew as Lord Maynor brushed from his mind what must have been momentary cobwebs arising from the prolonged efforts of his challenge.

"Ranevargar, you will give me access to your Pearl and end these futile attempts at interference. Your submission is inevitable."

Resplendent in full ceremonial dress, Lord Maynor left his helpless captive and strode from the room, his Ruby shedding a glowing aura of confidence. The moment the old fool's shields caved from unrelenting pressure, the High Castle would follow.

Ranevargar, with mind shields firm against unprecedented pressure, reached with the facility of his newly restored abilities through his strengthened Pearl link and communicated a direct message of wellbeing to every Realm Guardian. Through the resounding joy, an imperative called Kan and a host of other Griffins to fly at full speed to join him.

*   *   *

Rhys linked arms just before the giant protective barrier of skin settled in place, and the gesture was a happy moment interrupting all the other things Kieran was thinking about.

"I can feel Maurice moving, Kieran. We're going to ride a Dragon and we can't see."

Kieran mind-spoke to everyone. *"Maurice is preoccupied with getting his body ready to fly and I don't want to distract him till he's in the air. We'll watch through Krol's eyes for a while."*

Vision of Maurice's huge form moving through the cavern entrance filled the group's minds and Kieran smiled at the sheer amazement.

"Sorry. We didn't think about practising that."

"Unreal, Kieran ... Isn't Krol meant to be getting a piggyback ride?"

"When we're outside, Tan. The entrance would scrape him off."

"Of course it would. I'm too amazed to think properly. Everything is sort of extra clear?"

"That's Krol's different eye structure. Just wait till we switch to Maurice. His eyes are even more interesting."

No one said anything because Maurice was now gone from view and Krol himself was approaching the entrance. He wasn't happy with all the rain, but he understood he'd be out of it soon.

"Sheba, Kieran. It's still a downpour."

"Yes, but nothing compared to ten minutes ago, Rhys. Wow! Look at Maurice!"

"Look at us you mean, Kieran. My mind's flipping because I know we're there, but here feels like from where Krol's seeing ... What's he doing?"

"His body's too heavy to leave the ground by itself and he's activating energy to help ... I'll make the energy glow so you can see for yourself."

With his wings quivering strangely and flexed to the maximum, Maurice was already an unbelievable sight. The sudden appearance of a blue glow illuminating every part of his body brought mental gasps of astonishment.

"*Holy cow! ... I mean Dragon. Is that the way you see the energy in him, Kieran?*"

"*Sort of ... He's moving his wings around to adjust to the feel of his new size.*"

"*Here we go everyone. It's take-off time.*"

"*Krol's not piggybacking.*"

"*Not till Maurice is in the air, Tan. That's a lot easier for both of them.*"

The energy suffusing Maurice's body changed in some strange way and to Kieran's perception disappeared. For everyone else Maurice rose vertically before making his first massive wing beat.

"*Holy moly! Vertical takeoff. Is he doing that with the energy you showed us, Kieran?*"

Another powerful beat changed the sense of lift to forward motion and the vision relayed from Krol confirmed Maurice was securely airborne.

Kieran, linked in his special way, saw the rush of achievement and success momentarily eclipse Maurice's every other thought.

"*Yes, Kieran. I revel in the moment. We are on our way and when my flying awareness is rebuilt we race. We race to help the Maker.*"

"*Do you need any more energy? I was shocked at how much your launch used.*"

"*Not for flying, but as soon as Krol is with us I will renew the storm building.*"

"*Maurice has disappeared, Kieran.*"

"*Not for long, Rhys. Krol will catch him soon.*"

Krol launched and, in a coordinated moment while Maurice travelled in a smooth glide, was soon grasping a protruding ridge with his powerful talons.

Maurice worked to rise through the cloud and rain and, with breathtaking suddenness, Krol's view showed clear blue sky. With a change of aspect they looked down on a dazzling white bank of cloud.

"*Unreal, K!*"

It *was* breathtaking and Kieran interrupted his complicated juggle of thinking to take it in, swapped to Maurice's vision, because Krol's view was mostly either clear sky or the ridged back he was gripping, and smiled at the collective mental gasp as the prospect below broadened with extra life and clarity.

"*Oh my! Is this how Dragons normally see, Kieran?*"

"*It's normal for Maurice, Mr B, and as far as I know he's the only Dragon in existence. He's definitely the only one ever for the Realms.*"

"Well, yes, of course. I framed my question without thinking ... There's the edge of the storm."

Kieran saw Maurice's intention and sent a mental warning.

"Whoa! Wild ride for the next few minutes everyone, while Maurice tests his manoeuvrability and flying skills."

"Wild? Will Krol be able to stay on?"

Kieran didn't answer because the whole world revolved with a body roll, lost gravity with a short vertical dive, then lurched frighteningly sideways with a powerful bank and return to level flying.

"Holy hell! The rollercoaster left the tracks."

Again Rhys got no answer, because Maurice's call for directions was suddenly strong in Kieran's mind. He started to look for landmarks below and realised his ground-hugger perspective wasn't the best help.

"Check Krol's aerial memories and retrace the journey we made, Maurice. His viewpoint will suit you better than mine."

"Yes, of course. Thank you, Kieran."

A few moments later Maurice veered slightly, the power and rate of his wing beats increased with determined purpose, and his vision blurred.

"Why can't we see properly, Kieran? Is anything wrong?"

Kieran, as puzzled as Rhys and everyone else, switched to Krol's perception and saw absolutely nothing. His eyes were tightly closed.

"Wow, Rhys. Maurice is protecting himself with a special membrane and the only way Krol's eyes can cope with the speed is to keep them closed tight."

"Too fast for Krol? Gods! He doesn't even close them for power dives."

"The Maker is calling for great speed, Rhys. He needs us."

Wondering why he hadn't heard anything, Kieran rushed to check the Pearl link and was staggered by what he saw. His dismay registered with everyone before he could contain it and four concerned queries came at once.

"Sorry, everyone. Ranevargar's shields are fighting an unbelievable attack and I can't understand why I didn't feel it start."

"Will they hold, Kieran? Didn't you give him extra energy?"

"Um! ... Hang on ... The Pearl link's different too. I see ... He's done something to keep it hidden from Maynor while he uses it more strongly for himself. Wow! No worries about the shields, Mr B. He's got them backed up with the new energy I sent to the Grove."

"Can you see what's going on around him? If his shields are on there must be some other reason he called to Maurice for speed. Speak to him."

"I can't. He's in that deep-think he told us he needed."

"What's he thinking about?"

"It's too fast and way too complicated for me, Rhys. He's using his Pearl link though and I can follow that ... Sheba! He's called the Griffins to a rendezvous and they're coming from everywhere."

"All of them?"

"Almost ... about fifty, Mr B."

"Then there really must be another big change, because he needed them to look after the Realm when he was taken."

Tan spoke up. *"He must be properly reconnected with his Realm then, and that means he's not worried about Maynor interfering. Can you see what's going through the Pearl besides the shield energy, Kieran?"*

"You're way ahead of me, Tan. Hang on ... Yes, the link's busier every time I look at it."

"The Maker was strengthened by our contact and refreshes his mind with knowledge lost to my quietening. Kieran, I will need your assistance for the Boundary crossing. I am too occupied with storm generation to properly recall the way of it."

Rhys's explosion of incredulity expressed the group's astonishment. *"The Boundary? You've got to be kidding, Maurice. We can't be near it yet."*

"Ten minutes, Rhys. Our speed is considerable."

"Holy hell! Everything happens too quickly. That means Maynor's Castle is only a few minutes after that ... Kieran, we've got ten minutes to figure out how to get to Ranevargar. Maurice is too big to fit through any doors and those Power Masters can stop Krol and the rest of us."

"Be calm, Rhys! The Maker will be with us to guide our every action as soon as we pass the Boundary. His knowledge of the High Lords and the tactics they can employ is unsurpassed."

Kieran's mind raced and he kicked himself for assuming the flight to the Boundary would allow far more time for thinking ahead. If only he'd accessed Maurice's sense of progress. No, forget that. Think ahead.

"Ranevargar is paralysed and his abilities restrained by a golden helmet, Maurice. Will you be able to protect us while we deal with that? They point rod things that make us helpless. Could they affect you while you're flying?"

Maurice's mental snort of amusement was vastly reassuring. *"Kieran, I am a Realm Ruler and Protector. Let them try. It is time to close the storm channel of power and prepare for the Boundary crossing."*

The inflow of pure white energy ceased instantly. That, at least, was straightforward. Kieran's stomach lurched as Maurice slowed and headed downward. The protective eye membrane retreated and vision returned with a startling view of the Wall ahead. What?

"Maurice, we've always kept physical contact and walked through before.

I don't know what will happen if we're flying."

"Quickly! Show me! Landing will slow us and necessitate another accumulation of power."

Kieran filled his mind with his procedure for the previous crossing to Maynor's Realm.

"Yes, I see. The physical bond is important for your interesting method of transition. It is maintained and strengthened and, along with Krol, now includes me. Call the protection of your Opal and impose the image of our destination on all our minds, Kieran. That way the crossing will be seamless."

The Wall loomed, and Maurice's flight slowed dramatically and swerved to a parallel course while the red protective shielding built to completion. Another swerve brought the familiar change of reality, a short blurt which quickly cleared.

"We're through? What happened to all the disorientation?"

"This Boundary is no longer Unordered, Kieran."

*   *   *

"Kieran! Wonderful! You have arrived sooner than I expected."

The passage through the Boundary Wall was forgotten with this immediate and enthusiastic mental greeting as Kieran shared in a great five-fold mental cheer then watched joyous communication from Maurice and Krol.

"Ranevargar, thank goodness you're back with us. So many things happened and then Maurice flew so fast we're totally unprepared about what to do."

"My apologies, Kieran, but it was critical that I absorbed my first communication with Maurice. Maurice, slow your flight while with we discuss our strategy."

"Slow? Maurice said you called for speed."

"I felt it necessary to have Maynor focus all his attention and resources on me, Rhys, and your early arrival will give me a welcome respite when the shock of Maurice's presence shakes his confidence. Kieran, when you leave Maurice to release me from this prison you will be vulnerable to the arts of Maynor and his Court. I have devised a protective strategy which uses your demonstrated abilities but also requires your utmost cooperation."

Kieran was taken aback. Ranevargar had doubts about his cooperation? Hmm. It was something about that utmost. *"Why the qualification, Ranevargar? We're here to free you."*

"You have willingly opened your mind to me, Kieran, but this would be a step beyond, where I take complete control and act through you."

"Is it dangerous?"

"Not at all. It is a way for me to share our strengths and hold you secure against his every effort."

"I do trust you, Ranevargar. Go ahead."

"Wonderful, but first I must ask you to call stores of power for yourself and Maurice."

Kieran's assent was interrupted by a powerful probe questing against Maurice's mind shield.

Ranevargar spoke to everyone through Kieran's group link. *"Maynor sees Maurice. Listen everyone while I explain our approach."*

* * *

High above Lord Maynor's Castle keen Coarser eyes registered distant movement and instantly focused on the anomalous form moving across the sky. The perception of size and shape triggered vast alarm and a plummeting flight for the security of the home roost. The mind riding comfortably along for the routine patrol struggled for a moment to accept the reality of the image before raising alarms and firmly turning the Coursers towards the approaching impossibility.

Lord Maynor's anger at the old Lord's strangely effective provocation swayed to annoyance with an unwonted call for attention from the Castle rookery. Annoyance became puzzlement when the attendant image registered. Puzzlement morphed instantly into disbelief as Maynor seized control of Courser minds for a direct view.

Size and staggering shape filled his mind, a shape only seen in legends from the Human World. Memory of a conversation between the High King and Uirebon triggered, firmed, and with it came a partial understanding. This must be the failed Construct sent to order the Unordered Realm ... Ranevargar, interfering again! Well, whatever its fearsome appearance, no Construct could be a match for a Realm Lord in the exercise of power. Yes. Neutralise the Construct then give attention to denying Ranevargar the now certain use of his Pearl and ending his perverse interference.

Maynor reached with the redirected strength of thirteen Power Masters only to batter futilely against an aggravatingly familiar shield, and saw, with sudden alarm, that the passage of the Construct would have it above the Castle in minutes. Nexus power switched from Ranevargar to help repel the approaching form, again with no apparent effect.

Communication spread through the Castle as a threat warning reached every denizen.

The great structure of Castle Wards, dormant and unnecessary for the challenge against the High King, sprang to blazing life and, with apprehension an unwelcome and unexpected visitor to his thoughts, Maynor made his way to the closest battlement and directed resources to bolster his defences. He hastily sought an answer to the dilemma now facing him. The Wards would hold against physical entry, that was certain, but holding them strong would need the resources being used to subdue Ranevargar and acquire control of his Pearl.

"Ready our triads and assemble with haste in the Castle Courtyard."

The command, sent to his advisors and the thirteen Power Masters, received instant response from those inside the Castle and a delayed response from those transfixed by the spectacle above.

From his strategic battlement, High Lord Maynor again fought apprehension — a rare emotion for a High Lord — suppressing it with the force of his position and determination.

Let it wheel! Outside the Wards it could have little effect on those within, and the strength of his own call would rally the Court and steady everyone else.

"It is but a Construct and thus subject to the will of every High Lord. The Castle Wards hold it at bay."

Throughout the Castle the paralysis of wonder and worry lifted, partially, and after two more calls from their High Lord, almost completely. Yes, the High Lord was right. The gigantic shape circled dauntingly but did nothing else. With regard constantly shifting between the Wards and the mighty wings spread above, movement and purpose returned to the Castle denizens and its powerful visitors.

"Double the call on your reserves and transfer directly to me."

Thirteen alarmed Power Masters struggled to comply, with torrents of energy depleting their special gemstones at barely controllable levels, torrents of energy infusing the High Lord's Realm Stone with an aggregation of great power.

A terrible sound reverberated from above, a roar of challenge and defiance, chording primal fears within the Power Masters and all who heard it.

The call ceased abruptly as Maynor made the relatively simple change of rendering the Wards impenetrable to sound.

"Hold firm! That was nothing but sound, an expression of frustration against our Castle Wards. It can no longer affect us."

Suppressing his own reaction, Maynor exhorted the Power Masters to resume their energy transfer. Despite the immediacy of the construct above, the real solution must be subjugation of Ranevargar's mind and access to his Pearl, the only feasible controlling link to the Dragon.

The shaken Power Masters rallied but attention was wrenched to the great form above, suddenly limned with a brilliant nimbus of blue glow and descending with obvious purpose.

With wings spread in aggressive display, the massive Construct floated to land gently at the Ceremonial Entranceway to the Castle, a broad opening now blocked by the impenetrable Ward barrier. With a futile show of aggression, a massive front limb lifted high and reached to gouge at the shimmering barrier with savage, glinting claws. A blaze of light flared with the contact, along with a frightening scream of rage and pain.

Let it rage. Let it suffer. Let Ranevargar see how pointless was his interference.

A second and greater flare brightened the sky as, rising on its hind legs, the Construct gouged again, this time with both limbs. The scream increased then, unaccountably, ceased while a blue glow of power encased the now-poised claws, and then its body, with the same nimbus of its eerie descent.

What? Was it controlling its pain? The sudden silence and calmly deliberate pause gave Maynor a whisper of apprehension. Power was being applied. Applied with purpose?

Claws raked a vertical pathway down the barrier, peeling away layers of shimmering red while the Ward blazed with the stress of trying to hold its integrity.

Impossible! The whisper became a wind.

Maynor sent bolstering energy, but the Dragon repeated the double gouge, slicing now with apparent ease and without sign of pain. Methodically and inexorably, the claws cleared an opening large enough to accommodate the rest of its body. Head and shoulders moved into the gap and stilled.

Stilled? The blue nimbus intensified then washed, like a wave, through the whole Ward structure. Glowing blue absorbed shimmering red, Castle protection collapsed and the Construct, followed by one of Ranevargar's Flying Guardians, moved purposefully along the Ceremonial Entranceway to the Castle Courtyard.

Shaken by the failure of unassailable Wards, Maynor rushed from the battlement and joined his Power Masters to watch five figures scramble down the construct's spine and range themselves in front of the Guardian.

Transported by the Dragon? Brushing aside his confusion at this unexpected development, Lord Maynor silently instructed the Power Masters to use the rods which had been so effective at the encounter in

Ranevargar's Grove. Ten raised hands jerked in a reflex of release as their instruments radiated with a discordant blue glow. Maynor looked with disbelief to the triads functioning behind the Power Masters. Taken from Aglaron in Ranevargar's Central Grove and bound to his control, their partial dampening fields were having no effect.

Taking personal control, Maynor directed thirteen power flows to the same purpose. A great head lowered and golden eyes directed a gaze which sent his senses reeling.

"Cease, Maurice! Leave this to me."

The eyes blinked lazily, the head lifted, and Maynor's mind was released to a new shock of understanding.

Keryth? Keryth commanded the Dragon? No, more than that. The implication was overtaken by the sight of Keryth, one glowing blue hand clasped against his chest and the other pointing with a gesture of command at the Power Masters.

Thirteen flows of power ceased.

Thirteen Power Masters divested themselves of precious rubies.

Thirteen Power Masters knelt in submission while the Dark Child darted in a quick collection trip.

Shock compounded on shock for Lord Maynor at this revelation of yet another ability beyond comprehension. Three centuries developing control and direct mastery of power overmatched by an elf barely out of childhood, an elf whose mind and abilities he had studied carefully for months?

Realisation shook him to the core. A creature capable of ignoring the mightiest Wards in Faerie and freezing the mind of a High Lord at a glance, itself controlled by an elf who could wrest control from a Master of Power with a single hand gesture, meant the end of ambition.

Maynor studied the youthful figure watching him with an air of expectance and, assuming an aspect of command, closed the distance between them.

"You impose your presence here against my authority as Lord of this Realm. What is your purpose for this intrusion?"

Keryth took a small, confronting, step forward and Maynor quailed before an aura of command which reduced his own to a shadow.

"I am here for my friend, taken and held in full mockery of that very authority you claim. I am here to make you accountable to the High Court. I am here to end this destructive and unlawful Challenge. Do you wish to dispute my actions?"

Seconds passed, indecision and desperation raged as anger surged against this callow youth so confidently pronouncing the end of ambition.

Using the ruby energy gathered to lance at Ranevargar, adding the full force of free Nexus energy still under his control, Maynor struck, not Keryth but the Warrior at his side, the Warrior who meant so much. A foolish strike, springing partially from the lingering notion of leverage, and partially from an impulse for retaliation.

The Warrior jolted, startled, then laughed at the soft blue glow suddenly outlining his whole body.

"Enough!"

There was no laughter in the command which rang so clearly through the courtyard.

Keryth gestured again and Maynor watched the energy battering pointlessly against the Warrior disappear, watched keys of control unique to his mind alone dissolve, and watched the great flow of free energy return to the Nexus.

*   *   *

Recovering quietly while the High Castle Wards regained strength and stability, Uirebon jolted with startlement when his liege suddenly leapt to his feet, a purple aura of power radiating from his chest and wonder lighting his countenance.

"The Nexus energy has returned. Maynor no longer controls it."

"My Lord, make haste to construct new keys of control. It must be some mistake on his part."

"New keys are locked in place, Uirebon, readied on your earlier advice. Maynor still has formidable power, but with this energy returned we will eventually prevail. Ride with me again while we seek understanding. This is *not* a mistake Maynor would make."

"Maynor raised his Castle Wards. Even with the Nexus energy we cannot pass."

An instant of checking revealed the Wards were again inactive, and a hasty refocus showed thirteen quiescent pools of ruby energy and a flow of instantly familiar power.

"Maynor expends his personal energy for some reason. How quickly can we arrange a far-seeing?"

"Within minutes, my Lord, but only with the support of your Nexus energy."

"Yes, of course. I—"

An urgent request for communication seized the High King's attention and, recognising a member of the purloined triad, he gave wary acceptance.

"My Lord, the bonds of my compulsion are broken and I witness events my mind struggles to accept. Use me to view the confounding of Lord Maynor."

Aglaron reached ever so carefully, in case this was some devious ploy, into the open mind and, finding nothing but thoughts of relief and wonder, accessed the flow of vision. The wonder transferred to his own mind.

"Uirebon, watch with me. One of our lost triad members offers the witness of Maynor's undoing ... The sight is beyond belief and I need your help with understanding."

From a vantage point of no more than eight or ten metres, the watcher's sight presented an image definitely beyond belief, and way beyond comprehension. Lord Maynor was kneeling to Keryth.

*   *   *

Thirteen rubies, with centuries of painstakingly gathered energy, contained uselessly in the clothing of the Dark Child, Free Nexus energy, the foundation for all his ambitions, taken with little apparent effort, Lord Maynor clasped his Stone of Power and gathered again the authority of a Realm Lord.

"Leave my Realm. Only the High King has the right to dispute my command in this place."

"The right you denied your fellow Realm Lord? The right granted to the holder of a Realm Stone? Kneel in submission while my companions release Lord Ranevargar."

"Submission? I cannot. I am a Realm Lord."

There was no hand gesture this time, but when Keryth's eyes closed in fierce concentration, Maynor steeled himself. The expected mind assault didn't occur and, for the long moments before the Heir opened his eyes, nothing appeared to happen.

"Choose, Maynor!"

Choose between submission and some alternative?

Understanding came, along with fear and horror, when every link with his Court and the Power Masters dissolved to nothing. With rising panic his hand tightened at his chest where the call for protection was encountering a strange void.

A choice between losing his Realm Stone and submission was no choice at all, and Maynor dropped to one knee.

Keryth nodded a brief acknowledgement before turning to his companions, and a degree of connection with the Power Stone returned. Along with relief came a wash of understanding that Keryth had no actual interest in taking his Realm Stone, as well as a realisation that submission to such power and ability was in no way demeaning.

The Warrior and the Dark Child, accompanied by a peculiar sound, moved and disappeared through a Castle doorway, then every eye in the Courtyard followed suit when Keryth and his two remaining companions lifted their heads skyward.

The Flying Guardian trumpeted a clarion call to a host of plummeting aerial forms. The great chorus of answering calls stirred awe in every watcher as widespread wings changed plunging velocity to wheeling watchfulness with coordinated precision. Two Guardians detached and descended to land and eagerly greet the first Guardian and then the group of three.

*   *   *

Watching Rhys and Woorawa leave to face three Fetches would normally have had Kieran worried to the core, but ceding total control in this incredible manner meant any emotions expressed through his mind and body were Ranevargar's choice.

In the strangest experience ever he'd helped Maurice through the Castle Wards, caused the Power Masters to freely offer their energy rubies for collection, and forced Maynor to submission.

He'd made little communication with Ranevargar, who was totally preoccupied with insuring everything went according to the plan he'd hastily outlined in the minutes of final approach, but the discovery of the Fetches guarding Ranevargar's room, and seeing the proposed solution, had warranted a full intrusion. The answer, interrupted several times, came with assurance.

"Woorawa and Rhys will overcome any troubles, Kieran. The chant will confound the Fetches and allow Rhys to employ his Spook rope. Maurice will be watching and, if necessary, he will enclose them with the barrier he developed to repel power-formed creatures ... I need you very close to Maynor to maintain control, and because the watching Realms must be impressed with a sense of your confidence and ability. My Griffins arrive with powerful intentions of retribution against my captor which I need to calm. This partnership succeeds beyond my expectation."

Kieran turned his eyes to the sky — well, Ranevargar turned them — and at the same time passed a mixed message of joyful greeting and stern command to the vengeful host. Savage screams ceased abruptly and, while Kron and Kan landed, fifty watchful Guardians wheeled in spectacular display.

*   *   *

Maynor watched with renewed bewilderment when Keryth made greeting with two new Guardians, then gestured one arm skyward with a slow, circular movement. The fierce calls quieted and every Guardian assumed a coordinated formation of watchful control. Keryth could call on so many of Ranevargar's constructs and bring them unnoticed through the Realm Boundary? The rage of the single Guardian at the Central Grove had been easily contained by the Power Masters, but the angry power massed above?

"Lord Maynor, when Lord Ranevargar joins us we leave to speak with the High Court. You will accompany us and remain under my protection. Advise your Court and ready yourself for the flight."

Accompany? Protection? Flight? Thoughts and actions unfeasible mere minutes previously. Maynor accepted the implied release and rose to his feet. With all the resources backing his challenge stripped utterly away, an accounting with the High King was inevitable ... But right now? And flight with a Dragon whose glance could drown all will, or a Guardian angry at its maker's abduction? Maynor looked to the clearly amused young elf, then, perversely, hesitated, looking for an appropriate form of address.

"Yes, Lord Maynor. We fly because we must. The portal structure of Faerie is degraded to the point of ruin, drained of energy in defence of the High Castle. Choose your attendant and approach the Guardians."

Maynor hesitated again, because the primary Guardian had turned to seize an animal carcass attached to one of its companions, and beak and talons were working to rend and transfer gobbets of flesh.

"Hold a moment, lest in his hunger he mistakes you for a tasty morsel."

Maynor, with a distinct feeling this was a jest at his expense, held his dignity by gesturing for his principal Power Master.

The avid feeding left every mind with the appearance of Ranevargar, carefully supported by the Warrior and the Dark Child. A golden helmet dangled from the Warrior's hand and every eye in the courtyard watched the trio make its way slowly forward — slowly because Ranevargar was clearly relying on strong arms to keep him erect. Maynor, vastly relieved he'd made sure the Realm Lord's physical needs had been carefully tended, considered the strange stillness and half-closed eyes and wondered with new apprehension what accounting he would face for traumatising the old Lord.

A rumble of Dragon voice, counterpointed by the recognition calls of every Guardian, shook the Courtyard, and the Heir, discarding all authority, ran to enfold the shaky Realm Lord in welcoming arms.

Life and awareness returned as Ranevargar rallied and responded with smiles and obvious pleasure at the enthusiastic reception. Maynor watched excitement transform to quiet watchfulness when Keryth exchanged the formal double wrist clasp of welcome then directed the Warrior and the Dark Child to resume their support.

Words, softly spoken, but clearly heard in the hushed courtyard brought Maynor to a new puzzlement.

"Authority over your Realm is returned. I relinquish my temporary Stewardship."

To Maynor's great wonderment, Keryth produced from a compartment of his strange garb the very reason for holding Ranevargar captive.

He had reached through the Castle protections and taken Stewardship of Ranevargar's Realm? The Pearl glowed green at Ranevargar's touch and the old elf stood transfixed for what Maynor knew was a time of communion with his Realm. Keryth murmured to his companions, then cast his view around the courtyard while Ranevargar was ushered to a meeting with his Guardians.

Fixing his attention on one of the triads behind the Power Masters, Keryth nodded as if in recognition and raised a greeting hand.

"Gather the full High Court, my Lord, and prepare for our arrival."

That Aglaron was watching was no surprise to Maynor, the members of the commandeered triad would certainly seek to communicate with him when the holding bonds dissolved, but was Keryth discerning a link between an elven adept and the High King? Maybe it was a clever application of probabilities? No, there had been certainty in the manner of address.

* * *

Aglaron shared a startled look with Uirebon. "Keryth knows we watch?"

"Possibly an educated guess, my Lord, if he was aware the triad was yours."

"There was no guesswork involved. He turned without hesitation to the eyepiece and made a proper greeting."

"I agree, my Lord, along with a formal call to gather the full Court."

"What can have happened to my son, Uirebon? He looks well, apart from that outlandish costume, but he wields authority like a toy and displays abilities I wouldn't have considered possible."

Through the eyepiece came vision of preparation for flight.

"Maynor was divested of power with a hand gesture."

"My Lord, control of power is a straightforward matter compared with the assumption of Ranevargar's Pearl for temporary Stewardship of a Realm ... And why does he offer Lord Maynor protection? The mysterious Gemstone gifted by the Ancient People must be a factor, as well as Lord Ranevargar who ... What can that mean?"

Vision showed Lord Ranevargar assisted to a standing position on the shoulders of the Warrior and the Dark Child, with both hands resting in what to Uirebon looked like benediction on the lowered head of the Dragon Construct. A green glow of energy encompassed the whole group.

"That is Ranevargar's energy signature and he expends it copiously. The purpose is beyond me, but from the rapt expressions of those with him, it must be highly significant ... We cannot call a Full Court. Lady Narello cannot be present. Uirebon, I am gravely uncertain about this meeting. In this human persona, Keryth does not know me."

Uirebon, at a loss for a worthwhile response, remained silent.

Ranevargar's foot shifted slightly and Rhys adjusted his shoulder to keep him steady while he made the physical contact with Maurice that was essential to complete the return of his lost memories.

A quick glance at Woorawa showed him staring upwards through the green glow to where Ranevargar's hands were resting just below Maurice's golden eyes. They'd used this same tactic for Kieran, but the appearance of the glow and the sense of joy spilling from Maurice was making this yet another incredible experience. A shared experience too, because Kieran, in his not-K voice, had called for the group physical contact he liked for special situations, and everyone was gathered close in the space between Maurice's mighty legs. What was Woorawa thinking? A glance had shown the usual half-smile that made you feel like smiling along with him. *Gods!* So different to the intense concentration of a short while ago when the mystery of his chant had stilled the three Fetches directing fear and submission at them, and held them motionless long enough to dispel with a super-charged Spook rope.

Kieran's hand tightened on his shoulder. It felt good but quickly relaxed. Did it mean something? Probably, but it was hard to tell while Ranevargar was controlling him. Well, he'd be himself again when Maurice started flying. How long was this contact going to last? It must look weird to all those elves gathered in the courtyard. Kieran's grip tightened again.

* * *

Amazing! The awareness of all the unbelievable things Ranevargar had had him doing was overridden at the moment when Ranevargar's hands make contact with Maurice and the flood of joyous communion between Realm Lord and Construct filled their minds. Information poured both ways and, linked in this uniquely complete way, Kieran watched the already unfathomable complexity of Ranevargar's mind blossom and expand yet again.

With an understanding that the ultimate trust he'd given was being returned, Kieran watched memories and lost abilities return and refresh in Ranevargar's mind. Unbelievable memories — there was the method for creating a new Maurice, strange knowledge of the interaction between the Outer Realm Boundaries and the Chaos they held at bay, and, yes, there was the knowledge of portal construction. There was even a memory of Ranevargar monitoring and directing Nexus energy: the High King's prerogative. How far back did these memories extend?

"Later, Kieran. Maurice and I have finished our exchange and it is time to move. I will relinquish control when we are airborne and Maynor is separated from the resources of his Castle and Court."

The green glow disappeared, Ranevargar dropped, quite nimbly, to the ground, and Kieran listened to himself take charge again.

"Lord Ranevargar, the High King has made summons for a High Council and I ask for your company as sponsor and friend."

"That will be both an honour and a pleasure, Kieran. Will I travel with you or with my Guardian?"

"Your Guardian has striven mightily for your release, and bearing you to the High Castle would be a well-deserved honour."

Ranevargar nodded and moved towards Krol.

"Woorawa, instruct Lord Maynor and his attendant in the use of a Guardian harness and helmet, then return to the Dragon."

Woorawa gave a startled look, then beckoned to Maynor and ran to Kron and Kan.

Kieran pointed to Maurice with a gesture of authority and called the full channel of power he would need for this difficult takeoff from the confines of a courtyard. A great nimbus of blue glow surrounded Maurice's head then flowed like a river of light to cover both wings while the real power was taken and readied for use.

"Lead the way, Rhys. These Castle elves and any others watching will see that in the Realms the five companions are riders and friends of the Dragon. We will awe them with the spectacle of his takeoff."

Rhys gave Kieran a look of recognition that he knew it was really Ranevargar speaking, then turned to give the nearby scaly leg a few friendly whacks. "Give them all something to remember, Maurice. A short burst of the eye treatment should do it."

Maurice's head lowered and a message must have passed, because Rhys's face lit up with one of his cheeky grins. He turned again, pointed, and twelve Power Masters and the triads behind them dropped involuntarily to their knees as the eyes of the Dragon engulfed their will. Three more hand gestures subjected the onlookers from the three remaining Court sides to the same gaze before Rhys's blithe wave of dismissal released them all.

"Thanks, Maurice."

Maurice's head inclined in acknowledgement.

The climb up Maurice's back through the shimmering blue glow was a brief, surreal impression in the minds of the Court watchers, overridden completely when unseen power lifted him high enough above the Castle ramparts to allow unhindered wing beats.

*   *   *

As if in response to his wishes, vision of the Castle below filled Tan's mind as Dragon eyes watched Krol and the other two Guardians launch from the courtyard and pour strength into the task of gaining height and then positioning themselves slightly behind. Fifty other Guardians shifted their watchful circling to a double V of convoy flying.

"My friends, we fly to a meeting of the High Court. I will continue to act through Kieran till I am certain of Lord Maynor's full compliance."

"Is Kieran all right?"

"Yes, Rhys. He will be himself soon, but I need his strength to monitor a number of things first. He should be with you in a matter of minutes."

"Why is Maynor receiving our protection?"

"He goes to face the High King, Tan, but the protection is necessary for Kieran's wellbeing. Maynor has a hold over his unshielded mind which we need to guard against."

"We?"

"Yes, Mr B. Together, Kieran and I are formidable. As you know, he has abilities that are beyond me, but my contact with Maurice is returning my own unique abilities and combined we are, as I said, formidable."

"Have you recovered the knowledge about portals?"

"I have, Tan, and as soon as we are clear of all this complication Kieran will be able to master the necessary techniques. The news is not all good, however. The conflict between Maynor and the High King has seriously damaged the underlying portal structure and delay is inevitable while it is repaired."

"You are trying to be gentle with us, Ranevargar. How lengthy is the delay?"

"I can't make a definitive response, Mr B, as there are many factors for consideration, but the delay could well be significant ... Lord Maynor is seeking to covertly manipulate Kron's mind. Excuse me. Kieran will be with you shortly."

Except for the gift of vision through Maurice's eyes, Ranevargar's presence went, and Tan fought to contain his disappointment.

Significant? Surely that must mean a long time? *No! Don't dwell on it. Wait and see what Kieran has to say. He'll work something out.*

The wait went on and on, with the only input the passing view of the Realm below.

Maurice's occasional head twist checked on the Griffins behind, with Krol and Ranevargar at the apex of the formation and Kron and Kan flanking.

All the riders' faces were hidden behind the protective helmets, but Maynor was very distinctive with the finery of his red leathers. What did Ranevargar mean by a hold? Surely Kieran's shields would keep him safe? And Woorawa's mysterious chant was strong enough to hold three Fetches? How had Ranevargar known that?

And what about this High King they were flying to meet? Tan remembered Ranevargar describing him as the most powerful elf in all of Faerie. If he wasn't angry, he might be able to help with the portal ... It might be a good idea if Kieran and Ranevargar joined up again to face him.

Whoa! The world suddenly rotated, the view went crazy, steadied to show the ground below rushing towards them, then changed to clear sky. A wash of pleasure was a message that Maurice was revelling in his flying.

"Yo, everyone! Maurice is just venting for a bit."

"Kieran!"

Tan joined the excited, fourfold mental shout.

"Yep! It's me, while Ranevargar gets himself together. He's taking control again before we get to the High Castle, so they don't argue with us."

"Gets himself together?"

"Yes, Mr B, we've had so much stuff to watch he hasn't had a proper chance since his physical contact with Maurice."

"You sound like you're all right, Kieran, but it was pretty weird when Ranevargar was controlling you, like you were a different person."

"It was weird for me too, Rhys, but it was a good weird and it sure worked. I can hardly believe some of what we did."

"Some? Don't you mean all? The only thing that looked like it was you was the blue glow when Maurice powered up for flying again."

"One of the biggest things was when we made Maynor kneel, Woorawa, and that was all me. Ranevargar hasn't got a clue how I can directly take over a Realm Stone, and it was me protecting Rhys when Maynor threw all that ruby energy at him."

"When you made me glow blue and Woorawa collected all those rubies? I didn't feel a thing."

"Maynor was desperate by then, Rhys, but Ranevargar knew he wouldn't

give up without trying something, so he got me to reinforce everyone's shields."

"What did Ranevargar mean about Maynor having a hold over you?"

"I don't know. I only learnt about it when he answered your question, Tan, so it was a shock to me too. We're having a planning time once we cross the High King's Boundary and I'm sure I'll find out then."

"Another Boundary? The Opal is sure working overtime."

"It never stops. The energy channel from the Nexus place is permanent, Woorawa, and I am not used to that yet, but I won't need the Opal for this Boundary, because the High King will open it for us."

"Are you sure? Bringing a Dragon and fifty Griffins through will need an awful lot of power, and I thought he had none left."

"I don't know, Mr B. We gave him back his Nexus power, so that probably covers it."

"You should have kept it in case he tries something else against us."

"It's needed to help the Realms keep working properly, Rhys. Ranevargar didn't even think of keeping it."

"Right! Well, the Opal's probably better anyway. What's going to happen with the High King?"

"We told him to summon his High Council, so I guess they'll decide what to do about Maynor's Challenge."

"Ha! Is that all? What about the kidnapping and all the other stuff they've done to us? Are they going to keep doing that?"

"They wouldn't dare! We've got Ranevargar and Maurice and all these Guardians backing us and I'll throw a zillion tons of Opal energy at them if they even look like trying."

Kieran's determination and conviction was so strong Mr B got goosebumps.

"Yay! Way to go, Kieran! Make them all kneel like Maynor did."

Rhys's suggestion built a mental image which morphed Kieran's determination into the first feeling of amusement in quite a while.

"The ruler of Faerie and all his Realm Lords getting their knees dirty? Doubts, Rhys!"

"One look from Maurice and they'd be on their stomachs, not just their knees ... and then they can say why they're after us."

"Ranevargar already knows a lot, but we haven't had a chance to talk about it."

"He knows?"

"Maynor must have told him things while he was still a prisoner, Mr B, which is a bit curious."

"It's even more curious that he's kept it to himself. Hasn't he shared every-thing else that's happened?"

"I can't believe how much he's shared, Mr B. When we're a double mind I can see every single thing he's thinking."

"Double mind?"

"That's the main way I see it, Tan. He can use everything I know as well as everything he knows, and even put them together for things neither of us can do."

"That doesn't sound right, like getting something for nothing."

"I knew how to soak up the energy from the Rubies, Tan, and Ranevargar can't do that, but there's no way I could take instant control of thirteen Power Masters' minds. The double mind put all that together in one smooth action."

"I see ... I think I see."

Woorawa pushed in. "Soaking up energy instead of calling it, Kieran? You've never talked about that before."

"That's because I forgot I could do it. Ranevargar knew from watching my memories of how I fought off the big mental attack at home and he got me to do it again." Kieran laughed. "And you can't make me practise it because it only works when someone's attacking with lots of energy."

"Yeah! I'll talk to Maurice and Ranevargar then. They can attack you."

"That is a great idea, Woorawa. It is an excellent skill which I would like to learn."

"Maurice! You've been listening?"

"Of course, Woorawa. The Maker is incommunicado while he re-estab-lishes what was lost. Kieran would have to provide the energy for any prac-tice, because I have none to spare myself, but it would be a valuable exercise for all of us."

"Hey! Will your eye thing work against this Council we're meeting?"

"I'm sure it will, Rhys, but we must be very careful to follow the Maker's lead in the coming situation. We deal with the High Council of all Faerie, not simply one rebel Realm Lord. He has dealt with powerful personali-ties for many centuries and he has the knowledge and skills to negotiate outcomes which will benefit all ... Yes, all, Rhys, including our own group. The goodwill and assistance of the High Council could well be vital to our endeavours."

"What if they try to take Rhys again? They were all part of it, Maurice."

Dragon amusement washed through everyone. "My reaction as his protector, let alone any redress from the Maker/Kieran merge, would be burnt into their memories forever, Tan. A meeting of the High Council will, however, be free of any such petty conniving."

"Do you think Maynor will end up in prison?"

"Never, Rhys. That is not the elven way."

"Yes, it is! Ranevargar was treated much worse than just prison. His body was paralysed and his mind was trapped by that helmet. Maynor should get a taste of his own treatment."

"My own reaction would be to take his mind in thrall till he willingly undertook re-education, but Maker/Kieran placed him under their protection ... Look ahead. The High Realm Boundary Wall is visible."

Since everyone was seeing with Maurice's vision the looking was already happening, but interpretation was independent.

"Purple?"

"Yes, Rhys. I think it is just a signifier for the High King ... like Kieran's blue."

Woorawa laughed. *"Kieran's blue wouldn't work very well for a Wall. It's the same colour as the sky."*

"It would for dawn and dusk. It'd be totally specco then."

Mr B interrupted. *"I'm more interested in whether the colour uses much power. It might mean the High King hasn't got enough energy to try something. What do you think, Kieran?"*

"I don't know anything about the Boundaries except how to get through them, Mr B ... Do you know, Maurice?"

"Not without accessing and studying the Maker's knowledge. Don't be concerned about the High King, Mr B. The Maker is confident that nothing untoward will happen."

Kieran was surprised. *"Are you talking to him, Maurice? My link shows his mind's working at about a thousand miles an hour."*

"No, Kieran. He passed a tentative plan of action while we were in communion. We will hear from him soon though, as the Boundary crossing is now only minutes away."

"How long from the crossing to the High Castle?"

"I'm not sure, Tan. The High Realm is new territory for me, but my understanding of its relative size means that even at this slow speed we will be there soon."

"Slow? Are the Griffins struggling to keep up?"

"No, Rhys, but I am constantly monitoring Krol because, although the food brought by his companions has helped, his strength is not recovered."

"What? Is he all right? Kieran, we should have boosted him back at Maynor's Castle. Get him to land on Maurice's back again."

Kieran, as concerned as Rhys for Krol's wellbeing, reached to check.

"He's flying at about two-thirds effort, Rhys, and he's proud as anything

to be carrying Ranevargar and leading all the other Griffins. He's coping, so he'd be mad as a snake if we change that, and Ranevargar's helping him somehow ... It's like Maurice's power takeoffs ... But I don't know how Ranevargar's doing it."

"He told us about that back at the Groves, Kieran."

"I know, and Maurice does it with his takeoffs, but that's built in. Ranevargar's applying it to Krol externally."

"Gods! The Wall is clearer. Purple makes it look amazing."

That focused everyone's attention on the looming Boundary.

"It's different, Kieran. Are you or Maurice screening out all the normal effects?"

A clear voice supplied the answer. *"Very different, Mr B. It is structured without the disturbing effects of a natural Boundary."*

"Ranevargar! Is your brain unjumbled yet?"

"Never, Rhys. By the time I sort out one problem three more have taken its place, but I am much recovered, thank you."

"What about your body? We can give you another health boost when we land. Your legs were pretty wonky."

"Wonky ... I see. Yes, they were, but riding Krol is a wonderful stimulation for both my mind and my body."

"Great! ... Are you going to tell us about any dramas before you go all weird again with Kieran?"

"I will be working with Kieran for an exceedingly dramatic presence, Rhys, but apart from facing ten Fetches there should be nothing threatening."

"Ten!"

Kieran was as startled as everyone till he checked. *"Ranevargar's learning about stirring, Rhys. The Fetches won't be after us ... They're kind of ceremonial guards for the High King ... How do you know that, Ranevargar?"*

"I made brief contact to confirm the Boundary is ready for our passage, Kieran, and to inform the High King that for Maurice's inclusion the Council meeting should convene in the Great Courtyard."

"I will be included, Maker?"

"Of course, Maurice, as advisor to Kieran and as the sole and primary Guardian of a reawakened Realm."

"Wow! Neat, Maurice! They'll sure listen when you've got things to say."

"Indeed they will, Rhys, but at this meeting Kieran's voice will speak for us all."

"Like at Maynor's Castle?"

"Yes, Tan, but with even more authority. The Realms must see that his position cannot be questioned."

Mr B voiced the thought in everyone's mind. *"More than with Maynor?"*

"Yes ... But the Boundary looms and Kieran and I must make ready."

Ranevargar's voice went silent and Rhys understood that Kieran was now embarked on a joint experience with Ranevargar that was even more important than the rescue at Maynor's Castle.

The view swivelled to the rear and showed all the Griffins bunching into a tight group and moving close. Krol was so close he'd only have to manoeuvre a couple of metres and he'd be able to take the piggyback hold. Oh boy! The close piercing gaze of fifty Griffins sure was an awesome sight.

"Don't worry, Rhys. I will protect you if the Boundary sends them into a frenzy."

What? Was he serious? No, it was more stirring. *"Hey! You're watching my thoughts!"*

"Of course, Rhys, as you all agreed. I am your backup while Kieran and Ranevargar are otherwise occupied."

Rhys didn't answer for a moment because Maurice's convoy check finished and he turned his attention to the fast-approaching Boundary.

"Is that Wall for real?"

"Definitely, Rhys. We are about to pass through it.

"I mean it's ... it's beautiful."

*   *   *

Ranevargar did something which tightened their mindlink so much that Kieran lost his general link with Rhys and the others. No, not quite. It was still there but suppressed.

"Yes, Kieran. Your shields protect us from any outside intrusion, but you might need privacy for the heavy decisions ahead of you."

"How heavy? I don't like the sound of that."

"I can see no way for you to leave the Realms in the near future. The great Realm-wide portal system has been so drained of power that its very struc-ture has degraded to the point of collapse."

"The Opal can put the power back."

"Yes, Kieran. It can return the power and optimise the process, but I am afraid the repair itself is a time-consuming growth process which could take several years."

"Years! That's way too long."

"Very much so, especially for Tan and Woorawa, when you take account of the different time rates."

"Time rates?"

"A day in Faerie equates to more than four in the Human World."

"What? We've been away for ... over a month? That's unbelievable. Ranevargar, that's eight or nine home years before the portal's ready. We'll have to find another way."

"I don't know of any. Kieran, I now have the details of how you came to be in the Human World."

"The way you say that means I really am an elf. Is the High King truly my father?"

"He believed he was paving the way for his Heir."

"Me? High King? That's crazy!" The qualification registered. *"Why do you say believed?"*

"Widderkin are not accepted at any level in Courts of the Realm and you were being conditioned to have a proper outlook."

"My own father would do that to me? It's not conditioning, it's brainwashing, and that's ... barbaric."

"Don't judge too harshly or too hastily, Kieran. The strictures of our underlying culture are powerful indeed."

"I do judge. It's cruel and unforgivable."

"Far too hasty, Kieran, since you willingly agreed to the conditioning yourself."

"No, I didn't ... That doesn't feel right. Ranevargar, are you sure?"

"I can assure you it is, and you will see for yourself when I show you the information I have drawn from Maynor."

"I didn't have Rhys then."

"No, you had someone else. Someone who meant as much to you as Rhys does."

"They couldn't have."

"Of course they could."

"Well, it still doesn't feel right. Who was it?"

"His name is Pethron."

"Is?"

"Of course. He hasn't been disposed of."

Ranevargar's 'is' rang in Kieran's mind with a strong presence. *"He's still involved somehow?"*

"Very much so, Kieran. For the Realm, and for your brightest prospects, he agreed to lose you."

"I wouldn't have agreed. You'll have to show me before I can accept it's true."

"It happened, Kieran, but you are right. You wouldn't have agreed, so why do you think you did?"

"*I wouldn't, but I did? It's mind tricks again, isn't it?*"

"*The most devious and adroit strategy of mind manipulation I have ever encountered.*"

"*That means Maynor ... Maynor worked on my mind so I agreed?... That doesn't make sense either. If I became eligible that would make it harder for him to be High King.*"

"*Your conditioning was a ploy to gain mastery of Nexus energy — a very successful ploy.*"

"*Ye gods! I was a pawn for his power game?*"

"*As the game turns I would describe you as a knight rather than a pawn. Along with the High King, the Lore Master and Lady Narello, Maynor manipulated every major player in the Realms.*"

"*Why this roundabout way of telling me?*"

"*How does the knight piece stand in your judgement, Kieran?*"

"*Um! Right! I see! ... I can't judge the High King and not myself when he was tricked as much as I was, you mean?*"

Relief, and then satisfaction, played across Ranevargar's mind, along with a sense of a new respect. "*Yes, Kieran, and, I hope, acceptance. My primary concern is that alienation will hurt both you and your father. Beyond that is the need for harmony and cooperation while the Realms recover.*"

"*I can accept how the High King acted, Ranevargar, especially if I agreed to it, but it's weird too, because my memories tell me I don't even have a father. Do you think I'll remember him when we meet?*"

"*Not a chance. Lord Maynor worked on your mind for months, crafting and reinforcing your current persona with exceptional brilliance. He holds your elven memories in much the same way you held mine.*"

"*I don't like that.*"

"*Neither do I. It is one of the reasons we have him under our protection, and before he returns to his Realm we must do something about it.*"

"*We?*"

"*Well, mostly me, but it will be best if he believes it is you.*"

"*Are we going to call on the Opal much?*"

"*You anticipate me. Yes, we need you to appear unassailable again, and a demonstration of that mysterious new channel would be particularly valuable.*"

"*No worries. What are you going to do with it? That's an awful lot of energy.*"

"*It will be most impressive, Kieran.*"

"*Will I call ... What was that?*"

"*We passed the High Realm Boundary. We must merge. Watch and take full note of every word and action made by the High King and the three Realm Lords."*

"Three? There are only Uirebon and Maynor."

"With our aid, Lady Narello could well make a surprise appearance."

* * *

The High King surveyed the rush of preparation as the Great Courtyard was readied for an outdoor Council.

"Warn everyone that the central area must be clear well before the Dragon makes its landing and make clear that close sighting could well cause paralysing fear." Aglaron turned and switched to normal speech. "What do you make of Ranevargar's call for this unconventional meeting, Uirebon? Anything more than inclusion of the Construct?"

"An interesting thought, my Lord. It does make the proceedings open to every interested observer. Maybe your son wants all the Realms to hear any decisions."

"I am heartened that he has called a Council. Against the strength he demonstrated at Maynor's Castle, we could deny him nothing."

"I am heartened too, my Lord, and particularly by his association with Ranevargar who would, by nature, be a steadying influence."

"Yes, there was great joy shown at his release."

Despite knowing the arrival was still minutes away, Uirebon scanned the sky. It was hard not to with almost every elf gathered at the Courtyard sides doing just that.

"What do you make of that moment when Maynor dropped to his knees?"

"Beyond the shock of an act so much against his nature and position? Yet another mystery, my Lord, but a very powerful mystery whatever its nature. Maynor made no apparent effort at resistance."

"We could well be subject to the same treatment."

"I don't believe so, my Lord. The manner of Keryth's call for a Council implies a degree of respect for our forms of governance. As does bringing Maynor to face a formal Council."

"I wonder ... what other matters might he bring to the Council?"

"Our actions regarding his treatment and his companions, you mean? I hope Ranevargar has advised him of the Court's attitude to Widderkin and the wisdom of discretion."

Aglaron shook his head. "The authority he can command renders discretion meaningless and he has always been strong to act on his convictions."

"We don't know that, my Lord. He reacts with the persona Maynor gave him."

"Maybe, but his actions against Maynor were not those of any human."

"You think he might challenge the long established conventions of our Courts?"

That brought a strong reaction. "Challenge! That is laughable, Uirebon. He is a new force in the Realms. Maynor's Court knelt at a glance from the Dragon and ours would do the same. For all we know this High Council meeting could be his platform for a formal challenge to my position."

After a startled look Uirebon shook his head. "He is too young, my Lord, and he has no experience. Your plan after Maynor's conditioning was for four hundred years of carefully developing his management skills and expertise with every Court in the Realms. I don't believe he will consider it."

"I would agree, if we faced Keryth, but almost from the beginning this persona of Maynor's has had strength and determination beyond our ability to manage."

"I see. Yes, there are too many unknowns. We can only—"

The clarion call of the warning bell peeled from the highest Watchtower, cutting off every conversation and turning every eye to the sky. Lesser bells from the multitude of other towers and Castle spires joined with a riot of ringing. Shaking his head against the sound, Aglaron sent a call for silence and raised an arm to indicate the direction of approach. Watchers in the towers observed the oncoming phalanx with growing incredulity and so much alarm that Aglaron had to make a call for calm.

"Quell your fear. Despite their appearance these visitors are guests, arriving under the aegis of the High Court."

A monstrous form swept across the sky, shocking Aglaron and Uirebon, who'd already seen it, with no less force than the host of gathered elves. *Truly monstrous.* A hasty probe faltered against a glowing aura and failed.

"This is not the real Dragon, Uirebon. We saw it in Maynor's courtyard."

Uirebon could only gasp because the passing of the Dragon revealed formation after formation of countless flying Guardians filling the sky.

"This is a display of power, my Lord, some kind of projection. That Dragon would not fit in three of our courtyards, and to my knowledge Ranevargar supports a population of some fifty or sixty flying Guardians. Can you see any flow of energy?"

"Yes, centred on the Dragon's back, a flood of energy."

The Dragon returned, slowly descended with outspread wings to the Courtyard, and steadily diminished in size till it landed and folded its wings. The four flying Guardians which landed in its wake — a spectacle of great wonder with the increasingly rare occasion of a visit from their Realm Lord — held but a moment of attention as every gaze returned to watch the glowing creature cast its eyes in a careful scan of everything around. The huge golden orbs rested for a moment on Aglaron, switched to the five power adepts arrayed behind him, then switched again to the silent Fetches each was controlling. A deep but soft rumble passed a message of recognition and warning.

"My Lord, alert everyone to look at the Dragon's eyes with no more than a passing glance lest their minds are caught."

"Maynor's people weren't caught till the Warrior directed it and the Dragon added intent to his gaze ... Ranevargar dismounts."

Maynor and his Power Master were also dismounting, but once again attention turned to the Dragon, where the blue aura was suddenly brighter and flowing with a strange impression of life. A figure appeared and looked purposefully around the courtyard in much the same manner as the Dragon had. Four more figures emerged and made their own survey, this time with nothing more apparent than ordinary curiosity.

The first figure, clearly Keryth despite the clothing which emphasised a curiously human aspect, held both arms wide and, astonishingly, levitated to glide smoothly to meet with Ranevargar beside the flying Guardian. Aglaron looked for Uirebon's reaction.

"Another blatant display of strength. One of my Centres studies this ability with rare application because of the profligate call on power."

Aglaron nodded, wondering how Keryth could possibly have become a master of yet another extraordinary ability.

The four remaining figures made a more normal descent, scrambling with the confidence of familiarity from the Dragon's back and moving to join Ranevargar. The Warrior briefly rested a hand on the old Realm Lord's brow then, curiously, turned with Keryth to do the same thing to the flying Guardian.

Uirebon spoke softly. "My Lord, it has the appearance of a minor ritual, but I think we just witnessed the laying on of hands. Ranevargar's incarceration would have been a sore trial for any elf. He couldn't support himself after his release and he now stands steady."

To Aglaron's mind the degree of recovery was yet another puzzle for consideration. The old elf had transitioned from apparent frailty to capably flying from Maynor's Castle, but there was also something different about his general demeanour, a subtle air of confidence and vitality. Uirebon must be right ... But what of the Guardian? Why would it be singled out for a healing?

Maynor, holding himself with a degree of dignity, moved with his representative to join Keryth's quiet approach. Aglaron gave him a piercing gaze but was distracted by the actions of the Guardian when, with a cry of what must be satisfaction, it launched with partially spread wings past two of its companions and lunged for one of the carcasses attached to the fourth. With a display of ravenous hunger the flesh was rent and rapidly devoured.

"High King Aglaron, I thank you for calling this High Council and making accommodation for the needs of my friends and colleagues."

The formality of this greeting from his own son filled Aglaron with a sense of wrongness and great unease, and at the same time brought the realisation that he was indeed about to treat with an unknown personality.

"Under the aegis of the Council I welcome you here in the interests of harmony and resolution. My own welcome is personal and unconditional, with a deep yearning for understanding ... How should I address you?"

"Yes, that is a confusion. Call me Kieran." His voice softened and became personal. "I am more than one person, my father, as you well know. Your actions have brought complication to all levels of our lives. Before the Council convenes, and in complete privacy, I have important knowledge to share with you and Lord Uirebon."

Aglaron, affected and conflicted by the mix of personal and detached, watched Kieran change his stance and project his presence through the Courtyard. Aglaron managed to resist the impulse to take a backward step of deference in the face of so much authority.

"Know that by the working of this ancient Realm Stone the Lost Realm is no longer lost. The Unordered Realm is now ordered and under my Stewardship. For the harmony of all Realms the High Council should recognise my place at this table as that of a Realm Lord."

The mantle of authority dropped as bewilderingly as it had appeared, and into the astonished hush came a conversational request.

"I and my party have urgent need of amenities and refreshment. May we take advantage of your hosting?"

Aglaron hurriedly gestured for escorts and watched all eight visitors guided through the main entrance.

"That was somewhat unnerving, Uirebon, but also reassuring."

"More than somewhat, my Lord. Having to call him Kieran rather than Keryth will be a complication. Every Court in the Realms will seek an explanation. That assumption of authority, and it's almost instant casting aside, was more than unnerving, and was, in my mind, another message of hidden power."

"Hidden? Every elf present recognised its force. I could barely contain my own impulse to show deference."

"Yes, my Lord, but I have a sense it was wielded as a mere tool of the moment. We were shown a glimpse of great knowledge or experience."

"Again, you understate, Uirebon. Not only has he announced Stewardship and Restoration of the Lost Realm, that artefact he wields is the instrument which realigned the Nexus."

Uirebon stared at his liege in great wonderment. "Keryth ... I mean Kieran, is part of that? My Lord ... I am lost."

"Yes. But along with that unnerving authority he also showed a clear intention for harmony."

The Warrior and the Dark Child reappeared and, after a backward glance and survey of the Courtyard, moved eagerly to the food-laden tables at one side. The Warrior turned to stare intently at Aglaron then, deliberately dismissing him, shared a chunk of honey-bread with his companion.

"There was aggression and displeasure in that look, Uirebon."

"Yes, but controlled and rather overridden by his interest in the food."

"Look at them, Uirebon. That is more than ordinary hunger, and the Guardian was almost desperate. There is a story of hardship. I wonder how long they were in the Unordered Realm?"

Two more companions appeared and moved quickly to the tables.

"Long enough to require rationing their food supply it would seem. My Lord, have you considered your approach with Maynor? He has been brought here to answer for his actions."

"My immediate reaction is harsh but not considered, Uirebon, and the protection he has been granted is a puzzle. It limits the consequences available and, more importantly, means we lack the information to make a proper decision. We will learn more, either from the private communication or in the Full Council."

Keryth/Kieran appeared, accompanied by Lord Ranevargar, and, with a look indicating his purpose, joined his companions. Maynor and his attendant also appeared and, after a question to their escort, were guided to a place at the formal Council table.

"Maynor appears subdued, my Lord, and clearly concerned by the presence of the Dragon. His head turns toward it constantly."

"And then returns to Keryth with even more concentration. I have images, from the memory of the triad eyepiece, of Maynor's Castle Wards flaring and collapsing to nothing when the Dragon forced its way through them. Maynor is constrained by powers beyond him. Of course he is subdued. I watch the Dragon with much the same wariness ... Do we know anything of its abilities?"

"Apart from it being Ranevargar's final attempt at creating a Construct, very little. It has been hidden for over six hundred years in the Lost Realm."

"You must have something stored in one of your study Centres. Its effects when it was active were significant for every Realm."

"There will certainly be historical notes about those effects, but I doubt there will be knowledge of the Dragon itself. You know how guarded Ranevargar has always been about his skills of life mastery. I—"

Uirebon stopped speaking, held by the Dragon's direct gaze till its head abruptly lifted.

"It knew we were discussing it?"

"Maybe, Uirebon, but something distracts it. Look, Keryth is also distracted."

And, indeed, the young elf was suddenly frozen with concentration. His arm lifted and a glowing blue layer appeared above the length and breadth of the Courtyard. Understanding came to Aglaron as he recognised the all-too-familiar emanations of a Chaos Incursion. While he frantically called for defensive Nexus power, he watched the blue layer enfold the Incursion with a living net then steadily contract till it became a single point of brilliant light which disappeared completely.

Every disbelieving eye rested on the young figure while the glow at his chest dispersed and his concentration turned to immediate awareness. The raised arm moved to point at Maynor.

"Your influence over Lady Narello manifests, with a display of her displeasure at your reduced situation and annoyance for the exclusion of her physical presence. Inform Lady Narello that despite this ill-considered outburst her position in this Council is a right and a responsibility. Further, inform her that I will facilitate her presence."

Maynor nodded, and in the strained silence Keryth spoke to his companions, gathered an assortment of food from the table, linked arms with the Ranevargar in a curiously significant way and looked to the High King.

"Stand with me, Uirebon, while I return the Nexus energy I called. Keryth approaches for an informal discussion."

"Of course, my Lord, but how should we treat with him? With every minute that passes I feel more inadequate as a Lore Master."

"As do I in my role of High King."

A certain dryness in Aglaron's tone helped Uirebon repress his feelings of inadequacy.

"He commands the situation, Uirebon, so we follow his lead and treat as he treats ... Ranevargar looks tired and withdrawn again."

Keryth and Ranevargar paused, turned toward Maynor momentarily, then finished their approach.

Keryth passed his assortment of food to Ranevargar and, brushing his hands clean, extended both arms for a full double wrist clasp. He smiled at its completion, repeated the action with Uirebon then reclaimed his food. Quite casually, he bit and chewed the corner of a piece of honey-bread while he watched Ranevargar make the double clasps.

"We have been eating nothing but Ranevargar's travel bread for days now, Father, so honey-bread is extra delicious. Rhys's stomach started rumbling when he saw all the good food."

Taken aback to be talking about a rumbling stomach, as well as the easy setting of a relaxed conversation, Aglaron looked to the four companions. "Rhys is the name of the Warrior? He certainly attacks his food with gusto."

"Warrior? Is that what you call him?"

"Ever since he suffered hurt to protect you from Maynor's Challenger."

"Challenger?"

"His name is ... Geston. Maynor did not expect the challenge would be expressed with physical violence and vitriol."

"Father, your description touches a chord in my heart. You do not know it, but Rhys saved all of us by facing an Unordered Monster with nothing but a Spook rope ... a restraint cord."

This was not the time for disbelief, but the expressive pause while Aglaron tried for acceptance did just that. "... How can that be possible?"

The High King, as well as Uirebon, reeled with shock as they shared the memories now projected to their minds. Aglaron had confronted these Monsters himself, on several rare occasions, but always buffered by distance and powerful wards straining to keep him protected. The images of this first-hand encounter, frightful as they were, paled beside the cruel emotions of horror, fear and desperation that came with them. Aglaron shuddered and without thought reached to touch Keryth's arm.

"Through all the Realms your companion, Rhys, is now formally titled the Warrior."

Keryth nodded. "Thank you. It is fitting." Curiously, he now laughed. "When he finds out, he'll probably call you a twit."

"A twit?"

"It is human for idiot ... High King, the Council is delayed for a time till Lady Narello arrives. We must speak privately."

Aglaron looked to Uirebon, but all he saw was shared puzzlement.

"Lady Narello?"

"Maynor informed me she readies herself. Her representative here will take her aspect."

"I see, a mental link combined with a projected image?"

"No, Lord Uirebon, a more elaborate process with all the properties of a physical as well as a mental presence."

"I don't understand."

"Lost knowledge from Lord Ranevargar, Lore Master. One of your study Centres will have it stored in a dusty tome … Lord Maynor is searching for ways to influence the outcome of this gathering, so spare me a moment while I instruct Maurice to keep an eye on him while my attention is here."

Uirebon voiced more puzzlement. "Maurice? One of your companions has an alternate name?"

"Ranevargar's name for my Dragon is almost two sentences long, so Rhys renamed him."

Keryth turned slightly, and Uirebon blinked when the Dragon directed its attention toward them … then wondered why Ranevargar's Construct was also referred to in terms of ownership.

Maynor rose to his feet, stared at the Dragon, then stood motionless for several seconds.

"Will you accept a temporary shield while we speak? I have information you will prefer to hear in private."

"My privacy shields have never been passed, but please add your own. Uirebon will be even more fascinated than I to experience the puzzle of your shields … Kieran."

A hint of amusement and, more improbably, understanding came through the mental link. *"Your shields have been passed, High King … Father, I know myself as Kieran and understand I am Keryth. You know me as Keryth but understand I am Kieran. Address me as you will in private, but for now I am formally Kieran."*

The unsettling comment about his shields joined with all the other unanswered concerns when a curious structure imposed itself on the improved personal shield Uirebon had so recently developed. The background hum of Castle-wide mental activity cut to a silence deeper than that of his personal sanctum. Slightly uneasy, Aglaron felt Uirebon's disbelief as he tested the impervious shield.

"This feels like a mental prison."

"Yes, Lord Uirebon, but you can dissolve it at will with this trigger."

The trigger appeared. Aglaron felt Uirebon's smile of regret as his curiosity had to be dampened for more pressing concerns.

"Please understand that I see and feel your care and concern, Father, but I cannot return the bond that has been taken from me. Indeed, until I reached Lord Maynor's Castle, I was exceedingly angry with the forces tearing at those I care for and wanted only to return to my home and be left alone. With Lord Ranevargar's assistance, I saw that the harsh judgement I made against you I should also make against myself."

Uirebon felt the need to intercede. *"Your father intended only the best for you, Keryth. You should not judge him harshly."*

"How I judge the High King is for me to decide, Uirebon. For the matter of my conditioning I now hold him blameless."

This announcement, given with powerful conviction and an iron will, registered clearly with Uirebon ... and Aglaron.

"His mind was manipulated, Lord Uirebon, as was yours, and as was mine. All of us succumbed in varying degrees to Lord Maynor's subtle art."

Aglaron broke the short mental silence. *"All of us, Keryth? Uirebon knew of the influence and cleansed himself."*

"Yes, all, Father. Barely out of my basic training I was easy prey. Uirebon may be cleansed but, as with you, Maynor has pathways to influence he can still access."

"Are you sure?"

"Certain. When has a High King shared the keys to Nexus power with anyone but the Lore Master? Why does Lord Maynor's Realm receive more energy assistance than any other? Other matters demand I leave the High Realm when the meeting finishes, but before I go I will work with Lord Maynor to ensure all his controls are cleared."

"Keryth! Must you leave? This alienation saddens me."

Kieran wasn't in control, but the strength of his father's concern warranted an intrusion. *"Ranevargar, can we stay for a while? It's more important to him than any of his ruler stuff."*

"Yes, Kieran, his concern is deep, but you need time free from scrutiny to consolidate your position and consider your own needs. I suggest we offer him strong reassurance."

Ranevargar was right, as usual, and Kieran returned to observing.

"Pardon, Father. I was thinking. I cannot stay, but know that you are welcome to visit at the earliest opportunity."

"Visit? Yes, I will, as soon as possible."

"My Lord, the Realms require attention and such a visit will make heavy demands on your time."

"We have a new Realm Lord, Uirebon. It is incumbent on me as High King to foster the best possible relationship with the High Court. This is my priority."

Ranevargar/Kieran reacted instantly. *"Wonderful! Let us meet at Ranevargar's Central Grove one week from now."*

Aglaron gave immediate agreement. Uirebon puzzled at the practicality.

"My Lord, re-enabling portal travel would take power from vitally important repair and recovery needs, and a company of steeds would take at least five days of forced journeying to reach Ranevargar's Central Grove. It would be wiser to meet as we do now."

"We will travel by steed then, Uirebon. My Court will undertake every necessary task."

Ranevargar/Kieran intervened again. *"The portal system has collapsed beyond any simple repair, and re-establishment will take years of rebuilding. Till then, Lord Ranevargar offers you seven of his Guardians to provide transport throughout the Realms. The journey to his Central Grove will take an hour, not days."*

Aglaron turned to Ranevargar, standing quietly beside Keryth while the private conversation continued, spoke his gratitude and received a simple nod of agreement.

A clear and very expressive laugh sounded through the Courtyard, turning every head to the food tables.

Keryth looked then smiled. *"Maurice likes to make Rhys laugh."*

"You can know the Warrior's mind through this shield?"

"Of course, Lord Uirebon. I will not be cut off from my companions for any reason, not even while Maurice guards them. Father, you should know that when the Court convenes, Ranevargar intends to ask that I be formally titled as High Lord so my place at the table is beyond question. It matters not at all to me, but Ranevargar insists that your support for his sponsorship would set a harmonious tone for everything that follows."

Aglaron marvelled at what he was hearing. *"You feel the need to ask? With Maynor's Challenge ended, a Realm restored, and the Nexus a new wonder, my support is complete and unquestioning. Lord Maynor will recognise your standing whatever displeasure he holds. He has no choice after giving you submission. Lady Narello might equivocate from lack of knowledge and your youthfulness. What say you, Uirebon?"*

Uirebon's quiet consideration before offering Kieran his support surprised Aglaron and pleased Ranevargar.

"My Lord, I sense that within this deep privacy there is a strong expectation to speak openly. Keryth is clearly more than qualified for the title of High Lord and does have my support. I have serious reservations though. I perceive him as your son, the elf we sent to the Human World, but the Dragon was larger than the Castle itself, the same Dragon now watching

in the Courtyard. With such mastery Keryth could well be presenting in the form designed to touch your heart. He demonstrates abilities unknown or rare to the Realms and wields power as if it were a toy. And how can he proclaim himself a Realm Lord? That is a Stewardship granted only by the High King. The unknowns are seemingly endless."

Wariness rose in Aglaron's mind and he gave Kieran/Keryth regard, both physically and mentally. *"Are you Keryth? Uirebon expresses real concerns."*

"Lord Uirebon, your station as Lore Master and advisor to the High King is truly deserved. Yes, father, I am Keryth. More accurately, I am Kieran with a recent understanding of my origin as Keryth. Information drawn from Lord Maynor's mind shows both how and why this came to be. I don't claim to be a Realm Lord. I AM a Realm Lord. Almost of its own volition my Opal aligned itself with the Nexus and restored order to the Lost Realm. Lord Ranevargar conjectures that my Opal is one of the six original Realm Stones, a Realm Stone that was lost when its holder left the Realms. For your own certainty, Uirebon, I invite you to observe how my Opal connects me."

Uirebon studied the structure now revealed with increasing interest. Yes, Keryth was incontrovertibly a Realm Lord. There was the pattern, much like his own, linking Lord to Stone and to Realm. But also with a strange relegation of control. The Dragon, under Keryth's authority, was actively managing the basic functions of the Realm ... and other functions?

The patterns passed from view and Uirebon refocused his attention. *"The Dragon is a wonder, Keryth, but much of what it can do is new to me."*

"As it is for me, Uirebon. At the Central Grove there will be time for extensive discussion. And, Father, I have no proper understanding of the abilities I have unaccountably developed. It is clear that my Opal is the primary cause, but how that can be is a mystery. According to Lord Ranevargar, a Realm Stone will augment existing skills and abilities, not provide completely new ones."

"You don't understand your own abilities?"

"How can I? I have the human perception and understanding that the things I do are the fantasies of entertainment and storytelling. I discuss with my companions whether this is even real or part of an extraordinary dream."

"What of the power you wield? That is no dream."

"It's unlikely nature could be regarded as strengthening the idea that this is all a dream."

Aglaron gave a curious look. *"I don't accept that I could be the figment of someone's imagination."*

"The power is also an enigma. Until I awoke Maurice I thought it was all

part of my Opal, but now there are three distinct sources. My Opal energy, energy from the Nexus, and another exceedingly powerful flow which, while it comes through the Opal, has a strange sense of otherness. Lord Ranevargar says it is new to the Realms and suggests that Lord Uirebon, in particular, might be able to find some explanation ... Maurice will require power to leave the courtyard, so join and watch while I help him."

Aglaron and Uirebon had watched and marvelled at these power flows as outsiders and from afar. Joining with Keryth and experiencing the call itself and the answering torrent of energy was astonishing.

In the Courtyard a reservoir of energy formed above the Dragon then dwindled as it was seized and stored. When the call finished Aglaron was too amazed to respond, and Uirebon had so many questions he hardly knew where to start. He glanced at Lord Ranevargar standing so quiet and reserved beside Keryth.

"I have no explanation, but I agree with Lord Ranevargar. There is a feeling of otherness, but how can you control so much power?"

"I don't know. I nearly lost it the first time. Ranevargar says it is a natural ability, but my Opal must be involved."

"Lost it?"

"A term for panic, Uirebon. The volume and strength was overwhelming, but we will explore all this and more at the Central Grove. Time defeats us ... Father, I must insist, regardless of my own inclination, that Lord Maynor keeps full independence of mind and skill. I give surety against any unlawful Challenge and suggest you draw on his extraordinary capability with heavy demands for assistance and restitution."

"I plan to pass his Realm Stone to a new Realm Ruler."

"That was my first thought, but I now agree with Lord Ranevargar that that path would not be in the interests of the Realms, and most unwise. After yourself there is no elf in Faerie with so much capability and drive. Use it."

Uirebon expressed his disagreement. *"Maynor's abilities are pale shadows against the light of your own, Keryth."*

"I have my own path to decide, Uirebon."

In the courtyard Lord Maynor looked toward them with obvious purpose.

"Our private talk must end. Maynor informs me that Lady Narello is waiting. Father, a proper meeting with my companions must wait till you reach the Central Grove. The press of events has given me no opportunity to clear the strong animosity they all hold."

Aglaron wanted a different approach. *"I should face them myself, Keryth.*

I know almost nothing of your doings after you broke Maynor's hold and disappeared. Surely you can delay your departure?"

"*I cannot. I need time with my friends, with Ranevargar, with Maurice, and time to set the foundations for my Realm. Lord Ranevargar will help me smooth the way for a congenial and far more memorable meeting at his Grove.*"

There was no time for a reply. The special shield dissolved along with the sense of openness and inclusion, leaving Aglaron and Uirebon with a curious anticipation as to what Keryth meant by memorable.

"Amazing, my Lord. Despite his direct and personal manner he remains unreadable."

"Yes, Uirebon, though I have a sense he is driven in ways he keeps to himself ... Lord Maynor looks distracted."

Uirebon turned his attention from Keryth, who was partially supporting Ranevargar while they rejoined their companions, to watch Maynor repeatedly turn his head between the Dragon, the Warrior and the tall elf Lord who was Lady Narello's permanent representative to the High Court.

"More than distracted, my Lord. I would say apprehensive. I think the Dragon's attention is unsettling him."

"Yes, but Lady Narello's consul is— Oh!"

The consul shimmered strangely, blurred, then morphed disconcertingly from his tall male form to Lady Narello's shorter and very female presence.

Uirebon, probing without success for the normal traces of a projection, watched her rapid survey and quick recovery while two hands grasped the chair in front of her as if testing its reality. A storm of indignation gathered and, after pausing at the presence of the Dragon, turned on the High King.

"What manner of summons is this, Aglaron? You call a High Council without warning then demean me by asking my arch rival to facilitate my presence ... And what of my consul? Is he subsumed in some manner?" She touched her face and then the robe she was wearing. "This is not the link I expected. Explain yourself."

Aglaron was about to answer when Keryth murmured something and a laugh took the attention of everyone in the courtyard, the same laugh that had sounded once already.

"Wow! She's really feisty. Is this the other Realm Ruler, Kieran?"

Lady Narello's features suffused with colour as she turned toward the food tables.

Oh my! Aglaron braced for the reaction.

"Is that a human who makes mockery?" Lady Narello's imperious frown added intention to her rising voice. "If you don't call due account for the happenings in this Court then I will." Her arm raised in gesture.

"Desist, Narello!"

The strength of Aglaron's command rocked Lady Narello with shock.

"Theatrics have no place here today. The Warrior has my respect and protection in every corner of every Realm. Leave him be or the demeaning you pretend could well be exacted beyond your expectation."

Lady Narello recovered somewhat. "I am a Realm Ruler, High King, and above any real demeaning."

"So you might believe, but the Warrior has other protections. Face the Dragon and make the same threat."

More recovered, Lady Narello disdained to even look at Maurice. "You project an image of a mythical creature to impress us with your own ceremonial splendour while saying there is no place for theatrics?"

A further laugh interrupted whatever else she was about to say. "The Witch from the West! Melt her, Maurice. She thinks you're an illusion."

Lady Narello turned her full gaze to study the source of such blatant ridicule ... Curious clothing, a watchful manner cloaked by a carefree pose, hidden strength and a sense of connection with those beside him. A light mental probe rebounded from a strangely disturbing shield.

Caution! Caution! Caution! Ignore the challenge and acknowledge the unknown.

With a reversal of manner she gave a minimal nod of acknowledgement, then addressed the High King. "Why does this strangely clad youth who challenges me so curiously have your protection, and why are he and his companions here?"

Aglaron, distinctly aware that the Dragon had been on the verge of taking some action, showed his instant approval. "Wisely considered, Lady Narello. The Warrior is companion to the Lord of the now-restored Lost Realm, who is friend and master of the Dragon, holder of a Stone of Power and the instrument of intervention against Lord Maynor's unlawful Challenge. Observe the Dragon's eyes if you need to test its reality."

Aglaron watched Lady Narello's disbelief grow with each revelation to complete denial, temper with doubt because of his authority, then resolve with intent. "Lady Narello, beware!"

Confident eyes lifted to regard the golden pools of instantly disconcerting awareness. Lifted, then unaccountably lost all volition and locked in place ... *Beautiful! Oh so beautiful!* A wash of calm and wonderful peace replaced any concern for power and position with a rapture of adoration.

"Maurice, that's enough!"

As the words penetrated, the ocean of calm vanished. Lady Narello lowered the arms reaching for beautiful oblivion with shocked awareness as identity returned. The High King spoke truly. Never again would she willingly gaze into those eyes, but right now the imperative was to acknowledge her release.

The Warrior was smiling with satisfaction. It would be wise to revise her manner toward him. That thought was lost with surprise at the speaker next to him. Her first thought was that High King Aglaron presented himself in youthful guise. The likeness was powerful but, no, there were subtle differences. Shaking the lingering effects of those dreadful eyes, she considered the High King's startling revelations. Well, he was certainly the High King's son, though out of place in that drab clothing, and the Dragon enchantment *had* ceased at his word. Repressing every hint of haughtiness, she expressed her thanks with a courteous bow of acknowledgement.

The bow was returned with understanding and confidence, unsettling, even jarring, from one so young. "Beware the eyes of my Dragon, Lady Narello. He protects my friends and my Realm with a puissance new to Faerie. Open your mind so we can speak privately."

"Open?" Power flared instinctively to strengthen her shield walls. "I am a Realm Ruler. That is not proper."

"Very well."

A puzzling structure overlaid her barriers and a clear communication sounded.

"We have privacy while your deeper thoughts are still your own. Lady Narello, you are ignorant."

Shocked that shields strengthened by her Stone of Power meant nothing, Lady Narello sensed this was no derogation, just a clear statement of fact. Well, that was immediately evident, but the implication was all-encompassing rather than immediate.

"In some ways we are all ignorant. You have my full attention ... Rather, you demand my full attention."

"Yes I do, for a time and for your own enlightenment. Lord Maynor has been manipulating your mind for centuries."

"No!"

"Every decision made in that period has been to Lord Maynor's advantage."

This simply wasn't credible, especially coming from a youth who had barely finished his basic training if her scant knowledge of Aglaron's son served correctly, but the certainty was too powerful to ignore.

"Would you prefer to hear it from Maynor, or will I show you directly."

Thoughts churned with confusion and alarm.

"*Show me directly? With such an ability you could substitute any manipulations with your own.*"

"*I'm not interested in such toyings. I have serious matters to attend to.*"

The matter-of-fact dismissal of a working capability to change the inner workings of a Realm Ruler's mind as something akin to play was so startling to Lady Narello that she now accepted the High King's every claim, and indicated the need to see anything being offered.

The young elf nodded his approval and touched the gemstone now glowing softly at his chest. "*Follow my path to the deeper levels of your mind, Lady Narello, and watch while I highlight the subtle network imposed on the processes you employ for decision-making. I don't have the key to clear it yet, but Lord Maynor will do that when the Council finishes.*"

Lady Narello watched gentle tendrils probe deeper and deeper, till they accessed a level new to her, then steadily reveal a complicated set of structures entangled all around with a red-hued network.

"*See, Lady Narello, this is a work of great mastery, nurtured with great care for a long time.*"

"*All that mesh of red subverts my decisions? Leeching me of independent thought? Destroy it. It is demeaning beyond any acceptance.*"

"*See how close it twines? If I destroy it now there will be damage to your own processes. The safe manner of release is keyed to Lord Maynor's mind. All will be well if you wait.*"

"*Waiting leaves me open to influence while we are in Council.*"

"*I have warned him against using any such influence. He heeds me.*"

"*He may appear to heed you, but if the High King decides through this Council to diminish him he will, by his nature, resist. He controls great reserves of power.*"

"*Lady Narello, he heeds me. The power you ceded him is gone.*"

"*I face censure from this Council then?*"

"*The High King understands your actions well. He himself learnt just now that, along with Lord Uirebon, his own decisions have also been manipulated.*"

Hearing that the High King was unlikely to hold her responsible for actions initiated by Maynor brought a resurgence of Lady Narello's normal confidence. "*The High King? And he learnt this from you?*"

"*To his great surprise, Lady Narello, along with knowledge of certain other events which I would like to share with you. Everyone is waiting for us. Listen carefully.*"

*   *   *

"**Desist, Narello!** ... The Warrior has my respect and protection in every corner of every Realm."

What the hell! Rhys stared, completely startled by the unexpectedness of the statement. *Protection? Respect?* Not fair. How could he keep giving him dirty looks after that? What had Kieran/Ranevargar been telling him?

He glanced wonderingly at Kieran/Ranevargar, then forgot all that when the High King told Lady Narello that Maurice was not an elaborate projection and challenged her to face him. She didn't think he was real? ... She didn't.

She turned, stared directly at Maurice, lost every bit of forcefulness and relaxed with a dopey kind of look. *Oh my!* She was completely out of it.

"Maurice, that's enough!"

Kieran's strong call ended the eye-hold and with her will and force returned, she focused every bit of attention on him and the High King. Rhys saw her intense concentration and nudged Woorawa's arm.

"Look at that. It's Buddha time again. We could yell in her face and she wouldn't even notice."

The nudge was returned. "Kieran too. He must be telling her all the stuff she needs to know."

"Well done, Rhys. You helped Kieran change your group from a distraction to her strongest priority."

"Do you know what's happening now, Maurice?"

"They are behind a privacy shield like the one used with the High King and Lord Uirebon, Rhys, so, like you, I have to wait. My best guess would be exactly as Woorawa says."

"Too much waiting ... Did this lady really think you're just a projection?"

"She did, Rhys, and I also thought it rather curious. Her decision was automatic, as if projection was a normal expectation. It may be that the High King is proficient in the art and makes projections a feature of these high occasions."

"Ranevargar's pretty good at them. He made a giant Griffin out of camp-fire flame to thank Woorawa for his ceremony on the first night after we met him."

"More than good, Rhys. With the return of his abilities he is now a master. It wasn't apparent to you, but every denizen here saw me as larger than the Castle itself, a feat of projection beyond my own abilities."

"You can do projections?"

A touch of amusement came with Maurice's reply. *"You thought the elements you experienced with Kieran's challenge were real? Of course you didn't."*

"That was unreal. The dirt crushing me was too much and my feelings took no notice of what my brain was telling me."

"I have a suggestion you might like to act on, Rhys. Krol's hunger has been temporarily assuaged, but not his thirst, and a good drink would help him cope with the flight to the Maker's Grove."

Rhys was shocked, and this time it was a loud yell sounding through the Courtyard rather than his distinctive laugh. "Water! We need five buckets of water."

The hosts who had conducted them inside when they first arrived responded to the urgency in his voice and ran, actually ran, to comply. The friends, except for Kieran/Ranevargar, jolted in startlement.

"Water?"

"For Krol, Woorawa. We haven't looked after him properly. He should have had a drink back at Maynor's Castle and he's got to fly all the way to Ranevargar's Central Grove as soon as this meeting's over."

"That's where we're going next?"

"According to Maurice."

Maurice answered to all of them. *"That is my understanding at the moment, unless some outcome causes a change ... Rhys, Krol's needs aren't as critical as you think."*

"Yes, they are. Ranevargar was helping him on the way here ... That was quick."

The hosts, not even knowing what the water was for, arrived in a rush with extra buckets and Rhys redirected them.

"Woorawa and Tan, will you give Krol the water? Mr B and I will stay to support Kieran while his brain's not here."

The whole Courtyard was now treated to the spectacle of Krol being tended by Woorawa, Tan, and seven hosts with water buckets.

Lord Uirebon watched with the High King. "The Warrior is direct in his manner, my Lord. The ceremony of a High Council meeting is not a primary concern for him."

"Refreshingly direct, Uirebon, and it is interesting that he holds the Guardian in such high regard. But look at his manner with my son. The bond is clearly as strong as it was with Pethron. Our meddling will be very confronting for Keryth."

"Meddling?"

"Yes, Uirebon. That is how Keryth regards it, and, with the luxury of hindsight and Maynor as a focus for blame, so must we."

"My Lord, you should turn your mind to Maynor. Keryth's request that he keep full independence of mind limits how the Council might treat him."

"Very limiting indeed, but we will hear Keryth's specific proposals in Council before deciding anything."

"If he retains his Realm Stone a future Challenge is inevitable."

"And that is a great concern, given his willingness to ignore proper convention, but with a valid Challenge I am confident he cannot match me ... not for a long time."

"Extraordinary!"

Aglaron turned to Uirebon with a puzzled look. "The prospect of another Challenge, you mean?"

"No! No! All the happenings we find ourselves in, the mystery of the situation and the changes ahead for the Realms. There is so much to consider and instead we have more to challenge us ... Look at Lady Narello. Her force and independence is completely distracted by whatever Keryth is telling her."

"As it was with us, Uirebon, and, I think, with the same privacy shields ... I am unnerved that I gave Maynor more than his fair share of free energy. It is clear confirmation of the manipulation I still find hard to accept."

Lady Narello turned toward them and with full courtesy made a formal bow. Keryth did the same and, after a glance at the Dragon, Lord Maynor followed suit. Lord Uirebon, drawing into himself, mustered all the dignity of a Realm Lord for his own bow.

"The High Council convenes."

*   *   *

Rhys, watching the High King and Uirebon approach, grabbed Kieran's arm protectively when a volume encompassing the official table began to glow with a translucent sheen of a deep and vibrant purple.

"Sheba! What's this? Are you all right, Kieran?"

"Completely, Rhys. My talk with Lady Narello went well and the meeting begins. The glow is just the High King's show to impress everyone watching. Hold Ranevargar's arm as well as mine so we can get a boost. The next little while will be hard work, but after that we'll be out of here and we can talk."

Rhys moved to Kieran's other side. *"Is this you talking, Kieran? It's getting hard to tell."*

"Not quite, Rhys. Kieran is coming through partially while I gather myself for this last effort ... It is time to take our seats at the Council table."

Kieran and Ranevargar moved and sat next to each other, and when Woorawa and Tan arrived in a rush, the four companions stood ranged behind them. Maurice's great bulk moved just enough to position his head directly above. The High King took his place in the elaborate ceremonial chair just opposite, with Lord Uirebon on his right hand side, and Lady Narello, then Lord Maynor, on his left.

"It looks like us against them, Maurice. Is there some reason it's organised like this?"

"The Maker sits with Kieran to present him to all the established Realm Rulers and propose his recognition as one of them. It is a formality, because without it he technically has no voice in the Council."

"Technically?"

"The High King has already accepted him, so he will be heard anyway, but Lord Maynor is going to protest."

"After everything that's happened to him? He's crazy!"

"No, Rhys, he is very clever. While he sits at the Council table he has complete independence of mind and protection from interference of any kind."

"Ha! He breaks all the rules himself then hides behind them ... You're not sitting at the table. You can go into his mind and stop him making any stupid protests."

"I could, but I won't, Rhys. The act of sitting at the table signifies Kieran's agreement and if I do anything contrary it will reflect badly on him and, worse still, make it look as if he doesn't fully control me."

Rhys twisted to look up at the daunting head above. *"Does he really control you, Maurice, or is part of it because he woke you up and you're friendly because of that?"*

"Both, Rhys. The Maker designed the challenge specifically so that he and he alone would ultimately be able to harness my powers and the extensive abilities I have been imbued with, so the trust the Maker has placed with Kieran is extraordinary, especially with the strange power he commands."

"What's strange about it? Isn't all the energy the same, except he's got more than anyone else?"

"No, not at all. There are very clear differences, which I understand quite well, between energy from the Nexus and the energy he normally calls with his Opal. The pure white energy has qualities I don't understand."

"Gods! Everything's complicated."

"Indeed! Especially when you consider Kieran can also influence Chaos energy and the forbidden energy of the life force."

"Chaos energy? He's never said anything about that."

"I watched him counter elements of it which are inherent to all the Realm Boundaries."

"The red protection thing? He doesn't know how he does that."

"More talk later when we have time for proper attention."

And indeed, the purple glow was now limning Aglaron.

"This Council is called to consider our response to the illegal Challenge for the High Throne and all its ruinous consequences."

Maynor leapt to his feet. "My Lord, your claim of illegality has no foundation and prejudges any proper finding. My Challenge broke no laws because, apart from convention, there are none."

All attention turned to the Lore Master, who carefully considered before giving his answer. "I believe Lord Maynor is technically correct, my Lord."

Aglaron scoffed at this. "Technically?"

"A formal declaration of the rules of Challenge would be subject to the whim of any individual holding your office. With convention, any contention is bound by the expectation of every Court in the Realms. Convention takes far more profound precedence."

Aglaron gestured at Maynor's seat. "This High Council is called to consider the unconventional Challenge for the High Throne and all its ruinous consequences. Lord Ranevargar, your presence is a rare occurrence and the Court gives you full welcome. I understand you have an urgent proposal for us."

Rhys watched Ranevargar rise slowly to his feet and, when Kieran stood to support him, rushed to hold his other arm.

"Well done, Rhys! My apparent tiredness is a striking contrast with Kieran's youth and strength."

"You sneaky old codger! I thought it was real."

Ranevargar had started speaking aloud now, but a hint of amusement whisked through Rhys's mind. "I gratefully accept your welcome, High King. I propose that this Council should formally recognise Kieran as High Lord. The Realm that was lost is now recovered. That which was dead is returned to life."

Rhys couldn't believe it when Maynor leapt to his feet again.

"My Lord, I object. Convention demands you choose an accepted Lord of the High Realm, not a youth with no knowledge or experience."

The High King's open laugh cleared Rhys's renewed anger at Maynor's arrogance. "Maynor, your call for convention may seem clever, but in this situation it is nothing short of ridiculous. All at this table, save Lady Narello, witnessed your own submission to knowledge and authority beyond your own. The title is nothing more than recognition for the wondrous change to the Nexus and the renewal of a Realm." Aglaron raised his voice to address every being present and watching, and Rhys was completely startled by the accompanying, impossibly familiar, gesture. "Know that from now and henceforth all of Faerie recognises Kieran, sponsored by Lord Ranevargar, as High Lord and Ruler of the newly restored Realm."

Rhys didn't even hear. All his attention was on the face of the regal elf just across the table. Take off that silver crown of office, bypass the distraction of magnificent vestments, and the features and manner held disturbing elements.

The High King gave a smile and nod of invitation to speak and Rhys's mind stopped and went into overdrive at the same time. Not believing, he looked at Kieran. No, he couldn't be interrupted at the moment, so, with his mind practically screaming for understanding, Rhys made a silent call.

"Maurice, I must be going crazy. The King looks like Kieran and he just smiled and moved like him. Is he projecting an image to confuse us or something? It's creepy."

"The gesture had the same effect on all your companions, Rhys, and their minds, like yours, are searching for an explanation. There is no projection that I can detect and I daren't distract Kieran or the Maker ... Wait!"

"Lord of all Faerie and fellow Realm Rulers, the mantle of Stewardship was, without warning, given to me and I formally thank you for your recognition. I also thank Lord Ranevargar for his sponsorship and kind support. His debilitating treatment since the Challenge presses the need for a speedy return to the tranquillity and healing calm of his Central Grove. My Lord, before this Council makes any decision there is background information I must make clear. Grant me leave to address Lord Maynor."

Aglaron's startlement, shared by everyone around the table, passed instantly. "Of course."

Kieran — Kieran/Ranevargar really — augmented his aspect of authority and turned to Maynor. "Lord Maynor, you will stand while I speak."

This was high drama and Rhys watched as Maynor's reluctance to accede to this direct challenge gave way to wary acceptance.

CHAPTER 6

Kieran held Maynor with direct eye contact.

"Now that they know the extent of your manipulations to the workings of their inner minds, your standing with those at this table has fallen low, perhaps beyond recovery. Nevertheless, for reasons of my own, I lay it on this Council to leave you with full command of your mind and your Realm."

Rhys, shocked out of his brain, held back a yell of protest, then almost smiled at Woorawa's gasp of disbelief and Tan and Mr B's stare of frozen disapproval.

"Steady, Rhys. Trust in Kieran and the Maker."

There was no time for a response because Lady Narello, indignation radiating with palpable force, leapt to her feet in angry protest. "High Lord Kieran, that is beyond acceptance. Lord Maynor subverted my mind. He must make recompense. Without re-education he will certainly worm his way into our thoughts and make a Challenge for the throne again. He must suffer—"

Midsentence, she froze momentarily then, with a sedate nod, resumed her seat.

"Wow! Kieran/Ranevargar must have said something pretty powerful."

"Lady Narello, your concerns are cogent indeed, but by the convention we have just affirmed, Maynor has the right of Challenge. Now that he is aware of them, Lord Uirebon will develop ways to counter the tricks of manipulation. The matter of Challenge must be set to rest while the Realms recover. Lord Maynor, state your intentions clearly."

"Intentions? I don't understand."

"Yes, you do. Challenge now or vow to make none for a period of five decades."

Now it was the High King leaving his seat, not with Lady Narello's leap of indignation but with a gathering aura of the dignity and authority these Realm Lords seemed able to switch on and off at will. Well, Kieran could do it better than any of them. Whoo! More drama. Rhys's eyes darted back and forth, then settled on Maynor's intense concentration.

"Maynor is torn with temptation, Rhys. If he prevails against Aglaron, the

Council will be bound to give him fealty and he will be above consequence for everything he has done."

"Is he strong enough to win? The King looks kind of unreal."

"The High King's look is a projection, Rhys, but Maynor's aggregation of great external power for his unconventional Challenge indicates he knew his personal strength would not be a match."

"I hope he goes ahead then."

"You do? Ah! You want to see him defeated."

"I want to see him whipped like a puppy."

"You conjure strange imagery with your thoughts, Rhys. Whipping a puppy?"

Maynor studied the High King's force of presence, and very willing readiness, before turning back to Kieran. "If I Challenge successfully will you offer proper fealty?"

"Of course … and immediately institute my own formal Challenge."

"For the wellbeing of my Realm, I accept your terms, but …" Turning suddenly to address Lady Narello, he raised his voice. "He is Widderkin! The High King's proclamation is invalid because, no matter his strength, this youth cannot be accepted as a Realm Ruler. He is Widderkin!"

Lady Narello swayed strangely, then rose in her place, a storm cloud of indignation transforming her features. She pointed dramatically at Kieran. "This revelation changes everything and demands I support Lord Maynor's objection. Deny him the title. No ruler can be Widderstricken. Never in all the history of the Realms has this been allowed." She turned her attention to the High King. "I insist."

"What's wrong with her, Maurice? She looks crazy."

"Maybe …"

"Calm yourself, Lady Narello. Your views are strong but unfounded. If Lord Uirebon agrees with Ranevargar's proposal your objection is noted but overruled."

Uirebon nodded his assent and the whole assembly jolted in startlement at Lady Narello's scream of rage, then watched, transfixed, as her hands and arms moved with rapid gestures of power.

"Holy hell! Maurice, she is crazy. What's she doing now?"

"Calling another Chaos creature … Her mind is not her own."

Rhys didn't answer because now the High King and Lord Uirebon were also on their feet, gesturing as well, with what must be a counter for the quivering emanation springing to life beside them.

"She's attacking and it feels like a mini version of the Wall. Are we safe?"

"I would have thought not, but the Maker/Kieran are expressing no

concern ... I believe they may have been expecting something like this."

A quiet but powerful flow of assurance from Kieran/Ranevargar quelled all the companions' rising alarm as the sense of weird unreality grew stronger and stronger. Purple coruscations, backed by the yellow of Lord Uirebon's power, sparkled in brilliant display against increasing disorientation from the growing, writhing form.

"It's too strong. The High King's losing."

"Lady Narello has great knowledge of Chaos energy, Rhys, but the Maker/ Kieran is ready. Watch!"

And indeed, Kieran's arm left its support of Ranevargar and pointed with gentle but very deliberate intent at Lady Narello. The purple and yellow instantly gained strength as Lady Narello froze in place, transfixed with unseeing eyes. The Chaos incursion now shrank and disappeared, leaving all eyes studying the strangely disturbing statue aspect that Lady Narello had taken on.

"Lady Narello is without blame, Aglaron. The Chaos creature was called by a compulsion beyond her control, a hidden compulsion which Lord Maynor will remove before I release her mind to return to us."

Maynor shook his head in denial. "Lady Narello called the incursion, I—"

"Maynor."

Those listening sensed reproval, warning, command, all conveyed with the utterance of a single word. Maynor heard more, quailed visibly, then hastily nodded his compliance.

"Yay! That's better. One word from Kieran stops all his blathering. Can you see what happened, Maurice?"

"I saw no use of power, if that's what you mean, Rhys. Just a reminder of the consequences of resistance."

"Every last vestige of influence and compulsion must be removed, Lord Maynor. Proceed so we can continue with the business of this Council."

"The process is lengthy and requires long and deep concentration and you have placed her in a mind state I don't understand."

"Use your emergency strategy and she will be with us in minutes."

Utter disbelief crossed Maynor's features. "My strategy? How can you know of that? I ..."

The disbelief faded to acceptance, and with a resigned nod of compliance his eyes closed again.

In the silence that followed Uirebon shared his own disbelief with the High King.

"Can this really be Keryth, my Lord? Maynor's demonstrated mastery

of mind manipulation is clearly overmatched. We worked close and long with him before he went to the Old Continent, and while his potential was evident his skills were basic."

"You know very well he is Keryth, unfathomable and transformed somehow, strange in this human persona you have given him. Behind all the differences though, Kieran has the personality and traits of Keryth. I have decided I trust him completely." Irony flashed. *"Not that I am in a position to do anything else."*

"Have you considered the possibility he might have manipulated our own minds in his favour?"

"A possibility with no probability of execution. Kieran has influenced my thoughts with persuasive explanation and discussion and no other means."

Aglaron stopped this communication because Maynor's deep concentration was clearly finished.

"Lady Narello."

The motionless form softened, then transformed with the return of awareness and obvious bewilderment, and turned to Kieran. "What ... what happened? I was consumed with anger and suddenly I feel at ease."

"I quietened your mind. You were compelled to call a Chaos incursion against us, so I quietened your mind while Lord Maynor removed his web of influence and restored your mind to independence."

"The red web? It is gone?"

"Yes, the deep web which has influenced your decisions for more than a century."

Lady Narello shook her head. "How can it be possible. I make my own decisions and my mind has strong protections."

"You think so? Why, then, did you decide to cede control of all your great Power Masters to Lord Maynor?"

"I ... It was ... I don't know."

"What was the purpose of the power displays at your mutual Boundaries?"

"Lord Maynor made contest and I responded in kind. I ..."

"And yet you gifted him with energy drawn countless times from the Outer Chaos."

"I ..."

"Yes, Lady Narello, the control was insidious and masterful, but know with certainty that your mind is now your own."

Lady Narello turned her gaze on Maynor.

"Whoa! Look at that, Maurice. She's not happy."

"Yes, Rhys. Maynor is increasingly isolated."

"What was that quieting thing when she froze? Do you know how to do that?"

"I don't know everything the Maker knows, Rhys, but I hope he will gift me such useful knowledge at some stage."

Rhys's communication with Maurice was now completely interrupted because, in front of the whole assemblage, Kieran's arms were suddenly enfolding him in a great bear-hug. His eyes widened at the unexpectedness, and with a happy rush of exuberance he lifted Kieran off his feet and whirled him a full 360° before looking to see if there was any message as well. Kieran gently bumped foreheads then, after a tingle-raising look, took his hand and turned to those watching from across the table.

"Yes, Lady Narello, I am indeed Widderstruck. Accept it or not as you will, but know that my Realm is Widderfriendly, and my friend and companion will expect any visitor to respect that."

Rhys felt strange when every eye turned on him. That stopped with Kieran's soft laugh.

"Not these four. They are more than friends." His head lifted to the great golden eyes watching so keenly from above and behind. "Maurice is the Guardian of my Realm, the protector of those who come with good heart, and foil against those who don't. Maurice is the greatest Guardian, awoken to full potential after six hundred years, and a new thing. Maurice, now my friend and companion, is the one who will test intent."

Rhys expected Maurice to make a great roar or rear in acknowledgement with a spread of wings, but instead he lowered his head to receive a gentle touch from Kieran's free hand. *Wow!* Somehow it was more significant than any display of power.

"Yo, everyone! That's cleared up mostly everything from our side. We'll sit down now while the Council works out what it's going to do about Maynor. Ranevargar and I have to get him by himself for a while, but then we're out of here."

"Is that you, Kieran?"

"About 90% for a while, Rhys. This mind-sharing stuff is amazing, but it's really hard work and Ranevargar is relaxing as much as he can while the Council talks."

"What's going on with the High King? He acts like you, and Maurice says it is not a projection or some kind of trick."

"Yeah! Ranevargar knows everything, but I haven't found out properly myself yet. Part of it's why we need a special session with Maynor, but it's scary complicated and we'll have a big talk as soon as I get it worked out."

"Scary?"

"Not danger scary ... Whoops! Here comes Ranevargar again, Lady Narello's freaking out and we'll have to calm her down again. She looks and

feels like she's physically here, but she's not and it needs our double mind to sort it out."

Lady Narello, who had once again risen from her seat, sat down, closed her eyes briefly, then nodded to the High King with a look that said that whatever she'd been about to say didn't matter.

Aglaron took over and made a series of pronouncements which no one even questioned. In fifteen minutes the meeting was all over and Rhys (along with Mr B, Tan and Woorawa, as he found out later) was wondering why they'd even needed a meeting about Maynor being confined, along with a lot of gobbledygook limitations, to his own Realm for the next fifty years, most of them about repairing damage caused by the Challenge.

Ranevargar/Kieran offered four of the gathered rubies with their great store of energy as a help, but otherwise said very little till the High King pronounced the meeting finished.

"High King, other matters are calling us, but before we leave Lord Ranevargar and I will speak privately with Lord Maynor. Will you grant us a warding?"

Aglaron looked surprised, then hurriedly agreed. At Kieran's signal, Maynor moved to join them near Maurice, where they all disappeared inside an opaque curtain of purple glowing light. Rhys smiled at the curious expressions across the table, then shared a look with Woorawa, Tan and Mr B before trying for his own answers.

"Why can't we see them, Maurice? Do you know what they're doing?"

"I have no idea, Rhys, apart from the fact that it is something extremely important. The High King has simply provided the privacy Kieran/Ranevargar asked for."

"Can you see through it?"

"Yes, but then it wouldn't be private."

"Ha! What's the use of a Dragon who won't do what I tell him?"

"I abase myself at the feet of the mighty Warrior."

Woorawa turned in his seat to give Rhys questioning look. "What's funny, Rhys?"

"Nothing, just Maurice being cheeky."

"He never gives me cheek. He's really clever, isn't he?"

"Ha very ha!"

Mr B and Tan turned now. "Shush, Rhys! Everyone's listening. You'll give them a weird impression of Maurice."

"Too bad! Little pigs have big ears."

Mr B nodded because, in essence, he agreed, then wondered if the exchange of smiles between the High King and Lord Uirebon meant they

knew they were the target of Rhys's comments.

With a little nod the High King leaned forward and spoke softly. "Yes, Mr B. The gathered Court listens and marvels at the audacity of a welcome visitor likening their High King to a piglet. Surely, if you were in our position, you would seek to gather every morsel of information you could?"

"Rhys didn't really call you piglets. It's a saying."

"Of course, but curious words can effect curious consequences."

Mr B puzzled on that and glanced for Rhys's reaction. *Embarrassment? Maybe a little worry?* The puzzling stopped because when the High King's hands moved gracefully in front of him, the features of the closest attendant wavered and grew a pig snout. *Oh my!* The hand movements continued and every head around the Courtyard was suddenly a porker watching, with twitching ears and a bristly snout. Curious consequence was for sure, and Mr B wondered if the raised eyebrows and questioning look now directed at Rhys was the precursor for the next logical consequence. *Ha!* Rhys's startled look and sudden strong inwardness meant he was probably yelling to Maurice for protection.

He was.

"Quick, stop him, Maurice. He is going to do it to me."

"The mighty piglet wants protection from the cheeky Dragon?"

"Look at him. You can see it in his eyes."

"I most certainly can. Hold ... I think Mr B is giving his support."

"Think?"

"Yes, he says I should save your bacon. Isn't that support?"

"Very funny!"

Mr B dodged the great whack directed at him. "What was that for?"

"Making weak puns!"

"Only in my mind. I didn't expect Maurice to pass it on."

"Relax, Rhys. For a moment there the High King was strongly inclined to direct a projection only your friends could see, but he wasn't sure how you'd react."

"You're watching what he's thinking?"

"Only his surface thoughts, while the Maker is busy behind the privacy ward."

"Wow! Does he know you're looking? Don't you have to get permission? Ranevargar always does with us."

"This could hardly be called a normal situation, Rhys, but he is aware of my observation and thinks it is Kieran."

"What? You're listening with Kieran's signature or something?"

"Yo, Rhys! Why don't you turn around and gaze into my golden eyes for a while?"

The sound of Kieran's mental voice made Rhys twist towards the purple glow till the golden eyes part registered properly.

"Holy hell! Don't do that, Maurice. It's too ... I don't know ... too weird."

Maurice's familiar mental voice returned. *"Yes, Rhys, quite disturbing for a recipient, and I only employ it at the Maker's request."*

"Is it hard to do? You must be good if you're tricking the High King."

"If he looked carefully he'd know, but he holds his mind wide open for Kieran and the Maker in the hope of gleaning information. Kieran's actions have challenged his understanding of what is possible in the Realms."

"And he finds time to think of making me look like a piglet? He should turn Maynor into a snake or a headless chook or something."

"Against the protection Kieran has granted and his own guarantee? Hardly. Your reaction has impressed him though."

"Impressed? With me?"

"He is enjoying your slight indignation and comparing it with the image Kieran/Ranevargar gave him of the Monster being destroyed by a Spook rope. Of course he is impressed."

"Well, don't tell him I yelled for you to protect me then."

Rhys checked the purple privacy ward again, but there was no sign of anything happening, then took one of the pieces of honey-bread Woorawa was offering around. So nice after days of trail biscuits. Yes, their next food time might be quite a while yet if Maurice was held to Griffin speed. He looked around and took in the strong sense of expectancy from the hushed onlookers crowding the edges of the Courtyard and wondered what they were thinking about. It must be Maurice mostly, especially with Kieran and Ranevargar and Maynor hidden from view and the High King and Realm Lords across the table sitting so quietly. *Gods!* There were elves lining balconies at every level.

"These are momentous events, Rhys, not least of which is my presence, and all are wondering what it means."

The surprise of Tan leaving the group and walking around the table to approach the High King pushed a query about numbers from Rhys's mind.

"What's he doing, Maurice? Did you get a message from Kieran or Ranevargar?"

"It's his own initiative, Rhys, quite impromptu. Apparently he has decided to talk to the High King while we are waiting."

The High King twisted awkwardly in his seat then, when Tan inclined his head in a low-key gesture, stood to return in kind.

"You are the High King of all the Realms?"

Surprised at this statement of the obvious showed clearly. "I am indeed, young human. And you are Tan, companion to Kieran?"

"Friend, rather." The High King's head lifted when Tan continued. "Lord Ranevargar asserts that you have integrity. Will you be kind to Kieran and give him respect?"

Rhys grabbed Mr B's arm and called to Maurice. *"He just kind of told the High King off. Will he be okay? The King's staring at him."*

"The High King is startled and uncertain and seeks advice on how to respond."

Indeed, Aglaron was in hasty communication with Uirebon.

"Is this a confrontation, Uirebon? What do we know of this youth.?"

"Only the information Maynor took while he had brief contact. Intelligence, thoughtfulness and a sense of calm are the clearest qualities. We know nothing else and those shields make him an enigma. His manner suggests nothing to me but a deep concern for your intention toward Keryth. Answer honestly and from your heart."

"Of course, but despite the air of compulsion I will be circumspect."

"For my part, Kieran has all the gratitude that is within me. My heart is open to him and the respect you seek already approaches the level of awe."

Tan nodded quiet acceptance and faced the Lore Master. "Lord Uirebon, Lore Master and Realm Ruler?"

Taken aback, it was now Uirebon's turn to stare. *"My Lord, I feel strangely vulnerable."*

A wisp of amusement accompanied Aglaron's reply. *"Answer honestly and from your heart, Uirebon, and it will pass."*

"I am both, Tan. What would you ask me?"

"The same question. Will you be kind to Kieran and give him due respect?"

Uirebon rose from his seat and spoke with formal intensity. "Kindness is a curious request to make of a Realm Lord, friend of Kieran, but I offer it in what measure I can. The respect due for the reclamation of a Realm is beyond me, but what I am able to offer I also do so in full."

"Maurice! What the hell's going on? They look like naughty kids in front of their teacher."

"Quiet, Rhys. This is beyond me, and every detail and nuance must be gathered for the Maker/Kieran's consideration."

"But ..."

"Lady Narello, Realm Ruler?"

Rhys, Mr B and Woorawa exchanged disbelieving glances as the formula repeated.

"The anger of my ignorance was calmed with kindness, friend of Kieran. I am honoured to offer kindness and respect in return."

Tan's head inclined slightly with his third nodded gesture of acknowledgement, then he walked around the table and, ignoring the wondering looks from Mr B, Rhys and Woorawa, sat in his chair and closed his eyes. Woorawa's puzzlement was instantly concern and, dropping to the seat beside Tan, he pulled him close with an arm across his shoulders.

"Is everything all right?"

Tans eyes opened and he was himself again. "That was ... strange."

Mr B was kneeling in front of him and Rhys, one hand resting on his head in case he needed healing, was yelling Woorawa's same question at Maurice.

"All I see is the bewilderment you all share. He wants to explain because your concern worries him. Listen."

"I'm all right, Woorawa. I think Kieran or Ranevargar must have done something, because I had to ask them their true thoughts."

Mr B expressed the watching friends' puzzlement. "True thoughts?"

"Yes, they all meant exactly what they said. The only ruler Kieran might have to worry about is Maynor."

At this point Tan looked at the said rulers with an expression which Aglaron interpreted as embarrassment and apology.

"What are we seeing, Uirebon? Keryth's quiet friend shows bewilderment for his own actions."

"My Lord, the more I see the less I understand. Mystery increases at every turn. There was an element of compulsion, but I discount Maynor as the source. Maybe Keryth sought a stronger affirmation of our intent?"

Aglaron dismissed that instantly. *"Keryth is eager to meet us at Ranevargar's Central Grove. We will seek an explanation then ... Observe the fierce support he receives, Uirebon. It is a real force."*

Keryth, no, Kieran, appeared through the purple privacy ward and, clearly startled, abandoned both Ranevargar and Maynor and rushed to join his companions. With his hand resting on the quiet friend's brow, his gaze turned to settle for a short time on the Dragon. Aglaron watched as what was clearly surprise ended with an assured nod and a lowering of tension. Tension?

"Keryth was preparing to act, Uirebon, and the Dragon calmed him."

Any reply was cut off by Keryth.

"Tan is now himself and the impetus for his curious but beneficial approach has passed. High King, our day has been overly eventful. Lord Ranevargar

needs the tranquillity and restoration of his Central Grove, and the day has been long and trying for my friends. Please assist Lord Ranevargar while he gives you control of seven Guardians. He offers three for the High Realm and two each for Lord Uirebon and Lady Narello while the portal structure is dysfunctional, though you may delegate them however you wish. Two protected Guardians will fly to Ranevargar's Central Grove after returning Lord Maynor and his attendant to his Realm."

Assist? Yes, he did look weary. Aglaron moved quickly and was touched by the smile of gratitude as Ranevargar accepted the offer of a supporting arm. Five days of mind and body paralysis was unconscionable and definitely warranted that quite pointed denial of any Griffin transport.

Sympathy and concern were deferred when an unexpectedly robust transfer of information pressed into his mind. Seven links, sparkling with life, sprang into being and along with them the keys for both communication and control. No, agreement to cooperate rather than control. The aspect of these Guardians made the Fetch constructs looked pale and dreary. Ranevargar's suggestion to check the new links resulted in a short but startlingly clear view from one of the Castle ramparts. With eyes like these the Coursers would be redundant.

Impressions and consideration would have to wait, though, because they'd reached the Dragon's flank. Ranevargar wished him well and, cutting off their communication, took the steadying hand of the Warrior to help with the climb. The Dark Child scrambled hurriedly to help, and after Pethron and the quiet one had followed, Keryth turned to Lady Narello, who wasn't quite able to hide her wariness at being so close to the Dragon, and extended both arms to offer the double handclasp of honour and respect. She accepted instantly, but Aglaron noted that, if anything, her wariness increased. The wariness changed to eagerness, even excitement, and Aglaron noted yet another thing to discuss with Uirebon. How could Keryth know that inclusion would be so important to Lady Narello? He'd only just recognised it in her himself. Were she and Keryth still in private communication?

"I am honoured, High Lord Kieran, though the prospect of a journey with these Guardians daunts me."

Keryth's smile indicated he understood she was far from daunted.

"Lord Uirebon."

Uirebon leapt for the offered handclasp, then closed his eyes in concentration while it lasted.

"Through Lord Ranevargar? Indeed, Lord Kieran. The prospect is exciting and the resources of my Realm will be stretched with assistance to the

Gateway Realm, but we will find a way."

Aglaron didn't wait for the offer of a handclasp. He made his own and invested it with all the authority and meaning he could. The personal communication he was yearning for came, not as words but as a wash of understanding, gratitude and admiration. The quiet words which followed were short.

"One week, Father!"

Keryth — no, it was still Kieran, despite the offered bridge — turned to the Dragon, then looked back again with a smile. "I will scramble this time. Maurice's ascent will be impressive enough as a display."

Aglaron watched the nimble climb and the lowering of the protective flap, then his thoughts turned so deeply inward that the astonishing ascent of the Dragon was lost to him till Uirebon later shared the memory.

*　*　*

Rhys's glance switched from Ranevargar, sitting in the luxurious fur lining Maurice's transport cavity, to watch and wonder if Kieran's swift approach meant anything more than eagerness to get going. A big smile and a quick hug as they readied themselves suggested this was Kieran without Ranevargar.

"It's mostly me at the moment, Rhys, and I'll be all myself as soon as Lady Narello is safely back in her Realm and Maurice is on his way."

"Is everything all right? You looked like you were in a hurry?"

"Everything's good, Rhys, except we're both gonked."

Maurice's protective flap started lowering and Kieran's smile grew even stronger at the concerned touch to his brow.

"That won't help, Rhys. It's our brains exhausted, not our bodies, and Ranevargar's going to put us both in a kind of trance for as long as we need to recover properly. Stay close. Maurice will take over while we're out of it."

"Out of it? You mean we won't be able to talk?"

"I know. There's so much to tell you, but it'll have to wait, because the trance will be like sleep, only deeper."

Rhys had a strange sense that all the others were sharing his disappointment. Well, Kieran must be talking to them too. The Courtyard took on a blue tinge and the conversation halted with the distraction of Krol launching skyward and all the Realm Lords moving hastily clear.

"We depart for the Central Grove. Rest and relax while we travel."

That was definitely Ranevargar's signature voice, and Rhys briefly wondered what was ahead. No, he was referring to their non-stop efforts since before daylight. Maurice's upward glance showed Krol joining the formation of Guardians as its silent wheeling changed to purposeful direction.

*   *   *

Everyone in the Courtyard watched in wonder as the blue-glowing Dragon, wings now spread in unmoving splendour, lifted silently clear of the Castle. Powerful wing beats initiated a dramatic bank of direction change and motion.

Aglaron, mind whirling with a gamut of thoughts and emotions, dismissed the wondrous images of the Construct and turned to Uirebon. "Keryth's conditioning distresses me, Uirebon, and he gave no indication of a resolution."

Empathy flowed.

"We will continue to know him as Kieran while he makes that resolution, my Lord. I suspect that private session with Maynor was connected in some way and I eagerly anticipate our meeting in a week's time."

"Yes ..."

Lady Narello disappeared as her elegant form morphed to that of her tall envoy, and Aglaron's contemplation was lost with the awareness of Maynor's silent attention.

"Maynor watches with his mind shuttered and an appearance of apprehension. Can he be expecting me to ignore Keryth's protection?"

"He knows you have cause, my Lord. Maybe he expects a negative, but technically acceptable, reaction of some kind."

"He knows me better than that. My clear displeasure and silent dismissal will be enough. Learn the way of communication with these wondrous Guardians while I dismiss him to his Realm."

At Aglaron's authoritative gesture, Maynor moved, with his Power Master, to the harnessed Griffins they'd arrived on and climbed into place. As soon as they were goggled and secure the Griffins received their release and climbed skyward.

"Astonishing. Their minds are shielded."

"Yes, Maynor has experience with their control, remember. Keryth wants them free when they've completed their task."

The High King pointed to seven Griffins perched at vantage points on the battlements. "The remaining Guardians have no restraints beyond an expectation of respect and care. We will make time to learn their ways as soon as possible, Uirebon. How long can you delay the return to your Realm?"

"Days, my Lord. My Realm was unaffected by Maynor's assault and all the need is here and in the Gateway Realm. My triads, with their indefinite stay, will assist as they can. Also, we must study the reconfigured Nexus."

"The Nexus? Uirebon, the Nexus functions as never before. Repair and restoration elsewhere must take priority."

"Of course, but Keryth expressly sought my help with knowledge of its working, as well as information about the history of his Realm."

"He did? And you wish to have this ready for our welcome? Then we will make it happen."

*   *   *

When Kieran's grasp on his arm lost its firmness the query rising in Rhys's mind was quickly cut off.

"Don't disturb him, Rhys. We must leave Kieran and the Maker to recover from their deep exhaustion. This time of travel will greatly help with their recovery."

"Time of travel? That sounds like it'll take a while?"

"Well over an hour, Rhys, if we stay with our Griffin escort."

"Is Krol all right? I can't believe how much he's been through today."

A slight adjustment of wing action lifted Maurice above the Griffins and Rhys quickly found Krol positioned near the end of the second formation.

"Why's he way back there? He's their leader."

"He accepts the assistance of formation flying on my instructions, Rhys. The food gave him a boost, but he needs more."

"Ranevargar told Kieran that Krol would be okay for two or three weeks."

"His memories show that he expended four or five weeks of normal effort in the five days of the quest."

"I don't know how he did it. Kieran knew when he was weary, but he never ever showed it."

"It was a joint effort, Rhys, and you are all weary."

An impression of Mr B very sensibly telling them all to relax and rest while they could, popped into Rhys's mind and made him smile.

"Close your eyes, Rhys. Mr B has just requested that I put you all to sleep till we approach the Grove."

*   *   *

Rhys blinked at the dark and stirred reluctantly. Not another one of

Woorawa's early get-ups? Every part of his body said it wanted to do nothing.

"It's late afternoon, Rhys, and I am not Woorawa."

Sleepiness slipped away.

"Maurice, what's happened now?"

"The Grove is close and I have woken you all to share in our approach. The Realm gathers to welcome the return of the Maker. Look."

The view through Maurice's eyes showed the Griffin escort winging its way above a strange multicoloured cloud, and the webs of drowsiness fled from Rhys's mind.

"How can there be so many?"

"The Guardians passed the news and the Realm responds. It is a wonder I thought you should all see."

It was a wonder indeed. So many birds that the ground below was blocked from view. A mass of dark birds wheeled in concert, with a change of direction causing a chain reaction of response. Rhys recognised them as one of the types of wading birds they'd seen so abundant in the lagoons beside the big lake. Awareness switched abruptly to Kieran resting quietly against his side.

"Yes, Rhys. Kieran and the Maker show no sign of awakening and I am not to disturb them unless there is a situation I can't handle."

There was a muffled laugh, which sounded like Woorawa. Treetops appeared far below when Dragon and Griffins left the massive flock behind and the convoy began to lose height.

"We must be getting close to the Grove?"

"Minutes, Rhys. This descent gives the Griffins a big increase in speed."

Maurice's view turned to the left and revealed another massive flock of birds.

"Are they all heading for the Grove?"

"Yes, Rhys. The abundance of life in this Realm is hard to comprehend. That is the seventh distinct flock we have overtaken."

Rhys pondered that till the vegetation below became the viewpoint.

"What sort of forest is that, Maurice? They can't all be Realm Trees."

Maurice's eyes focused finely for a moment.

"In my memory the Central Grove is a magnificent group of eleven trees, Rhys. The change after six hundred years is hard to comprehend, but those are definitely all Realm Trees, bordering the river, as far as I can see."

The Griffins wheeled and the new aspect, showing an end to the trees and the start of a familiar lake system, made Rhys want to yell with excitement. Maurice powered past the trees then veered and banked in a grand circle over the open plain and flared enormous wings to scoop air and touch down in a surprisingly elegant landing.

"Why the surprise, Rhys?"

Rhys, thinking about Kieran as their cover lifted, had other things on his mind. "What do we do about them? Will they wake up, or will we carry them down? The four of us can do it if we're careful."

Mr B, Woorawa and Tan were now standing next to him.

"They look too peaceful to move, Rhys. Maurice's fur is soft, and if he closes his flap again they'll stay comfortable."

"Mr B is right, Rhys. Nothing will disturb them here with me."

Tan and Woorawa were nodding their agreement.

"I suppose. After doing everything together it feels like we're deserting him ... I think I'll stay close."

"Unnecessary, Rhys. You are as close as a thought here in the Maker's Grove. The hosts are eager to welcome you and Kieran will contact you the moment he is ready."

Rhys turned at this mention of the hosts and his eyes widened. Host was the right description. There were so many of them ... And dwarfing them were five Panthers sitting regally on their haunches. He had to restrain his yell of greeting so as not to wake Kieran.

"Well, I suppose Maurice will be enough to look after him ... Let's go!"

*   *   *

More than an hour passed before Kieran's return to awareness kicked into action with a hasty check of everyone's wellbeing and whereabouts. *Ha! Lucky things.* They were all relaxing somewhere in warm water. A peek through Rhys's eyes showed Mr B next to him, all drowsy with his eyes closed. Woorawa was the same, and Tan's blissful smile was matched by the contentment pervading his mind.

"They are being well treated, Kieran, and we will join them when we are ready. How are you feeling?"

The channels between them were wide open, so this was a kind of acknowledgement rather than a real query.

"Kind of weird, Ranevargar. My mind feels like it's ready for anything and my body is all complaining and lazy."

The mental equivalent of a laugh flowed to Kieran.

"I am the other way round. My body has been deprived of action while my mind still wants to recover."

Kieran's automatic probe to check the state of Ranevargar's mind revealed the usual bewildering degree of complexity, a buzz of activity too fast to follow, then a wonderful mix of achievement and gratitude.

Whoops! He was looking way deeper than he'd meant to. His apology was cut off by a wash of welcome.

"Delve deep, Kieran. Our merge was successful beyond expectation, but several more practice sessions before the High King arrives would benefit us both."

"We need to keep him thinking I'm a sort of super Realm Lord?"

"A general precaution, Kieran, while you establish your independence."

"Yes, there's an awful lot to work out."

"Indeed, Kieran, and before you rejoin your companions there are serious matters you must consider and resolve. Some you have wisely held at bay for lack of proper information and some are new or only lightly considered."

"You mean about the High King? Everything you had me say to him is clear in my mind and we've got a week before we see him again, but you really mean Rhys, don't you?"

"I do, Kieran, but also Mr B. There is information I haven't yet given you."

After the deep sharing of the mind merge Kieran wondered how that was possible and it heightened some puzzles he'd mulled, rather briefly, after the first merge at Maynor's Castle. Was this the right time to air them? Yes, with serious things ahead it was.

"Ranevargar, I do trust you. You know that. But who are you really? Every time we do something you get more mysterious. Maynor's mind manipulation is kid-stuff compared to what you can do ... and you bypassed the High King's Nexus locks without even trying. I saw you ignore the golden helmet and make Maynor attack you instead of the High Castle ... And how come the other Realm Lords seem to think you're kind of harmless and helpless when you've been doing stuff they're clueless about? None of them could make a Realm Tree or a Guardian, let alone a Dragon Construct who can rule a Realm. Uirebon's the Lore Master and he was completely baffled at the way you brought Lady Narello to the Council."

There was more, much more, but Kieran stopped at the strange mixture of amusement and empathy flaring from Ranevargar.

"Kieran, I can only smile. Your questioning is mirrored by mine. The return of lost abilities and knowledge partially answers many of your questions, but it increases my bewilderment of who you are, or, rather, who you have become. My knowledge is ancient, garnered through the passing centuries that precede even Lord Uirebon's by a millennium. For almost five hundred years, till I sought greater fulfilment, I held, under another name, the keys to the Nexus."

"You were the High King and you gave it up?"

"Your grandfather was eminently suited to the position and won his Challenge convincingly. Kieran, you can take any Realm Stone at will. You call power unknown in Faerie. Rhys brings healing. Woorawa sings and overrides even my Dragon's power, and, just before we left the High Castle, Tan called truth from the High King."

"He what?"

"While we dealt with Maynor, Tan approached Aglaron, Uirebon and Lady Narello with an unknown aspect about him."

"An aspect? What does that mean?"

"I have no idea, Kieran. It was new for the Realms. Maurice recognised its significance and relayed his memories to us the moment we left Aglaron's privacy ward, but your mind was taxed and somewhat fuzzy by that stage."

Fuzzy! Rhys was going to love hearing that. Kieran peeked again, but Tan just felt like Tan. Yet another puzzle.

"Ranevargar, I haven't got a clue how all these things are happening, except that it has to be connected with my Opal, so it's all a mystery to me too ... but I haven't been hiding stuff like you have."

"There are no more secrets, Kieran. At the time I was concerned for your peace of mind while we confronted Maynor and Aglaron, but our merge has put an end to that"

"Ha! Now I'm not fuzzy it's okay to disturb my mind?"

A mix of concern and support washed strongly from Ranevargar.

"Are you Keryth, an elven prince with two hundred years of life and heritage ... or are you Kieran, a human mix of predominantly manufactured memories and a short half year of real life?"

Kieran was silent while he figured how to respond. *"I am both, Ranevargar ... You are saying I have to be one or the other?"*

"The information I gained from Maynor shows clearly that, with every case like yours, the sense of human identity was lost when the conditioning was reversed."

"You mean I wouldn't be me anymore?"

"In essence ... yes."

Kieran's response was a while in coming. *"That's ... that's like dying. I'd lose Rhys and everyone else. There's no way that's going to happen."*

More understanding flowed from Ranevargar along with a sense of sadness. *"And what of Keryth's life and love? That is as real as yours."*

"Love?"

"Of course, Kieran — the underlying situation that allowed all Maynor's manipulations."

Kieran went quiet when a new understanding sent his thoughts whirling. *"You said 'is', Ranevargar. You mean there's someone here in the Realms?"*

"Yes, there is, Kieran. Someone who means as much to Keryth as Rhys means to Kieran. Someone who sacrificed his love because he was cruelly manipulated into believing it was the best thing to do for you."

Puzzlement and curiosity passed with sudden and troubling understanding. *"This is what you were keeping from me?"*

"Yes, Kieran. Keryth was heart-bonded for two decades with Pethron, his quiet and gentle companion, till Maynor learned of the relationship and used it to further his own purposes."

"Pethron? It doesn't stir any memories ... and he wasn't in Aglaron's mind."

"You remember nothing of your elven persona, Kieran, and Pethron was a factor of great concern in Aglaron's mind."

Kieran jumped to the wrong conclusion. *"Why? Has he hidden Pethron somewhere and he's worried I'll be angry if I know?"*

"Steady, Kieran. That is an overly hasty judgement. Everyone knew with complete certainty, Maynor's contrived certainty, that they were acting in your best interest."

"So, he wasn't hidden?" A new and disturbing realisation grew in Kieran's mind. *"Is he waiting somewhere, still with a heart bond? I—"*

Ranevargar interrupted forcefully.

"Pethron currently has no memory of Keryth. He eagerly agreed to Maynor's suggestion that he watch and guide you through your time in the Human World. Your father and Uirebon believed he was there to test the efficacy of the conditioning, but Maynor was expecting to manipulate your underlying attraction as a way to ensure continued exercises with Nexus power."

"Underlying attraction? You mean ...?"

"Yes, Kieran. Pethron has been with you all along in the human persona of Mr B."

Kieran suffered a kind of mental speechlessness as the somewhat impersonal Pethron became the thoughtful and caring Mr B. *"This is awful, Ranevargar. If we get Maynor to reverse Mr B's conditioning and not mine it will be cruel and sad for him. What am I going to do?"*

"I won't instruct you, Kieran. The decisions you face are so weighty they must be yours and yours alone, but I do have some thoughts you might like to consider."

"Please. Share them with me."

"You have your own wellbeing, the wellbeing of your friends, and your relationship with your father, along with the restoration and future pathway for

*a Realm to take into account. Mr B must have a full understanding of that
pathway, because any decision about his own reconditioning should be his."*

*"I didn't mean I would make it for him, Ranevargar. You've been way
ahead of me, that's all."*

"I know you didn't, Kieran. Now what do you think of ..."

*   *   *

Rhys's steady stream of queries to Maurice about Kieran and Ranevargar
had at last brought a response that there were signs of stirring, and the
four friends, accompanied by a group of hosts, were making their way to
the clearing at the edge of the great Plain.

"How long since we left them, Tan?"

Tan checked his watch. "Just over two hours now. They must have been
even more exhausted than we thought."

"Yeah! I can't believe a healing boost wouldn't have helped."

Woorawa paused at a junction to check the alternative trail. "Another
track. I wonder how they stop themselves getting confused?"

"They wouldn't get lost on that one. It looks major."

Mr B agreed. "It certainly is, Rhys, and with all these hosts I'm not
surprised it looks so used, but they do live here, Woorawa, so it's probably
so familiar they don't even think about it."

"I wonder if they've got a location sense like Kieran's ... We'll probably
have more waiting while he gets cleaned up."

Mr B laughed. "Don't be so impatient, Rhys. We're meant to be relaxing.
The hot spring and fresh clothes will be a lot better for him than a boost ...
I think Ranevargar will take over looking after us."

Woorawa turned from checking the diverging trail. "He'll probably
confuse us with the hosts."

Rhys gave a disbelieving snort. "Get real, Woorawa! Is he going to think
one of the hosts painted himself black? You look like a dressed up lump
of coal."

Tan got rather indignant. "No he doesn't. These tunics look better on
him than they do on the rest of us. He's kind of ... distinctive."

Rhys grinned knowingly, while Mr B answered. "I agree with you, Tan.
Though he's kind of distinctive whatever he's wearing."

Woorawa shook his head, dismissing this nonsense.

After a few minutes the trail ended and the huge form of Maurice,
watching their approach with his great golden eyes, grabbed attention like
a magnet.

"Gods! He's so big and his eyes feel like they're sucking my mind away."

"Ha! Impossible, Rhys, even for Maurice. You can't suck anything out of a vacuum."

Rhys started to respond, but a mass of movement brought an excited yell instead. "Gryl!"

He started to run, but after a few steps the moving mass of five special Panthers enveloped him, and then the others, in their second effusive reunion of intimate head-butts and great, rasping licks.

"You great lump! I've already had a wash."

That just brought more licks and a rather amused communication from Maurice.

"More lumps, Rhys?"

Rhys's head turned and, after a parting neck hug, rushed to join Kieran and Ranevargar as they clambered from Maurice's back.

"Who are they, Ranevargar? I don't recognise these hosts, except for the distinctive-looking lump of coal that must be Woorawa."

"Stickybeak! Eavesdropper!"

The first moment of meeting, both mind and body and totally personal, spread to include all the friends, then changed, with Kieran's communication of shared accomplishment, to shared happiness.

"Yes, my friends, the Dragon Quest has succeeded and we are safe at home. Come with me, while Kieran is refreshed, to receive the acclaim of my Realm."

Rhys was reluctant — well, they all were really — to be apart from Kieran any longer. Kieran lifted his arm and sniffed as if disgusted.

"I'll be back as soon as I can. I really need a good cleanup and I'm not going to wait till after the welcome."

He gestured in Maurice's direction then hustled off with several of the hosts.

Rhys glanced at Maurice, wondering why they needed a welcome from him.

"Not just a welcome from Maurice, Rhys. Kieran was indicating the gathering behind him."

Ranevargar beckoned, then surprised the friends by nimbly returning to Maurice's back, beckoning them to follow, then ascending to the smooth standing area of the big skin flap.

Rhys was first, and with every step his astonishment grew. On the left, behind the day's five journey steeds, dozens more Panthers sat quietly on their haunches. To their right and hidden till now by Maurice's great body, were rank upon rank of Griffins. The goosebumps already rising in his hair ran down his neck when his eyes lifted to the multitude of animals gathered as far as he could see. Woorawa's gasp of disbelief was echoed in various ways by Tan and then Mr B. The friends stared while the silence around them pressed with uncanny force.

Rhys looked from Maurice's back, farther, and farther, to see where the enormous gathering of creatures finished. It didn't, and the enormity of the scene, coupled with the atmosphere of uncanny, expectant silence, set his heart racing, while his body stilled in a strange communion with the motionless horde. Tan grasped his hand and Mr B and Woorawa immediately pressed close and did the same, moving into Kieran's well-established support pattern for confronting dubious situations or sharing an energy boost. Rhys shivered with the strength of the bond then, realising something wasn't quite right, called a silent invitation.

"Ranevargar."

Ranevargar smiled happily and literally jumped to join the group and cover the little totem pole of hands with his own. His smile broadened and, with a nod which Rhys would never forget, returned his own gesture of inclusion. His green signature glow, softer than usual, outlined his body then flowed to surround the friends. A thank you feeling came with it which made everyone smile.

When one hand moved to indicate Maurice the glow flowed to him and the gratitude strengthened. Krol's head lifted when Ranevargar's hand directed the flow of glow, and happiness joined with gratitude. With a new smile, Ranevargar touched the place where he kept the pouch with his Pearl and gestured to all the other Griffins. The Panthers were next, then a mob, including George, of about thirty horses. The glow enveloped each new group like a softly rising mist, and with each new addition came a variation of happiness or gratitude. When Rhys, almost overwhelmed, thought they should all be part of this, an image popped into his mind of Kieran washing in warm water, with a happy smile and a swirl of soft green in front of his eyes.

"I am part of it, Rhys. Ranevargar's making sure of that and I'll be with you for the walk-through."

Rhys's attention returned to the green mist building around the host of creatures massed as far as his eyes could see. Ranevargar gestured again, this time to the Realm Trees, which blurred softly, with more green mist glowing eerily around every leaf and branch. Even the trees were thanking them? The glowing tree mist settled lower, then flowed down the great trunk to join the general glow and share a new sense of beneficence.

Ranevargar, joyous and radiant, waved broadly to the tree tops. For a brief moment Rhys thought Ranevargar must have magicked them with strange new life, but then the blur of moving vegetation took flight and revealed itself as a monstrous flock of silently wheeling white birds. Another flock, equally huge, joined from the side, then another and another. In the light from the sinking sun, patterns between white and dark shifted and shimmered with every swirl of movement, then, in a stunning moment, changed to the living glow of Ranevargar's green. The massive flock veered abruptly and Rhys watched as the ribbons of movement disappeared behind the Realm Trees.

Ranevargar nodded his raised head and the sky filled again, this time with myriads of tiny birds, already glowing.

Ranevargar's soft mental voice broke the spell of the surrounding silence. *"Flower and nectar birds, Mr B. We rarely see them because they live in the canopy."*

"How can there be so many?" Tan's question was an expression of wonder.

"The big flocks are still to come, Tan. This is the greatest gathering my Realm has ever seen."

"Big? There won't be enough room in the sky."

"They display for us till Kieran returns."

Kieran's voice, soft with wonder, interrupted. *"I am rushing, Ranevargar. Another ten minutes and I'll be with you, but I share the view through Maurice's eyes. It's ... I haven't got any words for it."*

The little birds cleared the sky, merging with the foliage and, ever so high above, a bank of glistening cloud rolled closer and closer. Maurice's eyes focused and the cloud was no longer a cloud.

Four physical gasps joined Kieran's mental one as new clarity showed the reality. The leading edge plunged downward and, like a waterfall in the sky, the main bulk flowed to follow. The vast mass moved lower, casting a shadow over the assemblage and deepening it to an eerie twilight before the mist of green turned dimness to soft radiance. Like a film show in reverse, the mass of birds, wading birds Rhys realised, now flowed skyward. The soft afternoon light returned and with it a jolt to their joined hands and a great smile as Woorawa indicated Kieran rushing towards them.

"He's glowing!"

"Everything's glowing, Rhys, including us."

"I know, but it's green and I'm used to blue. He stands out like he's got a spotlight on him."

With every eye that could see him watching, Kieran scrambled quickly up Maurice's back and, after giving Rhys an excited whack in the ribs, joined his hands to the top of the pile. Rhys's eyes lit up, but any response was forestalled when Ranevargar withdrew the hand that Kieran had covered and, in front of the great gathering, knelt on one knee and raised his arms in benison.

"Friends of the Realm, receive our thanks."

Rhys, Mr B, Tan and Woorawa all looked for Kieran's lead in how to respond, but all he did was look happy and cast his view over the gathering.

A deep, soft, rumble of sound intruded on the silence, pervading the senses with a strange stimulation. The rumble intensified, then amplified. Rhys, thinking the whole world was shaking with an earthquake, instinctively grabbed Kieran to hold him close ... What? He was smiling? Maurice's head twisted so golden eyes could regard them. His jaws opened and the rumble strengthened then, with a swing of his head, projected across the watching host. Sixty Griffins broke their silence with a loud scream of triumph and adulation. Panther Guardians raised their heads, and their roar, expressing challenge overcome and vast appreciation, quivered the friends to the core. They staggered under the tsunami of sound and emotion now flooding from the whole gathering.

Mr B, tears streaming from his eyes, took Tan and Woorawa's hands and lifted them high, and Rhys and Kieran instantly joined them for a group acknowledgement.

Ranevargar gestured now and green glow flowed from all directions to gather in a sphere of radiance which then floated to enclose the friends, flash with power and light, then absorb into their bodies. The sound subsided to a background roar while Ranevargar gave each of them a formal double wrist clasp and a gigantic hug.

"Walk with me a while, friends. Your day has been tiring and after eating we will sleep long and well."

"Sleep? With all this happening?"

"Yes, Rhys. Your energy boosts have sustained us through great extremity, but our inner reserves must have natural replenishment."

Ranevargar led the way down Maurice's back and headed toward Krol and the ranks of Griffins.

"When will we get the time to understand everything, Kieran?"

"We'll have a good talk tomorrow morning before our trip with the Panthers, but Ranevargar's right, Rhys. We've pushed non-stop for more than six days and your energy boosts hide how wrecked we really are. Ranevargar's got so much to talk about we'd be awake all night, but he says our recovery's a bigger priority."

Maurice broke into Rhys's mind. *"The Maker is particularly concerned that Kieran's extraordinary efforts of mind will compound with all the physical efforts. We can talk while Kieran sleeps, if you wish.*"

"*I heard that, Maurice, and no one's staying awake. I'm giving one of my sleep commands.*"

Woorawa laughed. "*You're outclassed, Rhys. Overwhelmed by the big guns.*"

"*Yeah! More waiting.*"

"*It's not really waiting. Kieran's sleep command makes the time pass in a blink.*"

Rhys wasn't listening. He rushed to greet Krol then watched as every Griffin sought the opportunity to gently touch its beak against Kieran's chest.

The Panthers were next, fifty or sixty of them gathered regal and proud while Gryl initiated a pattern of practically licking everyone's face off.

Ranevargar led the way, till the sunlight waned, through group after group of different creatures which all acknowledged Kieran, and then the rest of the friends, in some distinctive way. Flock after flock, wheeling overhead and filling the sky with sound this time as well as pattern, added to the unforgettable reception. George, in the company of twenty or thirty other horses, greeted Rhys with a happily wiffling sound, then turned to Kieran.

On the way back a noisy chitter-chatter delayed their progress when several hundred Joker birds descended to perch on heads, shoulders, arms, and the backs of nearby plains grazers. Woorawa and Rhys, smiling at their clownish bobbing, laughed outright at the sight of three of them friskily tugging at Ranevargar's hair.

When they neared the waiting hosts, Maurice's golden eyes bathed them with a sense of joyful inclusion, a far cry from the customary unfathomable pools, and it all became too much for Mr B. He grasped Ranevargar's hand, knelt on one knee, then lowered his forehead to rest a moment against the fingers he was holding.

"Lord Ranevargar, my heart is overwhelmed with joy and beauty."

Kieran shivered at the wave of empathy and understanding from Woorawa, Tan and Rhys, then watched with quiet awe as Ranevargar reversed the positions, tugging Mr B to his feet then kneeling to rest his own forehead against Mr B's fingers.

*   *   *

Kieran studied Rhys's features, relaxed so peacefully against the luxuri-ous fur covering the soft feather-filled sleeping base, and marvelled at the providence that had brought them together. Providence? How strange that Maynor's selfish machinations could bring such a gift. Kieran sent a thought to dim the bio-luminous blossoms, smiling at Rhys's earlier reaction when Ranevargar showed them how, and moved quietly through the narrow walkway grown to connect with the next sleeping area.

"Mr B! Wake up!"

Mr B resisted the call to wakefulness. Relaxed so completely by the comfort, the demands of his body for recovery, and the lingering imperative of the sleep command, it took Kieran several minutes of gentle insistence before he sat up with full awareness.

"Kieran? It's still dark. What's happening?"

"We need to talk, Mr B. Things are very complicated."

*　*　*

Rhys woke, wriggled clear of the covers and, trying not to disturb Kieran, climbed carefully over him and made an urgent rush to the curious little toilet alcove. *Whoa!* Too much of that nectar drink last night. What time was it? Lots of light streaming through the entrance vines ... It must be well into morning. Kieran looked so peaceful he might sleep for ages. Cuddling next to him would be nice ... No, that might wake him up, and after Maurice's admonishment about how sleep was extra important, that mustn't happen. *Hey, wow!* There were his Melbourne clothes, all clean and folded, just inside the entrance. Someone had sneaked them in.

"Rhys, you have woken early."

"Yo, Maurice. I didn't have a choice. Did you have a good sleep too? What's so funny?"

"After six hundred years of sleep, I hardly need more."

"You stayed awake? Do you even go to sleep? Krol and Gryl do."

"The physical portion of their bodies demands it. I will rest any part of me if it becomes over-taxed."

"Are the others showing any signs of waking up? Kieran looks like he'll be out of it for ages."

"No signs at all, and the Maker doesn't want them disturbed in any way, especially Kieran."

"Ranevargar's awake?"

"Yes, Rhys, but only just. He is making arrangements in preparation for your busy day. But partake of some food, then keep me company for a while."

"Partake? Why does everyone in the Realms sound like a walking dictionary? I thought it was just Ranevargar, but you're the same, and so was the

High King."

Rhys thought he felt a whisper of sensation in his mind.

"*My own vocabulary emulates that of the Maker, Rhys, but I suspect the formality of the Courts and the extended elven lifespans are probably factors.*"

"*You mean they live so long they can't help learning lots of words?*"

"*Hmm! Your succinct exposition demonstrates the differences in our speech patterns quite pointedly.*"

"*You're an idiot, Maurice! I know when you're taking the Mickey out of me.*"

"*And I know that being insulted and accused of extracting some hidden persona is, in fact, an expression of friendship.*"

Rhys, having moved to the shelter where a range of food was waiting, was now preoccupied with making his choices. Honey-bread was the best.

"*Yum! It's a pity you don't eat, Maurice. You miss out on all these delicious tastes.*"

"*No, I don't. The honey-bread tingles with sweetness and every bite insists another be taken.*"

"*What are you talking about? You told me you only eat power.*"

"*And so I do, but by courtesy of your generous permission I share the sensation and taste of food through you.*"

"*Hey! That's kind of weird, like eating without eating. What happens when the five of us are eating different food at the same time? Do the tastes all mix together?*"

"*Yes and no, Rhys. I would say it is much the same as listening to a group of people talking. You can hear them all, but for your own reasons, such as interest or need, you focus on the message coming from one individual at a time.*"

Rhys laughed. "*So when Woorawa drools over those yellow fruit things he gives off thought vibes that catch your attention?*"

"*Precisely, though your own vibes for honey-bread are even more striking.*"

"*What? Don't tell him that or I won't be able to call him a greedy guts anymore.*"

"*I am quite certain you will continue the practice regardless of anything I might say.*"

Before heading through the vines, Rhys reduced his cache of honey-bread from four slices to two, hesitated a moment to add one of the yellow fruits, then pretended he didn't hear the soft little whisper of '*greedy guts*' in the back of his mind.

His eyes adjusted to the brighter morning light. Good grief! Except for Maurice, the animals were all gone.

"*Yes, Rhys. The Griffins have returned to their mountain homes for the day and the Panthers are shepherding the other animals to their customary feeding places.*"

Rhys made his way to the great form crouching motionless on the edge of the plain. "*You look like a giant statue shining in the sunlight when you keep so still.*"

"*My body may be still but my mind is fully challenged, Rhys, and has been all night.*"

"*All night? Were you planning stuff with Ranevargar?*"

"*The Maker slept as deeply as you did, Rhys. I spent some of the time pondering and refreshing the knowledge and abilities the Maker restored, and a great deal more consolidating the foundations for Kieran's Realm.*"

"*What exactly does that mean? It can't really all be his, can it?*"

"*To all intents and purposes it is, Rhys. His mysterious Opal bestowed the Stewardship beyond any questioning.*"

"*Is a Steward different to a Realm Ruler?*"

"*It would surprise me if Kieran viewed his Realm in the manner of Maynor, Rhys, but that would be his choice.*"

"*No way! I wouldn't let him. He'll copy Ranevargar's way, because it's the best.*"

"*You wouldn't let him? Isn't that rather hasty? None of you have more than a passing experience of any Realm other than Dead World and this one.*"

Rhys laughed. "*Imagine trying to force Kieran against his will.*"

"*That is still possible, Rhys, even for me, though the consequences don't bear thinking about.*"

Rhys was amazed. "*No way! He beat you fair and square in the Challenge when you woke up, didn't he?*"

"*The Challenge followed a strict order where the Maker had guided his mastery of every step. He has learnt many new things since then, but in many ways Kieran is still a novice compared to other Realm Lords. Without the merge with the Maker he would have been very vulnerable.*"

"*Yes, they did explain that, but wouldn't his special mind shield protect him?*"

Rhys carefully placed his remaining pieces of food on the ground, slapped himself on the cheeks quite gently five or six times, then proceeded to alternate between kissing Maurice's massive leg and passionately moaning how he loved him so much he wanted to hold him forever. After four or five repeats he abruptly realised what he was doing.

"*Stop! Stop! This is weird.*"

"And very pleasant, Rhys. I didn't suspect you were such an ardent admirer."

Rhys stopped the peculiar behaviour and felt like himself again. Well, a rather stunned self. *"Holy hell! That was bizarre! You could do that to Kieran? Hey! What did you mean about a suspicion? I do admire you but … ardent?"*

"I'm sure I could, Rhys, though there are aspects about Kieran's mind which would make me very wary of any such attempt."

Rhys loved hearing this. *"What sort of aspects?"*

"His response can be both unexpected and overwhelming."

"Like when he called the White energy and nearly cooked you?"

"Precisely."

"You should try this stuff, but tell him first, Maurice, so he can learn about it."

"The Maker has plans to work closely with Kieran on many matters."

"What about the Portal system? Is that one of them?"

"I know with certainty that it is one of their highest priorities. The Maker has already visited the Oasis Grove to check his Realm Tree systems."

"What? He couldn't have. You said he's only just woken up."

"It was practically the first thing he did."

"Wow! That's a big change then. He used to wait for half an hour or more while he recovered enough."

"That change is your doing, Rhys. You healed him, and Kieran poured energy into his reserves."

"Hang on! The Portal system's meant to be broken?"

"The general system is. The Realm Trees are the Maker's unique energy-saving innovation and they function quite independently."

Rhys quite liked the idea that the other Realms were stuck with slow transport, then had an idea for Woorawa. *"We might be able to take Woorawa to the Ocean Grove again. He raved about the Dolphin Guardians and the islands just about every day in Dead World."*

"I will take you all this afternoon if time permits. I would like to see the ocean too."

Rhys's jaw dropped. *"You know how to portal?"*

The surroundings blurred and Rhys stared at familiar sparkling Oasis waters.

"Yes, Rhys. If the Maker's plans had worked all those centuries ago it would have been my preferred way of travel."

"Why? Isn't flying more exciting?"

"It is, but the energy required for each launch, as well as the time factor, makes it quite impractical."

"You could use launching platforms like the Griffins."

"Indeed, and I will establish many."

Rhys moved towards the Oasis, but with another blur the surroundings resolved to the Central Grove. *"Hey! That was too quick. I was going to check the water."*

"It was a practical test for my knowledge, Rhys, and most satisfactory, but the Maker informs me that Woorawa and Tan are awake."

"Well, about time!"

"Shall I inform them that despite the predations of a certain greedy guts, enough food remains for their breakfast?"

"No way! Tell them they have to suffer while they wait for Kieran and Mr B to wake up."

"Hmm! The response surprises me enough to pass it word for word ... I see ... Woorawa says that means you are awake and there is probably no honey-bread left."

"Typical! They'll be out here soon ... Why is our day going to be busy? Kieran said we're having a big talk, but that won't last the whole day."

"Have you forgotten the Panther ride? That will be extensive."

"Extensive?"

"Into the Grove with the Panthers, Rhys. This Central Grove can only be described as extensive ... Ah, here come Woorawa and Tan."

They were too, and Rhys grinned as he thought of a good greeting. *"When they get here, do the kiss you and love you thing. It'll be a good experience for them."*

"Are you sure? You continue to surprise me, Rhys."

Woorawa, holding two of the yellow fruits, gave Rhys a morning greeting then, with Tan, watched in astonishment as Rhys whacked himself five times on the cheek then repeatedly kissed Maurice's leg and proclaimed undying love for him.

"You idiot, Maurice. I meant them, not me."

"Hey, Rhys? Did you get enough sleep?"

Curses, everyone was too clever. Tan had just spoilt the whole slug-a-bed opening.

"That was meant to be you, but Maurice had a brain fade."

"You did say it would be a good experience for them, Rhys, and apart from a moment of concern it's clear they thoroughly enjoyed it."

Woorawa popped one of the yellow fruit into his mouth and Tan gave a 'please explain' look.

"Maurice has got all sorts of new abilities and he was showing me how Kieran might be vulnerable to other Realm Lords. He can portal the same as Ranevargar and Kieran too, and we just went to the Oasis Grove."

"Yes, Tan. It is possible to portal, but only within the Realm Tree system."

"If we get the chance this afternoon, Maurice is going to take us to see the Dolphin Guardians."

Woorawa's eyes lit up. "Where's Ranevargar? Is he still asleep? We thought he'd be here."

"Greetings, friends. Gryl approaches and I will join you when he arrives."

"Ranevargar! Did you have a good sleep ... and is Kieran all right? He's sleeping like a log."

"All is well with him, Woorawa, though he will sleep deeply for almost another hour."

"You know when he's going to wake up?"

"Yes, Tan. He happily accepted my offer to hold him in a deeply restorative sleep."

Rhys sent his strong approval. *"Neat! Is it better than his own sleep command?"*

"Very similar, Rhys, but with refinements."

"Did you do the same to Mr B?"

"No, but his mind is stirring, so he will be with you soon."

Rhys followed the sudden sweep of Maurice's head to the open plain and fixed on the rush of movement. *"Whoo! Look at them go! ... Are they racing?"*

"Indeed they are, Rhys. They are excited and extremely pleased to be spending the day with you."

Smiles took over as they watched the rapid approach.

"The whole day?"

Rhys answered. *"They're taking us on a trip into the Grove for some reason, Tan, like Kieran said."*

The meeting with Gryl and eleven other Panthers was tumultuous.

∗   ∗   ∗

Kieran, wide awake and feeling particularly alert after his prolonged sleep, didn't even try to restrain his smile at the curious setup of this important gathering. Ranevargar was relaxed against Maurice's leg, Gryl was crouched close, with Rhys sitting on his back and Woorawa and Tan against his side, while Mr B was leaning against the side of Maurice's grounded head. Ranged in a comfortable spread, the rest of the Panthers watched quietly like some kind of relaxed guard.

"Well, I slept longer than I expected, but we finally get to have our big powwow about everything that happened yesterday. The first thing to clear up is the portal situation. We already know it's seriously bad, but Ranevargar's hopeful we might be able to work something out."

"To take us home?"

"Yes, Tan. It won't be the big portal system, because that's going to take more than a year to recover, but he suspects there might be other ways we could use."

All eyes turned to Ranevargar.

"I currently have more knowledge of portals than anyone in the Realms, Tan, but there are vast stores of ancient knowledge tucked away in the study Centres of Lord Uirebon's Realm and we have tasked him to a major search for anything that might help."

"He's already looking?"

"Not personally, because he's assisting Aglaron, but he has sent word to every Centre in his Realm, making it a first-order task."

"First order? For his whole Realm?"

"Yes, Rhys. We impressed its importance on him yesterday and he commanded it even before we left the High Castle. He is eager to help in any way possible, as well is being intrigued in his own right."

"Do you think there's much hope of finding another way?"

"I do have hope, Mr B. Certainty is very low indeed, but Kieran and his Opal have a habit of surprising us and may well do so again."

Tan broke in. "That makes a lot of sense to me. Kieran and the Opal brought us here without any help, so they should be able to go the other way. Why don't we go back to Maynor's Emperor trees where we arrived and Kieran can learn that as a focus, like he does for proper Realm Trees. Home in Melbourne must be strong enough in his mind for the other focus."

Ranevargar's approval washed through everyone. "I have pondered that possibility, Tan, and it is certainly worth trying."

Tan's head lifted. "There's a strong 'but' isn't there?"

"I am afraid so. Kieran did seize it for himself, but that transfer used the damaged system and can't be repeated till it is functioning again."

"The Realm Tree portals are independent. Could you build something the same only bigger?"

"I have re-established enough of my lost knowledge to let me build new portals, Rhys, but only within my own Realm. When Kieran is proficient, I hope we can work together to extend the range between Realms."

Kieran boggled, along with everyone else. "Me? Build my own Tree portal?"

"Yes, Kieran, you certainly have the ability and it may well be a necessary skill for a return to the Human World."

"There aren't any Realm Trees at home."

"One step at a time, Rhys."

Tan linked arms with Woorawa. "Woorawa's got one."

Woorawa squeezed the link. "We'd have to get it home first, Tan, but I don't see how we can plant it. I think it will be better to give it to Kieran for his new Realm."

Kieran was shocked. "No way, Woorawa. It's a special gift."

"I know, Kieran, but I've been thinking about it a lot. Imagine what would happen if a 300m-high tree grew in the desert. You couldn't hide it, and scientists and tourists from all over the world would converge on it. And doesn't it need power like yours, and those Tree Managers to help it grow properly?" He turned to Ranevargar. "I feel guilty, Ranevargar, because you said it's for my people. You see what I mean though, don't you? We could keep it as a seed, but that's wasting all its potential."

Ranevargar regarded Woorawa for several seconds before speaking, very formally, into everyone's silent curiosity. "What I see, Woorawa of the Ancient People, is wisdom. What I see, Dark Child, is a mantle of Stewardship for your people and your friends." He relaxed and smiled at Woorawa's dumbfounded expression. "I think your years of darkness allow you to see things clearly, young Woorawa, but Kieran accepts the spirit of your gift and no more."

Feeling a bit left behind, Kieran nodded the agreement Ranevargar was clearly expecting.

"Kieran doesn't need it, Woorawa, and there will be ways to address any concerns you have about its planting."

"You couldn't hide it, Ranevargar, not when it gets that high."

"A Tree Manager can direct its growth in any way Woorawa wishes, Rhys."

Rhys looked at the nearby giant bole. "All that? Where would it go? Sideways?"

Tan got all enthusiastic at that idea. "It could grow like a Banyan tree. I've read about big ones with hundreds of trunks."

"A tree with more than one trunk?"

"Yes, Woorawa, they're all connected. The tree sends an aerial root to the ground and it grows till it's like a new trunk ... Could the Manager do that?"

"With no trouble at all, Tan."

Rhys had another look at the Realm Trees. "It could spread for hundreds of metres in every direction with all that mass, but what about power to help it grow? Could Kieran give it some?"

Kieran got excited now. "Of course I could, but I won't need to. Woorawa has already got tons."

"I have? What do you mean?"

"The rubies in your pocket. You can keep one. That should be plenty ... Shouldn't it?"

Ranevargar smiled. "Plenty indeed, Kieran. Enough to stimulate the early growth of hundreds of trees in fact, but you have a misconception that all Realm Trees need power. In fact they grow naturally and produce their own power. I designed them that way, and they only need external power when they are managed for special purposes."

Woorawa touched the pocket with the rubies. "A ruby's no good to me, Kieran. How would I use it?"

"Easy! We just make it automatic, like the reserve for your shield ... Does that stimulation have much effect, Ranevargar?"

"An enormous effect, Kieran. With constancy and a good water supply you could effect decades of growth in a single year."

"Whoo, stop everyone! We were talking about how to portal home and we've got sidetracked to Realm Trees."

Ranevargar nodded. "You're right, Rhys, but they do relate. As I was saying, I consider the mastery of Realm Tree portals as Kieran's best foundation for any other method that might arise from Lord Uirebon's search, and skill with their growth is definitely part of that."

"Oh boy! That means a lot of heavy sessions for you and Kieran."

"Very heavy sessions, Rhys, across a broad range of topics."

Rhys nodded knowingly to everyone else. "Hours and hours of Buddha stuff to strain his brain."

"Not just his, Rhys."

Rhys, about to commiserate with Ranevargar, suddenly realised the reference was to his own brain, but Woorawa had something on his mind.

"I don't understand, Ranevargar. Surely the seed pod would help Kieran learn about growing Realm Trees?"

"It would, Woorawa, but he doesn't need yours when my Central Grove will supply as many as he requires."

"Lots of them?"

"Yes, Woorawa. Maurice has been readying the foundations for life in Kieran's Realm, but he is eager to return and proceed once he knows Kieran's vision."

Rhys was nodding, because of his earlier talk with Maurice, but

Woorawa, Tan and Mr B had to take it in.

"Decide on a vision for the whole Realm? We're here to help with that right now?"

Kieran jumped to his feet and spoke with great earnestness. "I'm thinking we could make it basically like this Realm, but with any changes we like."

Rhys jumped up to keep with Kieran. "I think that's a great idea. Everything we've seen here is awesome."

Ranevargar smiled at the word. "Thank you, Rhys, but my focus has primarily been to provide a sanctuary and I think you should consider other features."

"Like what?"

Tan spoke up. "I don't know how much prejudice there is, but what about making it a sanctuary for Widderkin elves? Kieran already made a big deal about that at the High council."

Kieran and Rhys looked at each other with big grins.

"Good thinking, Tan."

"Well, there aren't any towns here and that might need a big change if they've been living in Castles or towns, or on farms like the ones we saw near Maynor's Castle."

Kieran looked to see what everyone else was thinking. "Hmm! Tan's right, Ranevargar. Would it be hard to have different kinds of living areas like that?"

"You would need them anyway, Kieran, but how extensive they are is your real decision. There are a variety of what you would call towns in this Realm, Tan. Living in Realm Trees doesn't suit everyone, so there are alternatives. There are communities of artisans and crafters too."

"Artisans?"

"For the basic amenities, Woorawa. Clothing, pottery ... Your carry packs and the saddlery we will be using today, for example."

Mr B looked very thoughtful. "This will all be extremely complex, Ranevargar. How long before the Realm could be habitable? We didn't see even one plant the whole time we were there .... let alone a Realm Tree ... And how big is it? The mountains kept going way into the distance."

Rhys got excited at this. "Gods yeah! They looked enormous too ... And what about oceans? We hardly know anything."

Ranevargar raised an eyebrow in case Kieran wanted to answer. "Yes, Rhys. The mountains, unique in size and extent, are called the Great Range, and there are oceans as well as vast plains. Compare the size of the new Realm with what you know of mine. The time needed to make it habitable depends on the resources available and the power Kieran can use to stimulate them."

Kieran nodded, because Ranevargar had already given him a basic overview. Everyone else went silent while they processed this.

"What resources? There's nothing there ... except water from the storms."

"Ranevargar's helping us, Rhys. Well, helping Maurice really, because I haven't learnt enough yet, and tomorrow we're going to the Realm with a whole lot of seeds for the area where we started to climb up to Maurice's cavern."

"The pass with the riverbed?"

"A flood of water came down yesterday and when the weather's properly organised it'll be a permanent river ... Ranevargar, we can't do everything at once, so I think it makes sense to concentrate our efforts on getting that one main area really well established."

Rhys jabbed Kieran in the ribs. "You've been planning stuff with Ranevargar without telling us again, Kieran. What does established mean?"

"I can't do it myself yet, Rhys, but Ranevargar and Maurice can help things grow extra quickly."

"Like the little plant growing out of the table?"

"More a general application of power to ensure germination and optimum growth for the locations Kieran chooses, Tan, except for any Realm Trees which will receive special attention."

Woorawa pounced on that. "Kieran *will* need pods then?"

"Yes, Woorawa, and that is the purpose of our Grove trip today. There are almost eighty pods ready to collect."

Along with everyone else, Kieran stared at Ranevargar in disbelief. "What?"

"Kieran, I now have the vigour to generate new pods, but until they are ready this is all I can offer. For the Realm structure you have been discussing that is barely a start."

"Eighty Realm Trees feels like a great number to me."

"Not at all, Mr B. Maurice has already discussed his need for a system of portal Groves with Rhys, and just ten outlying locations would require half of those pods. A three-layer Grove near our mutual Boundary would take another eleven, leaving a scant thirty for a Central Grove."

Woorawa looked to the nearby Realm Trees. "There's nothing scant about a Realm Tree."

Mr B had something to say. "It depends how you look at them, Woorawa ... How many shelters can a Realm Tree have, Ranevargar?"

"It would be possible to grow dozens, Mr B, but in practice it is rarely more than four or five."

Mr B continued. "See, Woorawa, thirty Realm Trees would be very limiting ... What's the population of your Realm, Ranevargar? Do you know how many hosts there are?"

"They're in his Pearl network, Mr B. He knows exactly."

"If I counted them, Kieran ... There are thousands, Mr B, though not all are hosts. Along with the towns we discussed there are families, wardens, and a range of other individuals sharing this Central Grove."

"What's the point of the three-layer Grove, Ranevargar?"

"I plan to establish a new Grove close to Woorawa's waterfall, Mr B, to reduce the travel time to our mutual Boundaries, and an adjacent Grove in Kieran's Realm would be an invaluable help for Maurice's resource management."

Unexpectedly, Rhys thought that was funny. "You could call it ... the Waterfall Grove ... Or even the Woorawa Grove."

Woorawa went all embarrassed and tried to change the subject when everyone showed their agreement. "How long will it take before new Realm Trees can turn into portal trees?"

"Decades with normal growth, but with special attention a number of selected trees could be ready in nine or ten months."

"What about technology? Would that be part of your Realm, Kieran?"

There was a collective gathering of thoughts at Tan's return to the Realm vision discussion.

"What do you mean?"

Tan lifted his wrist and indicated his watch. "Well, this definitely works, but we've never seen anything like it."

Every eye swivelled to Ranevargar who paused thoughtfully before answering. "The successful functioning of the Realms relies on deep study of the mind, Tan, with years of training in the manipulation of Nexus power and other forms of power. Our extended lifespan is also related to focusing inward rather than outward to the physical world. For my own Realm I like to maximise the diversity and importance of living things. Discuss this with the other Realm Lords when they visit and you will see deep discomfort and disdain for the material path."

"Wow! That's kind of confronting, Ranevargar. I love parts of our technology, like computers and communication, but we don't manage it very well. Lots of our natural life is dying because of it."

Ranevargar frowned. "There are sanctuaries provided, Woorawa, surely?"

Tan answered this time. "There are, but lots of people think power and money is more important ... What about money, Kieran? Will you have that in your Realm?"

"Whoa! I haven't even thought of money since we got here, Tan. Do you use it, Ranevargar?"

There was an extended pause while Ranevargar accessed five sets of understandings.

"Not really. It seems to be an accumulation of resources or even indirect power. I see from your own thoughts that you used it mainly to gain the food and shelter which is abundant and free here. For Maynor, and maybe Lady Narello, it would equate to the accumulation of power, for Uirebon the stores of knowledge. The High King would regard it as irrelevant."

Kieran turned to Tan. "Well, if it's power I'm richer than anyone in the Realms."

"Hey, yeah! Imagine if you could swap your power for money at home. You'd be the richest student at college."

"There is no need to imagine it, Rhys. With the power Kieran commands he can have any resource he desires."

"Back in Melbourne? What's he going to do? Walk into a bank and zap the manager to give him money?"

Mr B shook his head. "That's hardly ethical, Rhys ... Banks are a system for managing money, Ranevargar ... But remember when Kieran found every bit of glass in the room just by thinking about it, Rhys? He could do the same with precious things if he was in the right location."

"My God! You could go to an old goldfield and use your GPS thing to find nuggets."

Kieran gave a very wary answer. "I suppose so, but it seems too easy, like I'd be cheating."

Mr B was forceful. "Not at all, Kieran, and think how useful extra finances would be? Woorawa could fly home more frequently, and Tan's car is your only transport."

Ranevargar's audible laugh came with a mental wash of amusement. "Kieran, accumulation of such a resource is so minor a thing it is irrelevant. Turn your attention to the main purpose of this meeting."

Kieran wondered why it was funny till he saw Ranevargar's appreciation of how new this was and the leaps of understanding still ahead.

"We'll all adapt, Ranevargar, but you're right and we should move on. Rhys knows a bit and so does Mr B, but the shock of seeing Aglaron's features and familiar mannerisms matching mine was a real jolt, and I wish I'd been able to prepare you more. I had some warning from watching Maynor's talks with Ranevargar, but it was so confronting I couldn't accept it."

"We didn't believe it either, Kieran. We decided it was a weird mental projection to confuse us ... He really is your father?"

"Yes, Woorawa. Ranevargar's knowledge of Aglaron for over 1400 years didn't match with him arranging for my mind to be conditioned, and he only found out the full truth when he made a deep interrogation of Maynor."

Rhys released his proprietary grip on Kieran's arm and gave him a giant hug. "Ranevargar told us you might be an elf that very first day, but I don't care. You're always Kieran to me."

There was silence while everyone watched Kieran's deep emotion settle to a happy smile which lingered long on Rhys then turned to include everyone else.

"You're all so amazing!"

Woorawa broke the new silence. "What's going on, Kieran? Your own father sends you to Melbourne and makes all this stuff happen, and you've changed from being so angry you'd throw a zillion tons of Opal energy at him to helping him and inviting him here? It must be a major change, because Rhys hardly reacted either, and yesterday he wanted Maurice to eat him or make him grovel on his stomach."

Kieran's arm tightened its hold on Rhys. "Too much has been going on, Woorawa, and I only found out the real truth yesterday when we were crossing the High Realm Boundary and Ranevargar merged to get ready for the big meeting. Aglaron only thought he wanted to send me away and it never would have happened if I hadn't persuaded him it was the best thing to do."

"You?" Woorawa thought his exceptionally good hearing must be playing tricks, but Tan's gasp and jerk of disbelief said it wasn't.

"Yes, Woorawa. I didn't believe it either, but Ranevargar showed me how Maynor manipulated my mind into believing it was the only way to help my father and the Realms."

"Your father was reluctant?"

"Originally, yes. He was deeply troubled that I was Widderkin, but Ranevargar's convinced that without Maynor's influence he would have come to accept it."

Woorawa looked to Ranevargar. "Maynor could have that much influence? You told us the High King's got the strongest mind in all Faerie."

"Maynor manipulated every Realm Lord, Woorawa, except for me, who he regarded as irrelevant. His influence over Aglaron was insidious and very cleverly developed through support and, indeed, friendship for at least three centuries."

Rhys shook his head in disgust. "Every Realm Lord? Gods! He's done all the stuff with the Challenge, dragged us here and paralysed you for days, and now you're telling us he was messing with everyone's minds as well. I don't understand this, Ranevargar. None of us do. How come he gets off so easy? He's back in his Castle, ruling his Realm like nothing happened."

"Aglaron, Uirebon and Lady Narello feel exactly as you do, Rhys, but, understanding there must be considerations outside their knowledge, they bowed to Kieran's will. The High King would have taken Maynor's Realm Stone and his Realm, and Lady Narello wanted his mind wiped and rebuilt."

"What considerations? They must be pretty important."

"Important indeed! Kieran's conditioning is so uniquely keyed to Maynor's mind that, until we can discover an alternative, we need his faculties healthy and unchanged."

"You're kidding! What happens to Kieran if Maynor dies or something else goes wrong?"

"Kieran's elf persona would be lost. All his memories and identity would be gone. A loss Kieran could not face with you and your companions."

"Maynor's a mongrel."

"The consequences for Maynor are not as minor as you think, Rhys. Centuries of planning and effort have come to nothing. He is denied any part in matters of the High Court. His role as advisor is no more and he now lives with the bitter understanding that his greatest ambition can never be realised."

"Why not? At the Council they said he could make another Challenge after fifty years."

Ranevargar laughed. "And then face Kieran, who can force him to kneel with little effort? No, Rhys, he knows that path is gone."

Tan looked very concerned. "Do you have much hope that you'll discover a way round the keying, Ranevargar, in case he does something with it out of spite or revenge? It might be important."

"With time I will find a solution, Tan, but you're right, it's so much of a concern I've done a little coercion of my own, to make sure the thought doesn't enter his mind."

"You can manipulate the manipulator? Neat!"

"Yes, Rhys, using skills recovered with Maurice's awakening."

Tan turned to Kieran. "What was the point of sending you to Melbourne for the conditioning, Kieran?"

"That was sneaky clever, Tan. Because it was outside the Realms it was a way for him to learn about controlling the Nexus Power and it worked perfectly."

Rhys, who'd been listening closely, brought another laugh to the discussion. "Until he got too big for his britches and tried to clobber Kieran's shields."

Ranevargar had a dampener for this enthusiasm. "Not really, Rhys. He was as surprised as Aglaron and Uirebon by the unexpected strength of Kieran's resistance, but that resistance actually accelerated his plans to gain access to, and then control of, the Free Nexus energy. It wasn't until the astonishing moment when he tried to take the Opal that he was truly clobbered."

Tan had another question. "There's more I don't understand, Kieran. The brainwashing was working till Rhys and the Opal got involved, so he wouldn't have needed extra energy."

"More sneaky plotting, Tan. He had a supporting plan to interfere with the Widderkin conditioning and make extra interventions necessary."

Rhys got a funny look. "Interfere? Is that something to do with me?"

Kieran gave him a squeeze. "You would have helped his plans if you weren't so special, Rhys. No, he brainwashed another elf to do that. Another elf who my father and Uirebon thought was being sent to look out for me and test how well the conditioning was working."

Rhys turned to look directly at Kieran. "How was he meant to do that? Seduce you or something?"

"Not in a nasty way, Rhys. He would just be friendly and helpful and every time my Widderkin nature responded Maynor would have cause for a reinforcement session."

"Friendly and helpful? How come we don't know him then?"

"We do, Rhys. Maynor sent the nicest person you could ever imagine."

"Well ..."

Woorawa, his features burning with understanding, scrambled to his feet and rushed to give Mr B a hug. Tan, startled for all of two seconds by Woorawa's desertion, raced to join them.

"What? Are they right, Kieran?"

"Triplets, Rhys! Maynor chose so well it wasn't just me who responded."

Kieran watched Rhys's initial astonishment change to a moment of wry acknowledgement that he had indeed responded, then, after a longer time of consideration, build to anger. His body stiffened and he stared at Mr B with reddened cheeks.

"Kieran, that's just ... evil. Brainwashed and sent to Melbourne? Is he all right? Can you fix it? What does he want to do?"

"Steady, Rhys. He's completely all right and he doesn't want the conditioning removed. We had a big talk last night and he's coming back to Melbourne with us."

Anger and concern were replaced with delight as Rhys rushed to add his hugs to those of Woorawa and Tan.

Mr B laughed while he struggled with a barrage of questions he couldn't answer.

"When will you reveal the full story, Kieran? I have a sense that secrets are not in the best interests of your group."

"Me too, Ranevargar, but not just yet. There's already too much happening."

"Yes, that is wise. All of them are feeling the need to be brought properly up-to-date."

"Everything just got a lot more complicated!"

"The big question has dawned with Woorawa, Kieran."

And indeed, Woorawa was nudging Tan and directing attention towards Kieran.

"You said back to Melbourne, Kieran, which we all expect, but how does that work if you're an elf and the High King's son and a Realm Ruler? When you get your memories back you might have to stay here."

"I'm not going to get them back, Woorawa. Ranevargar's looked carefully at how Maynor's conditioning works, and reversing it means I stop being me and I turn into a two hundred-year-old elf called Keryth. I told Ranevargar that losing Rhys and the rest of you would be the same as dying."

Woorawa once again broke the long silence that followed. "Well, we don't want another Kieran. It's hard enough keeping up with this one."

Tan took a hold of Woorawa's curly dark hair and tugged him toward Kieran. "You just take that back, Woorawa, Dark Child. Kieran's ours whatever set of memories he's got."

Everyone was smiling now, especially Woorawa, because, despite sounding so different, they were really saying the same thing.

"Help! Physical violence! Control him, Kieran. He's ripping my hair out."

Downward pressure, very gentle really, because he was happily complying, took Woorawa to his knees.

"Now, beg for forgiveness."

"Please forgive me, Master Tan."

Tan's mock severity gave way to a smile. "Hopeless! Kieran, you're surrounded by drongos. Can you fix him?"

Surrounded was right, because Rhys and Mr B were also crowding close. Rhys held his hand out and everyone instinctively joined for an energy zap.

"Extraordinary, Maurice! They respond with nonsensical behaviour and somehow strengthen every bond between them."

"They rally to Kieran's leadership?"

"More than that. Tan took the lead this time and Kieran followed without question. And the others take the lead according to the occasion."

"Puzzling."

"Puzzling indeed."

Rhys tackled Tan, who, while wrestling him to the ground and exhorting Woorawa to tie his hair in knots for a payback, was himself tackled by Mr B and set upon by Kieran, who wasn't going to miss any of the playful roughhousing.

"Another expression of bonding, Maurice."

Rhys paused and, cued in some way, all five sets of features turned with clearly expressed invitation.

Maurice's eyes blinked rapidly and his mighty chest quivered with amusement. *"Bonding, Maker? What will you do?"*

"How can I refuse?"

*   *   *

Rhys absentmindedly stroked his fingers through Kieran's hair as they relaxed close to the dancing flames from the little campfire. Kieran's eyes had drifted shut and he appeared to be dozing, and Rhys couldn't blame him.

What a day! The excitement and wonder of the four-hour Panther ride along the trails of the ever-changing Central Grove had been eclipsed by the portal to the Oasis Grove where Maurice, keen to see the ocean for himself, had flown the whole group to meet a pod of Water Guardians.

It had been a mix of fun, interest and effort, with Ranevargar loading Kieran up with so much related information Rhys was impressed his brain hadn't exploded.

"I wonder how many different foods they grow?" he mused out loud, but in a whisper. "That meal was so good it's no wonder they're all vegetarians."

"Who knows, Rhys. It must be lots, because all those different Realm Trees we saw probably have their own range."

"I wonder why Ranevargar's making a big deal about our practice time? Tomorrow sounds unreal and we should be having an early night if we're leaving at sunrise."

"You're just a slug, Rhys. How much sleep do you want?"

"Am not! I was up ages before you this morning, Woorawa, and I swam a lot further than you did too, so that means you're the slug ... And so are Tan and Mr B ... You're all slugs."

"Ha! What about Kieran then? He slept in longer than any of us."

"That's different. He needs more beauty sleep than the rest of us."

Tan made circles against his head to say Rhys was crazy, and Rhys's resultant chuckle disturbed Kieran, who opened his eyes and blinked sleepily at them.

"Turn him into a pillow for real, Kieran. He just said you're ugly, and at least as a pillow he can be useful."

Rhys didn't make a comeback, because at that moment Ranevargar entered the circle of light and sat next to him.

"What've you been up to, Ranevargar? Watching the campfire's making us all feel lazy."

"Planning tomorrow with the hosts and the Griffins, Rhys. They've been preparing all day for our early start."

Woorawa laughed. "Rhys thinks we should sleep in for three extra hours before we leave."

"Very wise! I will arrange things so we meet him in the afternoon."

"What? I ... Leave Woorawa behind. He's the one making up stories."

Ranevargar nodded, as if agreeing with both of them, then turned serious. "I would like very much to watch one of your special stories, Woorawa, as well as re-establishing the pattern of nightly practice you developed for everyone."

The relaxed atmosphere snapped to curiosity and strong attention.

"You and Kieran have been dropping into Buddha moments all day and that must be better training for him than our basic stuff."

"Not at all, Rhys. The basic stuff, as you call it, is the foundation for everything he learns and does, and is fundamentally important, but something extraordinary is puzzling me and it is you four I want to watch rather than Kieran."

Rhys's laugh startled everyone. "Hang on to your brains, everyone. For Ranevargar to say it's extraordinary after everything else that's happened means it's a real doozy."

Mr B put it all together. "Something extraordinary, beyond everything we've been involved in, Ranevargar? Whatever do you mean?"

"You are all changed, Mr B. Maurice pointed out something with Rhys which set me thinking."

Rhys sat up when every eye settled on him, nearly dislodging Kieran. "Me?"

Woorawa laughed. "Now it's definitely going to be a doozy."

Ranevargar nodded and continued. "Yes, Rhys. Ask Tan a question."

Wondering where this could be going, Rhys did just that. "Um! Do you know what Ranevargar's talking about, Tan?"

Tan shook his head then, with everyone, looked to Ranevargar.

"Good! He's in your mind. Now, without speaking aloud, ask him something else."

A frown creased Rhys's brow. "No way, Ranevargar. You know I can't do that."

"To the contrary, Rhys. I have watched you make contact with Maurice on a number of occasions during the day."

"That's not me. That's him listening, like he always does, and hearing my thoughts."

"Try with Tan. Call to your mind the pattern you use with Maurice then project your question to Tan in the same way."

Well, it was crazy, but ... *"Can you hear me, Tan?"*

Tan's head lifted with an emphatic nod ... then he turned to Ranevargar.

"Tan answered in his mind, Rhys. At this stage it appears you can send but not receive. Try with Kieran now."

"Is this for real, Kieran?"

"Wow! As clear as a bell and it came without me watching your thoughts. Try it with Woorawa and Mr B."

When two more heads nodded Rhys, totally bewildered, turned to Ranevargar. "This is real telepathy, Ranevargar. Where did it come from? You said I'm not an elf."

"My first thought was a transfer of ability through your intimate bond and close association with Kieran, but while it works with Mr B, it definitely doesn't for Tan and Woorawa."

"Mr B can do telepathy too?"

Kieran saw the bigger picture. "Everyone can do ... something?"

"Yes, Kieran. I have been studying everyone's memories, Maurice's in particular, and it is clear that everyone has gone through some kind of change. Tan called Truth from three Realm Lords yesterday in a manner gentle but undeniable. The power of the chant Woorawa used to render the combined strength of three Fetches meaningless made the backup precautions Maurice and I were convinced we would need completely unnecessary, and Mr B has a new feel of underlying capability. Mr B, hold out your right hand and when I surround it with my green glow I want you to tell it to grow and spread to your arm."

Mr B stared at his glowing hand for a while before shaking his head. "I think you must be wrong, Ranevargar. Nothing happens."

"It does, Mr B. I withdrew my support for the glow and it is still there."

Mr B moved his left hand to make a cup shape with his palms and watched the glow slowly spill across.

"Holy cow! This is incredible. What was your second thought, Ranevargar?"

"My second thought, Rhys, was that maybe everyone was affected by being so closely involved in Maurice's challenge, but, along with a number of other conjectures, I have discarded that and settled on a moment in Maurice's cavern which is both distinctive and strong in all your memories."

"Everything in the cavern is distinctive and strong, Ranevargar."

"Of course, Tan, but this moment was so striking it prompted Rhys to describe you as a pack of angels, and Woorawa to say you all had halos."

"When the White energy came? Hey, I do remember feeling weird when it covered us all."

Rhys laughed, expecting the weird bit to be thrown back at him, but everyone was too busy making their own recall.

"I remember it gave me goose bumps, Ranevargar, but by that stage it was just the next event of many. What makes you think it was more than a glow?"

"Kieran and Maurice were both frantically working to control the energy, Mr B, but they each have a peripheral memory of all of you stand- ing transfixed for long enough to be unusual."

"I don't remember that."

"None of you do, Rhys, and that makes the moment even more unusual."

Tan added his thoughts. "Well, whenever it happened, it's surely come from the Opal. It keeps doing amazing things."

"And that only adds to the puzzle, Tan. The renewal of Dead World leaves little doubt in my mind that Kieran's Opal is the lost Realm Stone, a Realm Stone now imbued with great mystery."

Tan offered an even more striking thought. "Woorawa's people looked after it forever, Ranevargar. Maybe that has something to do with why it's different?"

"Woorawa's people are an enigma to the folk of Faerie, Tan, but that must be a possibility."

Woorawa was immediately the centre of attention. "Uncle Burrimul said it was always preserved in the clay container, so that doesn't sound like anyone used it or did anything to it."

Kieran pulled out the Opal. "See what happens when you hold it, Mr B. If your elf abilities are waking up, anything could happen."

"That's distinctly scary, Kieran." Mr B grasped the Opal, stared at it warily for a few seconds, then relaxed. "I think it's warm, like the first time, but I'm not sure."

"Make it glow."

"How? Ranevargar gave me a glow to start with."

"Sort of tell it with your mind. That's all I do."

"Glow blue ... please!"

A soft glow appeared, along with wondering looks from all around.

"Wow, Kieran! I thought the Opal only worked for you."

Kieran gave Mr B a big grin. "Sorry for being tricky, Mr B, but it worked perfectly, and Rhys is right. The Opal didn't do anything, so that means you made the glow."

"Are you sure?"

"Completely, Mr B. Let go of the Opal and tell Woorawa's head to glow."

"Are you sure? I just said that ... It can't be so easy ... Glow blue, hair ... please!"

Woorawa took in all the smiles and nods and touched his hair as if some colour might rub onto his hand.

"Do it to Tan, Mr B, so I can see what it looks like."

Mr B managed without using his voice this time and felt a wave of approval from Ranevargar.

"With no vocal prop you demonstrated control of location as well as colour. Change them both and increase the brightness."

Gryl blinked curiously when everyone looked at him through heavily slitted eyes and hands raised protectively.

"Oh my! Sorry everyone. I didn't expect so much."

The glare softened, and for the next few minutes Ranevargar guided Mr B through a set of activities he should practice.

"Now, everyone, I'd like to see what happens with your mind battles. When was the last time you organised a practice, Woorawa?"

"Um ... three nights ago. Last night Kieran used his sleep command on us, and the night before that we thought sleep was more important and Kieran had other things to do as well."

"He certainly did. Kieran, start with Tan. Whatever change occurred with him is beyond my ability to detect."

Tan responded. "There mightn't be a change, Ranevargar. I don't feel different."

"You called Truth from three Realm Lords, Tan, in a manner unknown to the Realms. Can you recall any similar strange moments before this?"

"The only strange things in my life came after I moved into our share house."

Kieran gave the usual signal and carefully pressed till Tan's mental resistance reached its limit, marginally better but not significantly different.

"That's pretty much the same, Ranevargar. D'you want us to try again? We usually do."

"Not tonight. Tan remains a mystery, so let us see what happens with Rhys."

"You won't see much. I've got the least resistance of all."

"I doubt that is still the case, Rhys."

Ranevargar was proved right when, a few moments later, Rhys happily stirred Tan and Mr B for being mind wusses, then, shortly after that, pretended great chagrin when Mr B proved even stronger.

The chagrin lasted about two seconds.

"Mr B's an elf, so that counts as cheating. What about Woorawa? Am I anywhere close to him?"

Kieran shook his head. "He's got a sort of natural resistance to start with, Rhys, but when he adds the chant he learnt from Burrimul he's way stronger."

"Hey! The chant helps all of us. Give me another go to see what difference it makes."

Kieran thought that was an interesting idea and worth exploring. "Rhys is right, Ranevargar. We should test it."

"We should, Kieran, but particularly with Woorawa. I am expecting we will see a significant change."

"From the way the Fetches froze?"

"Yes, Rhys. That chant overrode the three power adepts supporting them. Battle without the chant first though."

Woorawa was really eager and he flexed his arm muscles at Rhys. "Watch and learn from the experts, Mr Wuss!"

Maurice sent a quick question to Ranevargar. *"What is a wuss, Maker? Rhys and Woorawa have both used the term."*

"I just looked for my own understanding, Maurice. While it appears to be a derogatory term for a timid and ineffective personality, Woorawa uses it for comradely encouragement."

"Rhys an ineffectual personality?"

"Woorawa only says it because it is obviously not true."

Woorawa readied himself for the push from Kieran and, knowing it was going to be overwhelming, consciously held back the impulse to use Burrimul's chant ... Why was he starting with so little pressure? Maybe he wanted a slow build-up, so Ranevargar could see what was going on? Kieran's head lifted, as if in surprise, and the pressure strengthened till

Woorawa needed to close his eyes for proper concentration. *Whoa! Hold on for just a bit longer. Yikes! Enough.* The pressure disappeared and now-open eyes showed Kieran and Ranevargar staring at each other.

"What? It was easy at the start, Kieran, but then it was the usual pattern."

"No, it wasn't. The start was close to your usual finish, and the end was a level you only reach when you're chanting." He shook Rhys's linked arm. "He can call you a wuss whenever he likes, Rhys. If I did that to you, you'd be a gibbering idiot."

Rhys was too impressed to even think of a comeback.

"Wow! He must be off the chart when he chants then ... Can you do the chant now, Woorawa, or did Kieran blast you too much?"

No comeback? No cheeky smile? Wondering if he'd missed something, Woorawa looked to all the others and saw a mix of surprise and curiosity.

"Kieran didn't blast me, Rhys. He was careful as ever."

"Yes, he did. I could feel it ... Scary!"

Kieran was puzzled. "You must have imagined it, Rhys. Burrimul taught me how to focus in on one person, and Ranevargar pushed me to practise really fine control, so I know for sure there wasn't any spill over."

Ranevargar was really interested. "You felt the pressure against your own mind, Rhys?"

"Not really. But I could sort of see it against Woorawa, and it was big."

Ranevargar nodded thoughtfully. "Another change, apparently. Let us see what effect your chant has, Woorawa, and I will watch what is happening with Rhys as well."

Kieran wasn't happy. "Hang on, Ranevargar! I have to push way harder when Woorawa's chanting and if that gets through to Rhys it could knock him unconscious. Can you do something to protect him?"

"Of course, Kieran, but I am sure he won't need it. Proceed as normal and if there is any need I will intervene."

There was nothing normal about the pressure Kieran had to use.

"Is this what you expected, Ranevargar? Chanting's making his barriers stronger, but I can't see any change in them."

The mental exchange was needed because Woorawa's chant was so strong.

"He ignored the efforts of three Fetches at Maynor's Castle, so the extra strength is a given, but, like you, I can't see what he is doing. Stress him, very carefully, Kieran, and see if that reveals anything."

"Are you sure? I think he's got so strong I might have to use the Opal."

Ranevargar was clearly startled at this and caution rose in his mind. *"That strong? We are in unknown territory. Don't use your Opal."*

Woorawa's chant went silent. "What happened? All the pressure stopped."

"You're doing something new, Woorawa, and we haven't got a clue what it is. I can't get any stronger without using my Opal and that makes us nervous."

"Us? You mean Ranevargar's nervous too?"

"Yes, your resistance should crumble and it doesn't. Your chant does something we can't see, something it only started doing yesterday."

"That doesn't make sense. This chant is exactly what Uncle Burrimul taught me. It hasn't changed even one bit."

Ranevargar nodded. "Yes, and that means the change must be within you."

Rhys piped up. "Wow! Looks like *you're* the kryptonite, Woorawa."

Kieran wondered at the shared grins. "What's that supposed to mean?"

"When you went gliding through the air at the High Castle Woorawa made a joke and it's come back at him."

"That wasn't me doing that. Ranevargar made it happen."

"Ha! Only because he hasn't taught you yet."

A long rumble of contented sound brought new smiles as everyone turned to look at Gryl's half-closed eyes.

"D'you want us to do any more practice, Ranevargar? He thinks it's time we all went to sleep."

"Hours more, Kieran."

That surprised everyone till he smiled ... He'd been smiling at things all day.

"But not tonight. Gryl's message is a timely one."

"What about Woorawa's campfire dance? I've seen that on your mind all night."

"It has been, Kieran, but we already have more than enough to consider for one day."

Everyone started moving, then Tan spoke. "I'm a bit puzzled about your White Power theory, Ranevargar. You've been with Kieran at least three times when he called it, so maybe it's changed you too?"

Kieran was impressed. "Is that possible, Ranevargar? And Aglaron and Uirebon were riding our minds when we called it for Maurice."

Ranevargar addressed Tan. "Your ideas challenge us again, Tan. I am still struggling to accommodate all the changes brought by Rhys's healing and my renewed contact with Maurice, let alone anything beyond that. I haven't noticed anything unexpected though. The prospect of the High King or Uirebon with some new ability is fascinating indeed ... There is one unique difference that comes to my mind, Tan. That moment when you all stood transfixed. Something to consider.

Chapter 7

Woorawa's mind boggled. The trip involving the joint effort of a Realm Tree portal for fifty Griffins loaded with life bombs, hosts and warders, a convoy flight to the Boundary, then a crossing and another flight to familiar territory had all been exciting, but the long, glittering ribbons of water replacing tracts of barren land made it hard to accept that one storm, massive as it had been, could bring so much change. Now, below, a small river flowed in the valley where they'd crossed the dry bed.

"This is unbelievable, Maurice. How can there be water still flowing after two days?"

"Remember the strength of the deluge, Woorawa. Huge quantities of snow and ice were carried to milder levels and they continue to thaw and supply this system that will become permanent lakes and swamps."

Maurice banked and descended to land on a large knoll rising from the surrounding sea of mud and pools and water. The protective flap lifted and everyone watched with their own eyes as the convoy of Griffins and riders made their landings.

"Ranevargar, fifty Griffins seemed like a lot when we left, but they're tiny really when you compare them to the area we saw through Maurice's eyes."

"Very tiny, Woorawa, and the hosts will only seed this immediate area which Kieran and Maurice have chosen as their Central Grove. The land-based seeds have been selected for their rapid growth and profuse seed production characteristics."

"Land-based? Are they going to put seeds in the water too?"

"Of course, Tan. Water plants will be the base for prolific growth of water creatures and everything that depends on them ... We can talk while we move. Time is in short supply."

Woorawa smiled at how nimbly Ranevargar led the way down Maurice's back. If the High King saw him now, the tired old elf image would be totally wiped.

Every Griffin and rider suddenly turned toward them.

"What's that about, Kieran?"

"They're listening to Maurice, Woorawa. He's assigning them exact areas, so there's no overlap. They're going to rest for a while and then half of them will concentrate on the nearby water areas and the rest will work close to this new Central Grove we're establishing. Krol and Kron are loaded for the next storm area and they'll be riding piggyback on Maurice to get there, and then I'd like Rhys and Tan to spread the seed while Ranevargar establishes the Realm Tree Grove."

"Will we be there for long? I'd like to take a turn."

"We want you involved in every Realm Tree planting, Woorawa, in case it helps with your own Tree back at Mparntwe."

"Helps? What does that mean? I can't do anything with Realm Trees."

"Ranevargar still thinks I'll be able to link you so you can send power and help its growth."

Woorawa gave Kieran a puzzled look. "I haven't got a clue about controlling ruby energy."

"We'll get a necklace for one of the ruby stones and then you'll learn."

Ranevargar interrupted. "It is not as unlikely as it sounds, Woorawa. Kieran has already given you a similar arrangement for your shields."

"I suppose ... but that's all automatic."

"Yes, and this would be too, unless we can find some way to give you a degree of mastery, but it's all just conjecture till Kieran develops at least a rudimentary skill with Realm Trees."

"... Airy fairy!"

"Bong him on the head, Kieran. We don't want him making fairy jokes."

Ranevargar sensed more than one level of amusement, but time was passing so he collected the first Realm Tree pod from the pack Rhys was carrying, gouged a shallow furrow, then set it into a carefully spread life bomb and covered it with a mound of soft, wet soil.

Tan was really curious. "I know they're clumps of especially good dirt, Ranevargar, but why do you call them life bombs?"

"The soil of Kieran's Realm is sterile, Tan, but, with moisture and the new conditions, the myriads of tiny life forms existing in the bombs will proliferate explosively and spread fertility. Without them the plants cannot access the nourishment they need."

"Sounds like science to me."

"Knowledge, Rhys. Link hands, everyone, while Kieran and I merge to activate the life within this pod."

"All of us?"

"Yes, Tan. We will share this experience."

The merge was brief and very intense, and while they moved to the next location Ranevargar guided Kieran through what they'd done.

"That was my demonstration, Kieran. When we merge for the next pod

I will direct your mind to make the activation."

"Like a kind of forced learning?"

"In a way, Rhys. It will establish a pattern which I expect Kieran will very quickly master."

"He's a genius with patterns. They just click in for him."

Ranevargar nodded; then he collected another pod and bomb and pointed. "Over there, Woorawa. Set the pod in the same manner as the first one."

*   *   *

When Kieran activated the fifth pod without any help, a giant smile lit Ranevargar's features.

"It is the first of many steps, Kieran, but it shows you will eventually be able to manage any aspect of Realm Tree growth you care to learn. Take Rhys and Mr B with you and we will split for the six remaining pods. Maurice will be well pleased, because this puts us ahead of schedule."

*   *   *

Woorawa's mind boggled at the sight of the massive bank of dark storm clouds covering three adjacent mountain peaks, lightning flickering brilliantly and constantly in contrast, with curtains of rain draping against the middle and lower slopes. This was a new storm, started when Maurice took to the air and built to his high-speed mode over half an hour ago, and they were seeing it because Kieran requested Maurice to slow enough to use his normal eyesight rather than the blurred vision through the protective membrane. No wonder this was called the Great Range. According to Maurice there was still about twenty minutes of rapid travel before they reached where the Range curved to flank the ocean before veering inland again.

"These mountains are a lot higher than Maurice's cavern, Ranevargar. The floods will take longer to reach the plains."

"Yes, Woorawa, and with the size of that storm there will be a staggering amount of water spreading across the plains for days and days, and with eight other storms planned we will need a whole series of seed expeditions and a dedicated group of hosts and Griffins to stay and work with Maurice."

"Will all the storms be as big as this one?"

"We've stopped storming so I can take in what's happening with this section of the range, Woorawa. As soon as we build up speed we'll be at it

again, because Maurice wants every bit of White Power we can manage. The next storm's even bigger than this one, because it has to supply three dry river systems which reach hundreds of kilometres across the plain."

Maurice increased speed and obligingly made a steady 360° scan. *"Have you seen enough, Kieran? We still have a great deal of ground to cover."*

*   *   *

Woorawa's mind boggled at the stark beauty of the panorama so far below: wrinkled ocean butting broken cliffs where mountains met water, white ribbons of sand way in the distance where the Range veered inland again, and the glitter of the newly standing water and river systems that were their destination.

Maurice dived, and Woorawa smiled at the muffled exclamations of excitement as his friends responded to the tummy lurch and whirling change of viewpoint relayed from Dragon eyes.

"How many pods for this Grove, Ranevargar?"

"We are approximately halfway along the Great Range, Woorawa, and Kieran and Maurice are initially developing a basic Grove as a staging point."

A basic Grove meant four trees, so it would be a relatively short stay.

"We won't be staying long, but make sure you stretch your legs because we only get one more stop after this before we rendezvous with the Griffins back at the Boundary crossing."

Maurice landed, and Ranevargar did the pod planting because, although he was present, Kieran was totally preoccupied with calling White Power and helping Maurice use it for yet another distant storm.

*   *   *

Kieran rested his head on Rhys's shoulder and closed his eyes for a moment of happy relaxation while everyone waited for Woorawa to return to the campfire.

Ranevargar was a real taskmaster — friendly and enthusiastic, yes, but so keen to see progress with everything they did that Kieran had to call for time out when the strain of concentration went for too long. Mr B laughed at every break, saying it was a kind of payback for the Maths coaching sessions where Kieran's intensity had pushed their time way past anything normal.

The two-hour morning session with a Tree Manager had been a

draining, slow motion process of establishing the curious rapport necessary for communication with the hybrid plant/animal construct, then recognising and locking in the patterns for a number of basic instructions. Ranevargar likened it to learning a new language: a strange language that was needed for intercession with a Realm Tree's growth. At the end of the session, Rhys was blown away when, following Kieran's instructions and completely independent of Ranevargar's help, the Tree Manager formed a small hollow in the living timber. Ranevargar's excitement at this achievement had spread contagiously to everyone else who'd been watching the process so patiently.

The next hour was a long-distance mind session with Maurice and the growing Opal network and, because there was nothing to see, Ranevargar sent the rest of the group for a ride on Gryl and three other Panthers.

The afternoon was taken up with a Tree Portal to the Mountain Grove, then a Griffin ride to four separate caves where Ranevargar quickened and invested proudly guarded egg clutches with the initial instalment of the power that would bring about the first new Griffins in six hundred years.

After an early evening meal they'd moved to the campfire for an extended group practice session, with Woorawa supervising and Ranevargar giving pointers to help everyone improve. Now, waiting while Woorawa was off preparing for this ceremony that he'd informed everyone he was calling his Dragon dance, Kieran was appreciating his first lazy moment for the day.

"It must be something special. He usually just makes it up as he goes. Has he told you anything about it, Tan?"

"Not much, but I know it's a big deal for him because he's been having thinking moments about it all day."

Rhys laughed. "Kieran and Ranevargar's Buddha trances must be contagious. You'd better be careful or you'll be infected next, Tan."

Everyone rolled their eyes in mock disgust. Thinking moments were a given with Tan.

"Thinking moments? Well, that means you're safe, Rhys."

Mr B's jibe got no response, because Rhys had a question he'd been meaning to ask for ages.

"How long will it be before the Griffin eggs hatch, Ranevargar?"

"Three weeks, Rhys, but it will be at least an extra week before you can meet the hatchlings."

"How come?"

"Maternal instinct. It's very powerful with Griffins and we will have to wait till Krol knows it is safe to invite us."

"Wow! What about him and the other males then?"

"They enter the caves with great caution, Rhys, carrying gifts of food. If you ask Krol for permission, he might let us watch with his vision."

"Well, I—"

A soft but deep humming sound turned every eye to watch the indistinct movement approaching from the direction of the Realm Tree.

"Oh! ... My! ... God!"

Rhys's amazement was universally shared, and above his own wonder, Kieran sensed Gryl's head lift uneasily till the approaching apparition entered the flickering circle of campfire light.

Seemingly luminous of their own accord, two golden eyes fixed each watcher in turn before settling on Ranevargar with fierce intensity. The hum strengthened and, complemented by half a dozen hosts tapping on rhythm sticks, sounded a querying pseudo-roar. Clad in a black, traditional-style loose loincloth disconcertingly matching natural skin colour, the figure froze on the spot with limbs reaching in entreaty to the ruler of this Realm. Lines of striking white ran down the front of all four limbs and spread to fingers and toes in surreal imitation of Draconian talons.

Kieran's hair stood on end as the supplication to Ranevargar failed and the frozen creature stirred and reached, with new and stronger longing, directly toward him.

After one more questioning roar a chant started, a new chant, soft and distinctive with a hint of a rumble, and Woorawa began to move.

Spirit consumed him. Spirit flared with every step as a Dragon awoke. Fire burned as eyes and mind opened after an age of darkness. Fire blazed in the four elements of a mighty challenge. The fire of pain spread to the watchers as flesh writhed with the torture of first movement. Again movement ceased and, accompanied by the evocative new chant, the Dragon spirit, arms outstretched, in poignant entreaty, looked for help in healing.

Rhys, dazed and entranced, swayed in earnest agreement. Quivering wings spread with growing vigour as frozen myth transformed to joyous reality. Woorawa, Dragon spirit, danced the expression of a curious elevation and first powerful wing beats. In Kieran's stunned mind the campfire became the world below Woorawa's wheeling motion till, with arms somehow kept widespread in a startling aerial body flip, the restored Construct brought everything to a stop.

The dark chest glistened in the firelight, heaving for air till Woorawa, returning to the world, opened his eyes, made a little bow, then looked for acknowledgement.

None came.

The silent onlookers, taken out of themselves, slowly and reluctantly made their own returns while eyes outlined with glowing yellow moved between them with increasing puzzlement. Woorawa's hesitant touch on Tan's arm brought rapid eye blinks, a head lifted in awareness and an expression which looked like disbelief.

"Tan! It's me! ... What's wrong?"

Tan's lips parted, but a rush of movement interrupted and Rhys, yelling incoherently, hugged an increasingly bewildered Woorawa, whirled him in a joyous circle, then released him to stare with happy disbelief while everyone else swamped him with their own hugs and strange exclamations. Even Ranevargar?

"Did I do something weird or have you all gone crazy?"

"It wasn't weird, Woorawa. It was amazing. You turned into Maurice."

Woorawa had to smile at everyone's eager agreement. "Um! That's the whole point, Kieran."

"No it's not. It was so real I don't believe it. My eyes could see it was you, but my brain said it was Maurice."

"I was flying, actually flying, except I knew I wasn't. I didn't know dancing could be so good. It totally sucked me in."

Rhys was raving about dancing?

Mr B spoke next. "Rhys is right, Woorawa. I felt Maurice's pain and then his ecstasy as strongly as when it happened. Did you practice that in secret to get it so perfect?"

"I've been thinking about it all day, Mr B, but we've been too—"

Kieran, surprised by the abrupt cut off, followed Woorawa's surprised gaze to Tan, who was standing with his eyes closed and body unnaturally still. *What?* A frisson of apprehension banished his excitement, then strengthened with the shock of being unable to sense any thoughts or feelings.

"What's happened to him, Ranevargar? He's kind of gone."

"We have mystery compounded with mystery and I am more than bewildered, Kieran. Merge with me while we seek answers."

With a rush of clarity and skill, Kieran joined all his Tan patterns with Ranevargar's experience and mastery in a careful and intricate probe which found nothing at all.

"This is beyond us, Kieran. He— His eyes have opened."

"You have the gift of dance, Child of the People. Use it as your heart and mind decree." Tan's eyes closed again, momentarily, then, along with a head shake, blinked open. "That's the best dance you've ever done, Woorawa, and your yellow eyes are unreal ... What?"

The merged probe rushed for assessment.

"He is himself again and completely unaware of the incident. Whatever it was caused no harm."

"You went funny, Tan. Why did you say I've got the gift of dance like it was a big deal?"

Tan turned to Kieran. "Was I talking, Kieran? I don't remember."

Rhys made a loud blat of disbelief. "He's got the Buddha look, Tan. You did speak, and he's thinking about it ... So's Ranevargar."

The merge dropped and Ranevargar spoke straightaway. "Woorawa and Rhys are right, Tan. You responded to the mystery of the dance with your own mystery. Kieran and I merged to try and understand, but your mind was closed to us while you made your pronouncement."

"Pronouncement?"

"Yes, Tan. Exhortation even. The message and its delivery held authority. 'You have the gift of dance, Child of the People. Use it as your heart and mind decree.' Those were the words you used."

"Child of the People? Where would that come from. It's true, but it's not what I'd say."

Woorawa leapt, literally leapt, to put a reassuring arm round Tan's shoulders, and Ranevargar smiled.

"There is nothing wrong with your mind, Tan. Kieran and I checked as soon as you returned to yourself. I am convinced this is your own special gift, given by the White Power as a match for your insight and integrity, a gift which surfaces for pivotal moments, such as Woorawa's Dragon dance."

Everyone nodded except Woorawa. "You're calling my dance a pivotal moment?"

"Absolutely, Woorawa. I thought it was the new strength in your chants, but now I think that must be a side effect. No one can dance with such power. Every one of us was held in a transcendent experience until your ending released us."

Kieran added his thoughts. "Ranevargar's right, Woorawa. Your dancing has always been special, but this was so much more. I don't even know how to describe it."

"I do. It's in lots of the stories I've read. We were spellbound."

Mr B spoke up. "Rhys is right, Woorawa. It's a wonderful description of how your dance affected us, and it does follow Ranevargar's idea that it has extended a gift you already had."

Woorawa released Tan. "The longer we stay here the stranger everything gets, Tan. I wonder if we'll stay different when we get back home?"

Tan had no answer, of course, so attention turned to Ranevargar again.

"I strongly suspect you will, Woorawa, all of you. These are mysteries from knowledge paths different to any we know in the Realms."

"Kieran's Opal's involved and that's linked to the Realms."

"Part of it is, Mr B, but somehow it has acquired properties beyond those of other Realm Stones. I hope and expect that Lord Uirebon's searches will help us with useful information about the Realm Stones and the early history of Kieran's Realm."

"And portalling. They're looking for anything about that too, aren't they?"

"You know they are, Tan."

"Yes, but we haven't heard anything yet."

"We will, most likely when Uirebon arrives with Aglaron, but his archives are large and it takes time and dedication to access them."

"Technology would really help, Ranevargar. If the information was stored in computers they could find what they were looking for in a few seconds."

By now everyone understood that Ranevargar's pause was really a search of their memories for understanding.

"Interesting, Woorawa ... How long would it take to transfer millennia of archived knowledge to these devices?"

Kieran laughed. "Forget it. It would take decades even for trained people ... Do you think Woorawa's dancing will get stronger if he does lots of practice, Ranevargar?"

"I have no idea, Kieran, but if it is part of the nightly routine we will find out soon enough."

"There's no if. His ceremonies are one of the special things we're not going to miss out on."

Ranevargar nodded agreement to Kieran's heartfelt outburst. "Has dance always been a part of your life, Woorawa?"

"Longer than I can even remember according to Uncle Burrimul. He says I responded to music and campfire ceremonies even while I was learning to walk, but it became really important when my eyes stopped working. It was a way to feel like I was doing what everyone else was doing, but then it changed so I was kind of in the story being told. It felt nice to be fairly good at something too."

Kieran nearly died of shock. "Fairly good! What a joke, Woorawa. At the Visitors' Centre you were the leader, and you were so brilliant we were shocked when we found out you couldn't see."

"You would dance for special visitors at this centre?"

"Our ways are not understood very well, Ranevargar, and it is an opportunity to show them to people."

Rhys interrupted. "They're not special visitors, Ranevargar, they're anyone who turns up, and most of them are pig ignorant. I was, till Mr B took us to the power rocks at Gariwerd."

"Power rocks? The wild place where Kieran sensed heat?"

"It was unreal."

Ranevargar hesitated then shook his head. "There are too many fascinating things to discuss and consider, Rhys, but right now I need to try to understand Woorawa's new gift."

"Do you still think it's because he's always been special at dance that it's now turned magic?"

"It is a conjecture, Tan ... Will we have the opportunity to see another dance tomorrow, Woorawa?"

Woorawa grinned while he shook his head. "No! Because tomorrow night you won't be watching. I'll plan it so you're all in it. You too, Ranevargar. Your worn-out old elf disguise doesn't work with us, and the hosts found this ochre substitute, so we can make it even better. How busy are we tomorrow?"

"Far too busy to be daubing the ruler of this Realm with coloured clay."

The grin got wider. "I'm going to make you into a Griffin."

Ranevargar made a little bow of acceptance. "Apparently I am without choice. Kieran's determination to master everything he can about portalling will involve a morning of deep concentration and practice and another session with the Tree Manager, then we ready new resources for our next expedition to his Realm. I did notice Woorawa's interest in our food harvesting, and since our 'Buddha' moments will be extensive, the rest of you might like a guided expedition through the upper reaches of our Realm Trees."

*　*　*

"I don't believe this. We can cross to another Tree when we're this high up?"

"Only if you wish to collect a good supply of fresh yellow fruit, Rhys. Providing you pay proper attention it is quite safe."

"Nothing's safe when it's three hundred metres to the ground, Pentar, and we haven't been climbing around like monkeys all our life. How old are you lot anyway, if that's not a rude question?"

"I am 112 years old, Rhys ... What is a monkey?"

Whoops! Another non-Realm reference. Rhys looked past Pentar to where Woorawa was happily shaking his head.

"Another holdup, Rhys. Make some mental images and don't move while you're distracted."

Their guides, protectors really, in this Tree world were all insatiably curious, and any chance reference involving back home started a chain of questions. Pentar's eyes lit up.

"Wonderful! I have never been there, but we have many similar tree creatures and their Guardians in our rain forest areas."

"More Guardians? What are they like?"

Whoops! Another holdup while an image of an imposing creature displayed in the four friend's minds.

"Wow! Something like a gorilla, but not really. How big are they, Glaryl?" Rhys questioned Woorawa's guide because it was her image.

"Your head would just reach his middle. He appears ungainly, but his movement through the trees is so graceful it gives the impression of flying."

Woorawa pointed. "Stop talking, everyone, and start moving. We'll only see half what we planned at this rate. Lead the way, Rhys."

"You want me to lead? That's your job, Woorawa."

"I'm sticking close to Tan. He doesn't like heights."

"Rillanor keeps me confident, Woorawa. Her mindlink tells me where to step and what to hold, and there's so much vegetation it completely disguises the height."

*   *   *

Rhys stirred reluctantly, gently removed Kieran's arm and carefully climbed across him to gain the comfort of the little alcove. What was the time? Light through the vines looked strong.

"You are the first to wake, Rhys. You should drink less."

"I know. I like it too much. Hang on while I grab some food, then I'll be with you."

Ignoring the 'greedy guts' mind whisper, he poured a goblet of the red drink, chose a strip of the meaty-tasting mushroom stuff, then, along with two slabs of honey-bread, collected a yellow fruit and headed outside.

"After yesterday's effort, I deserve it, Maurice. We left at dawn and got back from Kieran's Realm in the dark."

"We did cover a wearying distance, but it was a wonderful day, Rhys, with all the basic Realm Tree groves started, the last of the great storms over, and the vegetation at our Central Grove augmented and proliferating."

"No more storms?"

"Not energy-induced storms. Enough snow and ice has been thawed and

redistributed in liquid form to support a permanent weather cycle."

"Have you felt any effects from the White Power? Ranevargar's convinced it did stuff to us, and you used it five times yesterday."

"I have the same conviction, Rhys, but our careful monitoring found no change other than my increasing facility with using power which is, undoubtedly, a practice effect."

"Will Kieran keep giving you White energy? He hasn't said anything about it."

"I expect he will, though the Maker, not knowing where it comes from, has concerns which Kieran doesn't share."

"Wow! They actually disagree about something? That's a first."

"I would describe it as a differing viewpoint rather than a disagreement."

"Do you need much more energy, Maurice?"

"I have never needed it, Rhys. Kieran's Realm is now in harmony with the Nexus and receives the same energy support as every other Realm. I want it, though, as every bit extra helps to speed the restoration. The storms have saved decades and the Maker's commitment is doing even more."

"Ranevargar loves helping, though. Every one of us felt his happiness at the green patches spreading so well, and when we saw that the Realm Tree pods had sprouted into seedlings it was straight-out excitement."

"It was, Rhys, but seeing the results of his efforts gave Kieran an even greater sense of achievement, along with a new understanding of his domin-ion over the Realm."

"When he went quiet? I thought it was a Buddha moment with Ranevargar."

"He was linking with every Realm Tree seedling to check for health and progress."

"What? Even the ones at the staging point Grove?"

"They are in his network, Rhys, so the distance is immaterial."

"I should be used to that, because he used to use Ranevargar's network to talk across the Boundary to the Guardians when we were on your quest ... Hey! Is this another thing that's special with Ranevargar? No one's said anything about the other Realm Lords having a network."

"It is, Rhys. He developed it to improve his Stewardship."

"D'you know how long that is? He used to be the High King till he got sick of it."

"More than twenty centuries."

"Unreal! I wonder why he keeps quiet about his age? He told us the Realms think Lord Uirebon's the oldest elf ... Hey! That doesn't add up. If he's been Realm Ruler for twenty centuries it's obvious he's older than Uirebon."

"You're right. I don't understand."

Amusement and Ranevargar's presence flashed into Rhy's mind. *"Curiosity leads you down curious paths, Rhys. The numbers do add up, as far as the Realms are concerned, because nine hundred years ago my name and persona changed and I was appointed as the only suitable successor to my old and apparently failing previous identity ... And now that you know that, I will have to wipe your mind."*

"Ah! ... You will?"

"Not really. Kieran's shields protect you from prying minds, and my skills with misdirection are well and truly recovered."

"Kieran told us the other Realm Rulers don't know how complicated you really are, Ranevargar. Are you going to tell him why?"

"I won't have to, Rhys. He has been deep enough into my mind during our merges to figure it out for himself."

"Ha! Another cagey answer. So what're you doing at the moment?"

"I am preparing my mind with various approaches to help with Kieran's big effort this morning. Krol carried me to my lookout and he is keeping me company while I think."

"Is it going to be hours of mind stuff again?"

"It will be the last uninterrupted opportunity for several days and we want to make the most of it."

"Is that because you'll be too busy or because you don't want the High King to see what's going on?"

"Mostly because we will be too busy, Rhys ... Kieran is stirring and wondering where you are."

"Yo, Kieran! I'm outside with Maurice. Grab some food and get out here."

"Yes, boss!"

*   *   *

Kieran smiled at the mixture of support and anticipation from the watchers sitting quiet and still after Ranevargar's admonishment for no distraction of any kind while he went through this final and most difficult process.

The two focus points had been easy. The main Central Grove was so familiar from frequent use as to be second nature. This new focus location at a far end of the Grove was quickly fixed after a short time of observation and association.

Changing a cluster of four ordinary Realm Trees to special Portal Trees was way beyond his ability, but he'd merged with Ranevargar to watch and develop familiarity with how the transformation took place.

This last step was to build a completely new spider structure and permanently link the locations. Ranevargar had been a wonderful teacher, but his perception of the link as a type of river had meant lots of translation attempts before the building process would work for the shimmering silken link that Kieran saw in his own mind. Tendrils of blue-tinged power reached the length of the Grove, connected, locked in place then, under Kieran's directing mind, slowly and steadily gave substance to a shimmering new portal link. *Now, check all the length for integrity and apply a surge of power to make the location locks permanent, end the flow of energy from the Opal and watch.* Yes, a new spider link, firm and steady, reached invisibly all the way to the main Central Grove. Kieran opened his eyes and wiped his brow.

"It's done, everyone, and it looks good. Do you want to check it, Ranevargar?"

"It is more than good, Kieran. It is beautiful and we will all check it."

The no distraction time was obviously over, so Rhys spoke up. "It's really done? You can concentrate for half an hour and there's a Portal all the way back? And how do the rest of us check it, Ranevargar? It's invisible."

"A practical check, Rhys. Kieran will take us to the Central Grove and back."

"Back too?"

"Yes. Kieran will be well practised after repeating the procedure for the other Groves."

"You're kidding! There's ten of them. That's five hours. His brain'll be wrecked."

"The half hour will reduce with repetition, Rhys, quite dramatically I expect, but you are right about the effort. One more link today will help lock the pattern in place."

"Ranevargar's right, Rhys, and I want to do it while it's fresh in my mind. Let's make the next one the Oasis Grove, so we can stay for a good relax."

*   *   *

"They're only a few minutes away, everyone. Their Griffins are all excited about coming home and they're building up speed with their descent."

"You're in the Griffin's minds, Kieran?"

"Ranevargar is, Rhys, and I'm sharing. Woo hoo! He just took over and told them to make a power dive so it's a memorable arrival."

"Memorable? As if! They'll take one look at the Guardians and they'll forget everything else."

Kieran could only agree. A speedy descent on a Griffin steed would be breathtaking at any time, but the honour-walk through the proud Panthers and Griffins ranged for formal greeting would have to be on the verge of daunting. Ranevargar had decided that his best substitute for the pomp and ceremony of a grand castle would be the atmosphere generated by attending ranks of Guardians, and thinking back to his own first heart-stopping moment, Kieran wondered how the visitors would react to forty giant felines as well as a matching number of Griffins.

Woorawa insisted that even a single Realm Tree was far grander than any castle, but Ranevargar, knowing the ways of elven courts, said a close encounter with his Guardians would align with their traditions more effectively.

"How are you feeling, Kieran?"

Rhys tightened their linked arms while he searched the sky. "I haven't suddenly got nervous, if that's what you're wondering, Rhys. I just want everything to go well, and I know it will because Ranevargar's really in charge."

They'd talked this through between them stacks of times in the last few days, because of the strange one-sided relationship to Aglaron during the visit.

"What about you, Rhys? Are you worried he's going to make you look like a piglet?"

The arm link became a quick shove in the side.

"He won't, but don't remind him. If he finds out how funny Maurice and Mr B thought that was, he might try it ... I wonder if he's got a sense of humour? Has Ranevargar said anything? Being a High King probably makes him serious."

Maurice joined in. *"A curious thought, Rhys. I haven't noticed the mantle of rule affecting Kieran's propensity to smile."*

"Kieran's different. Aglaron's old."

The sky-scanning broke off as every eye turned.

"Whoops! That came out wrong. I didn't mean you, Ranevargar. You smile all the time."

"I find I can't stop myself, Rhys, when you suggest that age will curb Kieran's laughter."

"No! No! I—" A tiny piglet trotted from somewhere behind the companions and leaned adoringly against Rhys's leg. "... That's not real! Ranevargar, don't you dare leave it there."

"Me, Rhys? I am far too ancient to even consider such frivolity ... But look, our visitors arrive."

Seven Griffins plummeted from the sky, then, with joyous calls and the spectacular grace which always amazed Kieran, spread their wings to shed speed and land with precision.

Seven hosts moved to help the riders dismount, and in short order the three Realm Rulers gathered and, clearly taken aback while they adapted to the proximity of the Panthers, began their walk through the unique honour guard.

The companions stayed with Maurice while Kieran and Ranevargar advanced to meet them.

"Welcome to my Realm, High King, Lady Narello and Lord Uirebon. I hope your visit will be enjoyable and enlightening."

"Welcome, Father and fellow Rulers. We have much to discuss and much to do."

*   *   *

A light privacy ward surrounded the group, somewhat surprising the newly arrived Realm Lords.

"Thank you, Lord Ranevargar. The excitement of the journey and that unexpected descent was surpassed by the most unusual honour guard we have ever experienced. And thank you, Kieran. I am eager to know your thoughts on matters of the Realms, and heartened by this opportunity for some time together."

A full round of double wrist clasps took place, then, with the assurance of a detailed discussion later, Kieran gave an overview of some of his personal decisions. That done, he dropped the privacy ward and deferred to Ranevargar, who gestured for the three rulers to meet the companions.

"High King, this is Rhys, so aptly designated the Warrior. Without him, Kieran would not have been able to manage Lord Maynor. I commend him to you and suggest you make a point of giving him your attention. Be warned, though, he is prone to well-natured irreverence."

Rhys almost protested, but the High King was already offering the double wrist clasp.

"Rhys, I have been anticipating this meeting and I do look forward to any time we can share."

A firm double grip, along with an eyebrow lifted in an oh-so-familiar manner, sent assurance flowing through Rhys. *Oh my God!* He actually even felt like Kieran. The greeting he'd prepared was gone from Rhys's mind so, thoughts whirling, he gave a nod, then wondered at the downward glance.

"An interesting companion, Rhys. Is this the irreverence Lord

Ranevargar warns of?"

Wow! This guy's personality was so strong. Rhys looked for Kieran's reaction, but saw only his typical grin. With a new mental double-take he saw an older, more discreet version of the very same smile. Hmm! Aglaron knew this was Ranevargar's doing and he was enjoying it. Ha!

"Ranevargar's got a fixation for animals. He's the one being irreverent, so you have to be ready for anything ... And I hope we get some time too."

Ranevargar blinked and the little pig disappeared.

"Greet Woorawa, High King. He met Kieran and Rhys under the strangest of circumstances and instantly befriended them. It was his people who gifted the Realm Stone."

The High King gave the clasp, spoke interestedly with Woorawa, did the same for Tan and Mr B, then stood quietly while Lord Uirebon and Lady Narello made their own greetings.

Ranevargar pointed past Maurice to the base of the mighty Realm Tree. "My hosts will escort you for a restorative break, then we will share some refreshments before we visit our new portal focus."

Uirebon's head lifted in query.

"Kieran established it yesterday, Uirebon, as part of his search for an alternate way to the Human World. We are hopeful your searches will further help us."

"We have made significant headway with the early history of Kieran's Realm, but knowledge of the portal system is proving elusive."

He obviously had more to say, but the High King moved to accompany the waiting host elves.

Tan was disappointed. "That didn't sound very hopeful, Kieran."

Ranevargar answered. "This is as I expected, Tan, but have faith in the diligence and cooperation between Uirebon's scholars."

"Cooperation?"

"Yes, Woorawa. Every reference, however slight or seemingly inconsequential, will be shared and traced to its source. The process will be slow, but I am quite confident that something will eventually turn up."

"What's with the piglet? You left it there."

"The High King was nervous about meeting you, Rhys, and a smile helped him."

"Nervous of me? You said yourself that he's the strongest elf in all the Realms ... and there's no way he's scared of anyone."

"He is *not* scared of anyone, Rhys, but your bond with Kieran gives you a rather unique influence on the only person who does give him concern. He is delighted that you like him though."

"I do, too, but how would he know? Is he going into my mind?"

"Not without an invitation. He is a master at reading people, Rhys, and you are more open than most."

"Lady Narello didn't say much."

"Her mind is totally engaged, Mr B. She is keenly aware of how little she knows and hungers for information."

"They didn't react to the Panthers as much as I expected."

"It didn't show, but they were all exceeding impressed, Mr B, and the High King gave acknowledgement."

"It's pretty weird that this is the first time they've seen a Panther when you've had them for so many centuries."

"They have all seen the Panthers, Rhys, but from afar, and until now they regarded them as just another specimen in my interesting collection of animals and of little importance to their Realms."

"Until now?"

"Yes, Tan. Close association with the seven Griffins has changed their understanding."

Rhys looked to Krol, now crouching close to Maurice, and laughed. "Riding a Griffin would change anyone's understanding."

"Indeed, Rhys, but the mental cooperation has been the new and significant experience."

"Will it be a problem for you if they understand too much, Ranevargar?"

"How so, Tan?"

"Well they mightn't leave you alone any more. What if they pester you to give them constructs or want to learn how to make their own?"

"Lord Uirebon, in particular, is already wondering how to approach me for all of that. I will be most cooperative."

"What does he want to learn?"

"Everything he doesn't understand, Tan, and while I will be able to help him with much there will be even more disappointment."

"I meant in particular."

"That is extensive. Foremost in his mind at the moment is great wonder regarding my constructs, Maurice in particular, and he was intrigued just now to hear that we have established a new Tree Portal."

"Ha! I bet they all are, now they can't zap themselves wherever they like."

"Will you show him how to make Tree Portals, Ranevargar?"

"That will be one of the disappointments, Mr B. I can teach him how to use an existing Tree Portal, but creating his own requires an ability he doesn't possess."

"Could he find someone somewhere in the Realms with enough ability to do it for him?"

"It is possible, but rather unlikely, Mr B. "

"Unlikely, hey! Trust Kieran to break all the rules. Uirebon will turn green when he finds out it was Kieran who made the new portal."

Woorawa laughed. "Not really, Rhys. They've seen Kieran do all sorts of special stuff. This'll be just one more ... What will you do if they ask you for their own Realm Trees, Ranevargar?"

"They already have them. You call them Emperor trees."

"Could they make them into proper Realm Trees?"

"Not at all, Woorawa. They can't develop Tree Managers, and the further change to Portal Trees is beyond them."

"Why do they even have the Emperor form then?"

"The Emperor form provides a natural focus for the main Portal system."

"So that's why Maynor didn't take Rhys straight to his castle?"

"Indeed, Woorawa. He was at the end of his resources and took the path of least resistance."

"When will Uirebon be able to tell you what he's discovered about Kieran's Realm, Ranevargar? He said it was significant."

"Yes, that has intrigued me. After demonstrating Kieran's new portal link we have several hours of relatively free time at the Oasis Grove for discussion and relaxation."

"Relaxation? That's a joke! With those high-powered minds, Kieran won't be able to relax for a second."

"Yes, I will, Rhys. When we've had a good talk you're going to tell me it is time for a swim and a rest."

"I will? Neat idea! I wonder if they'll join in, or make it an opportunity to talk to Maurice?"

"Maurice will be enjoying the Oasis with us."

"Wow! I can't wait to see that. Does he even like water?"

I will look to you to teach me the enjoyment I see so clearly in your mind, Rhys.

"You big lump! You'll probably make the Oasis feel like it's all tidal waves."

Ranevargar pointed to Aglaron walking briskly to rejoin them.

"He didn't wait for the others?"

"His mind is focused on Kieran and he is eager to spend as much time as possible with him, Tan."

Rhys replied. "Wow! The next few days are going to be interesting."

*   *   *

"Everyone? Without assistance?"

"Kieran continues to surprise, High King. The Realm Trees provide some assistance, but he made this translation with his own resources."

Aglaron regarded the Realm Trees, the companions, a group of attendants, the Flying Guardian, which evidently had some special association with Rhys, and, dwarfing them all, the curiously-named Dragon Construct. He calculated the amount of Nexus energy he would need for a similar translation and then shared his wonder with Ranevargar.

"Kieran is driven to become a Portal Master, High King, for the sake of Woorawa and particularly Tan, who yearn for home and family, and his efforts have given him proficiency. When we visit his Realm you will see how he is establishing his own network of Tree Portals to help Maurice."

"His own Realm Trees, Ranevargar? I don't understand. Lord Uirebon advised me that Realm Trees are unique to your Realm and require a special type of attention which only you can give."

"Until Kieran arrived, Uirebon was right. Tomorrow you will observe for yourself how his affinity with life manifests in the response all creatures in my Realm give him."

"Affinity for life? That is a family trait, strong in myself, and strong in the Royal Consort. Is it possible I could be trained in the care of Realm Trees?"

"Affinity, to some degree, is almost universal, Lord Aglaron, and I have noted your pleasant rapport with my assigned Griffins. Ride my mind to understand what is needed."

Aglaron, thinking he was already linked, was surprised and then delighted when a strange and wondrous mental vista opened and drew him in. A new link firmed and he realised he was watching Ranevargar and himself from above. His elven eyes registered a group of the ubiquitous, amusing head-bobbing birds and locked on one in particular.

"This is curiously disconcerting, to be observing my own observation, Ranevargar, but this is a basic skill."

"Indeed. Watch."

An invitation flowed to the Joker bird's mind. Joker birds? Rhys's name for them? Blossoming eagerness for close association resulted in a swooping flight, then pleasure to be perching on a raised wrist. Realisation came. The command he himself would have used had been replaced with an aura of welcome, an aura new to his experience, and one Ranevargar was expecting him to copy.

"I can't do that. I have no basis to make a start."

Ranevargar's free hand rested against soft green feathers, and Aglaron, sharing a mysterious flow of energy, watched feather-pigment transform to brilliant orange, then, after a moment, return to green.

"Kieran radiates such an abundance of what your mind understands as an aura that he actually represses it to reduce the attention it brings. And he is learning to use it rapidly."

"He always had a way with animals, but none of his mentors noted anything really unusual about it."

"His Opal is more than a Realm Stone, much more, and I am hoping Uirebon's research will help us with understanding."

"The Opal has wrought the changes?"

"There is a definite association, but the more I see the more puzzled I become. Tonight you will witness a power from beyond the Realms, a power which will hold you in thrall."

Wariness surged. *"What manner of power, Ranevargar? I am averse to having my mind bound in any way."*

"Woorawa will dance."

Aglaron wondered momentarily if this might be an example of the irreverence ascribed to Rhys? No, Ranevargar's thought was earnest. *"Whatever can you mean?"*

"There is mystery, such as you have never known, expressed through the grace and power of his movement, my Lord. You will find yourself, as Rhys describes, spellbound."

A brief sense of Ranevargar's own reaction to Woorawa's dance came before he continued.

"My Lord, it is my belief that a mystery beyond our understanding entered Faerie with Kieran and his companions. Power rests with each of them in a guise appropriate to their nature."

"Do you mean the vast power which continually manifested in Kieran's Realm?"

"That is Kieran's doing. He worked with Maurice to speed the restoration of his Realm, but, apart from the unimaginable quantities, that power has properties akin to our own Nexus. The other powers are different. Woorawa walked through a barrier built by Maurice and froze three of Maynor's Fetches simply by singing. Tan is even more disconcerting. At first, as you have experienced, I thought he had the power to call truth, but now I know it is more than that. Rhys had power even before he met Kieran, but, in a passing moment, acquired a level of mind-to-mind speech which takes decades of training for our young to master."

"A passing moment? Surely there was something significant involved?"

"Yes. I was describing the rapidity of the event, but if I am correct the changes all occurred with Kieran's first summoning of that White Power he

demonstrated for you and Uirebon."

"Uirebon and I were shaken by its puissance and mystified as to its origin."

"As am I, High King, and the amount you saw him call for Maurice's elevation pales against the torrents released for his Realm storms."

"You believe the White Power confers abilities?"

"I do, but only on that singular occasion. I have been present many times when he has called it without experiencing anything except wonder."

"Lord Ranevargar, you do reveal wonder upon wonder, but what of my son? He is clearly a wonder in his own right, but this artificial persona has severed our blood-bond, and the new mantle of power and responsibility makes him unreadable. Does he fare well?"

Ranevargar passed a rapid assurance to Kieran, then built a privacy ward for himself and Aglaron. *"Kieran has entrusted me with the task of giving you assurance and enlightenment about all the complications of his situation and intentions."* Ranevargar acknowledged Aglaron's puzzlement. *"Yes, you would prefer to hear it personally from Kieran, and you will have many opportunities to do just that, but only I know the full story."*

"Another puzzle?"

"No, the outcome of a particular decision Kieran wants you to know and hold private."

Aglaron gave instant agreement.

"High King, Kieran will live in the Human World with Rhys until their time together comes to a natural end. He will then return to the Realms and, with certain provisos, resume his life as Keryth. In the meanwhile, he will make visits according to his situation and the re-establishment of the Portal system."

Aglaron, understanding the time differential, was impressed. A full and happy century of life for Rhys translated to less than twenty-five years of Faerie time, a blink relatively.

"What provisos has he set?"

"Currently, the removal of his persona would mean the loss of his deep bonds and all his Kieran memories. That is a loss he will not accept, but it is also a loss I am confident we can avoid by studying the conditioning process."

"You have that confidence when Maynor holds the knowledge and skill?"

"Kieran helped me gather Maynor's knowledge and, with Lord Uirebon's help, I believe we will find a way to assimilate a conditioned persona instead of losing it."

"Did you have this knowledge at the Council Meeting? It was by Kieran's command that Maynor cleared Lady Narello of all his manipulation."

"Some of it, High King, but the greater part was taken in that private discussion just before Maynor returned to his Realm."

"So that was its purpose? Uirebon and I wondered."

"There was more. We made it very clear that Maynor should hold to all the Council's directives."

Ranevargar was pleased to see the High King's instant recognition of a new element.

"Both of you? That was not apparent at the time."

"Your son wields great strength, High King, but he lacks knowledge, and it was my long experience as a Realm Lord that helped him counter Maynor and guide the Council."

There was a long pause.

"This explains many things, Ranevargar, but why the misdirection?"

"When the extent of Maynor's manipulation was first discovered there was no other course. We faced a strong probability that Kieran's standing would be rejected by the Council."

"Reject my own son? He ended the Challenge I was losing and restored a Realm."

"You ordered his conditioning."

"Yes, I see ... For all you knew, the High Council could have become a scene of conflict."

"The potential was there, as evidenced by Lady Narello's actions, but we were well prepared. Kieran had us uniquely shielded and Maurice was augmented and ready to intervene."

"The Dragon was augmented?"

"He is not invulnerable. Without Kieran's assistance the breaching of Maynor's Wards would have destroyed him."

Aglaron paused for thought once again. *"Lord Ranevargar, I am fully thankful for everything you have done, but this indicates it was your will and wisdom directing the High Council and, I suspect, guiding Kieran's actions. It also confirms Lord Uirebon's recent conjecture that you have been hiding knowledge and wisdom behind a mask of age and failing strength. Now you reveal yourself?"*

"Yes, High King. Kieran and I discussed this at great length and we are persuaded that you will respect my wish for isolation and apparent disregard for matters outside my Realm."

"'Persuaded' has a curious force to it."

"Yes, a consequence of the very powers we have been discussing. Kieran and I didn't see it ourselves, but Maurice recognised its unusual nature and carefully observed the detail of Tan's interaction with you three Realm

Rulers. We regard your willing promise of respect and friendship as a truth calling, and more than enough reason to give you trust."

"Lord Ranevargar, not only will I respect your wish, I will subtly cultivate it throughout the Realms. I am puzzled at how such a given applies with Kieran."

"Mr B will remain a companion, but chose to do so without knowledge of his deep Widderkin bond. Kieran and Rhys made the same choice and asked for your trust in not revealing it."

"Of course, but what of Lord Uirebon and Maynor?"

"We trust Uirebon. Maynor will forget."

"He will?"

"Maurice and I will make a visit. As things stand, Kieran's persona is keyed directly to Maynor's mind and we need to transfer that to Maurice for safekeeping."

"I wondered how Kieran would resolve the dilemma with Pethron. You advised him?"

"Only that he should discuss it with Rhys. He had already spoken with Mr B by the time we shared our thoughts."

"He wishes to formalise this trust with me?"

"He wishes to offer trust on a personal level because, though his memories tell him otherwise, you are his father."

Ranevargar dismissed the privacy ward and indicated all the enquiring looks.

"Kieran is ready to transport us to the Oasis Grove."

*   *   *

Uirebon felt the eagerness of the gathering to hear what he had to offer and noticed the particular intensity of the quiet companion.

"Information about the Realm Stones was relatively easy to find, because they are so fundamental, and because many ambitious Court Lords commissioned personalised treatises on their function and properties. We found a surprising amount of variation in the way they have been used through the ages, but almost no variation with their physical description. Kieran's Opal matches the Opal described as one of the six so closely we are certain they are one and the same."

"The same six through the ages, Uirebon?"

"Always, Lord Ranevargar. Any loss would result in a dead Realm and there has only been the one occurrence of that."

"And have you learnt much of the history of Dead World?"

"In essence, no. There is a plethora of description about its daunting and dangerous characteristics and almost as much conjecture about the disappearance of the ruling Realm Lord, but the death process itself has never been explained."

"That sounds interesting about the Realm Lord. Can you tell us some of it, Lord Uirebon?"

"Certainly, Mr B. One recurring theory posits that the Realm Lord was lost when he dabbled in experiments trying to control Chaos Energy."

All attention turned to Lady Narello.

"All such experiments are dangerous and the knowledge my Chaos Masters have gained has been hard won. Even when all known precautions are followed, disappearances occur. The theory has merit in my opinion."

"Another theory suggests the Realm Lord failed to return from a trip to the Human World and a third claims there was a secret banishment from the Realms after an effort to wrest control of the Nexus from the reigning High King."

Woorawa became quite excited. "The second theory fits with the story my uncle told us about where Kieran's Artefact came from."

"Artefact?"

"Yes, Lord Uirebon. It's what my people called Kieran's Opal while we were guarding it."

Ranevargar took over. "I agree with Woorawa. I think we can preclude the first theory, because if Chaos took a Realm Lord, his Realm Stone would undoubtedly have gone with him. The other theories both match Woorawa's story of a possible elven lord influencing matters in the Human Realm."

"Lord Ranevargar, I have no knowledge of this story."

"It is not mine to tell … Woorawa?"

Woorawa was eager. "My people pass knowledge through storytelling, Lord Uirebon, and my uncle shared this story as the reason Kieran was gifted with the Artefact. Burrimul and the other Elders discussed my wondrous healing and decided Kieran must be a Great One passing through our country, a Great One with the healing and other powers described in one of our ancient stories."

Eyes turned to where Kieran was nodding his head. "It was embarrassing being called a Great One but Burrimul spent a whole day with us before he made up his mind, watching and testing me with things I couldn't believe."

Woorawa continued. "Uncle Burrimul became extra certain there was a connection to the Great One when the guard song for the Artefact helped him resist Kieran's Medusa look." Woorawa laughed at the puzzled looks. "That's Rhys's name for the way Kieran can scare people just by looking at them. Medusa was a legendary creature who had snakes instead of hair and her gaze could turn you to stone. Kieran doesn't do that, but his look sure can make you feel petrified."

"We call it the Game of Will, Woorawa, and Kieran was always a strong player ... Does your uncle's story describe the visitor using such a look?"

"Not exactly, High King, but it does say he had abilities that were so hard to resist they had to call a great gathering of healers to take the Artefact away from him."

"Sounds like a Maynor going to Central Australia and trying to take over."

Aglaron looked to Uirebon and Ranevargar. "I agree with Rhys. Who else but a misguided Realm Lord would seek power in the Human World?"

Uirebon gave his attention to Woorawa. "Is there other detail to the story, Woorawa? Apparently your people identified the Artefact as the source of power and had the knowledge and strength to take it."

"Not really. Uncle Burrimul might know more, but we only heard about the conflicts and the big gathering of healers to end it."

"Despite the High King warning him, Maynor made an unsuccessful attempt to influence you before you joined Kieran. He would have been far more wary if he'd known your people could take a Realm Stone."

Woorawa's head lifted, as did all the companions. "Yes, they did, didn't they? It's really amazing, because Ranevargar told us that here in the Realms only a High King in full control of the Nexus can do that."

Aglaron queried Ranevargar. "You are well informed on one of the lesser-known functions of my office, Lord Ranevargar. That is knowledge I thought restricted to my Lore Master and my Principal Advisor."

"Knowledge I gleaned in the dim past, my Lord, knowledge which no longer holds."

"You mean because Woorawa's people also have the ability?"

"It would seem they do, Lord Uirebon, but a third force is now in play, a force which, contrary to all my experience and understanding, could take your Realm Stone in a passing moment and with little effort."

"A riddle? You mean my death?"

"No, Lord Uirebon. I mean Kieran. If he wished to control your Realm Stone you would have as little effect in resisting him as Maynor did."

Three Realm Lords stared in shock. Aglaron recovered first. "You took Maynor's Ruby, Kieran?"

"Not fully. Just enough to show him that I could ... He didn't like it."

"So that was why he knelt in submission? Astonishing. But how could you know you had such an ability?"

"Ranevargar and I were experimenting with our Realm Stones and it kind of just happened. I'll show you if you like, without going all the way of course."

Rhys's laugh sounded in the deathly silence that followed. "Don't do it, Aglaron. Ranevargar turned so white he gave us all a fright when Kieran did it with his Pearl."

"I will heed your advice, Rhys. Just the thought makes me uncomfortable ... But maybe my own Realm Stone, with its unique connection to the Nexus, is a different story?"

Ranevargar spoke with certainty. "Having watched the process with Maynor, my Lord, I judge the difference would mean little."

Lady Narello shook her head with an expression somewhere between doubt and concern. "This ability diminishes the security of our tenure as Realm Lords, Lord Kieran. In the wrong hands it would be a threat to the Council and to the High King."

"Don't worry about it, my Lady. Except that it's connected with my Opal, I haven't a clue about where it came from, and I know I can't pass it on. I shared the pattern with Ranevargar and it wouldn't work for him."

Ranevargar acknowledged the searching look from Lord Uirebon. "Yes, Lord Uirebon. I tried with no iota of success. The process, though appearing simple, was completely beyond me."

"Simple? Surely not?"

Kieran explained. "I never found it hard, but all the practice I had when Ranevargar was kidnapped made it almost automatic."

"You took control of Ranevargar's Realm Stone while he was with Maynor?"

"Well, Ranevargar offered it to me, really, when we worked out what to do, but I did have to go to Maynor's Castle to actually take it, because the Realm Boundaries interfered with my calling."

"Lord Kieran, I am increasingly bewildered. What does calling a Realm Stone mean, and how could you penetrate the Castle Wards?"

Ranevargar rested his hand over his Pearl. "Our visitors know nothing of this venture, Kieran. Share the moments of Krol's dive and your actions to protect my Pearl. Those memories will outshine any explanation or even a demonstration."

"Hey, include the rest of us, Kieran. You told us, but you've never shown us the memory."

The imagery transferred, and into the minds of the stunned tableau of recipients came Maurice's message.

"Krol flew mightily, Kieran. Do you realise how close you came to the Castle protections?"

"You mean the Wards? I didn't even know they existed, but when I call like that they don't matter."

"Calling? This is a new thing. Can you do it with all the Realm Stones?"

"Not straight off, Uirebon. I have to take a significant level of possession before it will work."

Uirebon's thirst for knowledge was too strong. "Lord Kieran, despite the wariness Rhys advises, I am eager to observe this process of possession and ask for a trial with my own Realm Stone."

"No worries! We'll make time for sure. But not today, because we're taking a break before we go back to the Central Grove."

"My thanks, Kieran ... If you do go so far as to try a calling, I suggest Lord Ranevargar should be with us. It is, after all, an instance of portalling and one of your expressed priorities."

"Hey! We're a pack of dead heads! ... Kieran, Uirebon's right. Why didn't we think of that?"

Through the low level of mind sharing Kieran and Ranevargar were holding for the visit came a two-way flow of excitement and surprise. Rhys was right. How could they have overlooked something so obvious?

"Lord Uirebon, we'll make some time tomorrow morning before our activities at the Lake Grove. Your new perspective might be valuable indeed."

Uirebon was really pleased, but his curiosity was still strong. "Also, what can you tell us of the guard song, Woorawa? I am puzzled that a song can resist any expression of power."

In a moment a rhythmic voice projected strongly and three startled Realm Lords watched Woorawa, with a curiously graceful movement, rise to his feet and face the High King. The eerie sound strengthened in force, if not in volume, and, following an unseen cue, Tan leapt to join in. Seconds later Kieran and Rhys, then Mr B and Ranevargar, were beside them, augmenting the strange chant.

A shiver of sensation passed through Aglaron's body and he, too, rose as something unknown pressured against him. The Dragon's voice came reassuringly into his mind.

"The companions are joined in their practised version of the guard song, High King, and Woorawa invites you to carefully test each of them with your Game of Will."

Aglaron immediately decided to project authority rather than fear and, since it was his invitation, started with Woorawa. It required effort to push through the strange barrier of the chanting, but then Woorawa signalled for an end with his hands and made a reluctant bow. Rhys and Tan were easier, then, surprisingly, so were Kieran and Ranevargar. The chanting finished and everyone sat down.

"The chant makes me feel as if I am pushing my Will through a fog of obstruction, Lord Ranevargar, but the strength to disable a Fetch is not in it. And, most unexpectedly, I reached you and Kieran."

"Woorawa used a different chant and a different frame of mind on those occasions, my Lord, and Kieran and I relied solely on the chant. The game would escalate otherwise."

"I see."

Aglaron took in Rhys's oh-so-confident smile and did indeed see an expectation that in a full contest he could end up grovelling at Kieran's feet.

"You have taken this chant for your own purposes, Ranevargar?"

"Kieran and his companions regularly practice their abilities, my Lord, and I am privileged to participate as well as advise. You will all learn a range of chants during your visit. You will see why when Woorawa presents his Dragon dance tonight."

"Um! The Dragon dance is still there, but I'm changing things so everyone's involved."

Uirebon's head lifted. "Everyone? You would have three Realm Lords join a dance they know nothing about?"

Rhys piped up. "Five Realm Lords, Uirebon. You won't be able to stop yourself. I'm a real klutz at dancing, but when Woorawa sucks you in, it doesn't matter a scrap."

Kieran leaned happily against Rhys. "In Realm Lord terms, Rhys just proclaimed he's a clumsy dancer but Woorawa draws him in so strongly he forgets his inhibitions."

Rhys leaned back just as happily while he answered. "Uirebon, you'd better find some new portalling stuff soon, so we can get home before we all turn into walking dictionaries. Kieran's already caught it off Ranevargar."

"You're a twit, Rhys. You make it sound like a disease. How do you expect Uirebon to understand crazy slang words?"

"Crazy? Since when is speaking normal crazy?"

"Klutz isn't normal. It's probably the first time anyone's heard it in the Realms, and you made it sound like Woorawa was slurping spaghetti when you said sucked in."

"Is that so? Well, you called me a twit, and I bet they've never heard that either, so you're crazy too."

"Which proves I haven't caught Dictionary Disease from Ranevargar."

Ranevargar smiled at the rather bewildered Realm Lords. "I have learnt that this is called stirring, Uirebon. It is a curious communication pattern where derogatory statements are in fact an expression of friendship."

"And what of this Dictionary Disease? It has a sense of derogation about it."

Ranevargar continued. "Our speech patterns have a tendency for over elaboration and precision according to the companions' perception."

Rhys laughed. "He means we speak more plainly, Uirebon."

"I see, and very directly too ... Lord Kieran, how much of your power do you delegate to the Dragon? Sharing control of a Realm is new to Faerie."

"As much as he needs, Uirebon. He knows how to manage all the things it will take me years to learn."

"And does he connect to the Nexus through your Opal?"

"Sort of. I'll show you— Aggh! What's that for?" 'That' was the dig in the ribs he'd just received from Rhys.

"You're not showing him anything, Kieran, not till you've had some relax time. You've been doing brain stuff all day and we're going for a swim. Uirebon can talk to Maurice while we're in the water."

"Not today. I am joining you in the Oasis."

Joining wasn't quite the right word, because everything stops when a mighty Dragon suddenly breaks from his watchful statue demeanour and bounds exuberantly to disrupt the shimmering calm of the water.

"Holy cow! Look at that! Come on, everyone! You too, Ranevargar ... and bring the visitors with you."

*　*　*

Kieran and Rhys were having catch up time before going to sleep, sharing their thoughts about the day's activities and, in particular, the way the visiting Realm Rulers had involved themselves.

"It was a really interesting day, Kieran. What do you think of them? Apart from your father, I mean."

"Apart? Why leave him out, Rhys?"

"Well, the more I watch him the more he's like a version of you. Tan reckons you must have grown up fairly close to him when you were little, because you've got so many of the same mannerisms."

"I have? Like what?"

Instant laughter. "Like the tiny angle you tilt your head and lift your eyebrows kind of unevenly for a questioning look."

"Do I do that?" A little grunt of self-amusement followed. "I felt it happen now that you've made me conscious of it. Have I done it all the time?"

"Yeah! But it's so natural we never noticed till Aglaron did exactly the same thing and Tan called it a mannerism."

"Tan does notice things the rest of us miss. I wondered why that description didn't quite feel like it was yours. So if you're leaving Aglaron out that means you like him?"

"Kieran, of course I do. He might be the High King of all Faerie, but he was one of us for Woorawa's story at the campfire. He set the example for Uirebon and Lady Narello to join in, and his wonder and excitement when it finished carried every one of us with him."

Kieran nudged his head against Rhys's shoulder. "That's for sure. Ranevargar always says he has the most powerful personality in the Realms, and he let it loose for Woorawa."

"Ha! Uirebon won't be questioning any more how a song and dance can be effective against power. He was gobsmacked."

"Lady Narello was more than gobsmacked, Rhys. Ranevargar noticed her wiping away tears, and when he sneaked a peek to make sure she was okay she was simply overwhelmed."

"How did he see that? It was dark."

"Not with his eyes. He uses our mind merge to monitor how they're reacting to everything."

"All the time? Why aren't you wrecked?"

"We would be if it was full on, like with Maynor and the Council, but we've had lots of practice since then and this is just a smidgen of merge ... And I like Uirebon and Lady Narello more and more as time goes on too. It's weird, like they're different people to the ones we were so angry with."

"Me too. I can hardly believe I called Lady Narello the Wicked Witch. Did you see her splashing water in Maurice's face at the Oasis? She should have melted."

Kieran twisted his head, rather awkwardly, towards Rhys. "What's that supposed to mean?"

"We'll have to get you reading more when we get home, Kieran, or watching movies. It's one of the best bits of the story. When the Wicked Witch of the West gets water on her she melts."

"Weird!"

There was a quiet time for a while.

"Well, I'm gobsmacked too. I wonder if Woorawa's dances will be the same when we're outside the Realms."

"I reckon they will, Kieran. They work for Tan and me and we're not elves ... We didn't learn much new from Uirebon, did we?"

"About getting home? No. It was all interesting, but disappointing about portalling ... Woorawa knows best, so we'll have a big talk with him about how to keep Tan from worrying too much."

"Yeah. Good thinking. I reckon he'll be okay while this visit lasts ... It'll be an interesting day tomorrow too. Did you see the looks from Uirebon and Lady Narello when Ranevargar said we'd all be riding Panthers while we're out on the plains?"

"No. Did they look nervous? And you left Aglaron out again."

"Only because he looked eager instead of wary like the other two."

"That'd be right. He likes his association with the Griffins Ranevargar loaned him so much we think he's going to ask if he can keep one permanently."

"Association? Does that mean something special?"

"Yes. It's not a bond like you've got with Krol and Maurice, but he does understand and admire them in a different way to Uirebon and Lady Narello, who kind of look on them as transport and not much more."

"Like your King of the Animals thing?"

"I suppose. He did tell us it runs in the family."

"Ha! When he sees you with the animals tomorrow, he'll blow his mind with how far it runs."

"I don't think that's all me, Rhys. It must be one of the things the Opal enhanced."

"The eagle and the honeyeater came to you before you had the Opal ... Hey, I wonder if the Realm animals react extra strongly because it's been built into them with Ranevargar's network?"

"That makes a lot of sense. We'll find out as soon as we get back to Melbourne."

After the contemplative pause that brought, Rhys went on. "It might work well for Aglaron if he had a permanent Griffin at the High Castle."

"It would, but he'll be disappointed because Ranevargar won't him give him one, at least not permanently."

"Why?"

"They're Guardians, Rhys, and being away from Ranevargar and their Realm is too hard for them. If the seven he's got now aren't swapped after three or four weeks they'll start pining."

"Have you got much Buddha stuff with Ranevargar tomorrow?"

"Lots, and all before we start anything else. There's too much to practice and learn and it'll be extra complicated because Ranevargar's invited Uirebon to be part of it."

"Uirebon? Why?"

"We're going to experiment with his idea about calling Realm Stones and he said we could use his."

"He did too ... so why are we talking?"

"What?"

"You should be sleeping. You won't stop all day tomorrow and you'll be wrecked again."

Kieran smiled at the concern. "Yes, boss!"

*   *   *

"Lady Narello appears drawn to the quiet companion, Uirebon. She watches his every action and speaks with him at every opportunity."

"Yes, and presses him to visit her Realm if ever there is an opportunity. Her motive is simply concern for his wellbeing. They were in conversation when his deep longing for family revealed itself momentarily and touched a chord of empathy."

"With Lady Narello?"

"Indeed, my Lord. Her own words, and she herself was somewhat surprised when it happened."

"So, you discussed this with her?"

"Yes, my Lord, or I should say she discussed it with me."

Aglaron considered. "Maynor has much to answer for. This positive aspect of Narello we have not seen for centuries. Did she share the moment with you?"

Uirebon relayed the memory.

"I see. No wonder Kieran has so strongly prioritised their return to the Human World ... Uirebon, what are your observations about yesterday's astonishing journey to the new Realm?"

"The flight itself, with Maurice, or the wondrous spectacle of growth revealed to us?"

"Any, but in particular your primary impression."

"So much, my Lord. At first it was puzzlement that Ranevargar's extraordinary mastery over living things has somehow never caught the attention of any other Realm. That was quickly replaced by surprise at the extent of their restoration progress."

"Surprising at first sight, Uirebon, but not when you think on it. What else would you expect from the joint efforts of two full Realm Lords and a Construct gifted with much of the knowledge and skills of his maker?"

"It is those efforts I regard as the most striking feature of all. The more I think on it the more it gains in significance. Kieran and the Dragon are bound to the Realm, but Ranevargar is not. Their joint restoration plan outlines expeditions like that of yesterday for several years, admittedly less frequently with progress, but organising all those Griffins and hosts we saw yesterday is an extensive commitment."

"Strong bonds have developed between Ranevargar and the companions, Uirebon, but I see what you mean. Are you thinking he should give more assistance to the Gateway and High Realms?"

"Not at all, my Lord. That is our responsibility, and Ranevargar has willingly offered to reduce his share of the free Nexus energy."

Aglaron laughed his agreement. "He is a canny elf, Uirebon. The offer is greatly appreciated, of course, but his Realm sacrifices nothing when you consider Kieran's gifts of Power."

"Cunning indeed, when you also consider his changed situation and independent source of power."

"Independent? I don't understand."

"Maurice explained it to me, my Lord. The Realm Trees were designed with the ability to store a minute portion of their life force and eventually build a reserve sufficient to allow his awakening. As it turned out, five hundred years of accumulation wasn't enough, but that steady flow is now available for Ranevargar to use in any way he chooses."

"Realm Trees, providing power for five hundred years and we had no knowledge of it? Have we been so complacent?"

"I don't believe so, my Lord. Maynor was undoubtedly an increasingly powerful influence, but I begin to wonder if Ranevargar's isolation and apparent decline was, in fact, a purposeful strategy."

"I am certain of it, Uirebon. He has already stated quite forcefully that everyday matters of Court and Realm management are for others. As I see it, his concerns are completely consistent with the imperatives of his highly individual viewpoint ... Uirebon, I have not yet heard the details of Kieran's calling of your Realm Stone."

"Thoroughly disturbing, my Lord. The warning Rhys gave was an understatement, and only Kieran's constant assurance kept me going. He started by placing his Opal in my hand and inviting any examination I could manage ..."

*   *   *

Aglaron sat close to the Dragon with Lady Narello and Uirebon, and took regard of Ranevargar's host elves arriving round Woorawa's camp-fire. Word of the previous Dragon dance had clearly spread, along with Woorawa's happy invitation that anyone was welcome to watch or join in. Ranevargar, Tan and Mr B were propped comfortably against a massive foreleg. Kieran and Rhys were involved with Woorawa somewhere and Aglaron wondered what that meant. Ranevargar and the two companions must have some idea, because their smiles and constant checks were building an air of happy expectation.

"Woorawa told us the tone will be different tonight, because he hopes to see everyone smiling, and at the moment we are reacting to involuntary protest and laughter projecting from Rhys."

Aglaron's curiosity had no time to develop because weird, raucous yells, screeches or whatever, whipped every head to the three figures capering toward them. Well, two were capering. Woorawa in the lead, was capering, yes, but in a manner so graceful it was riveting. More calls broke the hold and, startled, the High King felt his features stretch in instant amusement. With some subtle difference, Woorawa, with those painted golden eyes, was the Dragon again, while Kieran and Rhys, hardly recognisable beneath their copious body paint and strange costumes, looked completely ridiculous. Oh no! So much purple paint and the gawky cloth crowning Kieran's head was a clear representation of himself in leathers and the Crown of Office he'd worn at the High Council.

Aglaron's indrawn breath of startlement spluttered explosively with the realisation that the awful mess of coloured paint and mangled elven tunic was Rhys in the guise of Lady Narello. *Oh my!* Her eyes might be wide and apprehensive, but her smile was another story.

Woorawa now headed for the big group of helpers who'd followed them out and, while he set them going on the sound sticks with a lively rhythm, Kieran and Rhys made little sorties to mock any smiling onlooker who caught their attention. Woorawa added a chant to the mix of sound and, when it was established, moved closer to the campfire.

For several minutes Aglaron was lost to the laughter and happiness conveyed through every nimble step and quirky body movement. He came to himself and laughed aloud when two figures joined in a clumsy imitation which, somehow, only strengthened the atmosphere.

For the next half hour the gathering laughed in delight as a little piglet snuffling up to the High King, Lady Narello flinging a container of water in the Dragon's startled face, and a series of other indignities toward the visitors were played out. Interspersed, and reinforcing that atmosphere, was the repetition of Woorawa's happiness dance.

*   *   *

Kieran took in the honour guard of Griffins and Panthers waiting to make a formal farewell to the Realm Rulers with a sense that, apart from its striking nature, it was even more appropriate this time round.

Rhys, who'd originally claimed he'd look too posh and formal in the leathers he'd been gifted from the High Council, surprised everyone by deciding to wear them as a mark of respect for the High King. He sure looked impressive — well they all did — but his slightly taller stature and solid build made him look ... magnificent.

A pang of wonder touched Kieran. The unassuming student of old was standing by his side, changed so much but somehow still the same. Did he himself look impressive in his blue leathers? He had a peek through Maurice's eyes and thought he did, but looking at yourself from outside always felt a bit strange. Maurice's thought came to him.

"Your companions all regard your appearance as matching that of the High King, Kieran, except for Rhys who thinks you outshine everyone by a 'million miles'. Our three visitors, so accustomed to seeing you in your human garb, all see it as bestowing an appropriate mantle for the authority that is yours. While the High King and Uirebon converse with the Maker, Lady Narello approaches to offer her thanks and make yet another invitation to visit her Realm, particularly Tan."

"Lord Ranevargar, you have my gratitude for facilitating this extraordinary visit and revealing some of the wonders of your quiet Stewardship. Just five days of companionship and challenging activity has renewed our spirits. On a personal level, I have no way to express my gratitude for offering Kieran the sanctuary of your Realm and personally assisting him with a level of effort that, frankly, we don't understand."

"There will be more visits, High King. That is very clear in both Kieran and Rhys's minds.

My support for Kieran and his unfathomable companions is a pittance against their efforts on my behalf." Ranevargar turned to Uirebon. "Your understanding will grow with time, Lord Uirebon. The new harmony in the Nexus already speeds your efforts to help your friend restore his Gateway Realm, and that is but one of the changes they have wrought ... High King, rest assured that while your son's heart might be tied to Rhys's world, his bond to the Realms will be ever present in his mind. His intention is to make visits as frequently as his human studies allow."

"Human studies? Will they be of any value in helping him grow in the Stewardship of his Realm?"

"That is irrelevant, my Lord. The companions all see the college as their appropriate life path and, for his time in the Human World, so does Kieran. You must remember that his viewpoint is human rather than elven at present."

Aglaron pondered this a moment.

Ranevargar, peeking below the surface thoughts, was deeply pleased to see the High King's determination to outface any unacceptance of Widderfolk.

The eyes of the companions, Lady Narello, and the golden orbs of the Dragon settled expectantly on them.

"It is time, my Lord."

Three rulers moved through the honour guard of Griffins and Panthers, then halted when Rhys broke the formal atmosphere and raced to offer an entirely appropriate double hand clasp.

"We know you're crazy busy with all your Realm stuff, Aglaron, but come back as soon as you get a chance. We all think your visit was really neat."

Aglaron was lost for words, not because of the strange allusion to neatness, and not for long, but because of the emotions of acceptance radiating so clear and genuine in place of the confrontation and distrust of a few short days ago. *Amazing!* Tan's description of 'what you see is what you get' was so apt. No wonder Kieran was drawn to him.

"I don't know about neatness, Rhys. I regard this visit as a wild and wondrous time of speaking with a Dragon and Griffins willing to protect you with their lives, a time of seeing joyful companionship and staunch loyalty, and a time to begin to marvel at the healing and renewal you have helped bring to the Realms. We will certainly return."

Aglaron broke off and smiled because Rhys was waving his hands in negation at what he clearly regarded as 'talking dictionary' stuff.

The group joined the rest of the companions for a round of double hand clasps charged with far more than formality. The transport Griffins were all waiting, but Aglaron hesitated, this time really lost for words, and watched Kieran intently till he raised a hand.

"Hold, Father. I have a thank-you gift for your visit."

Aglaron shook his head. "There is no need, Kieran. The visit has been more than enough."

Kieran waved his hands in a strikingly similar manner to Rhys's dismissal of a few moments ago. "It's no big deal and it'll help with all your repair work. Let me see the rubies, so I can charge them up properly."

Aglaron reached to the secure pocket and glanced at Uirebon. "I have entrusted Uirebon with one to use as he sees fit, and the other three I keep close at all times."

"Yes, it was Uirebon's discussion with Maurice about the way he's been helping with your Gateway Realm that told us how handy the rubies are for projects that call on lots of power in a short time. Maynor threw stacks of their energy against the High Castle Wards, and since then you've used almost as much yourself, so topping them up makes sense. Last night Tan told us we're handing one over to Lady Narello as well, since they wouldn't exist without her, and she's got her own plans for rebuilding now that she's out of Maynor's control."

Lady Narello's features lit up with astonishment and Kieran thought she was going to bow to him. She didn't. She turned and gave Tan the most formal and meaningful gesture of respect any of them had so far seen. Aglaron, presenting his three rubies, was clearly impressed.

"Kieran, are you sure about this? The rubies store great quantities of power."

"I'm going to call the White Power, because there's so much of it, and also because Ranevargar thinks my Opal has a limit ... Woorawa?"

Woorawa hastened to present the remaining rubies, and Rulers and companions formed a loose semicircle to watch this major happening.

Barely suppressing a grin, because he was making this dramatic, Kieran held up his Opal and made it shimmer with all the colours of the rainbow. The repeated calls for Maurice's mega storms had set the process so securely in his mind he could trigger it almost automatically, but he hadn't called for a while and Ranevargar's constant coaching with other power flows meant this was an opportunity to watch from a more practised viewpoint.

A tentative probe made Kieran's smile bigger and he opened the surface level of his mind so Uirebon could watch the calling.

"What's with your Opal, Kieran? It didn't look so specco for the other White calls."

"I'm just making a point that my Opal is the critical source, Rhys."

Power coalesced round the Opal and, giving form for the eyes that wouldn't otherwise see anything, Kieran directed shimmering white streams to flow to the four gems now in the High King's hand, as well as Woorawa's nine.

Whoo! Thank goodness for all the practices. This was big, and the rubies were absorbing the energy at a slower rate than it was arriving. The coalescence increased its size rapidly and, seeing all the wary expressions,

Kieran dimmed the glow.

"Sheba, Kieran! Is that meant to happen?"

"It's a temporary reservoir, Rhys, like I did with Maurice when he couldn't take the power in fast enough. I'm looking to see why the rubies don't work like Realm Stones … Looks like it's built in and we'll have to be patient."

The merge with Ranevargar made a private communication. *This is trickier than we thought, Ranevargar. The test last night with Opal power didn't show this problem.*

"Slow the take-up rate for the rubies, Kieran, but let the reservoir build till there is enough to fill them."

"Slow?"

"Yes, as a precaution. I can see that the structure for power control within the rubies is stressed and, while it seems quite steady, it was never designed for such a rate. A few patient minutes is called for and might prevent the loss of a functioning ruby."

Kieran slowed the ruby intake rate till the stress disappeared and hastened to explain the sudden growth of the glowing reservoir. "We need to take a couple of minutes extra, Uirebon, to protect the rubies from overload."

All eyes were drawn to the shimmering power cloud and, on a whim, Kieran directed it to take the form of a perfect sphere.

"Holy Moses! That's unreal!"

"I'm just experimenting, Rhys. Ranevargar likes me trying new things."

"Wow! What sort of stuff can you do with it? It's like a big version of when you made your first blue glow."

Kieran was distracted by this interesting thought till, realising the power cloud now held as much as the rubies could take, he ended the call. The globe turned blue, then moved in a purposeful circle.

Kieran laughed. "Ranevargar says you're brilliant, Rhys, and I have to try as much stuff as I can before the globe drains into the rubies. Any ideas?"

Rhys's eyes lit up. "A zillion! Turn it green and make it look like Woorawa's tree frog."

A giant, 8-metre frog floated above.

"Whoa! Too big! Make it Woorawa size."

The frog quivered, but didn't change.

"It won't shrink."

"That's different to your glow. What about separating it into three frogs?"

That involved building two new reservoir structures, re-distributing the power and reforming the frog shapes, but it wasn't difficult.

Ranevargar spoke. "Disregard the frivolity, my Lord. Rhys's suggestion to manipulate this energy form is an opportunity for observation and learning we can't ignore ... Kieran, can you release one of the frogs to my control?"

"I don't see how. It's linked to my Opal till I release it as normal power, and that would need one of our ordinary reservoirs."

Uirebon interrupted. "You seem to be saying that this power is uniquely Kieran's unless he transforms it?"

"Apparently so, Lord Uirebon, though it may be unique to his Opal rather than himself."

"Amazing! ... Lord Kieran, the third frog is visibly shrinking?"

Kieran reintroduced visibility to the energy flowing into the rubies. "That's why, and we've only got a few minutes before the rest of it's gone. Any ideas to try before we farewell our visitors?"

*   *   *

Woorawa stared with real astonishment at the startling changes to Kieran's Central Grove and linked arms with Tan in the hope that a hurry on and a closer look would help lift the lagging spirits brought on by the brick wall Ranevargar and Kieran had run into with their portal studies.

"Look at that, Tan. The Realm Trees must be at least a half metre taller than they were five days ago and there's not a single patch of bare ground close to them. Ranevargar must be right about the life bombs going to the periphery instead of close to the Realm Tree roots."

Tan made a blatant show of shaking his head as if he was clearing cobwebs, and smiled at the concern implicit in the arm link. "All that flying, where I think too much, turns me into a gloomy guts about the time going so quickly at home. Just as well there's so much happening that snaps me out of it ... Half a metre? You're kidding."

There was no kidding about it, and Tan did snap out of it, because Ranevargar, Kieran and Rhys were already about to scramble from Maurice's back to the grass carpeting the ground.

Kieran made a quick check to see they were following okay, then started a flat-out race to beat Rhys to the primary Realm Tree.

Tan knew that Woorawa wanted their own race, so when his feet touched the ground he put on a fake look of astonishment and pointed in the opposite direction.

"I don't believe it! Look at that!"

Completely taken in, Woorawa turned to check and was caught by this sneaky ploy. It didn't make any difference to the end result, because he was so fleet-footed, and being called a sneak and a cheat and dumped on the ground was an even bigger spirit-lift for Tan.

These hijinks ended quickly though, because Kieran and Rhys were checking the growth of what, as the Primary Tree of this Central Grove, would be the main focus point for all of Kieran's Realm. *Wow!* This was a first. Rhys knelt so Kieran could stand on his shoulders then, holding the slim trunk for support, carefully stood so Kieran's upstretched arms could reach the greatest height. It was only just enough, and Tan repeated himself, this time for real.

"I don't believe it! It's accelerating! That's more like a metre than half a metre ... in just five days!"

Ranevargar, looking very pleased, gave an explanation. "The root system is the reason, Tan, along with our special stimulus. It will be as big as the above-ground section of the tree and drawing on the nutrients from the extra life bombs."

Tan knew this. They discussed the details of what was happening with every five-day visit, but seeing it for real had so much more impact.

Kieran jumped nimbly down and joined Ranevargar for a short Buddha moment to renew the stimulus energy. This was Ranevargar's specialty and they would tend every tree in the Grove before doing anything else. Rhys pointed back at Maurice.

"Come on you lot. We'll leave them to it and unload the seed packs for when the Griffins catch up."

Maurice had been a pack horse today, because the new seeds being introduced to the lakes and waterways were bulkier than usual and carrying enough was too big a task for the supporting Griffins and their riders. Tan glanced at the sky. It would be another half hour at least, but the convoy of fifty Griffins approaching and then manoeuvring to land was always impressive and a sight he looked forward to. A short while later, when Rhys was sharing his excitement at the difference in the river water, Woorawa gave Tan a nudge.

"Watch this. I bet he'll want us all to try swimming in it."

And sure enough, after pointing out some tiny plants and carrying on about how clear the water looked, he knelt and checked the temperature.

"Hey, everyone! It's warmer than it used to be. We should try it out."

Mr B wasn't so sure. "The convoy will be here soon and then we'll be too busy. I don't think there'll be enough time."

Rhys laughed. "You're too practical, Mr B. This is our chance to make history."

"History? Having a swim is making history?"

"The first swim in a whole Realm for nine thousand years is definitely history."

Well! It was too, and Tan decided he definitely wanted to be part of it.

"Come on! We'll make it quick."

Woorawa pulled his shirt off. This was going to happen. Rhys rushed to do the same, then stopped at Mr B's strong headshake.

"Save it for later, Rhys, the Griffins are close and Kieran might like to share the moment."

Rhys grimaced. "Of course he would. I got carried away. Put it on the agenda for our first relax time, Mr B."

Mr B didn't answer, because, like Tan and Woorawa, he'd turned to search the sky.

Two hours later the companions, along with a number of the hosts, had a christening ceremony — a brief one, because Rhys's evaluation of the water temperature had been overly optimistic, and even quicker when Kieran suddenly started treading water.

"What? Are you chickening out?"

"Ranevargar's just been contacted by Lord Uirebon and he says it's important ... Rhys, your christening swim is now official, but we need a powwow. Follow me."

There was an instant exodus and a few minutes later everyone was gathered in front of Maurice.

"A researcher has discovered a section with references to portals which is intriguing but very hard to understand. Uirebon is going to fly his Griffin to the study Centre to see what he can figure, but he suggests we might be able to help."

"What? Meet him in his Realm?"

"Maurice will fly us there tomorrow ... No, Tan, we can't manage today, but we *will* make an early start."

Maurice's thought came strongly. "*We can make a night flight, Maker, if the Centre isn't located too far from Lord Uirebon's Boundary and Kieran can provide me with an energy boost.*"

Kieran was keen. "As much as you like, Maurice."

CHAPTER 8

Secure under the travel flap while Maurice powered his way across Uirebon's Realm, the companions woke from the short but deep sleep Kieran had imposed on everyone. Even Ranevargar had insisted on being included, after the long journey to the Boundary Wall, the transitioning of Griffins and hosts to their home Realm, then another Boundary transition and a hasty sharing of food before starting this flight to join Uirebon.

Kieran checked for Uirebon's pattern with his GPS mode and then Maurice's sense of location.

"Watch through Maurice's eyes, everyone. We'll be there in a few minutes."

Eager minds marvelled at the clarity of the moonlit landscape passing so far below, dark patches of forested area contrasting with what must be grassy plains or cultivated areas.

"Has Uirebon learnt anything new yet, Kieran?"

"We'll ask him in person, Tan, but I doubt it. He only arrived from his home base about half an hour ago."

"Base? Isn't it a Castle?"

Ranevargar's thought came through. *"Think of a loose, sprawling castle without ramparts and towers, Tan, then add an endless series of underground storage and filing levels."*

"Endless?"

"Not really, but under Uirebon's Stewardship they have been steadily extending for almost 1400 years."

"Will this outpost Centre be very big?"

"We'll see for ourselves, Rhys. The outpost designation suggests otherwise, and Uirebon thinks of it as ancient."

Maurice's flight slowed and dipped, taking everyone's attention to a scatter of sparkling lights.

"Uirebon gives us guidance to a clear landing area among the trees, and I sense a group of some thirty attendants with him."

* * *

Uirebon made a gentle, though somewhat hurried, introduction to the little community, then turned to the elf at his side.

"Lord Kieran, this is Bantellar, the young researcher whose findings have brought us here in such haste. After more than a decade of searching the archives of many Centres for any early records referencing the Nexus, he was directed here, where delving through an old and unclassified section led to the discovery of a collection of scripts relating to the adepts and their work."

Kieran, smiling broadly, double grasped the wide-eyed elf with an eager and friendly grip. "These adepts, Bantellar, are they connected with portals in some way?"

Bantellar looked with diffidence to Uirebon and Ranevargar, but they both nodded for him to go ahead. "My Lord, it was the adepts who built the Nexus and brought us here with knowledge and skills now lost. The portal system connecting our Realms and linking to the Human World is one of their great legacies. My scripts are very hard to understand, but within their general treatment of the Nexus itself, I have been puzzled by consistent references to some related form of translation."

Through the partial merge they always maintained in the presence of another Realm Ruler, Kieran felt Ranevargar's alert level escalate.

"Related, Bantellar? Do you mean related by more than the general use of power?"

"I do, my Lord. There is a sense of ... specificity ... which warranted a response to Lord Uirebon's alert."

Rhys laughed, then hurriedly explained himself. "I'm not laughing at Ban, Ranevargar. I'm laughing because it's more dictionary talk."

"In this case, Rhys, it is more than appropriate, and even more exciting. A form of portal bound specifically to the Nexus is a possibility I have never heard of ... Is this new for you, Uirebon?"

"Completely, and it was this very wording which convinced me I should call Lord Kieran."

Rhys grimaced and grinned at the same time. "Well, I take it back then, Ban, and we'll make 'specificity' the theme for the day."

"Thank you, Lord Rhys ... I think. What is a dictionary?"

Rhys gave him a funny look. "Are you kidding me? A book of words and their meanings."

"Now I understand. You thought I sounded like a lexicon."

Ranevargar took over. "Ignore Rhys's preference for simplification and generalisation over clarity and finesse with the communication process, Bantellar. Are your scripts close at hand?"

Bantellar looked to Uirebon. "They are ancient, my Lord, and need the attention of a Master Restorer before they can be freely handled. Let me show you."

Kieran, still holding Ban's arm and showing his eagerness, started moving. "How serious is their condition, Ban? Will we be able to look at them without causing any damage?"

"My Lord?"

Ranevargar explained for the companions. "Lord Uirebon is a Master Restorer, Kieran. With the use of power, he will renew and reinvigorate any fading ink or brittle vellum. It is an unusual skill requiring innate ability and years of training, and vital for preventing the loss of stored knowledge ... How many Master Restorers do you have, Uirebon?"

"Five, including myself, plus one other who gives service at the High Castle."

Uirebon answered a barrage of questions while the group moved down three flights of stone steps then along a corridor with smooth rock walls lit at regular intervals by softly glowing white crystals. Tan was so intrigued he paused and wondered if they could be touched.

"There is no heat, Tan. It is a simple version of Kieran's blue glow that is used for lighting in all Realms but mine."

Tan's question about the crystals was forgotten because, just ahead, Bantellar was gesturing for Uirebon to enter a doorway.

"The records are in the old scriptorium on the left, my Lord, but after you repair them we can move to a study area."

"Scriptorium? Gods! Some of the novels I read are coming to life. I've got this image of old scribes dipping goose feathers in special ink and writing stuff on rolls of parchment with the light of a big candle flickering close by."

Uirebon turned with a smile. "Some of us are old, Rhys, but not all. Bantellar is much the same age as Kieran. Our pens are carefully crafted metal. Vellum outlasts parchment by centuries, and candle fumes would be highly deleterious in the long-term. Otherwise your image has a degree of accuracy."

Uirebon turned back to Bantellar who now led the way through another entrance and passed a long stretch of old stone shelving to a curious alcove.

"I have puzzled over four of the best-preserved scripts, my Lord, but in all there are twenty-seven works in this collection."

"Twenty-seven? Really? A number of Power. Fascinating! ... And these four at the front are the ones you have examined?"

At Bantellar's nod, Uirebon held his palms ever so gently above the old scripts and closed his eyes.

"Watch only, Kieran. The pattern is delicate and even a trace on the power flows could be too much interference."

Everyone stood silent, sensing there was no place for distraction of any kind, and watched till the capsule of soft yellow glow disappeared. Uirebon blinked and gave his head a little shake.

"Ancient indeed, Bantellar. Take them to the study area and find your references while I restore the full collection."

Bantellar gave the scripts to Rhys and clearly enjoyed his look of concern.

"This way, my Lord. They are now sturdy enough to cope with even the roughest of handling."

Kieran felt Rhys's pleasure at the blatant stir. The comeback was a pretended trip on a non-existent step and an exaggerated save from dropping which drew the moment of concern it was meant to. All that was forgotten when Bantellar selected one of the scripts and, setting it down, started purposefully leafing through. Out of interest, Tan opened another script and started examining it. His curiosity turned to complete amazement.

"Woorawa, feel this. It's perfect. Uirebon said it was ancient, but these pages feel like they've just been made."

The amazement spread and Kieran was really impressed. "Is this permanent, Ranevargar? Or will it revert when the effect of the power fades away?"

"My understanding is permanence, Kieran, but ask Bantellar."

Bantellar lifted his head from his close attention. "These scripts, restored by the art, will endure beyond our lifetimes."

"I wonder if Rhys might learn to be a restorer?"

Every heard turned and stared at Tan.

"Me? You mean Kieran, don't you?"

"No. This restoring is a kind of healing and you're the only one of us who can really do that."

"Healing? What d'you reckon, Ranevargar? It does make sense."

"Tan is presenting us with yet another fascinating idea, Rhys. It certainly does have a comfortable sense of feasibility, but your healing gift is exceedingly rare, and to my knowledge, completely unstudied ... You reject this idea?"

"No. I reject the idea of my brain getting turned inside out by a group of elf doctors ... Do you have doctors?"

"We call them healers or healer adepts ... But enough. Bantellar is distracted."

"Puzzled rather, Lord Ranevargar, but I have located the primary reference."

Ranevargar's head bent in perusal. Other heads closed in a circle of attention.

"Hm! The language is archaic. Can you or Lord Uirebon give it sense?"

"Yes, my Lord. 'The call of a Nexus translation may be instituted through a Power Stone.' It continues with outlines of a range of Nexus properties, but this reference is a direct statement."

"Read it again, please."

"The call of a Nexus trans—"

"Hold till I can read with you." Uirebon interrupted as he hurried close.

"Yes, all the scripts are restored. Start again, young Bantellar. Lord Ranevargar radiates great excitement."

"'The call of a Nexus translation may be instituted through a Power Stone.'"

Ranevargar spoke first. "Uirebon, that reference is more than specific. It is definitive. Do you see it as I do?"

"I do, but Bantellar's skill with this wording is practised and superior to mine."

"And what does it mean by Power Stone? Can that be a Realm Stone?"

"I suspect so ... Bantellar?"

"Without any doubt. Most ancient scripts reference the Six that way."

"Lord Uirebon, this young scholar is a treasure ... How much authority can we give to these scripts?"

"Again, I defer to Bantellar."

"The author held a position we would now call Lore Master and is the most respected scholar of that time."

"Hey! Is all this going to help us?"

"Not in itself, Rhys, but it notes a form of portal linking Realm Stones and the Nexus, a form which may be independent of the damaged main system ... Bantellar, you said the references were consistent. Do any of them give other information?"

"Not really, but the repetition and wording conveys a feeling that the process was familiar to the author. I have only examined four scripts so far, but in one of them he describes in great detail the process of redirecting free Nexus Energy on a temporary basis, and in another he sets out a teaching method for tracing a Nexus power flow."

"Are you saying it is a characteristic of this scholar to elaborate where he has expertise?"

"Very much so, Lord Ranevargar, and since the purpose of the collection is clearly to set out the properties and processes of the Nexus, I am confident that the problem will be to find the information rather than whether it exists."

"You found a number of references, Bantellar. Will any of them help narrow a search?"

"Not directly, but three of them do refer to particular scripts which until now were too fragile to handle."

Mr B interrupted. "How long has it taken to work through these four scripts? Lord Uirebon gave the impression it's been years."

"That is for my Nexus studies in general. It has been not quite a year since I discovered this collection."

"That still sounds like an awful obstacle from our point of view. If it takes a year for four scripts, it's going to take forever for the other twenty-three. And we can't help you because we can't even read them."

This brought a tense silence, and when the companions' eyes flicked to see Tan's reaction, Ranevargar hastened to speak.

"It is not as bad as that, Mr B. Bantellar's studies have been general until now, so a targeted search will be very different. If we start with the three reference scripts, we ..."

Ranevargar's speech stopped as every head turned to watch Tan's receding back.

Oh no! He must be upset at this letdown after the build up of anticipation from Uirebon's call. Kieran started after Woorawa, halted at a message from Ranevargar, and then sent his own mental command.

"Stop, Woorawa! He's not upset at all. He's not even there. Don't interrupt him."

Woorawa whirled and hurried back to the bewildered group. "What do you mean he's not there? More delay is bad news, and I want to be with him."

"It's the special thing again, Woorawa. We can't sense his mind."

"But he's by himself. What if I just go and watch without interfering? That should—"

Woorawa whirled again, because everyone's eyes had snapped to Tan's returning figure.

With quiet deliberation and no acknowledgement of anyone around him, he moved the open script to one side and replaced it with the one he was carrying. His hand hovered in a curiously meaningful fashion then manipulated the pages, with deft purpose, to a section some third of the way in.

"Here."

His finger rested a moment, he blinked, and then, with a little head-shake, returned to ordinary awareness. His finger jerked from the script and he took in the staring eyes.

"What? Did I go funny again?"

Woorawa laughed and gave him a big hug. "You sure did! You walked out on us and brought back that new script."

Tan leaned to peer at the manuscript which was now the centre of attention, only to be jostled by Ranevargar's excited approach.

"Bantellar, you saw where Tan's finger pointed. Fix the page and place in your mind and start reading. This will be what we seek."

Bantellar, moving closer, looked from Ranevargar to Tan and then, lost for words, to Uirebon. Kieran rushed to explain.

"We don't understand either, Bantellar, but we've seen Tan do strange things a few times now. I know it seems impossible, but check, please, if it's what we think it is."

Bantellar looked at Tan in wonder. "Lord Kieran the wonder of your Dragon landing is now surpassed by your more wondrous companion."

Rhys leapt to drape an arm over Tan's shoulder. "You said it, Ban, and it's right even without the weird stuff. Now, have a look and tell us if we're all carrying on about nothing."

*   *   *

Kieran smiled as the light of excitement brightened Uirebon's features and every step of the process so carefully set out in the thirteen pages following Tan's mind-bending finger point came to functional readiness. He'd felt the same excitement of success twice now, first through the merge with Ranevargar's ever-so-cautious application, and then with his own trial.

"You have it now, Uirebon. You used the locking pattern with precision. Would you like my supervision for another trial?"

"There is no need, Ranevargar. The pattern is straightforward once demonstrated, but how did you have knowledge of it?"

"I didn't, but I understood its purpose and simplified the more complicated mechanism I use to make my Tree Portals safe."

"Simplified?"

"Yes, this form can be used by any Realm Lord you choose to teach."

"I see."

He did too. He'd spoken at length to Maurice about Tree Portals and understood the special affinity that was so strong in Kieran and Ranevargar.

"This is amazing, Ranevargar. It's a baby version of your Tree Portals except it uses a power line to the Nexus instead of a proper spider net."

"And highly susceptible to interference, Kieran. Without the locking pattern I would be wary of using it."

"I think Uirebon should follow after us, in case something turns up we haven't expected. He hasn't got any experience with this kind of portal."

"I agree."

"Ranevargar, before we commit we should warn the High King."

"No, Uirebon, we won't wake the High King. Our own day has been overlong and we need rest ... What do you think, Kieran?"

Everyone looked keen and ready, but a quick peek showed underlying weariness. A boost from Rhys would counter that, but proper rest was far more sensible.

"We'll sleep deeply till two hours past dawn and then attempt a crossing to the High Castle."

"Deeply?"

"Yes, Rhys. By my command."

"Bossy boots!"

Kieran turned to Uirebon. "It's a one-way trip too, so that will give Maurice time to get there. That way we can bring you back here afterwards, or wherever you want to go."

"Wonderful! But, Lord Kieran, what of your companions? The script describes this as a single-person transfer."

"Tree Portals have a group pattern which I am confident will work but, beyond that, I have a method of my own."

The companions all gave a puzzled look.

"You do?"

"Yes, Rhys. When we do our group handhold it's a lot more than just holding hands."

"Okay, but why can't Maurice come with us then? He's always part of our group for Border crossings and Tree Portals."

"The Nexus chamber is underneath the High Castle, Rhys, and this transfer takes us right there. Maurice by himself is bigger than the arrival space, so I shudder to think what would happen if we all transferred at the same time."

"Whoa! I'm glad someone's thinking specifically. Is there plenty of room for the rest of us?"

Uirebon, familiar with the Nexus chamber, shared an image. "Sheba! That's the Nexus? It looks like a mass of old quartz rock. I was expecting some kind of giant gemstone."

Kieran had a similar idea, but quickly built a degree of understanding. "It is not opal or amethyst, Rhys, but quartz *is* a crystal, so your idea still works."

Mr B added his knowledge. "Amethyst actually is quartz, Kieran. It's a translucent form with traces of iron, and quite a few other gemstones are also forms of quartz. Tiger eyes and topaz are two that I remember out of quite a big list."

"Quartz? Are you sure?"

"I looked up gemstones, Rhys, because I wanted to know about black opal, and one article said quartz and opal are both made of silica. Ranevargar's Realm Stone spoils your idea though, because a pearl isn't really a gemstone."

"What do you mean?"

"Didn't you think the Nexus might be a giant Realm Stone?"

"Wow! That is radical!"

Ranevargar came in. "Not really, Rhys, though I would invert the premise and liken a Realm Stone to a miniature Nexus ... Bantellar, please guide us to somewhere we can rest. There are too many ideas flowing."

*　*　*

The group stared. Plain old quartz it might be, but the volume and order of the glowing hexagonal structure was striking in its own right.

The first few seconds of their arrival was no different, as far as Kieran could tell, to the reorientation after an ordinary Tree Portal, and the physical contact and fierce group protection had been unnecessary.

"*Well done, Kieran. A faultless translation. I will signal for Uirebon.*"

"Hey, Ranevargar. That felt like every other portal ... Sheba! It's glowing. Is that power coming out of it?"

"Yes, Rhys, the shift felt natural because of Kieran's proficiency. The glow you see is simply the light I am providing ... Clear the stone platform, everyone, and I'll send the okay to Uirebon."

Kieran smiled, because Ranevargar must be catching the group speech patterns, then did his own staring while he moved. The others couldn't see, but there *was* power coming out of the Nexus, radiating in six beautiful flows through some kind of filter. What was that about?

"*It is beautiful to anyone with the ability to see, Kieran, and that filter is a management tool the High King controls.*"

"*I have the strangest feeling that it's like when you stare at Maurice's eyes for too long.*"

"You can sense that? It has always been too subtle for me."

Ranevargar strengthened their merge enough to access Kieran's particular perception.

"Power workers visit this underground chamber for specific and temporary purposes only, Kieran. Prolonged stays result in a steadily increasing reluctance to leave."

"Like an addiction, or hypnotised like with Maurice?"

"Hey! Don't forget the rest of us. What's the big mind talk about?"

"Sorry, Rhys. We're talking about the weird way the Nexus feels like Maurice's eyes, and what happens when people stay close for too long."

"Something happens? Is it serious and how long is safe?"

"A curious dependency develops, Mr B, but only for those able to work with Nexus power. Kieran and I would be safe for days ... Ah! Here is Uirebon, and the High King is also rushing to meet us."

Mr B missed Uirebon's arrival, because his attention was with Ranevargar, but there was no missing his excited exclamation.

"Wonderful, Ranevargar! I had to use more power than I expected, but the translation itself is almost casual."

Ranevargar's reply was lost when a brilliant glow lit an entrance-way and Aglaron, practically running, emerged and rushed to grasp Kieran's arm.

"Wonder of wonders! With all the complications and calls on your life, I expected no visit to the High Castle. How is this possible, Keryth? Uirebon's message that you were about to arrive was a delightful but bewildering surprise. How is this possible and how long can you stay?"

His grip tightened and, understanding that just for this moment he was Keryth, Kieran returned the greeting with a quick impulsive hug.

"Thank you, Father. Lord Uirebon contacted us yesterday with news, and when we rushed to his remote Centre we unearthed knowledge of an emergency portal linking a Realm Stone to the Nexus."

"Emergency?" Aglaron gathered himself. "Welcome, everyone. What a pleasant surprise this is. Uirebon, with a little more warning I would have been better prepared."

Everyone was smiling, but it was Rhys's laugh that now caught Aglaron's attention.

"Yo, Aglaron! It's good to see you again. We stopped Uirebon from waking you up in the middle of the night, and then Kieran kept us zonked till just before we tried this new portal thing. It's not really an emergency, but we all got so excited about the discovery we had to see if it worked."

Uirebon hurried to explain. "Yes, my Lord, it is extraordinary. There was an element of risk in the process as translated by our young researcher, which leads us to believe it was likely used only in times of great need, but with Lord Ranevargar's modification it is safe for any Stone Holder to use."

"Any Stone Holder, Uirebon?"

"Yes, and if there is time before the Dragon arrives I will guide you through the process."

"Maurice will be here again? Wonderful! The Castle will be in turmoil, but of excitement this time, rather than dread. Kieran are you hopeful this development will help you find a way to the Human World?"

"I was for a while, but now I don't see how. It's a simple version of the process for Tree Portals, so we haven't really learnt anything new. My biggest hope is that Bantellar might find something else in the adept scripts."

Ranevargar shook his head emphatically. "I disagree quite strongly, Kieran ... Bantellar is the young researcher, High King ... Think of the ways Tan's gift has manifested. Every occasion has been significant, even if we haven't quite understood why, but this time it was more than extraordinary, as if we were being guided."

He broke off to explain Tan's finger point to Aglaron.

Tan lifted hands in an 'I haven't got a clue' expression when Aglaron stared at him in wonder.

"Guided? Who by?"

"I have no idea, Rhys. The number of happenings using knowledge foreign to the Realms is enough to make me wonder if some agency is working through the Opal."

"Which happenings? Aren't they all Realm stuff?"

"No, Rhys. Look at our mysterious mind shields. No one in the Realms could build them, and even Kieran doesn't fully understand how he makes them. His natural affinity with the life around him has developed at a rate beyond explanation. And you have inexplicably developed facility with mind speech."

"That's because of all the practice Maurice pushes me through."

"I doubt that. Demonstrate your progress by asking Lord Uirebon about training periods in the Realms."

"Can you hear me, Lord Uirebon? I'm only used to speaking like this with Maurice and my friends."

"Your communication is clear and capable, Rhys." Uirebon continued aloud. "With variations according to natural ability, Rhys's current level would typically require several decades of training. Inexplicable is an understatement ... Lord Ranevargar, could the agency be a legacy from our ancient adepts?"

Ranevargar paused to consider. "A fascinating idea, but I think it unlikely. The happenings we have witnessed are not from fields of knowledge we normally associate with the adepts. Do you know of any reference to an adept calling truth without a contest of will ... or accession of unknown knowledge?"

Uirebon shook his head. "No reference at all."

Rhys laughed and moved to give the nape of Tan's neck a friendly squeeze. "I do! We'll wait for the sun and the moon to line up at midday, then we'll feed him bird guts." Rhys laughed even more at the looks this brought. "They were called oracles and they used stones or bones or sacrifices to read the omens and answer questions. We'll call him the Oracle of Melbourne."

"Rhys is a lot more than just a funny face, High King. He has a love of books and reading, and he makes reference to a famous oracle called the Oracle of Delphi."

Rhys's jaw dropped. "Ouch! Watch your back, Mr B. That hurt."

The High King, taking in the smiles of the companions and the hint of a twinkle in Ranevargar's eye, understood there was no hurt at all. "I see, Rhys. You think Tan might be an oracle?"

"Not exactly. The knowing stuff sort of fits, but not the truth calling. Some of the oracles were bound to the truth, but I've never read about any who could control it in someone else."

Uirebon was looking puzzled. "A curious piece of partially relevant information, Rhys?"

Rhys laughed yet again. "I wasn't showing off my super knowledge, if that's what you mean, Uirebon. I was thinking how handy it would be if there was a way to set Tan going ... We could ask him about Mr B's face and find out whether it was a steam roller or a meat mangler ... Or we could get an answer for what to do next."

Mr B made a happy fist.

Kieran felt a burst of extra admiration.

Smiling, the High King said, "Ouch! I felt the hurt myself, Mr B."

Tan grabbed at Rhys's hand where it was still holding his neck. "I agree with Ranevargar about an agency. Sometimes it *has* felt like we're being protected and kept together. Kieran knew absolutely nothing about portals, but we came to the Emperor trees, and when we entered the Boundary Wall the red protection looked after us. I don't think I've got a special gift either. The weird things I've done could all be an agency using me to send us help. Kieran, it mightn't feel like a we've made any progress, but I think we have and just don't realise it." Tan faltered at the quiet, fixed attention. "What? Don't you agree? It's just a background theory that fits with Ranevargar's idea."

"Tan, it makes real sense, but you said it so earnestly we wondered if you were in Oracle mode."

Tan made a wry grimace at the knowledge he was now stuck with a new nickname. "No, it was all me ... Did you see anything different, Ranevargar?"

"I did wonder enough to have a peek, Tan, but you are clearly yourself and giving us cause to think in your customary manner. Do you have any thoughts or feelings about how we might proceed?"

"Not really ... except we *have* all been brought here to the Nexus. Maybe the Nexus is another step on the way."

The four Realm Lords exchanged glances and Aglaron answered. "I see what you mean about cause for thought, Ranevargar. I will willingly share the methods of Nexus control with you and Kieran if it will help in any way."

"You know more about the Nexus than he does, Ranevargar."

"But you don't, Kieran, and it is a gesture of trust and cooperation you would be wise to accept."

"You would show me how that filter thing works? Wonderful!"

Kieran looked round the Nexus chamber and turned to the companions. "This is special, everyone, but it means Buddha time for four of us ... What are those wall panels? Are they worth looking at?"

Uirebon almost spluttered. "Those engravings are a legacy from the time of Separation, Kieran. There is worth for all to see."

"What about the Nexus? We all want a proper look at that first."

"What do you mean, Rhys?"

"Well, will it turn radioactive or zap us if we touch it while you're fiddling?"

"Fiddling? Apart from investing inexperienced tinkerers with the permanent seeming of a giant frog there should be no adverse effects."

Rhys shared a look with Kieran. Uirebon was most definitely catching on.

The Buddha time, some twenty minutes, was definitely enlightening, and particular rewarding when Aglaron transferred control of the free Nexus energy to check Kieran's understanding.

"Direct a portion of the High Castle supply to Lady Narello's Realm while you apply a fresh set of locking keys ... Yes, just so ... Kieran, did you learn that mastery of power flows from Ranevargar?"

"Mostly. He made me practice really fine control, but a couple of times I

was clobbered by overloads and had to figure how to cope for myself ... Did you see that? Lady Narello's pushing the extra against her Outer Boundary."

"Every Realm Ruler is hungry for energy, Kieran, especially while so much is allocated to repairing the Gateway Realm. That push will be helping one of her Chaos Masters. Uirebon and I have tasked her to more deeply understand the link between Chaos energy and Chaos incursions."

Kieran returned control to his father and marvelled at his easy manner with it. *"How do you do that, Father? I had to concentrate like anything."*

"Time makes it as natural as breathing, Kieran. After 1200 years I am only aware of the control when I consciously bring it to mind."

"Can anyone except Realm Rulers take over if you want them to?"

"Anyone who has been adequately trained in the art of Power, Kieran, though none with the facility of a Stone Holder. Uirebon's Triad Masters would manage for a time and, with guidance, so would Narello's Power Masters."

"I'd like to understand more about triads, Uirebon. The one you had with you when Ranevargar was kidnapped was strong enough to block our portal."

Aglaron, eager to help, jumped in. *"Uirebon's best triads are currently resident in the Castle, Kieran, actively managing some of the more important repairs in my Gateway Realm. A visit would be well worth your time. One of them is dedicated to overseeing the—"*

"KIERAN! OVER HERE! QUICK!"

The strength of Rhys's yell, mental as well as oral, dissolved the construct of shared communication and had three Realm Lords trailing in the wake of Kieran's rush to where Tan was kicking at the base of one of the engraved wall panels.

"He must be in weird mode. He just started kicking a couple of seconds ago. Is he all right?"

A segment of panel cracked and fell away, and Tan took hold of the section next to where it had been and tugged with fierce determination.

Kieran's hurried peek probed at the strange, impenetrable identity barrier recognised from Ranevargar's close observation during the fingerpoint episode. "He's all right, Rhys, and it's definitely Oracle mode."

A larger piece came away, and when Tan discarded it to tackle a new section, Aglaron edged close and helped him.

"Look! A recess. This is important."

Woorawa joined the dismantling and left no room for anything except watching. With a satisfied grunt, the High King passed another piece to waiting hands, started a joint effort with Woorawa, then froze along with everyone else when Tan folded backwards into a sitting position and stared in bewilderment at the proceedings.

"I suppose I must've gone strange again, but why are you wrecking that beautiful panel?"

"Because you started it, Tan. Woorawa noticed it was a different material to all the others and we were discussing why when all of a sudden you were kicking it."

"Mr B's right, Tan. We were all shocked, because you were wrecking something precious, and then Aglaron came rushing over to help you."

Aglaron started loosening a new piece. "Of course I did, Rhys. It could only be important ... and look at the recess. I can already see part of another panel."

Woorawa gave Kieran a look which told him to keep an eye on Tan, then added his strength to Aglaron's waggling.

Kieran gave Tan a big smile and helped him to his feet, then, knowing he was completely all right, turned to watch another piece dislodged and passed back to Rhys.

"You've done it again, Tan. What I can see so far is covered in dust and cobwebs, but it's definitely another panel."

Uirebon moved to where Tan had been, then dodged when Aglaron levelled a calculated kick at the section stubbornly resisting his hand manipulation. Rhys gave a yell of approval which cut off when the largest piece yet cracked and fell.

"Sheba! Put some glow on it, Kieran. It's hieroglyphics or something."

It was definitely something, but it took more dismantling, and Uirebon making a curious cleaning pass with his hands, before it was revealed properly.

Not unexpectedly, Rhys broke the contemplation. "Is it a star chart?"

"No way, Rhys. Look at those perfect hexagons. I think it must be a geometric model of something."

"I suppose, Mr B! What can that double circle stand for then?"

Uirebon made a soft, attention-gathering sound, and Kieran felt a tingle of excitement at his nod and smile. "I am finally able to make a contribution. Tan has unearthed what could very well be the original form of a rare but important diagram which has three main interpretations. The foremost sees it as a representation of our Realm structure, with the six outer hexagons modelling the six Realms and the inner hexagon standing for the central High Realm or even the Nexus itself."

"Wow! That's fits perfectly."

"Nearly, Rhys. The second interpretation sees it as a theoretical representation of a Nexus of Nexuses ... similar to the compounding effect of a triad of triads, but more far reaching."

"That fits too. What about the third idea? Is it as good as the first two?"

"Until now it has been regarded as a less likely interpretation, with that inner central hexagon standing for this Nexus and the outer hexagons representing six other natural Nexuses."

"Natural? What does that mean? One hidden in each of the Realms?"

Ranevargar interrupted. "There is only one Nexus for the Realms, Rhys, constructed by the adepts for the Separation, but I have heard discussion that they used a model ... Uirebon, your 'until now' registered strongly with me. Do you see something new?"

"Yes, Ranevargar. The double lines describing the outer circle have long been a symbol for the Human World, usually centred with a small sun circle. In my mind this ties the outer hexagons to the Human World."

"Extraordinary! But where does this diagram lead? Tan acted with great purpose to reveal it."

Kieran, reviewing the three interpretations, and feeling Ranevargar's fierce concentration along with his own, started at Tan's soft voice.

"Um! I think I know. If Uirebon is right and each outer hexagon is a Nexus, we might have found a way home."

Afterwards, everyone was laughing because even Rhys was too dumbfounded to make any comment. Kieran broke first.

"Go on, Tan. You've lost us."

"Well, we've just learned you can portal to a Nexus, and now Uirebon says this panel shows there are Earth Nexuses. That would explain where your White Power comes from ... and we know you've got a link through your Opal."

"Hells! ... Holy! ... Bells! Are you in Oracle mode?"

Tan shook his head, and along with Mr B, Woorawa and Rhys, looked to see what the four heavies made of this.

Aglaron and Uirebon, not privy to the intense communication passing between Kieran and Ranevargar, were themselves watching with heightened anticipation.

"Ranevargar, it feels right."

"It does, Kieran, particularly the idea that the source of your White Power might be a Nexus. In hindsight it is a disturbingly obvious possibility. Examine your special link for any similarity with the link between our Realm Stones and this Nexus. I would like to help, but I can only see it through our merge."

Kieran was at a loss.

"I can't see it either. It's only there when there's a power transfer."

"Call power then, and study the link while it flows."

"Here? Now? It's a huge flood of power. What if it affects this Nexus?"

"Interesting thought! Control the flow. Reduce it to a moderate level."

"I don't think I can. It's always the same giant flood."

"You have never tried. You have always been eager to receive the copious quantity. Prepare yourself while I warn Aglaron."

"Well, all right, but strengthen our merge so I can use your experience."

"Tan, your suggestion is overwhelmingly sensible and Kieran is preparing himself to make a study of the link which carries his White Power. High King, when power floods this chamber, Kieran would like to disburse it to the triads and the Gateway Realm through your Nexus filter."

"The White Power? Yes, of course."

Rhys, staring at Kieran's inwardness, grabbed at Ranevargar's arm. "Hang on! Is Kieran all right? I hate when I can't help, and does sensible mean this could be the way back?"

"I fully expect so, and we will know one way or another very shortly. You would term it an extreme Buddha moment, Rhys, while he calls and controls the flow of White Power and examines the properties of the associated link."

To all the onlookers, Ranevargar's features transformed to match Kieran's. The Opal lit up. The familiar glowing cloud coalesced and the group switched attention to Aglaron's startled gasp. Ranevargar was too deep with his own concentration to make any response. Uirebon, avidly watching the White Power, closed his eyes at the High King's call for help in distributing the influx of abundant power.

Mr B and Woorawa moved next to Tan, and Rhys shook his head wonderingly.

"You've got all four Realm Rulers straining their brains to keep up with you. How did you figure that out so quickly?"

"It wasn't really that quick, Rhys, because last night I was kind of daydreaming for the Nexus to be at home instead of here. So when Uirebon said the hexagons could be Earth Nexuses, the connection was sort of already in my mind."

"That sounds funny."

"Why? It's true."

"I didn't mean that. I meant the daydreaming."

"I daydream a lot."

"So do I, but you said daydreaming at night, so it should be night dreaming, and that doesn't work either."

"Your mind works in mysterious ways, Rhys."

"Not as mysterious as Tan's, Mr B. Daydreaming at night sounds like the Oracle taking over."

The White Power shrank rapidly and Uirebon snapped to awareness.

"What's happening now, Uirebon?"

"Progress, Rhys. Kieran has learned control and the White Power is reduced to a trickle. Aglaron no longer needs my assistance."

Aglaron, smiling, was now also with them.

"Unbelievable! The triads are almost dizzy."

"Does it feel like Nexus power?"

"If you mean the White Power, Mr B, I don't know, because Kieran transforms it for us."

Kieran's Opal brightened for a short moment and stopped all conversation till it returned to the previous softer state.

"He did something that needed power."

That was obvious, but Mr B was really voicing the group feeling that it meant more progress.

The Opal flared again, even brighter, and a tinge of the red protection aura shocked the companions to full awareness. Mr B reacted first.

"Group contact, everyone, quick. Just in case."

Aglaron and Uirebon joined the rush to action, but the Opal softened and Kieran and Ranevargar surfaced to normality.

"Good thinking, everyone. We had to initiate the process twice before we got it right, and when we finally commit we'll definitely hold tight as a group."

"Finally, Kieran?"

"Yes, Tan, finally."

Woorawa rested his arm across Tan's shoulder, and Mr B voiced the clearly evident question. "So, when do we leave, Kieran?"

"We nearly left then, but we had to stop. According to the panel there are six possibilities for where we might end up, and we would have taken Ranevargar, my father, and Uirebon with us. My Realm has Maurice to look after it, but taking three other Realm Rulers is too complicated. Ranevargar thinks they might be able to get back, but we don't know."

"We can't leave before this afternoon."

Woorawa voiced his puzzlement. "Whyever not, Rhys?"

"Well, I'm not leaving without saying goodbye to Krol and Gryl … and George."

Woorawa and Tan exchanged a look and a nod.

"How close is Maurice?"

"*Close enough to worry about the High Castle Wards, Woorawa. Without Kieran's help I can't push my way through.*"

"You're listening in? You know what's happened?"

"*At Kieran's invitation. When I sensed a great flow of White Power I contacted him.*"

"Maurice is close enough to need your Wards lowered, High King."

Aglaron nodded, made it happen, then, after casting a thought, turned to Kieran. "My hopes for a longer stay are clearly dashed, Kieran. Can we speak while I tempt your party with the refreshments my people have been preparing in the Courtyard?"

"Briefly, Father, and the refreshments will be greatly appreciated ... but why not travel with us to Uirebon's Realm where you can learn the Nexus portal for yourself?"

Aglaron eagerly accepted and, sensing the tension of purpose, led the way out of the chamber.

*   *   *

"*That was a thoughtful gesture, Kieran. It meant a great deal to your father.*"

"*More than I expected, Ranevargar, but it was the best way to share some time with him.*"

Ranevargar was referring to Kieran's decision to speak with Aglaron for the duration of Maurice's return to Bantellar's study centre while everyone else had another forced catch-up sleep.

"*It was awkward that he was so open with his personal thoughts and feelings when he didn't know about our merge.*"

"*I don't think it was, Kieran. Public or private was clearly irrelevant on his part.*"

"*I suppose. Do you think he's carried away with this Castle project?*"

"*You need to experience the wonder of the Gateway Realm restored to have a proper understanding of his capabilities. The High King of all Faerie, not just a grateful and remorseful father, was expressing his gratitude. When the time is right a thousand artisans will strive to mould a Castle of surpassing magnificence.*"

"*A thousand? Is that your way to say it's a big deal, or do you mean for real?*"

"*Both, Kieran. Re-establishing a residence on the old site near the cavern signifies the importance of Maurice's place in your Realm, but its location will call for an extensive support network.*"

"*I suppose. Maurice wants to base himself up there, so it's just common*" *sense ... Ranevargar, the way this transfer process works means my Opal has to come with me and I'm still concerned my Realm might suffer without it."*

"I don't believe that will happen, but if it does you can return and leave your Opal with Maurice when the portal system is recovered."

"Leave it? I wouldn't want to do that."

"I would have the same reluctance if I needed to part with my Pearl, Kieran, but the strength of your connection means any physical separation is highly unlikely to be a real concern."

"Across the Realm boundaries is no problem, but out of Faerie might be a very different matter. You said so yourself."

"I did, but Woorawa's story of the contest between his people and the 'Great One' has lingered in my thoughts, Kieran, and I believe that the mysterious power they wielded not only severed the Holder's link, it also affected deeper functions of the Stone."

"That's amazing! You think Woorawa's people were strong enough to cause Dead World?"

"The strength is without doubt. The Realms have always regarded the Ancient People with wariness and respect."

"That's true. Aglaron and Uirebon explained about Maynor not being able to reach Woorawa and how they warned him off."

"And you're linked to that power now, Kieran, through deep association and even deeper friendship, and you should prepare yourself for involvement in matters unknown to any Realm dweller."

"Prepare? You make it sound like a big deal."

"Think, Kieran. An elder of the Ancient People gifted you with an Artefact of power and eager assistance. Your involvement can only be significant."

Kieran felt total agreement.

"That's for sure. Burrimul will want to know every little detail of what's happened."

"Hold nothing from him. Your mind shows him as wise, gracious, and very kind, and I suggest you continue to regard him as a mentor."

"They'll have a campfire get-together whenever Woorawa gets to Mparntwe, and I can't imagine what will happen when they see him dance ... Their brains will explode. ...You're my mentor, Ranevargar. We'd have been lost without all your help ... Do you think it will be hard to keep in contact if this process really does take us out of the Realms?"

"Our minds have become so attuned I expect even direct contact will be possible but, as with the home links through Tan and Woorawa, requiring significant concentration and effort. Maurice, at the apex of your Opal network, will be ever present in the background of your mind and with

minimal effort you can relay through him."

"Of course! Everything happened so suddenly I haven't properly thought it through. It makes me feel kind of guilty to be leaving when you've got so many things happening."

"Yes, desertion at the time of such need is unforgivable. I hope I can develop coping strategies."

Kieran had to smile because Ranevargar would absolutely have everything in hand.

"My first priority is always my Realm, Kieran, and while the renewal program for my Guardians is particularly exciting, helping bring life to your Realm only compounds that excitement. Another priority, in cooperation with Uirebon, will be a comprehensive study of Lord Maynor's mind manipulation methods. It is imperative for Uirebon, as Lore master, to be able to ensure the High King, or any other Realm Ruler, is protected from any insidious influence."

"Really? That's breaking your pattern of independence, Ranevargar."

"Yes, it will be an intricate, but necessary, path of association."

Kieran sensed something about a system of checks and balances, but Woorawa was now in Ranevargar's foreground thoughts.

"For reasons I don't fully understand, Woorawa sees extraordinary significance in the planting of his Realm Tree pod, and I hope you will be able to coax it to secure establishment."

Kieran knew the seed pod was precious as a gift to Woorawa, but there was a connotation of something else.

"Yes, Kieran, his gratitude is as forthright as his heart, but his constant questions about the pod convey a sense of almost ceremonial importance."

"Well, that sure fits with the way his people do things. His uncle made an event out of giving me the Artefact with special chants ... but Woorawa already knows we'll care for his Realm Tree, once he works out where to plant it."

"The Valley of the Eagles."

"What? No, that can't be right. There are some small rock pools ... but that's nowhere near enough water for a Realm Tree."

"He describes an underground storage with more water than even my Central Grove would ever need."

Kieran remembered one of the guides for the college trip describing how underground water was drawn to supply Mparntwe.

"Yes, I've heard about that, but I think it's too deep."

"Woorawa plans to use a mechanism which can tunnel through earth, and even rock, to whatever depth is needed."

"Tunnel? If he means a drill or a bore that's a big-deal project."

"With your backing there will be no doubt about its execution."

"We'll be backing each other for everything, Ranevargar. What do you mean?"

"I find myself wondering if your association with Woorawa and the Ancient People might call for more involvement than you expect. Tan made that strong exhortation for Woorawa to use his gift."

"I don't know why he said that. Woorawa's ceremonies are built into our life now, and they're too special to imagine them not happening."

"I can't either, Kieran, but the exhortation was to follow the 'dictates of his heart', which are clearly his companions and his family."

"And Woorawa ... But you're thinking in general terms, Ranevargar. It could also be a single event or issue that's especially important to him."

"Hmm. Yes. That could well be. And thinking back, it does more closely suit the tone and context of the moment. Kieran, have you given much thought to how you will reconcile your position and abilities as a Realm Ruler with your life as a student?"

"We talk about it between us all the time, with lots of 'what if' and 'hey you could' comments, but not really seriously. I don't think it will be as hard as my father thinks, because this persona tells me I'm an ordinary human student who's had all sorts of impossible things put onto me, rather than an elf with all sorts of mind training. We'll face any issues like that whenever they come to us."

"Of that I have no doubt. Now, you have had less rest than any of your friends and you saw how much they needed it, so put yourself to sleep."

* * *

The friends clambered from Maurice's back and into an onslaught of prolific licking and gentle head-butting from Gryl and his cohort of Panthers, which then turned into the excitement and happiness of one of their ever-so-meaningful mock battles.

Kieran, laughing at the soft tongue rasping the side of his head and helpless on his back beneath a great furry paw, watched as well as he could manage while Rhys and Woorawa made a determined but useless effort to free him.

"It's time to let me up, Gryl. The Griffins are coming."

They were too, but it would be another ten minutes before they arrived.

Gryl relaxed, released Kieran, and sat on his haunches, while Rhys hugged the column that was his leg and the others made a very tactile farewell. Kieran reached his hand to the crown of Gryl's head and rested it in the gesture of benison he'd learned from Ranevargar. At the same time he shared images of moonlight on the plains and the silver and black dappling of the track through the trees when they were rushing to the Realm Boundary.

"It's the beautiful memory that comes whenever I think about you racing with us, Gryl."

Kieran kept his hand where it was, because Gryl's soft throaty rumble and quivering muscles were too hard to resist.

Rhys laughed his happy laugh and massaged two big handfuls of neck fur. "The prince of Panthers turns to kitty putty. Does he understand we're leaving, Kieran? He doesn't look sad."

Kieran tried to sense that, but realised he didn't know enough. "He's definitely not sad, and the best I can tell he just thinks we're heading off for a while and we'll be back when we're ready."

Ranevargar approached. "Gryl shares my sentiments. We consider this a temporary parting rather than a goodbye. Rhys, turn your attention to another acquaintance who is somewhat daunted by the Guardians' actions."

"What?" Rhys looked around ... then charged off to where George, looking very sleek and conditioned, was watching expectantly.

Tan turned to Woorawa. "Rhys won't have animal friends around if the power link works like we hope."

Woorawa laughed, which was a surprise.

"What's funny about that?"

"It's not, Tan, but I thought of him turning up at college with Gryl or Krol and starting a panic ... Don't worry about Rhys and animals though. We'll probably have magpies or kookaburras sitting on our shoulders every time Kieran goes outside."

Tan laughed now. "And he'll call the magpie Maggie and the kookaburra Percy."

Woorawa canted his head knowingly. "That will be Percival, Tan, and it'll be a pelican not a kookaburra."

Kieran shared Ranevargar's bemusement at the smiles of acknowledgement passing between Tan and Woorawa. "What am I missing?"

Woorawa glanced to the full-on attention Rhys was giving George. "Rhys would be yelling at you for not reading enough, Kieran. Mr Percival is a famous pelican."

"He'll keep yelling at me too, because I reckon there'll be so much happening it will take me ages to even finish *Mysts*."

Kieran stopped talking because a rather subdued Rhys was approaching.

"Gods, Kieran! They're friends. I'll never look at animals the same way again."

None of them would. Kieran gave Rhys an arm nudge of shared understanding and pointed to where Griffins were approaching in the distance. "Wow! Get ready, Rhys. Krol's got something special."

"What? No, don't tell me."

All eyes focused and, Griffin speed being what it was, shortly watched the coordinated approach and graceful landing of the flight of Griffins. Krol was in the forefront, fearsome in aspect as always but also clearly welcoming.

Rhys's gasp was echoed. "They've brought the Grifflings with them!"

And indeed, from a number of backs, young heads were lifting to peer curiously at the strange new environment of giant trees, people, Panthers and the gigantic, golden-eyed form of Maurice.

The friends hesitated. Ranevargar, a smile in his voice, reassured them.

"Meet the newest Guardians, everyone. The maternal instinct is subsumed with pride, and homage is offered as a parting gift."

Rhys, unsure whether Ranevargar's statement *was* the meeting, or if it was the go-ahead for an actual approach, watched Krol twist his head to nudge the Griffling from his back. With an indignant *scrark* and a gangly spread of wings, the youngster moved to stand beside Krol.

Ranevargar gestured for everyone to move. "Rhys, go and meet Rhys."

Rhys, moving because of the gesture, halted when the words registered. "What?"

Kieran didn't understand either and wished their merge was active. Ranevargar was looking inordinately pleased.

"Make your physical greeting, Rhys. Krol sought advice for some way to express your special bond and I suggested giving your name to their dominant hatchling. I knew you would be honoured."

Kieran watched disbelief and wonder, felt building emotion through the light link he always kept, then smiled his own happiness as Rhys raced to greet Krol and the little Griffin.

Little? Well, compared to Krol, yes, but, already grown as tall as Rhys, he was developed enough in size and presence to command attention in his own right.

Knowing this was Rhys's time, everyone waited.

"How did they grow so quickly, Ranevargar? Was it a special stimulus thing like you use with the Realm Trees?"

"No, Mr B, just a natural growth spurt and an abundant supply of food. Those regular sessions I had were for their Guardian qualities."

Krol lowered his head and held it formally in position to receive a Griffin version of the gesture of grace Kieran had given Gryl. Rhys's happy laugh reduced the formality and at the same time added meaning.

Krol's head turned and there was a curious deep chirring sound. The little Griffin's head bobbed in a way that made Kieran think of the Joker birds, then lowered in a junior version of Krol's formality.

"That is so cool!"

Mr B's mouth opened in surprise and amusement. "Well, I agree with the sentiment, Woorawa, but ... cool? That would even sound funny coming from Rhys."

Woorawa wasn't one bit phased. "Which would be exactly why he'd say it, Mr B."

Talk became action because Rhys was beckoning everyone.

* * *

Five companions, kitted out with elven rucksacks packed chock-full, gathered close.

"We'll make a circle, everyone, and hold tighter than our usual hand grip. The red protection started building when we tested the start of this shift, so we might be in for a rough ride."

"Worse than Boundary Walls?"

"Probably, Rhys. If it works the way we want it to it's a lot more than a switch between Realms."

"Ha! I know how I want it to work, and it's not to end up somewhere in Antarctica."

That was from Ranevargar's thoughts that the North and South pole and the equator might be what he called Cardinal positions.

Conscious of the mix of trust, hope, and a certain amount of the trepidation he was feeling himself, Kieran nodded assurance to everyone and called for Ranevargar's merge and oversight in initiating this tested-but-never-completed process.

"Here we go, everyone. Hold tight."

A great roar sounded and every being gathered to send the friends on their way cowered in momentary shock.

Kieran's mind froze with his own shock till a message of affirmation, and indeed approval, came from Ranevargar, then began to function properly when the roar finished a few seconds later.

"It is an acclamation, everyone, not anger. Maurice announces your departure."

*   *   *

Kieran struggled to resolve the confusion of total darkness, returning reality, and a mix of pressure against both mind and body. A muffled expletive and the realisation that a knee was grinding into his stomach brought partial understanding. He called for light and a soft blue glow helped the press of bodies struggle upright. Rhys laughed as Mr B pushed Tan off his chest.

"Whoa! You blew that one, Kieran. D' you know where we are? What's wrong?"

"I don't know. It's not actually hurting, but it's sort of like a whole mountain's pressing on me. Hang on while I rebuild our shields. That was so major it wiped them all. Is everyone okay?"

Kieran knew they were, but answering would share the assurance.

"Are we in a cave, Kieran? It was so pitch black I thought my head wasn't working."

"Me too, Woorawa, and having Tan squirming on top of me made it even more confusing. Can you extend your light, Kieran? This little glow is giving me a closed-in feeling."

Extending was a better idea than extra brightness and Kieran sent a tendril of glow in the direction he was facing. Twenty metres away a sheer wall blocked everything.

"Well that doesn't tell us much, except that the stone's a weird colour. Try the other direction."

Kieran was already turning, but Rhys's colour comment sparked a thought. "The colour's from me, Rhys. My glow comes out blue unless I think about it. Have another look."

"Another look?"

Recognising a certain note in Kieran's voice, Rhys did just that. "So? It's white instead of grey-blue. It'll still block our— It's quartz! A whole wall of quartz?"

"It's not a wall."

Mr B broke the silence that followed. "It's too big!"

"I agree with you, Mr B, but it *is* a Nexus and it makes the Realm Nexus look like a toy. I felt it as soon as the red protection faded, but it's so different and overwhelming it's like I'm a grain of sand at the bottom of a whole ocean."

The wide-eyed looks expressed acceptance without real understanding.

Woorawa whirled to grab Tan's arm. "It *is* a Nexus, Tan, and if the panel was right it's an Earth Nexus ... Use your GPS, Kieran."

The urge to know more was almost a compulsion, but the question of their whereabouts, now immediate for everyone, took priority. What to use as a focus? Well, of course. Try the share house. Kieran couldn't help smiling.

"Something's funny?"

"The lounge came into my mind, Rhys, and the cardboard-covered window ... which isn't there ... but the house is ..." Kieran swivelled and pointed "... and it's that way ... a long way away."

Mr B spoke first. "That gives me a good suspicion, Kieran. Look for Burrimul."

With a quick new questing, Kieran's arm moved minimally to the right. His features lit up. "Better than good, Mr B. It's brilliant, because he's that way and he's not far. Tan, we're home!"

Tan's big smile said more than any words till the mix of emotions erupted with Rhys's yells of excitement and an assortment of hugs and expressions of wonder. Woorawa steadied first.

"This is the best, Kieran. I know you and Ranevargar were confident, but I couldn't help feeling it might be too good to be true. How close is Uncle Burrimul? Can you tell?"

"Not exactly ... I should have practised more. But I'd say about forty or fifty km. Are you ready to contact him?"

Woorawa nodded, then hesitated. "How? With real mind talk or a 'come and get us' feeling like our other assurances?"

"You know him best. Will mind talk freak him out?"

"Try it. It's hard to freak him out about anything. But what will we say? Apart from telling him we're back, I mean? Telling him we're in a cave somewhere close won't be much help."

Mr B added his bit. "Yes it will. Put your scouting brain into gear, Woorawa. If we're near your uncle that means Kieran's first direction was south and we're basically north-east. If he's got a vehicle he could make a start."

"He hasn't, but he could use the mini-bus from the Cultural Centre."

Rhys pointed at the surroundings. "He might need to bring an excavator so he can dig us out."

"The air's not stale, Rhys, so there must be an entrance somewhere."

"Hey! Good thinking, except if it's a crevasse or something in the ceiling. Gods! Imagine what this would be like without Kieran's light."

Every second was bringing new puzzles, and Kieran swept his glow in an arc, lingering on each of three definite openings in passing.

"Mr B can make a glow too, Rhys."

Mr B shook his head. "I know we'll have to explore, Kieran, but there's no way we're going to split into—"

"Sheba!"

Every gaze jerked from the third dark opening to Tan and the nimbus of soft white light surrounding him.

"Join with me."

It wasn't a command. It wasn't a request.

Discussing it later, everyone agreed with Mr B's description of a curiously nonthreatening compulsion to make the group join up.

Woorawa and Mr B, standing with Tan, lifted their arms. By the time Kieran and Rhys closed with a few automatic steps, they were outlined with the same soft aura. Without a question, Kieran completed the hand contact ... and blinked to awareness of Tan gazing at gully walls.

"Whoa! Unreal! We're outside."

That was Rhys, and a few steps away, Mr B and Woorawa were making their own survey.

"What did you do this time, Tan?"

"Me? Again? I thought Kieran must have done some kind of portal."

"You zapped us. The last thing I remember is seeing the halo thing round you. Where are we now, Kieran? Can you tell if we've moved far?"

Kieran's reply was slow, because he was checking everything again. "I don't know what Tan did, Rhys, but whatever it was this time it didn't affect our shields or anything! Burrimul feels about the same distance."

"What about the giant Nexus? Does your GPS work with that?"

It did, and Kieran pointed up the gully. "Somewhere in there and a bit more than a kilometre."

Woorawa left Tan's side and walked five or six metres.

"What are you doing?"

He pointed to the ground. "I'm wondering about footprints, Rhys. Gullies like this sometimes have shelters or caves at their head. Yes, I can see fresh marks in this sandy place. I don't think it was a portal." The scout hurriedly moved a few metres to another sandy patch. "More scuff marks. Tan dream-walked us out."

Tan looked at the wondering expressions. "Dream-walking?"

Mr B answered. "I've never heard of it, Tan, but it's a better description than sleepwalking. What time is it on your watch?"

"Twelve past nine in the morning, Mr B, but why? It doesn't mean anything."

"Just for a reference. Look at the shadows. The sun's behind the hills, so it must be early morning or late afternoon."

Kieran understood straightaway and did the Melbourne and Burrimul comparison again. "Melbourne is east so the sun is in the west."

Woorawa, returning from his sortie, took in the conclusion that it was late afternoon. "Kieran, I think we're close to one of the elders' secret places. Contact Uncle."

For the next while the friends watched Kieran's expression vary through intense concentration, moments of stillness, several smiles and a number of nods.

With happy impatience, Rhys turned to Woorawa. "It's turned into a gossip session about your funny singing and dancing. That's why he's smiling."

Woorawa didn't need a comeback, because Kieran was with them again.

"And I might have been telling him how you were nearly a roast chook. He did freak, Woorawa, but only for a few seconds, and then it was my turn to freak when he said he was expecting us."

"What? How come?"

"The regular reassurances made him really confident. At any rate, I showed him a mind picture of this gully and he knows exactly where we are. He's on his way, Tan, and he'll be here in less than an hour."

Tan answered in a curiously distant manner. "Life is about to become interesting."

MPARNTWE

Mirri and Jarra join with an AI to fight
for a future which includes everyone ...

PETER WOOD

www.ingramcontent.com/pod-product-compliance
Lightning Source LLC
Chambersburg PA
CBHW022013120726
47902CB00012B/14